READER'S
DIGEST
CONDENSED
BOOKS

READER'S DIGEST ASSOCIATION (CANADA) LTD.
CONDENSED BOOKS DIVISION
215 Redfern Ave., Montreal, Que. H3Z 2V9
Editor: Deirdre Gilbert
Assistant Editor: Anita Winterberg
Design: Andrée Payette
Production Manager: Holger Lorenzen

Reader's Digest Condensed Books

In this volume

HIDDEN RICHES
by Nora Roberts

Dora Conroy loves a bargain.
A young Philadelphia antiques
dealer with a taste for the unusual,
she's just wrangled a good deal
on a collection of novelties
at an auction. But she's unnerved
when her new assets become
a magnet for murder. Before
long, Dora and her neighbor,
rugged ex-cop Jed Skimmerhorn,
find themselves matching
wits against an international
smuggler. And discovering, too,
that there might be more between
them than either of them ever
bargained for. / Page 7

PHOENIX RISING
by John J. Nance

Like the legendary phoenix—the
bird reborn from its ashes—a new
luxury airline has just begun flying
under the old Pan Am name.
But sinister forces are conspiring
to clip the fledgling's wings.
Promised financing disappears, and
the company's airplanes become
targets of sabotage. Can Elizabeth
Sterling, Pan Am's bright financial
officer, and Brian Murphy, its
chief pilot, stop the plotters
in time? Or will their dreams for
Pan Am, like the phoenix, go down
in flames? A riveting new thriller
with an unmistakable ring
of authenticity. / Page 157

ROOMMATES
My Grandfather's Story
by Max Apple

A touching, true story about the
oddest of odd couples: Rocky,
the scrappy old baker, and
Max, his bookworm grandson. For
years they shared a household—not
to mention laughter, tears, battles,
and heartaches. It was often a closer
relationship than either of them
wanted, especially when a new
friend came into young Max's life.
But it was a bond that strengthened
them both. And when tragedy
struck, a very old man discovered
he had a new job: holding a
family together. / Page 321

WHITE HARVEST
by Louis Charbonneau

The Alaskan coastal tundra looks
forbidding and desolate, but it fairly
teems with life: seabirds, fur seals,
and walruses. Yet where these
animals congregate, poachers are
sure to follow. And the quarry this
time is the biggest prize of all—a
magnificent old walrus whose tusks
alone will bring a fortune in the
Hong Kong market. But two people
stand in the poachers' way: John
Mulak, a tough old Eskimo, and
Kathy McNeely, a spunky wildlife
scientist. The author of *The Ice*
has written a crackling adventure
tale of the wild. / Page 445

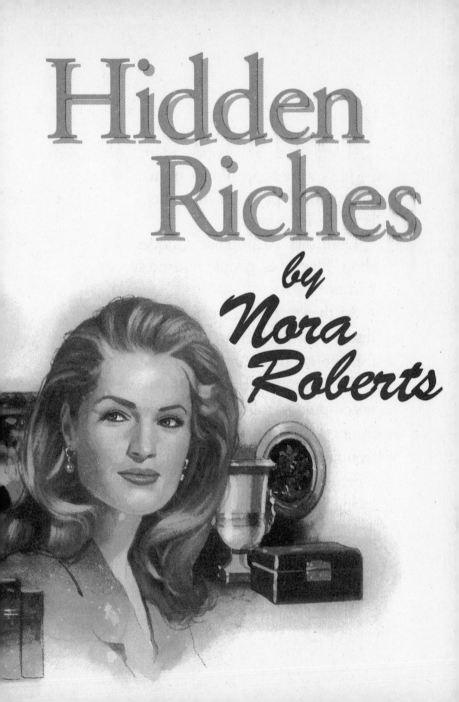

Jed and Dora are worlds apart. Jed's an ex-cop hiding from his troubled past. All he wants is to be left alone.

Dora owns a popular antiques shop. She loves people and noisy parties.

So they're both surprised to discover a smoldering attraction for one another. And when Dora becomes the target of an unscrupulous collector, Jed's instincts are to protect her. The trouble is, he's not sure which he's more afraid of: losing Dora—or loving her.

PROLOGUE

HE DIDN'T want to be there. No, he hated being trapped in the elegant old house, prodded and pinched by restless ghosts. It was no longer enough to shroud the furniture in dustcovers, lock the doors and walk away. He had to empty it and, by emptying it, purge himself of some of the nightmares.

"Captain Skimmerhorn?"

Jed tensed at the title. As of last week he was no longer captain. He'd resigned from the force, turned in his shield, but he was already weary of explaining it. He shifted aside as the movers carried a rosewood armoire down the staircase, through the grand foyer and out into the chilly morning.

"Yes?"

"You might want to check upstairs, make sure we got everything you wanted put in storage. Otherwise, looks like we're done here."

"Fine."

But he didn't want to go up those stairs, walk through those rooms. Even empty they would hold too much. Responsibility, he mused as he reluctantly started up. His life had been too crowded with responsibility to ignore one now.

Something nudged him along the hallway toward his old room, where he had grown up. But he stopped in the doorway. Hands jammed into his pockets, he waited for memories to assault him.

He'd cried in that room—in secret and in shame. And when tears had dried, he'd plotted in that room. Useless, childish revenges that

9

had always boomeranged on him. He'd learned to hate in that room.

Yet it was only a room. It was only a house. He'd convinced himself of that years before, when he had come back to live there as a man. And hadn't he been content? he asked himself now. Hadn't it been simple? Until Elaine.

"Jedidiah."

He flinched. He'd nearly brought his right hand out of his pocket to touch a weapon that was no longer there.

He relaxed and glanced at his grandmother. Honoria Skimmerhorn Rodgers was wrapped in mink, discreet daytime diamonds at her ears. Her eyes, as vivid a blue as his own, were filled with concern.

"I'd hoped I'd convinced you to wait," she said quietly.

"There was no reason to wait."

"But there's a reason for this?" She gestured toward the empty room. "A reason to move out of the family home?"

"Family? We were never a family here, or anywhere."

Her eyes hardened. "Pretending the past doesn't exist is as bad as living in it. What are you doing here, Jedidiah? Tossing away everything you've earned, everything you've made of yourself? Perhaps I was less than enthusiastic about your choice of profession, but it was your choice and you succeeded. You made more of the Skimmerhorn name when you were promoted to captain than all your ancestors did with their money and social power."

"I didn't become a cop to promote my name."

"No," Honoria said quietly. "You did it for yourself against tremendous family pressure—including my own. I saw you turn your life around, and it awed me." She studied him, this son of her son. He had inherited the bold good looks of the Skimmerhorns. Bronzed hair, tousled by the wind; a lean, rawboned face taut with stress; the tall, broad-shouldered build; the defiant blue eyes.

"I might have had reservations when you moved back in here alone after your parents died, but it seemed you'd made the right choice again. But this time your solution to your sister's tragedy is to sell your home and throw away your career? You disappoint me."

"I'd rather disappoint you than be responsible for the life of a single cop. I'm in no shape to command." He looked down at his hands, flexed them. "I may never be. And as for the house, it should have been sold years ago. After the accident. It would have been sold if Elaine had agreed to it. Now she's gone, too, and it's my decision."

"Yes, it's yours," she agreed. "But it's the wrong one."

Rage sizzled in his blood. He wanted to hit something, someone. It was a feeling that came over him all too often. And because of it, he was no longer Captain J. T. Skimmerhorn of the Philadelphia Police Department, but a civilian. "Can't you understand? I can't live here. I need to get out. I'm smothering here."

"Then come home with me. At least for the holidays. Give yourself a little more time before you do something irreversible." Her voice was gentle again as she took his rigid hands in hers. "Jedidiah, it's been months since Elaine—since Elaine was killed."

"I know." Yes, he knew the exact moment of his sister's death. After all, he'd killed her. "I appreciate the invitation, but I've got plans. I'm looking at an apartment today. On South Street."

"An apartment." Honoria's sigh was ripe with annoyance. "Don't bury yourself in some miserable room, Jedidiah."

"The ad said it was quiet, attractive and well located. That doesn't sound miserable. Grandmother"—he squeezed her hands before she could argue—"let it be."

She sighed, tasting defeat. "I only want what's best for you."

"You always did." He suppressed a shudder, feeling the walls closing in on him. "Let's get out of here."

1

ISADORA Conroy absorbed the magic of the empty theater as she stood in the wings of the Liberty Theater, watching a dress rehearsal for *A Christmas Carol*. As always, she enjoyed Dickens, but also the drama of edgy nerves, of creative lighting, of the well-delivered line. After all, the theater was in her blood.

Her large brown eyes glinted with excitement and seemed to dominate the face framed by golden-brown hair. That excitement brought a flush to ivory skin, a smile to her wide mouth. The energy inside her small, compact body shimmered out. She was a woman interested in everything around her, who believed in illusions. Watching her father rattling Marley's chains at the fear-struck Scrooge, she believed he was no longer her father, but the doomed miser wrapped for eternity in the heavy chains of his own greed.

Then Marley became Quentin Conroy again, veteran actor, director and theater buff, calling for a minute change in the blocking.

"Dora." Hurrying up from behind, Dora's sister, Ophelia, said, "We're already twenty minutes behind schedule."

"We don't have a schedule," Dora murmured, nodding because the blocking change was perfect. "I never have a schedule on a buying trip. Lea, isn't he wonderful?"

Lea glanced out onstage and studied their father. "Yes."

Dora beamed. Leaving the stage hadn't diminished her love of it, or her admiration for the man who had taught her how to milk a line. She'd watched him become hundreds of men onstage—Macbeth, Willie Loman, Nathan Detroit. She'd seen him triumph and seen him bomb. But he always entertained.

"Remember Mom and Dad as Titania and Oberon?"

"Who could forget? Mom stayed in character for weeks. It wasn't easy living with the queen of the fairies. And if we don't get out of here soon, the queen's going to come out and tell us what might happen to two women traveling alone to Virginia."

"Relax, honey," Dora said to her sister. "He's about to take five."

Which he did, on cue. When the actors scattered, Dora stepped out to center stage. "Dad, you were great."

"Thank you, my sweet. I think the makeup is an improvement over last year."

"Absolutely." In fact, the greasepaint and charcoal were alarmingly realistic; his handsome face appeared just short of decay. She kissed him lightly. "Sorry we'll miss opening night."

"Can't be helped." He did pout a little. Although he had a son to carry on the Conroy tradition, he'd lost his two daughters—one to marriage, one to free enterprise. "So my two little girls are off on their adventure." He kissed Lea in turn.

"Oh, Lea!" Trixie Conroy, resplendent in her costume, complete with bustle and feathered hat, rushed out onstage. "John's on the phone, dear. He couldn't remember if Missy had a Scout meeting tonight at five or a piano lesson at six."

"I left a list," Lea muttered. "How's he going to manage the kids for three days if he can't read a list?"

"Such a sweet man," Trixie commented when Lea dashed off. "The perfect son-in-law. Now, Dora, you will drive carefully?"

"Yes, Mom."

"It's an awfully long way to Virginia. And it might snow."

"I have snow tires." Dora gave her mother a kiss. "And a phone in the van. I'll check in every time we cross a state line."

"Won't that be fun?" The idea cheered Trixie enormously. "Oh, and Quentin, darling, we're sold out for the week."

"Naturally. A Conroy expects no less than standing room only."

"Break a leg." Dora kissed her mother again. "You, too, Dad," she said. "And don't forget you're showing the apartment later today."

"I never forget an engagement. Places!" he called out, then winked at his daughter. "Bon voyage, my sweet."

Dora could hear his chains clanging when she hit the wings.

To Dora's way of thinking, an auction house was very like a theater. You had the stage, the props, the characters. As she had explained to her baffled parents years before, she wasn't really retiring from the stage. She was merely exploring another medium.

She'd already taken the time to study the arena for today's performance. The building where Sherman Porter held his auctions had originally been a drafty slaughterhouse. Merchandise was displayed on an icy concrete floor, where people who were huddled in coats and mufflers wandered through, poking at glassware and debating over paintings and china cabinets and carved headboards.

Isadora Conroy loved a bargain. She'd always loved to buy and all too often had exchanged money for objects she had no use for. But it was that love of a bargain that had led Dora into opening her own shop, and the discovery that selling was as pleasurable as buying.

"Lea, look at this." Dora offered a gilded cream dispenser shaped like a woman's evening slipper. "Isn't it fabulous?"

Ophelia Conroy Bradshaw lifted a single honey-brown eyebrow. "I think you mean frivolous, right?"

"Come on, there's a place for ridiculous in the world."

"I know. Your shop."

Dora chuckled. Though she replaced the creamer, she'd already decided to bid on that lot. She noted the number. "I'm really glad you came along on this trip, Lea. You keep me centered."

"Somebody has to. Still, I feel guilty being away from home this close to Christmas. Leaving John with the kids that way."

"You were dying to get away," Dora reminded her. Tossing one end of her red muffler over her shoulder, Dora crouched down to check a lady's cherry wood vanity. "Honey, it's only been three days. You'll be home tonight, and you can smother the kids with attention, seduce John, and everybody'll be happy."

Lea rolled her eyes and smiled weakly.

Dora straightened, shook her hair from her face and nodded. "I've seen enough for now. We'd better get some seats before— Oh, wait!" Her brown eyes brightened. "Look." Dora scurried across the floor.

It was the painting that had caught her attention. It wasn't large, perhaps eighteen by twenty-four inches, with a simple, streamlined ebony frame. The canvas was a wash of color—streaks of crimson and sapphire, a dollop of citrine, a bold dash of emerald.

Dora smiled at the boy who was propping the painting against the wall. "You've got it upside down."

"Huh?" The stock boy turned. "Uh, no, ma'am." He turned the canvas around to show Dora the hook at the back.

"Mmm." When she owned it—and she would—she'd fix that.

"This shipment just came in."

"I see." She stepped closer. "Some interesting pieces," she said, and picked up a statue of a sad-eyed basset hound curled up in a resting pose. No craftsman's mark or date, but the workmanship was excellent.

"Frivolous enough for you?" Lea asked.

"Just. Make a terrific doorstop." After setting it down, Dora reached for a tall figurine of a man and woman in antebellum dress, caught in the swirl of a waltz. Dora's hand closed over thick, gnarled fingers. "Sorry." She glanced up at an elderly, bespectacled man.

"Pretty, isn't it?" he asked her, grinning. "My wife had one just like it. Got busted when the kids were wrestling in the parlor."

Dora smiled back. "Do you collect?"

"In a manner of speaking." He set the figurine down and his old, shrewd eyes swept the display—pricing, cataloguing, dismissing. "I'm Tom Ashworth. Got a shop here in Front Royal. Accumulated so much stuff over the years, it was open a shop or buy a bigger house."

"I know what you mean. I'm Dora Conroy." She held out a hand. "I have a shop in Philadelphia."

"Thought you were a pro." Pleased, he winked. "Don't believe I've seen you at one of Porter's auctions before."

"No. I've never been able to make it. Actually, this trip was an impulse. I dragged my sister along. Lea, Tom Ashworth."

"Nice to meet you."

"My pleasure."

"Have you been in business long, Mr. Ashworth?" Lea asked.

"Nigh onto forty years. The wife got us started, crocheting doilies and scarves and selling them. Worked side by side in the shop till she passed on in the spring of '86. Now I got me a grandson working with me. Got a lot of fancy ideas, but he's a good boy."

"Family businesses are the best," Dora said. "Lea's just started working part time at the shop."

"Lord knows why. I don't know anything about antiques."

"You just have to figure out what people want," Ashworth told her. "And how much they'll pay for it."

"Exactly." Delighted with him, Dora hooked a hand through his arm. "It looks like we're getting started. Why don't we find seats?"

Ashworth offered Lea his other arm and, feeling like the cock of the walk, escorted the women to chairs near the front row. Dora pulled out her notebook and prepared to play her favorite role.

The bidding was low but energetic. Dora bought the cherry wood vanity, snapped up the lot that included the creamer/slipper and competed briskly with Ashworth for a set of crystal saltcellars.

"Got me," he said when Dora topped his bid yet again.

"I've got a customer who collects," she told him.

"That so?" Ashworth leaned closer as the bidding began on the next lot. "I've got a set of six at the shop. Cobalt and silver. You got time, you drop on by after this and take a look."

"I might just do that. Now, here we go." Spotting the abstract painting, Dora rubbed her hands together. "Mine," she said softly.

BY THREE o'clock Dora was in front of Mr. Ashworth's shop, adding half a dozen cobalt saltcellars to the treasures in her van.

"It was great meeting you, Mr. Ashworth." She offered her hand. "If you get up to Philadelphia, I'll expect you to drop by."

"You can count on it. Take care of yourselves. Drive safely."

"We will. Merry Christmas." Dora climbed into the van.

15

With a last wave she started the van and pulled away. She smiled as she saw Ashworth standing with his hand lifted in a salute.

"What a sweetheart. I'm glad he got that figurine."

Lea shivered and waited impatiently for the van to heat. "I still can't believe you bought that hideous painting, Dory. You'll never be able to sell it. At least you only paid fifty dollars for it."

Dora shrugged. "Fifty-two seventy-five."

With a sigh Lea settled back. "This time tomorrow, I'll be baking cookies and rolling out pie dough."

"You asked for it. You had to get married, have kids, buy a house. Where else is the family going to have Christmas dinner?"

"I wouldn't mind if Mom didn't insist on helping me cook it."

"Maybe Will can distract her. Is he coming alone or with one of his sweeties?" Dora asked, referring to their brother's list of glamorous dates.

"Alone, last I heard. Dora, watch that truck, will you?"

Dora gunned the engine to pass a sixteen-wheeler. "So when's Will getting in?"

"He's taking a late train out of New York on Christmas Eve."

"Late enough to make a grand entrance," Dora predicted. "Oh, I just remembered. That new tenant Dad signed up is moving in across the hall today. I hope Dad remembers to be there with the keys. You know how absentminded he is when he's in the middle of a production."

"I know, which is why I can't understand how you could let him interview a tenant for your building. Just don't be surprised if you end up across the hall from a psychopath."

Dora smiled. "I specifically told Dad no psychopaths." She swung toward the exit ramp, imagining unpacking her new possessions. The very first thing she would do, she promised herself, was find the perfect spot for the painting.

HIGH in the glittery tower of a silver building overlooking the cramped streets of L.A., Edmund Finley enjoyed his weekly manicure. The wall directly across from his rosewood desk flickered with a dozen television screens—CNN Headline News and one of the home-shopping networks. Other screens were tuned in to offices in his organization so that he could observe his employees.

But unless he chose to listen in, the only sounds in the vast sweep of his office were the strains of a Mozart opera.

Finley liked to watch. His top-floor office gave him the feeling of power, and he would often stand at the wide window behind his desk and study the comings and goings of strangers far below. In his home, far up in the hills above the city, there were television screens and monitors in every room. And again, windows where he could look down on the lights of the L.A. basin. Every evening he would stand on the balcony outside his bedroom and imagine owning everything, everyone, for as far as his eye could see.

Edmund Finley—a tall, spare, distinguished-looking man in his early fifties who looked much younger—acquired. And once he acquired, he hoarded. His office reflected his taste for the exclusive. A Ming vase graced a marble pedestal. Sculptures by Rodin and Denécheau filled niches in the white walls. A Renoir hung above a Louis Quatorze commode. Two high glass cabinets held a stunning and esoteric display of *objets d'art:* carved snuff bottles of lapis and aquamarine, ivory netsukes, Dresden figurines, Limoges ring boxes, African masks.

His import-export business was enormously successful. His smuggling sideline more so. After all, smuggling was more of a challenge. It required a certain finesse and a ruthless ingenuity.

"You're all done, Mr. Finley." The manicurist placed Finley's hand gently on the spotless blotter on his desk. He smiled down at his buffed nails.

"Excellent work." Taking a gold money clip from his pocket, Finley peeled off a fifty. "Merry Christmas, dear."

"Oh, thank you, Mr. Finley. Merry Christmas to you, too."

Still smiling, he dismissed her with a wave. Before the door had closed behind her, he had swiveled in his chair and, through the stream of sunlight, studied his view of Los Angeles.

Christmas, he thought. What a lovely time of year. One of goodwill toward men, ringing bells and colored lights. Of course, it was also the time of desperate loneliness, despair and suicide. But those small human tragedies didn't touch or concern him. Money had catapulted him above those fragile needs for companionship and family. He could buy companionship.

The knock on his door made him turn as he called out, "Enter."

17

"Sir." Abel Winesap, a small man with the heavy title of executive assistant, cleared his throat. "Mr. Finley."

"Do you know the true meaning of Christmas, Abel?" Finley's voice was warm. "Acquisition. A lovely word, don't you agree?"

"Yes, sir." Winesap shivered. What he had come to report was difficult enough. Finley's happy mood made the difficult more dangerous. "I'm afraid we have a problem, Mr. Finley."

"Oh?" Finley's smile remained, but his eyes frosted.

Winesap gulped in fear. He knew that Finley's frigid anger was lethal. It was Winesap who had been chosen to witness Finley's termination of an employee who had been embezzling. And he remembered how calmly Finley had slit the man's throat with a sixteenth-century jeweled dagger. Betrayal, Finley believed, deserved quick punishment, and some ceremony.

Nervously Winesap continued with his story. "The shipment from New York, sir. The merchandise you were expecting . . ."

"Has there been a delay?"

"No. That is, the shipment arrived today as expected, but the merchandise . . ." He moistened his thin, nervous lips. "It isn't what you ordered, sir. Apparently there was a mix-up somewhere."

Finley placed his pampered hands on the edge of the desk. "Where is it?" His voice was a chilly hiss.

"In receiving, sir. I thought—"

"Bring it up. Immediately."

"Right away, sir." Winesap escaped, grateful for the reprieve.

Finley had paid a great deal of money for the merchandise, and even more to have that merchandise concealed and smuggled. Having each piece stolen, disguised, then transported from various locations to his factory in New York. Why, the bribes alone had run close to six figures. To calm himself, he poured generously from a decanter of guava juice. And if there had been a mistake, he thought, steadier, it would be rectified. Whoever had erred would be punished.

There was a knock on his door. "Come," he snapped out, and waited as one of his receiving clerks wheeled in a crate. "Leave it there. And go. Abel, remain. The door," he said.

Winesap scurried to shut it behind the departing clerk and walked back to the crate. "I opened it as you instructed, Mr. Finley." Gingerly he dipped his hand into a sea of shredded paper. His fingers trembled as he pulled out a china teapot.

Finley took the teapot, turning it over in his hands. It was English, a lovely piece, worth perhaps two hundred dollars on the open market. But it was mass-produced, so to him it was worthless. He smashed it against the edge of the crate and sent shards flying.

"What else?"

Quaking, Winesap drew out a swirling glass vase.

Italian, Finley deduced as he inspected it. Handmade. A value of perhaps one hundred and fifty dollars. He hurled it against the wall.

"Where is my merchandise?" he demanded.

"Sir, I can't— I believe there's been . . . an error."

"An error." Finley's eyes were like jade as he clenched his fists at his sides. DiCarlo, he thought, conjuring up an image of his man in New York. Young, bright, ambitious. But not stupid, not enough to attempt a double cross. Still, he would pay dearly for this.

"Get DiCarlo on the phone."

"Yes, sir." Winesap darted to the desk to place the call.

Systematically Finley destroyed the rest of the crate's contents.

2

JED Skimmerhorn wanted a drink. But he wasn't going to get one until he'd finished carting boxes up these rickety back steps and into his new apartment.

Not that he had a lot of possessions. His old partner, Brent Chapman, had given him a hand with the heavier pieces of furniture. All that remained were a few cardboard boxes filled with books and assorted junk. He wasn't sure why he'd kept that much. Then again, he wasn't even sure why he'd found it so necessary to move across town into an apartment. It was something about fresh starts. But you couldn't start fresh until you'd ended.

Turning in his resignation had been the first step—perhaps the hardest. The police commissioner had argued, refusing to accept the resignation and putting Jed on extended leave. It didn't matter what it was called, Jed mused. He wasn't a cop anymore. Couldn't be a cop anymore. He'd given fourteen years of his life to the force. It had to be enough.

Jed elbowed open the door to the apartment. He slid the boxes across the wooden floor before heading back down the narrow hallway toward the rear entrance.

He hadn't heard a peep from his neighbor across the hall. The eccentric old man who had rented him the place had said that the second apartment was occupied but that the tenant was as quiet as a mouse. It certainly seemed that way.

Jed started down the outside steps, noting with annoyance that the banister wouldn't hold the weight of a three-year-old. The steps themselves were slick with the sleet that continued to spit out of the colorless sky. It was almost quiet in the back of the building. Though it fronted on Philadelphia's busy South Street, Jed didn't think he'd mind the noise and bohemian atmosphere, the tourists or the shops. In any case, it would be a dramatic change from the manicured lawns of Chestnut Hill, where the Skimmerhorn home had stood for years.

Through the gloom he could see the glow of colored lights strung on the windows of neighboring buildings. It reminded him that Brent had invited him to Christmas dinner. A big, noisy family event that Jed might have enjoyed in the past. There had never been big, noisy family events in his life—or none that were fun.

And now there was no family. No family at all.

He pressed his fingertips to the ache at his temple and willed himself not to think of Elaine. But memories knotted his stomach.

He hauled out the last of the boxes and slammed the trunk with a force that rattled the reconditioned Thunderbird down to its tires. He wasn't going to think of Elaine or Donny Speck or regrets. He was going to go upstairs, pour a drink and think of nothing at all.

Once inside, Jed dumped the last box onto the oak table in the dining area. The apartment was echoingly empty, which only served to satisfy him that he was alone. One of the reasons he'd chosen it was because he'd have only one neighbor to ignore. The other reason was just as simple: it was fabulous.

He imagined the old building had been converted into shop and apartments sometime in the '30s. It had retained its lofty ceilings and spacious rooms, the working fireplace and slim, tall windows. The trim was walnut and uncarved, the walls a creamy ivory.

He unearthed a bottle of Jameson's, three-quarters full. He set it on the table. He was shoving packing paper aside in search of a glass when he heard noises. His hands froze. He turned, trying to locate the source of the sound. He thought he'd heard bells. And now laughter, a smoky drift of it, seductive and female.

His eyes turned to the brass open-worked floor vent near the fireplace. The sounds floated up through it. There was some sort of antiques shop beneath the apartment. It had been closed for the last couple of days, but it was apparently open for business now.

Jed went back to search for a glass and tuned out the sounds.

"I REALLY do appreciate your meeting us here, John," Dora said.

"No problem." Lea's husband huffed a bit as he carted another crate into the overflowing storeroom. He was a tall man with a skinny frame, and an honest face that might have been homely but for the pale eyes that peered out behind thick lenses. He smiled at Dora. "How did you manage to buy so much in such a short time?"

"Experience." She had to rise on her toes to kiss John's cheek; then she bent and scooped up her younger nephew, Michael. "Hey, frogface, did you miss me?"

He grinned and wrapped his pudgy arms around her neck.

Lea turned to keep an eagle eye on her two other children. "Richie, hands in your pockets. Missy, no pirouetting in the shop." Lea sighed, smiled. "I'm home." She held out her arms for Michael. "Dora, do you need any more help?"

"No. I can handle it from here. Thanks again."

Dora herded her family outside, then locked up and engaged the security alarm.

Alone, she turned and took a deep breath. There was the scent of apple and pine from the potpourri set all around the shop. It was good to be home, she thought. She lifted the box that contained the new acquisitions she'd decided to take to her apartment upstairs.

She unlocked the door that led from the storeroom to the inside stairway while juggling the box, her purse, her overnight bag and her coat. She was halfway down the hall when she saw the light spilling out of the neighboring apartment. The new tenant. She walked to the open door and peered in.

She saw him standing by an old table, a bottle in one hand, a glass in the other. The room itself was sparsely furnished with a sofa, an overstuffed chair and some weight-lifting equipment. But she was more interested in the man. He was tall, with a tough, athletic build. He wore a navy sweatshirt and Levi's. His hair was a bit unkempt, falling carelessly over his collar in a rich shade of ripening wheat. In contrast, the watch at his wrist was either an amazingly good knockoff or a genuine Rolex. His face seemed grim.

Before she had made a sound, she saw his body tense. His head whipped around, and he pinned her with eyes that were hard, expressionless and shockingly blue.

"Your door was open," she said apologetically.

"Yeah." He set the bottle down, carrying the glass with him as he crossed to her. Jed took his own survey. A pretty, oval face, slightly pointed at the chin, with an old-fashioned roses-and-cream complexion; a wide, smiling mouth; big brown eyes that were filled with friendly curiosity; a swing of sable-colored hair.

"I'm Dora, from across the hall," she said. "Need any help?"

"No." Jed closed the door in her face.

Her mouth fell open. "Well, welcome to the neighborhood," she muttered. She unlocked her own door and slammed it behind her.

Dora dumped her things on a settee. Marching to her candlestick phone, she decided to call her father and give him an earful.

Before she'd dialed the number, she spotted a sheet of paper with a big heart-shaped happy face drawn at the bottom. Dora hung up the phone and began to read. "Izzy, my darling daughter."

Dora winced. Her father was the only one who called her that.

> The deed is done. Well done, if I say so myself. Your new tenant is a strapping young man who should be able to help you with any menial work. His name, as you see on the copies of the lease, is Jed Skimmerhorn. I found him fascinatingly taciturn. I couldn't think of anything nicer to give my adored daughter than an intriguing neighbor.
>
> Your devoted father

Dora couldn't help smiling. The move was so obvious.

"Sorry, Dad," she murmured. "You're in for a disappointment."

Setting the note aside, she skimmed a finger down the lease until she came to Jed's signature and dashed her own name on both copies. Lifting one, she strode to her door and across the hall and knocked.

When the door opened, Dora thrust the lease out, crushing the corner against Jed's chest. "You'll need this for your records."

He took it. Her eyes weren't friendly now, but cool. Which suited him. "Why'd the old man leave this with you?"

Her chin tilted up. "The old man," she said in mild tones, "is my father. I own the building, which makes me your landlord." She turned on her heel and was across the hall in two strides. With her hand on the knob she paused, turned. "The rent's due on the twenty-first of each month. You can slip the check under my door and save yourself a stamp, as well as any contact with other humans."

She slipped inside and closed the door with a satisfied snick.

JED spent a satisfying ninety minutes at the gym around the corner the next morning, lifting weights and burning away most of his morning-after headache in the steam room. Now, feeling almost human, he craved a pot of black coffee. He pulled his key out of the pocket of his sweats and let himself into the hallway. He heard music, the rich-throated wail of Aretha Franklin. At least his landlord's taste in music wouldn't irritate him, he mused.

He noted her open door. An even trade, Jed figured, and wandered over. He knew he'd been deliberately rude the night before, and he thought it wise to make peace with the woman who owned his building. He nudged the door open a bit wider and stared.

Like his, her apartment was spacious, high-ceilinged and full of light from the front windows. That was where the similarity ended. He'd never seen so much stuff crammed into one single space. Glass shelves covered one wall and were loaded with knickknacks. There were a number of tables, each of them topped by glassware and china. A floral couch was loaded with colored pillows that picked up the faded tones of a large area rug. A Multan, he recognized. There'd been a similar rug in his family's front parlor for as long as he could remember. To complement the season, there was a Christmas tree by the window, laden with colored balls and lights.

It should have been messy, Jed thought. Instead, he had the impression of having opened some magic treasure chest.

In the midst of it was his landlord. She wore a scarlet suit with a short skirt and a fitted jacket over her nifty little body. Jed leaned against the doorjamb as she propped the painting she'd been hold-

23

ing on the sofa and turned. To her credit she managed to muffle most of the squeal when she spotted him.

"Your door was open," he told her.

"Yeah." She shrugged. "I've been recirculating inventory this morning—from up here to downstairs." She crossed the room and stood beside a pedestal dining-room table, pouring what smelled gloriously like strong coffee from a china pot into a matching cup. Dora set the pot back down and lifted a brow. Her unsmiling lips were as boldly red as her suit. "Is there something you need?"

He nodded toward the pot. "Some of that wouldn't hurt."

Saying nothing, Dora set down her cup, went to a curved glass cabinet and took out another cup and saucer. "Cream? Sugar?"

"No."

When he didn't come any farther into the room, she took the coffee to him. His eyes were hard and inscrutable.

"Thanks." He downed the contents of the fragile cup in two swallows. He looked back at the painting, studied it for a moment. Bold, he thought, like her color scheme, like the punch-in-the-gut scent she wore. "You know, that's upside down."

Her smile came quickly, brilliantly. She had indeed set it on the sofa the way it had been displayed at auction. "I think so, too." She went over and flipped it.

Jed narrowed his eyes. "It's still ugly, but it's right side up."

"The appreciation of art is as individual as art itself."

"If you say so. Thanks for the coffee." He handed his cup back.

"You're welcome. Oh, Skimmerhorn?"

He stopped, glanced back over his shoulder.

"If you're thinking of sprucing up your new place, come on down to the shop. Dora's Parlor has something for everybody."

"I don't need anything."

Dora was still smiling when she heard his door close. "Wrong, Skimmerhorn," she murmured. "Everybody needs something."

Cooling his heels in a dusty office of Premium Shipping wasn't how Anthony DiCarlo had pictured spending this morning. He wanted answers, and he wanted them now.

More to the point, Finley wanted answers yesterday. The phone call from L.A. the day before had been crystal clear. Find the merchandise within twenty-four hours or pay the consequences.

DiCarlo had no intention of discovering what those consequences were. He looked at the big clock—less than fifteen hours.

Through the wide glass panel stenciled with an overweight Santa, he could see more than a dozen shipping clerks busily stamping and hauling. DiCarlo sneered as the enormously fat shipping supervisor with the incredibly bad toupee approached the door.

"Mr. DiCarlo, so sorry to keep you waiting. As you can imagine, we're pretty frantic around here these days." Bill Tarkington waddled around his desk to his coffee machine. "Some coffee?"

"No. There's been an error, Mr. Tarkington," DiCarlo said, his fury clear. "An error that must be corrected immediately."

"Well, can you give me the specifics?"

"The merchandise I directed to Abel Winesap in Los Angeles was not the merchandise that arrived there." DiCarlo took the shipping invoice from his inside breast pocket.

"That's an odd one." Tarkington rattled the keys on his computer. "That was to ship out on December seventeenth. Yep, yep, there she is." He sipped some coffee. "Oh, wait, I remember. We provided the crate and the packing, and you supervised. So how in the world did merchandise get switched?"

"That is my question," DiCarlo hissed, slamming the desk.

Tarkington hit a few more keys. "That shipment went out of section three. Let's see who was on the belt that day. Ah, Opal."

"I want to speak to her."

Tarkington leaned forward and flicked a switch on his desk. "Opal Johnson, please report to Mr. Tarkington's office."

THE nightmare that had plagued Opal for nearly a week was coming true. The tall, striking black woman had worked three double shifts last week and was late one day. She was so rushed that she mixed up the invoices. "I'm sorry. I dropped them. I thought I put everything back, but I wasn't sure." She sobbed now to DiCarlo as she stood before him. "I went through all the paperwork yesterday. There was only one other oversized crate that came through that morning. I wrote down the address." She fished it from her purse. He snatched it. "Sherman Porter, Front Royal, Virginia."

DiCarlo slipped the paper into his pocket. "I'll check this out."

25

3

AT THE main counter in her shop, Dora put the finishing touch of a big red bow on a brightly wrapped box. "She'll love them, Mr. O'Malley." Dora patted the box containing the cobalt saltcellars.

"Well, I appreciate your calling me, Miss Conroy. I don't know what Hester sees in these things, but she sure sets store by them."

"You're going to be her hero. Happy Christmas, Mr. O'Malley."

"Same to you and yours." He walked out, a satisfied customer.

There were half a dozen customers in the shop, two being helped by Dora's assistant, Terri Starr, who was also a member of the Conroys' acting troupe. Dora skirted the counter.

"Oh, miss?"

Dora turned, smiling. There was something vaguely familiar about the stout matron with lacquered black hair.

"Yes, ma'am. May I help you?"

She gestured toward a display table. "Are these doorstops?"

"Yes, they are. Of course, they can be used for whatever you like." Automatically Dora glanced over as the bells jingled on her door. She merely lifted a brow when Jed walked in. "Several of these are from the Victorian period," she went on. "The most common material was cast iron." She lifted one in the shape of a basket of fruit. "This one was probably used for a drawing room."

"My niece, Sharon, and her husband just moved into their first house," the woman said. "I'd like to get them a house present."

"Was there a reason you had a doorstop in mind?"

"Yes, actually. My niece does a lot of sewing. It's an old house, you see, and the door to her sewing room won't stay open. Since they have a baby on the way, I know she'd want to be able to keep an ear out." Still, she hesitated. "I bought Sharon a chamber pot here a few months ago for her birthday. She loved it."

That clicked. "The Sunderland, with the frog painted inside."

The woman's eyes brightened. "Why, yes. You remembered."

"I was very fond of that piece, Mrs. . . ."

"Lyle. Alice Lyle."

"Mrs. Lyle, yes. I'm glad it found a good home." Dora tapped a finger to her lips. "If she liked that, maybe she'd appreciate something along these lines." She chose a brass figure of an elephant. "It's Jumbo," she explained. "P. T. Barnum's?"

"Yes." The woman chuckled as Dora passed Jumbo to her. "He's perfect." She took a quick, discreet glance at the tag dangling from Jumbo's front foot. "Yes, definitely."

"Would you like him gift-boxed?"

"Yes, thank you." She picked up the sleeping hound Dora had purchased at auction only the day before. "I think I'll take him along, too—a nice, cozy watchdog for the nursery. You do take Visa?"

"Of course. This will just take a few minutes. Why don't you help yourself to some coffee while you wait." Dora gestured to a table that was always set with tea and coffeepots and trays of pretty cookies. She carried the doorstops back to the counter. "Christmas shopping, Skimmerhorn?" she asked as she passed him.

"I need a— What do you call it? Hostess thing."

"Browse around. I'll be right with you."

Jed wasn't completely sure what he was browsing around in. The packed apartment was only a small taste of the amazing array of merchandise offered in Dora's Parlor. Bottles of varying sizes and colors caught the glitter of sunlight and begged to be handled. Tin soldiers arranged in battle lines fought beside old war posters.

He wandered into the next room and found it equally packed. Teddy bears and teapots. Cuckoo clocks and corkscrews. A junk shop, he mused. Idly he picked up a small enameled box decorated with painted roses. Mary Pat would like this, he decided.

"Well, Skimmerhorn, you surprise me." Dora smiled and gestured toward the box he held. "You show excellent taste. That piece is a Staffordshire, circa 1770." There was a laugh in her eyes. "It goes for twenty-five hundred."

"This?" It didn't fill the cup of his palm.

"Well, it is a George the Third."

"Yeah, right." He put it back on the table with the same care he would have used with an explosive device. The fact that he could afford it didn't make it any less intimidating. He grunted and scanned the room, afraid to touch anything now. "Maybe I should just pick up some flowers."

"That's nice, too. Of course, they don't last." Dora was enjoying his look of pure discomfort. "Tell me a little about our hostess so that I can help you select something. Is she the athletic, outdoors type or a quiet homebody who bakes her own bread?"

"She's my partner—ex-partner's wife. She's a trauma nurse. She's got three kids and likes to read books."

"All right. We have a busy, dedicated woman. A hostess gift. It shouldn't be too personal. Something for the house." She walked to a corner resembling an old-fashioned pantry. "This would do nicely." Dora took down a footed wooden jar trimmed in brass.

Jed frowned over it. "What's it for—like cookies?"

Dora beamed at him. "It's a biscuit jar. Victorian. This one's oak, from about 1870. A practical and ornamental gift, and at forty dollars it won't cost you more than a dozen long-stem roses."

"Okay. I guess she'd get a kick out of it."

"See? That wasn't so painful. Can I help you with anything else?"

"No, that's it." He followed her back into the main room. The place smelled cozy, he decided. Like apples. There was music playing softly. He recognized a movement from the *Nutcracker* and was surprised that he suddenly felt relaxed. "You actually make a living out of all this?" he asked her.

Amused, she unfolded a box. "People collect, Skimmerhorn. Didn't you ever have comic books as a boy, or baseball cards?"

"Sure." He'd had to hide them, but he'd had them.

She lined the box with tissue, working quickly, competently. She glanced up to find him staring down at her hands.

His gaze lifted, locked on hers. He'd felt something watching her work that had gone straight to the gut, like a hot arrow. "Just like you played with dolls," he said.

"Actually, I never liked them much. I preferred imaginary playmates because you could change them into any character you wanted." With more care than necessary she fit the lid on, with its gold-embossed DORA'S PARLOR. "What I was getting at is that most children collect and trade. Some people never grow out of it. Shall I gift wrap this for you? There's no extra charge."

"Yeah, go ahead."

He moved down the counter to give himself some breathing room. The sexual tug he'd felt wasn't new, but it was the first time he'd experienced it because a woman had pretty hands. And huge brown eyes, he added. Then there was that smile, he thought.

Dora set the gaily wrapped package in front of him. "I hope your friend likes her gift." She watched as Jed left the shop.

An unusual man, she mused. The unusual was her stock-in-trade.

DiCARLO raced along the Van Wyck Expressway toward La Guardia Airport, dialing his car phone. "DiCarlo," he stated, flipping the phone to speaker. "Get me Mr. Finley." With his nerves bubbling, he checked his watch. He'd make it, he assured himself.

Finley's voice filled the car. "Mr. DiCarlo."

"I tracked it all down, Mr. Finley." DiCarlo forced his words into a calm tone. "Some idiot clerk at Premium sent our shipment to Front Royal, Virginia. I'll straighten it out in no time."

"I see. And what is your definition of 'no time'?"

"I'm on my way to the airport right now. I've got a flight booked into Dulles and a rental car waiting. I'll be in Front Royal before five, East Coast time." His voice weakened. "I'm handling all of this at my own expense, Mr. Finley."

"That's wise of you, Mr. DiCarlo. You do know how important that merchandise is to me, don't you? You will use any means necessary to recover it. Any means at all."

"Understood." DiCarlo was more than ready to do just that.

"THIS is quite a mix-up, isn't it?" While he asked this rhetorical—and to DiCarlo unamusing—question, Sherman Porter rummaged through his dented file cabinet. "Guess we'd have caught it here, but we had ourselves an auction going on," Porter continued. "Moved a lot of inventory." He opened another file drawer.

DiCarlo looked at his watch. Six fifteen. Time was running out.

"Here now, this looks promising." Porter unearthed a short stack of neatly typed invoices and handed them over.

DiCarlo took out his own list and compared. It was all there, he noted, torn between relief and despair. All sold. The china hound, the porcelain figurine, the abstract painting, the bronze eagle and the stuffed parrot. The enormous and ugly plaster replica of the Statue of Liberty was gone as well.

Inside his pocket DiCarlo had another list. On it were descriptions of what had been carefully and expensively hidden in each piece of merchandise. An engraved Gallé vase valued at nearly one hundred thousand dollars. An antique sapphire brooch, reputed to have been worn by Mary, Queen of Scots. The list went on.

Despite the chill of the room, his skin grew clammy. Not one item remained in Porter's possession. "Nothing left," DiCarlo said weakly.

"We had a good turnout," Porter said, pleased with the memory. "That shipment came in just minutes before we started the auction, and there wasn't time to do an inventory. Best I can say is, go through a mailing list of our customers, match up the names and addresses with the names there next to the stuff we sold. You can get in touch, explain things."

It would take days to round up Finley's stock, DiCarlo thought, sickened. Weeks.

Porter shuffled through a drawer and came up with the mailing list. "Go ahead, take your time. I'm not in any hurry."

TWENTY minutes later DiCarlo left, with one bright pinpoint of hope. The porcelain figurine was still in Front Royal, the property of a Thomas Ashworth, antiques dealer. Regaining possession of one piece quickly might placate Finley and buy time.

As he drove through light traffic to Ashworth's shop, DiCarlo worked out his strategy. Since Ashworth had paid only forty-five dollars for the figurine, DiCarlo was prepared to buy it back and include a reasonable profit for the dealer. Once he had the figurine, he would tell Finley everything was under control. With any luck Finley would have Winesap contact the rest of the list and DiCarlo would be back in New York to enjoy Christmas.

The scenario brightened his mood. It wasn't until he had parked in front of Ashworth's shop that his smile faded. Closed.

DiCarlo got out of the car and rattled the knob, pounding on the glass-fronted door. He raced to the display window, cupping his hands beside his face. He could see nothing but his own misery.

Finley would accept no excuses, he knew—nothing so vague as simple bad luck. Then DiCarlo saw the porcelain figurine of a man and woman in balldress. He clenched his gloved hands into fists.

He moved the car two blocks away. From his glove compartment he took a flashlight, a screwdriver, his revolver. He slipped them all into the pockets of his cashmere coat.

This time he headed up a side street toward the rear entrance of

Ashworth's shop. As he walked, his eyes darted from side to side, watchful, wary. It was a small town, and on a cold, blustery night most citizens were home. DiCarlo passed no one.

Nor did he spot any evidence of a security system. Moving quickly, he used the screwdriver to jimmy the door. The sound of splintering wood made him smile. DiCarlo slipped inside, shut the door behind him. He flicked on his flashlight, shielding the beam with his hand as he swung it right and left. To make the break-in appear to be a random burglary, DiCarlo smashed a milk-glass lamp and kicked over a table of demitasses. On impulse, for the thrill of stealing, he dropped a few cloisonné boxes into his pockets.

He was grinning when he snatched up the figurine. "Gotcha, baby," he murmured, then froze as light flooded into the shop from a stairway to his right. Swearing, DiCarlo squeezed himself between a rosewood armoire and a brass pole lamp.

"I've called the police." An elderly man wearing a gray flannel robe and carrying a nine iron inched down the steps.

For a moment DiCarlo was baffled as he smelled roasted chicken. The old man had an apartment upstairs, DiCarlo realized, and cursed himself for crashing through the shop. But there wasn't time for regrets. Tucking the figurine under his arm like a football, he hurtled toward Ashworth.

The old man grunted on impact, teetered on the steps, his bathrobe flapping over legs as thin and sharp as pencils. Wheezing, Ashworth swung the golf club. DiCarlo grabbed it and Ashworth pitched forward. His head hit a cast-iron coal shuttle with an ominous crack.

Disgusted, DiCarlo shoved Ashworth over. In the spill of the upstairs light he could see the flow of blood, the open staring eyes. Fury had him kicking the body twice before he pulled himself back.

He was half a block away when he heard the sound of sirens.

"You have news for me?" Finley said.

"Yes. Yes, sir. I have the porcelain figurine with me, Mr. Finley, as well as a list locating all the other merchandise." DiCarlo spoke from his car phone as he drove back toward Dulles International.

Finley waited a beat. "Explain."

DiCarlo began with Sherman Porter, pausing every few seconds. "There was a bit of a problem in recovering the figurine, sir. An antiques dealer in Front Royal had purchased it. His shop was closed when I arrived, and knowing that you wanted results quickly, I broke in to retrieve it. Mr. Finley, the dealer's dead."

"I see. So I assume you took care of this Porter."

"Took care of?"

"He can link you to the . . . accident, correct? And a link to you, Mr. DiCarlo, is a link to me. I suggest you snap the link quickly. After you've finished tidying up in Virginia, I'll expect you here, with the figurine. We'll discuss the next steps."

"You want me in California? Mr. Finley—"

"By noon, Mr. DiCarlo. We'll be closing early tomorrow. The holidays, you know. Contact Winesap with your flight information."

"Yes, sir." DiCarlo broke the connection. He hoped Porter was still in his office so he could put a bullet in the man's brain.

"REALLY, Andrew, *really,* there's no need for you to walk me up."

Andrew Dawd, a C.P.A. who considered tax shelters the height of intrigue, gave a hearty laugh and pinched Dora's cheek. "Now, Dora, my mother taught me to always see the girl to her door."

"Well, Mama's not here." She inched up the steps. "And it's late."

"It's not even eleven. You're going to send me off without a cup of coffee? You know you make the best coffee in Philadelphia."

"It's a gift." She was searching for some polite way to refuse when the outside door slammed open, slammed shut.

Jed strode down the hall. His scarred leather bomber jacket was left unzipped over a sweatshirt and jeans. His hair was windblown, his face unshaved—which suited the surly look in his eye.

Dora had to wonder why, at that moment, she preferred Jed's dangerous look to the three-piece-suited, buffed and polished accountant beside her. "Skimmerhorn," she said.

Jed summed up Dora's date with one glance as he fit his key into his lock. "Conroy," he said, and slipped inside and closed the door.

Andrew's well-groomed eyebrows rose. "Your new tenant?"

"Yes." Dora sighed. She unlocked the door and let Andrew in.

Frowning, he folded his overcoat neatly over the back of a chair. Too frustrated for tidiness, Dora tossed her mink, circa 1925, toward the couch on her way to the kitchen. While she ground coffee beans in the hand-cranked grinder, she glanced at Andrew.

"Why don't you go put on some music, Andrew?"

"Music?" His bland face cleared. "Of course. Mood."

Moments later she heard the quiet strains of an old Johnny Mathis recording. She thought, Uh-oh, then shrugged. If she couldn't handle an accountant who wore Brooks Brothers suits and Halston cologne, she deserved to pay the price. "The coffee'll be a few minutes," she said as she walked back into the living room.

Andrew was admiring Dora in the short black dress covered with bugle beads. Suddenly he glided over the rug and clamped her to him. Before she could comment, his hands grabbed her bottom.

"Hey!" Furious, she reared back, freeing herself.

"Oh, Dora, Dora, you're so beautiful, so irresistible."

He pressed her against the side of a chair. Dora felt her balance going. "Well, resist, or I'll have to hurt you," she said.

He only continued to mumble seductive phrases as he tumbled with her to the floor, ramming against the coffee table and sending several of her treasures crashing down. Enough was enough. Dora brought her knee up between Andrew's thighs. Even as he grunted, she popped him hard in the eye.

"Off!" she shouted, shoving at him. Groaning, he rolled, curling up like a boiled shrimp. Dora scrambled to her feet.

He heaved himself up. "You're crazy," he managed.

"You're right. Absolutely." She picked up his coat and held it out, impatience snapping around her. "Go away, Andrew."

He snatched the coat from her. "I took you out to dinner."

"Consider it a bad investment. I'm sure you can find a way to deduct it." She yanked open her door just as Jed opened his across the hall. "Out! And you're fired." Andrew scurried off, and Dora stood catching her breath. The quiet sound of Jed clearing his throat had her spinning back. He was grinning.

"See something funny, Skimmerhorn?" she said.

He thought about it. "Yeah." He leaned against the doorjamb and continued to grin. "Interesting date, Conroy?"

"Fascinating." Dora let out a long breath. "Want a drink?"

"Sure."

She went into her apartment and tossed her shoes aside.

He glanced at the broken china on the floor. That must have been the crash he'd heard. He'd had a bad moment deciding whether to intervene. Even when he'd carried a badge, he'd worried more about answering a domestic dispute than collaring a pro.

He looked over at Dora while she poured brandy into snifters. Her face was still flushed, her eyes narrowed.

"So, who was the jerk?" he asked.

"My former accountant." Dora handed Jed a snifter. "He spends the evening boring me into a coma talking about capital gains, then figures he can rip my clothes off." Pouting, she crouched over the broken bric-a-brac. "Look at this." She held up a broken cup. "This was Derby, 1815. And this ashtray was Manhattan."

"It's trash now. Get a broom or something."

She rose and went out to the kitchen. She came back waving a whisk broom and dustpan. "I bet the guy was an Eagle Scout."

"Probably had a change of underwear in his overcoat pocket," Jed said. Gently he took the broom from her.

Dora winced as Jed dumped a load of broken glass into a trash can. "Were you?" Resigned, she sat on the arm of the chair. The theatrics, it seemed, were over. "An Eagle Scout."

He dumped the last load, then sent her a long look. "No. I was a delinquent. Watch your feet here. I might have missed some."

"Thanks. So what do you do now?"

"You ought to know. I filled out an application."

"I didn't have a chance to read it."

He smiled. "I'm independently wealthy."

"Oh. So what do you do with yourself all day?"

"Nothing much."

"I could keep you busy. That is, if you're any good with your hands. What I mean is, I need some new shelves in the storeroom."

"Your outside banister's a joke," he said.

"Oh." Her lips moved into a pout. "Can you fix it?"

"Probably. I'll think about it." He was thinking about something else at the moment—about how badly he wanted to touch her. Just a brush of his thumb along the curve of her throat. He couldn't say why, but he wanted to do that, only that. Annoyed with himself, Jed set aside his snifter and moved past her to pick up the trash can. "I'll take this to the kitchen for you."

"Thanks." She had to swallow. There was something about the way the man looked at her that sent weird jangles through her system. Stupid, she told herself. It had simply been an exhausting day. She started toward the kitchen. "Really, thanks," she said again. "If you hadn't come in, I'd be kicking things."

"That's all right. I liked watching you kick him out."

She smiled. "Why?"

"I didn't like his suit." He stopped in the doorway.

With the smile still curving her lips, she glanced up. Jed followed her gaze and studied the sprig of mistletoe over his head.

"Cute," he said, and because he was a man who'd decided to stop taking chances, he started to move past her.

"Hey." Amused by the situation and his reaction, Dora caught his arm. "Bad luck," she told him. Hiking up to her toes, she brushed her mouth lightly over his. "I don't like to risk bad luck."

He reacted instinctively and brought his mouth down on hers in a kiss that had the blood draining out of her head. Her lips parted helplessly under his. It was quick—seconds only—but when he released her, she rocked back down on her heels, eyes wide.

He stared down at her for a moment, cursing himself and fighting a vicious urge to do exactly what the idiot accountant had tried.

"Lock your door, Conroy," he said softly. He walked out.

4

"WHAT are you so cranky about?" Lea demanded. She'd popped back into the storeroom to announce a five-hundred-dollar sale and had been greeted, for the third time that morning, by a short snarl.

"I'm not cranky," Dora snapped. "I'm busy." She was boxing up a place setting of Fire-King dinnerware, honeysuckle pattern.

"I know something's wrong." Lea crossed her arms. "Spill it."

There was no way Dora was going to admit that she'd let one kiss tie her up into knots. She wrapped the last cup in newspaper. "Where's that stupid packing tape?" She turned, then stumbled back against the desk when she spotted Jed at the base of the stairs.

"I came to see if you still wanted me to fix that banister," he said.

"Banister? Oh . . . oh, well. You have to get wood or something?"

He looked over when Lea firmly cleared her throat.

"Oh, Lea, Jed Skimmerhorn, the new tenant. Jed, my sister, Lea."

"Nice to meet you." Lea extended a hand. "Settling in all right?"

"Not much to settle. Do you want the banister fixed or not?"

"Sure, go ahead." Dora occupied herself by sealing the carton. "You can slip the bill under my door if I'm not around."

He couldn't resist. "Another hot date?"

She smiled sweetly and yanked open the door. With that, he sauntered out.

"That's the new tenant?" Lea whispered. She hurried to the door to peek through. "Who is he? Tell," she demanded. "Tell all."

"There's nothing to tell. I went out with Andrew last night and he made a pass at me. Jed met him when I was kicking him out."

"What does he do? Jed, I mean. He must lift weights or something to have shoulders like that."

Dora had dug up Jed's application. His last place of employment had been the Philadelphia PD. "He's an ex-cop."

"Ex?" Lea's eyes went wide. "He was fired from the force?"

"He resigned," Dora said. "A few months back. According to the notes Dad took when he called the commissioner of police, Jed's got a potful of commendations, and they're keeping his service revolver warm for him in hopes that he'll come back."

"Well then, why did he quit?"

"That didn't seem to be anyone's business," she said primly, but she was just as curious. She held up her hand to ward off more questions. "We'd better get back inside to help Terri."

"All right, but I feel good knowing you've got a cop right across the hall. That should keep you out of trouble."

Dora shoved her sister through the door.

UNDER any other circumstances DiCarlo would have felt foolish sitting in an elegant reception area holding a cheap porcelain statue in his lap. In this particular reception area, decorated with muted impressionist prints and Erté sculptures, he didn't feel foolish at all. He felt scared, bone scared.

He hadn't really minded putting a small-caliber bullet between Porter's eyes. But considering his string of bad luck, he wondered whether he had the wrong statue in his lap. It certainly looked like the one he'd seen packed into the crate at Premium Shipping.

"Mr. DiCarlo?" the receptionist said. "Mr. Finley can see you."

"Right. Sure." DiCarlo rose, hooking the statue under his arm.

Finley didn't rise from his desk. He enjoyed watching DiCarlo nervously cross the ocean of white carpet. He smiled coldly.

"Mr. DiCarlo, you have tidied up in the great state of Virginia?"

"Everything there is taken care of."

"Excellent." Finley gestured to his desk, so that DiCarlo set the statue down. "And this is all you've brought me?"

"I have a list of the other merchandise. And all the locations." DiCarlo dived into his pocket. "There were only three other buyers, and two of them are also dealers. I think it should be simple enough to go into those shops and buy back that merchandise."

"You think?" Finley said softly. "If you could think, Mr. DiCarlo, my merchandise would be in my possession. However, I'm willing to let you redeem yourself." He rose and ran a fingertip over the female face of the statue. "A hideous piece, don't you agree?"

"Yes, sir."

Finley picked up an unused marble ashtray from his desk and decapitated the woman. "An ugly cocoon," he murmured, "to protect sheer beauty." From inside the figurine he pulled a small object wrapped in bubble plastic. Delicately he unwrapped it, and DiCarlo saw what looked like a gold cigarette lighter, heavily ornate.

"Do you know what this is, Mr. DiCarlo?"

"Uh, no, sir."

"It is an etui." Finley laughed then, caressing the gold. "This small ornamental case was used to hold manicure sets or sewing implements, perhaps a buttonhook or a snuff spoon. This one is gold, and these stones, Mr. DiCarlo, are rubies. There are initials etched into the base." Smiling dreamily, he turned it over. "It was a gift from Napoleon to his Josephine. And now it belongs to me."

"That's great, Mr. Finley." DiCarlo was relieved that he'd brought his employer the right figurine.

"You think so?" Finley's emerald eyes glittered. "Oh, I'm pleased to have it, but it reminds me that my shipment is incomplete. A shipment, I might add, that has taken me nearly a year to accumulate." Finley caressed the etui in intimate little circles. "Tomorrow is Christmas Eve. You have plans, I imagine."

"Well, actually, yes. My family, you see . . ."

Finley's face lit up with a smile. "There is nothing like family around the holidays, Mr. DiCarlo. I'll give you until the first of the year— No, no, make it the second." His smile spread and widened. "I trust you won't disappoint me."

"No, sir."

JED couldn't say why he was doing it. He'd had no business going down to the shop that morning in the first place. He was perfectly content to spend his days working out, lifting weights, catching up on his reading. Lord knew what crazy impulse had had him wandering downstairs and somehow volunteering to fix the banister.

Now he was standing out in the cold, working on it. He was forced to work outside because Dora didn't have ten feet of unoccupied space anywhere inside. At least there was no one to bother him in the rear of the building, and he enjoyed working with his hands, liked the feel of wood under them. Once, he'd considered adding a small workshop onto the back of the house in Chestnut Hill. But that had been before Donny Speck. Before the investigation that had become an obsession.

And, of course, it had been before Elaine had paid the price.

Before Jed could switch off his mind, he saw it again. The silver Mercedes sedan sitting under the carport. He saw her blue eyes look with annoyance in his direction. He saw himself racing across the manicured lawn, between the rosebushes. Then the explosion had ripped through the air with a hot fist that had sent him flying back. He hoped she'd felt nothing after her fingers had twisted the key in the ignition and triggered the bomb.

Swearing, Jed attacked the new banister with the power sander. It was over. Elaine was dead and couldn't be brought back. Donny Speck was dead. And however much Jed might have wished it, he couldn't kill the man again.

And he was exactly where he wanted to be. Alone.

DiCARLO was feeling fine. His luck was back; the rented Porsche was tearing up Route 95. Boxed on the seat beside him were a bronze eagle and a Statue of Liberty, both from a novelty shop outside Washington, D.C., as well as the stuffed parrot from Virginia. After a quick detour to Philadelphia to pick up the last two items on his list, he would make it to New York in time for holiday celebrations.

The day after Christmas he would take up his schedule again. At this pace, he figured he would have all of Mr. Finley's merchandise in hand well before deadline. He might even earn a bonus.

He dialed Finley's private number on the car phone.

"Mr. Finley. DiCarlo. I've recovered three more items—two from D.C. and the other one from Virginia. I'm on my way to Philadelphia now. The last two items are in a shop there."

"Then I'll wish you merry Christmas now, Mr. DiCarlo. If you have something to report, you'll leave a message with Winesap."

"I'll keep in touch, Mr. Finley. Enjoy your holiday."

DiCARLO walked into Dora's Parlor fifteen minutes before closing. He noticed a statuesque redhead wearing a green elf's cap.

Terri Starr beamed at DiCarlo. "Merry Christmas," she said. "You've just caught us. We're closing early today."

DiCarlo tried a smile. "I bet you hate us eleventh-hour shoppers."

"Are you kidding? I love them." She'd already spotted the Porsche at the curb and was calculating ending the business day with a whopping sale. "Are you looking for anything in particular?"

"Actually, yes." DiCarlo took a look around, hoping to spot either the painting or the china hound quickly. "I'm on my way home, and I have an aunt who collects animal statues. Dogs in particular."

"I might be able to help you." Terri led him to a curved glass cabinet and took out an apple-green, carved foo dog, one of their most expensive jade pieces. "Gorgeous, isn't he?"

"I'm afraid my aunt's tastes aren't quite so sophisticated."

"Let's see, then." With some regret Terri replaced the jade. "We've got a couple of nice cocker spaniels in plaster."

"I'll take a look. Would it be all right if I just browsed around?"

"You go right ahead. Take your time."

DiCarlo saw the plaster cockers. He saw cloisonné poodles, blown-glass retrievers, but not the china hound. He kept his eye peeled for the painting as well. There were dozens of framed prints, advertising posters. There was no abstract in an ebony frame.

"I think I've found the perfect thing." Terri came up to him. "It's Staffordshire pottery, a mama English sheepdog and her puppy."

DiCarlo kept a pleasant smile in place even after he'd spotted the four-figure price tag. "I had something a little different in my mind, but this is Aunt Maria all over." He pulled out a credit card. "She used to have this mutt, you see," he continued as he followed Terri to the counter. "A brown-and-white spotted dog who slept curled up on the rug. I was hoping to find something that looked like him."

"Too bad you weren't in a few days ago." Terri nestled the Staffordshire in tissue paper. "We had a piece very much like that. In china, a spotted hound. It was only here a day before we sold it."

"Sold it?" DiCarlo said between smiling teeth. "That's too bad."

"It wasn't nearly as fine a piece as the one you've just bought, Mr. . . . DiCarlo," she added after a glance at his credit card.

"I'm sure you're right. I notice you also carry art."

"Some. Mostly posters and family portraits from estate sales."

"Nothing modern, then? I'm doing some redecorating."

"Afraid not. I haven't noticed any paintings."

While she wrote up his bill, DiCarlo drummed his fingers on the counter. If it hadn't been broad daylight, he might have stuck his gun under the clerk's pretty chin and forced her to look up who had bought the dog. Of course, then he'd have to kill her.

"Just sign here." Terri passed him the sales slip and his card. "I hope you and your aunt have a terrific Christmas, Mr. DiCarlo."

He'd go somewhere for a late lunch. When it was dark, when the shop was empty, he'd be back.

DORA gave Jed's door her best businesslike rap. She knew he would growl at her when he opened it. He didn't disappoint her.

His short-sleeved sweatshirt was damp with sweat. His forearms glistened with it. Scowling, he gripped the ends of a towel he'd hooked around his neck. "What do you want?"

She spotted his weight equipment scattered over the living area. "My phone's out of order. I need to make a call."

For a minute she thought he was going to shut the door in her face. Again. But he swung the door wider and stepped back. "Make it fast," he told her, and stalked away.

Dora juggled the phone, then swore softly. "Yours is out, too."

He looked at her, intrigued now rather than annoyed. "You always dress like that to talk on the phone?"

She was wearing a slithery jumpsuit in silver, with strappy spiked heels. "I have a couple of parties to drop in on. How about you? Are you spending Christmas Eve lifting weights?"

41

"I don't like parties. Why don't you run along?" He tossed the towel aside and picked up a barbell.

She sat on the arm of the couch, frowning, as she watched Jed lift his weights. She shouldn't feel sorry for him, she mused. And yet she hated to imagine him spending the evening alone, with barbells. "Why don't you come with me?"

The long, silent look he sent her had her hurrying on.

"It's not a proposition, Skimmerhorn. Just a couple of parties. It's Christmas Eve. A time of fellowship. You might have heard of it."

"Take off, Conroy."

She sighed, rose. "Enjoy your sweat, Skimmerhorn." She stopped. "What's that noise?" Her eyes narrowed in concentration.

He lowered the barbell and listened. "Someone down in the shop. The sound carries up through the vent."

She froze. "We closed hours ago. Terri left by three thirty." Dora's heels clicked smartly on the floor as she crossed to the door.

"Where are you going?"

"Downstairs, of course. Somebody must have cut the alarm and broken in. They're in for a surprise."

He took her arm and pushed her into a chair. "Stay there." He strode into the bedroom, then returned carrying a .38.

Her eyes rounded. "What's that?"

"It's a parasol. Stay in here. Lock the door." Jed closed the door behind him. It was probably Dora's assistant, he thought as he moved silently down the hall. But there was too much cop in him to take chances. And to dismiss the fact that the phones were out.

He reached the door that led down to the storeroom, eased it open. He heard a sound—a drawer closing.

A movement behind him had him braced and pivoting. And swearing under his breath. Dora was three steps back, a barbell hefted in one hand. Jed jerked a thumb. She shook her head.

He started down, going still when the third step groaned under his foot. There was a rapid series of pops, and the wall inches away from his face spit plaster.

Jed crouched, sprinted the rest of the steps, rolling when he hit bottom and coming up, weapon drawn in time to see the rear door slam shut. He hit the door at a run, went through low. The cold air bit into his lungs, like slivers of ice. He raced after the sound of running footsteps. After about two blocks, he heard the roar of an engine, the squeal of tires, and he knew he'd lost his quarry. When he returned, he found Dora standing in the small gravel lot, shivering.

Her fear had already turned to anger. "Your face is bleeding."

"Yeah?" He brushed at his cheek, and his fingers came away wet. "The plaster must have nipped it." He looked down at the barbell she still carried. "And what were you going to do with that?"

"When he wrestled you to the ground, I was going to hit him with it. Weren't you supposed to call for backup or something?"

"I'm not a cop anymore."

Yes, you are, she thought. In your eyes, in your moves. Saying nothing, she followed him toward the rear entrance of the shop.

"Ever heard of security systems?" he asked.

"I have one. It's supposed to clang if anyone tries to get in."

"Mickey Mouse," Jed said in disgust after one look at the mechanism. "All you have to do is cut a couple wires." He held out the frayed ends. "This guy took out the phone for good measure. He'd have seen by the lights that there was somebody upstairs."

Her teeth were chattering. "Then he was stupid, wasn't he?"

"Maybe he was in a hurry. Don't you have a coat?"

"Silly of me not to have thought to grab my wrap. What was that popping noise right before you took your heroic flight downstairs?"

"Silencer." Jed checked his pocket for loose change.

"Silencer?" The word came out in a squeak as she grabbed his arm. "Like in gangster movies? He was shooting at you?"

"I don't think it was personal. We'd better call this in."

Her hand slid away from his arm. "He could have shot you."

"Got a quarter on you?"

"I have a phone in my van."

He strode over to her van, shaking his head when he found it unlocked. He punched in Brent's number and waited two rings.

"Merry Christmas!"

"Hi, Mary Pat." He could hear children yelling in the background over a forceful recording of "Jingle Bells."

"Jed, you're not calling with a lame excuse about tomorrow?"

"No, I'll be there. M.P., is Brent around?"

"Right here, making his famous sausage stuffing. Hang on." There was a clatter. "Hey, Captain. Merry, merry."

"Sorry to bust in on your cooking, but we had a little problem over here. Break-in. The shop below the apartment."

"They get anything?"

"I have to have her check." He watched Dora shiver. "Took a couple of pops at me. Used a silencer."

"Jeez. You hit?"

"No." The bleeding on his cheek had nearly stopped. "He had a car close. From the sound of the engine, it wasn't an economy."

"Sit tight, Kemo Sabe. I'll call it in and be on my way."

"Thanks." Jed hung up and looked at Dora. "Come on." He took her frozen hands, warming them as they walked back to the shop. "You can take a look around, see if anything is missing."

He took a brief glance at the jimmied lock, then closed out the cold. After he'd switched on the lights, he simply stood and absorbed. The storeroom was crammed with boxes. Shelves held uncrated merchandise in no sort of order he could discern. Two file cabinets were in a corner. There was a desk, which seemed to be an island of sanity. It held a phone, a lamp, a porcelain pitcher stuffed with pencils and pens, and a Beethoven paperweight.

"Nothing's gone," Dora said.

"How can you tell?"

"I know my inventory. You must have scared him off."

"What about cash?"

"We deposit everything but about a hundred in small bills and change every night." She walked over to the desk, opened the top drawer and took out an envelope. "Here it is." She turned to check the files. "Look at this. These drawers are a mess."

He came to peer over her shoulder. "So he was after something in your files."

"It's just business stuff." Baffled, she ran a hand through her hair. "There's no reason for anyone to break in here for paperwork. A crazed IRS agent? A psychopathic accountant?" As soon as she'd said it, Dora bit her tongue.

"What was that jerk's name the other night?"

"Don't be ridiculous. Andrew would never do anything like this."

"Andrew what?"

She blew out a long breath. "I'll give you his name and address. Then you can go do cop things like harass him for an alibi."

"I'm not a cop."

"If it looks like a cop, sounds like a cop . . ." She dropped her gaze, then lifted it slowly. "You're tough, authoritative, a little mean."

"I can be meaner." He edged closer to her.

"Did I tell you I've always had this problem with authority?"

"Well, you're lousy at taking orders. I told you to stay put." She lifted her hand, rubbed her thumb over the cut on his cheek. "You scared me. Were you scared?"

"No. I love having people shoot at me."

"Then this is probably just a reaction we're having." She slid her arms around his neck and liked the fit. "You know, from the shock."

Her lips were curved when his mouth came down. He knew it was a mistake. Even as he steeped himself with her, he knew. Somehow she'd already dug a hook into his mind he'd been unable to shake loose. Now she was trembling against him. He drew back, wanting to clear his head, but she pulled him toward her.

He was still sane enough at that moment to hear the spit of gravel under tires outside and the rattle at the door upstairs.

"The troops are here." He took Dora by the shoulders and set her firmly aside. She saw in his eyes what he would continue to deny. He was a cop again. "Why don't you go put on some coffee, Conroy? It doesn't look like you'll make your parties after all."

She started up the stairs, her back to him. "And that's it?"

"Yeah. That's it."

DORA had brandy. Jed drank coffee. Wanting to ignore him as completely as he was ignoring her, she curled herself onto the couch and studied the cheerful lights of her Christmas tree.

She liked Jed's pal, though, Lieutenant Brent Chapman, with his wrinkled slacks and easy grin. He'd come in smelling of sausage and cinnamon, his heavy horn-rims magnifying mild brown eyes. His questions were slow and thoughtful, his manner reassuring.

No, there was nothing missing as far as she could tell.

No, there was nothing in the files of any monetary value.

Yes, the shop had been crowded the past couple of weeks, but no, she couldn't remember anyone acting suspicious.

Enemies? This brought on a quick laugh. No.

"Tell him about the bean counter," Jed ordered her.

"For heaven's sake. Andrew wouldn't—"

"Dawd," Jed interrupted. "Andrew Dawd, accountant. He put some moves on her, so she gave him his walking papers."

"I see." Brent scribbled the name in his dog-eared notepad. He would have liked to smile, but the gleam in Dora's eye warned him to keep a sober countenance. "It wouldn't hurt to talk with him," Brent pointed out gently. He picked up one of the cookies she'd spread on a pretty fluted dish. "Great cookies."

"Thanks. Why not take some home? You've got kids, don't you?"

"Three." In a knee-jerk reaction Brent reached for his wallet to show off pictures. While Jed rolled his eyes and paced away, Dora rose to admire the children's snapshots. There were two girls and a boy, all spit and polish for school pictures.

"That's Carly. She's ten," Brent said. "Fifth grade over at Bester Elementary."

"My niece Missy's in fifth at Bester, too." They beamed at each other. "I bet they know each other."

"That wouldn't be Missy Bradshaw, would it?" Brent asked.

"Yes, that's right."

"She's been to the house a dozen times. They live a block over. Missy's parents and my wife and I are in the same car pool."

"Would you two like to be alone?" Jed asked.

"Tell me, Brent, is he always so crabby?" Dora said.

"Pretty much." He tucked his wallet away and rose. "But he was the best cop I ever worked with, so you can feel safe with him."

"Thanks. I'll get those cookies." She walked to the kitchen.

"Some landlord," Brent commented, and wiggled his eyebrows.

"Get a grip. How soon will you have anything on the slugs?"

"It's Christmas, Jed. Give the lab boys a few days."

Dora walked back in, carrying a paper plate covered with foil.

"Thanks, Miss Conroy."

"Dora. You will let me know if you find out anything?"

"Count on it. You just relax. Merry Christmas."

"I'll walk you out." Jed nodded to Dora. "I'll be back."

As they walked down the hall, Brent said, "You've been here what, about a week? How'd you get her mad already?"

"It's a gift. Look, why do you figure a pro would break into a junk shop and rifle a bunch of paperwork?"

"That's the sixty-four-dollar question." Brent walked through the rear door, sucking in his breath at the slap of wind.

"And what would anyone look for in the files of a junk shop?"

Brent opened his car door. "You can take the boy off the force, but you can't take the force out of the boy."

"I take a personal interest when somebody shoots at me."

"Can't blame you for that. We miss you downtown, Captain."

"Save it." He wasn't in the mood for a lecture or a pep talk or a guilt trip. "Let me know what comes through."

"You'll be the first." Brent climbed into the car.

Jed headed back inside. He wanted to make certain Dora was locked up for the night before he went back downstairs for another look. Just as an interested civilian, he told himself.

"They've cleared out," he told her when he breezed through her open door. "You can count on Brent. He's a good detail man."

"Terrific. Listen, I've got to ask. I know what you'll say—not to worry, it was just one of those freak things that happen. But I have to ask anyway. Do you think whoever was here before will be back?"

Jed studied her face. There was a strain in her eyes she'd done a good job of hiding up until now. "I don't know," he said flatly.

"Great." Dora closed her eyes, drew a deep breath. "I should have known better than to ask. If you can't figure out what the guy was doing here, how can you tell if he'll be back or not?"

"Something like that." He could have lied, Jed told himself, uneasy that her cheeks had gone pale. "Look." He rose, and surprised them both by reaching out to tuck her hair behind her ear. "I don't think you've got anything to worry about tonight. You need to go to bed, tune out. Let the cops do their job."

"Yeah." She shook her head. "I'll be out most of tomorrow—at my sister's. I'll leave you the number just in case."

"Fine. Lock up behind me. Okay?" He stepped into the hall.

"You bet. You, too. Lock up, I mean."

"Sure." He waited until she'd closed and bolted the door. Then he went down to take another look at the storeroom.

IN A pretty Federal town house shaded by stately oaks, a well-to-do matron was enjoying a glass of sherry and a showing of Bing Crosby's *White Christmas* on her big-screen TV.

47

At the sound of a quiet footstep behind her, Mrs. Lyle smiled. "Come watch, Muriel," she invited, addressing her housekeeper.

She didn't cry out when the blow came. The crystal wineglass shattered against the edge of the coffee table, splattering the Aubusson rug with blood-red sherry. Somewhere through the haze of pain that left her paralyzed, Mrs. Lyle heard the crashing of glass and a furious male voice demanding over and over, "Where is the dog?"

Then she heard nothing at all.

It was midnight when DiCarlo rode the elevator up to his Manhattan apartment. His arms were laden with boxes. He'd been lucky to find the receipt for the stupid dog, he told himself, and wondered idly if the bullets he'd sprayed up the stairs of the antiques shop had hit anything. Or anyone.

Not to worry, he thought. The gun was untraceable. And he was making progress. He had the bronze eagle, the plaster Statue of Liberty, the parrot, the china dog.

And a partridge in a pear tree, he thought, and chuckled.

5

"So . . ." Dora snacked on a raw carrot while Lea checked the Christmas goose. "Jed races out after the guy, waving a gun while I stand there like a Hollywood heroine, clutching my hands."

"Thank goodness you weren't hurt." Harassed by the number of pots simmering on the stove, the sound of her children wreaking havoc in the family room and the very real fear that her mother would invade the kitchen at any moment, Lea shuddered.

"The cops came and did all this cop stuff—Dad would have loved the staging—and asked all these questions." Dora purposely left out the part about the bullets. "It turns out Jed's ex-partner is your neighbor. Carly Chapman's father. She goes to school with Missy."

Lea lifted a lid and sniffed. "Oh, yeah. Brent and Mary Pat."

"Here's the good part. They're going to question Andrew."

"You're kidding. Andrew?"

"Jilted accountant seeks revenge by destroying woman's tax files." Dora ate a broccoli spear and shrugged. "When's dinner?"

"Twenty minutes. If we can keep Mom busy for—" She broke

off, swore under her breath as Trixie Conroy made her entrance.

Trixie always made an entrance, whether it was onto a stage or into a market. She'd dressed for the simple family dinner in a flowing caftan of bleeding colors that billowed around her willowy form. Her hair, cropped gamine-short, was a bold red. Her milk-pale face was striking. The blue eyes were lavishly lashed.

"Darlings!" Trixie's voice was as dramatic as the rest of her. "It's so lovely to see my two girls together. Oh, and those glorious aromas. I do hope you're not overheating my meatballs, Ophelia."

"Uh . . . no, of course not." Lea had stuck them under the sink, with hopes of palming them off on the dog later.

"Perhaps we should put them out now, as an appetizer."

Since she couldn't think of a good ruse, Lea sacrificed her sister. "Mom, did you know someone broke into Dora's shop last night?"

"Oh, my baby. Oh, my lamb." Trixie rushed to Dora.

"Why don't you take Mom in the other room, Dora? Sit down and tell her all about it."

"Yes, yes, you must." Trixie gripped Dora's hand. Dora glared at Lea before she was yanked into the fray.

The Bradshaw family room was in chaos. Toys were strewn everywhere. There were shouts and yips as a remote-control police cruiser, operated by Michael, terrorized the family dog, Mutsy. Will Conroy, looking very New York in a dark silk shirt, entertained Missy on the spinet. Richie and his father were glassy-eyed over a Nintendo game, and Quentin was well plied with eggnog.

"Quentin." Trixie's stage voice froze all action. "Our child has been threatened."

"I wasn't, Mom." Dora eased her mother into a chair. "The shop was broken into. They didn't get anything. Jed scared them off."

"I'd've shot him dead." Richie fired an imaginary weapon.

"Dora, you called the police?" John asked.

"Yes." She scooped up Richie. "And the investigating officer is the father of your good friend, frogface. Jody Chapman."

"Jody Chapman!" Richie made gagging noises.

"She sends her love." Dora smacked her lips. The resulting din of groans and shrieks had her convinced the crisis had passed.

"Willowby!" Trixie cut through the noise. "You'll stay at Isadora's tonight. I won't feel safe if your sister's alone."

49

"No problem," Will said.

"Mother knows best." Quentin rose to kiss his wife's hand.

Will grimaced. "What is that stench?"

"Dinner," Lea announced, swinging through the kitchen door. "Sorry, Mom, I seem to have burned your meatballs."

A BLOCK away, Jed was trying to ease himself out the door. He'd enjoyed Christmas dinner at the Chapmans' more than he'd anticipated. It was hard not to get a kick out of the kids, who were still enthusiastic over their Christmas loot. Impossible not to relax with the scents of pine and turkey and apple pie sweetening the air.

But there was no way to avoid comparing the homey family scene with his own miserable childhood memories of the holiday. The shouting matches. Or worse, the frigid, smothering silences.

Mary Pat was heaping turkey leftovers into a Tupperware container. "Tell me about this landlord of yours, Jed. Brent said she's gorgeous. Why don't you bring her over sometime?"

"I pay her rent; I don't socialize with her."

"You chased a bad guy for her," Mary Pat pointed out.

"That was reflex. I gotta go." He picked up the food container she'd just sealed. "Thanks for dinner."

Her arm around Brent's waist, Mary Pat waved good-bye to Jed's retreating headlights. "You know, he needs someone in his life."

"He needs to come back to work."

WHEN Jed knocked on Dora's door a little after nine on the day after Christmas, the last thing he expected was to hear a man's voice saying, "Wait a minute." There was a thud, a curse.

Will, a flowered sheet wrapped around his thin frame like a toga, and favoring the toe he'd just smashed, opened the door with a sneer. "If you're selling anything," he said, "I hope it's coffee."

She sure could pick them, Jed thought nastily. First an accountant with overactive glands, now a skinny kid barely out of college.

"Isadora," Jed said, and showed his teeth.

"Sure." Mindful of the trailing sheet, Will moved back so that Jed could step inside. "Where the heck is she?" he muttered. "Dora!"

Jed noticed, intrigued, the tangle of blankets on the sofa.

"You're not getting in here until I dry my hair." Dora stepped out

50

of the bathroom, dressed in a terry-cloth robe and armed with a hair dryer. "You can just— Oh." She spotted Jed. "Good morning."

"I need to talk to you for a minute."

"All right. You met my brother?"

Brother, Jed thought, annoyed with his sense of relief. "No."

"The guy in the sheet is Will. Will, the guy who needs a shave is Jed, from across the hall."

"The ex-cop who chased off the burglar." Will's sleep-glazed eyes cleared. "Nice to meet you."

"Here." Dora passed Will the hair dryer. "You can use the shower." He headed off, trailing the sheet.

"My mother thought I needed a man in the house after the break-in," Dora explained. "We can talk in the kitchen."

She put a kettle on to boil. Then she scooped coffee beans into the grinder and ran it before she spoke again.

"So how was your Christmas?"

"Fine. I've got a guy coming by around noon to hook up a new security system. He's a friend of mine. He knows what he's doing."

"A friend. Incredible. You might have discussed it with me."

"You weren't around. You need real locks on the doors."

Her lips pursed, Dora measured coffee into a filtered cone. "I'm debating whether to be amused, annoyed or impressed."

"I can pick up the locks at the hardware. I'll bill you."

That decided her. Her smile turned into a quick laugh. "Okay, Skimmerhorn. Go make our little world safe. Anything else?"

"I figured I might measure for those shelves you want."

"As it happens, we're not opening until noon today. Why don't you set the table for breakfast? Will makes terrific crepes." Before he could answer, the kettle shrilled. Dora poured boiling water over the coffee. The smell was all it took.

"Where do you keep your plates?" he asked.

"First cupboard."

"One thing," he said, opening the cabinet. "You might want to put some clothes on." He sent her a slow smile that had her throat clicking shut. Dora poured her coffee and walked toward the bathroom.

"Smells good." Will strolled in, now wearing jeans and a sweater. His hair, lighter than Dora's, had been blow-dried into artful disarray. "Hey, would you mind switching on the tube? CNN, maybe. I haven't heard what's happening for a couple of days." Will poured both himself and Jed a cup before rolling up his sleeves.

He measured ingredients and stirred with careless finesse. "So this burglary thing. Do you think it's anything to worry about?"

"I always worry when somebody shoots at me."

"Shoot? What do you mean 'shoot'?"

"A gun. Bullets." Jed sipped his coffee. "Bang."

"She didn't say anything about shooting." He dashed into the living room and down the hall and opened the bathroom door.

Dora nearly poked her eye out with her eye pencil. "Will!"

"You didn't say anything about shooting, Dory."

She sighed, giving Jed a hard stare over Will's shoulder. "Thanks loads, Skimmerhorn."

"Don't blame him." Incensed, Will took Dora by the shoulders and shook. "I want to know exactly what happened. Now."

"Then ask the big-nosed cop." She gave Will a shove. "I'm busy," she said, and shut the bathroom door, deliberately locking it.

Will turned toward Jed. "Fill me in while I make breakfast."

"There's not much to tell." There was a sick feeling in Jed's gut. It didn't come from running over events while Will whipped up apple crepes. It came from watching the brother and sister together, in seeing Will's concern and anger—emotions that came from a deeply rooted love, not simply from family loyalty.

"So that's it?" Will demanded. "Some joker breaks in, messes with the files, takes a couple of potshots and runs away. Why?"

"That's what the police are paid to find out. Look, she'll be safe."

"What kind of a cop were you?" Will asked.

"That's irrelevant, isn't it? I'm not a cop now."

"Yeah, but . . ." Will trailed off, frowning down at the crepes he scooped onto a platter. "Skimmerhorn. Name sticks in the mind. I remember something from a few months ago. I'm a news junkie. Captain, right? Captain Skimmerhorn. You blew away Donny Speck, the drug lord. 'Millionaire cop in shoot-out with drug baron.'" Will remembered the headline. He would have pressed, but there was more. The assassination of Skimmerhorn's sister with a car bomb. "I guess anyone who could take out Speck ought to be able to look out for my sister."

Dora came in to answer the ringing kitchen phone. "Hello. . . .

Yes, Will's here. One minute." Dora fluttered her lashes. "Marlene."

"Oh. I might be awhile." Will took the phone from his sister.

"Why didn't you tell him the whole story?" Jed asked Dora.

Dora kept her voice low. "I didn't see any need to worry my family. They tend to be dramatic under the best of circumstances. My mother would have called the CIA, hired two bodyguards named Bubba and Frank. As it was, she stuck me with Will."

"He's all right," Jed said just as Will made kissy noises into the phone. Jed savored the crepes and grinned into his coffee.

Dora rose. "Since he's busy, I'm turning off the television." She had nearly tapped the OFF button when a bulletin stopped her.

"There are still no leads in the Christmas tragedy in Society Hill," the reporter announced. "Prominent socialite Alice Lyle remains in a coma this morning as a result of an attack during an apparent burglary in her home on December twenty-fourth. Mrs. Lyle was found unconscious. Muriel Doyle, the housekeeper, was dead at the scene. The two were discovered by Mrs. Lyle's niece. A police spokesperson states that a full investigation is under way."

"Oh, Lord. I know her. She was in the shop before Christmas, buying a gift for her niece. She bought a couple of doorstops. Her niece was expecting a baby." Dora shuddered. "How awful."

"You can't take it inside." Jed got up to turn off the television.

"Is that what they teach in cop school?" she snapped, then immediately shook her head. "Sorry. That's why I never listen to the news." She struggled to shake off the mood. "I think I'll open early."

"It's tough when they're not strangers."

"It's tough when they are. Is that why you quit?" Dora asked.

"No. I'll head out to the hardware store. Thanks for breakfast."

Dora merely sighed when the door closed behind him. "Will, when you finish your call, do the dishes. I'm going to the shop."

"I'm finished." He popped out of the kitchen. "You're full of secrets, aren't you, Dory? How come you didn't tell me that your tenant was the big bad cop who took down Donny Speck?"

"Who's Donny Speck?"

"Jeez, what world do you live in? Speck ran one of the biggest drug cartels on the East Coast—probably the biggest. He was crazy, too. Always the same MO—a pipe bomb triggered by the ignition. Jed whacked him in a real old-fashioned gunfight."

"Killed him?" Dora asked through dry lips.

"I think he got a medal for it. It was all over the news last summer. The fact that he's the grandson of L. T. Bester, Incorporated, got him a lot of press, too."

"Bester, Inc.? As in large quantities of money?"

"None other. Real estate, Dora. Shopping malls. Philadelphia doesn't have too many loaded cops."

"Then why would he be renting a one-bedroom apartment?"

Will began to clear the table. "The way I see it, the wealthy police captain is taking some downtime. Last summer was pretty hairy. The Speck investigation kept him in the news for months. Then when his sister died in the car explosion—"

"Wait." She gripped Will's arm. "His sister?"

"They figured it was Speck, but I don't think they ever proved it."

"Oh, that's horrible." Paling, she pressed a hand to her stomach.

"Worse—he saw it happen. Pretty tough. The tabloids got a lot of play out of it, too. The sister'd been divorced three or four times. The parents used to have public brawls. There was stuff about Jed getting in scrapes as a juvenile. You know how people like to read about wealthy families suffering."

"No wonder he wants to be left alone," Dora murmured. "But that's not the answer." What she didn't know about Jed Skimmerhorn could apparently fill a football stadium. She leaned over and kissed Will's cheek. "Lock up when you leave. See you New Year's?"

"Wouldn't miss it."

THE Conroy woman was asking for trouble, Jed thought grimly as he sent the power saw ripping through a board. He wasn't scared of her. Damned if he was. But she sure made him nervous.

He'd be stupid not to admit he liked the way she looked. She wasn't any wilty pushover, either. He admired the way she'd taken on the accountant, her fists raised and fire in her eye. Jed caught himself grinning.

He wasn't going to let her get to him. After all, he mused, he'd been raised to be suspicious and aloof, in the best Skimmerhorn tradition. His years on the force had only heightened the tendency.

Jed gathered up the lumber and headed back inside. She was in the storeroom, sitting at her desk. Before he could come up with an appropriately sarcastic comment, he saw her face. Her cheeks were dead white, her eyes dark and gleaming.

"Bad news?" he said. When she didn't answer, he set the lumber aside. "Dora?" He stepped in front of the desk.

She lifted her face. One of the tears swimming in her eyes spilled over and slipped down her cheek. She blinked, spilling another.

"What is it?"

Battling fiercely for control, she shook her head.

"Do you want me to get your sister?" he asked.

"No." Dora pressed her lips together. After a moment she sniffled and said, "I met this other dealer on a buying trip right before Christmas. I just called down there to see if he had this piece my last customer wanted." She took a long breath. "He's dead. He was killed during a burglary last week."

"I'm sorry."

"I only met him once. I outbid him for a couple of lots. Lea and I went by his shop after the auction." Her voice broke. "He was killed the next night. That was his grandson on the phone."

"Did they catch the guy?"

"No. I don't know the details. I didn't want to ask. How do you handle it?" she demanded, gripping Jed's hand with an urgency that surprised them both. "How do you handle being close to the horrible, day in and day out?"

"You don't look at things the same way as a civilian. You can't."

"Did you leave because you stopped looking at things like a cop?"

"That's part of it." He pulled his hand away, distanced himself.

"I don't think that's a good reason."

"I did."

"Interesting choice of tense, Skimmerhorn." She rose, wishing her stomach wasn't still so shaky. "You should have said 'I do'— unless you've changed your mind. I've got to go talk to Lea now."

6

DORA loved a party. It didn't matter if she knew a single soul, as long as there was music, interesting food and plenty of people.

As it happened, she knew a great many people attending the winter ball. Some were friends; some were customers; some were patrons of her family's theater. She mingled, moving from group to group to exchange pecks on the cheek and fresh gossip. Though she'd taken a chance wearing a strapless white gown, the press of bodies comfortably heated the room.

"Darling, you look fabulous." Ashley Draper, a social climber of the first order, swooped down on Dora in a cloud of Opium.

Dora was amused by the air kiss. "You look radiant, Ashley."

"You're a dear to say so, even though I know I'm a bit washed-out. The holidays are so fatiguing, aren't they? We missed you the other night at the Bergermans' Christmas Eve."

"I was . . . unexpectedly detained."

"I hope he was worth it," Ashley purred, then grabbed Dora's hand in a crushing grip. "Look. The grande dame herself. Honoria Skimmerhorn Rodgers. She rarely puts in an appearance here."

"Who?" Dora craned her neck but lost the rest of Ashley's explanation the minute she saw Jed. "Surprise, surprise," she murmured. "Excuse me, Ashley, I have to go see a man about a tux."

And he did look fabulous in it, she mused as she circled the ballroom to come up behind him. "I know," she said at his shoulder. "You're undercover for the force." She caught his soft oath as he turned. "What is it—a ring of insidious pâté burglars?"

"Conroy. Do you have to be everywhere? It's bad enough I have to be here at all without—"

"Jedidiah!" Honoria's authoritative voice halted any complaints. "Have you lost whatever slight degree of manners I managed to teach you? Introduce your friend to your grandmother."

"Grandmother?" Dora said.

Honoria stood nearby. Her snowy hair was softly coiffed around her face, and her Adolfo gown of royal blue set off her eyes and stately figure. Diamonds glittered at her throat, at her ears.

Dora took her narrow-boned hand. "I'm delighted to meet you, Mrs. Skimmerhorn. It destroys my theory that Jed was hatched from a very hard-shelled, very stale egg."

"His social graces are lacking." Honoria studied Dora with growing interest. "And it's Mrs. Rodgers, my dear. I was briefly married to Walter Skimmerhorn but rectified that as soon as possible."

"I'm Dora Conroy, Jed's landlord."

"Ah." There was a world of expression in the single syllable.

"Grandmother." Very deliberately Jed took her arm. "Let me get you some hors d'oeuvres."

"I'm capable of getting my own." Just as deliberately, she shook him off. "Dance with the girl, Jedidiah."

"Yeah, Jedidiah," Dora said as Honoria swept off. "Dance with the girl. Your grandma's watching." She tugged on the sleeve of his tux.

Jed took her arm. "Don't you have a date around here?"

"No," Dora said as they shifted into dance position. "I don't usually like to bring a date to a party. Then I'd have to worry if he was having a good time. I prefer having one myself." The orchestra was playing a silky version of "Twilight Time." "You're a nice dancer, Skimmerhorn. Better than Andrew."

"Thanks a lot. Andrew's clean, by the way. He was at his office Christmas party."

"Of course he's clean. He washes behind his ears."

"Why did you ever go out with him in the first place?"

"He was talking about the new tax law. I was terrified not to." She tilted her head and smiled. "So are you having a good time?"

"I hate these things." It was a shame, he thought, that Dora felt so incredibly good in his arms. "You probably love them."

"Oh, I do."

He slid a hand up her back, encountered bare skin. "Do you ever go out at night in anything that doesn't glitter?"

"Not if I can help it. Don't you like the dress?"

"What there is of it." The song ended and another began, but he'd forgotten he didn't want to dance with her. Honoria glided by in the arms of a distinguished-looking man. "You look okay, Conroy."

"My, are you exuding charm for your grandmother's sake?"

Her smile encouraged one of his own. "She liked you."

"I'm a likable person."

"No, you're not. You're a pain in the neck." He stroked his hand up and down her bare back. "A very sexy pain in the neck."

"I'm getting to you, Jed." And her heart was pounding, just a little, as she trailed her fingers along his neck.

"Maybe." Testing them both, he brushed her mouth with his.

"Absolutely," she corrected. Her stomach fluttering, she kept her mouth an inch from his. "We could go home together tonight. Or"—she tried to smile—"we could be friends first."

"Who said I wanted to be your friend?"

"You won't be able to help yourself."

"How do you figure that?"

"Because everyone needs a friend. Because it's hard to be alone in a room full of people, but you are."

After an inner struggle he rested his brow against hers. "I don't want to care about you, Dora. I don't want to care about—"

"Anything?" she finished for him. When she looked up into his eyes, her heart broke. "You're not dead," she murmured.

"Close enough." He pulled himself back. "I want a drink."

She went with him to the bar, ordered champagne while he chose Scotch. "Tell you what." Her voice was light again. "We'll try something new. I won't give you a hard time—and vice versa."

He studied her. "What's left?"

"We'll be agreeable, have a good time. Let's check out the buffet."

They went over together. She heaped food on her plate, then generously held it out to share. He plucked a cube of cheese from her plate while she sampled a thumb-size spinach pastry.

"Try one of these, Skimmerhorn," she said with her mouth full, and picked up another pastry. Before he could accept or refuse, she had it up to his mouth and in. "Great, huh?"

"I don't like spinach." He washed it down with Scotch.

"I used to be the same way, but my father got me hooked on it by singing 'Popeye the Sailor Man.' I was twenty," she said earnestly. "And naïve." When his lips quirked, she lifted her glass in toast. "There now. You look so pretty when you smile."

"Jed." A hand clamped on his shoulder. Jed braced, turned.

"Commissioner," Jed said, both his face and voice neutral.

"Good to see you." Police Commissioner James Riker gave Jed a quick but thorough study. What he saw obviously pleased him, as his thin, dark face creased in a smile. "You're keeping fit, I see. How was your Christmas?"

"Fine." Because he couldn't ignore Riker's pointed look toward Dora, Jed did his duty. "Commissioner Riker, Dora Conroy."

"Hello." As both her hands were full with a plate and a champagne glass, Dora beamed him a smile instead of a handshake.

"I hope you'll forgive me, Miss Conroy," Riker said, "but I need to steal Jed for a minute. The mayor would like a word with him."

Dora gave way. "Nice to have met you, Commissioner Riker."

"My pleasure. I'll only keep Jed a moment."

Oh, he really hated this, she mused as she watched Jed walk away. A man faced a firing squad with more enthusiasm.

Feeling for him, Dora wondered if she could find some way to distract him when he returned, to turn whatever emotions the commissioner and the mayor managed to stir up into a different channel. She wandered away to get a refill on her champagne.

Five minutes later Jed strode over to the sitting area with cushy chairs and potted plants, where Dora had seated herself. She grinned at him. "Give me a kiss, will you?"

"Why?"

"Because I'd like one. Just a friendly one."

He touched his lips to hers. "Friendly enough?"

"Yeah, thanks."

She started to smile, but he shifted his hand, cupped it around her throat. He lowered his mouth to hers again. She felt a rush that left her limp. His kiss was slow, cool, devastatingly controlled. When he drew back, she kept her eyes closed, absorbing the flood of sensation. Her heart was still pounding in her ears when she opened her eyes. "Jeez" was all she managed to say.

"Problem?" Jed asked her.

"I think so." She pressed her lips together. "I think . . . I'll go." Her knees wobbled when she stood. It was very difficult, she thought, to be in charge of a situation when your knees wobbled.

7

THE new security system on Dora's building brought DiCarlo a great deal of irritation. He'd hoped to get in and out of the storeroom by midnight. For surely if the Conroy woman had bought the painting, it was inside, regardless of what the idiot redheaded clerk had told him on Christmas Eve. Now, with the sturdier locks, he'd be lucky to be inside by midnight. And worse, a cold and nasty sleet was beginning to fall.

At least there were no vehicles in the graveled lot, he thought as he worked and shivered—which meant no one was home. He could still be in New York by morning. He'd sleep the entire day, then catch a late flight to the West Coast. Once he'd handed over Finley's toys, he'd fly back to New York for a rollicking New Year's Eve.

When the final tumbler fell, he gave a little grunt of satisfaction. In less than fifteen minutes he was certain that the painting was not in the storeroom. Using self-control, he curbed the urge to wreck the place. He did another thorough tour of the shop, automatically picking up a few small trinkets as he went, including the jade foo dog that the redhead had tried to sell him.

Resigned, DiCarlo went upstairs. The lock on the door at the top of the steps was basically for looks. He was through it quickly.

He listened, heard nothing. No radio, television, conversation. Still, he moved silently down the hall. Three minutes later he was inside Jed's apartment. That search was over almost before it began. There were no paintings on the wall, none tucked into the closets. He found nothing under the bed but a dog-eared paperback and a balled-up sock. He did find the .38 in the nightstand of some interest but, after a brief examination, replaced it.

DiCarlo was in Dora's apartment in a matter of seconds. She hadn't bothered to lock it. The search here was a different matter. There were several paintings, but no abstract on the wall.

He moved into the bedroom. He barely had time to react when he heard the front door open. By the time it slammed, DiCarlo was hidden deep in the closet behind a colorful assortment of outfits.

"I have to be crazy," Dora said to herself. She peeled off her coat and yawned. How did she let her parents talk her into it? Still muttering, she walked straight to the bedroom. Her plans had been to spend a quiet, relaxing evening at home. But oh, no, she thought, and switched on the Tiffany lamp beside the bed. She had to fall into that old family trap of the show must go on. Was it her fault that three stagehands had come down with the flu? "Absolutely not," she decided as she undressed. "I didn't give them the flu. And I didn't have to jump in just because I have a union card."

Dora sighed. She had spent hours handling props and scenery. She'd even reluctantly enjoyed it. Standing backstage and listening to the voices echo, feeling a vicarious pride when the cast took their curtain calls. After all, Dora thought, what's bred in the bone . . .

Through the crack in the closet door DiCarlo had an excellent view. The more he saw, the more his annoyance at being interrupted faded. The woman who was now stretching at the foot of the bed was wearing only a couple of lacy black swatches. Very nice, DiCarlo thought, and smiled in the dark. Very nice, indeed.

She'd changed his plans, but DiCarlo prided himself on creative thinking. Once she'd gotten into bed, DiCarlo figured, it would be a simple matter—using his .22 automatic—to convince her to tell him where the painting was. And after business, pleasure. He might not even have to kill her afterward.

Dora shook back her hair, rolled her shoulders. It was as if she were posing, DiCarlo thought. His blood surged.

The pounding on her door had Dora jolting. In the closet DiCarlo's breath hissed out in a combination of rage and frustration.

"Hold on!" Dora shouted. She struggled into her white terrycloth robe. Switching on lights as she went, she hurried out to the living room. She hesitated with her hand on the knob. "Jed?"

"Open up, Conroy."

"You gave me a start," she said as she opened the door. "I was just—" The fury on his face stopped her. She stepped back.

"What did you think you were doing?"

"Uh . . . going to bed," she said carefully.

"Cut the nonsense." Jed yanked her into the hall. "I know when my place has been tossed." Enraged, he shoved her up against the opposite wall. Her muffled cry of surprised pain only added to his fury. "What were you looking for?" he demanded.

"Let go of me." She twisted, too terrified for denials.

"You figure because you've got me churned up inside, you can paw through my things anytime you want?" He dragged her stumbling after him. "Fine." He slammed his door open, shoved her inside. "Take a look now. Take a good one."

Her breath shuddered in and out. "You're out of your mind."

Neither of them heard DiCarlo slip down the hall and away. They stood two feet apart, with Dora tugging with a shaking hand at the robe that had fallen off her shoulder.

"Did you think I wouldn't notice?" He moved quickly, grabbing her robe by the lapels. "I was a cop for fourteen years."

"Stop it!" She shoved against him. The sound of her robe ripping at the shoulder was like a scream. Tears of terror and rage sprang to her eyes. "I haven't been in here."

"Don't lie." But a seed of doubt now squeezed through his fury.

"Let me go." She tore free. Slowly, waiting for the tiger to spring again, she backed away. "I just got home. Go feel the hood of my car. It's probably still warm." Her voice sputtered in time with her heart. "I've been at the theater all night. You can call, check."

He said nothing, only watched her edge for the door. She was crying now—fast, choking sobs—as she fumbled with the doorknob.

"Stay away from me," she whispered. "Stay away from me." She fled, leaving his door swinging open and slamming her own.

He stood where he was, waiting for his heartbeat to slow. He hadn't been wrong. Someone had been inside. He knew it. His books had been moved, his gun examined. But it hadn't been Dora.

Sickened, he pressed his hands to his eyes. He'd snapped. He'd been waiting to snap for months. Wasn't that why he'd turned in his badge?

He'd come home after a miserable day of dealing with lawyers and accountants and bankers, and he'd snapped like a twig. And if that wasn't bad enough, he'd terrorized a woman. Why her? Because she'd gotten to him. He took a long breath and walked over to Dora's.

At the knock she stopped rocking on the arm of the chair. Her head jerked up. She scrambled to her feet.

"Dora, I'm sorry." On the other side of the door Jed shut his eyes and knocked again. "Let me come in, will you?" The silence dragged on, tightening his chest. "I swear I won't touch you. I want to see if you're okay, that's all." In frustration, he turned the knob.

Her eyes widened as she watched it rotate. Oh, Lord, she thought in panic. She hadn't locked it. A little sound caught in her throat. She lunged for the door just as Jed opened it.

She froze, and he saw wild fear on her face. Slowly he lifted his hands, palms out. "I won't touch you, Dora. I want to apologize."

"Just leave me alone." Her eyes were dry now, but terrified.

He couldn't walk away until he'd eased that fear. "I hurt you."

"Why?" Her hand clenched and unclenched on the neck of her robe. "You owe me why."

It was a hot ball in his throat. But she was right. "Speck tossed my house a week after he killed my sister." Neither his face nor his voice gave away what it cost him to tell her. "He left a snapshot of her and a news clipping about the explosion on my dresser. He just

63

wanted me to know he could get to me, anytime. He wanted to make sure I knew who was responsible for Elaine. When I came home tonight and I thought you'd been in, it brought it back."

She had a beautifully expressive face. He could read every emotion. The fear, and the anger to combat it, faded away. In their stead were flickers of sorrow, understanding and sympathy.

She lowered her eyes. "When you kissed me last night, I thought something was happening with us." She lifted her gaze again, and her eyes were cool. "But it can't be, or this wouldn't have happened. Because you'd have trusted me. And that's my mistake."

"I can move out if you want," he said stiffly.

"It isn't necessary, but you do what you want."

Nodding, he stepped back into the hall. "Will you be all right?"

For an answer she closed the door gently and turned the lock.

SHE found the flowers on her desk in the morning. Daisies, a little wilted and smelling of far-off spring, were stuffed into a Minton vase. Sternly Dora ignored them.

He hadn't moved out. That much had been clear from the monotonous thud of weights bumping the floor. As far as she was concerned now, Jed Skimmerhorn was a paying tenant. Nothing more. No one was going to terrify her, threaten her and break her heart, then lure her back with a straggling bunch of daisies.

Since Terri and Lea were handling the shop, she took out her accounts book and prepared to work. She sneaked a peek at the daisies and smiled. Then the sound of boots coming down the stairs had her firming her lips and staring at her electric bill.

Jed hesitated at the base of the stairs. "If you're going to be working in here, I can finish up those shelves later."

"I'll be here for a couple of hours," she said, not glancing up.

"I've got some stuff to do downtown." He waited for a response, got nothing. "Do you need anything while I'm out?"

"No."

"Fine. Great. Then I'll finish the shelves this afternoon. After I go out and buy myself a hair shirt."

Dora lifted a brow, listened to the door slam. "Probably thought I'd throw myself in his arms because of the flowers. Jerk." She looked over as Terri stood in the doorway wringing her hands.

"Dora, did you take the jade dog? The little Chinese piece?"

"The foo dog?" Dora tapped her pen on the desk. "No. I haven't circulated any inventory since before Christmas. Why?"

Terri gave a breathless laugh, a sickly smile. "I can't find it."

"It probably just got moved. Lea might have—"

"I've already asked her," Terri interrupted.

Dora pushed away from her desk. "Let me take a look around."

Lea was busy showing tobacco jars to a customer when Dora and Terri entered the shop.

"It was in this cabinet," Terri said quietly. "I showed it Christmas Eve, right before closing. I'm positive I saw it here yesterday."

"All right." Dora patted Terri's shoulder. "Let's look around."

Even the first glance was alarming. Dora made sure to keep her voice calm and low. "Terri, have you sold anything this morning?"

"A tea set—the Meissen—and a couple of cigarette cards. Lea sold the mahogany cradle and a pair of brass candlesticks." Terri's already pale cheeks went whiter. "Is something else gone?"

"The vinaigrette, the enamel one that was on the bonheur." Dora controlled a curse. "And the inkwell that was beside it."

"The pewter?" Terri turned to the delicate desk and groaned. "Oh, no."

Dora shook her head and did a swift tour of the entire shop.

"The Chelton paperweight," she said a few moments later. "The Baccarat perfume bottle and the Fabergé desk seal." That one, priced at fifty-two hundred dollars, was tough to swallow.

"We haven't had more than eight or nine people in all morning," Terri began. "Oh, Dora, I should have watched more carefully."

"It's not your fault." Though she felt sick with anger, Dora slipped an arm around Terri's waist. "We can't treat everyone who walks in like a shoplifter. We'd end up shoving all our stock behind glass. It's the first time we've been hit this hard."

"Dora, the Fabergé."

"I know. I'll report it to the insurance company. That's what they're for. Terri, go take your lunch break now. Clear your head."

"Okay." Terri blew her nose. "Aren't you mad?"

Dora's eyes snapped. "I'm furious."

Terri left her alone in the small side parlor.

"Honey, I'm sorry," Lea said when she stuck her head in.

"Don't worry. I'm insured. Look, close up for an hour. Go get some lunch. I want to go in the back and have a tantrum."

Lea took one look at the glint in Dora's eyes. "I'll lock up."

8

JED wondered if going back to his old precinct for the first time since his resignation was just another way to punish himself. He could have met with Brent elsewhere and avoided the wrenching reminder. But Jed walked into the place where he'd spent eight of his fourteen years on the force, because he knew he had to face it. After the way he'd spun out of control the night before, he admitted there were plenty of things he was going to have to face.

Everything was the same. The air still smelled of spilled coffee and stale smoke—all with an undertone of disinfectant. The sounds—all familiar. Ringing phones, raised voices. Walking in without his weapon strapped to his side made him feel naked. He nearly walked out again, but the only way through it was ahead, he decided.

Jed stopped at the desk, waited until the sergeant turned. "Ryan." The man had shoulders like a bull, but he also had the face of a teddy bear. When he spotted Jed, that face creased into a smile so big his eyes seemed to disappear into the folds of ruddy Irish skin.

"Captain." He grasped Jed's hand. "Really good to see you."

"How's it going?"

"Oh, you know. Same old same old." He leaned companionably on the desk. "We miss you around here, Captain," he said. "Goldman's okay as an acting captain. I mean, he pushes paper with the best of them, but let's face it. The man's a fool."

"You'll break him in."

"No, sir." Ryan shook his head. "Some you do, some you don't. The men knew they could talk to you, straight. With Goldman you gotta tippytoe through regulations and procedure."

Whatever Jed felt about Ryan's easy flow of information, he kept to himself. "Is Lieutenant Chapman in?"

"Sure. I think he's in his office. You can track him down."

To get to Brent, Jed had to walk through the bull pen. His stomach clenched each time his name was called, each time he was forced to stop and exchange a word. Each time he forced himself to ignore the speculation, the unasked questions. By the time he reached Brent's door, the tension was rapping at the base of his neck like a dull spike.

Brent was sitting at his overburdened desk, the phone at his ear. "Tell me something I don't know," he was saying. He glanced up, and the irritation in his eyes cleared. "Yeah, I'll get back to you." He hung up. "You were in the neighborhood, thought you'd drop by, right?"

"No." Jed sat down. He didn't want to ask, to get involved. But he had to. "Is Goldman being as big a jerk as Ryan claims?"

Grimacing, Brent rose to pour two cups of coffee from the pot on his hot plate. "Well, he's not exactly Mr. Popularity." He gave Jed a cup, then leaned against his desk. "Come back, Jed."

Jed lowered his eyes, slowly lifted them again. "I can't, Brent. I'm a mess. Give me a badge right now and I don't know what I'd do." He had to stop. "Somebody'd been in my place last night."

"You had another break-in over there?"

Jed shook his head. "This was slick. A couple things out of place, a drawer shut when I'd left it partway open—that kind of thing. I'd been out most of the day settling Elaine's estate. After that, I went to a movie. I came home, took one look around and went after Dora." He sipped his coffee. "I mean I went after her, Brent. Saw the crime, made the collar. I pushed her around."

Stunned, Brent stared at Jed. "You didn't—hit her?"

"No. I scared the heck out of her, though. Scared myself. I just snapped. Dora didn't go into my apartment. So who did?"

"Might have been a return from whoever broke in the other night. Looking for something to lift. What about the security?"

"I looked it over. Couldn't find anything. This guy's a pro, Brent. Could be a connection to Speck, somebody who wants revenge."

"Speck wasn't the kind to inspire loyalty after death." But, like Jed, Brent wasn't willing to dismiss the possibility. "I'm going to do some checking. Why don't I put a couple of eyes on the building?"

Jed nodded. "I'd appreciate it. If somebody wants me, I wouldn't like to have Dora caught in the middle."

JED was surprised to find Dora still huddled over her desk when he returned. It didn't surprise him that she ignored him as she had that morning, but this time he thought he was prepared.

67

"I got you something."

Jed set a large box on the desk in front of her. When she glanced at it, he had the small satisfaction of spotting curiosity in her eyes.

"It's, uh, a robe. To replace the one that got torn last night."

"I see." When she looked up at him, the curiosity had been replaced by glittering anger. "Skimmerhorn, you think that a bunch of pathetic flowers and a robe are going to clear the path?"

She rose and slapped her palms down on the box. She paused.

"Keep going," Jed said quietly. "Get the rest of it out."

"All right, fine. You muscle your way into my apartment, flinging accusations. Why? Because I was handy, and because you didn't like the way things were moving between us. You didn't even consider that you might be wrong—you just attacked. You scared me. And worse, you humiliated me because I just took it." Wearily she lifted a hand to push back her hair. "Look, I've had a rough day—"

She broke off when he took her hand. She stiffened, but he gently straightened her arm. "I can keep saying I'm sorry. That doesn't mean a lot." He released her, tucked his hands away in his pockets. "I hurt you. And I don't know how to make it up to you."

He started for the steps.

"Jed." There was a sigh in her voice. "Wait a minute." Sucker, she admitted, and flipped open the top of the box. The robe was nearly identical to hers but for the color. She smoothed a finger down the deep green terry-cloth lapel.

"They didn't have a white one. You wear bright colors, so . . ."

"It's nice. I didn't say I was forgiving you. I'm just not comfortable feuding with the neighbors."

"You've got a right to set the rules."

She smiled a little. "You must really be suffering to hand over that kind of power."

"You've never been a man buying women's lingerie. You don't know about suffering. I am sorry, Dora."

"I know. Really, I do. I was nearly as mad at myself as I was at you this morning. Before I could cool off, we had some trouble in the shop. So when you came back, I was ready for blood."

"What kind of trouble?"

"Shoplifting." Her eyes hardened again.

"Are you sure it was all there last night when you closed up?"

That stiffened her spine. "I know my stock, Skimmerhorn."

"You said you'd got in just before I did last night. And you were upset when I left you. You were still upset this morning. I don't suppose you'd have noticed if anything was missing from upstairs."

"What are you talking about?"

"Somebody was in my place last night."

He saw the doubt on her face.

"I'm not saying that to excuse my behavior," he went on. "Somebody was. Cops see things civilians don't. I have an idea that some of Speck's men had dropped around to hassle me, but it could have been somebody looking for some trinkets. Let's go take a look."

"What about the alarm system, those locks you put in?"

"Nothing's burglary-proof."

"Oh." She closed her eyes briefly as he took her hand and pulled her up the stairs. "Well, that certainly makes me feel better."

"Let's just check it out. Got your keys?"

"It's not locked." His look made her bristle. "Look, ace, the outside door's locked, and I was right downstairs."

He bent down to examine the lock, saw no obvious signs of tampering. He opened the door and scanned the room. "What happened to the painting? The new one you hung over the couch?"

"The abstract? I took it over to my mother."

"Jewelry?"

She crossed to the bedroom. She opened a camphorwood-and-ebony chest that sat on a lowboy. "It looks like it's all here." She took out a velvet pouch and shook out a pair of emerald earrings. "If anybody was going to rifle through here, they'd go for these."

"Nice," he said after a glance. It didn't surprise him that her bedroom was as crowded and homey as her living room. "Some bed."

"I like it. It's a Louis the Fifteenth reproduction. I bought it from a hotel in San Francisco. I couldn't resist that headboard."

It was high, covered with deep blue brocade and gently curved at the top. She'd added a quilted satin spread and fussy pillows.

"I like to sit up late and read with a fire going." She closed the jewelry box. "Sorry, Captain. I don't have a crime to report."

He should have been relieved, but he wasn't. "Why don't you give me a list of the stolen goods? We—Brent—can have some men check out the pawnshops."

"I've already reported it."

"Let me help." He ran a hand down her arm. She didn't back away. So he was forgiven, he thought. That simply.

"All right. It wouldn't be smart to turn down the services of a police captain over a simple shoplifting. Let me—" She started forward, but he didn't move. Her heart stuttered in her chest with an emotion that had nothing to do with fear. "The list's downstairs."

"I think you should know, you were right," he said.

"That's good to know. What was I right about this time?"

"I was tangled up about what was happening between us."

"Oh." It came out shaky. "What *was* happening between us?"

His eyes darkened. "I was wanting you. It was making me a little crazy. If you want to pay me back solid for last night, all you have to do is tell me you're not interested."

"I think . . ." On a weak laugh she pushed both hands through her hair. "I'm going to consider your offer carefully and get back to you."

He hadn't expected to fluster her, but he was enjoying it. "You want to have dinner? We could discuss the terms."

"I can't. I have a date—with my nephew. Richie's at that stage where he detests girls, so every now and again I take him out to the movies. A kind of guys' night out. Sitting through *Zombie Mercenaries from Hell*—that makes me one of the guys."

"If you say so." He grinned. "Maybe we'll try guys' night out tomorrow, then. Why don't we go get that list?"

When they'd passed safely out of the bedroom, Dora let out a small relieved breath. She was definitely going to think this over—as soon as some of the blood returned to her head.

DiCarlo might have enjoyed his luxurious suite at the Ritz-Carlton with its soft king-size bed and fully stocked bar—if he'd had the painting in his possession. Instead, he fumed. Without the ill-timed arrival of the man in that other apartment, DiCarlo figured he would have had the painting—or known its whereabouts.

He hesitated to call Finley. There was nothing to report but failure, though he still had until the second of January.

He chewed on a nut and washed it down with the Beaujolais left over from his lunch. It baffled him that the man knew his apartment had been searched. Since the man suspected the woman next door had been in his apartment, DiCarlo's plans didn't change.

He'd do exactly what he had planned to do the night before. Only this time he knew he'd kill the woman when he was finished.

THE temperature had dipped to a brisk fourteen degrees under a dazzling night sky splattered with icy stars and sliced by a thin, frosty moon. The shops along South Street were locked up tightly, and traffic was light.

DiCarlo spotted the police cruiser on his first circle of the block. His hands tightened on the wheel. He hadn't counted on outside interference. He drove around aimlessly for ten minutes. By the time he'd circled around to South again, DiCarlo had his plan formulated. He pulled to the curb in front of the police car. Taking a Philadelphia street map out of the glove box, he climbed out of the car.

"Got a problem there?" The cop rolled down his window.

"I sure do." Playing his part, DiCarlo grinned sheepishly. "I don't know where I made the wrong turn, Officer, but I feel like I've been driving around in circles."

"Thought I saw you drive by before. Where you trying to get to?"

"Fifteenth and Walnut." DiCarlo pushed the map into the window.

"No problem. Make a left on Fifth. You'll run right into Walnut at Independence Square. Make another left."

"I appreciate it, Officer." Smiling, DiCarlo pressed his silenced pistol against the uniform's breast. Their eyes met for less than a heartbeat. There were two muffled pops. The cop's body jerked, slumped. DiCarlo checked the pulse. When he found none, he quietly opened the driver's door with his gloved hands and straightened the body into a sitting position. He rolled up the window, locked the door, then strolled back to his own car.

DORA was disappointed that Richie hadn't taken her up on her invitation to sleep over. It seemed her nephew had had a better offer, so she'd dropped him off at a friend's after the movies.

The simple fact was, she didn't want to be alone.

No, she corrected, she didn't want to be alone and a few easy steps away from Jed Skimmerhorn. No matter how attractive and charming he'd been that afternoon, he was a crate of dynamite set with a very short fuse. She didn't want to be in harm's way when and if he exploded again. She turned into the little gravel lot behind the shop.

His T-Bird was gone. Dora frowned a moment, then shook her head. For the best, she thought. If he wasn't around, she couldn't think about knocking on his door and inviting trouble. Her boots crunched over the gravel, clattered up the back stairs. After entering the code into the alarm system, she unlocked the door, then secured it.

She decided to make an early night of it. A pot of tea, a fire and a book—the perfect remedies for a troubled mind.

She let herself into her apartment and turned on the Christmas tree. The cozy colored lights never failed to cheer her. She took off her boots and coat and put everything into her hall closet.

She padded into the kitchen to heat the kettle. Her hand on the tap jerked as a board creaked in the other room. She stood frozen—water splashing into the sink—listening to her own racing heart.

"Get a grip, Conroy," she whispered. Imagine, letting a silly film give her the willies. The building was settling, that was all.

Amused with herself, she put the kettle on to boil. She walked back into the living room and stopped dead. It was pitch-dark, with only the thin backwash of light from the kitchen illuminating the silhouettes of furniture. Which, of course, made the dark worse.

But she'd turned the tree on, hadn't she? Of course she had. A fuse? Maybe the tree lights had shorted. Shaking her head at her overactive imagination, she started across the room.

And the kitchen light went out behind her.

Her breath sucked in on a gasp. Slippery little fingers of fear slid over her skin. She didn't move, listening to every sound. There was nothing but her own drumming heartbeat and shallow breathing. Lifting a hand to her head, she laughed. A bulb blew, that was—

A hand clamped over her mouth. Before she could think to struggle, she was yanked back against a hard body.

"Now you stay real quiet." DiCarlo kept his voice at a whisper. "You know what this is?" He loosened his grip enough to slip his gun against her. "You don't want me to have to use it, do you?"

She shook her head, squeezing her eyes tight.

"Good girl. Now I'm going to take my hand away. If you scream, I'll have to kill you."

When he removed the hand from her mouth, Dora pressed her lips together to stop them from trembling.

"I watched you the other night, in the bedroom, when you took off your clothes." His breath quickened. "You're going to do that little striptease for me again, after we take care of business."

She groaned, repulsed. Tears burned in her eyes. She thought she'd been scared the night before with Jed. But that was nothing compared with the ice-edged horror that clawed through her now.

"You cooperate, and we'll get on fine." He slipped the barrel of the gun under her sweater, sliding it around. "Now you tell me where the picture is, and I'll take the gun away."

"The picture?" Her frantic mind whirled. She'd cooperate. But she wouldn't be powerless. "I'll give you any picture you want. Please move the gun. I can't think when I'm so scared."

DiCarlo lowered the gun. "Just tell me where it is."

"All right." She cupped her left fist with her right hand. "I'll tell you." Using the force of both arms, she rammed her elbow into his stomach. He grunted with pain as he stumbled back. Dora heard a clatter behind her as she raced out the door.

Her legs felt numb with fear. She fell into the hall, nearly lost her footing. She'd reached the rear door and was dragging at the lock when he caught her. She screamed and turned to claw at his face.

Swearing, DiCarlo hooked an arm around her throat. "We're not going to be able to be so nice now, are we?" He cut off her air and began to pull her backward toward the dark apartment.

They both heard footsteps pounding up the stairs. With one desperate swipe DiCarlo smashed the fluted hall sconce and waited in the shadows.

Jed came in low, weapon drawn.

"Toss it down," DiCarlo hissed, jerking on his arm to make Dora choke. "I've got a gun at the lady's back."

Jed could see the outline of Dora's face and hear her struggle for air. With his eyes on DiCarlo he crouched, set his gun on the floor. "She won't be much of a shield if you strangle her."

"Stand up. Hands behind your head. Kick the gun over here."

Jed straightened, linked his fingers behind his head. He nudged the gun halfway between himself and Dora. "Sorry," Jed said. "Looks like I missed the extra point."

"Back against the wall, damn it." DiCarlo was beginning to sweat now. Things weren't going the way they were supposed to.

He began to sidestep down the hall toward the open door, with Dora between him and Jed. When he reached for Jed's gun, he pulled her down with him to retrieve it, loosening his hold.

Even as Jed prepared his move, she sucked in her breath. "He doesn't have a gun," she gasped out, and threw her body back.

Her foot hit the .38, sent it out the door. Jed dragged her aside and braced for DiCarlo's attack. But DiCarlo ran. Jed tackled him at the door. They went through together in a tangle of limbs. The banister cracked in two jagged pieces under the weight. By the time they'd hit the ground, Dora was down the steps in search of the gun.

A blow glanced off Jed's kidneys. Another caught him low in the gut. He plowed his fist into the other man's face and saw blood.

Dora let out an outraged howl when DiCarlo grabbed part of the broken banister and took a vicious swing that missed Jed's face by inches. She ran and leaped on DiCarlo's back. She bit down on his neck and drew blood before he flung her aside.

Pain exploded as her head hit the edge of a step. Dora reared up, then blacked out completely as she crumpled to the ground.

WHEN she opened her eyes again, everything swam in and out of focus. And it hurt. Dora tried to slip back into the void.

"No, you don't. Come on, open up." Jed tapped Dora's cheeks until he had her moaning and opening her eyes again.

The room revolved like a carousel. "My head." She touched a tentative hand to the back of her head and hissed in reaction.

"How many fingers?" Jed held a hand in front of her face.

"Two. Are we playing doctor?"

Though he worried about a concussion, at least her vision and speech were clear. "I think you're okay." The flood of relief was instantly dammed by temper. "Not that you deserve to be, after that idiotic piggyback move. What were you doing, Conroy?"

"I was trying to help." It all came rushing back. Her fingers gripped his. "Where is he? Did he get away?"

"Yeah, he got away. I'd have had him if you . . ."

Her eyes narrowed, dared him. "If I what?"

"You went down like a tree. I thought you'd been wrong about the gun. It turned out all you'd done was crack that amazingly hard head of yours."

"Well, why didn't you go after him?" She tried to shift, noticed she was wrapped in a crocheted afghan.

"I guess I could have left you unconscious, freezing, bleeding."

"Oh." She glanced around the apartment. "He did have a gun before. I don't know what happened to it."

"It was under the table. I've got it."

Her smile was weak and didn't last. "You've been busy."

"You took your sweet time coming around." He took her hand again, too gently for her to refuse. "Tell me what happened. Exactly."

"I guess you were right about somebody breaking in yesterday. It seems he was in here, too. I didn't notice anything moved or taken, but he said he'd seen me undressing." She hesitated.

He recognized the signs—humiliation rushing through the fear, shame jockeying with anger. "Dora, Brent's on his way. I can have him call in a woman officer if it would be easier for you."

"No." She took a deep breath. "He must have been hiding in here. I went right into the kitchen to make tea—I left the water boiling."

"I took care of it."

"Oh, good. I'm fond of that kettle. Anyway, when I came back in here, the tree was off. I'd just turned it on, so I figured it had shorted or something. I started to go fix it, and the kitchen light went off. He grabbed me from behind." Her voice started to shake. "I would have fought back, but he put the gun under my sweater."

He gathered her close, easing her throbbing head onto his shoulder, stroking her hair. "It's all right now."

"He was going to rape me." She closed her eyes and burrowed in. "I took this self-defense course last year, but I couldn't remember a thing. He kept saying I just had to cooperate. I got so mad because he thought I wasn't going to do anything to protect myself. I rammed my elbow into his stomach and I ran. Then you came in."

"Okay." He didn't want to think of what might have happened if he hadn't come in. "Did you know him?"

"I don't think so. I got a good look at him outside, but he wasn't familiar." She let out a breath. "Your new banister's busted."

"I guess I'll have to fix it again. Got some aspirin?"

"Bathroom medicine chest." She smiled when she felt his lips brush against her temple. "Bring me a couple dozen, will you?"

He brought out the aspirin and some water, and she downed the pills. She winced at the knock on her door. "Is that the cavalry?"

"I imagine. Stay here."

She watched him, her eyes widening as she saw him reach for the gun hooked to his jeans. He stood at the side of the door. "Yeah?"

"It's Brent."

"It's about time." He yanked open the door, furious all of a sudden. "What kind of cops are you putting on these days when an armed rapist can stroll right by them and break into a building?"

"Trainor was a good man." Brent's mouth was tight and grim. He saw Dora on the couch. "Is she all right?"

"No thanks to Philadelphia's finest. If—" Jed broke off. "*Was?*"

"Dead. Twice in the chest, close range."

Dora saw the look they exchanged. "What is it? What?"

"I asked Brent to put a man on the building in case whoever broke in came back. He came back. And the cop's dead."

"Dead?" The color in her cheeks washed away. "He was shot, wasn't he? Was he married?"

"That's not—" Jed began.

"A man was outside trying to protect me. Now he's dead." She started up off the couch. "I want to know if he had a family."

"He had a wife," Brent said quietly. "Two kids in high school."

Hugging her arms, she turned away.

"Dora." Jed started to reach out. "I want you to sit down. And run through the whole thing again, step by step."

She pushed back her tousled hair. "I'm going to make coffee."

Later they sat at Dora's dining-room table going over her statement point by point.

"Funny he'd come back—we've got to figure three times." Brent checked his notes. "And taking out a cop to get inside. Not the pattern of your usual rapist."

"He kept talking. He said . . . I forget. He said something about a picture."

"He wanted pictures?" Brent asked.

"I—no. He wanted a specific picture, wanted me to tell him where it was," Dora said. "I wasn't really listening then."

"What kind of pictures do you have?"

"All sorts. Family pictures, snapshots. Nothing interesting."

"It doesn't fit," Jed said. "A guy doesn't kill a cop, then walk across the street to rape a woman and raid her photo album."

"Did you get a good enough look for a make?" Brent asked.

"Six foot, a hundred seventy," Jed replied. "Dark hair, dark eyes, slim build. He had on a cashmere coat, gray, and a navy or black suit with a red tie. Funny, a guy wearing a suit and tie for a rape."

"It's a funny world." Brent rose. "Tomorrow I'd like you two to come down to the station and work with the Identi-Kit. It's a little toy we have to help put together a composite. You need some rest, Dora. If you think of anything else, you call—anytime."

"I will. Thanks."

When they were alone, Dora stacked the dishes. It was still difficult to look Jed in the eye. "I haven't gotten around to thanking you."

"You're welcome." He put his hands over hers. "Leave them." He then tipped her head back to examine her eyes. What he saw was simple exhaustion. "Go to bed."

"I'm not tired. The coffee will probably keep me awake. . . ."

Gently he laid his hands on her shoulders. "Do you want me to call your sister? Your father or your mother?"

"No." Dora plugged the sink, flipped on the water. "I guess I'll have to tell them something tomorrow, and that'll be bad enough."

She wasn't fooling with dishes out of a sense of neatness, he knew, but because she was postponing that moment of being alone again. At least that was something he could take care of.

"Tell you what. Why don't I bunk out on the couch for tonight?"

With one indulgent sigh she shut off the tap. "Thanks."

He put his arms around her. "Don't thank me. I might snore."

"I'll risk it. I'd tell you that you could share the bed, but—"

"Bad timing," he finished.

"Yeah." She eased away. "I'll get you a pillow."

9

SHE looked good, really good, in the morning. Dora slept sprawled on her stomach. Her hair, tousled from the night, was swept back from her cheek. Her skin was like smooth white silk. She looked enormously appealing.

Jed walked over, set his mug of coffee on the nightstand, then sat on the edge of the bed. "Isadora." He shook her shoulder lightly.

She made a sound of annoyance and turned over on her back. The movement slithered the thick quilt down past her shoulders. Her flannel gown was an eye-popping blue. Jed made out two little pink appliqués that looked like pigs' ears. Curious, he lifted the quilt. Sure enough, a fat pink pig face grinned back at him. He dropped the quilt and shook her shoulder again.

"Isadora," he whispered close to her ear. "Wake up."

"Go away."

Grinning, he leaned closer and captured her mouth. That had her eyes springing open. Dazed, she lifted a hand to his shoulder.

Jed murmured, "You awake now?"

"Oh, yeah. Wide." She cleared her throat.

"Who am I?"

"Kevin Costner." She smiled and stretched her shoulders. "Just a little harmless fantasy of mine, Skimmerhorn."

"Isn't he married?"

"Not in my fantasies."

Jed leaned back. Her eyes were heavy. "How's the head?"

She lay still, taking inventory. "It hurts. My shoulder's sore, too."

"Try these." Jed held two aspirin in his hand.

Dora took the pills, then the mug of coffee he offered.

She sipped again, sighed. "I can't remember the last time anyone brought me coffee in bed." Smiling, she tilted her head and studied him. With his hair damp from a shower and his chin shadowed with stubble, he made a very appealing picture. "You're a tough one to figure, Skimmerhorn."

He took the hand she pressed to his cheek. "Listen to me." He spoke carefully. "You don't know me. You don't know what I'm capable of or what I'm not capable of. The only thing you can be sure of is that I want you, and when I'm certain you're a hundred percent, I'm going to have you. I won't ask."

"There's no need for that, since I've already answered yes. I also know you're not warning me. You're warning yourself."

He let her hand go and rose. "We've got other things to deal with today. What are you doing about the shop?"

"We're closed today."

"Good. We've got to get down to the station house. Get yourself together, and I'll make some breakfast."

"Can you?"

"I can pour milk on cold cereal."

"Yummy." She tossed the quilt aside as he started out.

"Oh, Conroy," he said over his shoulder, "I like your pig."

DiCarlo paced his New York apartment. He hadn't slept.

He couldn't go back to Philadelphia. The dead cop was one thing, but the two witnesses had seen his face well enough for an I.D. And they'd tie him to the dead patrol. He'd need to go underground. A couple of months, six at the most. He had plenty of contacts, plenty of liquid cash. He could spend the winter in Mexico, swilling margaritas. Once the cops finished chasing their tails, he'd return.

The only hitch was Edmund J. Finley.

DiCarlo studied the merchandise he'd stacked against the wall. They looked like sad, neglected presents. The parrot, the eagle, Lady Liberty, the china dog. Counting the figurine he'd already delivered, that made five out of six. Anyone but Finley would consider that a success.

It was only one lousy painting, he thought. He'd given it his best shot. He had a black eye, a split lip and sore kidneys. His cashmere coat was ruined. As soon as he had time, he was going to make that shipping clerk, Opal Johnson, pay for her mistake.

In the meantime he figured he would approach Finley businessman to businessman. After all, Finley knew one had to take losses along with profit. First put him in a cheery mood by personally presenting him with the four newly recovered items; then elicit sympathy and admiration by detailing the specifics. He'd explain about the cop, too. Surely a man like Finley would understand the great personal risk taken by icing a badge.

Not enough, DiCarlo admitted, and picked up his ice pack to press it against his bruised cheekbone. It was just as well he was too busy to celebrate New Year's Eve.

He would use good faith. He would offer to put another man on the job, at his own expense. Surely that was an offer that would appeal to Finley's business sense. And his greed.

Satisfied, DiCarlo went to the phone.

"I THINK HIS FACE WAS JUST a little longer." Dora watched the computer-generated image change on the monitor to the quick rattle of the operator's fingers on the keyboard. "Yeah, that's it. And thinner, too. Maybe his eyes were heavier—more lid."

Jed moved behind her chair. "Thin out the lips and nose," he ordered. "The eyes were deeper set. Square off the chin some."

"How do you do that?" Dora whispered.

"I got a better look at him than you, that's all."

No, that wasn't all, she thought. He'd seen what she'd seen, but he'd absorbed and filed and retained. Now she was watching the image of her attacker taking shape on the monitor.

"Now deepen the complexion," Jed suggested, narrowing his eyes, focusing in. "Bingo."

"That's him." Shaken, Dora reached over to hold Jed's hand. She smiled weakly. "That *is* him. That's incredible."

"Give us a printout," Brent told the operator. "We'll see if we can come up with a match."

"I'd like a copy for Lea and Terri, too." Dora got to her feet. "In case they notice him hanging around near the shop."

"We'll get you one." Brent nodded to the operator. "Why don't you come back to my office for a few minutes?" He took Dora's arm, guiding her out of the conference room and down the hall. Jed followed.

Brent opened his office door and ushered Dora inside. "Oh, I got a call from your mother. An invitation to your parents' New Year's Eve bash tomorrow at the theater."

She'd all but put it out of her mind. "I hope you can make it."

"We're looking forward to it." Brent cleared his throat, pushed up his glasses. "Well, until we run this guy down," he said, watching from the corner of his eye as Jed paced, "we'll put a couple of guards on your building."

"I don't want anyone else put at risk," she said.

"Dora, there isn't a man in this precinct who wouldn't volunteer for the duty. Not after Trainor. This guy's a cop killer. Which is why it was easy for me to put a rush on ballistics. The bullets they took out of Trainor matched the ones we dug out of your wall."

"Surprise, surprise," Jed muttered.

"I've got a case to build." Brent polished his glasses on his wrinkled shirt. "I'm sending out the ballistic report to other precincts throughout the city and the state. Something might match."

It was a good move, Jed thought. "Where's Goldman?"

"In Vail," Brent said under his breath. "Skiing. A vacation."

"Son of a gun. He's got a dead cop at his feet—one of his own."

Brent snatched up his shrilling phone. "Call back," he barked into it, and slammed it down. "Look, I hope Goldman breaks his butt. Maybe then you'll get off yours and come back where you belong. The morale level around here's about knee-high." He stabbed a finger at Jed. "What are you going to do about it?"

Jed didn't speak, didn't dare. Instead, he turned and walked out.

Brent looked at Dora, grimaced. "Sorry."

"Don't worry about it." Actually, she'd found the entire incident illuminating. "I'd better go after him."

"I wouldn't."

She only smiled. "See you tomorrow night."

SHE caught up with him half a block away. She trotted up beside him, matched her stride to his.

"Nice day," she said. "The temperature's up a bit, I think."

"You'd be smart to stay away from me right now."

"Yeah, I know." She tucked her hand through his arm. "You're not really mad at him, you know."

"Don't tell me what I am." He tried to shake her off, but she hung on like a silk-covered burr. "Get lost, Conroy."

"Impossible. I know my way around this neighborhood too well."

Jed stopped, turned. "You're not going to quit, are you?"

"Nope. I can keep this up indefinitely." Reaching down, she tugged up the zipper of his jacket. "Brent's frustrated because he cares about you. It's tough being cared about, because it loads all this responsibility on. You've had a potful of responsibility there, I imagine. It must be a relief to toss it out for a while."

It was tough to hold on to his temper with someone who understood so perfectly. "I had reasons for resigning. They still hold."

"Why don't you tell me what they were?"

"They're my reasons."

"Okay. Want to hear my reasons for leaving the stage?"

"No."

"Good. I'll tell you." She began to walk again, leading him back around the block. "I liked acting. I was good, too. The reviews were terrific. But it wasn't really what I wanted to do. I wanted my own shop. Then, about five years ago, I got an inheritance from my godmother. I took the money and a couple of courses in business management. When I told my family what I was going to do, they were upset. They loved me, but they wanted me to be something I couldn't. I wouldn't have been happy in the theater. So I did what was right for me. It took a long time before I adjusted to the responsibility of being cared for, worried over and loved."

For a moment Jed said nothing. It surprised him that he wasn't angry any longer. Sometime during Dora's monologue his temper had dissipated and blown away on the wind of her persistence.

"So the moral of your story is that since I don't want to be a cop, I shouldn't get mad because a friend wants to guilt me back."

Dora stepped in front of him. "No, you missed it entirely. I made a choice that my family didn't agree with, but that I knew was right for me. You're a cop down to the bone. You just need to admit you made the right choice in the first place."

He snagged her arm. "Do you know why I left?" His eyes weren't angry now, but dark and, to Dora, frighteningly empty of emotion. "I didn't have to kill Speck. I pushed the situation to the point where I knew one of us would die. It turned out to be him. I used my badge for personal revenge. Not for the law. For myself."

"A human frailty," she murmured. "I bet you've had a heck of a time adjusting to the fact that you're not perfect. Now that you have, you'll be a better cop when you put that badge back on."

He tightened his grip on her arm. "Why are you doing this?"

For a simple answer she grabbed him and pulled his mouth down to hers. She tasted impatience in the kiss, but there was something else twined with it. It was need—deep and human.

"There's that," she said after a moment. "And I guess we'd have to say that despite what I've always considered my good common sense, I care about you, too." She watched him open his mouth, close it again. "Take responsibility for that, Skimmerhorn."

Turning away, she walked the few steps to the car, then took his keys. "I'm driving."

He waited until she'd unlocked the passenger door. "Conroy?"

"Yeah."

"Same goes."

Her lips curved as she gunned the engine. "That's good. What do you say, Skimmerhorn? Let's go for a ride."

10

FINLEY's home was a museum to his ambitions. High in the hills over L.A., it was built by a film director whose love of elaborate construction had outreached his means. When Finley purchased it, he had immediately installed an elaborate security system, an indoor lap pool for those rare rainy days, and a high stone wall around the property. Finley was a voyeur, but he objected to being watched.

As in his office, the walls in every room were white, as were the carpet, the tiles and the bleached-wood flooring. All the color came from his treasures. Every table, every shelf, every niche, held some masterpiece he had hungered for. When one began to bore him, as they always did, Finley set about acquiring more.

He was never satisfied.

Finley was waiting in the master bedroom. Paintings by Pissarro, Morisot and Manet graced the white silk walls. The furnishings here were lushly ornate, from the Louis XVI boulle bureau to the cabriole nightstands. Overhead, a trio of Waterford chandeliers sprinkled light. The sixteenth-century four-poster was a massive oak affair, complete with tester, headboard and footboard.

He flicked on the monitor. He watched as the cook prepared lunch in the kitchen—the pheasant salad he'd requested.

Finley switched the monitor to the drawing room. He watched DiCarlo sip at the club soda, rattle the ice, tug at his tie. That was good. The man was worried. Overconfidence bred mistakes. He supposed he should let the poor boy off the hook soon. After all, he had brought the merchandise two days ahead of deadline.

Perhaps he wouldn't have his arm broken after all.

DiCARLO tugged at his tie again. He couldn't shake the feeling that he was being watched. He took another swallow and laughed at himself. Anybody would feel as though he was being watched, DiCarlo decided, if he was stuck in a room with a hundred statues and paintings. All those eyes. Painted eyes, glass eyes, marble eyes.

DiCarlo rose to wander the room. It was a good sign, he thought, that Finley had invited him to the house rather than the office. It made it friendlier. Over the phone Finley had sounded pleased. DiCarlo figured he could smooth over the missing painting.

"Mr. DiCarlo, I trust I haven't kept you waiting overlong."

"No, sir. I've been admiring your home."

"I'll have to give you the grand tour after lunch." Finley scanned DiCarlo's bruised face. "Dear me. Did you have an accident?"

"Yes." DiCarlo touched the back of his neck. The memory of Dora's bite had him steaming all over again. "Nothing serious."

"I'm glad to hear it. I hope your plans for the holiday haven't been upset by this trip. I didn't expect you for another day or two."

"I wanted to bring you the results as soon as possible."

Finley smiled as the door chimes echoed down the hallway. "Ah, that will be Mr. Winesap. He'll be joining us to inspect the merchandise. Now, I hope you'll both forgive me, but I must see my treasures," he said as Winesap entered. "I believe they were taken into the library." He gestured toward the door. "Gentlemen?"

The library smelled of leather and lemon and roses. The roses were arranged in two tall Dresden vases set atop the mantel. There were perhaps thousands of books in the room. The ubiquitous monitors were hidden behind a trompe l'oeil panel of a bookcase.

"And here we are." With a spring in his step Finley walked to the library table and picked up the parrot. As instructed, the butler had left a small hammer, a knife and a large wastebasket. Finley took the knife and neatly disemboweled the parrot. "Ah, here," he said, opening a velvet pouch. The lightest of tremors passed through him when he let the sapphire brooch drop into his palm. It was set in an intricate gold filigree encrusted with diamonds, a deep cornflower-blue stone of more than eight carats, square-cut and majestic.

"Worn by Mary, Queen of Scots," Finley told his guests. He stroked the stone, turned it over to admire the back. "It was part of the booty good Queen Bess took after she'd had her pretty cousin executed. It shall have a place of honor." He set it gently aside. Like a spoiled child on Christmas morning, he wanted more.

The engraved Gallé vase in the bowels of the Statue of Liberty thrilled him. He cooed over it. Finley's eyes had taken on a glassy sheen that had Winesap averting his own in faint embarrassment.

From within the base of the bronze eagle, Finley released a box and tore the padding aside. The box itself was rosewood. But the lid was the treasure, a micromosaic panel commissioned in imperial Russia for Catherine the Great. Signed by the artist, it was a wonderfully delicate reproduction of the imperial palace fused onto glass.

"Have you ever seen anything more exquisite? The pride of czars. Now it's mine. Mine alone."

"It's a beauty, all right." DiCarlo hated to interrupt, but it was time to make his pitch. "I'm happy to have played a part in bringing you your merchandise. Of course, there was some difficulty—"

"I'm sure." Finley waved him off before the mood was spoiled. "But we must finish here." He used the hammer on the dog, bursting its belly open. The hound gave birth to a solid-gold cat. "It's said to have been a gift from Caesar to Cleopatra," Finley explained softly. "A beautiful piece."

His hands shook as he set it down. "And now, the painting."

"I, uh . . . there was a little trouble with that, Mr. Finley."

"Trouble?" Finley's smile remained fixed on DiCarlo. "I don't believe you mentioned any trouble."

DiCarlo's cheeks flushed. "I wasn't able to bring it on this trip, Mr. Finley. As I started to tell you, there was a problem." He explained about the three break-ins, reminding Finley that the first had resulted in the recovery of the china hound. He highlighted his personal risk in the search for the painting. "It would be dangerous for all of us for me to return to Philadelphia now. I do have a contact I can put on the matter—at my own expense, of course. I'm sure you'll be patient. I see no reason why the painting can't be in your hands within, say, six weeks."

"Six weeks." Finley nodded, tapped his forefinger to his lip. "You say you shot a police officer."

"It was necessary. He was watching the building."

"Mmm. And why do you suppose he was doing that?"

"I can't be sure." Sincerity in every pore, DiCarlo leaned forward. "I did overhear an argument between the Conroy woman and her tenant. It might be that she asked for police protection."

"Interesting that she simply didn't have him evicted," Finley commented—very very pleasantly. "Shall we dine, gentlemen?"

They enjoyed the pheasant salad along with a chilled Pouilly-Fumé in the formal dining room, with its sun-swept garden view. Finley kept the conversation away from business. He spent an hour playing jovial host, generously refilling DiCarlo's glass himself.

When the last drop of wine and the final morsel of dessert had been consumed, Finley pushed back from the table. "I hope you'll forgive us, Abel, but Mr. DiCarlo and I should conclude our business. Perhaps a walk around the grounds?" he said to DiCarlo.

DiCarlo patted his stomach. "I could use a walk after that meal."

Finley led DiCarlo out into a solarium, through the atrium doors and into the garden. Their shoes crunched lightly over the smooth white stones on the garden path, and they stopped to admire the view. Finley stood looking out over the Los Angeles basin, drawing deeply of the fragrances around him. Flowers—early roses, jasmine. The tang of freshly watered mulch and clipped grass.

"Your plans, Mr. DiCarlo?" Finley said abruptly.

"What? Oh. I put my man on it. He'll snatch the Conroy woman, put on the pressure until she leads him to the painting."

"And then."

"He'll whack her, don't worry." DiCarlo smiled a little, professional man to professional man. "He won't leave any loose ends."

"Ah, yes, loose ends. Most inconvenient." Finley bent over a rosebush, sniffed delicately at a pale pink bud. When he straightened, he held a pearl-handled revolver in his hand. And he was smiling again, charmingly. "It's best to snip them off."

He fired, aiming just above DiCarlo's belt buckle. The sound echoed over the hills and sent terrified birds screaming skyward.

DiCarlo's eyes glazed with pain. He pressed a hand against his belly as his knees crumpled beneath him.

"You disappoint me, Mr. DiCarlo." Finley didn't raise his voice, but bent low to let the words carry. "Did you take me for a fool?"

He straightened and, while DiCarlo writhed in pain from the gunshot, kicked him. "You failed!" Finley shouted, and kicked again, again, screaming over DiCarlo's groaning pleas for mercy. "I want my painting. It's your fault, your fault I don't have it."

Finley replaced the revolver in his pocket. He brushed dust from his sleeve as he walked back toward the solarium.

"Winesap!" he snapped.

"Sir." Winesap tiptoed in, folded his nervous hands. He'd heard the shots and was very much afraid of what was coming next.

"Dispose of Mr. DiCarlo."

Winesap's shoulders slumped. He glanced through the glass wall to where DiCarlo was lying on his back. "Of course, Mr. Finley."

"I realize that tomorrow's a holiday, Abel," Finley said. "So I'll ask that you focus your attention the following day on gathering all the information you can on this Isadora Conroy in Philadelphia." He sniffed. "I'm afraid I'll have to take care of this matter myself."

11

THE lobby of the Liberty Theater was fashioned in Gothic style, with yards of ornate plasterwork, pounds of curlicues and gremlins decorating the gilded molding. Over the doors that led into the theater itself were bronze masks of Comedy and Tragedy.

Tonight the area was packed with people who all seemed determined to be heard above the din. The space smelled of perfumes and smoke, and popcorn erupting cheerfully from a concession stand. The guests' attire ranged from white tie to torn Levi's. Through the open doors Jed could hear the band tear into a blistering rendition of the Rolling Stones' "Brown Sugar." The winter ball, he mused, it wasn't.

The houselights were up. He saw people crowded in the aisles, dancing or standing, talking and eating, while onstage the band pumped out rock. In the box seats and mezzanine and into the second balcony were still more partygoers, shooting the noise level toward sonic with the help of the theater's excellent acoustics.

Jed set about trying to find Dora. If she hadn't left for the New Year's party so early, with the excuse of being needed to help set up and keep her mother away from the caterers, he could have come with her, kept an eye on her. He didn't like the idea of her being alone when her attacker was still loose. Though he could hardly call a gathering of this size being alone.

Jed sipped Scotch and worked his way toward the stage.

Then he saw her. She was sitting on the edge of the stage, dead center, in what had to be an avalanche of sound, holding what appeared to be an intimate conversation with two other women.

She'd done something to her hair, Jed noted. Piled it up on her head in a tangle of wild curls that looked just on the edge of control. She'd painted her eyes up so that they looked as sultry as a Gypsy's. Her lips were a bold red. She wore a black-and-silver jumpsuit with long sleeves and sleek legs that fit like a second skin. She might have left the stage, but she still knew how to lure the spotlight.

He wanted her. For a moment that desire blocked out everything else. Setting his glass on the armrest of an aisle seat, he pushed his way forward against the current of people.

"But he's a method actor, after all," Dora said, grinning. "Naturally, if he's going to pitch the product, he'd want to—" She broke off when hands hooked under her armpits and lifted her up.

She got a quick glimpse of Jed's face before he covered her mouth with his. Her heart was stuttering when he released her.

"Well, hi." She staggered, put a hand on his arm for balance. In her spike-heeled boots she was nearly eye level with him, and his look was intense. "Glad you could make it. I—uh—this is . . ." She turned to her two friends and went blank.

"Excuse us." Jed pulled her to a corner, where they didn't have to shout. "What do you call that thing you're wearing?"

She glanced down at the cat suit. "Sexy. Do you like it?"

"I'll tell you when my tongue rolls back into my mouth."

"You have such a way with words, Skimmerhorn. Do you want a drink, some food?"

"I had a drink."

She took Jed's hand and led him backstage, where another bar and a buffet were set up. He opted for club soda, while Dora chose champagne. She glanced down at his drink. "You don't have to play designated driver, you know. We can cab back."

"I'll stay with this." He reached out, cupped a hand under her chin. "I want a very clear head when I make love with you tonight."

"Oh." She lifted her own glass with an unsteady hand. "Well."

He grinned. "Run out of lines, Conroy?"

"I . . . uh . . ."

"Isadora!"

Jed saw a statuesque redhead in a glitter of green that slicked down a regal body, then frothed out in stiff fans from the knees to the ankles. She looked exotically like a ferocious mermaid.

Blessing Trixie's timing, Dora turned to her mother. "Problem?"

"That caterer is a beast. He refused, absolutely refused, to listen to a word I said about the anchovy paste."

It had been Will's shift to keep their mother separated from the caterer. Dora took a quick glimpse around. "Where's Will?"

"Oh, off with that pretty girl he brought from New York," Trixie said. She tossed up her hands and drew in a deep breath.

"Mom, you haven't met Jed."

"Jed?" Distracted, Trixie patted her hair. Her face transformed when she took her first good look. Subtly she angled her chin and swept her mink lashes. "I'm thrilled to meet you."

Jed kissed her hand. "The pleasure's mine, Mrs. Conroy."

"Oh, Trixie, please," she crooned. "Otherwise I'll feel old."

"I'm sure that would be impossible. I saw you perform *Hello, Dolly!* last year. You were magnificent."

Trixie's cheeks pinked with pleasure. "Oh, how kind of you."

"Mom, Jed's the tenant Dad found for me."

"The tenant!" Instantly, maternal instincts outweighed flirtations. "Oh, my dear, dear boy! I am so completely, so irrevocably in your debt. You saved my darling Isadora from that horrible burglar." Trixie kissed both his cheeks. "We'll never be able to repay you."

Jed narrowed his eyes at Dora over her mother's shoulders.

"There you are, passionflower." In white tie and tails, Dora's father swaggered up. Quentin gave his wife a lingering kiss that had Jed's brow raising. "I've come to claim my bride for a dance."

"Of course, dear." Trixie slipped her arms around him. Quentin winked, dipped his wife, then tangoed her away.

"Passionflower?" Jed asked after a moment.

"It works for them."

"Obviously." He couldn't remember ever seeing his parents exchange even an impersonal embrace, much less a smoldering kiss.

"You never mentioned you'd been to this theater before," she said, drawing his attention back to her. *"Hello, Dolly!?"*

"You didn't ask."

"Come on, I'll show you around," Dora said. "The building's mid–nineteenth century. It used to be a popular music hall." She headed away from the stage, down one of the narrow corridors.

As the evening wore on, Jed stopped questioning the fact that he was enjoying himself, and he didn't feel any impatient urges to leave early. When he ran into the Chapmans in the first balcony, he concluded that they were also enjoying themselves.

"Hey, Jed. Happy New Year." Mary Pat kissed him, then leaned on the rail again to watch the action below. "What a party."

Jed checked out her view. A swarm of people, streams of color, blasts of noise. "The Conroys are—unique."

"You're telling me. I met Lea's father. We jitterbugged." Mary Pat's face flushed with laughter. "I didn't know I *could* jitterbug."

"Where's Dora?" Brent asked. "I haven't seen her."

"She moves around. Her brother, Will, wanted to dance with her." Brent looked down in his empty glass. "Let's go get a beer."

"Oh, no, you don't." Mary Pat grabbed Brent's arm. "You're going to dance with me, Lieutenant. It's almost midnight."

"Couldn't we stay up here and neck?" Brent dragged his feet as his wife pulled him along. "Listen, Jed'll dance with you."

"I'm getting my own woman," Jed said.

By the time the three had managed to elbow their way down to the orchestra level, the lead singer was shouting into the mike, holding up his hands for silence. "Listen up, everybody. We got one minute until zero hour, so find your significant other—or a handy pair of lips—and get ready to pucker up for the new year."

Jed cut through the crowd. He saw her, stage right, laughing with her brother as they poured champagne into outstretched glasses.

She turned to see that the band had full glasses to toast. And she saw him. "Will"—with her eyes on Jed's, she pushed the bottle at her brother—"you're on your own."

"Get ready, people!" The singer's voice boomed out over the theater. "Count with me now. Ten, nine . . ."

She walked to the edge of the stage, her heart beating hard.

"Eight, seven . . ."

She leaned down, put her hands on Jed's shoulders.

"Six, five . . ."

The walls shook. He gripped her waist, and she stepped off into the air and hooked her legs around him.

"Four, three . . ."

Inch by inch she slid down his body, her eyes locked on his.

"Two, one . . ."

Her mouth opened to his in a deep kiss. He continued to lower her from the stage to the ground. Even when she stood, her body remained molded to his. He took his mouth from hers but kept her firmly against him. Her eyes were half closed.

Quentin bounded up and swung an arm around them. "Happy New Year, *mes enfants.*" He kissed Dora, then Jed, with equal enthusiasm. Before Jed could adjust to the shock, Trixie descended on them.

"I love celebrations," she said. There were more kisses, lavishly given. "Will, come here and kiss your mother."

Will obliged, leaping dramatically off the stage and catching his mother up in a theatrical dip. He then turned to Jed.

Braced, Jed held his ground. Will only grinned. "Sorry, we're a demonstrative bunch." Despite the warning, he gave Jed a hard, tipsy hug. "Here's Lea and John."

Thinking of survival, Jed stepped back but was blocked by the stage. He gave up, accepting it philosophically when he was kissed by Lea and embraced by John—whom he'd yet to meet.

Watching his reactions, Dora laughed and found a glass of champagne. Here's to you, Skimmerhorn. You ain't seen nothing yet.

WHEN dusk began to fall, Winesap went out to the garden and his grisly task. It was easy to block the routine from his mind. He had only to imagine it was he who lay staring sightlessly at the sky.

He spread a large painter's cloth over the white stones. Crouching, breath whistling through his teeth, he rolled DiCarlo's limp body over and over until it was centered on the cloth. Then he carefully removed DiCarlo's wallet. He decided to burn it, money and all, at the first opportunity. With the resignation of the overburdened, he meticulously checked the rest of DiCarlo's pockets to be certain he'd removed all forms of identification.

Faintly, from a second-floor window, he heard the strains of some Italian opera. Finley was preparing for an evening out, Winesap mused. After all, tomorrow was a holiday.

THE night was clear as glass, the air brittle. Inside Dora's apartment the warmth, and the music from the stereo, might have lulled her to sleep after the party.

But Jed had taken her hand in his for the short walk to the bedroom, had switched on the bedside lamp to look at her.

Her breath shuddered out when he touched his lips to hers. Tenderness was the last thing she'd expected from him, and the most devastating gift he could give. Her lips parted beneath his, accepting, even as her heart jammed in her throat.

Her head fell back. He continued to play her lips delicately. "You're shaking," he murmured, trailing his lips down her face.

"That's you."

"You could be right." He brought his mouth back to hers, deepening the kiss until pleasure swam giddily in her head.

"Let me turn down the bed," she whispered.

But when she shifted aside, he drew her back against him, nuzzling the nape of her neck. "That can wait."

His hands were on her midsection. "I don't think I can."

Jed slid his hands up her sides, down again, wanting every inch of her. Her heart gave a wild leap, and she abandoned herself to the flood of sensations.

"Dora, you look terrible."

"Lea, what would I do without you around to boost my ego?"

Unfazed, Lea studied her sister's pale face and shadowed eyes in the morning light. "Maybe you're coming down with something."

Dora walked around the counter as a customer came in. She put on a sunny smile. "Good morning. May I help you?"

"Are you Dora Conroy?"

"That's right." Dora knew she looked wan from lack of sleep, but this woman looked near collapse. "Would you like some coffee?"

"I'd love some, but I'm not supposed to drink it." She laid a hand on the gentle mound of her belly. "Tea would be nice. Just black."

"Why don't you sit down?" Taking charge, Dora guided the woman to a chair. "We're all starting a little slow this morning. After-holiday fatigue." When a young couple strolled in, Dora gestured for Lea to see to them. Then she poured two cups of tea.

"Thanks. I'm Sharon Rohman," she told Dora.

"Oh." It hit her all at once. She sat down and took Sharon's hand. "You're Mrs. Lyle's niece. I'm so sorry about what happened. The last time I called the hospital, I was told she was still in a coma."

"She came out of it last night. But she's still critical." Sharon lifted her cup, then rattled it back in the saucer without drinking. "The doctors can't say if or when she'll recover."

Dora's eyes stung in response. "It's a dreadful time for you."

"We've always been close." She brushed at a tear with the back of her hand. Then she took a deep breath. "Miss Conroy—"

"Dora."

"Dora. I came by to thank you for the lovely flowers you sent to the hospital. The nurses told me you've called several times about my aunt. But I don't know how you're connected."

"We only met briefly. She bought a few things here right before Christmas." Dora didn't have the heart to tell Sharon they had been gifts for her and her baby. "I liked her," Dora said simply. "And it bothered me that she'd been hurt so soon after she'd been here."

"She was shopping for me, wasn't she?"

"She's very fond of you." After a moment's hesitation Dora made a decision. "Would you like to know what she bought?"

"Yes, I would, very much."

"She said that you sewed. She bought you a Victorian doorstop so you could keep the door open and hear the baby in the nursery."

Sharon smiled softly. "A brass elephant—like Jumbo?"

"Exactly."

"We found it in the corner of the living room."

"She picked up a doorstop for the nursery, too. A china dog."

"Oh, I didn't see that. It must have been broken. Whoever hurt my aunt also shattered the gifts she'd wrapped, and a great deal of her things as well. It looked as though he'd gone crazy. I suppose he had to be, to kill one old woman and leave another for dead?" But she shook the question away. "I'd like to take her something this morning. Could you help me pick something out?"

"I'd love to."

"WHAT was that all about?" Lea asked as Sharon got into her car.

"That was Mrs. Lyle's niece—Mrs. Lyle was the woman who was attacked on Christmas Eve. She's just come out of a coma."

Lea shook her head. "It's awful to think that someone could break into your home that way."

A quick shiver raced up Dora's spine as she remembered her

own recent experience. "Awful," she agreed. "I hope they find him."

"In the meantime"—Lea turned Dora to face her—"back to you. Why do you look so exhausted when you had yesterday off?"

"I haven't a clue. I spent the entire day in bed," she said, a smile playing around her mouth.

"Oh," Lea said, drawing the word out. "The light dawns. Just whose bed did you spend the day in?"

"My own." Then she grinned. "And it was incredible."

"Really?" Lea was all ears. "Okay, spill it."

"Well, Jed's . . . I can't," she said, baffled. "This is different."

"Uh-oh," Lea said, and grinned, ear to dainty ear.

The door rattled. "Hi!" said Terri. "Busy morning?"

Dora turned to her. "You could say so. Listen, there's a new shipment in the back. Why don't you unpack it. Then I'll price it."

Terri shrugged out of her coat on her way to the storeroom.

"We're not finished, Isadora," Lea said.

"We are for now, Ophelia." Dora kissed her cheek.

"Dora." Terri poked her head out of the storeroom. The copy of the computer-generated picture of DiCarlo was in her hand. "Why do you have a picture of the guy who came in Christmas Eve?"

"What?" Dora struggled to keep her voice even. "You know him?"

"He was our last customer. I sold him the Staffordshire—the mama dog with pup."

Dora's heart danced in her chest. "Did he pay cash?"

"No. He charged it."

"Would you mind digging up the receipt for me."

"Okay. He had some Italian name," Terri added. "Delano, Demarco, something." Shrugging, she closed the door behind her.

"DiCarlo," Brent said, handing Jed a rap sheet. "Anthony DiCarlo, New York. Small-time stuff: larceny, a couple of B and E's. Did a short stretch for extortion, but he's been clean for nearly six years. NYPD faxed this to me this morning. Shouldn't be too hard to find out if our boy has an alibi for the other night."

"If he has one, it's fantasy. This is him." Jed tossed the file photo onto Brent's desk. "Maybe I should take a trip to New York."

"You look pretty relaxed for a man who wants to kick butt."

Jed's lips twitched. "Do I?"

"Yep." Leaning back, Brent nodded. "That's what I thought." He grinned. "Dora's quite a woman. Nice going, Captain."

"Shut up, Chapman," Jed said mildly on his way out.

JED went straight up to his own apartment, stripped down to gym shorts before settling on the bench press. He had to decide how much to tell Dora. She had a right to know it all. But if he knew Dora, she'd want to do something about it. One of a cop's biggest headaches was civilian interference. Not that he was a cop, he reminded himself, keeping up a steady rhythm with the weights.

Some poking around in New York wouldn't infringe overmuch on the official investigation there. If he could do something tangible, he might not feel so . . . He scowled. Just how did he feel?

Useless, he realized. Unsettled. Unfinished. Nothing in his life had ever really had a closure, because nothing had ever really been open to begin with. It had been easier to keep himself shut off. But this was about protecting the woman across the hall. The woman he'd begun to feel something for.

He didn't stop lifting when he heard the knock, but his lips curved when she called his name.

"Skimmerhorn, I need to talk to you."

"It's open."

She walked in, looking all business in a hunter-green suit. "Oh." Her eyebrows lifted as she scanned his body stretched out on the bench, muscles rippling and oiled with sweat. Her heart did a fast somersault. "Sorry to interrupt your male ritual."

"Did you want something, Conroy?" Jed rattled the barbell back in the brace.

"You won't be so cranky after I tell you what I found out." She paused, dramatic timing. "Terri recognized the magic computer picture. He was in the shop on Christmas Eve. His name is—"

"DiCarlo, Anthony," Jed interrupted, amused, as Dora's jaw dropped. "Last known address East Eighty-third Street, New York."

"But how did you . . . Darn. You could have at least pretended to be impressed with my skills as a detective."

"You're a real Nancy Drew, Conroy." He went to the kitchen, took a jug of Gatorade from the fridge and gulped it from the bottle. "You did okay. The cops just work faster. Did you call it in?"

"No." Her lip poked out. "I wanted to tell you."

"Okay, spill it, Nancy."

"Well, Terri said DiCarlo was very smooth, very polite. He said he had this aunt he wanted to buy a special gift for. Terri said she showed him the foo dog—which I'm now sure he helped himself to when he broke in." She scowled over that a minute. "She said he was a snappy dresser and drove a Porsche."

"I want to talk to her. Is she downstairs?"

"No. We're closed. You could catch her at the theater later. Curtain's at eight. We can grab her backstage between scenes."

"Fine."

Dora followed him as he walked toward the bedroom. "But what good will it do? I've already talked to her."

"You don't know the questions to ask. He might have said something. The more we know, the easier it'll be in interrogation."

THEY arrived at the Liberty Theater in time to hear nurse Nellie demonstrate how to wash a man out of her hair. Dora had taken Jed through the stage door and into the wings. Her father was there, mouthing the lyrics and pantomiming the moves.

"Hey." Dora pinched his cheek. "Where's Mom?"

"In wardrobe. Jed, my boy. Glad you came by." He pumped Jed's hand while keeping an eye onstage. "Light cue," he muttered under his breath, then beamed at the glow of a spot.

"We just dropped by to see how things were," Dora said, and shot a warning look at Jed. "And I need a minute with Terri at intermission. Shop business." She slipped an arm around her father's shoulders and was soon as absorbed in the staging as he.

Jed hung back, more intrigued by Dora and Quentin than the dialogue onstage. Their heads were tilted together as they discussed the scene. Quentin's arm wrapped around her waist.

Jed experienced a sensation that shocked him. It was envy. Had he ever felt that easy affection with his own father? he wondered. The answer was very simple and very bleak. No. Never.

The scene ended. There was applause, and then sudden chaos backstage as Dora caught Terri coming offstage.

"I need to talk to you for a minute."

"Sure," Terri said. "How about that dance number?"

"You were great." With a nod to Jed, Dora steered Terri briskly past the stagehands to a corner of the dressing room.

Dora commandeered a stool. "Sit down, Terri. Get off your feet."

"You don't know how good that feels."

"About DiCarlo," Dora began.

"Who? Oh, the guy from Christmas Eve."

"What did he buy?" Jed asked her.

"Oh, a Staffordshire figure. Never even winked at the price. It was for his favorite aunt. I thought he might bite on the foo dog, too, because he was looking for an animal."

"An animal?" Jed's eyes sharpened, but his voice was cool.

"His aunt collects statues of dogs. He really wanted a dog like the one his aunt had had that died." She shifted toward the mirrors to freshen her lipstick. "I thought how we'd had that china piece that would have been perfect. You know, Dora, the one you picked up at that auction. You'd already sold it, though."

Dora felt her blood drain. "To Mrs. Lyle." She needed to get out. Needed air. "Thanks, Terri." She fumbled for the door.

Jed caught up to Dora at the stage door just as she was pushing through and drawing in deep breaths of air.

"Shake it off, Conroy." He held her by the shoulders.

"I sold it to her." When she tried to jerk away, he merely tightened his hold. "And the day after he found out—"

"You sell lots of things—that's what you do. You're not responsible for what happens to the people who buy them."

"I can't be like that!" she shouted at him, and struck out. "I can't close myself off that way. That's your trick, Skimmerhorn."

That twisted in his gut. "You want to blame yourself, fine." Gripping her arm, he pulled her toward the car. "I'll take you home, and you can spend the night beating yourself up over it."

"I can get myself home."

"You wouldn't get two blocks before that bleeding heart of yours splashed on the sidewalk."

Her temper snapped. She rounded on him, leading with her left. He dodged it, yanked out his keys and unlocked the car door.

She got in and closed her eyes, listening to him stalk around the car, open the door, slam it shut. The fury drained out of her, and she shut her eyes a moment. "I'm sorry, Jed."

He drove out of the lot, a cool look in his eyes. Then he took her hand, lifted it to touch to his lips.

She mustered up a smile. "I'm glad you're not mad at me."

"Who said I wasn't? I just don't want to fight when I'm driving." He lapsed into silence a moment. "About Mrs. Lyle," he began. "I'm going to need to check on her condition. If she comes out of the coma, she might put some pieces together for me."

"Us," Dora corrected quietly. "She's awake. Her niece, Sharon, came by the shop this morning and told me. But I won't let her be interrogated after what she's been through."

Tires spat out gravel when he turned into the lot. "Do I look like the Gestapo, Conroy?"

Saying nothing, she snapped down the door handle and climbed out. He reached the steps before her and blocked the way.

"Dora." Searching for patience, he took her hands. "I know what I'm doing. I'll be careful with her. Trust me."

"I do." Watching his face, she linked her fingers with his. "Completely. This whole thing has shaken me up some, that's all."

A bit shaken himself, he kissed her. He didn't like to ask. He didn't like to need. But he did. "Stay with me tonight."

The worry cleared from her eyes. "I was hoping you'd ask."

"HE MURDERED the housekeeper for a little china dog," Dora said. They were at the elevators. They had just come from visiting Mrs. Lyle in the critical care unit. She was frail and weak but lucid.

"Not much doubt of it," Brent said. "But that's not the end of it. The bullet that killed Muriel came from the same gun that killed Officer Trainor. Matched the ones we dug out of the plaster at the shop."

"So he came back for something else." Calculating, Jed stepped into the elevator. "The dog wasn't it—or wasn't all of it."

"But the piece wasn't valuable or unique," Dora murmured. "It wasn't even marked. I only bid on it because it was cute."

"You bought it at an auction." Slowly Jed turned the possibilities over in his mind. "Where?"

"In Virginia. Lea and I went on a buying trip. You remember. I got back the day you moved in."

"And the next day you sold the dog." He took her arm when they reached the hospital lobby. "There was a break-in at the shop, Mrs. Lyle was attacked, then another break-in. What else did you buy, Dora?"

"At the auction? A lot of things. I have a list at the shop."

"What did you buy right before the dog, and right after?"

She was tired down to the bone. Her temple throbbed. "Jeez, Skimmerhorn, how am I supposed to remember?"

"Conroy, you know everything you buy, everything you sell and the exact price. Now what did you buy before the dog?"

"A shaving mug, swan-shaped." She snapped the words out. "Circa 1900. Forty-six dollars and seventy-five cents."

"And after the dog?"

"An abstract painting in an ebony frame. Primary colors on white canvas, signed E. Billingsly. Final bid fifty-two seventy-five—" She broke off, pressed a hand to her mouth. "Oh, my Lord."

"Right on target," Jed muttered.

"A picture," she whispered, horrified. "Not a photograph—a painting. He wanted the painting." Dora's cheeks were the color of paste as she groped for Jed's hand. "I gave it to my mother."

JED, Dora and Brent had dropped in on Trixie and picked up the painting. They'd chosen to work in Dora's apartment rather than the storeroom because there was both room and privacy. No one had mentioned that Brent hadn't insisted on taking the painting, or the information he'd gathered, to his superior, Goldman. It was an unspoken fact that Brent still considered Jed his captain.

Jed removed the frame from the canvas and set it carefully aside. "Nothing to the frame. We'll let the lab boys take a look."

"Can't be the painting itself," Dora said. "The artist is an unknown—I checked the day after I bought it."

Jed turned the painting over. "The canvas is stretched over plywood. Get me something to pry this off with, Conroy."

"You think there might be something inside?" In the kitchen she rummaged through drawers and brought out a screwdriver. "A cache of drugs—no, better. Diamonds. Rubies, maybe."

"Try reality," Jed suggested, working at the plywood backing.

"It has to be something worth killing for, and that's money," she insisted.

"Nothing," Jed muttered as he examined the backing he'd removed. "No secret compartments."

"That's odd. The back of that canvas has a lot of age to it," Dora said. "I suppose Billingsly could have painted over an old canvas."

"Sometimes people paint over paintings to smuggle them."

"You think there's an old master behind there?" Amused, Dora shook her head. "Now who's dreaming?"

But he was studying the splashes of red and blue. "We need to get this paint off, see what's under it."

"I have some stuff in the storeroom that should work. Give me a minute." Dora went downstairs, returning moments later with a drop cloth, a bottle and several rags.

Jed took the bottle. "What's in here?"

"A solution I use when some idiot has painted over stenciling." She knelt on the floor to roll back the rug. "We need a careful touch. Give me a hand with this." Brent crouched and spread the cloth, and Dora handed Jed a rag. "I'd start on a corner if I were you."

He knelt beside her, dampened the rag and, working in slow, delicate circles, removed the end of the signature, then the white primer. "Something's under here." He gently removed more of the primer. "Pay dirt."

"What is it?" Dora crouched close to the corner. "Monet." She whispered the name, as though in church. "Claude Monet. I bought a Monet for fifty-two dollars and seventy-five cents."

"I'm not much of an art buff," Brent said, "but even I know who this guy is. I don't think anybody would have painted over the real thing unless it was being smuggled. I'll see if there've been any art thefts that included our friend here."

Jed looked at Brent. "You'll have to take this to Goldman."

"That's the next step."

"I shouldn't ask you, but I'm going to."

"How much time do you want?" Brent asked, anticipating him.

"Time enough to check out the auction house in Virginia and find the trail." He kept his voice even.

Brent nodded, picked up his coat. "Watch your back. See you, Dora."

"Bye, Brent." She stayed where she was a moment. "Why don't you book us a flight for Virginia. I'll be packed in ten minutes."

"I don't want you with me," Jed said. "It could be dangerous."

"Fine, I'll book my own flight."

"You know, you're a pain in the neck."

"So I've been told."

12

IT WAS raining in thin, chilly sheets when Jed drove into Front Royal after the flight into Dulles. Dora chatted away on the drive, her easy voice and casual observations relaxing him.

She used the visor mirror to freshen her lipstick. "Make the next two rights," she told him. "There's a parking lot in back."

Jed pulled up into a slot beside a battered Ford pickup. "Remember, Conroy, you're not here on a buying jaunt."

"I know, I know." She rolled her eyes as they climbed out of the car. "And you'll ask the questions," she continued. She hooked her arm through his and started for the rear door. "It won't be warm inside," she told him as he pulled open the metal door. "Mr. Porter has a rep for extreme frugality." Her eyes kindled. "Wow, just look at all of this stuff. I think that's a Maxfield Parrish print."

Jed snagged Dora's arm. "Where are the offices?"

"In the front, to the right."

He hauled her along. The office was open but empty when they reached it. Curious, Dora poked her head inside.

"May I help you?"

Jed turned to the tidily dressed woman with glasses hanging from a gold chain. "We'd like to speak to Mr. Porter."

Helen Owings' eyes clouded and filled alarmingly fast with hot tears. "Oh," she said, and dug into her pocket for a tissue.

Before Jed could react, Dora had her by the arm and was leading her into the office, into a chair. "Can I get you some water?"

"No, no." Helen sniffled. "You couldn't have known, I suppose. Sherman—Mr. Porter's dead. Murdered." Her lips trembled.

"Oh, Lord." Dora groped for a chair herself.

"Right before Christmas. I found him myself. There at the desk."

"How was he killed?" Jed demanded.

"Shot. Through the head. Poor, poor Sherman."

"Do the police have any suspects?" Jed asked.

"No." Helen sighed and dropped her hands into her lap. "There doesn't seem to have been a motive. Nothing was taken, Mr. . . . ?"

"Skimmerhorn."

"Mr. Skimmerhorn. Did you know Sherman?"

"No. Miss Conroy is a Philadelphia dealer. We're here about items that were auctioned on December twenty-first. Miss Conroy bought two pieces. We're interested in where and how you acquired them."

"Well . . ." It wasn't regular to reveal sources, but Helen couldn't find any harm in it. "Do you remember the lot number?"

"F-fifteen and F-eighteen," Dora said dully. She'd remembered something else, something that made her stomach roll.

Helen rose and went to the file cabinets. "Oh, yes. The F lots were from the New York shipment. A small estate sale." She smiled, taking the folder to the desk. "To be frank, the quality was not what I'd expected. Conroy . . . Yes, you purchased both pieces."

A knock on the door interrupted her. "Miz Owings? We got a question out here about that Early American dry sink. People are in a hurry."

"All right. I'll be right there." Helen rose, smoothed down her hair, her skirt. "Will you excuse me just a minute?"

Jed waited until she'd walked out before picking up the file himself. He scanned the lists, the inventories, the prices, then simply pocketed what he felt was relevant.

"What are you doing?" Dora demanded. "You can't do that."

"It'll save time. Come on. We'll make copies, then send the originals back." He took her hand, but this time she didn't try to linger. Once they were outside and in the car, Jed took her chin in his hand. "Okay, spill it. You went white as a sheet in there."

"I remembered Mr. Ashworth. He was the dealer I met at the auction that day. He bought a piece from that shipment."

"The guy who was killed during a burglary," Jed murmured. "You said his shop was around here."

"Yes, just a couple miles away, in Front Royal."

"Then that's where we're going next. Can you handle it?"

"Yes. But I want to call my shop first. I don't want Terri or Lea anywhere near the place. I want it closed."

"Okay." He took her hand. "Okay."

JED HAD HOPED TO MAKE THE TRIP to Virginia and back in one day. There was no question of doing so after visiting Ashworth's shop. Dora said nothing when he checked into a hotel near the airport. The fact that she'd said little throughout the rainy ride from Front Royal concerned him nearly as much as the information they'd gleaned from Tom Ashworth's grandson. In addition to Ashworth's death and the damage done during the break-in, the porcelain figurine of a man and a woman had apparently been taken.

Jed unlocked the hotel-room door, set the overnight bags aside, then pointed Dora toward a chair. "Sit down. You need to eat."

"I'm not hungry."

He picked up the phone and ordered two steaks, coffee and a bottle of brandy. "Thirty minutes," he said when he hung up.

"I . . . I think I'll have a bath," she said numbly. She rose, picked up her bag. "Don't you feel anything?" she asked in a voice cracking with fatigue. "At least three people are dead. People I care about might be in danger simply because they work for me. And you order dinner. Doesn't it make you scared? Doesn't it make you anything?"

Jed met her eyes levelly. "Yeah. It makes me mad. Go take your bath, Dora. Tune it out for a while."

Wearily she turned away. She closed the door behind her.

He swore under his breath. She was disappointed in him—that's what had been in her eyes. And it mattered too much to him.

He heard the water running in the tub, then called Brent.

"It's Jed."

"What have you got, Captain?"

"A couple of dead guys." Jed automatically kept his voice low and told Brent what he knew. "I've got the name of the guy who sent the shipment down from New York," he concluded. "I'm going to check him out tomorrow, in person. Franklin Flowers, Brooklyn address. Any more on the painting?"

"Still working on it."

"Are you taking any heat on this?"

"Nothing I can't handle. Goldman decided to take an interest in Trainor's shooter. Did an interview in front of the courthouse."

"We'll dump DiCarlo right in his lap."

The disgust in Jed's voice gave Brent hope. "If we can find him. Our boy seems to have gone underground."

"Then we'll dig him up. I'll call you from New York."

He hung up. The water had stopped running.

Dora was lying back in the tub while the hot water relaxed her body. It was more difficult to relax her mind. She kept seeing the way Helen Owings' eyes had filled. She kept hearing the way young Ashworth's voice had thickened when he spoke of his grandfather. She kept remembering how fragile Mrs. Lyle had looked. And she could feel the memory of the cool gun barrel against her skin.

Worse, she could still hear Jed's flat, dispassionate voice questioning the victims, and see his eyes, so gorgeously blue, blank out all emotion. No heat, no ice, no sympathy. Perhaps she'd been wrong about him all along.

The water cooled. Dora dried off carefully, then reached for her robe. Her hand brushed over the vivid green terry cloth. She'd let herself forget the gentle side of him, she realized.

Sighing a little, she slipped into the robe. She opened the door, letting out a flow of steam. Jed was standing at the window, looking out at the rain. The room-service cart was beside him, set for two. He turned to her.

"You're trying to make things easier for me." Why hadn't she realized that before? she wondered.

"I got you some fuel, that's all." She looked fragile and lovely. He started to pull out a chair, but she was crossing to him. Her arms went around him, her body pressed close, she buried her face against his neck. He held her like that, his hands stroking her back.

"I was scared," she murmured.

"Nothing's going to happen to you."

"I was scared of more than that. Scared you wouldn't be here to hold me like this when I needed you to. Or that if you were, it would be because it was a job you couldn't graciously avoid."

"I don't worry about doing anything graciously."

She laughed. "I know. But I got in your way. Pushing you to feel things you can't afford to feel if you're going to do what you have to do. Wanting you to have feelings for me you don't want to have."

"I don't know what I feel for you."

"I know that, too." She lifted a hand to his cheek. "Tell me what we do next," she said.

"We go to New York in the morning."

"You said 'we.' You're making progress, Skimmerhorn."

"Just saving myself an argument."

"Uh-uh. You like having me around. You might as well admit it." She smiled gently. "I like having you around, too."

He caught her wrist, held it. "Maybe you shouldn't. Maybe you should be running hard in the other direction. What you need to understand is that I may not be able to give you what you want."

"It occurs to me, Skimmerhorn, that you're more worried I might be able to give you exactly what you want."

DORA had always loved New York—its unrelenting pace, its energy. The sidewalk vendors, the blatant rudeness of the cabdrivers.

Jed swore as a cab cut him off with a coat of paint to spare.

Dora beamed. "Great, isn't it?"

"Yeah. Right."

"Oh, look!" She rolled down her window, craned her neck. "Did you see that fabulous outfit?" Dora narrowed her eyes to try to make out the name and address of the shop. "It would just take me five minutes if you could find a place to park."

He snorted. "I should have known better than to drive you through Manhattan. It's like offering a steak to a starving dog."

"You should have let me drive," she corrected. "I wouldn't have been able to look at the shops. Besides, you're the one who wanted to check out DiCarlo's apartment."

Jed made the turn onto Eighty-third. After a quick scan for a spot big enough to slip the rental car into, he double-parked. "I want you to wait here while I go in and check out DiCarlo."

"How come I can't come in?"

"Because I want the car to be here when I get back." He kissed her and got out. "Lock your doors, Conroy."

When five minutes passed into ten, and ten into twenty, Dora began to consider leaving Jed a note to pick her up at the boutique, when he jogged back to the car.

"The super let me into DiCarlo's apartment."

"So? What did you find?"

"Italian shoes, Armani suits, silk underwear. A checkbook with a balance of seven thousand, a porcelain Madonna and dozens of framed family photos." He started the car and headed downtown.

"I also found letterhead from E.F., Incorporated, based in L.A., with a branch here in Manhattan, a lot of paperwork from the same, and about a dozen messages on his phone machine. No one has seen him for more than a week, and his mail hasn't been picked up."

"Do you think he's still in Philadelphia?"

"He won't get near you, Dora. That's a promise."

Jed fought his way from Manhattan to Brooklyn Heights. By the time he found Franklin Flowers' address, he had fit together all the pieces he had so far, jumbled them and let them reassemble. He slipped smoothly into a parking spot.

"Looks like you're in on this one, Conroy. But don't forget—"

"I know. You'll do the talking."

They entered the shop. It was hardly bigger than the average living room and was crammed with merchandise ranging from ratty teddy bears to pole lamps. It was deserted. As the sign on the counter instructed, Jed rang a brass bell.

"One moment, please." A male voice came from behind a beaded curtain. Before Dora could finish her survey of a group of Avon bottles, Flowers came through the curtain with a rattle of beads. He was a big man, gone soft in the middle. Like his teddy bears, he had a round, homely face that radiated sweetness.

Jed took the lead. "Mr. Flowers?"

"Yes, I'm Frank Flowers." He sang the words, like a kindergarten teacher. "And what may I do for you today?"

"Do you know Sherman Porter?"

Flowers' jolly expression disintegrated. "Poor man. Tragic."

"You sent a shipment to him," Jed continued. "It arrived in Virginia on the twenty-first of December."

"Oh, yes." Flowers smiled sadly. "Who would have guessed it would be the last time Sherman and I would do business together?"

"There seems to be a question about the shipment. A painting."

"Painting?" Flowers frowned. "I didn't send a painting."

"The abstract, signed E. Billingsly."

"Abstract?" Tilting his head, Flowers giggled. "Oh, my dear, no. I would *never* touch an abstract. They're so hard to sell."

"Do you have a list of the inventory you shipped?"

"Naturally. I'm a bear for organization. I'll be back in a jiff."

He disappeared behind the curtain and returned carrying two

107

files—one in yellow, the other in red. "I color-code, you see. The yellow will be what I purchased at the estate sale." He opened the folder and flipped through meticulously typed lists of merchandise. "Now that would have been . . . December twelve. Here we are. Woodlow estate, Catskills, December twelve. There's no painting."

Nor was there a china dog, Jed observed. Or a figurine matching the description of the one Tom Ashworth had died for.

"And this is one of my shipping files, specifically dealing with Sherman—the Lord rest him. As you can see," he said as he opened the red folder, "the top shipment was the last. Not a painting in sight." He grinned. "It must have gotten mixed up with my things after uncrating. Sherman, bless him, was a bit careless."

"Yes," Jed said. "I'm sure you're right."

"HE's wrong," Dora stated as she pulled open the car door. "I saw the stock boy setting up that entire lot. It had just arrived."

"Yeah." Jed took out his keys, jiggling them restlessly in his hand. "Not one item matches Flowers' list. Tell me this, Conroy. If you were smuggling a Monet and other illegal valuables—"

"I wouldn't have them shipped to auction," she interrupted, her eyes darkening with inspiration. "Somebody messed up. DiCarlo?"

"Might be. But the packing slips. The one in Flowers' file, and the one I lifted from Porter's. They were both from Premium Shipping." He started the car. "I've got some calls to make."

They stopped at a small Brooklyn restaurant. While Jed made his calls from the pay phone, Dora had coffee and a sandwich.

"Looks like the Monet's genuine." Jed sat down and pulled Dora's plate over. "They need to run tests, but it got a thumbs-up." He wolfed down a triangle of sandwich and signaled for coffee. "It turns out that everybody who bought from the shipment was robbed between December twenty-second and New Year's. In each case the piece they'd bought at the auction was taken. Sloppy jobs. And still no sign of DiCarlo. He's some sort of vice president of the New York branch of E.F., Incorporated. His staff claim not to know his where-abouts. His mother filed a missing-person report this morning."

"I have a theory," Dora said.

He grinned. "Playing Nancy Drew again?"

"Well, it's obvious to me there were two shipments. The one

from the estate sale and the one with the smuggled goods. Since we agree that it would have been impossibly stupid for DiCarlo to have purposely shipped off his loot to auction, the logical conclusion is that the two shipments were mixed up."

"Go on," he encouraged. "You're about to earn a merit badge."

"And since both packing slips originated from Premium, one could deduce that the mix-up happened there."

"Nice going, Nancy. Let's go check out Queens."

BILL Tarkington bounced up to his office door, beaming a smile. "Mr. Skimmerhorn?" He pumped Jed's hand. "And Miss Conroy. I apologize for making you wait. How about some coffee?"

Before Jed could decline, Dora was saying, "I'd love some."

Happy to serve, Tarkington turned to fill three cups and passed them out. "Now, then." He settled himself behind his desk. "You had some question about a shipment, didn't you?"

"That's right." Jed read what he'd copied from Flowers' invoice. "December seventeenth from a Franklin Flowers, destination Sherman Porter, Front Royal, Virginia. Number ASB five four four six seven."

"We'll just call that right on up. What was the problem, exactly?"

"The merchandise shipped was not the merchandise received."

Tarkington's face took on a pained look. "Oh, Lordy, not again."

"You had this happen before?" Jed demanded.

Tarkington punched keys. "The Christmas rush this year was unusually bad. December seventeenth, you said." His eyes brightened. "That could be it! There was another complaint about a shipment that went out that day. The client was very upset."

"DiCarlo," Dora said involuntarily.

Before Jed could snarl at her, Tarkington was beaming again. "Righto. Do you know him?"

"We've met." Dora kept an easy smile on her face.

"Isn't that a coincidence? I've done everything possible to locate Mr. DiCarlo's merchandise, and now it seems that the two shipments were misdirected. I'll contact him immediately."

"We'll take care of that." Jed scanned the computer screen over Tarkington's shoulder and noted the shipping clerk's name.

"That would save me an embarrassing moment." He slurped at

his coffee and winked. "We will, of course, reimburse both you and Mr. DiCarlo for all shipping charges."

"I was right," Dora said under her breath as they walked away.

"Pat yourself on the back later." Jed walked up to the nearest clerk. "Where's Johnson?"

"Opal?" The clerk jerked his head. "Over there. Line six."

"What are we doing now?" Dora asked.

"Checking tedious details."

Dora didn't find it tedious at all. They sat with Opal in the employee lunchroom and listened to her story. Because Dora was obviously fascinated and sympathetic, Jed sat back and let her play good cop. He'd have said she was born for it.

"Can you believe it?" The excitement was drumming again as they made their way across the parking lot. "She mixes up invoices, and we end up with a smuggled Monet." Dora grinned as Jed unlocked the car door. "Maybe I like police work after all."

"Stick with selling knickknacks," Jed advised.

"At least you could say I did a good job."

"You did a good job. Don't get cocky."

"I'm not cocky. All we have to do now is find DiCarlo."

"Leave that one to the big boys, baby. Time to step back."

And he had something else to check out now. Bill Tarkington's computer screen had been a font of information: the intended recipient of DiCarlo's illicit shipment was Abel Winesap of E.F., Incorporated, Los Angeles.

13

DORA was trying not to be annoyed. Any woman would be annoyed if she awakened alone in bed without a clue as to where her lover had gone or when he might be returning. She wasn't *any* woman, Dora reminded herself. They were both free to come and go as they pleased. She wouldn't even ask Jed where he'd been.

But when she heard the knock on the door, she tugged down the hem of her oversized sweatshirt and marched into the living room. "Okay, Skimmerhorn," she muttered. "This better be good."

She yanked open the door, turned and walked stiffly into the kitchen. "I woke up alone in bed this morning."

"Hold it. What are you talking about?"

"Nothing." Her voice was low and furious.

"Conroy." Caught between amusement and exasperation, he leaned against the doorjamb. "You're ticked because I went out?"

"Why should I be? I'm used to waking up in bed alone."

Baffled, he scrubbed his hands over his face. "Look, I got up early. I didn't want to wake you. . . ." Yes, he had wanted to wake her up, he thought. But it hadn't been to tell her he was going out. "I went to the gym for an hour, caught breakfast with Brent. We had some things to go over."

"Did I ask you for an explanation? Oh, forget it!" Disgusted with herself, she pinched the bridge of her nose.

"I really need to satisfy my curiosity," he said. "What does a woman wear under baggy football sweats?"

"Nothing important. In fact . . ." She laughed. "Nothing at all."

"There's a hole in the shoulder." He scooped her up, nuzzled her neck as he carried her to the bedroom.

"I know." They tumbled like wrestling children onto the bed. She sighed and slid her fingers into his hair.

He kissed her, twining a lock of her hair around his finger. The sun was bright through the open curtain, spilling generously over her face, her skin. "We could start a fire," Jed said, "and spend the rest of the morning in bed watching game shows."

"That sounds incredibly tempting, Skimmerhorn. Why do I have this odd feeling that you're trying to keep me out of the way?"

"Out of whose way?"

"Yours. You and Brent are working on something, and you don't want me to know what it is." He showed no reaction at all. She shrugged. "I'll find out anyway."

"How?"

She smiled. "I'll vamp it out of you."

"Vamp? You can't expect me to concentrate on Bob Barker or Vanna White after a statement like that."

"Bob Barker?" She laughed, so delighted with him she leaped into his arms. "Bob Barker? Skimmerhorn, I love you."

She started to kiss him senseless, when she felt him stiffen. Very slowly, very quietly her heart sank to her knees. "Whoops." She fought for a light tone as she untangled herself from him. "Wasn't

111

supposed to let that one out, was I? Sorry. Chalk it up to the heat of the moment."

He finally managed her name. "Dora—"

"No, really." Oh, Lord, she thought, panicked. She was going to cry if she didn't do something. "It was just a slip of the tongue."

His face was set, his eyes absolutely blank.

"Listen, Skimmerhorn, the L word comes real easy to me. My family boots it around like a football—you know us theatrical types." Her voice was excessively cheerful. "Why don't you start that fire. I'll make us something to snack on while watching game shows."

"You meant it, didn't you?" He said it quietly, and the eyes that had fastened on her face made it impossible for her to hedge.

"Yes, I meant it. And since it obviously bothers you so much, I'll be careful not to say it again. Ever. All right?"

No, it was far from all right. He couldn't pinpoint the moment when things had changed between them any more than he could pinpoint his own feelings. But he could do something to stabilize what was becoming a dangerous situation.

"Get dressed," he told her. "I want to show you something."

THE weather, at least, was promising. The sun beat hard against the windshield of Jed's T-Bird as they drove through the city, far from the rivers with their frisky breezes, toward Chestnut Hill.

He hadn't spoken since they'd started the drive. She didn't ask where they were going. She was almost sure she knew.

Far up the hill the trees were old and stately, the homes trim and elegant. Jed pulled up in a narrow driveway beside a lovely old Colonial. The brick had mellowed to a soft dusky rose, and the trim was a Wedgwood blue. Tall windows glinted in the strong sunlight.

It was a fine house, Dora mused. Beautifully maintained, strongly feminine, with its neat lines and dignity. She imagined it in the summer, when the roses would be sumptuously blooming. And in the fall, when the big leafy trees would burst into golds and scarlets. The picture was completed with lace at the windows and a dog in the yard. And because she imagined so well, her heart broke a little. She doubted very much that Jed saw the house as she did.

She alighted from the car. "This is where you grew up?"

"That's right." He led the way to the door flanked with lovely beveled glass inserts. When he'd unlocked it, he stepped back and waited for Dora to go in ahead.

The foyer was two stories, topped with a many-tiered chandelier that would graciously light the way up the grand oak staircase. The floor was tiled with large squares of black and white marble. Dora ran her hand over the gleaming newel-post at the base of the banister—a banister, she thought, fashioned for a woman's trailing fingers. She was curious where Jed had fit into the design.

"You're planning to sell it."

He was watching her carefully as she wandered from the foyer into the front parlor. "It's on the market." He stayed where he was when Dora walked over to study the scrubbed and empty hearth.

A fire would take away the chill, she thought. Absently she wandered out again and down the hall. She found a library, stripped of books; another parlor, with a view of a cobbled patio that begged for flower boxes; the dining room, vast and empty; and, finally, the kitchen, with its charming hearth and brick oven. But she found no warmth there, only the cold, echoing silence of an unwanted house.

"It's a pretty view from here," she said, to fill the void. There should be a sandbox in the yard, she thought, linking her tensed fingers together. A swing hanging from the big maple.

"You should see the rest of it." And once she had, he thought grimly, he hoped never to walk through the door again.

She caught up with him at the base of the stairs, where he had gone to wait for her. "Jed, this isn't necessary."

"Let's go upstairs." He took her arm, ignoring her hesitation. Jed inclined his head toward a door. "My mother's room. My father's was down the hall. As you can see, there were several rooms between."

She sighed. "Where was yours?"

"There."

Dora moved down the hall and peeked into the room. It was large and airy, bright with afternoon light. The windows overlooked the rear lawn. Dora sat on the narrow window seat and looked out.

"There used to be a chestnut tree out there," he said. "I'd go out that way at night, hitch a ride and go down to Market Street to raise hell. One night one of the servants spotted me and reported it to my father. He had the tree cut down the next day. Then he came up here, locked the door and beat me. I was fourteen." He said it without emotion. "That's when I started lifting weights. He wasn't going to beat me again. If he tried, I was damn well going to be strong enough to take him. A couple of years later I did. And that's how I earned boarding school, until I got kicked out."

"What about your mother?" she asked quietly.

"She preferred throwing things, expensive things. She knocked me unconscious once with a Meissen vase."

Dora nodded, swallowed. "Your sister?"

He shrugged. "They vacillated between treating her like a Dresden doll and an inmate. Tea parties one day, locked doors the next. Sharing the misery should have made us close, but somehow it never did. I got the call to go see Elaine from one of Speck's men. They wanted me on the scene when it happened. They knew she went out every Wednesday at eleven to have her hair done. I didn't. I was minutes away from her house, and annoyed at being summoned, when the dispatch came through with the bomb threat."

He paused a moment. "I was first on the scene, just as Speck planned. I could see her in the car as I ran. The roses were blooming," he said softly, seeing it all perfectly again. "She looked toward me. I could see the surprise on her face—and the irritation. I imagine Elaine was ticked off at the idea of the neighbors' seeing me run across the lawn with my weapon out. Then she turned the key and the car went up. The blast knocked me back into the roses."

"You tried to save her, Jed."

"I didn't save her," he said flatly. "That's for me to live with."

Dora sat quietly. Jed felt a jolt of surprise at how lovely she looked there with the sun pouring around her, her eyes calm and watchful, her mouth solemn. Odd, he thought, there had never been anything in this house he'd considered beautiful. Until now.

"I understand why you brought me here," she began. "You wanted me to see a cold, empty house, and you wanted me to understand that, like the house, you have nothing to offer."

"I don't have anything to offer."

"You don't want to," she corrected. "And considering the role models in your life, it's certainly logical. The problem is, Skimmerhorn, emotions just aren't logical." She tilted her head and the sun warmed her skin. "I told you I love you, and you'd probably have preferred a slap in the face, but there it is. I didn't mean to say it—or maybe I did." She smiled a little, but her eyes were dulled with sadness. "Let me tell you how I see it. Love's a gift, and can certainly be refused. I'm not asking for a gift in return. It's not that I don't want it, but I don't expect it."

She rose then and, crossing the room, took his face gently in her hands. There was a compassion in her eyes that humbled him. "Take what's offered, Jed, especially when it's offered without expectations. I won't keep throwing it in your face."

"You're leaving yourself open, Dora."

"I know." She kissed him—one cheek, the other, then his mouth.

"I'm not what you need." But he gathered her close and held on. Because she was so exactly what he needed.

"You're wrong." She willed the threatening tears away. "You're wrong about the house, too. You're both just waiting."

HE KEPT losing his train of thought. Jed knew the details he and Brent discussed were vital, but he kept remembering the way Dora's hands had felt against his face when she'd smiled and asked him to accept love.

"Jed, what's on your mind?"

Jed blinked, focused. "What? Nothing." He washed the mood away with some of the station house's atomic coffee. "Winesap looks like he's another underling. I still think we should approach the top man, Finley."

"What I can gather on the guy wouldn't fill a teacup," Brent complained. "He's the American ideal, a self-made man."

"Then a little digging shouldn't hurt him," Jed pointed out. "I want to take a trip to L.A."

"I thought that was where this was leading." Brent shifted in his chair. "Listen, the department wouldn't have diddly on this case without you. But Goldman's asking questions."

"I'm a civilian, Brent. There's nothing to stop me from taking a trip to the Coast—at my own expense, on my own time."

"Why don't you cut the crap?" Brent blurted out. "I know you've got a meeting with the commissioner in an hour, and we both know what he's going to say. Tell me you're coming back on the job."

"I can't tell you that. I *can* tell you I'm thinking about it." Jed rose and paced the room. "Lord, I miss this place. Isn't that something?

I miss the tedium, the stupid reports, the snot-nosed rookies. Nine mornings out of ten I reach for my shoulder harness."

"Hallelujah. Let me tell Goldman. Let me be the one."

"I didn't say I was coming back."

"Yeah, you did. What does Dora think about it?"

Jed's grin faded. "We haven't talked about it. It doesn't concern her." He headed for the door. "We'll touch base tomorrow."

IT WAS nearly midnight when Dora gave up the attempt to sleep, and bundled into her robe. Jed hadn't come home or called. Wandering into the kitchen, she put the kettle on to boil.

How could she have blown it like this? she wondered as she tossed a tea bag into a cup. Hadn't she known that a man would head for the hills when he heard those three fateful words? Nope. She hadn't known, because she'd never said them before. And now that she was in the real show, she'd rushed her cue.

Well, it couldn't be taken back, she decided. She was going to get on with her life—with him, she hoped. Without him, if necessary. She figured she could start now by going downstairs and putting her wide-awake brain to work. Carrying her tea, she headed out, remembering to lock the door behind her.

Once in the storeroom, she continued the tedious task of re-organizing the files DiCarlo had upended. The work absorbed her.

Jed stood midway down the stairs watching her. She'd set all the lights burning, like a child left home alone at night. She was wearing the green robe and a pair of purple socks. Each time she leaned down to read a piece of paper, her hair fell softly over her cheek. Then she would push it back, the movement fluid and unstudied, before she filed the paper away and reached for another.

She turned, caught a glimpse of a figure. Papers went flying as she screamed. "What are you doing?" she said furiously.

He came down to the base of the steps. "What are *you* doing, Conroy? It's after midnight."

"What does it look like I'm doing? I'm practicing the minuet."

He bent down, placed a hand over hers. "I'm sorry I scared you. I guess you were too involved to hear me." He tilted her face up toward the light. "You look tired. And you're cranky, too."

She straightened and drew a deep breath. "If I'm out of sorts, it's because I feel useless having to keep the shop closed; and deceitful, because I'm lying to my family."

"You don't have to be either. No reason not to open tomorrow, and you'd feel better if you came clean with your family."

She considered it. "I will open," she decided, "but I'm not telling my family. Not yet. It's for me to deal with."

He couldn't argue. He wasn't going to tell her about his decision to pick up his badge. Not yet. "Come upstairs. I'll give you a back rub."

Eyes narrowed, she stepped back. "You're being nice to me. Why, Skimmerhorn? You're planning on doing something you know I won't like." She raced up the steps after him. "It's something about DiCarlo, isn't it? About the painting, the whole mess."

He wondered if it was the coward's way out to give her that one part. "I'm going to L.A. to have a talk with DiCarlo's boss."

"Winesap?" Her brow creased as she concentrated. "That's who the shipment was supposed to go to, wasn't it?"

"The top man's name is Finley, Edmund G.," Jed told her as he unlocked his door. "I'll start with him."

"And you think he—Finley—was expecting the shipment, that he arranged for the smuggling?"

"Yeah. And I think I know enough about him to buy a ticket for L.A." He offered her a brief rundown.

"Import-export," she mused. "He's probably a collector. It's possible that he was unaware of DiCarlo's sideline. But if he isn't . . ."

He caught the gleam in her eye and bit back a sigh. "Don't think, Conroy. You can be dangerous when you think."

"But I am thinking. And what I think is, you aren't the one who should talk to Finley. I am."

"You're out of your mind. You're in no position to tackle something like this."

"On the contrary." She was warming up to the idea now, and began moving around the room. "I'm in the perfect position. I, after all, was the victim of his employee. I, the baffled innocent, will appeal to Finley's sympathies if he, in turn, is innocent and, since I, too, am a collector, to his imagination if he's guilty. In short, Skimmerhorn, this part is tailor-made for me."

"It's not an audition, Conroy."

"But it is, essentially. Jeez, when are you going to get some

117

furniture in here?" She scooted up to sit on the table, in lieu of a decent chair. "What was your plan, Captain? You would request a meeting to discuss the ugly situation informally, possibly soliciting his help to locate DiCarlo?" She waited for his denial or assent, and got neither. "Meanwhile, you'd be looking for a chink in his armor. While doing so, you'd get a firsthand view of his operation and develop an informed opinion as to his culpability."

"You sound like a lawyer," he muttered. "I hate lawyers."

She crossed her legs. "Now, how would I play this?"

"Dora, I don't have a handle on this guy," Jed said. "Walking onto his turf is risky. If Finley's involved, he's going to take one look and see through that pretty face of yours like plate glass."

"You don't trust me, Skimmerhorn. That's it, isn't it?" Her voice thickened and shook even as her eyes filled.

"It's not a matter of trust. Don't take it so personally."

"How else can I take it?" The first tear spilled over, ran a lonely trail down her cheek. Her eyes were glistening with more. "Don't you understand that I need to do something? That I can't just sit in the background after my home and I have been violated this way? I can't bear it, Jed. I can't bear having you think of me as some helpless victim who only gets in your way."

"Stop it." He awkwardly lifted a hand to her hair. "I don't think of you as helpless. You're just not trained to do this. If he suspects anything, the whole sting could fall apart before it gets started."

She sniffled, pressed her face to his throat. "Do you suspect?"

"What?"

"Do you suspect?" she demanded in a perfectly controlled voice. Leaning back, she grinned at him. "Fell for it, didn't you?" Laughing, she patted his cheek while he stared at her. "Don't feel too stupid, Skimmerhorn. I told you I was good. And that was just an impromptu performance."

"You ever turn on tears again like that, I swear I'll smack you."

She shrugged. "Be assured, Captain, that our Mr. Finley will see exactly what I want him to see."

She could do it. He hated the fact that he was certain she could.

"I don't want you hurt."

She softened all over—eyes, mouth, heart. "That's one of the nicest things you've ever said to me."

He set her down on her feet. "Conroy, I said I didn't think you were helpless, but I never told you what I think you are." She braced. "Important," he said simply, and melted her heart. "Very important."

By NOON the next day Dora felt at least one part of her life was shifting back into normal gear. The shop was open for business. When Lea walked in, Dora greeted her with a fierce hug.

Laughing, Lea untangled herself. "What's all this?"

"We're open."

"You never explained why we were closed."

"Too complicated," Dora said breezily. "I needed downtime."

"That break-in bothered you more than you let on. I knew it."

"I guess it did. Anyway, I may have to go to L.A. for a couple of days. There's an import business out there I may want to cultivate. I don't want to close the shop again." No reason to, she thought, since Brent was still pulling strings to ensure police protection.

"Don't worry about it. Terri and I can keep things going."

The phone rang. "Good afternoon. Dora's Parlor."

"I'd like to speak to Miss Isadora Conroy, please."

"Speaking."

"Miss Conroy." From his desk in Los Angeles, Winesap turned to his meticulously rehearsed notes. "This is, uh, Francis Petroy."

"Yes, Mr. Petroy," Dora said as Lea turned to greet a customer.

"I hope I'm not disturbing you, but I was given your name and number by a Mrs. Helen Owings of Front Royal, Virginia."

Dora's fingers tightened on the receiver. "What can I do for you?"

"It concerns a painting you bought at auction in December."

All moisture evaporated in her mouth. "Yes, an abstract."

"Exactly. A Billingsly. I'm a collector of abstract work. I specialize in emerging artists—in a small way, you understand. I was unable to attend that particular auction—a family emergency. It gave me some hope when Mrs. Owings informed me that the painting had been sold to a dealer rather than an art collector."

"Actually," Dora said, playing for time, "I'm a little of both."

"Oh, dear." He shuffled through his notes. "Oh, dear."

"But I'm always interested in a legitimate offer, Mr. Petroy. Perhaps you'd like to see the painting. It would have to be sometime late next week, I'm afraid." She paused and mimed flipping

119

through an appointment book. "My schedule's hectic until then."

"That would be excellent." Relieved, Winesap mopped his sweaty neck with a handkerchief. "What day would be good?"

"I could fit you in on Thursday. Say, at two?"

"Perfect." Winesap scribbled down the date.

"Is there a number where I can reach you if something comes up?"

"Certainly." As his notes instructed, Winesap gave the number for one of Finley's fronts in New Jersey. "During business hours."

"I understand perfectly. Next Thursday, then, Mr. Petroy." She hung up. "Lea, I have to go out for a while."

She found Jed in the storeroom, calmly painting shelves. "There you are." She paused for drama. "I made contact."

"With what?" Jed laid the brush across the top of the paint can.

"With whom, Skimmerhorn. I got a call from Mr. Petroy—only I don't think it was Mr. Petroy. It could have been DiCarlo, but—"

"Sit down, Conroy. Try a Jack Webb."

"A Jack Webb? Oh, just the facts." She imagined herself filing a report, and related the phone conversation precisely. "How's that?"

"What on earth were you thinking of, making an appointment to meet him without checking with me?"

She'd expected him to be impressed, not irritated. "I had to say something, didn't I? Wouldn't he have been suspicious if a dealer had seemed reluctant to meet with him? I checked on Billingsly. He doesn't even exist. There isn't any Billingsly."

"That's brilliant, Conroy. Just brilliant. But you should have put him off until I got back." He tucked his thumbs in his pockets. "Brent and I will work out how to handle Petroy on Thursday. We'll be back by then."

"Back? Are you and Brent going somewhere?"

"No, you and I are." He still wasn't happy about it, but she'd made an odd sort of sense. "We're leaving for L.A. tomorrow."

"I'm going to do it?" She pressed a hand to her heart, then tossed her arms wide and vaulted into his. "I knew you'd see it my way."

"I didn't. I was outvoted." He wasn't going to admit he'd recommended her idea to Brent.

"Whatever." She kissed him hard. "Tomorrow?" She stopped, frowned. "How are we going to make him want to see me?"

"Because you're going to call him. And do what you're told."

14

In Los Angeles, Winesap entered Finley's office with a worried frown creasing his face. "Mr. Finley, sir. Miss Conroy's on line two. She's waiting to speak with you."

"Is that so?" Finley closed Isadora Conroy's file, folded his hands on top of it. "An interesting development."

Winesap's hands twisted together like nervous cats. "Mr. Finley, when I spoke with her earlier today, she was quite cooperative. And I certainly never mentioned my connection with you."

"Sit, Abel." He lifted the receiver and, smiling, leaned back in his chair. "Miss Conroy? Edmund Finley here."

He listened, his smile growing wider and more feral. "I'm afraid I don't follow you, Miss Conroy. You're inquiring about one of my employees—Anthony DiCarlo? . . . I see. I see. I don't know if I'll be able to help. We've told the police all we know about Mr. DiCarlo's unexplained disappearance, which is, unfortunately, nothing. . . . Very well," he added after a moment. "I'd be happy to see you. Tomorrow?" His brows raised. "That is rather short notice. I'll see if it can be arranged. Will you hold? I'll give you to my assistant."

Finley punched the HOLD button. "Give her four o'clock."

"Yes, sir." Winesap took the receiver in his damp hand. "Miss Conroy? This is Abel Winesap, Mr. Finley's assistant. The only time that Mr. Finley has open is at four. . . . Yes? . . . You have the address? . . . Excellent. We'll be expecting you."

"Delightful." Finley nodded approval when Winesap replaced the receiver. "*Fools walk in,* Abel. I'm certainly looking forward to this. Clear my calendar for tomorrow afternoon. I want Miss Isadora Conroy to have all my attention."

"Tomorrow, four o'clock," Dora said, and turned to Jed. "He sounded puzzled but cooperative, pleasant but reserved."

"And you sounded on the verge of hysteria but controlled."

"There's something else." Though she wanted to, she didn't take his hand. Hers was chilled. "I think I just spoke with Mr. Petroy."

"Finley?"

"No." She forced a thin smile. "His assistant, Winesap."

121

DORA WAS PLEASED WHEN THE cab pulled up in front of the pink stucco Beverly Hills Hotel. "Skimmerhorn, you surprise me."

"The room's booked in your name." Jed watched Dora offer her hand to the doorman. "You have to put it on your credit card."

She cast a withering look at him. "Thanks a bunch, big spender."

"You want to advertise the fact that you're traveling out here with a companion?" he asked. "A cop?"

"You left out the ex."

"So I did." The tony lobby of the BHH didn't seem the right setting to tell her that the ex wouldn't apply much longer.

Dora covertly scanned the lobby for passing movie stars when she handed the desk clerk her card for imprint. "I'm going to bill you for this, Skimmerhorn."

"It was your idea to come."

True enough. "Then I'll only bill you for half." She accepted her card back and two keys. They went up to the room, where Dora walked over to the window to check out the view. "I haven't been in L.A. since I was fifteen, when my father did a part in a small, forgettable film with Jon Voight. I guess I'm an East Coast snob, because L.A. doesn't do it for me. It makes me think of unnecessary eye tucks and designer yogurt. Or maybe it's designer eye tucks and unnecessary yogurt." She turned back, her smile becoming puzzled when he only continued to stare at her. "What is it?"

"You're nervous."

"Of course I'm not nervous." She tossed her bag onto the bed.

He laid his hands gently over hers. "You've got a right to be nervous. I'd be more worried about you if you weren't."

"I'll be fine. Classic opening-night jitters, that's all it is."

Since she so obviously needed him to, he played along. "I'll order up some lunch; then we'll go over the routine again."

Dora flopped on the bed. "I hate heavy-handed directors."

Two hours later she stepped out of the bathroom, wearing a red suit that showed off every glorious curve. "I'd forgotten how much better you feel once you're in costume," she said. "There's just those little ripples of nerves that keep the adrenaline up."

"Just stick to the plan and try to remember everything you see," he told her. "Don't bring up the painting. You haven't got a clue about it. Try to go through Winesap. We're running him down, but I want your impressions."

"I know." She brushed her hair. "Jed, I know exactly what to do. It's simple. Simpler because I might have done just this if I hadn't known about the painting. It's a very logical step."

"Just watch your back."

"Darling, I'm counting on you to do that for me."

DORA was impressed with the decor of Finley's outer office, trying to pick up helpful clues. As she'd suspected, he was a collector, and their mutual interest would give them a firm foundation.

It was difficult to hang on to her nerves, though, and character, when she really wanted to walk over and examine some of Finley's treasures firsthand. She felt favorably toward anyone who put malachite vases and Chiparus figures in his waiting area.

She hoped Finley would prove to be in the clear. She'd love to develop a business relationship. But if he wasn't . . . That thought had the nerves creeping back. She brushed at her skirt, looked at her watch. It was four ten. How long was he going to keep her waiting?

"EXCELLENT," Finley murmured to Dora's video image. She was every bit as lovely as he'd expected from the newspaper photos Winesap had unearthed from old show and style sections. Finley enjoyed the way her hands moved around restlessly. Nerves, he thought, pleased. And despite the nerves, her eyes were drawn again and again to pieces in his collection. That flattered him.

He buzzed his receptionist. It was time to begin.

"Mr. Finley will see you now."

"Thank you." Dora rose, tucked her envelope bag under her arm and followed the woman to the double doors.

When she entered, Finley smiled and stood. "Miss Conroy, I'm so sorry to have kept you waiting."

"I'm just happy you could see me at all." She crossed the rug— that pool of white—and took his extended hand. Her first impression was one of vitality and health and of well-channeled power.

"What can we offer you? Some coffee, tea or perhaps wine?"

"Wine would be lovely." And would give her the prop of a glass stem to twist in her hands as she told her story.

"The Pouilly-Fumé, Barbara. Please sit, Miss Conroy. Be comfortable." In a move calculated to disarm her, he rounded the desk and took the chair beside her. "And how was your flight?"

"Long." Dora smiled. "Of course, I'll go back tomorrow."

"So soon?" His eyes glinted with a touch of curiosity. When the wine was poured, the secretary slipped soundlessly out. Finley raised his glass. "To your health, Miss Conroy, and a safe journey home."

"Thank you." It was beautiful wine, silk on the tongue. "I know it might sound foolish, coming all this way just to see you, Mr. Finley. But I felt compelled." As if overcome, she looked down.

"You're upset," Finley said kindly. "Take your time. You told me this had to do with Anthony DiCarlo. Are you . . . a friend?"

"Oh, no." There was horror in her voice, and in her eyes as she dragged them back to Finley's. She imagined DiCarlo's voice whispering in her ear to bring the revulsion into her voice. "No. He— Mr. Finley, I need to ask how much you know about him."

"Personally?" Thinking, he pursed his lips. "I'm afraid I don't know many of my branch employees as well as I might."

"He's worked for you for some time?"

"Six years, I believe." He sipped his wine. "I have studied his file since his odd disappearance, to refresh my memory. Mr. DiCarlo worked his way up the corporate ladder rather quickly. He showed initiative and ambition." He smiled. "The desire to better oneself— this is something I respect in an employee. I'm very much afraid of foul play. Mr. DiCarlo isn't a man to neglect his responsibilities."

"I think—I think I might know where he is."

"Really?" There was a flash in Finley's eyes.

"I think he's in Philadelphia." Dora took a quick sip of wine and her hand shook lightly. "I think he's . . . watching me."

"My dear." Finley reached for her hand. "Watching you?"

"I'm sorry. It's not making sense. Let me start at the beginning."

She told the story well, with one significant pause in which she described the attack. "And I don't understand," she finished, with her eyes wet. "I don't understand why."

"How horrible for you." Finley was all baffled sympathy while his mind performed rapid calculations. DiCarlo had left out significant details, he mused. An attempted rape and a knightly neighbor coming to the rescue. It did explain the bruises on DiCarlo's face.

As if overcome, Dora covered her face with her hand. "I'll never forget the attack. And I identified him to the police. He killed a police officer, Mr. Finley, and a woman. He left another woman for dead— one of my customers." The thought urged the first tear down her cheek. "I'm sorry. I've been so upset. I think he must be crazy."

"Miss Conroy—Isadora." He took her hand again, gently. "This is difficult for me to take in. The idea of one of my own staff attacking women, murdering police officers. It seems I misjudged Mr. DiCarlo badly. What can I do to help you?"

"I don't know. I guess if he contacted you . . ."

"My dear, I assure you, if he contacts me, I will do everything to lead the authorities to him." Finley heaved a sigh. "I'll say, with confidence, that you won't be bothered by Mr. DiCarlo again."

"I'll try to hold on to that. You've been very kind, Mr. Finley."

"Edmund."

"Edmund." Her eyes were guileless and trusting. "Just talking it out has helped. I'd like to ask, if you find anything, that you'd call me."

"I understand. Of course. I'm going to put our security team on this. If there's a trace of DiCarlo, they'll find it."

She closed her eyes, relaxed her shoulders. "I knew I was right to come here. Thank you." When she rose, he took both her hands.

"I'd consider it a favor if you'd have dinner with me tonight."

"Dinner?" Her mind went sheet blank.

"I don't like to think of you alone and upset. I feel responsible."

"That's very kind of you."

"Then ease my conscience a bit. And, I admit, I would find it very pleasant to spend the evening with a lovely young woman who shares my interests." Finley gestured toward a curio cabinet. "If you run an antiques shop, you'd be interested in my treasures."

"Yes, I am. I've already admired several of your pieces. The horse's head?" She nodded toward a stone figure. "Han dynasty?"

"Precisely." He beamed, a professor to a prize student.

"I love things," she confessed. "Owning things."

"Ah, yes. I have a brooch I'd like you to see." He thought of the sapphire, and the pleasure it would give him to taunt her with it. "So it is decided. I'll have a car get you at your hotel. Say, seven thirty."

"I . . ."

"Please, don't misunderstand. My home is fully staffed, so you'll be well chaperoned. But I don't often have the opportunity to show off my treasures to someone who recognizes their intrinsic worth. I'd love your opinion on my pomander collection."

"Pomanders?" Dora said, and sighed. If she hadn't been on a mission, she'd have agreed in any case. How could she resist a collection of pomanders? "I'd love to."

DORA strolled back into the hotel room, filled with the warmth of success. She found Jed pacing. "What took you so long?"

"It was only an hour. I was brilliant," she said, and wrapped her arms around his neck.

"I'll tell you if you were brilliant." He put a hand on top of her head and pushed her into a chair. "Tell me about Finley. Everything."

"Is there any coffee left?" She picked up a room-service pot, poured coffee, took a sip and told him.

"He really was nice," she concluded. "And properly shocked by my story. I, of course, played the part of the spooked heroine to perfection. He offered his security team to track down DiCarlo."

"What about Winesap?"

"The receptionist told me he was out of the office."

"If he's the one who's going to keep the appointment next Thursday, he couldn't afford having you see him."

"I thought of that. So I talked to the security guard in the lobby on the way out. I told him I'd seen Winesap's name on the board and that my father had worked with an Abel Winesap years ago. So I asked if this guy was tall and heavyset, with red hair. It turns out this Winesap is short and skinny and round-shouldered."

"Good girl, Nancy Drew."

"Thanks, Ned." Now came the hard part, Dora mused. She would have to work up to it carefully. "Finley has a whole wall of monitors in his office. Kind of creepy, you know. I guess he has security cameras everywhere. But he also had a Gallé lamp that made me want to sit up and beg. And a Han horse. That barely touches on it. Anyway, I'll see his personal collection at dinner tonight."

Jed snatched her wrist. "Play that back, Conroy. Slow speed."

"He asked me to have dinner with him." She walked over to the closet and brought out a little black dress with a glittery bolero jacket in red and gold stripes. "This is what I'm here for, isn't it? To gain his sympathy and confidence and to find out everything I can."

"I don't like you going alone. I don't have enough on him."

"You'll have more when I get back, won't you?"

He crossed the room to her. His face was set. "I never had anyone to worry about before. I don't like it."

"I can understand that. I'll be fine."

"Sure you will." He lowered his cheek to the back of her head. "Dora . . ." What could he say? he wondered. Nothing that was churning inside him seemed right. "I'll miss you tonight."

She was wonderfully touched. "It's always hearts-and-flowers with you, Skimmerhorn."

"Is that what you want? Is that what you're looking for?"

She smiled at him. "I've got a heart, thanks, and I can buy flowers anytime I like." To comfort him, she nuzzled her lips to his. "I've also got an hour before I have to get ready."

"Okay, Conroy. We'll go over the ground rules for your dinner."

DORA stepped off the curb and into a white Mercedes limo at precisely seven thirty. A single white rosebud lay across the seat.

Brushing the rose petals across her cheek, she looked up toward the window where she knew Jed would be watching. The car pulled smoothly away. Because she was looking back, she noticed a dark sedan cruise out into traffic behind them.

Dora closed her eyes and put all thoughts of Jed out of her mind. For the next few hours she was alone. She enjoyed the ride up into the hills and prepared for act two.

She'd expected Finley's house to be lavish. She wasn't disappointed. The sweeping drive up, the quick, teasing peeks of the building through screening trees. Then the full impact of stone and brick and glass simmering in the last fiery lights of the dying sun.

A well-set stage.

There was only a moment to appreciate the dolphin-shaped Adam knocker before the door was opened by a uniformed maid.

"Mr. Finley would like you to wait in the drawing room."

Dora didn't bother to disguise her admiration for the magnificent entrance hall. In the parlor she gave the maid a murmured assent at the offer of wine and was grateful when she had the glass in hand and was alone to worship.

127

When Finley joined her, she was mentally devouring a collection of netsukes. "I see you're enjoying my toys."

"Oh, yes." Eyes dark, she turned from the curios. "I feel like Alice, and I've just stumbled into the best corner of Wonderland."

"I was certain I'd find it pleasant to share my things with you."

"You've made my trip very worthwhile, Mr. Finley."

"Then I'm content." He walked over, placed a light hand at the small of her back. It wasn't a suggestive move. She had no explanation as to why her skin crawled under the friendly pressure. "Shall I give you the tour before dinner?"

"Yes, please." Agreeably, she slipped a hand through his arm.

He was erudite and entertaining, Dora thought. Why she was violently uncomfortable she couldn't have said. He took a greedy delight in all he'd acquired, yet she understood greed. It took all of her skill to play out her role as they moved from room to room.

"This is the pin I mentioned earlier." Finley offered her the sapphire brooch. "The stone is, of course, magnificent, but the workmanship of the setting, and, again, the history, add intrigue."

"It's beautiful." It was both beautiful and tragic. Tragic, she realized, because it would be forever behind glass. Perhaps that was the difference between them. She passed her treasures on, gave them a new life. Finley locked his away.

"It was said to belong to a queen," Finley told her, waiting, watching her face for a sign of recognition. "Mary, Queen of Scots. I often wonder if she wore it when she was arrested for treason."

"I'd rather think she wore it riding across the moors."

"And this." He now chose the smuggled etui. "This belonged to another queen with a sad fate. Napoleon gave it to Josephine. Before he divorced her for being barren."

"You give your treasures a sad history, Edmund."

"I find poignancy increases their meaning. Shall we dine?"

There was lobster bisque, and Peking duck so delicate it all but melted on the tongue. The meal was served on Limoges and eaten with Georgian silver. Dom Pérignon was poured into antique Waterford. Dora fought to relax and enjoy the meal.

"Tell me about your shop," Finley invited. "It must be exciting for you to buy and sell, to handle lovely things time and again. There's something innately satisfying about making your own business out of something you love. Not everyone has the courage. I believe, Isadora, that you have a great deal of courage."

Her stomach fluttered, but she managed to swallow the bite of duck. "I hate to confess, but I frighten very easily."

"You underestimate yourself. After all, you came here, to me." He smiled, watching her with eyes as sharp as carved jade. "For all you knew, Mr. DiCarlo might have been acting on my orders."

When she went pale and set down her fork with a rattle, he laughed, patted her hand. "Now I have frightened you. I apologize. It was merely said to illustrate my point."

She fisted and unfisted her hands in her lap. She'd never wanted to escape so badly in her life. "You must have marvelous contacts," she said. "Do you do much traveling and acquiring?"

He signaled for dessert, and a creamy chocolate soufflé was soon served. "Not as much as I'd like. But I take the occasional trip to the Orient or Europe. I even get to the East Coast from time to time."

"I hope you'll let me know if you're ever in Philadelphia."

"I wouldn't think of taking the trip without paying you a call."

After a few moments she rose to play her final scene, the contented guest taking a reluctant leave. "It was a wonderful meal, Edmund, a delightful evening."

"Believe me, it was my pleasure." He stood and kissed her hand.

She had the urge to rub her hand clean on her jacket. "Please, call me if you—if there's any news about DiCarlo."

"I will. I have a feeling it will all be sorted out very soon."

WHEN she returned to the hotel, Dora watched the limo drive away, then stood on the sidewalk and waited to calm down. She didn't want to face Jed until she had herself under control. Then she saw the dark sedan pull up across the street. She bolted into the lobby.

Jumping at shadows, Conroy, she berated herself while her heart roared in her ears. By the time she'd ridden up to her floor and slipped the key into the lock, she had herself back in line. She was even able to smile when she walked in and saw Jed scowling.

"Ah, you waited up for me."

"You're always good for a laugh, Conroy. You really—"

He broke off after he'd turned and gotten a look at her. He hadn't known anyone could appear so exhausted and still stand on both feet. She sat tiredly on the edge of the bed to pull off her dress and remove her hose, then slipped on a nightshirt.

"The house—it's immense. I've never seen so many museum-quality pieces in one place. It's a little empire." There were faint bruises of fatigue under her eyes. "He spooked me, Jed. He was a perfect gentleman. And being alone with him terrified me."

"Tell me." He combed a hand through her hair.

"He took me all through the house," she began. "And there was something odd about the way he showed off his pieces. A handful of them in particular. I could feel him watching me when I looked at them. I kept telling myself I was imagining it, because he was being so charming. We had this elegant dinner in this elegant room on elegant china. But it was like being defenseless."

"You were alone."

She yawned. "Not really—or not often. He has an army of servants. I wasn't really afraid that he'd hurt me. I was afraid he wanted to." She blew out a breath, grateful that Jed didn't tell her she was being a fool. "You might see what you can find out about a sapphire brooch—sixteenth century. The stone looked to be about eight carats, in a horizontal setting of gold filigree, with small, round-cut diamonds. He made a real issue of showing it to me."

"Fine. You did good."

She gave him a sleepy smile. "Do I get a detective's gold star?"

"That's gold shield, Nancy. And no. You're retiring."

She stretched out without bothering to crawl under the sheets. "I forgot. I saw this guy in a dark sedan pull out after the limo when we left. Then he drove up a few minutes after I got back."

"I've had you tailed all day. Local P.I."

She smiled. "You hired a bodyguard for me."

"I hired him for me," he said lightly.

After pillowing her head on her folded arms, she shut her eyes and was asleep. Quietly he turned down the covers and, lifting her, slipped her between the sheets. She never stirred. Jed turned off the lights, got in bed beside her and gathered her close to hold her.

THE phone shrilled beside them. Dora's heart shot to her throat. Jed shifted to grope for the receiver. "Skimmerhorn."

"Jed, sorry to wake you." There was an edge of excitement in

Brent's voice. "I've got something you might want to check out."

"Yeah?" Jed rolled over, switched on the light and picked up the pen from the nightstand.

"I just picked up a fax from the sheriff's department out there. A couple of hikers stumbled over a body a few days ago, wedged in a shallow ravine in the hills. There was enough left for a couple of prints. We can stop looking for DiCarlo. He's real dead."

"How long?"

"Given the exposure, sometime around the first of the year. I figured you'd want to talk to the coroner, the investigating officers."

"Give me the names." Jed wrote down the information.

"I'll fax the guys back," Brent continued. "Tell them that you were on a related investigation out there. They'll be ready for you."

"Thanks. I'll be in touch."

Dora was sitting up in bed, her chin resting on her knees, when Jed hung up the phone. "You've got cop all over your face."

"DiCarlo," he told her flatly. "They've found him."

15

SHERIFF Curtis Dearborne harbored an innate distrust of outsiders. Since he considered any member of the LAPD an outsider, an East Coast cop was an entity to be watched with extra care.

He rose from his desk when Jed and Dora entered, a towering, well-muscled man. His square, handsome face was serious, his handshake firm. "Captain Skimmerhorn, pretty handy you being out our way when we identify the John Doe."

Jed summed up his man instantly. "I appreciate your passing on the information, Sheriff. I'm sure Lieutenant Chapman filled you in on the mess we've got back home. Your quick work will be some comfort to Officer Trainor's widow."

It was exactly the right button. Dearborne's eyes frosted, his mouth thinned. "Sit down, Captain, Miss Conroy."

"Thanks." Stemming impatience, Jed took a seat. "I was told there was no identification on the body."

"Not a lick." Dearborne's chair creaked comfortably as he sat back. "But we ruled out robbery right off. The wallet was gone, but the guy wore a diamond on his pinkie, and a gold neck chain."

131

"I'd like a look at the coroner's report if that's all right," Jed began. "And any physical evidence you've gathered. The more I go back with, the better."

"I think we can accommodate you there. We've got the tarp and what's left of his clothes downstairs. If you want a look at the body, we'll take a run down to the coroner's."

"I'd appreciate that. Could Miss Conroy wait here?" Jed said.

"That's fine. You just make yourself comfortable."

"Thank you, Sheriff. I wouldn't want to get in the way," Dora said. "May I use your phone to make a credit card call?"

Dearborne gestured toward the phone. "Use line one."

"Thank you." There was no use being annoyed with Jed, she mused as they trooped off. In any case, she'd let her family know she was being delayed a few hours. She smiled. She wondered if Jed realized that Dearborne had called him Captain—and that Jed hadn't even winced. He'll have his badge back by spring, she predicted.

"Good afternoon. Dora's Parlor," Lea answered.

"You've got a great voice, honey."

She chuckled. "Hey, where are you? At thirty thousand feet?"

"No." Dora pushed back her hair. "Just taking care of a little business Jed wanted to handle while we were here. So we'll be taking a later plane. Everything there okay?"

"Fine. How did your meeting go with the import-export guy?"

"Oh." Hedging, Dora thumbed a file on the desk. "I don't think we'll be doing business after all. He's out of my league."

"Well, call me when you get in."

"All right. I don't imagine we'll make it before ten your time, so don't start worrying until after eleven." Dora idly flipped open the file. Her mouth went dust-dry as she stared down at the color photo. Her head buzzed.

"Dora? Dory? Are you still there? Shoot. Did we get cut off?"

"No." With a herculean effort Dora leveled her voice. "Sorry, I have to go. I'll call you later."

"Okay. See you tomorrow, honey. Safe trip."

"Thanks. Bye." Very deliberately Dora replaced the receiver. Her hands had gone icy cold beneath a sheer layer of sweat.

It was DiCarlo. There was enough of his face left for her to be sure of that. She was also sure that he hadn't died well. With numb

fingers she shifted the first police photo aside and stared at the second. She couldn't take her eyes away even when the buzzing in her head became a roar and her vision blurred.

Jed let out one concise oath when he walked in and saw her white face and the open file. Even as he strode toward her, he watched her eyes roll back. He had her sitting on a chair away from the desk and her head between her knees in two brisk moves. "Breathe slow." He slapped the file closed with his free hand.

"I was calling Lea," Dora said as her stomach heaved.

"Try a little of this." Dearborne held out a cup of water. Sympathy was in his voice. He remembered his first murder victim.

Jed kept the pressure light on Dora's head as he accepted the water. "Would you give us a minute, Sheriff?"

"Sure. Take your time." Dearborne closed the door behind him.

"I want you to come up real slow," Jed told her.

"I'm okay." But the trembling was worse than the nausea, and much more difficult to control. She let her head fall back against the chair and kept her eyes closed.

"Try some of this." He brought the cup to her lips, urging her to swallow. "I want you to feel better before I yell at you."

She looked away from him. "I wasn't playing detective."

"You have no business being this close, Dora."

"I have no business?" She set the cup aside and forced herself to stand. "The man inside that file tried to rape me. He would certainly have killed me. That brings me pretty close. Even knowing all that, I can't justify what I saw in those pictures. I just can't." She walked shakily to the door. "I'll wait in the car."

Jed waited until she was gone before he picked up the file and studied the photos. He swore at what Dora had seen.

"She okay?" Dearborne asked as he came back in.

"She'll do." He handed the file over. "I'd like to take you up on your offer of talking to the coroner."

"No problem. You can read the autopsy report on the way. It's interesting. Our pal had a heck of a last meal."

DORA refused the snack the flight attendant offered and stuck with icy ginger ale. "You haven't yelled at me yet."

Jed continued to work his crossword puzzle. He'd have preferred to read through Dearborne's reports again, but they would wait until he was alone. "It didn't seem worth it."

"I'd rather you did, so you'd stop being mad at me. And I think I'd handle it better if you told me what you found out. You've hardly spoken since we left L.A. Speculation can be worse than reality."

"There isn't that much to tell." He let the newspaper fall into his lap. "We know DiCarlo flew out to the Coast on New Year's Eve, rented a car, booked a hotel room. He didn't sleep in the room that night; he didn't return the car. That hasn't turned up yet, either. He'd also booked a flight for Cancún, but he didn't use the ticket."

"So he didn't plan on coming back east anytime soon." She tried to think it through. "Do you think he came out to see Finley?"

"There's no record of him going to the offices. There's no evidence to link Finley to any of it at this point. We know DiCarlo came to L.A., and he died there. He was murdered sometime between December thirty-first and January second—a gunshot wound to the abdomen. The bruises on the face, I put there myself."

"I see." To keep her voice steady, she continued to sip the ginger ale like medicine. "That's like no signs of struggle, right?"

"That's right, Miss Drew." He gave her hand an approving squeeze. She was toughing it out, he thought, and admired her for it. "The condemned man had enjoyed a hearty last meal that included pheasant, wine, and raspberries with white chocolate. Dearborne's going to have his hands full checking restaurant menus. There were also some white stones and mulch found rolled up in the tarp he'd been wrapped in. The kind you find in flower beds and around ornamental shrubs. Did Finley have gardens?"

"Extensive ones." She let out a shaky breath. "And he's very proud of them. I admired part of them from his solarium. They were neat and tidy, well mulched, with narrow pathways of white stone."

"You've got good eyes, Conroy. Now close them for a while."

"I think I'd be better off watching the movie." She reached unsteadily for the headphones, slipped them on and escaped.

In L.A., Winesap entered Finley's office, wringing his hands. "You wanted to see me, Mr. Finley?"

Finley gestured Winesap in. His eyes were blank as he sat back. "How long have you worked for me, Abel?"

Winesap moistened his lips. "Eight years now, sir."

"Eight years." Nodding slowly, Finley steepled his index fingers. "I've been thinking of you, Abel, all through the morning and into the afternoon. And as I did so, it occurred to me that over these eight years, I've had very little cause to criticize your work. You are prompt, you are efficient, you are—in most cases—thorough."

"Thank you, sir. I do my best."

"I believe you do. Which is why I find myself so disappointed today. You perhaps haven't read the morning paper?"

"Things have been a bit hectic," Winesap said apologetically.

"One should always make time for current events." With his eyes glittering on Winesap's face, Finley stabbed a finger at the newspaper on his desk. "Such as this. Read it now, Abel, if you will."

"Yes, sir." All but shaking in terror now, Winesap approached the desk and took the paper. The article Finley referred to, circled over and over again in blood-red ink, was headlined BODY DISCOVERED BY HIKERS. Winesap felt his bowels loosen.

Finley snatched the paper away. "I expected better from you, Abel. They will, of course, identify the body, and I will be forced to answer more questions. Naturally, I'm confident that I can handle the police. But really, you should have spared me this inconvenience."

"Yes, sir. I'm terribly sorry. I can't apologize enough."

"No, I don't believe you can. However, I will try to overlook this. You'll be leaving for the East in a day or two. I trust you'll handle Miss Conroy with more finesse than you handled Mr. DiCarlo."

Cautious, Winesap backed out of the room. "Thank you."

Finley leaned back as the door closed respectfully. He would have to keep a closer eye on Abel, he thought sadly. A much closer eye. If things got too sticky over DiCarlo, he would simply throw dear devoted Abel to the wolves like so much dead meat.

IT WAS good to be home in the simple routines of each day. Dora comforted herself with that and tried not to think of the meeting with Mr. Petroy she still had to face. At least Jed hadn't noticed her lack of appetite. She'd covered it well. Her eyes might have been shadowed, her skin pale and drawn, but with facials and creams and powders, she presented a very competent mask. She hoped it didn't slip until after Thursday.

DORA FELT A NEED FOR HER FAMILY. She indulged it by closing the shop an hour early and spending the evening at Lea's. The din from the family room soothed her soul.

"I think Richie's definitely improving on the trumpet," Dora commented.

Head cocked, Lea listened to the wet musical blats with a mixture of pride and resignation. "There's a band concert at school in three weeks. I'm saving you a front-row seat."

Dora slipped onto a stool by the counter. "I needed this."

Lea added another touch of burgundy to the stew she had simmering. "Something's going on." She frowned. "You've got that line between your eyebrows. And you're pale. You always get pale when you're worried about something."

Passing a hand over her face, Dora took a cleansing breath. "I guess I'm still a little jet-lagged. And my life's taken a few odd turns. I think I'll go home, take a hot bath and sleep for twelve hours." She started to move as the knock sounded on the back door.

"Hi." Mary Pat stuck in her head. "I came to pick up my share of the monsters." She listened a moment to the blare of the trumpet. "Ah, the patter of little feet. Wonderful, isn't it?"

"Have a seat," Lea invited. "Unless you're in a hurry."

"I'd love a seat. I've been on my feet for eight straight hours." She sighed. "Terrific news about Jed, isn't it?"

"What news?"

"About him coming back on the job." She missed Dora's blank look. "Brent's really flying. He detested Goldman, of course. Who didn't? But it's more than that. The department needs Jed and Jed needs the department. Now that he's made the decision to . . ." One look at Dora's face made Mary Pat stumble to a halt. "Oh, Lord. Did I jump the gun? When Brent told me, I just assumed you knew."

"No. Jed didn't mention it." Dora fought to work a smile onto her lips, but couldn't make it reach her eyes. "It's great news, though. I'm sure it's just what he needs. How long have you known?"

"A couple of days. I'm sure Jed planned to tell you. Once he, uh . . ." But she couldn't think of any handy excuses. "I'm sorry."

"Don't be. I really am glad to hear it." After sliding off the stool, Dora reached mechanically for her coat. "I've got to get going."

"Stay for dinner," Lea said quickly. "There's plenty."

"No, I have things to do. Say hi to Brent," she told Mary Pat.

"Sure." The door closed.

I⊤ WAS two o'clock in the morning. Jed paced his living room, strode through the door he'd propped open, and paced the corridor. As he had numerous times over the last four hours, he strode to the back door and stared out at the gravel lot.

Where was Dora? If she wasn't home in ten minutes, he would call in all his markers and put out an APB. Unless she was paying him back. It was a safe, even comforting, thought, so he played with it. Was this how she'd felt when he'd come in late without leaving any word? She wasn't going to get away with it, he decided. But he was reaching for his phone when he heard her key in the outside lock.

He was out in the hall and at the back door before she'd opened it. "Do you have any idea what time it is?" he demanded.

"Yes." She closed the door and locked it. "Sorry. I didn't realize I had a curfew." She walked past him, but he caught up with her at her apartment door and spun her around.

"Just a minute, Conroy. We'll forget the personal stuff for now. The fact is, you're a prime target, and it was incredibly irresponsible of you to be out of contact for half the night."

"I'm responsible to and for myself." She unlocked her door and shoved it open. "And as you can see, I'm perfectly fine."

He followed her in. "You had no right—"

"Don't tell me about rights," she interrupted, very cool, very calm. "I spent the evening as I chose to spend it."

Anger and resentment bubbled inside him. "And how was that?"

"Alone." She took off her coat and hung it in the closet.

"Conroy. You knew damn well I'd be half crazy with worry. I was about to call out an APB."

"Interesting, isn't it, the way those police terms slide right off your tongue? It's a good thing you're going back on, Captain. You make a lousy civilian." Her eyes were as dull as her voice.

"It's not official until next week." He spoke carefully, studying her. He'd never seen her eyes that cold. "How did you find out?"

"Does it matter? It's more to the point that I didn't find out from you. Excuse me." She brushed past him and into the living room.

He cursed himself for a fool. "So you're angry. But that—"

"No," she interrupted. "I'm not angry." Because she was unbearably tired, she sat on the arm of a chair. "You could say I've been illuminated, devastated, but I'm not angry."

The quiet resignation in her voice reached him. "Dora, I didn't do it to hurt you."

"That's why I'm illuminated. You didn't tell me, because you didn't think it was any of my concern. You didn't want it to be. It was a major decision in your life. Your life," she repeated with emphasis. "Not mine. So why should you bother to tell me?"

She was slipping away from him. He was standing two feet away from her and watching the distance grow by leaps and bounds. It terrified him. "You make it sound as though I was keeping it from you. I needed to work it out. I didn't think you'd understand."

"You didn't give me the chance, Jed," she said quietly. "Did you think I could have felt the way I did about you and not understand how important your work was to you?"

"It had nothing to do with you." As soon as the words were out, he knew they were ill chosen. "I didn't mean it that way."

"I think you did. I wish I didn't blame you for it, but I do. I know you had it rough, but you've been making your own choices for a long time. You chose not to accept my feelings for you, and you chose not to let yourself feel anything back." Her voice didn't waver. "I do blame you for that, Jed, and for hurting me. Since you're the first man who's ever broken my heart, I think you should know it."

"For heaven's sake, Dora." He started toward her, but she jumped up and stepped back.

"I don't want you to touch me now. I really don't."

His hands fisted. "Dora, I need you to stop this and be reasonable."

"I am being reasonable, believe me. The day after tomorrow you should be able to tie up the loose ends about the painting. Or most of them. You shouldn't need me after that."

"You know I need you."

Her eyes filled then, and she fought back tears. "You can't imagine what I would have given to hear you say that before. Just once. But I have to protect myself, Jed. When we're finished on Thursday, I intend to close the shop for a couple of weeks, take a trip someplace warm. That should give you time to find other accommodations and move out. I don't want you here when I get back."

"Just like that?"

"Yes."

"Fine." He had his pride. He wouldn't beg. "I'll go as soon as things are wrapped up." Because it hurt—it hurt unbelievably—he covered the wounds with a professional shield. "There'll be a team in tomorrow after closing. They'll set up the wires. We'll go over procedure when they're done."

"All right. I'm very tired. I'd like you to go now." She walked to the door, held it open. "Please."

It wasn't until he'd reached her that he realized his hands were unsteady. When he heard the door close behind him, he had the sick feeling that he'd just been shut out of the best part of his life.

"Whats's with you two?" Brent asked as Jed climbed into the surveillance van.

Jed ignored the question. "How's the sound?"

"Loud and clear." Though Brent offered the headphones, he was far from finished. "Loud and clear enough to hear the two of you talking in there like polite strangers. Don't you think she could have used a morale boost instead of a lecture on procedure, Captain?"

"Drop it." Jed checked the rear window of the van to be sure he had a clear view of the shop.

The radio crackled. "Base, this is unit one. A man answering subject's description just got out of a cab on the corner of South and Front streets. He's walking west."

"Showtime," Brent murmured, but Jed was already reaching for the portable phone. Dora answered on the first ring.

"Good afternoon. Dora's Parlor."

"He's half a block away," Jed said flatly. "I've got him in view."

"All right. Everything's ready here."

"Keep loose, Conroy."

"Sure."

"Dora—" But she'd already broken the connection. "Damn." He said it softly, finally, helplessly.

"She can handle it, Jed."

"Yeah. But I don't know if I can." He watched Winesap mince hurriedly down the sidewalk, shoulders hunched. "I just figured out I'm in love with her." He slipped on the headphones in time to hear the bells jingle as Winesap opened the shop door.

"Good afternoon." Dora smiled. "May I help you?"

"Miss Conroy? I'm Francis Petroy."

She let her smile broaden. "Mr. Petroy, I was expecting you." She walked to the door to flip the CLOSED sign around. Her eyes slashed to the van, then away. "Can I get you some coffee? Tea?"

"I'd love some tea." It might soothe his stomach more than the Alka-Seltzer he'd downed earlier. "Your shop is very impressive."

"Thank you. I like to surround myself with beautiful things. But you'd understand that."

"Excuse me?"

"Being an art collector." She offered him a cup. "You said you specialize in abstract, but you might find some of my nostalgia prints interesting." She gestured to a car manufacturer's sign for a Bugatti, which hung beside a Vargas girl. Watching him, she sipped her own tea. "But as an abstract buff, you'd be more interested in, say, a Bothby or a Klippingdale," she said, making up names.

"Yes, of course. Exceptional talents." The tea soured in Winesap's stomach. He'd really tried to be thorough by studying the subject, but all the names and pictures swam through his head. "My collection isn't extensive. Which is why I concentrate on the emerging artist. I'm very anxious to see the Billingsly, Miss Conroy."

"Then, by all means." She led the way into the side room. Jed had gotten an artist friend to work overtime to reproduce the painting. Now it stood in the pretty sitting room.

"Ah." The sense of satisfaction was so great, Winesap nearly wept. "It's everything I'd hoped for."

"Did you have an offer in mind, Mr. Petroy?" Dora asked.

"In mind, naturally," he said, trying to be coy. "I'd prefer if you'd set a price—for negotiation."

"Happy to. Why don't we start at two hundred fifty thousand?"

Winesap's prim mouth fell open. "You can't be serious."

"Oh, but I am. You look as though you need to sit down, Mr. Petroy." She gestured to a petit-point stool. "Now, let's be frank," she said. "You don't know diddly about art, do you?"

"Well, really. As I told you, I have a small collection."

"But you lied, Mr. Petroy," she said gently. "You haven't a clue

141

about abstract. Wouldn't it be simpler if we admitted we're both more interested in Impressionism rather than Expressionism?"

For a moment he didn't follow her. Then his pasty face blanched. "You know about the painting."

"I bought it, didn't I?"

"Yes. But that was a mistake." His frantic eyes widened. "No? You knew—knew all along about the Monet? You were working with DiCarlo? You—you cheated," he accused miserably. "I can't imagine why I was sorry he died so badly."

The image in the police photo flashed obscenely in Dora's mind. "So you killed him," she murmured. "For this."

But Winesap wasn't listening. "Now I have to clean up the entire mess again. I'm not happy about the two hundred and fifty thousand, Miss Conroy."

He rose. So did Dora. Even as he reached under his coat, two officers were bursting through the rear door.

"Freeze."

Winesap took one look at the guns pointing at him and fainted.

16

DORA watched as two officers escorted a babbling Winesap out of the shop. She sat down, not sure her legs would support her.

"Here." Jed shoved a cup of tea into her hands.

"Good idea." She knocked it back like water and felt it warm her jittery stomach. "I guess you guys got all you needed."

"We got plenty." He wanted to touch his fingertips to her hair, but he was afraid she'd cringe away. "You did good, Nancy."

"Yeah, I did." She lifted her eyes then, made herself meet his. "I guess on some level we didn't make such a bad team."

Brent swept in to kiss Dora. "You were brilliant."

"Thanks."

Jed felt his heart sag. "I'm going down to interrogation with Brent. Are you going to be all right?"

"I'll be fine. Go be a cop. It looks good on you." She softened the words with a smile. "I'd appreciate it if you'd call me, let me know what the result of the interrogation is."

"You'll get a full report," Brent promised her.

"In the morning." Steadier, she rose out of the chair. "I'm going up to sleep." She followed them to the door. Jed turned, closed his hand over hers on the knob. He couldn't help it. "I'd like to talk to you tomorrow, when you're feeling up to it."

She nearly gave in. Very nearly. There was as much hurt in his eyes as she was holding inside her. But a fast break was a clean one. "My schedule's a little tight, Jed. I've got an early flight to Aruba."

There was nothing in her voice, nothing in her face that offered the slightest opening.

"You move fast."

She gave his hand a quick squeeze. "Give 'em hell, Captain."

She closed the door quickly and turned the lock.

ONCE she got to Aruba, Dora promised herself, she'd do nothing but sleep. She'd bake this aching depression out of her body and mind with the sunshine. She went to lock the storeroom door and engage the security alarm, and then headed up to her apartment.

She took the tea tray into her kitchen to wash it. When she turned from the sink, she was standing face to face with Finley.

"I've taken you up on your offer of hospitality, Isadora. And may I say you have a charming home. Why don't we sit down?" Finley took Dora's arm and pulled her into the living room.

"How did you get in?"

"There was such a lot of confusion today, wasn't there?" He smiled as he pushed her into a chair. "I wasn't at all sure that Abel—Mr. Winesap—could handle this matter efficiently."

Finley took the chair beside her. He saw Dora's eyes cut toward the door, and shook his head. "Please don't attempt to run, Isadora."

She was certain she wouldn't get two feet. Her best bet was to play for time and wait for help. "It was you who sent DiCarlo."

"It's a long, sad tale. But I find you such good company." He settled back and began to talk. He told her about the carefully planned robberies in several different countries. The network of men and finances it required to operate a successful business—legally and illegally. When he reached DiCarlo's part in it, he sighed.

"But I don't have to go into that with you, do I, dear? You're an excellent actress. I realized after your visit to my office that you and DiCarlo had been in league together."

143

She was stunned. "You think I was his partner? What I told you in your office was the truth. He broke in here and attacked me."

"I'm quite sure you had a falling-out." His eyes narrowed. "Did you pit another man against Mr. DiCarlo, so that he came to me with a feeble excuse for not returning my painting?"

"You stole it. And I was never involved with DiCarlo."

"And when he didn't return," Finley continued as if she hadn't spoken, "you became concerned and decided to test the waters with me yourself. Oh, you were very clever. I very nearly believed you. There was just one doubt in my mind, which proved sadly true. You turned to the police, Isadora. Settling for a finder's fee."

Terrified, she sprang to her feet. "They have Winesap down at police headquarters. He'll be telling them all about you by now."

Finley considered, then moved his shoulders in elegant dismissal. "Perhaps. But Mr. Winesap will very soon suffer a fatal accident. I would much rather talk about how I can retrieve my painting. Surely the police have told you where they've secured it."

This surprised her. "I don't know where it is."

"Don't lie, please." He slipped his hand into the inside pocket of his Savile Row suit and pulled out a highly polished Luger. "Gorgeous, isn't it? Now, Isadora, where is my painting?"

She looked helplessly into his eyes. "I don't know."

The force of the bullet slammed her back against the wall. Even as the fire erupted in her shoulder, she didn't believe he'd shot her.

"I think you'd better tell me." Finley stepped to where Dora lay in a heap. "We'll give you a little time to compose yourself, shall we?"

Leaving her bleeding, he began to methodically examine her treasures, one by one.

"THE little fool sure did sing." Brent felt like singing himself as they turned onto South Street. They had just left Winesap at the police station.

"I don't like cutting deals with weasels," Jed muttered.

"Even for a big fat weasel like Finley?"

"Even for that." He checked his watch. "I'll feel better when I know that LAPD's picked him up."

"The warrant's in the works, pal."

There was some comfort in that. Some small comfort. "You

didn't have to come out of your way. I could have caught a cab."

"Nothing's too good for the captain. Not tonight. And if I were you, I wouldn't wait until morning to give a certain gorgeous woman the good news."

"She needs the sleep."

"She needs some peace of mind."

"She ought to get plenty of it in Aruba," Jed said.

"Come again?"

"Nothing." They turned onto South as light sleet began to fall.

"Now, then." Finley sat down again, pleased when Dora found the strength to sit up. The blood seeping out of her shoulder wound had slowed to an ooze. "About the painting."

Her teeth were chattering. She'd never been so cold. She tried to speak, but the words slurred. "The police . . . took it. Took it away." Her head lolled on her shoulder. The room was going gray. "To grandmother's house. Then away. I don't know."

"I can see you need incentive." He set the gun aside and reached for the gold buckle of his belt. He wrapped the end of the belt around his hand. "Now, Isadora, where is the painting?"

Dully Dora saw him pick up the gun and raise the belt.

"Door-to-door service." Brent whipped into the gravel parking lot. "If you had any heart, you'd ask me up for a beer."

"I haven't got any heart." Jed pushed the car door open and glanced back at Brent's engaging grin. "Sure, come ahead."

"You got any of that imported stuff?" Brent asked. "Mexican?"

They trooped to the steps. When they heard the thin cry, they each slapped a weapon into their hands and charged into the back door in a dead run. Years of partnership clicked seamlessly into place. When Jed kicked open Dora's door, he went in high, Brent low.

The faintest flicker of irritation crossed Finley's face as he whirled. Two police issues fired simultaneously. Two 9-mm bullets caught Finley high in the chest.

With terror singing in his head, Jed rushed to Dora. He said her name over and over like a prayer. "Hang on, baby."

There was so much blood, he thought frantically. When he looked at her wide dilated eyes and still, white face, he had one moment of horror, thinking she was dead. But she was shaking. He peeled off his jacket to cover her. "You're going to be okay, Dora."

"Use this." Brent pushed a towel into Jed's shaking hands and folded another to place under Dora's head. "Ambulance is on the way." He spared a glance at the body sprawled on the rug.

"Dora, listen to me." Jed used the towel to pad the upper wound. "Hold on. Just hold on." Then he could think of nothing else but to gather her close. "Please. Stay with me. I need you."

HE WOULD have wept if it would have helped. He'd tried everything else. Swearing, pacing, praying. Now he could only wait.

The Conroys were there. Jed wondered if Dora would be surprised at how tough they were. He doubted it. There had been tears and there had been terror, but they had all drawn together in the hospital waiting room while Dora was in surgery.

He'd waited for recriminations. They had given him none. Not even when he had stood, smeared with Dora's blood, and told them that he'd left her alone, left her defenseless, had they blamed him. He wished to heaven they had.

Instead, John had gotten them all coffee, Lea had gone down to wait for Will to arrive from New York, and Quentin and Trixie had sat side by side on the sofa holding hands.

After the second hour had crawled by, Trixie murmured to her husband. With his nod of agreement she went to sit beside Jed.

"She'll want lots of pampering, you know," Trixie began. "She was never sick often, but when she was, she expected everyone's devoted attention. Dora's never been one to suffer in silence." Gently she touched the back of his hand, then gripped it firmly. "It's so much harder to wait alone."

"Mrs. Conroy . . ." But he didn't have the words. He simply leaned against her and let himself be held.

They all rose to their feet at the quick slap of shoes on tile. Still in her nurse's scrub suit, Mary Pat stepped through the doorway. "She's out of surgery. It looks good. The doctor will be out soon."

It was then that Trixie began to cry, with hard, racking sobs. Jed's arms went around her automatically as he met Mary Pat's eyes.

"When can they see her?" he asked.

"The doctor will let you know. She's a tough one."

IT WASN'T UNTIL HE WAS ALONE again that Jed started to shake. He'd gone outside and sat down on the steps. The sleet had turned to a quick, light snow. There was something hypnotic about the way it danced in the streetlights. He stared at one beam of light as he waited for the tremors to subside. Then he walked back in and rode the elevator to the floor where Dora lay sleeping.

Mary Pat smiled at him. "Jed, you're soaked."

"I just want to see her. I know she's sedated. I know she won't know I'm there. I just want to see her."

"Let me get you a towel. Then I'll take you in." When Mary Pat was satisfied he was dry enough, she led him into Dora's room.

Dora lay still and white as death. Jed's heart careered into his throat. "Are you sure she's going to be all right?"

"She's stabilized, and there were no complications." Mary Pat didn't want to think about the amount of blood they'd had to pump into Dora or how long it had taken to get that feeble pulse to steady. "The bullet's out—and there's some tissue damage, but it'll heal. Why don't you just sit with her for a while. You'll feel better."

"Thanks."

"I go off duty in an hour. I'll check back."

But when she did, one look had her leaving them alone.

He was still there in the morning.

SHE awakened slowly, as if swimming toward the surface of still, dark water. Her hand flexed once in his, then lay still again.

"Come on, Dora." He brushed his fingers over her pale cheek. Her lashes fluttered; then her eyes opened. "Jed?"

"Yeah, baby. Right here."

She shifted, sending an arrow of pain radiating through her arm. Like the pain, memory burst back. "Finley shot me." She moved her hand to the fire blooming in her shoulder. "I'm in the hospital." The panic came quickly. "How—how bad?"

"It's all over now. You're going to be fine. You just need to rest." None of his fourteen years on the force had prepared Jed to deal with the pain clouding her eyes. "I'm going to get a nurse."

"I remember." Her fingers trembled as she groped for his. "He was in the apartment, waiting for me. He wanted the painting back. I told him I didn't know where it was, and he shot me."

147

"He won't ever hurt you again. I swear it." He pressed his brow against their joined hands. "I'm so sorry, baby."

"Don't leave me alone here."

"I won't."

THE next time he saw her conscious, she was surrounded by banks and bouquets of flowers. She was wearing something frilly and pink. But to Jed she looked horribly frail.

"How you doing, Conroy?"

"Hi." She smiled, held out a hand. "How'd you break in?"

"I pulled rank." He hesitated. Her hand felt as fragile as bird wings. Miserably awkward, he turned away to study the forest of flowers. "Looks like you ought to go into a different business."

"Great, isn't it? I love being fawned over." She shifted, winced. "So what's happening? Mary Pat tells me you kicked Goldman out early and went back to work."

"Yeah." He'd had to have something fill his days, or go mad.

"Can I see your badge?"

"Sure." He pulled out his shield.

She took it, studied it. "Pretty cool. How does it feel?"

"Right," he said as he slipped it back into his pocket. He kept seeing the stark white bandage beneath that frilly nightgown. "Listen, I just stopped by to see how you were doing. I've got to go."

"Before you give me my present?" She drummed up another smile. "That box you're holding? Isn't it for me?"

"Yeah, it's for you." He set it on her lap.

She reached for the fussy bow, then sat back again. "Give me a hand, will you? I have a little trouble using my arm."

He didn't move, but his eyes were eloquent. "They told me there wouldn't be any permanent damage."

"Right." Her mouth moved into a pout. "Like a scar isn't permanent damage. I'm never going to look the same in a bikini."

Turning abruptly, he strode to the window and stared blindly out. "I should have been there. You shouldn't have been alone."

"Brent says Finley slipped right through LAPD. Nobody could have imagined he'd waltz into my apartment and shoot me."

"It's my job to know."

"So, it's going to your head already, supercop." She was lifting the top off the box when he turned. "Well, you just can't be everywhere at once." Though her arm was beginning to throb, she dug happily into the tissue paper. "I love presents. I don't particularly care to get shot to— Oh, Jed, it's beautiful."

Completely stunned, she lifted out an old wood-and-gesso box, delicately painted and gilded with figures from mythology. When she opened the lid, it played "Greensleeves" softly.

"I had it in storage. I figured you'd get a kick out of it."

"It's beautiful," she said again, and the look she sent him was so sincerely baffled he felt foolish. "Thank you."

"It's no big deal. I've really got to go. You, uh, need anything?"

She looked at him. "I could use a favor."

"Name it."

"Can you pull some strings? I want to go home."

IT TOOK him several hours, but Dora finally laid her head down on her own pillow, in her own bed. She closed her eyes, sighed deeply, then opened them again to smile at Mary Pat. "Nothing against your workplace, M.P., but personally I hated it."

"You weren't exactly the ideal patient, either, kiddo." She wrapped a blood pressure cuff around Dora's uninjured arm. "But I'm not complaining; a few days of private duty suits me just fine." But Dora caught the quick frown over the blood pressure reading.

"What's wrong?"

"Nothing that quiet and rest won't fix."

"I've been quiet. I'm tired of being in bed."

"Live with it." Sitting on the edge of the bed, Mary Pat took Dora's hand—and her pulse. "I'm going to be straight with you, Dora. If Jed hadn't gotten you in when he did, you wouldn't be here to complain. It was close. You're entitled to moan and groan, but you're also going to follow orders. Or I'll report you to the captain."

Dora smiled a little. "You nurses have ranks?"

"I'm talking about Jed, dimwit. He's financing this operation."

"What do you mean?"

"I mean you've got round-the-clock home care for as long as you need it, courtesy of Captain J. T. Skimmerhorn."

"But I thought insurance was arranging it. He shouldn't feel guilty," Dora murmured.

"He feels a lot more than guilt where you're concerned."

Dora only shook her head.

When Mary Pat left the room, Dora reached for the music box. She opened the lid, closed her eyes and wondered what to do.

AT THE end of her shift Mary Pat marched across the hall and rapped sharply on Jed's door. When Jed opened it, she jabbed a finger into his chest.

"Couldn't you find the energy to walk across the hall and—" She broke off, scowling. "What are you doing?"

"I'm packing."

Darts of fury shot out of her eyes. "You're not walking out on her when she's flat on her back."

"I'm not walking out. She *asked* me to leave. It's only going to upset her if she finds out I haven't moved yet."

"You're an idiot. Can you tell me you're not in love with her?"

He glared. "No, I can't. But that's not the point. The doctor was real clear about keeping her free from stress."

"Have you ever told her you loved her?"

"I don't see that that's any of your business."

"I didn't think so." Impatient, she took a quick turn around the room. "Have you ever picked her wildflowers?"

"It's February."

She turned on him. "She needs to be wooed, Jed."

He felt a flush creeping up on his neck. "Give me a break."

"I'd like to break your butt. You almost lost her."

His eyes whipped around, sharp as a sword. "Don't you think I know that? I wake up every night remembering how close it was."

"Then do something positive. Show her what she means to you." She kissed him. "Find some wildflowers, Jed. My money's on you."

THE box arrived the following afternoon.

"More presents," Lea announced, struggling to shove the huge box across the living room to where Dora sat on the couch.

Dora leaned down to study the box. "No return address."

"Ah, a secret admirer." Lea attacked the packing tape. "Oh," she said, deflating when she opened the lid. "It's just books."

"Oh, my Lord. Carolyn Keene." Dora was down on her knees,

rummaging. "Nancy Drew—the complete set. And first editions. It's *The Clue of the Leaning Chimney, The Hidden Staircase.*" All at once she clutched the books and began to weep.

"Oh, honey, did you hurt yourself? Let me help you to bed."

"No." She pressed a book against her cheek. "They're from Jed."

"I see," Lea said carefully, and sat back on her heels.

"He went to all this trouble just to be sweet. Why is he being so sweet? He also sent me this bracelet. Why is he doing this?"

"Honey, don't you know when you're being romanced?"

"He's just feeling sorry for me. And guilty." She hitched back tears, blinked them away. "Isn't he?"

"The man I saw haunting that hospital wasn't there out of guilt." Lea reached over to tuck her sister's hair behind her ear. "Are you going to give him a break?"

Dora laid a book on her lap, running her hands gently over the cover. "Before I was shot, I broke things off with him. I told him to move out. He hurt me, Lea. I don't want him to hurt me again."

"It seems awfully unfair to make him keep suffering." Lea rose to answer the knock on the door. "Hi, Jed." She smiled, took his hand and pulled him inside. "Look who's here, Dory."

"Hi." Dora brushed at tears and managed a shaky smile. "These are great." Her eyes overflowed again. "Really great."

"Their value's going to plummet if they're water damaged."

"You're right. But I always get sentimental over first editions."

"I was just on my way out." Lea grabbed her coat and left.

"Listen," Jed said to Dora. "I've got the go-ahead to spring you for a while. You up for a drive?"

"Outside?" She scrambled to her feet. "And not to the hospital?"

"Get your coat, Conroy."

"I can't believe it," she said a few minutes later as she slid luxuriously into Jed's car. "No nurses. No thermometers."

"How's the shoulder doing?"

"It's sore." She opened the window just to feel the rush of air on her face. "They make me do this physical therapy, which is—to put it mildly—unpleasant. But it's effective." She jockeyed her elbow to a right angle to prove it. "Not bad, huh?"

"That's great."

"Everything all right at work?" she asked him.

"It's fine. You were right all along. I shouldn't have left."

"You just needed some time." She touched his arm, then let her hand fall away. It was time, she thought, to clear the air. "Jed, I know that— Well, before I was hurt, I know I was unkind."

"Don't. You were right. Everything you said was right. I didn't want you to get too close, and I made certain you couldn't. You were a main reason I went back on the job, but I didn't share it with you, because I would have had to admit that it mattered. That what you thought of me mattered. It was deliberate."

She rolled up the window. "No point in raking it up again."

"I guess it would sound pretty convenient if I told you that I was going to ask you for another chance, before you got hurt." He shot her a look, caught her wide-eyed stare.

"I'm not sure," she said, "what another chance might entail."

He was going to try to show her. He pulled up into the driveway, set the brake, then rounded the hood to help her out. Because she was staring at his house, she moved wrong and bumped her arm against the car door. Her gasp of helpless pain broke him.

"I can't stand to see you hurt." Shielding her arm, he gathered her close. "I just can't stand it. It rips at me, Dora. I thought you were dead. I looked at you on the floor and thought you were dead."

"Don't." She soothed automatically. "I'm all right now."

"I didn't prevent it," he said fiercely. "I was too late."

"You saved my life. He'd have killed me. He wanted to, as much as he wanted the painting. You stopped him." She lifted a hand to his cheek. He grasped at it, pressed it hard to his lips.

He stood there a moment, with the air cool and crisp, whispering through the trees. "You shouldn't be standing out in the cold."

"It feels great."

"I want you to come inside. I want to finish this inside."

"All right." Though she no longer felt weak, she let him support her as they went up the walk. She thought he needed to.

But it was he who was unsteady as he unlocked the door, opened it, led her inside. His nerves jumped as she gasped in pleasure.

She stepped onto the Bokhara rug. "You've put things back."

"Some." He watched the way she ran her fingertips over the rosewood table, the curved back of a chair, the fussy gilded mirror. "My landlord kicked me out, so I took a few things out of storage."

"The right things." She walked on into the front parlor. He'd put back a curvy pin-striped settee, a lovely Tiffany lamp on a satinwood table. There was a fire burning low in the hearth. She felt a surge of pleasure and of grief. "You're moving back in."

"That depends." He carefully slipped her coat off her shoulders, laid it on the settee. "I came back here last week. It wasn't the same. I could see you sitting on my window seat, looking out the window. You changed the house," he said. "You changed me. I want to move back in and make it work. If you'll come with me."

Dora didn't think the sudden dizziness had anything to do with her healing injuries. She lowered herself to the striped cushions. "You're going to move back here? You *want* to move back here?"

"Yeah, that's right."

"And you want me to live with you?"

"If that's the best I can get." He took a small box out of his pocket and pushed it into her hands. "I'd like it better if you'd marry me."

"Can I—" Her voice squeaked. "Can I have some water?"

Frustrated, he bit back on his temper and nerves. "Sure."

She waited until he was out of the room before she worked up the courage to open the box. She was glad she had, because her mouth fell open. She was still staring dumbfounded at the ring when he came back in carrying a filled Baccarat tumbler.

"Thanks." She took the glass, drank deeply. "It's a whopper."

He fumbled. "I guess it's overstated."

"Oh, no. There isn't a diamond in the world that's overstated." She laid the box in her lap but kept a hand possessively around it. "Jed, I think these past few weeks have been as hard on you as they have on me. I might not have appreciated that, but—"

"I love you, Dora."

That stopped her cold. Before she could gather her wits, he was on the settee, his hand over hers. "If you don't want to answer yet, Dora, I'll wait. I just want a chance to make you love me again."

"Is that what all this has been about? The presents and all? You were trying to undermine my defenses when I was down."

He looked down at their joined hands. "That about sizes it up."

She nodded, then rose and took the box with her to the window. She'd want tulips out there in the spring, she thought. And daffodils.

"Good job, Skimmerhorn," she said quietly. "It was the Nancy

Drew that really did it, though." She opened the box again and looked down at the bold square-cut diamond. "You exploited my weaknesses for nostalgia, romance and material gain."

Nerves screaming, he came up behind her to touch a hand to her hair. "I've got some flaws, sure, but I'm loaded."

Her lips curved. "That approach might have worked once, but I'm pretty well set myself, since I'll be awarded a fat finder's fee on the Monet. I might be greedy, but I have my standards."

"I'm crazy about you."

"That's better."

"You're the only woman I've ever wanted to spend my life with." He brushed a light kiss at the curve of her shoulder and throat and made her sigh. "The only woman I've ever loved, or want to love."

Tears burned her throat. "That's excellent."

"So does that mean you're going to fall in love with me again?"

"What makes you think I ever stopped?"

"And the marriage thing? You'll give it a shot?"

She grinned into the sunlight. It might not have been the world's most romantic proposal, but it suited her. It suited her just fine.

"I have a Chippendale bench that's waiting to sit in front of that fire, Jed."

He turned her around, brushing her hair back so that his hands could frame her face. He only had to see her eyes. "Kids?"

"Three."

"Good number." Overwhelmed, he rested his brow against hers. "There's a bed upstairs in the master suite. A George the Third."

"Four-poster?"

"Tester. Stay here with me tonight."

She laughed her way into the kiss. "I thought you'd never ask."

Though Nora Roberts is new to Condensed Books, she is certainly not new to romance readers. This best-selling author has published more than ninety novels—yes, ninety!—with twenty-six million copies of her books in print. Since she began writing some fifteen years ago, Roberts has won almost every award for excellence given to romance writers. And she was the first author inducted into the Romance Writers of America Hall of Fame, in 1986.

Nora Roberts

So what's the secret of her success? As Nora Roberts explains, many of her romances are really romantic suspense. "Relationship books are the most important to me," she says. She adds, deadpan, "But I really like to murder people. That's an awful lot of fun."

Roberts started writing when her two sons were very young, ages three and five, and the family was living in western Maryland. "We were snowed in during the blizzard of '79," she recalls. "So I really started writing to avoid murder/suicide. As soon as I started, I realized that writing was what I wanted to do."

The author grew up in Silver Spring, Maryland. Like Dora in *Hidden Riches,* she enjoys antiques and the stage—her father worked in television and the theater in Washington, D.C. But most of all, Roberts loves to garden. Her second husband, Bruce, whom she married in 1985, is a carpenter, yet he's often at her side, planting and pruning under the sun. "He doesn't know a pansy from a petunia—he really doesn't," she says affectionately. "But he loves being out there."

What's next for this talented writer? More romantic suspense novels with intriguing relationships, she says. She's already finished the next one. And, her fans will be pleased to hear, she has no intention of letting up.

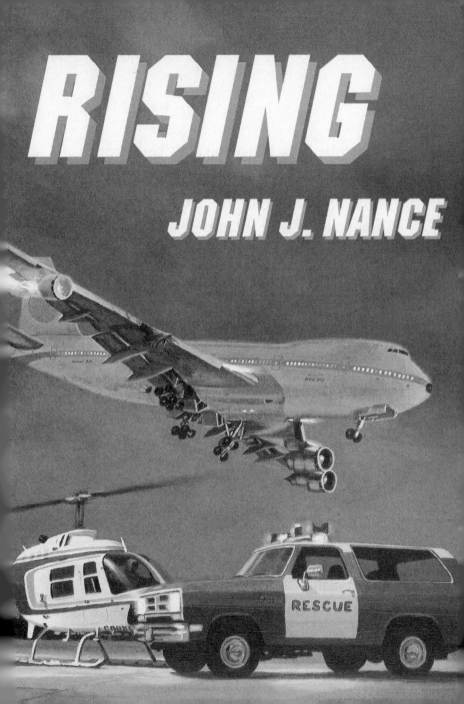

RISING

JOHN J. NANCE

Someone wants to destroy the proud new luxury airline. But who? And why? That's what the company's chief financial officer, Elizabeth Sterling, must find out. At stake is nothing less than the fate of a billion-dollar company—and the lives of everyone Elizabeth holds dear.

———————◅◦▻———————

"Veteran aviation novelist Nance has written what could turn out to be the *Airport* of the 1990s. . . . A superb novel."

—*Library Journal*

Prologue

Tuesday, February 14, St. Valentine's Day

ELIZABETH Sterling woke in a panic, with her heart racing and the distant roar of surf in her ears. In the darkness she grasped frantically for the fading image before her, trying to hold on to the tranquil feeling that had enveloped her so completely mere seconds before.

But the warmth was slipping away rapidly—and so was the man who had been with her on the beach. She watched him race away, recognizing slowly that he was only a fleeting character in a dream. In his place now was just the background roar that sounded like surf, tinged with the rich aroma of new and expensive fabrics. She was in a comfortable bed. But where *was* that bed?

"Mom? Are you awake?"

Kelly's sleepy voice floated in from somewhere above in the darkness, bringing Elizabeth's memory with it. That background roar wasn't surf, she realized. It was high-speed air passing just outside their window.

Elizabeth groped for a switch, flooding the lower regions of their small cubicle with light as Kelly lay unseen above, in the upper bunk. Squinting, Elizabeth tried to read the tiny numberless dial on her watch. Although the small hands seemed to show a few minutes past 2:00 a.m., she felt as if she'd been asleep much longer. Her subconscious had been lulled by the sounds of the slipstream at thirty-nine thousand feet as their airborne bedroom sped through the night toward the mainland of the United States.

"Where are we?" Kelly asked.

"Over the Pacific and at least seven hours out." They were supposed to arrive in Seattle, she recalled, at 9:30 a.m. "Try to get back to sleep, honey."

There was a singular murmur of assent from her fourteen-year-old daughter. Elizabeth smiled and leaned back, luxuriating in the opulence of the compartment and stretching her legs against the crisp percale sheets with the Pan Am logo.

I'd better wake up. I promised Ron Lamb I'd meet him at three a.m. Seattle time in the upper lounge.

The mattress was seven feet long—more than enough for her five-foot-six-inch height—with an identical bed just above. During the day the upper bed retracted neatly into the ceiling, while the lower one split into two plush first-class seats facing each other in the private compartment. Each of the roomettes was separated from the adjacent aisle by a wall of space-age glass, which could be turned opaque with the flick of a switch.

Not since the days of propeller transports had an airline embraced the concept of private airborne compartments, but the new Pan Am design had garnered worldwide attention—and full bookings. Equipped with television, air-to-ground telephone, and intercom, the compartment's only flaw was a traditional one: the communal bathroom and showers were located at the foot of the circular stairway leading to the upper deck.

A small concession at worst, Elizabeth figured, as she got up to dress. It was, indeed, the only way to fly—and Elizabeth felt a flash of pride that she had been a part of making it happen.

She glanced again at her watch.

Oh, Lord, it's not two; it's after four. I'm late!

THE inaugural flight of Pan Am's Seattle–Tokyo route was filled with expensively dressed guests and dignitaries, but in terms of importance to the airline, Elizabeth Sterling and her daughter were at the top of the list. Pan Am had flown them nonstop from New York to Tokyo on a competing carrier just so they could attend the inaugural party and join the flight back.

Ron Lamb, president and C.E.O. of the newly created airline using the venerable name of Pan American, had asked Elizabeth to meet him at 3:00 a.m., when they both presumed the party in the upper lounge would be over. Something important was up, and considering the immense amount of money involved in restarting worldwide operations, it couldn't be good news. Elizabeth had felt a shiver of apprehension—the same fear she'd felt for the entire eighteen months it had taken to construct the billion-dollar start-up package from her office in New York.

Ron Lamb was waiting for her when she topped the circular stairway. Extending back from the cockpit door some forty feet, the upper lounge was breathtaking. Pan Am had converted it into a luxurious club of leather and chrome, teakwood, and indirect lighting.

Lamb greeted her with a warm smile. He had silver hair, sparkling eyes, and a perpetual smile that made the small mustache he wore look slightly silly. Elizabeth had enjoyed working with him from the day he and his delegation of hopeful entrepreneurs had walked into her office at the investment banking firm of Silverman, Knox, and Bryson in New York to pitch their outlandish idea. Since at fifty-eight he was the former C.E.O. of two substantial airlines, even a wild idea from him was worth listening to.

But his idea had turned out to be far from crazy.

That had been just under three years ago, and now, with a year of highly successful operations under their belt, it looked as if "Pan Am: The Sequel" was going to make it. But with so much money at stake—not to mention her reputation in the financial community— it seemed like a continuous high-wire act without a net.

"Ron, I'm very sorry to keep you waiting."

He smiled. "I'm just glad you're here on the inaugural."

A flight attendant materialized with a freshly brewed pot of gourmet coffee on a silver tray, which also held a variety of pastries. Elizabeth followed Ron to a couple of leather chairs with a small table in between.

He sat opposite her and pulled a sheaf of papers from a battered brown leather briefcase, placing them on the table. "I've got the latest financial results and projections here for you to study. The good news is we're still ahead of schedule and gaining traffic."

"And the bad news?"

"William Hayes has resigned as chief financial officer."

"I hadn't heard." In working with Hayes, Elizabeth had found him secretive and not terribly sharp, but his departure shocked her.

"Well, it was sudden, and so is this," Ron Lamb was saying. "We want to hire *you* for the job. *I* want you, the board unanimously agrees, and the airline you helped to create needs you. I know it would mean resigning from your partnership, moving to Seattle, and uprooting your life and your daughter's life."

"To say the least. I'm not opposed to a change, but . . ."

"Okay, consider this, please. If you accept, this position will give you your very first full executive position in a publicly held corporation. Remember, Elizabeth, you're the wizard who built this financial structure, and you're the one to bring it to maturity. Hayes screwed around with the credit lines and lied to me and the board about it. That's why I need you. *We* need you."

1

Friday, February 17—La Guardia Airport, New York

THE ground dropped away beneath Elizabeth Sterling with stomach-churning suddenness as the helicopter leaped off the overcrowded airport and headed toward the south end of Manhattan Island.

Eric Knox was grinning at her behind the microphone boom of his headset. One of the senior partners of Elizabeth's investment banking firm and worth millions now, Eric could afford to commute by helicopter. Forty-two and single, he owned a mansion on eastern Long Island equipped with its own airfield. With the retirement of his father, he was now the Knox in the highly respected firm of Silverman, Knox, and Bryson.

They reached five hundred feet and began moving toward the East River as Eric gently banked the Jet Ranger left toward the heliport by the South Ferry dock, near their office building.

Elizabeth's eyes scanned the magnificent cityscape ahead. How could twelve years have passed so fast? The day she first drove into the city, she'd luxuriated in Manhattan's skyline. The years at Harvard Business School had been nothing short of brutal, especially for a widowed mother going through the lonely trials of raising a baby daughter alone. She had fallen in love with a fellow M.B.A. candidate—an ex–air force pilot named Brian Murphy—whom Kelly had begun to regard as her father. But Brian had had six months to go to his degree and couldn't accompany them to the big city when Elizabeth began her new job as an investment banker.

Nevertheless, New York had taken her in. First she had had the good fortune of finding an affordable flat in Greenwich Village. Then Brian moved in with them just before Christmas. When he left to fly for a start-up airline in Phoenix four years later, Kelly was inconsolable at losing the only father figure she had ever known.

Elizabeth's metamorphosis into a New Yorker had come all too fast. In the last few years the selfishness and pointlessness of her job had begun to gnaw away at her conscience. Every new stock issue or junk-bond package was publicly hailed as a benefit for the corporations involved, but she knew better. What she did for a living, she had finally admitted to herself, was similar to a financial shell game: she thought up ways to magically change the ownership of hard-earned corporate profits.

Then the Pan Am project had come along, fraught with the opportunity to create new employment and new, productive wealth. She had believed in it and fought for it and ultimately succeeded brilliantly. But afterward everything had snapped back to the same pointless routine.

Kelly had noticed her distress, but her associates had not.

I'm scared to leave, Elizabeth realized now, and I'm scared to stay.

As deftly as Eric had handled the departure, he made a perfect touchdown. The short walk to their building was taken at double time. Elizabeth smiled at the receptionist as she breezed through the double glass doors and headed for her office, with Eric in hot pursuit. She stood before the floor-length window by her desk, her thoughts suddenly far away, as Eric sat on the couch.

Eric watched her carefully as she stood with her back to him, her amber-blond hair cascading gently over her sculpted shoulders, the broad angles of her face turned from him but etched in his mind. Her nose was perfect—diminutive and slightly upturned—in balance with her broad mouth, which was set off by laugh lines.

But as Eric had discovered with secret pride years before—after hiring Elizabeth Sterling as much for her looks as her professional qualifications—any male that mistook her gentle female image for weakness rapidly slammed into a brick wall of determination.

"Why leave this behind, Elizabeth? Seattle's a backwater."

"I haven't decided yet." She turned.

"This new Pan Am could fail miserably, you know."

"I'll have a golden parachute."

"But you won't have *us.*"

"I know," she said softly. That part would be hard.

Saturday, February 18—Provincetown, Massachusetts

SATURDAY blew in on a freezing east wind accompanied by a full moon hung in a frosty indigo sky. Provincetown, no longer awash with tourists, had an intimate atmosphere, even in the cold.

It was 11:00 p.m. by the time Elizabeth and Kelly returned to their cottage from an evening of seafood. Kelly had already decided what her mother should do, and with a seriousness beyond her years she had sat Elizabeth down at the small kitchen table. "Mom, as long as we keep this place, moving is the right thing to do."

Elizabeth looked at her daughter with pride, realizing what a beauty Kelly was becoming. Her clear blue eyes and shoulder-length auburn hair were already attracting the attention of the awkward boys in her class. Kelly tossed her hair and smiled an odd little smile that made her look just like her father. Elizabeth felt herself weaken for a moment as she thought of Ted and how much he would have loved their daughter. She seldom thought about the drunk driver who had killed him, leaving a pregnant young wife with nothing.

Elizabeth shook off the memories and smiled back at Kelly. "You're sure you're happy with the idea?"

Kelly loved her grandmother, who lived in Bellingham, Washington, two hours north of Seattle. The move was an exciting change. The idea of free passes on Pan Am had filled Kelly's head with visions of endless trips to exotic destinations. Kelly nodded. "I'm sure."

When Kelly was asleep, Elizabeth pulled on a parka and slipped outside to brave the wind and think.

She sat on a driftwood log listening to the crash of the surf as she realized the decision had already been made.

Monday, February 20—Pan Am Headquarters, Seattle, Washington

RON Lamb replaced the receiver and sat back uncomfortably in his elaborate desk chair. It was 9:50 a.m. in Seattle and 12:50 p.m. in New York, and already four different stock analysts had called for reassurance that all was well with Pan Am—even as the new airline's stock sank on the market.

"Rumors!" Ron had roared at each of them with what he hoped appeared to be unshakable confidence.

The origins of the rumors were unimportant for the moment, but they would force him to stage a meeting for the airline analysts within a few days in New York, in a frantic attempt to calm them down. Already the black financial crepe of impending doom had been hung around the cornices of Pan Am's credit rating.

"We've gotta stop this, Ron." Joseph Taylor, chairman of the board, was staring at him from the leather couch across from the C.E.O.'s desk.

"I know it." Ron checked his watch again. Elizabeth Sterling was supposed to call in another ten minutes.

The chairman wasn't finished. "Ron, what's going on with the FAA? Are they after us, or what?"

Taylor, an imposing lump of a man at two hundred eighty pounds, had made a fortune creating an international chain of warehouse clubs. His considerable bank account and a lifelong devotion to the original Pan American Airways had made him the engine—and the chairman—of the corporation they had formed to refly the Pan Am name. But Taylor needed help finding airports, and knew nothing of what went on there. For the most part he stayed out of Ron Lamb's way.

Ron Lamb inclined his head toward the vice president of operations, Chad Jennings, who snapped to attention.

"Mr. Taylor, we don't think there's any sort of, uh, campaign to nail us on violations, but as you may know, a team of FAA inspectors descended on our Denver maintenance station last week and found parts records missing. Yesterday they called and claimed we were using the wrong minimum-equipment lists on the 747s and told us to brace for a large fine. They said they were responding to tips."

Taylor refocused on the C.E.O. "Sounds like one of our competitors may be setting us up, Ron."

The C.E.O.'s secretary appeared in the office doorway. "Mr. Lamb, Miss Sterling is calling from Massachusetts on line two."

Ron Lamb took a ragged breath and picked up the receiver.

"Okay, Ron, I'll take it. You've got yourself a new C.F.O."

"How soon can you get here, Elizabeth? We need you."

"Good Lord, Ron, I haven't resigned from Silverman, Knox yet."

"Well," he replied. "Can you come out here tomorrow—just for a quick orientation?"

"Yes, I can do that."

"Good. I'll have first-class tickets for you on our early afternoon flight out of Kennedy tomorrow. Bring Kelly if you like. Just give me one day to get you up to speed on some important items."

"Such as why the financial press thinks you're going belly-up?" She said the words in a breezy tone, but there was stunned silence from Seattle.

AT THE very moment Ron Lamb's office was emptying of Chairman Taylor and other Pan Am corporate officers in downtown Seattle, Pan Am's chief pilot, Brian Murphy, was engaged in a delicate balancing act: aligning his Boeing 767 flight simulator for a tough approach to fog-shrouded Anchorage, Alaska, while trying to figure out why his cellular phone was ringing. Finally he snapped on the autoflight system and reached for his phone.

The voice in his ear was familiar. "Brian? Is that you?"

He lurched forward in his seat involuntarily. "Elizabeth?"

"Yes, it's me. Where *are* you?"

"In the flight simulator. Where are *you?* In Seattle?"

"No . . . Cape Cod. But I'm coming to Seattle."

"Wonderful! When? For how long?"

"Maybe forever, Brian."

"What do you mean, Elizabeth? You aren't teasing me, are you?"

She told him then of the job offer and her acceptance and the impending move. Despite all the years and the supposedly final choices they had made, she missed him. She missed him more than she had ever let herself admit.

"I'm coming in tomorrow for a quick orientation," she said.

"Tomorrow? Damn. I have to be in D.C. We've, ah, had a few problems with the FAA I've got to take care of."

The word "problems" didn't register. The fact that she wouldn't see him for a few more weeks did.

Suddenly it seemed an eternity.

JAKE Wallace turned the time card over again in complete confusion. The imprint that showed that he had already clocked in for the graveyard shift was still there, the time of 9:54 p.m. showing clearly on the appropriate line.

But it was now 10:01 p.m.—and he had just arrived.

Jake glanced around the interior hallway of the sparkling new hangar, searching for an explanation. There were twenty-two other mechanics on the graveyard, and he was their foreman. Obviously, one of them had grabbed Jake's card by mistake.

He sighed and began looking through the time cards of his shiftmates, verifying the time stamp on each one until he had counted twenty-two properly clocked-in employees.

So much for the obvious explanation, he thought. He pocketed the time card and headed for job control.

Ed Washburn looked up from his computer screen with a characteristic grin, but received no smile in return from the bearded mechanic. As two of his crew came in the door, Jake waved the offending time card in front of Ed and explained the problem.

Ray McCarthy, who had overheard, raised his index finger. "That new man may have got hold of your card, Jake. He clocked in just behind me. He seemed surprised his card was already there."

Jake Wallace looked at Ed Washburn. Simultaneously they turned toward McCarthy. "*What* new man?"

He had worn the regulation white coveralls with the Pan Am logo, McCarthy explained, and introduced himself as Bill Somebody-or-other before asking for directions to the job control office. The man had come through the security door into the maintenance complex with McCarthy, and it was Ray who had punched in the security code and opened the door for them both. Five feet ten and of medium build, the new man had a mustache but an otherwise forgettable face.

"No one checked through here, and I wasn't expecting anyone new," Ed Washburn said. "Did he have an I.D. badge, Ray?"

Ray McCarthy tried to call up a memory of the man's identification card. There had been something there clipped to his pocket. He just assumed it was a Pan Am I.D. "I *thought* it was there."

They all stared silently at one another.

Washburn broke the silence. "Whoever he is, we'd better find this guy before he hurts himself or steals the coffee money. I wonder if someone in Seattle hired him and forgot to tell us."

The search began casually. But when a quick walk-through of the facility turned up neither an explanation nor a confused new-hire mechanic, Ed Washburn, as shift supervisor, began to get seriously concerned. He stepped up the search and alerted his boss at home. Robert Chenowith, the general manager of the maintenance base, jumped into his car and arrived in job control within fifteen minutes, equally worried.

Two dozen mechanics now roamed the hangar and connecting buildings, looking for the intruder. Someone had invaded their space, and the group was determined to catch him. All other work had ceased.

At first the search had centered around the only aircraft in the facility—Ship 612, a sparkling 747-200, which squatted in the middle of the giant hangar, bathed in sodium-vapor lights and looking magnificent. Ship 612 was due to be flown back to Seattle-Tacoma Airport (Seatac) the following morning, carrying the latest modifications to the compartment- and first-class sections.

By 11:30 p.m. it was obvious that whoever had crashed their gate was long gone. Every square inch of floor space had been checked and checked again, but the intruder wasn't there.

They turned, then, to the more sinister question: Regardless of who he was, did the intruder *do* anything to our airplane?

Two dozen people now began crawling over Ship 612, looking for anything unusual. But by 2:00 a.m. Ed Washburn declared it to be clean. With Chenowith's permission they terminated the search.

Chenowith now faced a dilemma of his own. His hand hovered over the telephone in job control as his mind calculated the percentages in alerting his vice president of maintenance in Seattle. He would be getting the man out of bed, of course, but for what?

Despite the nagging doubts, Ship 612 was clean. Now his people would have to drive themselves twice as hard during the remaining four hours of their shift to get the huge bird ready to fly back to Seattle. Chenowith read 2:45 a.m. on the wall clock as he quietly replaced the receiver, his decision not to call already made.

AT THE SAME MOMENT, SOME two hundred miles to the west, Pan Am's president and C.E.O. was sitting in the back seat of a rented limousine and rubbing his eyes. The multimillion-dollar advertising package Ron Lamb was supposed to help launch in little more than an hour was critical to Pan Am's success.

The inauguration date for the new globe-circling service was three weeks away, Ron reminded himself, and yet there was still much left to do.

The dark mass of the KOMO television building slid into place, and with a practiced rush of open doors the limousine driver delivered the airline president to the care of a studio technician. The man escorted him to a talk-show set and seated him in a comfortable chair. He fussed over an earpiece as he clipped a tiny microphone to Ron's tie.

Ron glanced around the darkened studio. There were several bright studio lights shining in his eyes, but the houselights in the background were turned off. He began concentrating on the briefing paper provided by Ralph Basanji, senior vice president, public affairs, and that triggered a mental review of the past week.

The meeting with the financial community in New York had been an inquisition, but he'd pulled it off—or so the feedback had confirmed. Ron's performance had quieted the waters for the moment. Elizabeth Sterling couldn't arrive a moment too soon, and Ron reminded himself that she'd be landing in Seattle this very evening to take over the financial reins at last.

"Mr. Lamb?" The sudden voice in his ear caused him to jump slightly as Ron reminded himself that the technicians back east were probably looking at him by satellite through the lens of the camera that sat some fifteen feet away.

"This is the director in New York, Mr. Lamb. We appreciate your getting up at such an early hour to be with us. We're going to run a taped report about your company; then we'll come back to the studio and to you about six minutes from now."

"Okay." Ron closed his eyes for a second and felt the butterflies begin to alight, one by one.

The familiar theme music of *Good Morning America* filled his ear now, and he took a deep breath and prepared to pump sunshine into the hearts of the flying public.

2

Wednesday, March 8, 8:07 p.m.—Seattle

BENEATH the high overcast that covered Puget Sound by sunset, a wispy veil of stratus now floated like an afterthought at three thousand feet. The diaphanous layer gently enfolded the nighttime city of Seattle, enshrouding a region of mysterious beauty and twinkling lights in multicolor hues.

Many of the newly airborne passengers marveled at the view as Ship 612—Pan Am Flight 10—slipped into the sky, making a lazy left turn toward Tokyo, some five thousand miles distant.

Wednesday, March 8, 8:40 p.m.—Pan Am Flight 10

FOR the last few minutes there had been nothing but a soft electronic hum in the earpiece of the captain's lightweight headset. It changed now suddenly, the businesslike voice of an air-traffic controller cutting through the void.

"Clipper Ten Heavy, say again your GUNNS estimate."

To Captain Jim Aaron, the radio channel had been quiet for so long that he'd begun to wonder if they'd lost contact with Seattle Center. But no, the controller was still with them and wanting to know when the 747 crew expected to pass over the invisible checkpoint called GUNNS, an oceanic intersection some three hundred sixty miles west-northwest of Washington State.

Judy Griffin, the copilot, raised her microphone to reply.

"Clipper Ten Heavy is estimating GUNNS at . . . ah"—Judy leaned to her left, her eyes searching the screen of the flight computer for the right number—"zero five two two Zulu, Seattle. We're level now at flight level three five zero."

There was a rustling of papers as the flight engineer, Patrick Hogan, handed the fuel plan forward for the captain's approval. The fuel would be tight. A nonstop flight from Seattle to Tokyo was just barely within legal range without a fuel stop in Anchorage.

Jim scribbled his initials on the log and handed it back. He turned to Judy and then to Patrick. "You two ready to rig for ocean running? Turn the houselights up, I mean."

Night flying in a dark cockpit made everyone sleepy, and once over the ocean, under positive control at high altitudes, there was no point in looking for other traffic.

They both nodded in unison, and Jim reached up to the overhead panel to flood the cockpit with light, when a soul-shaking thud thundered through the 747 cockpit.

The cockpit voice recorder duly recorded the time as 04:46:08 GMT—8:46 p.m. in Seattle.

CAPTAIN Jim Aaron felt as if something large and hard had hit the plane at high speed. The combination of sound, orange light, vibration, and the sudden yawing of the 747 overwhelmed him.

In a split second Jim's eyes were scanning the instrument panel. The fact that a cold, foggy mist had suddenly formed in his cockpit registered, but in the immense confusion of the moment he was trying to grasp everything at once and could focus on nothing.

The 747 immediately began to yaw dangerously to the right as the left wing came up. Jim's hands flew to the yoke, pulling instinctively as he rolled the giant Boeing back to the left.

Maintain aircraft control. That was the prime directive. *But the mist meant that—*

"Rapid decompression!" Judy was flailing at something on her right and trying to speak above the sound of a warning bell.

Rapid depressurization! We're depressurized! Jim Aaron understood instantly now. *Get your mask on, boy.* The voice of experience was suddenly echoing in his head.

Jim clawed over his left shoulder with his right hand, groping for his oxygen mask. There were precious few seconds left before lack of oxygen would doom him to unconsciousness. Finally he swept the mask over his head, and for the next few seconds all his energy flowed into the controls as he tried to right the airplane.

The unspoken fear that the 747 might be coming apart in midair sat like a cold specter on his shoulders. The controls felt mushy, and he found himself testing them, rolling the yoke left and right slightly to see if the airplane would respond.

There! The 747 was responding. They were still flying, but they were obviously in trouble.

We've got to turn back. We're still headed out to sea.

His eyes scanned the center instrument panel—the zeroed read-

171

ings on engine number three were all too obvious. Number four's instruments looked strange. It was hard to concentrate with all the noise. There was a loud, persistent ringing noise that had been there all along, he now realized. A bell. A fire warning!

Judy was pointing excitedly to the illuminated fire handle for number three, the inboard engine on the right wing. Jim could see a bright orange glow reflecting against the edges of the window frame. "Engine fire, number three!"

Judy nodded. "It's burning! We need to shut it down."

Jim grabbed the number three fire handle. He pulled hard, instantly shutting off the fuel supply to the engine, then punched the fire-bottle-discharge button to send a wave of fire-extinguishing foam into the surrounding cavities of the huge engine.

Gotta get down! He had to get the passengers to lower altitude, where everyone could breathe. Their oxygen masks were insufficient at thirty-five thousand feet. Only nineteen seconds had passed since the initial explosion.

"Emergency . . . ah . . . descent!" He couldn't seem to get the words out without a struggle, but Judy nodded again. He heard her voice on the overhead speakers as she talked to Seattle Center.

"Seattle . . . Pan Am Clipper Ten. We have a problem up here. We're going to make an emergency descent. We're turning back, leaving flight level three five zero now."

Jim Aaron pulled all four throttles and extended the speed brakes as he let the huge 750,000-pound aircraft bank to the right and start down.

The calm voice of the Seattle Center controller cut through the cockpit. "Clipper Ten, roger, receiving your emergency squawk. You're cleared to descend pilot discretion to ten thousand, right turn to a heading of zero nine zero degrees for now."

"Jim, number three's still burning!"

"Okay, ah, shoot the other bottle, Judy." He saw her hand react instantly, pressing the alternate fire-extinguisher button for the last fire bottle they carried in the right wing.

"Jim, we've lost some hydraulic systems." It was Patrick's muffled intercom voice.

Jim Aaron glanced over his shoulder at the flight engineer. Patrick met his gaze and leaned forward. "I just talked to the lead flight attendant. Everyone's frightened, but they're hanging on."

Jim nodded a thank-you and focused on the unwinding altimeter. They were descending through twenty-two thousand feet, the rate of descent more than eight thousand feet per minute.

"Jim, we ought to dump fuel if we're going back." The low, urgent voice was Patrick's.

Jim snapped his head around to look at the engineer's panel. *Where the hell are the hydraulics? I don't see pressure anywhere.*

He remembered that the 747 was following his control inputs, even if sluggishly. *I have to have at least one hydraulic system left. I couldn't be flying if I didn't have at least one.*

"Jim, I need to dump fuel," Patrick repeated.

Suddenly fuel didn't seem very important. Hydraulics did.

The controller's voice interrupted Jim's fragmented thoughts. "Clipper Ten, Seattle. Come right now to one zero zero degrees. State your intentions."

Judy punched the TRANSMIT button. "Seattle, we want vectors back to Seatac for an emergency landing."

Jim was still staring at the engineer's panel, trying to make the dead hydraulic systems live again. "Are we really down to one?"

Patrick looked up at the captain. "Systems two, three, and four are gone—no pressure and no fluid. All we have left is hydraulic system one. We *will* be able to lower the gear and fly the plane, as long as nothing happens to the—the last system."

Jim nodded. Okay, we're through sixteen thousand now, headed back east, he thought, as he began to shallow the descent and level the huge aircraft. He pushed the power up on the three remaining engines, startled to feel heavy yawing to the right again.

This damn thing flies like I've got two engines out on one wing. Judy pulled off her oxygen mask. Right. We're low enough now, he thought. He pulled his mask off as well, and turned toward Patrick. "Everybody can come off oxygen now. Patrick, tell the cabin."

The flight engineer nodded and reached for the PA as Jim rolled in still more aileron to the left, shaken at how much it was taking to keep the wings level.

The airspeed caught his eye. It was too low. *Something's wrong!*

"Judy"—he spoke without looking at her, his voice an urgent appeal of worry—"it feels like she's refusing to fly level at this

173

altitude on three engines. What's going on? Number three *and* four, looks like. I mean, they're *both* zero. Did we lose both?"

Judy's head snapped to the right for a look at the wing. For several moments she tried to make sense of the flames now roaring around the right outboard engine. "I think it's number *four* that's burning," she said. "But we never got a fire warning."

"We're out of fire bottles. We fired both of them on the right wing into number three." The voice was Patrick's.

"Patrick, go back and take a look out there at the right engines. See what we've got," Jim ordered.

The flight engineer took a large flashlight and rushed from the cockpit. He returned in two minutes.

"Boss, number three must have exploded. The engine looks to be gone, and—and number four *is* burning."

"Are we together, otherwise?" Jim was scared, plain and simple.

"No damage I can see," the engineer replied.

Jim glanced back at the flight instruments. Engines one and two, the two power plants on the left wing, were already just a hair below maximum power, yet he couldn't hold a safe flying speed and stay level at fourteen thousand feet. There was no choice but to keep on descending. With rising fear he pushed the yoke forward.

Immediately the 747 picked up a healthy rate of descent. But the realization on Jim Aaron's part was now unavoidable: *We're too heavy to fly level with only two engines. But if we can't maintain fourteen thousand, what* can *we maintain? How low do I have to get this tub before we can level off?*

Patrick's warning about having too much fuel coalesced at last. They had enough fuel to get to Japan, and it was dragging them into the water.

The captain turned to his flight engineer and fairly barked, "Start dumping!"

Patrick's answer was instantaneous. "We can only dump out of the left wing. I can't use the right dump mast with number four engine burning right next to it. That means our dump rate's half of normal."

Jim turned back to the panel. *If we didn't have the overcast down there, I could see the coastline by now.* As it was, only blackness filled the windscreen.

"We're through eight thousand," Judy intoned.

Jim knew the descent rate was slowing. But he still couldn't fly level. "How far out are we?" he asked.

"Fifty-two miles from Neah Bay," Judy replied. "But we've lost contact with Seattle Center. We're too low."

He let himself take a deep breath and straightened himself in the command chair. They were descending now through seven thousand feet and under control, but he wasn't doing it right. There were a thousand duties to perform, and here he was trying to play the game single-handedly—the brave captain flying the airplane and giving the orders. Now it was time to act like a crew commander.

"Judy, you take the airplane and keep us in the air while I work on the problems, okay?"

"Roger, I've got it." Judy took the yoke, astounded at the control pressures necessary to keep them going straight.

Jim then turned to the flight engineer. "Give me an assessment."

Patrick pointed to the right side of the jumbo. "Apparently number three engine exploded on us. I'm sure it threw debris everywhere, and it probably peppered number four with shrapnel."

"Why are we depressurized?"

"Well, number three probably machine-gunned turbine blades into our belly—you know, into the air-conditioning systems, and maybe even the landing gear. With that size explosion, no telling where all the pieces went or which engines ate parts."

"Are you saying it could have hurt the left engines, too?"

Patrick heard the strain in Jim Aaron's voice. They might make it on two engines, but they would have to ditch if they went down to one. A nighttime ditching in a 747 would probably be unsurvivable.

Jim's head throbbed with tension. "We're too low to fly over the Olympic Mountains. We're gonna have to follow the Strait of Juan de Fuca back in toward Seattle to keep clear of all terrain."

Judy had been staring at the forward panel while the captain talked. Suddenly her voice rang through his words. "Jim, we're losing number two!" Her left index finger was nervously tapping a small round gauge on the center panel, on which a tiny indicator needle was climbing into unacceptable temperature ranges.

"How in the hell . . ." Jim pulled the throttle for number two back halfway. Perhaps they could keep it running at part power.

"How much do we weigh now?"

175

The response was immediate. Patrick was monitoring the dump rate like a computer. "Six hundred forty-two thousand. With two engines and max power and a full dump rate, we should have been able to level at eight thousand. With one engine and half a dump rate, I don't think we can stay in the air long enough to dump down to, ah, flying weight."

Jim Aaron looked at his two companions. "Okay, we're not licked yet. If nothing else, we'll fly this ship like a ship in ground effect until we get rid of enough fuel to climb again."

Patrick was stunned. "We'll do *what?*"

"Ground effect. I've seen it done before over water."

Jim knew an airplane otherwise incapable of flight could hang above the surface at an altitude of up to half its wingspan on the very cushion of air it was compressing by the act of flying by.

"I'm guessing, but I think we have enough power. Provided number one hydraulic system holds and engines one and two continue to run, and provided the fire on the right side doesn't threaten the wing and there aren't any large freighters in the way, I think we can get as far as Whidbey."

Jim Aaron had never landed at Whidbey Island Naval Air Station, but he knew it was the only major Puget Sound airfield with a runway on the water. It was their only chance. Every other airport within range was too high above sea level.

Patrick leaned forward, his expression ashen. "What if we get all the way down to the surface and she won't fly in ground effect?"

"Then we ditch her," Jim said. "Not much of a plan, I'll admit. But it's all we've got at the moment." *And I'm not giving up yet!*

3

Wednesday, March 8, 9:10 p.m.—Seattle Center, Federal Aviation Administration Air Route Traffic Control Center, Auburn, Washington

To THE uninitiated visitor, the subdued lights and quiet background noises that filled the cavernous interior of the Air Route Traffic Control Center were unaltered. The long rows of radar display screens divided a work area occupied by a host of men and women wearing headsets and speaking quietly by radio to pilots scattered all over the skies of the Pacific Northwest. But to the senses of a veteran air-traffic controller, the atmosphere filling Seattle Center had suddenly become electric.

In a far corner, a small, solemn gathering could be seen standing behind the controller in charge of the airspace just west of the Olympic Peninsula. The man was trying once again to raise Pan Am Flight 10, whose call sign was Clipper Ten Heavy.

Three minutes had elapsed since the last transmission from the Pan Am jumbo, though the radar signal was still strong. It crawled across the screen toward the coastline of Washington State, but there was no answer from the occupants of the distant cockpit.

The controller's stomach was in a knot behind his polished mask of detachment. What was happening out there? It was a helpless feeling to sit in a windowless room a hundred miles distant, devoid of radio contact, watching a sterile version of the drama unfold as the 747's transponder dutifully reported their sinking altitude.

The controller glanced quickly at his shift supervisor, who had materialized by his side just after the Pan Am pilots had set their transponder to the emergency code of 7700—an act that set off an insistent alarm in Seattle Center.

"He's got a rapid depressurization and an engine loss of some sort, and an onboard fire, probably in the engine," the controller reported. "I cleared him to fourteen thousand and then to five."

"But he's now at two thousand!" The supervisor was incredulous. "What's he doing so low over the water? Where does he want to go?"

The controller shook his head in frustration. "He didn't say. I'm ready to vector him wherever he wants. But I've got to reach him first and then turn him. He's too low to go over the peninsula."

The controller punched his TRANSMIT button. "Clipper Ten Heavy, if you're hearing Seattle Center, change your squawk to seven six zero zero."

They watched the small data block on the screen. Finally the numbers changed to 7600.

"All right! He hears me." The controller jabbed the TRANSMIT button. "Clipper Ten Heavy, come left now to a heading of zero six zero degrees."

The supervisor's voice was in his ear once again. "How about bringing him down in Port Angeles?"

The image of Port Angeles Airport popped into the controller's

177

head. Port Angeles was on the north shoulder of the Olympic Peninsula, and it was the closest real airport to Clipper Ten if he planned to limp eastbound down the Strait of Juan de Fuca.

He turned to his supervisor. "That might do it. The runway is about sixty-three hundred feet. I think a 747 could get in there."

The supervisor turned to one of the other controllers watching the situation. "Jerry, call the Port Angeles manager. Tell him what we've got. Does he have enough people and equipment to handle it if he can't get her stopped in the available concrete?"

The supervisor already knew the answer, but they had to try.

9:15 p.m.—Seatac Airport

PAN American's vice president of operations, Chad Jennings, dashed up the escalator two steps at a time. He was late, and yet he might just make it after all. Elizabeth Sterling and her daughter were coming to town again, this time for good. He had met her two weeks before, when she came in from New York to finalize her new position. Elizabeth had technically become an officer two days ago, a senior vice president like him, but with a seat on the board, which was something he didn't rate as yet. Meeting her flight was a courtesy—and a smart idea in the corporate hierarchy of things—but being late was not.

The flight's E.T.A. was 9:25 p.m., but the flight crew had made it in a few minutes early. They were just nosing the 767 into the terminal as Chad covered the last few hundred feet to gate N-4. As he watched the Jetway being moved toward the aircraft, his cellular phone began to chirp.

Chad pulled the diminutive portable out of his inside coat pocket and punched it on, instantly recognizing the voice on the other end as that of a TV newsman from Seattle's Channel 7.

"Mr. Jennings, we know that your Flight ten has had some sort of explosion and is coming back. We know they've declared an emergency and may be on fire. Can you tell us anything more?"

Jennings was stunned. He had heard nothing. He pumped the newsman for information. The reporter relayed all he knew. They were sending their news helicopter to wherever the captain decided to land. The betting in the newsroom was that it would be one of several other airports closer than Seatac. Would Jennings like a ride?

Suddenly the urge to be as close as possible to the action overwhelmed him. "You say you'd come pick me up?"

"Yes, sir, we could, depending on where you are."

"I'm at Seatac, the north satellite."

"Our pilot will be there in a few minutes. He's already airborne."

ELIZABETH and Kelly had already left the Jetway when Chad found them. He filled them in, his face a mask of concern. "I'm going to meet a news station helicopter and try to be wherever our flight lands. I hate to say hello and good-bye, but I've got to run."

"How big's the helicopter?" asked Elizabeth.

"It's a Jet Ranger, I think," Chad replied.

"Okay, then take us with you. Rangers carry five. One pilot, one photographer, and three of us. We can get our bags later."

9:20 p.m. — In flight, Clipper Ten

CAPTAIN Jim Aaron had pushed the throttle for number two engine back up a bit, feeling the surge in power. And just as quickly the exhaust-gas temperature began climbing toward redline limits. It was no use. Jim pulled the throttle back to almost idle. It made sense to keep it running in case they needed a final surge of power. But either they got enough fuel dumped to fly on one engine, or they would have to put Ship 612 in the water.

He picked up the intercom handset and punched in the code for the lead flight attendant. Her voice filled his ear almost instantly.

"June, is that you?" June Digby was perhaps the most experienced flight attendant to join the new Pan Am, a pro with over thirty-two years in the air.

"It's me. What's happening up there?"

"June, I need you to get everybody ready for a possible ditching."

"The water down there, Jim—it's very cold."

"I know," he replied, replacing the handset.

Jim looked at his copilot. Judy was doing a magnificent job of holding the crippled 747 steady, but they were through fourteen hundred feet and still coming down at two hundred feet per minute.

"Clipper Ten Heavy, Seattle Center. How do you hear?"

Judy shook her head in disgust. "I've heard him for the last five minutes. I just can't talk to him. We're too low to reach his antennas with our radio, but his radio's powerful enough to get through to us."

Jim raised the microphone and replied once again, expecting nothing, and was startled when the controller's voice came back with open excitement. "Clipper Ten Heavy, read you loud and clear. Say your condition."

"I can't stay high enough to get over the terrain, so I'm going to fly over water the whole way. I need you to coordinate with the coast guard ship-traffic control people to keep us clear of big ships. We may be flying in ground effect as low as fifty feet."

A long silence ensued, and a somber voice came back. "Roger, Clipper Ten. We're establishing contact with the coast guard now. All search-and-rescue forces in the area are scrambling as well. We're checking on Port Angeles International as a possible airport."

"Port *Angeles?*" Jim knew he sounded shocked. He had never landed there. It sounded like far too small an airport for a 747.

"Roger, Clipper Ten. They've got sixty-three hundred feet, with a thousand-foot overrun, and are stressed for a jumbo."

"What's their field elevation?" Jim Aaron asked.

"Two hundred eighty-eight feet above sea level."

All three pilots looked simultaneously at the altimeters. They were under a thousand feet above the water now, and still descending. Port Angeles was seventy miles away.

Jim Aaron took a deep breath. "Get them ready, Seattle, but I'm not sure we can use it."

"Roger, Clipper Ten. What else can we do for you?"

"Just stand by, Seattle. And a few prayers would be in order, too."

Jim looked down at the navigation panel in front of him. Their altitude was now dipping under eight hundred feet.

"Unlike Port Angeles, which is at two hundred eighty-eight feet," Jim began, "Whidbey Island . . ."

"Is literally at sea level," Judy finished the thought. "It's also a hundred twenty miles away."

"I know it," he said simply.

9:35 p.m. — In flight, Chopper 7

Aboard the TV news helicopter, Chad Jennings huddled in the left front seat of the Jet Ranger with a phone to each ear. After some minutes he looked up and turned toward the pilot. "Okay, can you head for Port Angeles Airport? That's where he may come down."

The pilot nodded and banked the chopper to the left across Puget Sound. They had climbed in at Seatac. Chad took the co-pilot's seat, Elizabeth the left rear seat, Kelly the middle, and the photographer, the right rear.

As the pilot flew the chopper northwestward, Elizabeth thought back to something Chad Jennings had said while they waited for the helicopter. Pan Am was being targeted by the FAA for a host of violations. He suspected that a dirty-tricks campaign might be behind each one of the FAA inspections, which had turned up problems they didn't know they had. The thought that something more than financial problems faced her new company was chilling.

Another thing hung in the back of her mind as a dark warning of trouble: Jennings' reaction. It was as if this emergency threatening Clipper Ten was merely the latest in a long string of operational problems, none of which Ron Lamb had mentioned.

9:40 p.m.—In flight, Clipper Ten

"DON'T let me get below seventy feet, or bank over fifteen degrees, Judy." Jim Aaron's eyes were riveted on the instrument panel, his vision taking in the radar altimeter, which now showed a mere eighty feet above the waters of the Strait of Juan de Fuca.

Jim had pushed number two engine up a bit, bringing its exhaust-gas temperature right to the redline. Everything was in a state of precarious balance. They had already passed abeam of one ocean-going freighter, a ship with a superstructure tall enough to snag them out of the sky if they'd attempted to fly over it.

A coast guard rescue C-130 helicopter had found them and joined up overhead now, acting as a radio relay station when they hit blank spots in Seattle Center's coverage. The passengers had been briefed and prepared, and the flight attendants had reviewed their procedures. Everyone below crouched in a brace position. If he had to put it in the water, they were as ready as they would ever be.

Survival now depended on the skills and courage of the pilots of Clipper Ten to keep their ship flying without dipping a wingtip in the water and cartwheeling everyone to their deaths.

"Position, Judy?" Jim dared not take his eyes off the altimeter.

"Twenty-four miles from Port Angeles Airport."

Patrick's voice followed. "We're down to six hundred and eighteen thousand pounds. If I'm figuring it right, in about twenty minutes we should be light enough to gain some altitude."

Jim Aaron quickly converted the twenty minutes to sixty-four nautical miles. It wasn't enough. They would have to fly in circles off Port Angeles until they were light enough to climb to the four hundred feet needed to use Port Angeles Airport. Banking the aircraft much in such perilous conditions was unthinkable. One circle could take in a diameter of twenty miles.

Jim shook his head. "We can't make Port Angeles. We've got Whidbey dead ahead about eighty miles; we're aligned with the runway, and even if I can't gain ten feet, we can get her on the ground."

"Roger. I'll tell them." Judy's finger was already pressing the TRANSMIT button.

9:55 p.m. — In flight, Chopper 7

THE full magnitude of what was happening finally began to sink in. For the past twenty minutes Elizabeth Sterling's ears had been filled with technical facts of Clipper Ten Heavy's emergency, but it had all seemed rather impersonal. Until now.

As they raced north toward Whidbey Island Naval Air Station, the facts and images coalesced in her mind. She was a corporate officer of Pan Am. That, in effect, was *her* crippled airplane out there, loaded with passengers who had trusted *her* airline. Suddenly it all became personal and frightening.

The fact that whatever happened, Pan Am would now be seen as an airline with safety problems, sent more chills down her spine.

In flight, Clipper Ten

"PULL it up!" Judy's voice rang sharply through the cockpit as Jim Aaron pulled the yoke back quickly. The altimeter had dropped below fifty feet for a second, startling them. He felt the ship gain a little altitude, then reach the crest of the pressure wave they were flying, and begin to protest.

Yet it seemed they were getting light enough to nudge higher, out of ground effect. Slowly he let the rate-of-climb needle start up as the radar altimeter cracked through a hundred feet for the first time in many long minutes: 120 feet; 140 feet; then mushing into 160 feet as the airspeed dropped to 180 knots and stabilized.

"Hallelujah! I think we're going to get out of here." Jim's voice was hoarse.

"We've got to have at least a few hundred feet in the air approaching the runway threshold," Judy said. "When we lower the landing gear, we're gonna slow down big time and start sinking."

Jim Aaron checked the altitude again. They were still climbing, edging foot by foot through two hundred feet. Then he glanced at the others. "Okay, I think we should take it straight in to Whidbey and land it with whatever we've got. We've got to time it just right. Too soon and we sink into the water before getting to the runway. Too late and we touch down with the gear not fully extended."

Patrick leaned forward. "Boss, why don't we circle out here for a little while and keep dumping? Then we could get enough altitude to give us an edge."

Judy was shaking her head. "Patrick, number four's still burning out there, as far as I can tell. Not much, but some. I think we'd better get on the ground as quick as we can."

Jim Aaron had listened quietly. Now he spoke up. "Good point, Patrick. If I could approach at five hundred feet, I'd feel a lot safer." He glanced at Judy. "Okay, let's plan to make a wide circle as close to Whidbey as we can make it, out over the water."

"What would you think," Patrick said, "about my using the right-wing dump mast? It's far enough from number four engine. I don't think the fuel stream will catch fire."

"I say we try it," Jim said. "We need to get lighter fast. You violently object, Judy?"

She looked at the forward panel for a moment, then turned toward the captain and smiled thinly. "Not violently."

Patrick nodded and immediately flipped the appropriate switch, doubling the fuel-dump rate to five thousand pounds per minute.

The sudden sound of an engine fire warning bell rang through the cockpit almost immediately. Judy craned her head to the right, expecting new flames, but saw nothing as Patrick fairly yelled, "It's number two. That's nothing to do with my fuel dump."

"Is it really burning?" Jim Aaron asked. Patrick picked up the interphone handset and punched in the number of the aft flight attendant station as Judy scanned the engine instruments.

Patrick relayed a frightened report from the aft galley. "It's really on fire! They say there's a plume of flame coming out!"

Jim reached up and pulled the fire handle, then punched the fire-extinguisher button, watching with relief when the fire light went out. The aft galley confirmed there were no more flames.

There was also no more thrust from the inboard left engine. Clipper Ten's airspeed began dropping. With a sinking heart Jim realized that number two had been giving the critical edge of thrust they needed to get out of ground effect. Now it was gone.

Reluctantly he relaxed his back pressure on the control yoke to let the big ship settle back down to an altitude of seventy feet.

One engine left, and no options.

Whidbey Island Naval Air Station

WITH little more than twenty minutes' notice, the duty officer had accomplished wonders. Rows of fire trucks and rescue equipment lined the taxiways in their appointed positions now, flashing a silent staccato of red beacons into the night.

Three TV news helicopters were circling the naval base. More choppers—army, coast guard, air force, and private medical evacuation helicopters—were en route from various points.

In the control tower cab, the chief petty officer on duty lowered his field glasses and turned to his newly arrived commander, stabbing a finger at the western night sky. "There, sir. Use the glasses. You can see the beacons just coming in view, right on the surface."

Clipper Ten

THE fire on number two eliminated the idea of circling. The crew of Clipper Ten headed straight for the runway at Whidbey Island Naval Air Station, praying they could stay airborne that long.

Inch by inch Jim Aaron had once again nudged Clipper Ten up to two hundred feet above the water, on the power from a fire-walled number one engine alone, as fuel continued to spew into the night.

"Clipper Ten, Whidbey Tower. Winds are one six zero at eight knots."

The runway lights were in view now, dead ahead.

Nine miles remained. The three pilots could see the red-over-red visual-approach indicators as well, indicating they were dangerously below glide slope for a normal approach.

"Two hundred feet off the water, speed one eighty-five." Judy's voice came from the right. Her eyes were riveted on the instruments as Jim clawed for more altitude.

"Okay, Patrick, watch our timing," Jim said. "You tell me when."

"Remember," Patrick replied, "the gear may be damaged."

The captain nodded. "We'll land with whatever we have."

There was no possibility of a go-around. Clipper Ten was coming down one way or another as soon as the gear lever was moved to the down position.

"Two hundred twenty feet, speed one eighty knots."

Jim held the back pressure. He needed three to four hundred. They would lower the landing gear first, then the flaps.

"Two hundred fifty feet, airspeed's one seventy-five."

He could take it only to one hundred seventy. Jim nudged the yoke forward, watching the rate of climb begin to drop. Five miles. He could see the rows of flashing emergency equipment beacons ahead.

"Two hundred seventy feet, speed one seventy."

Four miles. Almost there. He couldn't get more than two hundred seventy-five feet, but the speed was back up to one hundred seventy-five now and climbing slightly.

"There's three miles, Jim."

"I don't think we're high enough. I may cancel the flaps," Jim said. *This is gonna work. We're gonna make it work.*

"Stand by on the gear!" Patrick's voice was taut with tension.

"Gear down." Patrick fairly yelled it, and Judy snapped the gear level down instantly. The sound of the nose-gear and body-gear assemblies coming off their up locks radiated through his senses. *Something*, at least, was happening down there.

Predictably, the airspeed began dropping. Jim lowered the nose, feeling the ship shudder and begin to descend, trading altitude for airspeed as the landing gear acted like speed brakes.

"Coming up on flap extension," Patrick announced.

"I'm not sure I want them," Jim said.

"Now or never!"

Jim traced through the possibilities. "Flaps five!" he barked.

Judy's right hand moved the alternate flap switches as her left hand positioned the main flap handle to five degrees.

Less than two miles now. But the threshold of the runway began to climb slightly in the windscreen. They were sinking too much!

"No more flaps," Jim said.

They were through one hundred fifty feet now. He needed to cross the threshold of the runway at fifty feet, but they weren't going to be that high.

One mile to go, and they were settling through one hundred feet and slowing.

Oh, God. We did it too soon! The cry echoed through his head as he tried to reinvent the laws of aerodynamics. Speed, altitude, airspeed. *Airspeed!* He could cheat with more flaps.

"All the flaps you can give me. Now!"

Judy complied instantly. He could feel the airspeed decaying with the monstrous braking effect of the giant, triple-slotted flaps.

As the threshold lights slipped beneath the nose, the stall warning began. They were too slow!

Jim pulled ever so slightly, increasing the pitch, holding the altitude, praying his wheels were still above the surface of a runway that was twenty-eight feet above sea level.

There was nothing left but to hold and hope.

No one aboard Clipper Ten felt the first contact between the rear wheels and the absolute edge of the runway overrun, but Jim Aaron heard the speed-brake handle deploying automatically and knew they'd touched something. The remaining tires of the extended main gear struts settled onto the hard surface one by one and rumbled onto the main runway.

Those in the emergency vehicles had watched in stunned silence as Clipper Ten thundered over the shoreline like an accident about to happen. But instead of flame and tumbling metal, there were wheels rolling across hard surfaces, as they were designed to do.

When it was obvious his machine was on the ground, Jim Aaron hit the brakes immediately, but Ship 612 barely slowed as they continued to barrel down the runway. At last he felt the brakes begin to grab. Agonizingly, Clipper Ten rolled off the runway and onto the overrun, its nose gear finally coming to a halt less than a hundred yards from the absolute end.

The fire trucks raced for the still burning number four engine immediately, spurting a greeting of fire-suppressant foam.

Within ten minutes the passengers and crew of Clipper Ten had evacuated the airplane, using the emergency slides. The huge Boeing now sat bracketed by several portable searchlights as emergency vehicles ringed the scene. The TV cameras broadcast live feeds from the various reporters on hand. Several times loud applause and cheers broke out from the rescuers and the rescued alike as various members of the crew came down the slides. Captain Aaron slid to the ground last, and the passengers broke out in applause and cheers once more.

On the western side of the runway, standing quietly by the empty Jet Ranger and holding her daughter's hand, Elizabeth Sterling watched the scene in shocked silence. She was shaking slightly, but she wasn't cold. The suspense had been almost unbearable. Looking up now at Clipper Ten, she suddenly felt very small and very out of place.

Do I really belong here? Do I really know what I'm doing?

Elizabeth felt Kelly snuggle against her. "Mom? Are you cold? You're shivering." Kelly was looking up at her, obviously worried.

"A little."

"Mom? They did a good job, didn't they? The pilots, I mean."

Elizabeth could see the bright portable lights of several TV photographers illuminating the vice president of operations. "Mr. Jennings used the word magnificent after they stopped, Kelly. He should know. It looked pretty impressive to me."

Kelly took in the same scene without a word, a smile spreading across her face. "If you hadn't done the money work, they wouldn't have an airline, right?"

Elizabeth nodded slowly as Kelly turned to open the door of the Ranger, reaching out to pull her mother inside.

"I'm real proud of you, Mom."

Moses Lake, Washington

ROBERT Chenowith watched the happy images from Whidbey Island Naval Air Station in pure shock. That was Ship 612. The same one that had been sitting in his hangar the night before. The same one that had been exposed to an intruder.

187

And the same one he had declared free of sabotage.

With a sigh Chenowith put his hand on the telephone. He had no doubt that his decision not to report the intruder to Bill Conrad, the vice president of maintenance, would be fatal to his career.

Apparently it had almost been fatal to Flight 10.

As he dialed the number in Seattle, he knew deep down that engine number three had not come apart by itself.

4

Thursday, March 9—Pan Am Corporate Headquarters, Seattle

ELIZABETH had hidden her anger well. Making a good first impression with the staff and fellow executives of Pan Am was the prime directive for the moment, but she was aching for the opportunity to get Ron Lamb alone. He had some serious explaining to do.

She hated facing an important day with less than four hours' sleep, but by the time she and Kelly had reached their new condo and settled down the previous evening, it was 2:00 a.m. By 5:30 a.m. the continuous dreams revolving around the momentous events of the night before had made sleep impossible. She had rummaged instead through the groceries they'd ordered in advance, finding coffee to brew and bread to toast. She took a shower then and left a long list of chores for Kelly before clearing the door as soon as the new housekeeper arrived.

By 7:15 a.m. Elizabeth was across the city on the fifty-sixth floor of the Columbia Center Building. Her office was beautiful. She left her briefcase on the mahogany desk and set off in search of Chad Jennings. In the middle of the night she had seized on what Jennings had told her about the FAA. She had accepted it as if Pan Am were completely guiltless. But were they?

By 9:00 she had briefed her assistant, her new secretary, the comptroller, and most of their people, reassuring everyone that the only changes she would be making in the next few months were strategic ones at the corporate finance level.

At 10:15 the executive committee of the board met. They had invited her, as a new board member, to attend. The agenda was urgent and worrisome, especially the news that yet another FAA inspection had been launched at the Seatac operations offices.

And finally, at long last, by half past eleven, Elizabeth was able to follow Ron Lamb into his office and close the door.

"Ron, I'm here now. What do I need to know?"

She had made up her mind in midmorning after getting a clearer picture from Chad Jennings. Pan Am's public image was in trouble, and it was affecting the markets. If Ron Lamb didn't level with her about the FAA pressures and other problems, the deal was off.

Ron began by outlining the same scenario Chad Jennings had detailed, leaving nothing out, and added a new twist.

"Politically, we have a problem in Washington, D.C. Someone may be, shall we say, energizing the FAA to lean on us real hard. We're successful so far, and we're taking traffic from some of the big boys, so I suppose retaliation is understandable. The major airlines would be much happier if the new Pan Am weren't around."

"How much trouble can the FAA cause?"

"Large fines, bad publicity, plus building the perception in the financial community that we're losing it."

"Ron, a month ago, flying in from Tokyo, you told me the previous C.F.O. had misled you and the board about the new loan agreements. What exactly did you mean?"

He had been dreading the question. It took a half hour to tell her the story of how the previous financial officer, William Hayes, had been seduced by the promise of a doubled credit line for less interest, in exchange for the sale and leaseback of the fleet.

"Essentially, we—the board and me—let ourselves be talked into accepting a risky agreement. We gave the lenders—the consortium of banks and institutions who financed the package—what amounts to the right to call the loan if they ever felt threatened."

"You *what?*"

"We sold the fleet at the same time and figured we'd always have enough cash in reserve. The provision limits their rights to calling the loan only if all consortium members agree that we have insufficient profits or assets to justify their continued trust that we can repay the loan."

"Ron, what did your general counsel say?"

"Jack Rawly begged us not to sign, because he felt we were giving them the sole right to determine what constitutes profits and sufficient assets."

"I agree with Rawly."

Lamb's hand went up, palm out. "Now, mind you, I don't for a minute think this consortium would ever hurt us, because they'd be hurting their own investment if they did."

"But they're already threatening, aren't they?" she asked.

Lamb nodded slowly. "Yes. They're worried about the rumors."

"Okay." Elizabeth got up and moved to the window. "We've got to get this paid off and get back to a normal loan agreement. The credit line I got you was for two hundred fifty million. This one's for five hundred million. How much have you borrowed on this?"

"Four hundred thirty million."

"Already?" Elizabeth felt her stomach sinking as she turned to face him. "And the equipment financing? Where did that money go?"

"That, too, has been a disaster. Hayes convinced us to sell the fleet of aircraft and lease them back, giving us considerable additional capital but vast monthly payments."

"Ron, I'm—I'm flabbergasted. You've snatched financial disaster from the jaws of solvency. I had this set up so your payments were low, your security was high, and you could ride out three years with heavy losses."

"There's more, Elizabeth."

How could there be? she thought. "What else?"

"If we're declared in default, the aircraft leases can be canceled."

Elizabeth searched Ron Lamb's eyes and saw a combination of desperation and contrition. He had made one gigantic mistake in trusting the wrong man as C.F.O., and now he wanted her to wave a magic wand and make it all better.

"Elizabeth, I know this is a gargantuan task. I know I made it seem rosier than it is. There are nearly two thousand people carrying our I.D. cards now. They've pinned their hopes on us. That's why I need you. *We* need you. Please don't run."

She nodded, taking a deep, ragged breath. "Okay, Ron. The first task is refinancing, and it's going to be a bear."

Thursday, March 9, 7:00 p.m. —Seatac Airport

ELIZABETH started to leave the ladies' room, then stopped once more and turned toward the mirror, adjusting her blouse and carefully coaxing a stray lock of hair back into place. She had spent more time deciding what to wear to greet Brian than she'd spent picking an outfit for her first day on the job—and Kelly had needled her unmercifully about it.

Kelly loved Brian. Plain and simple. Some of her earliest memories were intertwined with the warmth and humor and strength that the six-foot-one, square-jawed Irishman from Boston had brought to their tiny flat in Cambridge when she was just a baby and he and her newly widowed mother were struggling M.B.A. candidates.

Brian and Elizabeth never agreed to marry, but when he followed her to New York to work on Wall Street, then four years later decided to join an upstart airline in Phoenix as a pilot, the loss of his companionship was tough for Elizabeth to take. But to Kelly, then age eight, Brian's departure had been the end of life as she knew it. When her strong-willed mother had refused to chuck her Wall Street career and follow Brian to Phoenix, an inconsolable Kelly had blamed that mother.

Brian was attentive over the years as best he could be from so far away—more so even to Kelly than to Elizabeth. There was no way Kelly was going to stay home and let her mother greet Brian Sean Murphy alone. And there was no way Kelly was going to be shy about the other major item on her agenda: marriage. Elizabeth was to marry Brian as fast as she could drag him to an altar. That was that.

ELIZABETH and Kelly watched as the blue-and-white 747 taxied majestically into the ramp area and turned toward the gate.

"There he is!" Kelly had spotted Brian. He saw them and waved enthusiastically from the cockpit.

It took forever to get the passengers out of the way and the crew up the Jetway, but finally Brian was there, calling to Kelly.

Kelly gave him a bear hug, hanging on with not a shred of dignity. Smiling, Elizabeth moved to embrace him just as she noticed someone else waiting.

"Captain Murphy?" The man was younger than Brian by several years, short and stocky, and Brian obviously recognized him.

Brian gave Elizabeth a quick hug and turned a friendly expression to the man. "Scott, what're you doing out here?"

The man held out an envelope. "Mr. Jennings wanted this delivered to you, sir, and asked you to call him as soon as you could."

They began walking toward the escalator then, Brian with one arm around Kelly, who was pulling his wheeled flight bags, the other around Elizabeth, who was hating every second of the intrusion. She wanted to hold him and kiss him and talk to him, not get blindsided by business.

"How did the inspection go?" Brian asked in a breezy fashion.

The man named Scott nervously motioned to the envelope. "Captain, you might want to take a look at that right away. We've got some real problems, sir. There were a lot of records missing."

Brian stood stock-still and stared at him. "Pilot records?"

"Yes, sir. The FAA is quite upset. Your secretary outlined it in a memo in there, and that's what Mr. Jennings wants to talk about."

Brian pulled his arms away from Elizabeth and Kelly and ripped open the envelope, scanning rapidly over the three-page memo.

"This is not possible." He glanced up at Scott and then stared at the paper again. "Thanks. I'll take it from here."

"Yes, sir."

"What is it?" Elizabeth asked after the man disappeared down the escalator.

Brian sighed. "I've got to get over to the office. The FAA pulled an inspection of our records this morning. If I can't find the missing ones, we may have to start grounding pilots instantly all over the system."

They drove him to the operations center, where he'd left his car, and he got out with a promise to come to the new condo as soon as he was through. He hugged Kelly again and kissed Elizabeth.

"I'm really sorry about this. I'll get there as quick as I can."

"Hey," Elizabeth said, forcing a smile, "we're on the same team now, kid. I expect you to work your tail off."

Brian leaned through the open window of Elizabeth's rental car and kissed her again, with greater depth and promise this time. "If I don't get this straightened out, I'll be working for the Mrs. Grace L. Ferguson Airline and Storm Door Company instead of Pan Am."

Thursday evening, March 9—Anacortes, Washington

BILL Conrad had arranged the meeting while driving the seventy miles north to Anacortes, which was connected by a single bridge to Whidbey Island. Jake Lovesy, the investigator in charge of the

NTSB "go team" probing Clipper Ten's close call with oblivion, had agreed to meet Pan Am's maintenance chief at a small restaurant in the diminutive harbor town at 9:45 p.m.

The orders for dinner placed, Bill lowered his voice and leaned closer to the man who was a veteran with the National Transportation Safety Board. "Jake, let me summarize this. We have reason to believe our airplane, and number three engine in particular, was sabotaged the night before last in our Moses Lake hangar with some sort of explosive device."

The NTSB man sat quietly, probing Bill Conrad's face. They were a study in contrasts—Lovesy a trim man in his early forties with a full head of sandy hair, a mustache, and a penchant for crisp suits and monogrammed shirts; Conrad a balding veteran approaching sixty who always looked as if he'd been sleeping in his clothes.

Conrad related the embarrassing saga of the intruder. When the story was finished, Lovesy twirled a swizzle stick in his alcohol-free Bloody Mary. "You've got an intruder with access, I'll grant you that. What you lack is hard evidence that anything but internal failure seized and scattered that engine. Is there plastique residue on the shop floor? A blasting cap? Wire? Something? Anything?"

"We've got nothing except a collection of broken parts about eighty miles off the coast, in several hundred feet of salt water. That would tell the tale."

"Look," Jake Lovesy said suddenly, shifting in his chair, "I agree this one flew apart with an unusual vengeance. I also promise we'll get the FBI in on this and comb the wing and what's left of the pylon for any evidence of explosives. We find any, I'll buy the idea."

"Jake, I—"

"Bill, I've been around this business long enough to know that the publicity is already hurting you. But I can't go public with speculation on a bomb or sabotage without something more than what you've given me."

"The publicity is hurting a little," Bill began. "At least don't deny the possibility if the media should ask you—"

Lovesy was shaking his head. "Don't do it. Don't—repeat, *don't*—put the media in my face with questions about sabotage before we have hard evidence. Go get that engine out of the water if there's any way you can do it. Air-traffic control will have the radar track, and I'll bet we can locate the impact point from the tapes."

"Already have," Bill said. "Friend of mine at Seattle Center spent hours with the tapes, and he found a radar return headed for the water just after the explosion. He's got the exact coordinates."

"Good. Go get the sucker."

Thursday, March 9, midnight—Downtown Seattle

KELLY had succumbed to fatigue and sleep in the new condo when Brian phoned. Elizabeth read ten past twelve on her watch as she picked up the telephone.

"I'm sorry, Elizabeth. I'm going to be here all night, I think."

"You haven't found them?"

"Nothing. And I know those files were there."

"Brian, you've been awake since Tokyo. You can't think straight when you're that tired. Go to bed. At least get some sleep on your couch in the office."

A long sigh filled the phone. "Okay. A few hours, then. Can we take a rain check and spend tomorrow evening together?"

"Tomorrow's not possible. I've got my mother coming to town to pick up Kelly for the weekend."

More silence, then a chuckle. "The weekend, huh? Even if I'm unemployed by Saturday, I can't pass this up. How about Saturday evening at your place, m'lady?"

"I thought the gentleman would never ask. Bring wine. Bring yourself."

5

Friday morning, March 10

THE tip had come into the newsroom of United Press International at around 4:00 on Thursday afternoon.

By 1:00 a.m. eastern standard time the story was in motion and being picked up in early morning news operations worldwide, including CNN.

By 9:00 a.m. in New York, the story had begun to depress the price of Pan Am stock, and at 9:15 eastern—6:15 Seattle—time two stock analysts had issued an emergency sell recommendation on Pan Am.

Elizabeth Sterling turned on her TV and saw the Pan Am logo hovering over the shoulder of the CNN anchor.

"The new Pan American Airlines, whose Seattle–Tokyo flight suffered a catastrophic multiple engine failure on Wednesday and had to make an emergency landing after a harrowing flight at wave-top level, is reported this morning to be the subject of a special investigation by the Federal Aviation Administration. Sources close to the FAA have told CNN that major fines in the millions of dollars are pending against the newly formed airline for alleged violation of training and other operational regulations, including serious maintenance violations."

By the time Elizabeth arrived on the fifty-sixth floor of the Columbia Center, two TV crews were waiting. She had brushed by them and entered the inner sanctum when Ron Lamb, a thoroughly panicked look on his face, materialized.

Lamb gestured for her to follow him to his office. She entered and moved to one of the chairs opposite his desk as he closed the door. There were papers spread across the usually neat desk, and Ron scooped up a couple before turning to Elizabeth.

He was breathing hard, she noticed.

"You all right, Ron?"

"No." He shook the papers, sat on the edge of his desk next to her, and studied his shoes. "I'm going to have to call an emergency board meeting on this, I think."

"What?"

"An hour ago I got a call from the lead bank of the revolving-credit-line consortium—the one you're going to try to replace. They heard the news this morning, and they've panicked."

"Okay, Ron, so they've panicked. What did they say?"

"They froze the revolving line at its current balance. We've got a bond payment due on the twentieth of this month. We have to make that payment, and without the credit line, I don't know how we're going to find the money."

"How much?"

"We owe, and must raise, eighty-five million dollars."

"What?" Elizabeth sat back in the soft leather chair.

"I'm sorry, Elizabeth. We've got about forty million in the accounts right now, but that's operational money. We spend that, we can't pay our bills."

"And if we don't pay the debentures and someone in that consortium declares us in default, poof."

"Yeah. Poof."

BRIAN Murphy looked at his watch. He had made an appointment with Larry DePalma for 10:00 a.m. It was less than fifteen minutes' drive from Pan Am's Seatac base to the FAA's Northwest Mountain Region headquarters, but Brian preferred being early.

Larry DePalma's second-floor office was not hard to find. Larry was waiting for him, but not alone. In the corner was Larry's boss, Ken Schaffer.

Brian shook hands with DePalma and Schaffer. They kept the small talk to a minimum, and within minutes he had their full attention. "Larry, I'll say it plain and simple," Brian began. "Someone stole our files—pilot files and training files for nine captains. Coincidentally, they happen to be our most experienced men. There's no way those files could have been misplaced accidentally."

DePalma looked up, meeting Brian's eyes. "We had a tip, Brian, that you folks had been shortchanging the training. We were told that where your operations specifications require a full four hours of simulator time for the 747 captain recurrent training session, your check captains have been cutting it down to three hours."

"That's baloney," Brian shot back. "We did nothing of the sort!"

"Okay," Larry continued. "So we organized an unannounced inspection. When we did a routine check of the records for the captains who've gone through the recurrent training in the last five months, we discovered the folders had been removed."

Brian fought to contain his anger. "We didn't pull those files, Larry, if that's what you're implying."

"I didn't say you did. I merely—"

"But your implication is clear. So let me ask you gentlemen"—Brian turned to Schaffer—"to consider an alternate conclusion. Assume someone wants to set up Pan Am for an embarrassing situation. Now, what better way for that someone to accomplish his

197

goals than to phone in a tip to you, then go steal the very records the tip concerned? We can't prove we're innocent, because the records are gone, and on top of it, *we* end up looking like we're trying to hide something by apparently concealing the records."

Larry DePalma shook his head. "Brian, either we find those records or some acceptable proof that those nine captains have been trained in accordance with your training manual, or you've got to ground them and retrain them."

"That is ridiculous! I brought a computer printout showing that everything's been done properly, and if you want it, I'll—"

"Won't be acceptable, Captain Murphy." Schaffer's voice stabbed at him from the corner. "That computer file could easily have been altered. Now, we'll let you reconstruct and recertify those hard-copy records if you can show us independent proof— simulator instructor logs, classroom logs, that sort of thing."

Brian whirled on Schaffer. "You know damn well that'll take days. In the meantime I'll have to ground all these guys worldwide."

Schaffer shrugged. "You're already in violation for not having the records in place for us to inspect."

"Mr. Schaffer," Brian hissed, his eyes flaring as he fought to bring himself under control, "if someone out of our control has stolen those records, we are *not* in violation."

"Well, Captain, I guess that's our determination, not yours. Besides, you said someone *out* of your control might have stolen those records. But someone *within* your control might have been involved, too."

"That's a ridiculous suggestion. The culprit's I.D. card could have the FAA's emblem on it as easily as Pan Am's."

Larry DePalma's voice shot across the desk. "Anger and accusations are going to get us nowhere."

"I need forty-eight hours to prove to you that we're guiltless in this." Brian looked over at Schaffer, who met his gaze with a neutral expression and a single word.

"No."

BRIAN Murphy worked hard at self-control in aggravating circumstances. He practiced it now all the way to the FAA parking lot. He climbed calmly into his car, closed the door, and finally permitted himself to slam his fist into the padded dashboard. "Dammit!"

There was a cellular phone in the car, and he turned to it now, dialing his secretary. All nine of the affected captains would have to be pulled off the line. The possibility of delayed flights was very high, a fact he had avoided facing until now.

Brian accelerated for the short ride back to Seatac. Something was nagging at his mind. *The question is not how or why the records were taken, but by whom. If I can find out who, I can find out why.*

He pictured the file cabinets at the office. They were locked at night with a combination kept by several people, but they were open during the day.

Is there any way to figure out when this was done? he wondered. *Wait a minute. One of the guys was in the simulator just a few days ago. The last date of entry in the computer could tell us something.*

Brian realized he was sitting forward against the steering wheel, anxious to get back. If there was a trail, he was going to find it.

3:30 p.m. — Pan Am Headquarters

THE fallout sparked by the FAA's announcement of a fine at noon had rolled through the fifty-sixth floor, leaving everyone stunned. Elizabeth had spent the day on the phone, it seemed, in order to deal with the life-or-death crisis of the credit line and bond payments. She had called Eric Knox in addition to a dozen other friends on Wall Street in an initial search of the money market, preparing the way to find eighty-five million dollars by March twentieth. Eric had been out, but now he was on the line.

"Hello, beautiful former partner. Ready to come home?"

"Seriously, Eric, I'm in the middle of a real-life corporate crisis. And—and it's a bit frightening."

She told him about the loan she needed to arrange, asking for help and guidance if possible. Eric promised to do what he could, and then the conversation dropped back to the personal level.

"Elizabeth, technically you're still a partner."

"Eric, I can't walk out on these people."

"Yes, you can. They didn't tell you everything they could have told you, and you're entitled. They're too weak to fight."

"Eric, you know me better than that. I made a commitment."

"Think about it. Call me night or day. I miss you."

6

WHAT struck Captain Dale Silverman most about the new Denver airport was how empty it seemed. Even now, at midnight, as he and his copilot taxied one of Pan Am's two 767s—Ship 102—toward one of the Jetways, the place looked like a thoroughly modern ghost town. A lone figure wearing white coveralls appeared beneath the docking lights with a pair of lighted wands and waved them in.

By the time Dale Silverman remembered his reading glasses, his crew and all their baggage had been loaded into the hotel van. He hated to admit he needed glasses, but without them he'd be too blind to deal with flight paperwork in the morning.

"You guys go on and get checked in and send the driver back for me. I left something on board."

As he passed through the boarding lounge, headed for the Jetway, he noticed through the window that the lights of the cockpit had been turned back up to full bright, which was curious.

A mechanic he had never seen before greeted him from the door of the cockpit as he approached the front of the 767. "Hello, Captain. Forget something?" the mechanic said breezily.

"My glasses," Dale replied. "Be out of your way in a second."

"No hurry, sir," the man said. "I'm just waiting for the fuelers."

That explains the cockpit lights, Dale thought. He's going to refuel her tonight. He hadn't recognized the small logo on the man's coveralls. Probably the logo of a contract service outfit, he supposed.

Silverman entered the cockpit and reached over the left seat, relieved to find his glasses still sitting where he'd left them, right by his flight bag. *What the hell?* He'd already put his flight bag on the bus with the rest of the crew, hadn't he?

That corner of the cockpit was shaded by the seat, and he had to look closely to see what was there. It wasn't his flight bag. It was the mechanic's tool kit, along with two rack-mounted electronic black boxes apparently destined for his airplane.

"What're the boxes for?" Dale asked as he left the cockpit.

"Routine swap-out for one of the computer components. Your people back in Seattle requested it."

"Okay. Sorry to hold you up." Dale smiled at him and left.

He was halfway to the hotel before the mechanic's words coalesced in his mind. Why would Pan Am order components swapped at a station without Pan Am maintenance, unless there had been a write-up he'd failed to notice in the log.

He resolved to ask the copilot about it in the morning.

Saturday afternoon, March 11—Downtown Seattle

ELIZABETH looked at her widowed mother—at fifty-nine still trim, blond, and attractive. She was a sweet lady, one who had always stood by her daughter and granddaughter no matter what.

"You sure you two have everything?" Elizabeth asked almost wistfully. She had hovered around the door of the condo as her mother and Kelly loaded the minivan downstairs. She found herself wishing she could take time to go, too.

Virginia Sterling stopped in the doorway with two bulging pillowcases pressed into use as impromptu bags: one for Kelly's dirty clothes, the other stuffed with odds and ends—the result of the decision they'd made together last night. Kelly would attend school in Bellingham until early June. Elizabeth had bristled at first at her mother's suggestion, but the logic was irrefutable. She knew deep down that the Pan Am battles ahead of her would leave Kelly a work orphan. With Elizabeth's mother so close, that made little sense, as Virginia had pointed out.

Kelly gave Elizabeth a final hug at curbside, and waved to her from the passenger seat as the van disappeared into Seattle traffic.

Elizabeth found herself standing there for a few minutes deep in thought, feeling suddenly very good on what had become an unseasonable and almost balmy Seattle day. Brian was due in two hours, at 5:00 p.m. She had just enough time to bathe and freshen up.

Saturday, March 11, 3:00 p.m.

PAN AM's maintenance chief, Bill Conrad, had been home for only a few hours' sleep each night since Clipper Ten's close brush with oblivion. The fatigue showed on his face now as he stepped through the cramped doorway of a salvage barge and back into the sunlight of a Saturday afternoon. The large, unshaven owner followed him out, clanging the door closed behind them.

"I could have her on site in about two days, Mr. Conrad. Once they find it, I can haul it up."

Bill thanked him and returned to his car. He punched the number of Operations Vice President Chad Jennings into his car phone as he backed through the unkempt waterfront yard and turned around.

Jennings was on his new sailboat in Puget Sound when he answered his maintenance chief's call. Jennings sounded distracted, and possibly a bit drunk, as Conrad filled him in on the bottom line: finding the sunken engine and bringing it up was going to cost a minimum of fifty thousand dollars and probably a lot more.

"So do I have your authorization, Chad," Conrad asked, "to contract for a salvage operation that's going to cost that much?"

"Tell me again why we need it?" Jennings asked.

Bill Conrad shook his head in silent disgust. *Pay attention, man. You're supposed to be the executive in charge.*

He explained it again: the refusal of the NTSB to pay for such a mission; the refusal of the NTSB even to admit publicly that sabotage was a possibility; and the growing publicity pointing fingers at the competence of Pan Am maintenance.

"I don't know, Bill. That's an awful lot of money."

Conrad could hear ice cubes tinkling against a glass in the background and the murmur of a feminine voice. "Just a second," Jennings said, and the sound of a hand covering the mouthpiece reached Conrad's ears. Jennings, he knew, was newly divorced and showing, at age forty-two, all the signs of a midlife crisis resolved at the expense of his family. Bill Conrad had tried to avoid the gossip about Jennings, but at fifty-eight, with a stable and happy thirty-three-year marriage, he couldn't help being put off by the rumors about the younger man. Chad Jennings had supposedly walked out on a wife and four children in Dallas and paid incredible sums to some high-priced legal talent who had successfully manipulated the court into leaving him with most of the assets.

Conrad negotiated the on-ramp to southbound Interstate 5 as Jennings came back on the phone. "Okay, Bill, sorry. You were asking for money? No, you were asking for authorization to spend up to fifty thousand, right?"

"At least."

"Okay, go ahead, you got it. Call me back on Monday."

The phone rang again almost immediately, and Conrad punched it on, fully expecting to hear Chad Jennings' voice with second thoughts. Instead, a Seattle newspaper reporter introduced himself and asked for an interview on the NTSB's search for answers to Clipper Ten's accident.

"No," was Bill Conrad's reply. "If you'd like, I'll give you the number of our public relations department, and you can—"

"I know about the sabotage, Mr. Conrad." The words echoed around the car before Bill Conrad was able to compose an answer. "We had a tip that someone broke into your 747 at Seatac and fooled with the engine the night before the accident."

"I've heard no such rumor regarding Seatac," he said, walking the razor edge of the truth.

"Okay, but I've heard you're urging the NTSB to look into sabotage. Talk to me, Mr. Conrad. You're the maintenance chief."

"And not the P.R. man, which is why I have nothing to say."

"If you change your mind," the reporter said, "my name again is Adrian Kirsch, and here's my number. Please write it down."

It was a useless gesture, Bill told himself, but he did it anyway. Deep down he wished that Kirsch or someone else *would* tell the public that all the bad press was nothing but a rush to judgment.

Pan Am maintenance wasn't at fault. Or so he hoped.

Saturday, March 11, 5:00 p.m. —Downtown Seattle

BRIAN was early, and Elizabeth was ready, greeting him at the door with a long, sensuous kiss. Both of them had been through so much tension the previous two days, they were determined to put their problems behind them for a few hours and enjoy this evening.

They had closed the door when the phone rang. Reluctantly Elizabeth answered the call as Brian took the bottle of wine he'd brought to the kitchen.

"It's a tough sell, Elizabeth, I won't kid you," Eric Knox was saying. "Pan Am's reputation on the Street took a harpoon yesterday, and I was almost laughed at when I pitched the need for a short-term loan. I think you need to get back here tomorrow and be ready to hit the bricks Monday morning."

"*That* hard a sell? Okay. Okay, I'll come in Sunday."

"Elizabeth, you may not win this one. Just be prepared."

She replaced the receiver as Brian materialized beside her with two crystal goblets of zinfandel wine—her favorite. He held his glass with his left hand, sipping the wine and lightly running his right hand through her hair as she told him about the call.

She didn't notice the faraway look in his eyes until he spoke suddenly. "I've missed you, Elizabeth," he said.

She smiled, remembering the warm security of being enfolded in his arms. He had carried her emotionally through a thousand doubts and terrors in those early years.

She looked up at him, getting lost in his eyes. "I've missed you too," she said. "I could never let myself dwell on it, because . . ."

"I know," Brian replied. She felt his large hand brush her cheek. She turned to nuzzle it, kissing his palm and enclosing the back of his hand in hers before leading him out on the balcony.

The sun was still swimming above the horizon beyond Elliott Bay, its low angle creating a softened light that painted a warm glow on their faces as they stood watching the Bremerton ferry churning away to the west.

"Beautiful, isn't it?" she asked.

"Incredibly," he said, "and the scenery out there's nice, too."

"Brian! Honestly." She turned to him. "I've made beef bourguignon. Come on, my long-lost lover, and let me feed you."

Dinner was magnificent, just as she had planned it. With the usual Puget Sound evening chill in the air, they built the inaugural fire in the new condo's fireplace and settled back together on the white leather couch.

"I never thought we'd ever live in the same area again," he said. "I never thought we could ever make it work again."

"Can we now?" she asked.

"Oh, honey," he said. His hand cupped the back of her head, and she felt herself being drawn forward gently as he leaned to kiss her.

Their kiss had become impassioned, when the ringing of the phone cut through the moment.

"Don't answer it," Brian said. "Please."

"I have to."

"Let the answering machine earn its keep. We're busy." His mouth closed on hers again as the machine snapped on.

"Elizabeth, this is Ron Lamb," the message began. He sounded exhausted and beaten. "Uh . . . I've been on the phone with some of the bondholders, people I know, trying to work something out in principle." The message continued on, somewhat rambling.

And it was obvious to Elizabeth that if Ron Lamb went too far with the phone calls on his own, he could prejudice her efforts.

Brian's embrace slackened a bit. He could feel Elizabeth drifting away as she looked toward the machine. She turned back to him suddenly. "Brian, I need to talk to him."

He smiled and nodded, letting her twist over the back of the couch to retrieve the phone.

"Ron? Elizabeth. I just came in and heard your voice."

There was a grateful response on the other end, and she sat back down, not noticing that Brian had moved around behind her with a mischievous grin.

"Who did you talk to?" she asked.

Brian could hear the company president's voice as a series of squawks through the earpiece as he bent over to kiss her neck.

Elizabeth said something to Ron Lamb. There was another long soliloquy from his side of the conversation as Brian moved around to the other end of the couch to face her.

"Ron, let me explain what I'm planning to do."

As she launched into a detailed analysis of her game plan, Brian leaned forward and slowly began to caress her. She stroked his head in response, but there was no break in the meter of her voice, until one of her routine murmurs of acknowledgment—what had been intended as an um-hum—became an extended um-m-m-m-m.

"Ron"—she took a deep breath—"I, ah, better call you back in a few minutes."

Brian felt her reach to replace the phone. She would come to him now. That was the Elizabeth he knew—sensuous and responsive. But instead, she sat up.

"No business tonight, remember?" Brian said. "We agreed."

"I have to do this, Brian. Duty calls. I have to call the man back." She patted his face. "It won't take long."

Brian struggled with himself, fighting down irritation as she placed the call to Ron Lamb and tried her best to keep it short. But the conversation went on for twenty minutes. She was trying to finish up when Ron mentioned the name of Irwin Fairchild.

"Ron, what did you say? What was that name?"

"Irwin Fairchild. He's an acquaintance who's been helpful with advice over the last year or so."

"Who introduced you?" she asked, suspecting the answer.

"It was our previous C.F.O., Bill Hayes. Why does that interest you, Elizabeth?"

"Nothing. I'll tell you later. I've got to go."

"Okay. Good night."

She murmured good night and replaced the receiver. Her mind was racing with the implications of Ron's having been influenced by Irwin Fairchild. There was no way that could be an accident. William Hayes had been something more than a poor financial officer. He had been an instrument for someone else's purpose.

But what purpose, and to what end?

"What did Lamb say to you this time?" Brian asked her.

"He mentioned the name of a man who's a notorious manipulator on Wall Street. It's a name I know well. A major deal I put together was destroyed by this guy."

"So?"

"So if this man is involved with Pan Am, we could be in even more trouble than I thought."

He leaped to his feet and started pacing the floor.

"Elizabeth, can't you put away business for a while? You *used* to be able to do it, but now I get to play second fiddle to corporate concerns on the first evening we've had together in years."

"Brian, I'm trying to save your job, too."

"Well, thank you, ma'am, but kindly do it on Monday. Okay?"

"Brian, listen to me. If I'm a little preoccupied right now—"

He whirled on her. "A *little*?"

"Brian, come hold me."

He continued pacing. "What exactly is the financial problem you've got to solve next week?"

"I really shouldn't go into it. There are things that are more or less privileged information, and I'm a corporate officer."

He looked at her with an expression she had never seen before— a combination of hurt, anger, and frustration.

"And I'm just a peon, right? A stupid working stiff."

"Brian, cut it out!"

"I hadn't paid attention to the rank difference. I didn't think you would either, Miss High-and-mighty. But you obviously have."

"Brian—"

"Elizabeth, I'm sorry," he said. "I love you. But I don't know if I can live with you—or you with me."

7

Sunday, March 12—Tacoma, Washington

BILL Conrad collapsed the antenna of the cordless phone and slammed the instrument back in its cradle. "Bureaucrats," he muttered as he paced around the living room of his home.

On the coffee table, faxed copies of half a dozen clippings from Sunday newspapers lay in haphazard profusion, some merely hinting at potential Pan American maintenance incompetence, others actually raising the issue of how safe Pan Am really was.

He had called Jake Lovesy again, begging him at least to tell the media about the intrusion at Moses Lake. But it was clear that the NTSB was not going to publicly acknowledge the possibility of sabotage—even though Lovesy hinted broadly that the FBI might already have found something "interesting."

If what had happened to Ship 612 was sabotage, and if it was a professional job, as Jake Lovesy had suggested, there was no reason to believe that the saboteur had gone away—or given up. And next time the crew might not be able to bend the laws of aerodynamics and get themselves back on the ground safely.

No one else, though, seemed to see the urgency. Chad Jennings was only mildly alarmed and had even questioned the extra money for the added security precautions his director of maintenance had ordered. Bill had approached the president as well, but even Ron Lamb wouldn't believe it until the NTSB formally agreed that someone had purposefully monkeyed with a Pan Am airplane.

No, no one was listening, so it was up to him to force the issue.

He grabbed the phone once more, fumbling for the scrap of paper that held the number he had decided to call. He was drumming his fingers restlessly as the last ring was replaced by the voice of a Seattle *Chronicle* reporter. "Adrian Kirsch."

"Mr. Kirsch? This is Bill Conrad of Pan Am."

ELIZABETH pushed through a gaggle of commuters blocking the
subway exit, checking her watch as she walked. Fifteen minutes to
go. The crowd between her and Grand Central Terminal's main
concourse was heavy, but not unmanageable.

Eric's lengthy memo had been hopeful. He'd obviously spent
most of Saturday putting together a list of the sources most likely to
be persuaded to loan Pan Am eighty-five million dollars. He had
also contacted several of them and left a list of their home phone
numbers for her to reach Sunday night from his loaned condo.

In typical fashion Eric had left the papers on a bedside table,
along with a bottle of Dom Pérignon Champagne, with a note
reading, "In case of success, break seal."

Elizabeth had paused to buy a copy of *The New York Times* on
boarding the subway but had yet to open it. The dossier on Harold
Hudgins—her first appointment—was more important reading.
He was one of the principals in a consortium of investors consisting
mostly of U.S. banks. For them, eighty-five million would be a drop
in the bucket. And he'd indicated to Eric that Pan Am was not an
unwelcome applicant.

She pushed through the heavy doors and turned left, northward
onto Lexington Avenue, letting her leather briefcase flop against
the side of her black cashmere coat. There was a gray overcast,
with the temperature in the fifties, and the winds were whipping
through the canyons of Manhattan.

As she moved toward the target building on East Forty-fourth,
she forced herself to avoid looking up at the renamed building once
owned by Pan Am. It towered like a specter on her left—a monolith
of scorn for someone who would seek to raise the dead.

A bank of television screens swam into her peripheral vision as
she hurried past an electronics shop. She was startled to see her
company's logo filling each set, and she came to an instant halt,
pressing her nose to the storefront. The logo receded to an over-
the-shoulder box as the morning-show host began a story she
couldn't hear.

Elizabeth quickly pushed through the door of the shop and
found the volume control on one of the sets.

". . . Conrad, director of maintenance for the newly restarted airline, has revealed that the National Transportation Safety Board is investigating the possibility of sabotage in last week's near disaster involving a Pan Am 747."

Bill Conrad's face looked haggard as he appeared live from a Seattle TV studio. The word sabotage caught her cold. No one, not even Ron Lamb, had mentioned such a possibility, nor had anyone told her about the intruder at the Moses Lake facility.

Who would want to sabotage us? she wondered.

Conrad answered the first few questions cautiously. He vigorously defended Pan Am maintenance, but when asked how an intruder could have gotten into a Pan Am hangar, he stumbled badly. It was obvious he hadn't thought about the implications of his argument. If Pan Am *had been* sabotaged, that would prove they had failed to provide adequate security for their airplanes. Either way, Pan Am looked guilty, sloppy, and perhaps less than safe.

When Elizabeth was ushered into Harold Hudgins' office, she was relieved that he had apparently not seen the interview.

It took an exhausting two hours of discussion, but Elizabeth left around 11:00 a.m. with real hope. Hudgins promised to spend the rest of the day on the loan and have an answer for her in the morning. His words had rung like sunshine through the mist: "I think we've got a deal here; I just need to cement it together."

The pain of trying to walk in high heels the twenty blocks to her next appointment finally reached Elizabeth's consciousness, and she hailed a cab. She'd been out of contact all morning, but now she opened her briefcase and pushed the POWER ON button on the small cellular phone Ron Lamb had obtained for her in Seattle.

A chirping sound erupted from the phone almost immediately, signifying an incoming call from the company president. She reported the progress in the first meeting before asking Ron why no one had bothered to tell her about the sabotage possibility.

"Elizabeth, *I* didn't even know until Thursday, when Conrad told us, and *he* hadn't known the details until that morning."

In the back of her mind the memory of Brian's infuriated speculation that someone had sabotaged their training files suddenly merged with Conrad's statements.

"Call me, Elizabeth, day or night, if you make any progress. I'm not sleeping anyway," Ron said as he rang off.

There had been an intrusion at Moses Lake, stolen files in the Seatac operations center, the suspicion of sabotage on their 747, and something else. Oh, yes. The anonymous tipster with a penchant for calling FAA headquarters in Washington, D.C. *This isn't bad luck; it's all part of a pattern.* The abrupt insight left her feeling shaken.

The next banker she was going to see had been alerted to an upcoming NTSB news conference on CNN. He had a TV in his office and had it turned on as he showed her in. They watched together as a distinguished man approached a podium and introduced himself as Joe Wallingford, chairman of the NTSB. Holding a piece of paper he had taken from a small manila envelope, he began to speak.

"The impression was left this morning on national television that the NTSB might have access to certain information regarding the Pan American Flight ten incident last week—information suggesting possible sabotage—and might be sweeping it under the rug.

"It so happens that as Mr. Conrad was speaking this morning, the FBI's crime lab was delivering to us a report that indicates— and I quote—'Residue removed from the lower right wing of the subject aircraft by FBI personnel under NTSB supervision has been found to be of a metallic nature foreign to any metallic alloys used in the construction of the subject aircraft.'

"In other words, folks, the small shard of metal found impaled in the underside of the wing raises a real possibility of sabotage. When we have more information of the exact alloy, and so on, we'll release it. The FBI remains fully involved in this case."

Elizabeth was shocked. That *was* confirmation of sabotage, wasn't it? Surely that would help her win over someone in the financial quarter.

But the banker had been looking for an excuse to declare Pan Am too hot to handle. "We saw the name change on that building once," he said, motioning uptown to the old Pan Am tower. "And that's enough of a warning about putting money in airlines."

There were more exploratory meetings in the financial district that afternoon. But by 5:30 it was obvious to Elizabeth that Hudgins was the only viable possibility so far.

Okay, I'll have faith that it's a go from Hudgins in the morning and I'll get a good night's sleep and— Who am I kidding?

The subway carried her back to Eric's neighborhood. Inside the condo she shucked her shoes and settled down with the phone to call Kelly and her mother.

"Kelly doesn't have to be in school until next Monday," her mother said. "I thought we'd fly somewhere. You mentioned passes?"

"On Pan Am? Sure. How about coming to New York, Mom?"

"Well, maybe. Let me see what Kelly wants."

"Call my secretary when you're ready. I'll tell her to give you first-class passes."

Elizabeth promised to call the next evening, then dialed Ron Lamb's office in Seattle. The day had been a constant battle, he told her, with little good news to report. Scores of reservations were evaporating, presumably at the hands of frightened passengers.

"Maybe I'll have some good news in the morning," she told him.

"Praise the Lord and pass the money," he replied, a tired chuckle in his voice.

There was one other call she had been waiting to make, but she hesitated, half dreading it. She longed to talk to Brian but was afraid she'd hear that same cold edge in his voice.

Fatigue was making her foggy. She set the alarm for midnight New York time and decided to take a nap. *Then* she would call Brian.

Monday night, March 13—Pan Am Operations, Seatac Airport

BRIAN Murphy sat down heavily behind his desk and rubbed his eyes. It was 9:10 p.m., and the duty to get a decent night's sleep before report time at 11:00 in the morning was pressuring him almost as much as the hunt for the thief who had stolen the pilot files.

There was no way he wanted to pilot a Boeing 767 to Frankfurt and back in the middle of a crisis. But with nine captains grounded and recertification of their training records still a day away at best, it was either take the flight or let crew scheduling cancel it for lack of 767 pilots, costing the company tens of thousands in revenue.

He thought of calling Elizabeth and decided to wait. What could he say to her anyway that he hadn't already said on Saturday night? He had acted like a spoiled brat, a stupid idiot, and a male chauvinist piglet all rolled into one.

He decided to call Kelly at her grandmother's. He was surprised when Elizabeth's mother joined them on an extension and asked for suggestions on where she and Kelly should fly.

"Well, I have to fly a trip to Frankfurt tomorrow as captain, and I've got a two-day layover there. If we've got seats left on the flight, why not come along with me on that one?"

"Frankfurt? Sounds wonderful, Brian," Virginia said. "Is that okay with you, Kelly?"

"Are you kidding? I can be packed in ten minutes."

"Good," Virginia said. "Then it's settled. What time should we be at the airport, Brian? When does the flight leave?"

"At three p.m. I'll call you at nine a.m. to coordinate things."

"I can't wait to tell Mom," Kelly said excitedly before hanging up.

Brian got to his feet and looked at the yellow legal pad on his desk. He had made some progress in trying to narrow down the field of who the thief could be. At least he had isolated the date the files were taken by backtracking through the computer's training records and looking for the last date of entry. It had to have been the previous Thursday. But there were scores of people who could have wandered in and rifled through the file cabinet, and he was at a frustrating impasse without some additional clue.

Brian turned off his light and headed down the carpeted hallway. Pan Am had built a beautiful facility for their operations staff, and he was proud of it. Everything was in its place and sparkling.

He came to a sudden stop and repeated the thought.

Everything in its place. Suppose everything isn't *in its place.*

He turned and headed back to the scene of the crime—the file room—with the name Willis running through his head.

They had two unrelated pilots named Willis—Art and David. Art was a copilot–first officer, while Dave was a captain. Dave Willis' file was one of the ones taken, but something had snagged Brian's memory earlier, when he had gone through the files himself.

He had no memory of having seen Art Willis' file either.

Brian spun in the combination on the newly installed file cabinet lock and pulled open the bottom drawer. Each file was color-coded according to crew position: red for captains, blue for first officer–copilots, and green for flight engineers. He paged through them, stopping in the spot where both Willis folders should have been.

Both folders were missing. Two files with the same name were gone, and one of them belonged to a copilot. Yet only captains had been cited by the FAA for missing training folders. Why hadn't the FAA complained about Willis the copilot, too?

Of course. Because the tipster told them exactly which captains were deficient, and those are the only ones the feds came in to check.

But if the thief had intended to turn in only captains, why did he take the copilot's folder in the first place?

Wait a minute. What if he pulled it by mistake, discovered his error, and just stuffed it back in at random?

Brian began searching through the folders again. Between the U's and the V's the name Willis suddenly popped into focus.

Brian stood there in disbelief for a second, stunned by the chance it gave him. "Gotcha, you son of a gun!"

He dashed to the break room for a paper towel, then gingerly pulled the file out, using the towel to avoid smudging any fingerprints. He opened it the same way, noticing that some of the papers within were upside down.

What else? The color-coded tab on the edge of the folder came into view as if lit by a spotlight.

Of course. Anyone who knew this filing system would never have made the mistake of grabbing a copilot's file. The person I'm looking for is not on my office staff and couldn't be one of the training pilots.

Brian carried the folder to his desk. It took several calls to roust out the FBI agent assigned to the NTSB investigation, and several minutes to get the man to agree to a late-night meeting.

"Whoever tried to murder our passengers and crew on Flight ten is probably the same person who took these files, and I think I've got fingerprints. I need you to lift the prints and run them through your central files in Washington, as well as compare them with our fingerprint files."

Fingerprinting had been required of all Pan Am employees before hiring, including the executive staff. If the culprit was a Pan Am employee, they'd catch him now for sure. And if the thief wasn't a Pan Am employee, well, at least they'd know.

Brian slid the folder into a larger manila envelope and headed for the door. The FBI agent had agreed to meet him at corporate headquarters in two hours. Sleep would have to wait.

8

ELIZABETH stretched luxuriously and rolled over, nestling her head in the pillow as filtered daylight played over her closed eyelids.

Daylight?

The numbers of Eric Knox's bedroom clock jumped out at her with accusatory intensity. *It didn't ring. I would have heard it.*

She had set the alarm for midnight to call Brian. Now it was 8:35 a.m. in New York, 5:35 a.m. in Seattle, and she'd missed the chance.

Elizabeth pulled on a bathrobe and padded to the kitchen to make coffee and toast. *I could call Harold Hudgins now. It's late enough.*

It was going to be an immense relief to hear him confirm the eighty-five-million-dollar loan, and by the time she dialed Hudgins' number, she was energized and eager.

At first she almost didn't recognize the cold, distant voice on the other end. "Harold, you indicated that you'd be finalizing things yesterday afternoon, so I decided to start the morning out with good news and call you. Good news in regard to the note."

"Oh. I see," he said. "Well, I *was* able to get to the various lenders yesterday, and I'm afraid they simply weren't interested."

"What about your assurances yesterday?"

"Now, listen, I gave you virtually no assurances of any kind—"

"Harold," she cut in, "I am not going to have the plug pulled on me without an adequate explanation. You clearly indicated this was very close to a done deal. I want to meet at your office in an hour."

There was a lengthy hesitation before he replied. "If you insist, but there's really nothing more to say."

Elizabeth ended the call, realizing she was shaking with a combination of anger and alarm. She showered quickly and picked out a gray silk business suit trimmed in black. Black patent shoes and handbag—along with the sterling silver jewelry that had become her trademark—would give just the right balance.

What in heaven's name am I going to do now? she thought as she finished dressing. Panic began to rise up, and she fought to contain it. She had a long list of friends and contacts who had yet to be called, and she knew Eric would help as well. All they really needed by the twentieth of March was a letter of intent. With that, she could buy the time from the bondholders for a delayed payment without going into default.

But the first problem on the list was Hudgins. Why the sudden reversal? Why the frostiness?

With a last look in the mirror, Elizabeth grabbed her briefcase and headed out the door. She was hailing a cab when the phone in Eric's apartment rang, activating the answering machine.

Tuesday, March 14, 9:55 a.m. — New York City

IRWIN Fairchild buttoned his overcoat against the cold and glanced around cautiously as he pushed through the revolving door. Slight of build, just under five feet six, with deep, sunken eyes submerged in a hawkish, cadaverous face, Fairchild was a caricature of the grim reaper. His limousine was right where he had instructed the driver to be, and he slid swiftly onto the plush back seat.

The limo began to glide away from the curb while Elizabeth Sterling watched from her taxi. They had pulled up just behind the limo as Fairchild came through the door. Now she paid the cabby and got out. *What was that snake doing here?*

Elizabeth walked into the building and headed for the security desk to announce herself.

"Which office, ma'am?" the guard asked.

Elizabeth found herself responding with a ploy she hadn't planned. "I'm Mr. Fairchild's assistant, and I need your help. He just sent me back in here with papers that have to be delivered to one of the offices, but I don't know the right one."

"If I can find which office he came from, will that do it for you?"

"Yes. He was just up there in an important negotiation."

The guard consulted his sign-in book. "Forty-fifth floor. Just sign here. Bannister Partners is the office. A Mr. Hudgins."

She thanked him and found the elevators. Fairchild and Hudgins together. What did that mean? Was it coincidence? Or could his presence here be connected with the abrupt refusal to set up an emergency loan to Pan Am?

Elizabeth got off on the forty-fifth floor and asked for Harold Hudgins. When he came out, there was no friendliness. He didn't show her back to his office until she insisted.

After ten minutes of noncommittal platitudes, Elizabeth got up to go, then turned to Hudgins. "I saw Irwin Fairchild when I was coming in. Are you two acquainted?"

Hudgins paused. "No. I mean, I haven't talked to him."

He extended a limp hand, and she ignored it as she left.

She was certain now. Something *was* going on between Hudgins and Fairchild, and whatever it was, it involved Pan Am.

Tuesday, March 14, 7:45 a.m.—Anacortes, Washington

ADRIAN Kirsch picked up the McDonald's coffee cup again before remembering he'd already emptied it. The small-town restaurant he'd parked in front of was already open for business, but he decided to wait for the NTSB man to arrive. The interview would be clandestine. At the field-investigator level you didn't talk to the media without risking your career. But Michael Rogers had agreed to take a chance.

An anonymous caller had rousted Kirsch from sleep at 2:00 a.m. "Ask the NTSB about the FBI report on the chromium," the man had said. "The chromium came from a wrench left inside the engine during the last teardown in Pan Am's maintenance shop."

"How do you know this? Are you an employee?"

"Not now."

"Why are you calling a reporter?"

"Because Pan Am's trying to claim they were sabotaged, when it had to be their own sloppy procedures. That's what happens when you treat people like dirt. They make bad mistakes. Then the company covers them up. I don't want this one covered up."

"You don't like this airline much, do you?"

"Pan Am's gotta pay for what Pan Am's done." The caller then disconnected.

Tuesday, March 14—Off the Washington State coast

BILL Conrad gripped the metal railing of the diesel-powered workboat as it pitched in heavy seas. The captain materialized beside him, pointing to the submarine tender holding its position exactly above the remains of Clipper Ten's number three engine. "There they are, Mr. Conrad."

Conrad pulled his heavy coat a bit tighter, bracing against the

216

stiff, cold wind, and turned to the captain. "What next?" he asked.

"Well, we've got the crane. Once the guys in the sub locate the engine, photograph it, and get the rigging in place, we'll haul it up."

The captain's radio crackled into life as one of the submarine's crew members reported back to the tender's bridge. "We've got it right in front of us now—one huge piece, at least. I can identify a part of a turbine wheel. The basic engine is smashed up rather badly, but the thing that holds it onto the wing—the strut—looks like it was ripped apart by some single-point force. The way the metal's splayed out, it looks like a bomb went off inside the strut."

Tuesday, March 14—New York City

AFTER leaving Hudgins' office in a combination of fury and fright, Elizabeth called Eric Knox. She told him of the Hudgins debacle, the Fairchild connection, and the collapse of all the contacts she had made on Monday.

"Elizabeth, grab a cab and get down here. We need to talk."

Eric was just hanging up from a call when Elizabeth walked into his office, shutting the door behind her and noticing the grim look on her former partner's face.

"We have a big problem here," he began.

"What do you mean?" She felt her stomach tighten in a cold void as they sat down on the couch.

"Elizabeth, this last-minute loan for Pan Am was a tough sell from the beginning. But what I didn't tell you over the weekend was that there's someone out there working hard to scare everyone away from lending Pan Am a penny. Someone, or some entity, has done an incredible job of anticipating our every move and poisoning the waters—and now I know how."

Eric went to his desk to pick up a piece of paper. He returned to the couch and sat down again. "Okay, you're the First National Bank, and I walk in some fifteen minutes before Elizabeth Sterling has an appointment, and I say, 'Pan Am's gonna hit you up for a loan. But before you decide, you'd better look at this.' Then I lay this little number in front of you."

The paper had been faxed. It was an FAA internal memo sent from the FAA general counsel to the FAA administrator, and it gave a legal opinion on the consequences of terminating the operating certificate of Pan Am. It was, the memo concluded, a drastic step, but it could be done.

"*This* is what I'm fighting?"

Eric nodded. "Apparently. Our old friend Lou Higginbotham said it had chattered off his fax machine Monday morning. He checked the FAA. That memo is real."

Elizabeth sat back. "Eric, we're dead."

"This doesn't mean they're going to shut you down; it's merely an opinion that they *could*. They've announced a fine instead."

"But as you said, no one here will lend us money, and without the money, we're in default as of the twenty-first."

"That's the key, Elizabeth. You used the word 'here.' Well, New York isn't the only place to borrow money. We have no reason to believe that whoever did this has poisoned the London market, and that's where you should head immediately. But you'll have to do it clandestinely, and that means not even your office should know."

"Why, on earth?"

"Elizabeth, you've got to realize that someone's been tracking you. Someone knew you were headed to New York."

Eric got to his feet and began pacing. "Could anyone have overheard us speaking on the phone over the weekend, or seen or intercepted the list I left you of who to call Monday? You didn't fax that list anywhere, did you?"

"No. And I didn't copy it. I only have the one copy you left for me, next to the Champagne bottle. And by the way, thank you. That was sweet."

Eric's head snapped up suddenly, his tone one of amazement. "*Where* did you say? Beside the bottle? Are you sure?"

"Yes. Why?"

"Elizabeth, I left those papers *under* the bottle, weighted down by it, so you couldn't miss them."

The two of them fell silent. "Eric, this scares me," she said at last. "I mean, we've seen industrial espionage before, but this . . ."

"That proves it. Someone's been tapping your phones and possibly tailing you. Okay"—he leaned against the edge of his desk—"here's what I recommend. You need to get to London. First, though, there's someone I want you to see. A fellow named Lloyd White, with Lloyd's of London. He's based here in New York."

218

She raised one eyebrow, and he raised the palm of his hand. "I know, Lloyd takes a lot of kidding about his name, now that he's doing underwriting for his namesake. But he was in investment banking over there and can steer you to the right people."

"So now what?"

"We get you out of here without being seen, and on the way to London. I'll arrange the ticket under another name."

The meeting with Lloyd White was arranged quickly. They would meet at The Players club, in Gramercy Park. Elizabeth let herself be driven from the basement garage of the building in the firm's limousine, the dark windows ensuring that anyone stalking her would have no chance of seeing her go by.

Lloyd White was waiting for her at a table near the back of the grand old club. In his early sixties, with an angular face set off by a full head of white hair, White had a patrician charm, and Elizabeth found herself liking him instantly.

"Eric has explained the situation," he told her, "and I think I can help." He handed her a lengthy list of financial firms and houses in London, four of them circled in red and one starred.

"You'll no doubt be somewhat startled to find that the chap I want to steer you to first is at my own Lloyd's of London. Alastair Wood is his name. A common chap, really, with the heart of a shark and only twenty-nine, but he's the best off-the-cuff deal maker around. He's got the cunning of a Fagin, though he's thoroughly honest. If he likes the challenge, he'll find a way to do the deal."

They talked strategy for nearly an hour before White reached into his pocket and produced a small notebook. "Now, there's one other thing you should do, Elizabeth. There is a chap up in Scotland who started his own airline in the Midlands and was roundly hated by the major European carriers and everyone else who believes in monopolies. Eventually they ran him out of business by a campaign that bears a striking resemblance to what you're going through."

"You mean someone interfered with his corporate borrowing?"

"No. I mean he and his little airline were subjected to a full-blown campaign of economic destruction. It took him eight years in the courts to win a massive lawsuit against the culprits. He's sitting up there near Inverness now with more money than he can ever spend, but he's still bitter, and what he learned the hard way about how such campaigns operate might help your company."

White wrote out the information and handed it to her. "A bit of a warning, though. Watch yourself around Laird MacRae. He's a raging chauvinist who believes a woman's place is in the kitchen and the bedroom, not the boardroom."

"He certainly won't like me, then," she said, smiling.

"Depends entirely on the context. In regard to your role as a female executive, he'll be outraged and hostile. In regard to your charms as a woman, he'll be intrigued and challenged." He winked at her as he got to his feet. "But by all means ring him up. He rarely leaves his Highlands estate these days, and it's certainly not likely he'd leave it for a wee lass, if you understand my meaning."

ELIZABETH found the limo waiting to take her to Eric's condo to get her things. It felt different this time, as if the realization that it had been penetrated by someone else made it feel dirty and contaminated.

She was ready to close the door behind her when the blinking message light on the answering machine registered.

It was the voice of Virginia Sterling. "Elizabeth, Kelly and I are going to Europe on Brian's Pan Am flight this afternoon for two days. We'll be back late Friday night. Take care, honey, and good luck. I'll call you when we get back to Bellingham."

Eric loved planning details of trips. His driver took Elizabeth to La Guardia, where she bought a decoy ticket on United. An airport security officer then escorted her through back rooms and a maze of corridors to Eric's waiting helicopter. In fifteen minutes they were approaching JFK Airport, and within an hour she was sitting in the first-class section of a 747 heading for London.

Tuesday, March 14—Anacortes, Washington

ADRIAN Kirsch had all but taken up residence in the back alcove of the restaurant, where the pay phones were located. With a deadline looming, there was no time to drive back to his Seattle newsroom to do the research.

The NTSB's fieldman had been some help, but not much. Michael Rogers claimed he didn't have a copy of the FBI lab report. Neither could he confirm their exact metallurgical findings other than to say that chromium was found on the fragment taken from the right wing of Pan Am Clipper Ten, just above the area where number three engine had fragmented.

Kirsch hadn't told Rogers about the anonymous call at first. But he had to turn over the information. He wasn't a lawyer, but he was damned nervous about sitting on such an accusation as a wrench in the engine. When he was sure Rogers had said as much as he was going to, Adrian told him the details of the call.

Rogers had feigned disinterest. "We get a lot of tips," he'd said. "It was probably a crackpot."

Logic had guided Kirsch from there. The anonymous tipster had said that the chromium came from a wrench left in the engine. If there was no other way chromium could have normally been in or around a 747 engine, then the presence of the stuff would tend to validate the possibility. At least it would indicate that something foreign to the engine had been inside when it exploded.

He'd spent two hours on the pay phones hunting down metallurgical experts, two jet engine mechanics, a tool and die company, and several others. At last he felt he had enough confirmation. At 11:00 a.m. he called his editor, who decided to go with the story.

By midafternoon the story was gaining nationwide attention, alerting the public to the possibility that there was something more to the drama of Clipper Ten than the NTSB, the FBI, or Pan Am had yet admitted.

Tuesday, March 14, 3:30 p.m.—Seatac Airport

CAPTAIN Dale Silverman was beat. The flight in from New York was the last one he was scheduled to fly for a week, but as he put his flight bag in his assigned locker in the Seattle pilot lounge, he remembered that he had one more duty to perform.

Brian Murphy's office was just down the corridor of the Pan Am operations center, and he headed that way now. He'd thought about the situation all weekend. He had expected to see an entry in the logbook Saturday, when he and his crew had returned to their Boeing 767 at Denver's airport for the flight back to Seattle. After all, he had seen the mechanic and his tool kit on the flight deck the night before, along with a couple of rack-mounted electronic boxes he assumed were to be swapped with their counterparts in the

221

electronics bay. But there was nothing in the aircraft's maintenance log, and the operations supervisor claimed no work had been done.

Brian Murphy's secretary was at her desk and recognized Silverman immediately. "Dale! How're you doing, Captain-san?"

"Ah'm jes' fine, ma'am," he responded in a feigned Texas drawl. "High yew? Is the head birdman in?"

She shook her head. "Nope. The head birdman has gone to Frankfurt. He took off thirty minutes ago. Anything I can do?"

He could tell her the story, but there was something unsettling about the whole thing that only a fellow captain would fully understand. "That's okay. It'll wait. Probably nothing anyway."

9

Tuesday, March 14, 11:32 p.m. — In flight, Clipper Forty

THERE it was again.

Brian Murphy stared at the CRT screen that covered the forward center instrument panel and waited. The computer-driven engine instrument displays had flickered a second time, all the information scrambling for a few seconds before returning to normal.

He leveled an index finger at the engine readouts and addressed the copilot. "Tyson, did you see that?"

"What's the problem?" First Officer Tyson Matthews asked.

"The engine displays turned to garbage for a split second, then recovered."

Tyson shook his head. He hadn't seen it.

Brian's gaze remained on the panel, though he had to fight the urge to rub his eyes. I'm fatigued, he admitted to himself. It had been nearly 2:00 a.m. when his head had hit the pillow after combing through the Pan Am personnel files. He had provided the FBI agent with all the fingerprint files for those with authorized access to Pan Am pilot records. Now any other prints the FBI lab might find on First Officer Willis' folder would have to belong to the thief.

Brian refocused his attention on the center panel. There were three main displays, two of them identical flight instrument displays for the pilot and copilot, and the center screen. The engine readout displays on the center screen remained mockingly normal, but he could feel himself getting apprehensive. Forty-one thousand feet below them was a frozen wilderness. The barren, frigid nature of it had always made him uneasy.

Brian thought suddenly of Kelly and her grandmother back in compartment class, and a feeling of immense guilt rolled over him. He had enticed them into coming along—the three most important people in Elizabeth's life on the same airplane.

Without a whisper of warning, the engine display screen exploded in gibberish again. Just as abruptly it returned to normal, leaving both pilots stunned.

"I sure saw *that!*" Tyson said. He looked down at the flight computer to double-check their position. "We're just north of Hudson Bay," he told the captain.

Brian chuckled. "And if we decided to pop in somewhere and have maintenance take a look, which way would we head, Tyson?"

"About a thousand miles in any direction but north."

A warning chime resonated. On the forward CRT screen a computer message—RIGHT ENGINE THRUST REVERSER NOT LOCKED— suddenly appeared. Then, as quickly as it had illuminated, the thrust-reverser warning light went out on its own.

The flight instruments seemed to have returned to routine readouts, but both pilots were now on full alert.

"Look at that." Tyson pointed to the engine gauge display. The engine instruments—displayed as small colored round dials on the computer screen—were also showing strange readings. Every thirty seconds or so the scrambled data they had seen before would return in an artful burble of colors.

"Is there a circuit breaker that could explain this?" Brian asked.

The copilot began searching the breaker panels and shaking his head. "I don't know, boss, but it's probably not dangerous. We'll want to get the system fixed in Frankfurt, though."

Brian started to agree, but the raucous sound of an engine fire warning bell rang through the cockpit at the same moment. Brian's full attention snapped to the annunciator panel. Number one engine on the left side, according to the indications, was burning.

Tyson silenced the fire alarm as Brian looked to the left, pressing his nose against the side-window glass in an effort to see the engine. "I think you'd better run back to the cabin and look the engine over. I don't believe it's on fire. Not with all the weird indications."

Tyson was already headed for the cockpit door when the number-two-engine fire warning came on.

"Jeez!" Tyson jumped with alarm as he looked back up front and watched Brian cancel the audible warning. Bright red lights were now glowing in both fire handles.

"Now I know this is a false alarm," Brian said over his shoulder. "But go ahead and check the right engine, too."

The door closed behind Tyson, and Brian picked up the radio microphone. "Iqaluit, Clipper four zero."

"Go ahead, four zero," the controller answered.

"Ah . . . just checking to see if you were still there, Iqaluit."

A Canadian accent gave a cheery reply. "We're here, all right."

Tyson was back through the cockpit door and strapping into the right-hand seat again. "Nothing. No trouble on either engine."

At the same instant, both fire lights extinguished simultaneously—almost as if some unseen hand had flipped off two switches down in the electronics compartment, one deck below.

Two minutes passed without a flicker; then the center screen suddenly went dead, and both pilots began to feel something new and disturbing—they were slowing down.

Brian's right hand gathered the throttles and shoved them forward as far as they'd go. There was no response. "We've lost both engines," he said, his heart racing. "Emergency restart. Airstart 'em!"

Tyson grabbed for the overhead switches to fire the ignition plugs in both engines in the hope of restarting quickly.

Brian was watching the airspeed decay. "I'm, ah, gonna set up a glide here. Around two hundred twenty knots, I think."

Tyson nodded, and Brian lowered the nose to stabilize the airspeed, as the rate-of-climb indicator began a slow descent.

Tyson was hanging on both restart switches. "Nothing, Brian."

"I'm gonna start the APU." Brian's hand shot to the upper panel and toggled the auxiliary power unit in the tail into the start mode, and within a minute there was a steady run indication from the diminutive jet engine.

"Okay, we have electrical, hydraulic, flight controls, and cabin pressure. Now we need engines," Brian said.

"Brian, we're coming through thirty-nine thousand. If anything's happening out there, I don't feel it."

"Keep trying the restart," Brian said. "The problem may be our altitude. It may fire off when we get a little lower."

Then he yanked up the microphone. "Iqaluit radio, Clipper four zero. We've lost both engines and are now descending. If there's an emergency airfield within a hundred miles, please give us an immediate vector."

The radio crackled in their ear, a startled operator suddenly intense and concerned. "Clipper four zero, roger, copy your emergency. The nearest usable airfield is over three hundred miles from your position. I recommend a heading now of zero nine five degrees magnetic. You're a two-engine 767, is that correct?"

"That's right. We may need to think about an emergency landing."

"Brian? We need to let the passengers know," Tyson said.

Brian nodded as he scooped up the interphone handset and punched in the appropriate code. The response was nearly instantaneous from the lead flight attendant.

"What's up, boys? Why are we descending?"

"We've got a double engine flameout. We'll probably get them restarted when we get lower, but for now get the cabin ready for an emergency landing. Worst case, we'll have fifteen minutes."

The line clicked dead. He picked up the PA microphone and looked at Tyson with a question in his eyes. If just one engine could be brought back on-line, it wouldn't be necessary to scare the passengers. Tyson shook his head in the negative.

"Folks, this is the captain. We have a very serious problem, and it may be necessary to make an emergency landing. I've instructed the flight attendants to get you ready. Please cooperate."

That was enough. Brian snapped the microphone off and adjusted his descent rate to increase the speed a bit.

"We're through thirty-six thousand, and they're not starting, Brian. We're gonna have to do something fast."

"Okay. Give it a rest for two minutes." He waved at the overhead restart switches. "Let's—let's think options."

"We don't get one of these suckers started, we *have* no options," Tyson said. "We'll have to land on whatever flat spot we can find below, with gear down, and pray we can do it."

Brian started to grab the map, then remembered the radio. "Iqaluit radio, Clipper four zero. Still zero engines. We need your help. What's ahead of us about eighty miles? Are there any flat areas?"

The voice of the Canadian operator came back immediately. "We've been looking at that for you, sir. If you have to put it down somewhere, you'll want a lake."

"What's the weather below us?"

"Our remote station closest to the position is reporting winds out of the west at twenty knots, a solid overcast at three thousand feet, and temperature in Fahrenheit is, uh, minus forty-eight."

"Can you vector us to a big lake? I assume they're all frozen?"

"They're all frozen solid, and we have no radar here. Stand by."

They were below twenty-six thousand feet now, coming down at around fifteen hundred feet per minute. Brian calculated seventeen minutes and ninety miles left before they'd be out of options.

"Ah, Clipper four zero, if you turn back west to a heading of two seven zero degrees, we think you can find an area of many good-sized lakes."

"Roger, Iqaluit. We'll give you our final position and heading just before we . . . land." The word was hard to get out. He hoped it would be a landing. He had to believe it would be a landing.

There was a knock on the door. It was Jan, the lead flight attendant. "What—what's our situation?" she asked.

Brian looked her in the eye. "I won't mislead you, Jan. There's no airport out here, only frozen terrain and frozen lakes. We're going to try our best to find a lake. It could be rough. Very rough."

She nodded stoically and took a deep breath. "You'll remember to give us a PA warning to brace?"

"I promise," Brian told her.

She started to go, then turned back. "Oh, the woman and the young lady in compartment one who're friends of yours? The young lady says, 'Thumbs up,' and she loves you."

"Tell"—he had to clear his throat—"tell her I love her, too . . . and thumbs up."

Jan closed the door as the phrase rattled around Brian's head. How many times he'd used that to buck up Kelly when she thought she was facing some insurmountable hurdle. "Thumbs up, young lady. Only can-do attitudes permitted around here."

Tyson glanced at the altimeter. They were coming through fifteen thousand feet. The moonlight glinted off the overcast below, and it

was obvious they were only a few thousand feet from entering it.

"Okay, make a last check with Iqaluit. Give our position," Brian commanded. Tyson grabbed the microphone to comply.

Brian watched the ghostly shape of the undercast rising to gobble them, and lofted a small prayer. *Dear God, please help me do this! Please help us do this. Let Kelly get out of this okay.*

"Okay, the operator's been told. Rescue forces are already launching, he said." Tyson replaced the microphone and reached to the engine airstart switches for one final try.

They were into the clouds now.

Brian picked up the PA microphone. "Okay, folks, everyone in the brace position."

They descended through five thousand, then four thousand, with no hint of a breakout. "They said three thousand, right?" Brian asked.

"That's what they said," Tyson responded.

"Okay, Canada. Show yourself. Please," Brian muttered.

"Coming through three thousand," Tyson called out.

Nothing.

"Two thousand," Tyson said.

Still nothing.

"Turn on all the landing lights," Brian directed. Tyson snapped them on immediately. Nothing but illuminated clouds showed ahead of them, the light almost blinding as it reflected back.

"Twelve hundred feet, Brian. Wait a minute. We may be breaking out," Tyson called out, his voice tense with hope and fear.

The reflection of the powerful landing lights suddenly ended, the beams stabbing unimpeded into the Arctic night.

"We're at nine hundred, speed two ninety," Tyson called out.

"You see anything?" Brian asked.

"Not yet . . . not yet. I'm looking." Tyson's words were almost breathless. They needed a target. "Brian, there to the left. I can almost make out the surface. Come left forty degrees at least. You're coming through six hundred now and slowing."

Brian leveled at four hundred, listening to their airspeed drain away as Tyson's voice cut through the tension.

"There! Dead ahead I can see what looks like a lake."

Brian checked the airspeed. They were under two hundred forty knots now. "I don't see it!"

"Just ahead. See that angled shadow cutting across in front of us? And see the slight reflection on this side? That's got to be a lake."

Two hundred twenty knots. They were out of time, and Brian could see the shoreline—if that was what it was—moving toward them.

"We'll have to try it," Brian said. *Please let that be a lake.*

At two hundred knots he pushed the nose forward and called landing gear down. Tyson snapped the lever down, and the sounds of the gear extension process reached their ears.

"Flaps five," Brian ordered.

The gossamer shadow had become something more now. It could be a small ridge, or it could be a shoreline, but whatever it was, they were closing on it rapidly.

"You're four hundred feet, speed one sixty."

"Flaps . . . hell, all the way."

"Roger," Tyson replied. His left hand worked the flap lever as Brian pushed the nose over slightly, the landing lights now confirming that whatever was beyond that threshold was not a frozen lake.

"Damn! We're headed for the shoreline."

Brian banked the 767 to the left instantly. He had very little altitude but just enough airspeed. The shore angled away to his left.

"Come on, baby!" Brian spoke the words as his left foot mashed hard on the left rudder to skid the jetliner around. He was at forty degrees of bank now, letting the nose fall slightly as the lights aligned themselves with the shoreline and then moved left onto the lake surface.

"One hundred feet, Brian. We're gonna have to land it."

A snow-covered surface as flat as a griddle stretched ahead of them. Brian let the 767 settle into ground effect and come down slowly. At the last second he leveled the wings for touchdown.

The first indication that the wheels had kissed a solid surface was the realization that the radio altimeter was on zero. Neither of them had ever made a smoother landing.

Brian let the nose down to the surface then, and stepped on the brakes. Amazingly, they responded as the speed of the jumbo slowly decreased to under a hundred miles per hour.

The landing lights stabbed into the darkness ahead, but now there was a reflection of something dark moving in from the right—

the edge of the lake. If the aircraft should rocket off the ice and into that embankment, the landing gear and possibly the engines could shear off, causing a fire.

Brian steered left as far as he dared, and tromped hard on both brakes, checking the airspeed as it fell under fifty knots. They were slowing but were on a collision course with the black ground ahead.

Brian and Tyson both mentally braced for impact. Over a hundred feet behind them, the chattering brakes and skidding tires bit into the surface. The big Boeing shuddered and slowed.

Finally, in almost absolute silence, the nose wheel came to rest within eight feet of the potentially lethal eighteen-foot embankment surrounding the nameless lake.

At first both pilots sat in stunned silence.

Brian closed his eyes. *Thank you, Lord.*

"I think we did it," Tyson said.

Through the cockpit door the sound of applause, spotty at first, then energetic and heartfelt, filtered through.

They were safe. At least for now.

10

Wednesday, March 15, 7:15 a.m. — London, England

ELIZABETH was burning with impatience. The first-class sleeper seat had worked better than expected, carrying her to Heathrow Airport reasonably rested and ready to work, but she was blocked by the impenetrable wall of normal business hours. She could do nothing before her nine-o'clock meeting with Alastair Wood at Lloyd's.

Instead, she decided to stay in her hotel room and work on the battle plan. Pan Am had five days left, and she was determined to work her heart out up to the deadline.

A sudden swell of sleepiness rolled over her. She blinked and rubbed her eyes, trying to stay focused on the screen of her laptop computer as the thought of a warm shower became a siren song.

I guess I didn't get as much sleep as I thought.

She found herself undoing her earrings and unbuttoning her blouse, her legs propelling her toward the bath. She had just stepped into the cascading hot water when the phone rang. *Now what?*

The satellite call last night from the aircraft to Ron Lamb's home came to mind immediately. The fact that she was headed for London seemed to surprise Ron, but he had seemed truly shocked when she warned him in dire terms not to tell anyone else in the company where she really was.

The phone was on its fourth ring when she reached for it. She had expected Lamb's voice, but there was no way to anticipate the news that Clipper Forty was down on a frozen lake in Canada.

"Oh no, Ron. How cold is it up there? You say the airplane's intact?"

"Yeah. It's minus forty degrees or more, but fortunately their APU, the auxiliary power unit, is working fine. After they landed, an Arctic storm front moved over them, and the Canadian Forces rescue center is not sure they'll be able to reach them until it blows over."

"How long is that, Ron?"

"Could be three days or more. What's got us all scared is that APU. If they run out of fuel before rescue can get in there . . ."

"How could the engines just quit?"

"Our chief pilot—well, you know Brian Murphy, of course—Brian is dumbfounded, as is our chief of maintenance. Nothing like this has ever happened to a 767 before."

The mention of Brian's name caught her full attention. She could imagine him at that moment with a phone to each ear at the operations center. Brian was wonderful in a crisis.

"Ron, where *is* Brian Murphy? I may want to check with him."

There was a long pause.

"Elizabeth, Brian Murphy is the *captain* of Clipper Forty. He's on that frozen lake right now."

Wednesday, March 15, 3:00 a.m. EST—Clipper Forty

THE wind had come up as Brian sat on an armrest in the front of the first-class cabin and talked to the passengers on the PA. It had grown rapidly to gusts that shoved the 767 sideways at times.

"I'm going to be completely honest with you," he had begun. "Rescue forces are already on the way, but as you can hear and feel, there is a storm over us. It could be a while before they can find us or get aircraft in here to evacuate us."

Brian felt the eyes of every passenger on him. He was the man to whom more than two hundred forty people were looking for guidance and reassurance.

"Okay, here's the bottom line, folks. We'll hope to be here only for hours, but we'll work and act as if we'll be here for days. This is now a survival situation. Mutual cooperation and dependency—and teamwork—will be essential."

There were nodding heads.

"Let me take questions for a few minutes; then I'm going to pass out some paper. I'd appreciate it if each of you would write down your occupation, any military training, survival experience, whether you're a physician, or anything else I might need to know."

The passengers' confusion was apparent from their many questions. How could they be in a warm environment when they were stranded in the Arctic, with temperatures nearly fifty below zero?

"The APU, or auxiliary power unit," Brian explained. "It's a small jet-turbine engine in the tail of the aircraft. It gives us electrical power and heat, and we have enough fuel to run it for many days."

An elderly man a few rows from Brian began to raise his hand, then decided against it. His haunted look transmitted the question as clearly as if he'd spoken: What happens if the APU fails?

That answer, Brian decided, was best left for later.

After a few more minutes of questions, Brian excused himself and walked back forward through the compartment-class section with its two-person compartments. Virginia Sterling and Kelly had been assigned to compartment 1, just behind the cockpit. He found them now and hugged them both.

"You were terrific, Brian," Kelly said with tears glistening in her eyes. "I couldn't even feel the landing."

"I got your message, honey. It helped."

"Brian, is rescue really on the way?" Virginia asked him.

He meant to glance at her with a reassuring nod, but this was Elizabeth's mother, and he found himself unable to varnish the truth. "They are, Virginia, but I doubt they'll be able to find us just yet, or land. We may be here awhile."

THE nine flight attendants were all veterans, but none of them had ever lived through such a nightmare as the previous hour. With Tyson remaining in the cockpit to talk to Iqaluit, Brian called a staff meeting in the forward area. He praised his crew lavishly before getting down to organizational details.

"First, I mean it when I say we're a team, the passengers included. I need your every idea and suggestion; I need your strength as well. I'm still the captain. Tyson Matthews is second-in-command. Jan, your first flight attendant, is third-in-command. Anyone can communicate with me or Tyson or Jan at any time about anything." He took the time to smile and make eye contact with each of the flight attendants then, all of whom nodded in turn.

"Okay. First, communications. We have four satellite lines, as you know. We'll retain line one for cockpit use, but I want the other three used to let each passenger call home at our expense to let loved ones know they're okay.

"Next item: food and water. Take inventory of what we have in unserved meals, packaged food—everything, down to peanuts; then report back to Jan. Water use in the bathrooms has to be curtailed. Toilets are recirculating, of course, so those are unaffected."

A flight attendant raised her hand. "Sir, we may have people with medication needs. What if they need their luggage?"

He shook his head. "Not possible. None of us is tall enough to deal with the baggage compartments. Even if we could, at fifty below, whoever tried would be risking serious frostbite—and we'd have to open a door and use an emergency exit slide to get him to the surface. Don't forget our floor level is over ten feet off the ground. But let's see if anyone who needs medicine left it in their bags. I would think most of them have their medicine in their carry-ons."

Another heavy gust shoved the aircraft sideways, moving the wheels a few inches and pivoting the nose to the left. Brian looked at the group. They were all looking back at him quietly.

"Oh, one other thing. Even though we can't serve much in order to ration what we have, let's establish a regular meal schedule and try for some semblance of normalcy."

TYSON Matthews was on satellite phone link with Pan Am headquarters when the captain returned to the cockpit, but the radio was tuned to an aeronautical radio frequency.

"Clipper four zero, Rescue five. We've been in solid cloud cover since descending through twenty thousand. We'll continue to orbit, but until this storm lifts, there's nothing else we can do."

"Roger, Rescue. It's just good to know you're up there."

Tyson looked at Brian and shook his head sadly. "I think we gave them the wrong position, Brian. That C-130 made three passes over the coordinates we gave him, and I couldn't hear a thing."

Both men remained silent for half a minute, listening to the wind gusts roar at them through the cockpit windows.

Tyson spoke first. "Brian, everyone in our maintenance department keeps telling me there simply isn't any way that normal failure modes in the computers could cut off the fuel switches. No way."

"Do they have any ideas on how to get them running again?"

Tyson shook his head. "They have no suggestions yet, other than pulling the rack-mounted black boxes in the electronics bay below. But we don't have any tools to work on them, let alone the problem of going outside in these temperatures to get to the compartment."

Brian sat deep in thought for a few seconds, staring forward into the Arctic night, remembering the company decision to seal off the small floor hatch that normally connects the passenger compartment of a 767 with the lower electronics bay. On Pan Am a permanent bulkhead covered the hatch.

"You're right. I'd have to go outside to get in the electronics bay. And here we sit, totally dependent on that APU."

"Brian, on that subject . . . I hate to bring it up, but I checked the log for past problems with the APU."

"And?" Brian looked at him with an apprehensive expression.

"This APU's had a lot of maintenance troubles lately. It's not terribly reliable."

Wednesday, March 15, 11:35 a.m.—London

"ELIZABETH? Are you quite all right?" Alastair Wood had cocked his head and tried to meet her gaze, which had soared off through the glass windows of Lloyd's main floor and into space.

She snapped back to London and smiled at him, anxious not to discuss Clipper Forty. "Sorry. There's a lot on my mind."

Alastair Wood had turned out to be exactly what Lloyd White had represented: a young street fighter who had acquired the manners of a financier but who still had the heart of a shark.

"Where were we?" she asked.

"Well, I have a frightful amount of phoning to do to line up our chaps, but I see no reason why we shouldn't meet again in the morning to begin drawing up the papers."

"You're that sure?"

He laughed as he got to his feet and removed his glasses. "Well, the members of my syndicate have made a lot of money listening to me over the past four years. Your interest rate offer is excellent, and we've got security, so why not?"

She shook his hand warmly, but her mind was on an empty office she had seen as she came in. Could she use its phone for a minute?

"Certainly," Wood replied, showing her in and closing the door to leave her in privacy.

Elizabeth fumbled through her briefcase for the satellite access number to Clipper Forty. The number came up busy, and she tried again, hearing a ringing circuit on the third try.

The sound of a strained feminine voice rang clearly from the other end. "Clipper Forty."

"This is Elizabeth Sterling, chief financial officer of Pan Am. Could I speak with Captain Murphy, please?"

"Sure. Let me transfer you."

"Brian!"

"Elizabeth? It's good to hear your voice. Hold on."

In the background she heard Brian ask someone to go back to the cabin, and a moment later his voice came on the line again, much gentler now.

"Elizabeth, I—I had to fight to keep you out of my head on the way down." He paused. "I'm truly sorry for the other night. It scared me that I might not have the chance to tell you that. It kept eating at me. 'What if we don't make it? Will she know how much I love her?' "

Elizabeth had to clear her throat. There seemed to be a growing lump there. "I *do* know, Brian, and I feel the same. And I'm as much to blame for Saturday as you. Brian, when can you get out of there?"

Several thousand miles distant, Brian hesitated, his mind racing. "Honey, we're in a serious situation. It could get tough, but we'll be okay. As for your mother and Kelly, they're doing just fine."

Mom and Kelly? Suddenly she recalled her mother's words on

235

Eric's answering machine in New York: "Kelly and I are going to Europe on Brian's Pan Am flight."

"I, ah, knew they were flying to Europe, but I forgot they were with you."

"I'm sorry to shock you."

They talked for five more minutes before Brian called Virginia and Kelly to the cockpit for a short conversation with Elizabeth.

When the call was over, Elizabeth sat in the vacant office, still holding the receiver, a tide of conflicting emotions welling up inside. *I've got to get up there, be there when they're rescued.*

Elizabeth looked around suddenly, reminding herself where she was and what she was doing. There were five days left for Pan Am, and no one but Elizabeth could possibly carry the financial ball. In the Arctic wilds of Canada, there was nothing she could accomplish. But in London—by staying to finish her mission—she might be able to save an entire airline.

She had no choice.

Wednesday, March 15, 3:55 a.m.—Seattle

CHAD Jennings focused on the open hatch to the electronics bay of Ship 103, their other Boeing 767. He had breezed into the Pan Am hangar at Seatac in his Porsche, smelling lightly of bourbon.

A collection of men stood beneath the aircraft, including FAA, NTSB, and Boeing engineers. Bill Conrad introduced Jennings to those the operations vice president didn't know.

"Okay, Bill. What are we doing here at three a.m.?" Jennings asked.

Michael Rogers of the NTSB and the FAA man listened carefully as the maintenance chief explained to Jennings what he already should have known about Clipper Forty's engine failure.

There was no doubt now that Clipper Ten had been sabotaged with a bomb in the number three engine, and the NTSB was going to announce that to the world later on Wednesday. But was Clipper Forty a victim of sabotage, too?

Captain Dale Silverman stood quietly to one side, watching the proceedings with an ashen expression. A quick check had revealed that the man he had seen on Ship 102 in Denver on Friday night did not match the description of anyone working for

Pan Am and there had been no maintenance scheduled that night.

"There was no way," Bill Conrad explained to Jennings, "that anyone should have been changing electronic units like the black boxes Captain Silverman saw on the floor of that cockpit."

Jennings nodded solemnly. "And Ship one oh two . . ."

"Is the very one sitting on the ice slab above the Arctic Circle."

"Bill, look at this." One of the Boeing team leaned down through the hatch and motioned the maintenance chief over to the ladder beneath the electronics bay. Bill climbed in carefully.

"Okay, this is the main box controlling the center display. The way it feeds data into the adjacent systems, it could conceivably be programmed to cause havoc, but any normal circuit failure will simply drop that function out of the loop. We built it to fail-safe."

Bill Conrad fingered the ends of the plug. "If you wanted to bring down this airplane—cut off the engine—and you had this box and time to monkey with it, could you produce that result?"

"I guess you could. But once you remove the unwanted system, it should work again. One problem. You remove this box, you have virtually no engine indications."

Bill looked at the Boeing man. "Thanks, Phil. This may be our edge."

Bill climbed out and spoke to one of the Pan Am maintenance team. "Run a telephone line up to the electronics bay. We're gonna get Brian on the satellite connection and talk him through this—if he can find a way to get outside and up into the compartment."

A hand landed gently on Bill's shoulder. Its owner introduced himself as Loren Miller of the FBI. With the NTSB's Rogers, the FAA's man, and Chad Jennings in tow, they compared notes—Agent Miller finally coming to the inevitable conclusion.

"We have to assume," he told them, "that there is someone willing to commit mass murder by bringing down a Pan Am airplane any way he can. Whoever it is, he isn't finished. There is no way you people"—he gestured to Jennings and Conrad—"should allow a single additional departure without a massive security effort, including complete examination of every aircraft."

The FBI agent checked his watch. "My records will read, gentlemen, that you were warned about this as of four twenty-three a.m. Pacific standard time. I suggest you act immediately."

Phoenix Rising

Wednesday, March 15, 1:00 p.m.—London

THE message was waiting for Elizabeth the moment she opened the door to her suite. Call Ron Lamb at the office, whatever the hour. He answered his private line on the first ring, and she filled him in on the optimistic meeting with Alastair Wood.

Ron sounded grateful, hopeful, and agonizingly tired.

"You okay, Ron?"

There was a long delay in his answer. "My head's killing me, Elizabeth. I used to have migraines. I think they're back."

He told her of the security precautions, the schedule disruptions, and the pending NTSB confirmation that Clipper Ten had been bombed—and Clipper Forty more than likely sabotaged as well.

"Ron, could this all be connected? The financial interference and these emergencies?"

"I don't know. But if so, what force are we facing here?"

There were no answers, and they ended the conversation with mutual fears growing.

Elizabeth had appointments with several banks that afternoon. Things went well, but they needed more time than Pan Am had. She returned to the hotel, anxious to get back on the phone.

The lines to Clipper Forty were continuously busy, even after an hour of dialing. Elizabeth ordered dinner from room service and decided to hold off trying to get through to Brian again. There was another call she should make in the meantime.

She searched her notepad for the name—Creighton MacRae— and punched in the number. The phone rang nine times before a gruff voice with a distinct Highland accent rang through the line.

"Yes?"

She introduced herself and mentioned Lloyd White's name. "I was told by Mr. White that you were once head of your own airline company and that you're an excellent financier who can appreciate another professional's need for advice or assistance." She related in capsule form what was happening to her company and why she had been told he might help.

"White exaggerates. Did he also tell you I'm retired?"

"Yes, he did."

"My advice, Miss Sterling, is to go ring up someone in the busi-

238

ness of providing corporate financial advice. I'm finished swimming with sharks. Good night." The line went dead suddenly.

The jerk hung up on me. Elizabeth held the receiver out and looked at it in disbelief.

She dialed MacRae's number again. He picked up the phone instantly. "Yes, Miss Sterling?" he said.

"Are you always this insufferably rude, Mr. MacRae? Or is that a Scottish tradition? A gentleman doesn't hang up on a lady."

"Ah, but I was called by a self-proclaimed chief financial officer. Now I am to understand you're a lady? Which is it?"

"In my country it's possible to be both." There was a snort from Scotland. "Mr. MacRae, hear me out, and if you refuse what I'm going to ask, I'll leave you alone."

"If that's what it takes to dine in peace, by all means proceed."

"Okay," Elizabeth continued. "I know you won a large judgment after a long and torturous lawsuit against organizations and individuals who forced you to sell the airline it took you so much agony to build. The tactics that they used against you included financial sabotage, operational and financial interference, and even physical sabotage of your company's property. In addition, you uncovered a network of foreign companies that had joined in a collusive effort to wage the war against you. Does that about sum it up?"

"Well done, Miss Sterling. You obviously know how to absorb a briefing paper."

"Mr. MacRae, someone is now doing the same thing to us. If that in any way makes you angry, please have the decency to let me come to Scotland and discuss this further."

"When would you be coming, then?" he asked.

The question caught her off guard. "Ah . . . in a day or two."

"Call me then. I can only promise you a meeting in Inverness, you understand, but I will do that."

"That would be helpful. Thank you, Mr. MacRae, I really—"

"No need for thanks. Frankly, I'm just curious to see a hybrid lady vice president. May I get back to my supper now, Miss Sterling? My chips have gone stone cold."

"You may, Laird MacRae."

She disconnected before he could think of another reply. Lloyd White warned me, she recalled.

11

THE interior of Clipper Forty had been plunged into darkness, the cabin illuminated now only by the ghostly glow of the emergency exit lights. The howling of the wind outside rose to demonic levels as the Arctic void began sucking the heat from the Boeing 767.

Brian could hear the sound of the APU's turbine winding down as he headed for the cockpit. It was Tyson's watch. Why wasn't he restarting it? *How long have I been asleep? Could we be out of fuel?*

Brian burst onto the flight deck and saw the copilot holding a flashlight on the start switch while he tried to coax the turbine back into operation. Brian slid into the left seat, watching intently.

"I think we're going to get her back," Tyson said, the concern in his voice obvious. There was the unmistakable sound of a ragged acceleration as the turbine wheels spun up to operating speed.

"There." The APU stabilized, and Tyson's hand moved toward the electrical panel to reconnect its generator. Instantly they were awash in light, and heat coursed through the vents.

They sat in tense silence for nearly a minute, watching the gauges and listening. "What do you think?" Brian asked at last.

The copilot shook his head. "I don't trust it. I talked to the rescue forces about ten minutes ago. They don't expect any change in this storm for at least another thirty-six hours."

Brian gestured at the snow streaming past the window. "I'm going to have to go out there."

"Brian, you can't—" Tyson began.

"You heard Seattle," Brian continued. "If we can pull that box and find out whether someone's screwed around with it, we might be able to start the engines. Then we can live without the APU."

"We've been through this before, Brian. It would be a crazy risk. The windchill factor's close to a hundred below. We don't have a ladder to get up to the electronics bay, and you don't have the cold-weather gear."

Brian had been incredulous at first when the suggestion had come over the satellite phone. At the time maintenance was talking to him, all the cabin doors of Clipper Forty hung more than ten feet above the surface. Since then, the wind had pivoted the aircraft nearly ninety degrees. The tail and rear fuselage now hung only a few feet over the embankment. Suddenly, getting out and in without a Jetway or stairs could be fairly easy.

Brian took a long, deep breath. "I'll bundle up and cover every inch of skin. We'll toss out an empty galley food container to stand on. I'll just have to pull myself up into the compartment."

Tyson had opened his mouth to protest when the APU died once more. This time it took several attempts to get it restarted. Whatever opposition Tyson had felt to Brian's plan was overwhelmed by the very real fear of facing the Arctic cold without a source of heat.

WITHIN a half hour Pan Am's maintenance team in Seattle had reassembled in the Seatac hangar, the company's top avionics man sitting in the electronics bay of the company's other 767, wearing a telephone headset. Anchoring the other end of the satellite phone was Tyson Matthews in the cockpit of Clipper Forty, ready to relay instructions to Brian Murphy—provided Brian could get into the electronics compartment.

Brian zipped his coat over several layers of sweaters and opened the right rear door, letting the emergency slide flop out and inflate. The slide lay at a shallow angle on the frozen tundra that formed the perimeter of the lake. With help from two bundled-up flight attendants, he positioned himself and slid down the slide into wind and cold deeper and more frightening than anything he'd ever experienced. Then the flight attendants closed the cabin door behind their captain, leaving him alone in the alien world.

The electronics compartment lay a hundred and fifty feet ahead of him in the frozen gloom. With the cabin access hatch closed off, a small hatch in the belly of the 767, just behind the nose gear, was the only way in. If he could get inside, he could plug the headset he had stuffed in his pocket into an interphone panel and communicate with the copilot, one floor above in the cockpit.

The wind was an incredible torrent of icy fury sucking his body heat away at a furious rate. The lake ice beneath his feet seemed impossibly slick. The distance from the tail to the nose gear seemed to stretch into miles. Slowly he taught himself how to move forward without falling, moving step by step toward the nose strut.

All the warmth he had felt in the cabin was long gone, and the cold had penetrated his inner core. His toes felt slightly numb, as did his fingers in the inadequate leather gloves he had borrowed from a passenger. The need to get into the warmth of the electronics bay was becoming urgent.

The food carrier box he had dumped out the forward galley door had been blown backward. He retrieved it and positioned it under the compartment.

Brian stepped gingerly up onto the box, his numb fingers feeling in around the recessed door lever. He pulled with determination, but the handle stayed frozen in place. He put his entire weight on it then, lifting himself in the air, finally feeling the handle snap down and out of the recess. Suddenly the landing lights and the window lights went out. *The APU again.*

In near-total darkness—shaking and shivering violently—Brian twisted the handle, feeling nothing move in response. He had to turn it a full one hundred eighty degrees. His arms ached. Soon he wouldn't have the strength to support himself.

The sound of something distant distracted him. As he tried to decide if it could be the sound of the APU, the lights came back on.

Brian jerked at the handle then with renewed confidence, putting everything he had into it. His teeth gritted, he was rewarded at last as the hatch moved inward.

Then, feeling the warmth spill from the compartment above, he gripped the edge of the compartment and hauled himself up.

Brian closed the hatch from the inside and braced his back against an electronics rack, letting the heat radiate into his body. The shaking was severe now, but slowly it subsided. In the glow of several red and yellow indicator lights on various rack-mounted boxes, he managed to find the light switch.

Brian pulled the lightweight headset from his pocket and found the interphone panel, plugging it in. "Tyson, you there?"

"Yes. I've got them on the line. I'll relay when you're ready."

Thursday, March 16, 1:00 a.m.—London

ELIZABETH stared at the ceiling of her hotel suite and wondered what was really going on. The copilot of Clipper Forty had said that Brian wasn't available, but he wouldn't elaborate.

The fact that she could still reach them was comforting, but there was no hope of sleeping.

Elizabeth threw off the covers, reached for the phone, and dialed Ron Lamb's private office number. For some reason she let it ring twenty times, which was ridiculous. If he was there, he would have answered. Yet she kept on—physically startled when the receiver was suddenly raised, six thousand miles away.

"Ron? Ron, are you there?" she asked.

"Hee—heeah . . ." The sounds were human, but words weren't forming.

"Ron, this is Elizabeth. Are you okay?"

"Whaa . . . ?"

Elizabeth had her finger a millimeter from the disconnect button before she stopped herself. Instead, she grabbed the cellular phone. Within three minutes she had reached the emergency center in Seattle, giving them instructions on where to find the owner of the small voice on the other end of the phone connection to Ron Lamb's office.

For nearly fifteen tense minutes she listened to what sounded like the distant sound of labored breathing before there was a new noise—that of hurried footsteps and voices approaching.

She half expected someone to replace the receiver and cut her off. Instead, a worried guard picked it up. "Hello? Anyone here?"

"Yes." She explained who she was and asked what he was seeing.

"It's Mr. Lamb. He was on the floor behind his desk. The paramedics say it looks like he's had a stroke."

Wednesday, March 15, 9:00 p.m. EST—Clipper Forty

BRIAN Murphy sat with the opened electronics box in his lap, feeling helpless. Working by intercom with Tyson, who was relaying instructions coming over the satellite phone from the team in Pan Am's Seatac hangar, he had located the black box that controlled the engine instrument displays, and opened it. He could see nothing out of place.

Brian had already relayed the serial number on the case. Now Tyson was back on the intercom. "That box was stolen from United's bench stock in San Francisco. They want you to read the serial numbers of each circuit card."

One by one Brian pulled the electronics-laden cards and relayed the numbers. The sixth one held the key.

"Tyson, tell them this one looks funny, as if things have been resoldered sloppily. There's also a tiny device that doesn't look like anything else wired to the card. I couldn't see it before."

He read the serial number. It didn't match United's records.

They were discussing it when the lights went out again. Tyson's voice rang in his headset. "The APU's not starting, Brian. I've tried three times."

"Okay. Okay, let's think this one through. I'm going to plug this box back in without the bad component."

Working by flashlight, he pushed the box into place, carefully checking the connections, and then stopped. They might have only one chance. As long as the APU was down, the satellite phone was dead. But if they could restart the APU and keep it running for just a few minutes, they might get an engine started.

It would be a gamble.

"Tyson, why don't you try to fire off the APU again. If you get it going, immediately try to start engine number two. If she doesn't start in forty-five seconds, I'll yank this box out of here and you keep your finger on the switch."

"Let's do it," Tyson answered.

On the third attempt the APU caught. Both pilots held their breath as Tyson began the start sequence, talking Brian through every step.

"Okay. Moving the start switch. Nothing. . . . Nothing, Brian. This isn't cutting it."

"The fuel may be frozen, Tyson. Boost pumps on?"

"Yeah, they're on. Nothing. We've got nothing!"

Brian yanked the box back toward him, feeling the electronic connectors separate from those on the end of the electronics rack. Almost immediately Tyson was back in his ear.

"All my engine instruments dropped to zero."

"Don't stop," Brian yelled. "Keep going!"

From the right side of the aircraft Brian heard another noise now, the sound of vibrations starting up a long scale, from a very low frequency and climbing, accompanied by the sound of—

"We got it! Brian, it's starting. Number two— We've got it!"

THE CONTROLLED FALL FROM THE electronics bay to the ice, the struggle to close the hatch, the trip back to the rear door, and even the climb up the inflated emergency slide—all seemed minor inconveniences now that the comfortable whine of number two engine played in Brian's ears.

When he had returned to the cockpit, they decided to start number one as well. It took over a minute to start, but it ran. Brian explained the victory to the passengers, then reinitialized the satellite phone and reported the good news to Seattle, getting Bill Conrad on the other end.

"So it *was* a monkeyed-with card in the box?" Conrad asked.

"Looks like it to me, Bill. But this is an amateurish job." Brian turned the circuit card over in his hand. "Whoever put this in didn't care what it looked like, which tells me he didn't expect there to be anything left of us but wreckage."

Conrad told Brian of the confirmation that Clipper Ten's engine had been bombed and of the FBI's response.

Brian sat up suddenly in the captain's seat. "Bill, get the FBI agent and find out if he's finished running the fingerprint checks on my files. There's got to be a tie-in between whoever screwed around with our pilot files and what's happening to our airplanes." Brian laid out the details of his midnight search of the files.

"Brian, how's your fuel holding out?" Bill asked.

"Thirty-two thousand pounds. At present rate of consumption, with two engines running, we'd run out in fifteen hours, but we're going to alternate engines. That'll give us thirty hours."

Brian ended the call with Bill Conrad and stared into the void ahead. The 767 was now pointing toward the middle of the frozen lake, its far shoreline virtually invisible in the darkness.

"Tyson," he said at last, "that wind's pretty steady, isn't it?"

Tyson nodded. "Yeah. I've been reading thirty to forty knots."

"Okay, and it's possible that this lake is two or three miles long, right in the direction from which this wind is blowing. Okay so far?"

"What are you getting at, Brian?" Suddenly a small gleam of understanding flashed in the copilot's eyes. "An airplane with both engines running and enough fuel to—"

"To get to Gander or Goose Bay or Thule, or maybe even Montreal," Brian finished the sentence.

"But we've got to know what's out there."

"So we taxi out and look. Tyson, call the aft galley. Get Jan to jettison the emergency slide and lock the door. Let's secure the cabin, tell the folks, and get moving." Tyson reached for the interphone as Brian ran through routine control checks, feeling that he was in control again.

Wednesday, March 15, 11:00 p.m. EST—Clipper Forty

THE satellite phone call from Elizabeth came through as Brian taxied Clipper Forty back to the northeast end of the lake.

"Brian, I've been trying for hours to reach you. What's happening? How are you holding out?"

"We're not holding out. We're *getting* out." Brian filled her in on what they were preparing to do.

Elizabeth's head was swimming with a combination of elation and alarm. What did a blind takeoff from an Arctic lake in darkness involve? How dangerous was it? She spoke her worries aloud.

"Not as dangerous," Brian explained, "as waiting to run out of fuel. We can't stay here, honey. We're out of options. I'll call you back as soon as we're airborne."

The lake was at least four miles long and perhaps a half-mile wide, with the entire surface frozen solid and relatively smooth. They had taxied around for thirty minutes before Brian brought them back to their starting point.

Brian turned the 767 into the wind and set the parking brake. The airspeed indicator on his display screen was showing a steady thirty-five knots, with gusts to forty-five. The only thing they were missing was the center display and all the engine instruments.

"Ready?" Brian studied Tyson's face.

"Ready," the copilot confirmed.

"Okay, since we have zero engine indicators, we'll have to guess at everything. I'll push up the throttles to where the engines sound about right, holding the brakes until we start sliding; then I'll try to keep her steady on two zero zero degrees true heading down the lake until you call, 'Rotate.' Since we know we've got enough runway, I'd say let's get out of here."

"Amen," Tyson said.

Brian began advancing the throttles, the engine speed following,

246

the whine of the two high-bypass turbofans becoming a loud roar as the 767 began to buck against the restraint of the brakes. He released them as Tyson kept both his hands on the control yoke, holding it almost full forward to keep the nose wheel firmly on the surface of the frozen lake.

The airspeed leaped within seconds to eighty knots, then ninety, then a hundred. The frozen surface had seemed perfectly smooth while they were taxiing around at low speed, but now it became a washboard, bucking, bouncing, and vibrating the instruments as well as the occupants of the cockpit.

There was nothing in front of the windscreen but snow streaming past. No more than three hundred feet of lake surface ahead could be seen. They were accelerating blindly into a storm at over a hundred twenty miles per hour, with no hope of avoiding anything that might loom out of the ice fog ahead, and Brian longed to hear Tyson say the magic word.

"Rotate!" Tyson's voice finally filled the cockpit. Brian responded instantly, pulling the yoke and feeling the nose of the 767 rise smartly. The big Boeing bounded free of the surface then. He pulled to fifteen degrees nose up, and ordered gear up.

"Roger, gear up," Tyson responded.

As they climbed through six thousand feet, Brian retrieved the PA microphone. "Okay, folks, we're safely airborne and headed back to civilization."

Cheering and applause broke out through the cabin.

As soon as Brian had called Seattle, he dialed Elizabeth.

Some three thousand miles away, sitting on the edge of her bed in London, Elizabeth Sterling let her breath out as the phone rang. "Elizabeth?"

"Yes, I'm here, honey." *Thank you, God. Thank you.* Elizabeth ran the words in her mind as Brian's voice filled her ear again.

"We're going to Goose Bay, Labrador. We're all fine, Elizabeth. It's going to be okay now."

Thursday, March 16, 9:00 a.m.—Pan Am Headquarters, Seattle

CHAD Jennings stood at the door of Pan Am's boardroom. One by one he shook the hands of the departing board members, each of them grim-faced at the necessity of appointing an acting president

247

while Ron Lamb struggled against partial paralysis in a nearby hospital. Jennings kept a tight rein on his expression, cloaking the excitement he felt at his new position.

Joseph Taylor, Pan Am's rotund chairman, was last out the door, grasping Chad's hand in his meaty grip. "Okay, you've got the ball. Keep me informed—daily if possible. And if Ron can regain speech, you keep him in the loop. He's still the titular head of this thing."

"I will, Joe. Don't worry."

"Another thing," Taylor added. "Ron thinks very highly of Elizabeth Sterling. I'll admit she did a good job on setting us up, but so far all she's done is to go chasing around New York looking for money. Now I think . . ." Taylor noticed Fred Kinnen, vice president of finance and Elizabeth's assistant, standing close by.

"C'm'ere." Taylor walked Jennings toward Ron Lamb's office. They stepped inside, and Taylor closed the door behind them.

"Okay, here's the deal. Sterling's a smart financier, but I don't think she's gonna cut the mustard in forcing good ol' boys to loan us money, especially with Wall Street convinced we're in trouble."

"What's the point, Joe?" Jennings asked.

"Point is, that's your most important assignment. You start looking for a loan, too. Right now. We need eighty-five million by Friday, or we're all out of a job."

Thursday, March 16, 5:00 p.m.—Inverness, Scotland

ELIZABETH Sterling tightened the collar of her coat against the stiff north wind and pushed through a door into an ornate interior of dark wood laced with the aroma of beer. Creighton MacRae had been curt and specific. "The Phoenix at five sharp. It's a pub. Bottom of Academy Street."

Elizabeth hesitated, letting her eyes take in the men sitting or standing around in small circles. There were only three women in the room. Two were obviously wives or girlfriends; the third was a colorless woman with owlish glasses and clad in a tweed business suit, sitting primly by herself at a table, her briefcase lying open before her.

But where was MacRae? Elizabeth peered around the corner self-consciously, scanning the faces of the men, looking for one that might belong to Creighton MacRae. A young man at the bar returned her gaze with an expectant smile. No one, however, came forward to greet her.

She felt uncomfortable, but she forced herself to move into the room, selecting a small table a few feet from the woman in tweed.

The sudden presence of a neatly groomed man filling the doorway caught her attention. She guessed him to be six feet tall, in his late forties or early fifties. His dark hair was neatly combed, and his prominent eyebrows seemed to connect across his brow, framing a set of smoldering deep blue eyes. His mouth seemed to be frozen in a slightly amused expression. He stood there with confidence as he surveyed the room, then moved into it with forceful agility.

He was ten feet from her table now, and Elizabeth lifted her head in anticipation just as he stopped at the table to her left, his eyes focusing on the dowdy woman in tweed.

"Miss Elizabeth Sterling, I presume?"

The woman looked up in confusion. "I beg your pardon?" she replied, startled.

"If you expect me to call you Madam Vice President, you'll have a bloody long wait, lass," the man said.

The woman folded her hands on the edge of the table. "You've obviously mistaken me for someone else," she said.

MacRae stepped back a half step as his eyes noted Elizabeth at the same time slowly rising to her feet.

"Mr. MacRae, I presume?"

"Miss Sterling?" he managed. He turned from the other woman and muttered an apology as he moved toward Elizabeth.

After shaking hands, she spent a half hour explaining the perils of Pan Am, drawing a detailed picture of the changed loan agreements, the strange appearance of Irwin Fairchild in the equation, and the apparent sabotage campaign. MacRae seemed to be listening carefully to every word, with his eyes probing hers, but occasionally she saw his eyes flicker over her body.

Lloyd White had warned her, but she hadn't expected MacRae's instincts to lock on to her so obviously and so soon—and she certainly hadn't expected herself to respond to his interest, as she felt herself doing.

Unfortunately, it was dividing his attention. Though he appeared

to be listening, his obvious enjoyment of her femininity made her wonder how much he was absorbing of what she was saying. The mention of sabotage, however, changed all that.

MacRae began talking in urgent and angry terms about the battle to destroy his airline. He described how he had traveled the world for two years, trying to document who his enemies were, and preparing the monumental lawsuit he had eventually won and that had left him wealthy, if bitter.

"I knew, you see, that no one person or firm could have done the coordination necessary to deny me credit worldwide. But finding every company involved was quite a trick. I came to know computerized banking and communications systems very well. It's amazing what you can find out when you know where to look."

"Do you still have that network?"

MacRae smiled and nodded. "Aye, I do."

"Would you help us? As a paid consultant, of course?"

He sat back, as if seeing the executive under the exterior for the first time. At last he leaned forward, his eyes studying hers. "I had no intention of doing this, but you were right to think this would arouse my anger. I don't know what I can do for you, but I'll try."

"Your fee?" she asked.

He smiled. "Ever the financier, eh? Very well. I'll charge you two thousand pounds per day, plus expenses."

"Done. Ten days in advance, whenever you want it."

He raised his magnificent eyebrows in surprise and nodded with grudging respect at her decisiveness. "I'll bill you later."

Creighton MacRae seemed confident that whoever might be orchestrating a financial sabotage campaign against Pan Am could be discovered and neutralized. "We've got to find out who's doing it," he told her, "as well as who's bankrolling the effort."

"How about why?" she asked.

"If I find the *who*, you'll know the *why* automatically."

12

Friday, March 17, 7:45 a.m.—Inverness, Scotland

THE flight back to London departed at 10:00 a.m., but the phone by Elizabeth's bed at the Craigmonie Hotel rang at 7:45. She found an agitated Alastair Wood on the other end.

"It's bloody well coming apart, Elizabeth. Someone's got hold of a list of my people and has been faxing a devastating little packet of information to each of them, implying that you and Pan Am are lying about your performance and prospects."

"What's being said? And by whom?"

"I don't know who's responsible, but I have copies of what he's sending, and I've already faxed them to your hotel."

"Hold on," she told him. She looked at the rug by the door, spotted the papers, and leaped out of the bed to get them.

There were four pages, two of them appearing to be purloined Pan Am interoffice memos, and two purporting to be financial summary sheets for the previous four days. One memo was supposedly a note from Chairman Joe Taylor recommending to Ron Lamb a rapid Chapter 11 bankruptcy filing as the "only way out." Of the two financial summaries, one was the current weekly cash flow, which showed an airline in deep and potentially fatal trouble.

"These are all fraudulent, Alastair. I'll have my office provide the true ones in an hour. They'll show a totally different picture."

"I'm sure they will, but the problem is, they've already poisoned the waters. I've got two of my key participants ready to bolt."

"Can you have them come in for a meeting this afternoon? I can make the investors you've lined up feel better if you'll get them in a conference room by, say, one thirty p.m."

"It shall be done, dear lady. Have a good, quick flight back."

She snapped her notebook computer on now, pulling out the home phone number of her assistant Fred Kinnen.

"Hello?" The voice was sullen and sleepy.

"Fred? This is Elizabeth Sterling. I need some emergency help."

"Eliz— Oh. Are you still in London?"

The question froze her in her tracks.

"Fred, who told you where I was?"

"You did. I got a fax from you, remember? You asked me to send a packet of financial data to a number over there immediately."

She sank back on the bed. "Fred, I sent no such fax."

"But it had your *signature* on it." He sounded panicked.

"What exactly did you send, Fred? And to whom?"

"Well, I prepared a special weekly cash flow printout through today's close of business, along with a weekly traffic analysis." He had the name of the company and the fax number he had sent the materials to, and a copy of "her" fax with a forged signature.

"Okay, Fred, what did you send in the way of a memo?"

"You asked me to write one to Ron Lamb, just saying you were making progress, and send a copy to that fax number, and I did. I had no way of knowing it wasn't you."

Someone used it as a template and inserted their own language, Elizabeth thought.

"Get a pen, Fred. Here's what I need, and I need it in the next three hours, faxed to Mr. Alastair Wood at the following number." She gave him a list of financial summaries for the previous five months. "Those will show a prettier picture, I trust."

"Yes, of course. We were doing well until the past week. This week our load factor's been at forty-eight percent, but our director of reservations believes that's false. She thinks someone's worked a computer scam on us to show our flights as overbooked."

"Have her call me with the details. Call Joe Taylor at home. Ask him if he ever wrote a memo to Ron recommending Chapter Eleven. And have our entire finance staff stand by to provide figures, summary sheets, and whatever else I need to convince a roomful of doubting financiers that we're not really in trouble. Understood?"

"Yes, ma'am."

"Oh, and one other thing. Unless you actually hear my voice, don't follow any orders that supposedly come from me. If you get any more faxed orders over my signature, call me immediately."

She hung up then, checked her watch, and called Brian at his office, feeling a warm rush when his voice came over the line.

With Clipper Forty's passengers placed on other airline flights that would take them to Frankfurt, and replacement electronic components installed, Brian and his crew had ferried their 767 back to Seattle from Goose Bay, with Kelly and Virginia Sterling aboard.

While they headed for Bellingham, Brian had headed for the office.

She told him of the latest agony, including the upcoming briefing. "I don't know whether I can pull it off, Brian."

"Tell them the truth. Tell them," he said, "we're being attacked. But tell them that Pan Am has the opportunity for faster growth and greater monetary success than any other airline on earth. And tell them that eventually whoever is behind this will end up paying Pan Am hundreds of millions in damages."

That puzzled her. "You've got an idea, don't you? If you've got a theory, let me have it."

"You can't tell anyone this. They'd think you were paranoid. But ask yourself this: Whose profits do we threaten? We threaten the big three in North America, don't we? Which carriers own the biggest reservations systems and have the biggest bucks to sabotage a growing airline like ours?"

"Brian, that's crazy. There are foreign carriers with as much at stake, too. It could be any one of them."

"Elizabeth, I'm not saying that the leaders of those airlines or their boards would ever do anything like this, but somebody with money and some degree of sophistication is tearing us apart. The only reason I can see that happening would be to protect the dominance of the big three. Nothing else makes sense to me. There's no way a single nut case could plant a bomb in our 747, slip a reworked black box in my 767, and block you at every turn in the financial world. No lone wolf could be that clever or powerful."

"Have you told Ron Lamb? I'm sorry. I mean Chad Jennings." The thought of Jennings running the company still seemed very strange. He seemed competent enough, but Brian had already hinted at a darker side to the man's abilities.

"Not yet," he replied, "but I may. We've got to act fast before they finally succeed and bring one of our airplanes down in flames."

They ended the call, with Elizabeth feeling hunted again.

Later, as she was opening the door to leave, the phone rang. This time Creighton MacRae's voice filled her ear. "Miss Sterling?"

"Elizabeth. Please."

There was an uncomfortable hesitation. "Very well. Elizabeth, then. Call me Creighton."

"Thank you, Creighton. I'm in a rush for the airport."

"I'll be brief. I spent last evening in research, and I've some promising leads. I'm leaving this morning as well, but I shan't tell you where just yet. I'll be in touch in a few days. And Elizabeth—"

"Yes?"

"I must warn you of something. If your company is up against the level of adversary I believe you are, understand that they have enough money to corrupt anyone. Trust no one with information."

"Don't *trust*— What exactly does that mean?" She knew she sounded skeptical.

"Dammit, woman, it means don't confide in anyone you aren't absolutely certain of. I'm going to try to find you a new credit line, as well as a path to the enemy camp. But you'd be well advised to assume they're watching and listening to you at all times."

She sat deep in thought and said nothing. But she was overwhelmingly glad he was on her side.

THE flight to London was a blur of rapid note-taking as she tried to organize what to say. At Lloyd's, Alastair Wood greeted her with a stack of faxed financial reports from Fred Kinnen and a detailed briefing on the men who would be in the meeting, as well as background information on those who had yet to sign. Elizabeth took thirty minutes to prepare herself before Alastair showed her into the modern screening room and introduced her to the two dozen men who shook her hand and sat quietly staring at her.

All but five had already signed the loan agreement. As Alastair closed the door to the small theater, she walked to the front with a relaxed air and smiled, willing the shaking inside to go away.

"Gentlemen, I appreciate your coming on short notice. In a nutshell, someone is trying to sabotage our deal by misrepresenting our performance, our stability, and our potential for profit. The new Pan Am is *not* unprofitable. We are *not* failing as a business. And we are perhaps the brightest star in the airline constellation."

Alastair had the new information sheets from Seattle converted to overhead transparencies, and Elizabeth began showing them now, tracing the rising curve of business until the previous week. Then she ticked off the elements of sabotage, including the FAA violations, the physical tampering with two airplanes, the files, and the reservations systems, and outlined how the first C.F.O. had stupidly dismantled her carefully constructed start-up package.

There was a smile in the first row. Then another investor caught her eye and nodded. Many of them had been attacked in business, and they could identify with what Pan Am was experiencing.

She opened the floor to questions and fielded each one with ease. After an hour and twenty minutes the vast majority of the men were smiling and relaxed, and all but one of the critical five seemed satisfied. That man was portly and distinguished, and his voice rasped into the room with thundering authority.

"Young lady, nary a bit of this blizzard of paper with which you are attempting to inundate us has been counterchecked or endorsed officially by any independent auditor. Put another way, I've heard nothing I can well and truly trust. You may indeed be correct. And then again you may be selling worthless paper."

The poisonous comment settled over the audience like a shroud.

"Lord Richards," Elizabeth began, noting his surprise that she knew his name. "You were the driving force behind the successful growth of St. James Publishing through the acquisition of two old-line hardcover houses in New York." She was reaching to the bottom of her memory, marshaling a dozen half-read magazine articles and praying she wasn't overstepping her ability to recall the details.

"You, sir, in 1989, if I recall correctly, faced a massive difficulty on Wall Street when a major junk-bond issue was imperiled, and your empire seemed to be virtually teetering on the brink. In a series of meetings you told the financial community that your basic enterprises were well run and profitable. They almost didn't listen to you, and in fact a number of your backers bolted. You had to refinance—a process that cost you millions of pounds and months of time. Do I have my facts straight, Lord Richards?"

She held her breath as she watched his face. Finally a slow, sly smile began to spread across his craggy features as he answered, "Indeed you do, Miss Sterling."

"Good. Because my point is that those who believed you and stuck with you profited handsomely, and I have long admired you for not giving up in the face of opposition. In regard to the sound and profitable nature of your company, the world discovered that you *were* telling the truth."

She looked directly in his eyes. "And, sir, so am I."

THE PAPERS WERE FAXED TO Seattle to a surprised Chad Jennings, who signed them as acting president. By 4:00 p.m. Barclay's Bank had transferred via wire eighty-five million dollars in loan proceeds to Pan Am's main receiving account at Seafirst Bank in Seattle.

Friday, March 17, 10:00 a.m.—Pan Am Headquarters, Seattle

As ELIZABETH Sterling settled back in a first-class seat aboard a British Airways flight direct from London to Seattle, an exhausted Brian Murphy was sounding an alarm to a roomful of shocked executives at Pan Am headquarters. Ninety minutes after he started, they filed out of the boardroom in a daze—apparently someone was out to ruin the new Pan Am.

Chad Jennings was still in the boardroom, questioning Brian, when Ralph Basanji, Pan Am's public affairs vice president, arrived late for the meeting and caught corporate general counsel Jack Rawly on his way out the door. "Can you fill me in, Jack?"

Rawly nodded and motioned Basanji toward the elevators. "Basically our chief pilot thinks that all the things that have been happening to us could be a coordinated assault by someone seeking to protect big-three market dominance."

"What if he's right?" Basanji asked.

"He may be," Rawly shot back. "But to my way of thinking, we may have a problem here. Chad Jennings is buying this theory, and a few minutes ago up there he was talking about going public with his suspicions. I saw a look in his eye that has me spooked."

Ralph Basanji's mouth dropped open. "Going public?"

"He might. And he could trigger a massive lawsuit if he did."

BRIAN Murphy made a rapid departure from the Pan Am headquarters. His appointment with the FBI was set for 11:00 a.m. at the Federal Building, several blocks away. He was already late.

Agent Loren Miller and NTSB field investigator Michael Rogers were waiting for him in a small, utilitarian conference room.

"Okay, Brian," Miller began, "on the file folder we found only one print not attributable to your staff, and it was someone's single index finger. That print, however, is a bit strange. It's as if the guy took off a latex glove at one point and purposefully left a single print on the folder. It was clear, crisp, and pressed right into the fibers."

257

"Have you matched the print to anyone?" Brian asked.

"No. But wait. There's more." Miller pulled some papers from a transmittal folder. "We *have* found a better set of fingerprints on one of the circuit boards in that black box of yours."

Miller plopped the papers down in front of Brian. "The index fingerprint from your black box and the index fingerprint on your file folder belong to the same individual. The guy who rifled your files and most likely tipped the FAA also had contact with the circuit board that forced you down in the Arctic."

Mike Rogers took over. "You'll recall we found some pieces of chromium on the underside of the wing of Clipper Ten, the 747? You also know about the newspaper reporter who got a tip that a mechanic's wrench had been left in the engine?"

Brian nodded. "I saw the article. The little jerk tried to imply we were feigning sabotage to cover up our so-called negligence."

"Adrian Kirsch was the reporter," Rogers said, "but give the man credit. He reported the phoned-in tip to me before he printed it. We now believe that the man who called Kirsch was the same one who planted the bomb on Clipper Ten. He knew damn well there was no wrench in that engine, but he'd set it up to look that way."

"How?" Brian asked.

"We think the plastic explosive was wrapped around a real chrome-plated wrench and placed inside the cowling near the top of the engine. Whoever designed it was not a professional saboteur."

Brian nodded. "In other words, if you want to make Pan Am look incompetent, you do just enough damage to destroy the engine in a way that makes it look like mechanical failure, but you want the airplane to limp back so all this can be found out."

"Exactly," Rogers replied.

"By the same logic, then," Brian said, "the guy didn't expect I'd lose both engines in flight with what he did to the circuit board, which means he may have been trying to cause an in-flight abort and merely cost us money and public humiliation."

Brian sat impassively for a second as his mind turned over the possibilities. "It fits. Whoever did this was an amateur at sabotage, someone who was just trying to cause trouble for us, not kill people. In both cases, though, he went too far and screwed it up."

Miller cleared his throat. "There's one more item. The Bureau is of the opinion that someone on the inside is making this sabotage campaign much easier for whoever's carrying out the specific acts."

"A Pan Am employee, you mean?" Brian sounded alarmed.

"Or a former employee, which is equally possible."

RALPH Basanji slammed the door of his car and fumbled with the key, trying to calm down. He'd discovered that Pan Am's acting president had just done a telephone interview with a newspaper reporter and was now headed to a local TV station for an interview.

Chad Jennings was just getting to his feet when Basanji located him in a back room at KIRO television. "Ralph," Chad said with a saccharine smile.

"Uh, could we talk, please?" Basanji began.

"Sure. I'm finished here." The reporter and crew thanked him, and he walked out to the parking lot with Basanji.

When they were out of earshot, Basanji whirled on Jennings. "Chad, did you say anything in there about blaming other airlines?"

Jennings met Basanji's gaze and didn't blink. "Yeah, I did."

"What did you say?"

"The truth. That United, Delta, and American are trying to run us out of business with a dirty-tricks campaign."

Basanji closed his eyes momentarily and groaned. "You have a board of directors, Chad, and an executive committee, and they should have been in on this, as should I. We don't have any proof. What did you say about the 747 and the 767 incidents?"

Jennings smiled. "Nothing, of course. I'm not crazy."

They returned to the office separately, walking in on a frantic beehive of activity. Every telephone line seemed to be in use, with executives and secretaries alike awash in some new crisis.

Basanji caught the eye of an administrative assistant, motioned her over, and asked what was happening.

"The baggage-routing computer," she said. "It's gone nuts. Sometime this morning it decided to start sending every passenger's bag to the wrong location on different airlines. We've got"— she checked a computer printout—"fourteen bags headed for Bangkok on Thai Air, several dozen routed on United to all sorts of destinations, and"—she looked up at him over her reading glasses—"one lonely little cosmetic case bound for Katmandu, Nepal."

Ralph excused himself and slipped into his office, closing the door. There was a worse disaster in the making. The evening news would air on the East Coast in less than an hour, and Jennings' accusations would undoubtedly be a lead story. The legal department needed to gird for warfare.

He picked up the phone with a weary sigh and dialed Jack Rawly.

13

Friday, March 17, 4:45 p.m.—Denver, Colorado

THROUGH the huge western window of the two-story penthouse, the Rocky Mountains spread like a frosted tapestry of rock and snow beneath a cold azure sky dusted with cirrus clouds.

A lone figure clad in a silk bathrobe paced before the mountain panorama, cordless telephone in hand. His footsteps echoed from the surface of the oak floor as he navigated past a massive collection of signed, first-edition works on the American West.

"By the way, where the hell have you been?" The man growled the question into the phone. "I've been waiting for you to call back for the past three days. I sit here in Denver watching the news and hear that a 747 almost crashed because someone blew up an engine, and then a 767 loses both of its engines, and I can't help wondering if these little inconveniences might just be connected to you somehow. Don't forget this for a second. I haven't even *suggested* screwing around with the planes. Yeah. . . . Yeah. . . . You better not have had anything to do with—"

The man paused to listen.

"The woman's smarter than you thought she was. We lost her in New York, and it took days to find her again. She turned up in the U.K., and we tried to neutralize her efforts there, but we were too late. Now we go on to the next phase. It's time to finish this. Her ability to interfere is coming to an end. I've got a timetable, and I'm under more pressure than you'd ever understand."

The man picked up his coffee cup and took a sip as he watched an airliner climbing out to the west over the mountains.

"Let's just put it this way. We're on schedule, and the clients are happy. It should be over by the first. Now get back to work before somebody sees you hanging around a pay phone."

ELIZABETH rubbed her eyes briefly before reaching down to close her briefcase and carry-on bag, ignoring the irritated look of the customs officer as she waited for Elizabeth to clear her table.

She'd slept for hours on the flight from London, but not well. Now she lifted the bags, walked to the exit, and pushed through the doors—right into Brian's arms. She sighed deeply at last and rested her head on his chest. "I missed you so much."

"I missed you, too," he said gently.

Brian took her bags and pointed toward the underground shuttle to the main terminal. Elizabeth reached up and brushed Brian's cheek with her hand as the car began to move. "I want to go straight to Bellingham. Will you come with me? After what happened up there in Canada, I want all three of you with me."

He thought it over quickly and agreed. It was Friday night, and he'd done about as much as he could do before Monday.

"Thank you," she said, not taking her eyes off his. "So tell me what's going on?"

Brian lowered his voice. "In a nutshell, the FBI has evidence that whoever rifled my files also caused my engines to fail over the Arctic. Chad Jennings has gone public and accused United, American, and Delta by name of trying to run us out of business. It's the lead story on two of the three networks this evening, and sure to be all over the newspapers in the morning."

Elizabeth realized her mouth was hanging open, her mind racing to calculate the effect on the financial community, none of whom would believe that the big three could be behind Pan Am's problems.

"I need to get my briefcase and overnight bag from the office," Brian said. "You need to stop by the condo?"

She shook her head.

MARVIN Grade ignored the fact that he'd already retied his tie three times, and did it again. He wanted to look sharp and professional, so he had decided to wear his one remaining business suit. His fulminating hatred for the airline that had ruined his life had suddenly been emasculated by the reality that the company was

261

~~offering him a job.~~ It made no sense, but it was an answered prayer.

After the collapse of the original Pan Am, he had spent the following years in a mist of deep depression, alcohol, odd jobs, and overdue bills. When the new Pan Am started up, there had been hope again. He remembered all too well having been turned down. The shock left him nursing a dark hatred that grew like a cancer.

Grade's thoughts returned to the present. The Pan Am recruiter said to be at the Seatac operations center at 9:00 p.m. He slid behind the wheel of his old Chevy and fired up the throaty engine, checking his watch. *Eight fifteen. I've got forty-five minutes. Good.*

He accelerated slowly down the street, oblivious to a dark sedan sitting in the shadows a half-block away. As his taillights disappeared around the corner, the sedan's engine came to life, following at a discreet distance the same path Marvin Grade had taken.

BRIAN slowed as he drove his BMW across the double speed bumps at the entrance to the operations center parking lot.

"No gate guard yet?" Elizabeth asked, surprised.

Brian shook his head. "The guard box will be installed next week. Meanwhile, we've got a guard roving around with a radio."

Brian nosed the car into his marked parking space adjacent to the office building's main door.

"Why don't you run in, and I'll stay out here," Elizabeth said.

She locked the doors before reclining the seat and adjusting her head. It would feel good to catch a few minutes' sleep.

MARVIN Grade rolled into the Pan Am operations parking lot. He headed for the area in front of the main building adjacent to the hangar, as he had been instructed, and quietly selected a space to the left of an expensive-looking BMW.

Grade checked his watch. He had ten minutes. *I'll get out of the car in five minutes and walk in exactly on schedule,* he decided.

A chill shuddered through him. He reached over to turn up the heater, leaving the engine idling as he watched the time and waited.

ELIZABETH had slipped almost instantly into a deep sleep, but now, slowly, she swam back to the surface of consciousness. Without moving her head, she noticed the driver next to her and the odd fact that in an almost empty parking lot he would choose a spot right next to Brian's car. A creepy feeling began to grip her. The way the man sat hunched over the wheel and stared straight ahead was unnerving. That and the fact that the engine was still running.

A dark car entered the far side of the lot, triggering feelings of relief that she wasn't all alone. But the car stopped just inside the gate and sat there with the engine running. She watched with increasing apprehension as the driver killed his headlights.

A small voice began to whisper in her mind, *Get out. Now!*

She leaned over the driver's seat and found the trunk release. In one swift motion she opened her door and swept to the trunk to grab her briefcase—the instinctive need to protect the papers and the computer inside as great as the need to protect herself. She slammed the lid closed, noticing that the car in the distance hadn't moved and neither had the driver next to her.

Elizabeth moved toward the main door of the building. Fear clawed at her as she reached for the handle. It wouldn't open!

There was a sound from behind her now. She glanced over her shoulder and saw the shadowy figure behind the wheel look at his watch and then glance in her direction.

She rattled the door as hard as she could, finally pushing against it with her shoulders. The sound of a car door being opened reached her like a thunderclap. The man was getting out.

Panicked, Elizabeth began alternately pushing and pulling on the glass door, nearly falling backward when it flew open in her hands.

She rushed inside then, closing the door behind her and turning the lock. She headed down the hallway as fast as she could without running, her heart pounding, half expecting to hear the sound of smashing glass behind her.

She found Brian closing a file cabinet in his office. He looked up, startled at her wide-eyed appearance. "Elizabeth, you okay?"

As she opened her mouth to reply, the impact of a massive explosion shuddered through the office complex, accompanied by the sounds of breaking glass and crashing metal.

"What on earth was *that?*" Brian's voice was loud and panicked.

They reentered the hall together, moving toward the front of the building. The door had been shattered and thrown inward. Glass and flying metal had wrecked the outer reception area. They stepped gingerly over debris as they walked out into the parking lot. The flaming hulk of a car lay on its side to the left. Brian recognized it as the remains of his BMW. Where the Chevrolet had been sitting, there was only the twisted skeleton of a car, its interior on fire. People were beginning to converge from various directions. In the distance Elizabeth thought she saw the occupant of the dark-colored car get out and run toward the scene as well.

Brian's voice rang in her ears. "My God, Elizabeth, there was a bomb in my car!"

She realized she was shaking her head. His BMW was shattered, but the basic structure was still intact. The old car, however, had been literally blown apart.

"No. It was the car next to us. He was running his engine."

"There was someone in it?"

She nodded as her mind filled in the implications.

Brian's arms enfolded Elizabeth, and he swung her around to face him. "What made you— I mean, thank God you came in!"

"He scared me," she said, knowing there had been more to it.

"I guess I was wrong," Brian said quietly, stroking her hair and holding her tight. "They *are* homicidal."

Monday morning, March 20—Seattle

THE mood in Pan Am's corporate headquarters was dark. Elizabeth's attitude matched. They were under attack, and the weekend had been a joyless search for answers as she and Brian had huddled at her mother's house in Bellingham, the seriousness of the situation suppressing even Kelly's ebullient personality.

No one yet knew precisely why the car had exploded in the operations parking lot at Seatac. But the campaign against Pan Am seemed to have taken a very personal turn.

On Monday morning Pan Am's frantic executive committee called a board meeting to deal with the public relations crisis Jennings had unleashed. The articles and television reports about Pan Am's accusations against the big three had ballooned into a major story.

The big three carriers had each returned fire with a fusillade of bitter denials and furious denunciations, all laced with counter-threats of legal actions for defamation.

The board ordered Jennings to apologize or be fired. At first he refused, but just as quickly relented, retreating to his office to call the media for yet another round. Grumbling and furious, the outside directors milled toward the door, Joseph Taylor among them. Elizabeth was heading quietly for the same door when Taylor snagged the sleeve of her dress. "That was good work, getting the loan from London. I'll be frank with you. I didn't think you could do it."

She smiled at him. "I'll be frank with you, Joe. I wasn't sure I could either."

The board meeting had been over for less than ten minutes when Brian phoned from operations with the news that the Seattle police and the FBI had discovered the identity of the man killed in their parking lot. "Marvin Grade is the name. Get this. He was a former mechanic for the old Pan Am. Personnel says he applied to us for a job during the start-up a year ago, but wasn't hired."

"So he was just holding a grudge?" she asked. Elizabeth hadn't expected that possibility. She and Brian had both assumed the bombing was related to all their other troubles.

"Who knows? The police are searching his house right now."

"You reminded them about the dark car?" she asked.

"Yes. And they don't believe it was connected either. You said you saw the driver run toward us after the explosion? They say that shows that whoever was in the dark car wasn't involved. So it was probably a spectacular suicide—or an accident."

"What do you mean, an accident?"

"The guy brings a bomb into our complex, planning to install it in an airplane, but it blows up prematurely and kills him."

"Which would make him the saboteur," she said softly.

"It makes sense. A former mechanic who probably knew the 767 and 747. Anyway, we might know something after they search his house. I'll call you as soon as I hear anything."

Elizabeth hung up the receiver at the same moment she noticed an ashen-faced Fred Kinnen in the doorway holding some papers.

"Fred? You look like you're in shock."

"I am," he said, sliding the two-page fax across the desk to her.

She recognized the letterhead. It belonged to the lead bank of the consortium that provided Pan Am's revolving credit line.

"We've got seven days to repay one hundred forty million dollars," he said, "and half of the remaining balance at thirty days and sixty days, respectively, from the date of this notice. Otherwise, they formally declare us in default."

She saw his eyes fall and realized he was holding something back. "Fred? What do you know about this? What happened?"

"Jennings happened. Just after the board appointed Jennings acting president, the chairman took him aside. I couldn't overhear all of the conversation, but later Jennings told me that Taylor said he had no confidence you could get the money in time. Joe Taylor directed *him* to try to get the eighty-five million through other channels, including local banks—or so he claimed."

Elizabeth sat back, thoroughly stunned. "And, of course, the first thing they did was call up and ask questions of our current debtholders, tipping them off that we were desperate, and giving them all the excuse they needed to trigger this provision."

"Yes."

She looked down at the desk, formulating a battle plan. "Go get the general counsel, Jack Rawly, and ask him to come in here."

"How about Mr. Jennings?"

"We'll deal with him later."

By noon Elizabeth had relayed the news to Brian by phone. She was probably violating officer confidentiality, but it didn't seem to matter anymore. Brian was the only one she could really trust.

"If we don't repay one hundred forty million in seven days," she explained, "they declare us in default, the lessors reclaim the airplanes, and we're no longer an airline."

"What can you do?" Brian asked.

"I'll keep trying to negotiate, but Brian, I don't think they *want* to negotiate. This is part of the campaign, don't you see? I surprised them by getting the eighty-five million. When I did, they had to find another way to shut us down, and this is it."

"Then it's all but over," he said.

"Not necessarily. I could save us if I could replace the entire credit line."

There was another line holding for Elizabeth. She ended the call with Brian and punched the appropriate button, unprepared for Creighton MacRae's voice. "I want you to call me in thirty minutes from a public phone," MacRae said, and relayed the number.

"We've got a major crisis in progress. I can't leave the office."

"You want to solve that crisis? Then do as I ask. Please." There was a long pause before he continued. "Do you remember I warned that you might be dealing with a very powerful adversary?"

"I remember."

"Turns out I was right. Call me in thirty minutes, and don't be followed to whatever phone you use."

She left the office almost immediately and took the elevator to street level, walking north at a brisk pace as the cellular phone in her purse rang, with Brian on the other end.

"Elizabeth, Marvin Grade was our saboteur. They found plastic explosive, timing devices, false I.D. badges—the whole works—in his house, *and* electronic parts stolen from United in San Francisco. He was just too ham-handed to do things right, and he blew himself up accidentally. He wasn't after either of us."

"Thank goodness for that," she said, wishing she could sound more convinced. "But it doesn't explain all the other things, though."

"What? You mean the financial stuff?"

"*And* the interference with reservations, *and* our baggage computer, *and* the creepy thing in New York at Eric's apartment."

"Where are you?" he asked. "I can hear traffic."

"Heading up the street to a meeting," she lied. She decided not to mention Creighton MacRae. She promised to check in later.

Elizabeth put the cellular phone away and resumed walking, making certain no one was tailing her. She found the perfect pay phone, out of the mainstream. MacRae answered immediately.

"Can you meet me this afternoon in Vancouver?" he asked.

"I suppose so. Why not Seattle?"

"You're being watched in Seattle."

"Watched? You're sure?"

"Yes," he said. "Elizabeth, I'm in Houston, Texas, at the airport. I've got an old friend here who's interested in helping. We're flying up there in his jet in a few minutes. I've arranged for a financier from Hong Kong to meet us in Vancouver as well. Incidentally, I'm aware of what your acting president did last Friday. While he's correct that the interests of the three major airlines are involved, they're not responsible."

"I don't understand. You mean—"

"All three airlines stand to benefit greatly if Pan Am fails, but their hands are clean. Someone else is doing all this to protect his investment in the big three."

"Our enemy is a stockholder of all three airlines?"

"My guess is a huge, very rich company. In the meantime, you need money."

"More than you know." She filled him in on the cancellation of the revolving credit line.

"Very well," he said at last. "Then we're going to have to dance to their deadline. March twenty-seventh, you say?"

"Yes," she said. "The same day our new round-the-world service is starting from New York. Creighton, if we had anything we could take to court, we could get an injunction and stop the clock."

"I understand that. I just don't have the proof yet. It should be easier and quicker to get you the money to pay them off than to find enough evidence to make a court case this rapidly. People at that level are very good about covering their tracks."

"When do you want me to be in Vancouver?"

"First, get there without uninvited guests tagging along. Drive. Don't fly. And for heaven's sake, don't tell anyone at your office." He gave her the rendezvous address in Vancouver and rang off. They would meet in the Tai Pan Suite of the Delta Court Hotel at 6:00 p.m.

14

Monday, March 20—Seatac Airport

CAPTAIN Dale Silverman had been the only Pan Am employee to get a good look at the man who'd apparently sabotaged Clipper Forty's electronics in Denver on March 10. The description he'd given the FBI fit the late Marvin Grade like a glove. Silverman had been on a layover in Tokyo when he'd heard the news of Grade's death. Back home at last, the Pan Am captain stood at the bulletin board in the pilot's lounge at Seatac operations, intensely scanning a clipping about Marvin Grade's demise—a story containing a picture the local newspaper had obtained from Grade's ex-wife.

There was only one thing wrong.

Silverman removed the clipping and walked straight to Brian Murphy's office. "Brian, you got a minute?"

"Of course, Dale. What's up?"

"You've seen this picture?" Dale Silverman carefully placed the clipping on the desk and pointed to the face in the photograph.

"Yes. Why?"

"Brian, this is not the man I saw in Denver."

Monday evening, March 20 — Vancouver, British Columbia

ELIZABETH accelerated across the Cambie Bridge and into the heart of Vancouver. At sundown the premier metropolis of western Canada transformed itself into a rare and exquisite blend of man-made and natural beauty, and to Elizabeth, having grown up just to the south, in Bellingham, it was always like coming home.

Elizabeth took a parking spot on the street near the hotel, locked the car, and pulled her briefcase from the trunk—surprised when the routine act suddenly brought back the horror of Friday night.

A gaunt young man with Asian features answered the door of the Tai Pan Suite and introduced himself as Jason Ing from Hong Kong. Creighton MacRae had already arrived with Jack Bastrop, the owner of the Falcon 50 business jet that had carried them up from Texas. Both men got to their feet to greet her.

Elizabeth wasn't prepared for Jack Bastrop. He stood well over six feet tall, but the physically intimidating effect of his barrel chest and heavily jowled round face became even more pronounced when he extended a huge, beefy hand.

"Delighted to meet you, Miss Sterling," he said in deep, rumbling tones, relaxing her with a friendly smile.

Creighton's handshake in turn was proper. But she realized he had lingered a few seconds with her hand in his.

He motioned them all to the large couch. Elizabeth sat next to Jack Bastrop, with Jason Ing on her left. Creighton took the chair closest to her. "In brief," Creighton said, "Jack helped me when no one else would consider it. In the end, we didn't succeed, but—"

Bastrop raised his hand, and finished the sentence. "We didn't succeed, because the consortium against Creighton was far too well organized. I, too, have a score to settle. I'm equally incensed, and equally eager to block international bullying."

"You think there's a chance I'm fighting the same company?" Elizabeth asked.

Jack Bastrop looked at Creighton MacRae as if to ask how much he should tell her. MacRae nodded.

"Does the name Irwin Fairchild ring a bell?" Bastrop began.

She knew she looked shocked. "I saw him in New York last week, and yes, I know the felonious little snake all too well."

Jack Bastrop explained that Fairchild had been the operative who spent more than a year engineering the financial isolation of Creighton MacRae's start-up airline in Britain. "He was working," Bastrop continued, "for a group of corporations in the U.K., France, and Germany. When Creighton finally won his lawsuit, it was against that consortium, but Fairchild escaped liability. Yet he was the dirty-tricks facilitator—the financial triggerman. Now he's doing the same thing for another group. By the way, Fairchild does a lot of his money laundering through a bank in Hong Kong—a competitor of Jason's called the International Trading Bank, or ITB."

Creighton spread a hand-drawn chart on the coffee table. "Elizabeth, I want to give you a clear picture of what you're facing and why." He pointed to the names of United, American, and Delta along the bottom of the chart. "U.S. deregulation of the airline industry was an unmitigated disaster. The idea of zero government control of what is essentially a public utility destroyed the industry. It also created opportunities for fast-buck artists like Irwin Fairchild and others to steal billions and leave old-line airlines in ruins. What's left are the big three and a few successful niche carriers, like Southwest and Alaska. When your Congress finally decided to block foreign takeovers of U.S. airlines, that frustrated a powerful group of investors in Europe and Asia, who had been planning to cash in on the lucrative U.S. airline market. But those chaps didn't go away. They've now secretly secured a huge interest in each of the big three airlines—or so we believe—and you've become a threat to their plans."

"How," Elizabeth asked, "can anyone expect to make a killing just by owning shares in all three?"

"Because their plans are global. The consortium I ran afoul of had a master plan to hold monopolies in various world markets. If there were three carriers in a particular market or country, they would quietly buy up all three, and then slowly eliminate competition among them as they divided up the pie."

Elizabeth's eyes flared. "You're saying this is a worldwide plot?"

"No. This is a brilliant business plan, designed to create huge multinational transportation giants with monopolies all over the world and unlimited power."

"I had no idea," Elizabeth said.

"Just think of the potential if you could own and control major airports, and all sides of the transportation equation coming in and out of them—airlines, trains, buses, and all cargo shipments. You'd have an endless money machine and more power than many governments. Anyone who wanted to go anywhere or ship anything would ultimately have to deal with you."

"Could they really put such a thing together?" Elizabeth asked.

Creighton nodded. "The men running this type of organization think ten to twenty years ahead. They know that if they move slowly, they can change almost anything to their liking. The problem comes when you block them cold, as my airline did, or conceptually threaten their master plan, as I believe Pan Am has done. Then they move with frightening speed to protect their interests."

Creighton spread out his hands in an explanatory gesture. "Look at your situation in America, Elizabeth. The big three are no longer in real competition with each other. They essentially own the North American market, and they've been able to divide it up."

"And Pan Am is the skunk at that tea party?" Elizabeth asked.

"Quite right," Creighton agreed. "It threatens their control and their profits."

"But you said the big three themselves aren't behind this anti–Pan Am campaign."

"I'm sure they aren't. Oh, the three majors would be very appreciative if you'd just go away quietly. But they're far too ethical and concerned about being prosecuted themselves to ever engage in sabotage. I'm convinced they have no inkling of what some of their stockholders are doing."

"This unidentified company in Europe? Can we unmask them?"

Creighton hesitated, then nodded slowly. "It will take a lot of investigatory work, but the first order of business is to get Jack and Jason here busy finding you a credit line of five hundred million dollars by next Monday."

There was a chance, Jason Ing told her, that the money could be made available that fast. They would all have to move rapidly. Jack Bastrop, an independent Texas oilman, was willing to put up seventy-five million as part of a package.

"Jason represents a bank in Hong Kong that is a neophyte at airline investments," Creighton said. "But they have money in shipping and real estate all over the world. Whatever he puts together may be completely unconventional."

She took a deep breath. "As long as it's legal," Elizabeth said carefully, "I can't see why unconventionality would be a problem."

"Can you follow me to Hong Kong tomorrow?" Ing asked. The question took Elizabeth by surprise. Her inclination was to say no. The airline was unraveling around her. But without a new credit line or a hundred forty million in cash by next Monday, the new Pan Am would be yet another footnote in the corporate history books.

I have no choice, she told herself. The future of Pan Am once again came down to one person: Elizabeth Sterling.

"I'll book myself on the first flight out of Seattle."

"No!" Creighton's voice was a little too forceful, and he raised his hand in apology. "I think it would be far safer if you let me book you under another name. You mustn't be traced to Hong Kong or followed anywhere."

She looked at him, searching his eyes, wondering if she was imagining a slight edge of personal concern in his tone. She smiled and nodded. "Okay, we can work that out."

Elizabeth casually checked her watch. "I'm getting a bit hungry. Would you gentlemen consider joining me for dinner?"

"Jack's got another engagement, and Jason has a party to attend, but I'd be delighted to take you to dinner," Creighton said instantly.

She smiled as wryly as she could at him. "On Pan Am's expense account?"

He looked momentarily off balance, then recovered as he smiled back at her in shared understanding. "Eventually, of course."

ELIZABETH was in her element in Vancouver, and the discovery that Creighton MacRae had never visited the city before gave her an advantage that she found herself using with delight.

"There is only one appropriate restaurant for an evening like this," she told him when they had stepped out onto the lanai of the

Tai Pan Suite for a few minutes. "The Teahouse, in Stanley Park."

"I believe I've heard of it. The Teahouse, you said." He excused himself to make a reservation.

She insisted on driving her rental car, enjoying the opportunity to play tour guide as they navigated the short distance to the park. She paused on the overpass crossing the Lion's Gate suspension bridge, watching the traffic whiz by beneath them.

"Creighton, is Jason Ing a millionaire in his own right?"

There was silence for a minute. "He's very wealthy, and from a wealthy family in Hong Kong. He was planning on moving to Vancouver when Hong Kong reverts to China, and that's why he owns the hotel. But he's changed his mind."

"He owns the hotel?"

"Yes. He bought the hotel last year. By the way, there's a suite reserved for you at no cost."

Elizabeth turned into the restaurant parking lot.

Creighton examined the restaurant with obvious pleasure. "Rather like something out of the Victorian period in Covent Garden. Almost a greenhouse, with all that glass."

Their table by the western windows was perfect, the candlelight a warm complement to the twinkling lights of freighters at anchor in English Bay. The meal, too, was world class, as she had expected. As they talked, Elizabeth watched the candlelight play off Creighton's weathered features, and basked in his occasional smile.

With the dessert gone and coffee before them, Creighton replaced his cup and looked down a moment before letting his eyes rise to engage hers. "I must say, Elizabeth, you are without a doubt the most unique combination I believe I've ever encountered. You're feminine and businesslike at the same time—smart and hardened, yet soft and beautiful."

"I'm glad you approve," she said.

She felt wonderful, and she was quite sure he was the cause.

After dinner they walked together toward the water, hands pushed deep in the pockets of their respective coats, letting the conversation drift to more personal matters.

He was ten years older than she, and their childhood memories of the world were slightly out of sync. But he, too, had grown up in love with the seashore and the wind, and the gentle bite of cold sea breezes in early spring. They sat on a wooden bench, and he fell silent. Elizabeth saw again the reflective look she'd noticed several times earlier.

"There's a bit of the Heathcliff in you, Creighton MacRae," she said at last. "I hope that doesn't insult you as a Scot."

He glanced at her, surprised, and smiled. "Not at all. Though I'm neither a gypsy nor a foundling like Heathcliff."

"But you do plead guilty, I take it, to a brooding nature?"

"I was raised to be a vicar," he said, "and vicars are by nature brooding. At least my father was."

"What happened?"

His gaze turned to the bay. "Rebellious sons, determined to embrace the world and all the ladies within it, are hardly suited to a life of stern, unyielding drabness. I was determined to break loose. I decided I couldn't escape my father unless I escaped Scotland, too. Going to college in America seemed the perfect answer."

"Which university over here?"

He snorted softly and smiled. "The University of Texas, on a scholarship. Texas became a metaphor for freedom. Cowboys, wide-open spaces, limitless opportunities. It was a wonderful school, and I shot through a bachelor's and M.B.A. program in five years and headed back for London to be an airline executive—only to find that my American business degree impressed no one."

"Your M.B.A. didn't open doors?"

Creighton shook his head. "Not without the appropriate background and family. Three years later a gentleman named Freddy Laker took me in and taught me the practical side of business in Britain. And yet I've never really been accepted in that club."

"Would it surprise you if I said I understood? On the subject of not being accepted in the good old boys' club of American business, a female with an M.B.A. understands that problem all too well."

"We do have something profoundly in common, it seems," he said softly. "I'd never thought of that."

There was an electricity in his gaze, and she felt herself responding. This is silly, she told herself. I hardly know this man. There was only one way to regain control of the situation, and that was to end it. "I'm getting cold out here," she lied.

"Permit me to remedy that, Elizabeth." His arm moved expertly behind her, and his right hand gently gathered her in toward him.

She jumped to her feet suddenly. "I'm sorry, Creighton. I— It's getting late."

He stood slowly, smiling. "I didn't mean to startle you."

She laughed, but it came out a nervous giggle. "You didn't. I'm not sure what I was thinking. But we *should* go."

It would be better, Creighton pointed out as she drove them back to the hotel, if she left for Hong Kong on a Canadian airline from Vancouver. She could be tracked in Seattle, and the dirty-tricks group would have the airport staked out as well as her condo.

"You said I was being tracked. How do you know?"

"Let's just say Jack Bastrop has some friends in low places. One of them reported this morning that a West Coast security firm has been making a lot of money in the past few weeks following a particular female airline executive all over the map."

The same chill she had felt before worked its way up her back. "Okay, Vancouver it is."

He smiled. "I took the liberty of arranging the ticket. Can you leave with Jason tomorrow at ten a.m.?"

"Ten is okay. Are you coming, too?" She asked the question matter-of-factly, but she found herself hoping the answer was yes.

"No. I'm going to fly back to the East Coast with Jack. We've got a mountain of wire-transfer records to probe."

Creighton secured the entry cards to their two rooms from the front desk. They took the elevator to the top floor, where he handed her the electronic card-key.

"Our rooms are next to each other," he said with a casual air.

Elizabeth thanked him with a proper handshake for the dinner. Almost in unison they approached their respective doors, but she found herself fumbling with the key card. Without warning he put his right hand over hers and helped her move the card into the slot.

The latch clicked and the door swung open, but she turned to him instead. He caressed her face as his lips brushed hers; then he engulfed her in his arms. She rose to meet him, and the kiss intensified, warm and deep and long. She felt herself pull back ever so slightly, and their lips disengaged. She could feel his heart beating at a furious rate, or was that only hers? They stood, startled, looking at each other.

"Elizabeth, I . . . Why don't I want to let you go?" he said.

"I don't—don't know, but we must," she replied.

He let her pull back, his hands gently holding only her shoulders as he lowered his head and forced her to meet his eyes.

"We share a common door, Elizabeth. If you want anything, just tap on it."

She nodded, picked up her bag, and moved into the room, shutting the door without looking back.

ELIZABETH tried to ignore the sound of his moving around next door. She thought of Brian. She thought of Ron Lamb. She thought of anything she could to get her mind off him.

Resolutely she undressed and went to bed. She was anything but sleepy, however. Finally she got up and wandered toward the lights of nighttime Vancouver twinkling through the sliding door. She parted the sheer curtains with one finger, startled to see Creighton standing on his lanai, his hands gripping the railing, his head turned toward the harbor, the wind ruffling his hair.

Just for tonight, what would it matter? she thought.

But Brian's image reimposed itself, propelled by conscience and memory and loyalty.

She stayed in the shadows, watching, as Creighton turned away and walked back inside. Then she turned as well, slipping between the sheets of the king-size bed—alone and confused.

Wednesday, March 22, 2:05 a.m.—Bellevue, Washington

BRIAN Murphy sat at the kitchen table in his house and stared at a blank steno pad. Something about the riddle of Marvin Grade's death was just out of reach. He picked up a pen and drew the pad closer, writing the names of those Pan Am employees who had seen an intruder they couldn't identify as Marvin Grade.

The list was short: Dale Silverman and Ray McCarthy. He drummed on the polished glass table before adding the word "definite" to Captain Silverman's name and "unsure" to McCarthy's.

Whoever it was that Captain Dale Silverman found in the cockpit of his 767 in Denver on March 10, Silverman was certain it hadn't been the late Marvin Grade.

But the mechanic who had seen an intruder in the Moses Lake

hangar was *not* certain. It could have been Grade, he said, but it could have been someone else with a mustache and a similar build.

The feeling that Grade wasn't the man—or at least wasn't working alone—haunted Brian all Monday. Now the idea was robbing him of sleep for a second night. He picked up the pen again and wrote, "No computer equipment in house."

Brian had gone to Grade's house himself Monday evening with a flashlight and a screwdriver, half expecting to be arrested for breaking and entering as he forced his way in through the back door. Grade had supposedly rewired a sophisticated computer board from a stolen 767 black box. Yet Brian saw no home computers, no books on computer technology, and no collection of wires and switches of the kind amateur electronics buffs always have. Nor had there been any listing of such items on the FBI seizure report.

The sound of a passing jet broke his concentration. Brian looked at the kitchen clock. It was 2:21 a.m. He wished he could call Elizabeth, but there was no telling where she was. She had called saying she'd be out of town for several days.

He looked back at the steno pad and wrote the word fingerprints. If Grade had been innocent, how could his fingerprints have ended up on the file folder and circuit board? Not "prints," plural, but "print," singular, he reminded himself.

There was also the matter of the dark car that one of Grade's neighbors had seen lurking near Grade's house Friday night—the same type of car Elizabeth had sighted just before the explosion.

But why was Grade dead? Had he detonated the explosion accidentally as he was getting ready to slip into Pan Am's hangar and sabotage another airplane? Or . . .

Wait a minute. Wait just a minute. Brian began pacing, his eyes staring far beyond his kitchen. What if Grade *hadn't* come to sabotage another airplane? What if he'd had an attack of conscience and decided to tell Pan Am what was happening and what he'd done?

And what if his co-conspirator had found out?

The dark car fits, too!

Elizabeth saw it enter the Pan Am parking lot and just sit there with the motor running, a perfect position from which to detonate a radio-controlled bomb.

And killing Grade would have been a double benefit for his

co-conspirator; for with the sabotage supposedly a thing of the past, Pan Am would relax its security, which would leave the airline vulnerable to another attack.

Whatever the bastard is planning, he'll have to be quick about it. If Elizabeth doesn't succeed in getting the money, it's all over on the twenty-seventh anyway—five days from now.

Brian stopped in his tracks and replayed the previous thought. *That's it!*

He lunged for the phone and dialed Bill Conrad's home number. A sleepy voice finally answered.

"Bill? Brian Murphy. I'd like you to meet me at seven a.m. at Seatac. I know exactly when and where the bad guys are planning to hit us again."

Thursday, March 23, 8:00 a.m.—Hong Kong

ELIZABETH climbed into Jason Ing's limousine at the front door of the new Conrad Hotel in Hong Kong. They had arrived the previous evening after an eighteen-hour flight.

She had developed a deep appreciation of Jason Ing's capacity for work as they had negotiated and discussed their way across the Pacific, forging the basic agreement. Two hours out of Hong Kong he had smiled at long last, happy with the basic outline. The terms of the loan were a bit lopsided in favor of the lenders, but it would be Pan Am's salvation if they could fund it.

The offices of Cathay Alliance, Ltd., were an elegant blend of modern architecture and traditional mandarin decor. Elizabeth complimented them profusely as she and Jason entered the executive suite and a smiling secretary waved them into the large corner office that belonged to the board chairman. The office was empty.

Jason crossed the room and sat down behind the desk, delighted at Elizabeth's surprised expression. "I must apologize, Jason," she told him. "I didn't realize you were the chairman of this firm."

"You were polite not to inquire," he said. "I could have been a functionary, but you treated me like a chairman all yesterday."

After extensive introductions to the other officers of the company Elizabeth spent several hours with Cathay's legal staff, finalizing the form of the agreement.

At noon Jason Ing thanked the last of his departing staff and quietly closed the door of his office before turning to Elizabeth.

"I wanted a few minutes alone with you to discuss the source of these funds," he said.

"I'm not sure I understand, Jason. You were going to pool various sources for the money, were you not?"

Jason's voice was smooth. "We talked yesterday, Elizabeth, about the coming reversion of Hong Kong to Chinese ownership."

"I'm aware of the changes in general terms," she hedged.

"A few years ago we were planning to move to Vancouver. But when we put this company in play for sale, we found that certain, shall we say, interests presented us with an offer that, well . . ."

"Who was it, Jason?"

"Beijing. The Chinese government."

"Jason, are you saying that at least one of the principal investors in this loan, if we conclude it, will be the government of *China?*"

"Does this present a problem?" Jason asked. "I know you Americans are very upset over Tiananmen Square."

"Tiananmen Square has nothing to do with it, Jason. U.S.-certificated airlines are required by law to clear certain transactions with the Department of Justice in advance."

"Can't you get an expedited approval from your government?"

"I can try, but we're looking at a month at the minimum." Elizabeth got to her feet slowly and picked up her briefcase. "I need to make a lot of telephone calls."

BACK at the hotel, Elizabeth telephoned the airline's general counsel at home in Seattle, where it was 8:00 p.m. Wednesday. "Is there any way to accelerate the approval process?" she asked Jack Rawly, after telling him that the government of China was involved.

"Don't hold your breath," he told her.

"Then there's nothing we can do to stop a default on Monday?"

There was a long sigh from Seattle. "Elizabeth, at best I could buy us a day or two with a friendly federal judge. In the meantime, if you get any evidence whatsoever that our lenders have tried to hurt us illegally, let me have it."

"I will, Jack. Thanks."

She replaced the telephone receiver, feeling very alone.

The phone rang almost instantly, and she picked it up. It was

279

Fred Kinnen with news of an unsolicited offer of a new revolving credit line, received from a bank in Hong Kong called ITB. "I think they were fishing," he said. "They wanted an incredible amount of financial information sent by computer transmission, but the man who called Chad Jennings said they would consider a new six-hundred-million credit line."

Creighton MacRae's comment about ITB immediately popped into her mind. It was the bank used by Irwin Fairchild.

"Give them nothing, Fred," she said, "but fax me anything they've sent us in writing. I'll check it out here."

"Does it sound hopeful?" he asked.

She realized she was shaking her head. "It sounds sinister."

15

Thursday afternoon, March 23—Amsterdam, Holland

JACOB Voorster stood for a moment in the outer office of the managing director, his thoughts immersed in the damning evidence he had just given the head of Van Zanten and Vetter, Ltd.

He smoothed his neatly trimmed mustache and checked his appearance with a sideways glance in the full-length mirror to his left, pleased that he had looked thoroughly professional in the presence of the company's leader.

Voorster loved Van Zanten and Vetter. After thirty-three years of service it hurt terribly to have to turn in one of the officers—a senior director—and, by doing so, expose the firm to the possibility of international scandal. His eyes wandered to the polished, lovingly displayed artifacts from the two-hundred-year history of the old-line Dutch shipping company.

The managing director, Herr Frederick Ooest, had called him one of the most capable financial analysts VZV had ever employed. Ooest had listened intently as Jacob described his initial suspicions over his discovery of a sudden, unexplained transfer of millions of dollars to an American corporation from an obscure account—a transfer for which he could find no authorization. The managing director had also complimented him highly for working nights and evenings to track down the name of the VZV employee who had triggered those payments—and why.

And Ooest had promised swift action as he showed Voorster to the door. "I will need, Jacob, all copies and computer disks or anything else that contains material you used to compile your analysis. Everything. Immediately. And you will speak of this with no one, Jacob, inside or outside the company. That is a very solemn order."

Jacob Voorster nodded, and moved energetically toward the big double doors leading to the elevator lobby. He had done his duty. Now the managing director would see to everything else.

Friday, March 24, 9:50 a.m. — Hong Kong

As FAR as Elizabeth could tell from outward appearances, there was nothing unusual about the International Trading Bank of Hong Kong. It was simply a small commercial bank, mostly focused on international finance—but a bank, she reminded herself, somehow associated with Irwin Fairchild.

The assistant manager of international banking greeted her warmly when she walked into his office unannounced and asked to see the operation. Elizabeth had pulled her hair back, worn dark glasses, and presented herself as Ann Murphy, a wealthy widow from Atlanta with money to invest and the need for a correspondent bank in Hong Kong. As she expected, a low-level assistant was assigned to show her around. It took only a few dozen technical questions about the bank's computer banking system to bore the man beyond tolerance, causing him to pair her off with one of the bank's computer programmers as he fled to "other duties."

Elizabeth enjoyed the company of the programmer—a young Hong Kong woman who seldom got to meet the bank's customers. They sat side by side at a computer terminal in the woman's small office as she explained how the system could be used by a customer with a home computer. "So," Elizabeth asked, "I could call from Atlanta, using my computer, and move my money around, right?"

"Yes," the woman agreed with a smile, "from anywhere in the world. It's a simple menu-driven program even for our internal use." Her fingers flew over the keyboard, and a page of entry codes and passwords appeared next to a list of employee names.

She pointed to the screen and turned to Elizabeth. "My department is the only one that can open these security files, of course. But everything else is safely available on-line because we use a three-tiered entry-code sequence that's impossible to break."

She deleted the security-code display as she reached for a ringing telephone, and then excused herself for a minute, leaving Elizabeth alone with the computer terminal.

Elizabeth had memorized the keystrokes the programmer had used to open the security file. The possibility of searching ITB's files from a distance with her laptop computer and a telephone hookup was too enticing an opportunity to pass up.

She scanned the doorway, listening for footsteps. There were none. Elizabeth repeated the keystrokes, delighted that after a brief pause the entire list of security codes and passwords reappeared.

She looked at the doorway again, listening to the small noises from the hallway. For the moment the hallway was empty.

With her right hand Elizabeth took a notepad from the woman's desk, using a pen to scribble down the code and password sequences for two of the names listed. She was on the third group when the sound of footsteps reached her ears.

Suddenly the programmer was back in the doorway, smiling at her guest, unaware that the security codes were showing on her screen.

Elizabeth stood up abruptly, keeping the pad out of sight as she gestured down the hallway. "A young man came in here just a minute ago looking for you," she fibbed.

"A tall man? Balding and tall?" the programmer asked Elizabeth.

"Yes."

"Oh. Excuse me a minute." She was beaming. "That's my, ah . . ."

"Boyfriend?" Elizabeth offered with a sly grin.

The woman laughed self-consciously as she stepped from the room. The second the footsteps had faded down the hall, Elizabeth finished copying the last few digits and cleared the screen. She had slipped the pad in her purse by the time the woman returned.

"So, was he the guy looking for you?" Elizabeth asked, smiling.

"I know he was, but he wouldn't admit it. He's shy."

RETURNING to her hotel room, Elizabeth connected her laptop computer to the phone line. Her entry to ITB's main computer was almost instantaneous. As the programmer had said, everything was done with easily understood menus.

For a half hour she navigated around the different files, eventually finding one that promised to reveal stock ownership. With two short commands on her keyboard, the file poured through the phone line and into her computer's memory. She paused to open it and take a peek. The names of the principal stockholders were listed alphabetically. Elizabeth stared at them disbelief.

Irwin Fairchild's name was not there, but another name was: Nicolas Costas, the former chairman of the defunct Columbia Airline systems. Short and stocky, with silver hair, Costas was hated and reviled in airline circles. For years he had been a legend on Wall Street for his devastatingly successful attacks on organized airline labor and for his amazing ability to pull massive amounts of financing from thin air.

Nick Costas owned over eighty-five percent of ITB—which meant that he had to be behind any loan offer from the bank.

Elizabeth sat back, trying to figure out what Costas' ownership meant. Could ITB's sudden interest in offering money to Pan Am be an innocent commercial transaction? Or was Costas himself trying to manipulate them? But how and why?

She used the bank's search routines to look for any occurrence of the last name Costas. There were dozens of Costas accounts— checking accounts, investment accounts, savings accounts, transfer accounts, and more. She copied the files to her hard disk, then went back in search of more until the name was exhausted.

The menu prompt returned: ENTER SEARCH NAME.

The image of Irwin Fairchild popped into her head.

"Where Nick Costas slithers, Irwin can't be far behind," Elizabeth muttered to herself.

On a hunch she typed the name FAIRCHILD and hit ENTER. Suddenly listings for two checking accounts under the name of Fairchild, Irwin B., appeared on the screen. She copied the files to her disk.

But if she *had* uncovered a rat's nest, what other parts of it should she document?

Creighton MacRae believed some huge European company was behind the sabotage effort. She tried searches for various corporate customers of the bank, looking for companies headquartered in European cities and pulling in a long list of them.

She had finished the latest file transfer when her computer screen changed and a new message from the ITB computer took over:

YOU HAVE EXCEEDED ENTRY TIME OR DOWNLOAD ALLOWANCE. ENTER
APPROPRIATE EXTEND CODE WITHIN THIRTY SECONDS.

Elizabeth stared at the message. The bank's computer had probably been programmed to embed a security destruct program whenever data was downloaded to a distant computer. It had been triggered now. If she broke the phone connection without the host computer sending the right code sequence to cancel the program, it would work like a virus and destroy her data.

She had placed the piece of paper with the purloined entry codes next to the computer. Now she pulled it to her, remembering a strange reference on the bottom of the security screen, which had said something about inverting the codes. She had entered 3376 for the last of the three required code sequences. Would it be the first string or the second or third that she should invert?

Ten seconds left, she calculated.

Go with instinct, she told herself. The third sequence felt right.

Elizabeth typed in 6733 and hit ENTER, expecting the worst.

The screen went blank, and her heart sank. Then suddenly the normal prompt was back.

She paged carefully through the files and the data, finding it all there. She quickly ended the session, commanding a disconnect.

ITB's computer shot back a parting message:

THANK YOU MR. LEE. YOU WERE CONNECTED FOR 58:04 MINUTES, AND
YOU WERE CALLING FROM 521-3838.

Elizabeth stared at the screen for a few seconds before understanding its meaning. The computer thought it had been dealing with Mr. Chong Lee, an ITB loan officer.

She removed the phone cord from the computer and began looking through the downloaded files, relieved that she was dealing with only her computer now.

The Fairchild accounts appeared on screen with all the details of deposits and checks over the past year. There was one very large deposit for two hundred thousand dollars on March 13.

She had arrived in New York looking for an eighty-five-million-dollar loan on March 12. The coincidence was titillating.

She switched to Costas' checking accounts. There was a debit on one of them for exactly two hundred thousand dollars. It had been deposited directly into Irwin Fairchild's checking account.

There was no doubt. Nick Costas himself had made at least one large payment to a man she had caught interfering with a pending Pan Am loan.

She reached for the telephone. It was midnight back in New York, where Creighton MacRae was staying. He answered on the first ring, and she told him the story of ITB's loan offer and Nick Costas' ownership of the bank. MacRae said nothing until she was through.

"Elizabeth, Jack and I discovered that during the last year, each time your debtholders made large advances to Pan Am under the revolving-credit agreement, those very same sums of money were imported from a single offshore bank."

"ITB?"

"The same."

She told him then of her raid on ITB's computer. When she was through, Creighton's voice was in her ear again, carrying a new and urgent tone. "Elizabeth, get the hell out of there. Now! Come back to New York, and I'll help you take this to a judge."

"I need to check with Jason Ing first, because—"

He cut her off. "You've got to get out of there *now*. These people are powerful and ruthless, Elizabeth. They can have you arrested for breaking into their system. You've stumbled into the middle of a snake pit, so get out of there. Right now!"

He said good-bye, and they disconnected. The phone had been back on the cradle thirty seconds when it rang again. She picked it up, expecting to hear Creighton's voice once more. Instead, a high-pitched computer tone warbled in her ear. The ITB computer had found her room number and was trying to reestablish the link.

Elizabeth dropped the receiver back on the cradle.

It rang again, and she let it as she turned to the closet and began flinging her things into a bag. She zipped the overnight case with shaking hands, closed her briefcase with the computer inside, and yanked open the door to the hallway, gasping at the sight of Jason Ing standing just outside her door.

"Where are you going?" he asked in an amazed voice.

"Is your car here, Jason?"

"Yes, but—"

"Take me to the airport. Now. Please!"

Ing nodded immediately and joined her in a dash to the elevators and the lobby. She shot out the door and into the back seat of his limo. As they pulled away, two police cars rushed past them and turned into the entrance of the hotel.

"How close are we to concluding this loan, Jason?"

"Close. Cathay Alliance will loan you the one hundred forty million in an unsecured note by Monday. But we'll wait for your government's approval before bringing in funds from Chinese sources."

"I think we can go to court and block the creditors from calling a default now. That will give us some additional time."

At the airport, they found that a British Airways 747-400 was scheduled to leave nonstop for London in thirty minutes. Not until the plane had reached cruising altitude did Elizabeth relax. She checked carefully to make sure no one was watching, then opened her computer and used several spare diskettes from her briefcase to make copies of the most incendiary information she had purloined from ITB's computer. If something were to happen to her computer—or to her—the information had to survive.

Brian had once told her about an alcoholic steward who had for years hidden a flask of vodka behind the mirror in the rest room of a Boeing 727. There were removable panels in each rest room, Brian told her. She locked herself in one of the rest rooms and began searching the wall, finding a small latch that gave access to an inside compartment. She wrapped the diskettes in an airsickness bag and carefully placed them behind the insulation in the compartment.

She returned to her seat and picked up the satellite phone and called Creighton in New York.

"Elizabeth! Thank the Lord. Where *are* you?"

"On a British Airways jumbo headed for London. Why?"

"I just got off the phone with Cathay Alliance. Jason Ing was kidnapped outside the airport, and his driver was killed. I was afraid you—"

"What do you mean, kidnapped?" she interrupted.

"Hundreds of people saw it happen, but the police couldn't get there in time. So far there's no ransom call."

"I know what they want. They want me and what I've got in this computer. Creighton, there's a story our chief pilot tells about an

286

airline crew member and a flask of vodka. If anything happens to me, that story will lead you to copies of what's on my hard drive."

"I don't understand that, but I'm writing it down. When are you scheduled into London?"

"Ten p.m. tonight," she told him.

"Someone will meet you at the gate in London with the tickets on the next flight out to New York."

Friday, March 24, noon—Amsterdam

THE police inspector made one last note to himself before looking at Jacob Voorster. "For the moment you are free to go, Mr. Voorster. We will continue to gather the evidence, and then we will present it to a magistrate, who will decide whether or not you are to be arrested and tried for embezzlement."

Jacob's right hand fluttered above the scarred surface of the wooden conference table. "I did nothing. I've never taken a penny of my company's money."

The inspector gestured toward the door. "You will have a chance to present your arguments to a magistrate, not to me."

Jacob retrieved his overcoat and hat with shaking hands and walked through the door of the police station. He sat behind the wheel of his car for fifteen minutes, reliving the previous hour.

The police had been waiting for him when he arrived at his office, as had his immediate supervisor, who slammed a computer printout down in front of him. It listed the transactions of a bank account at Barclay's in London, now containing over three hundred thousand guilders, all of it coming from VZV payments of bogus invoices for stock investments that didn't exist. The account, which he had never seen before in his life, had been traced to him, they said. A passbook for the same account had been found in his desk. It had been planted there, of course, but he was fired instantly.

His mind filled with hurtful thoughts of disbelief and betrayal. It was the morning after he had turned in a senior director to the managing director. The connection—though he longed to believe otherwise—was obvious.

Not since his wife had died of breast cancer five years before had life looked so bleak. Jacob started his car and drove slowly home. He parked in front of his small suburban house and approached the front door, looking for signs of forced entry. He had been told to turn over all his office files and disks, and he had. But had they guessed he had copies at home?

Now the second set was the only hope to prove himself innocent. The house was pristine, and the damning collection of evidence was where he had left it, including the strangest evidence of all—VZV's purchase of a Hong Kong bank that had been subsequently all but given to Nicolas Costas. For what reason he didn't know.

It would be useless to fight VZV's trumped-up charges directly. VZV was too strong and clever and could create a hundred such fake accounts with correspondent banks. It came down to a matter of survival. To prove himself innocent, he would have to prove his beloved company guilty, and of a much greater crime.

The enemy of my enemy is now my friend. The paraphrased quotation rolled around in his head. He began stuffing the papers and disks into his briefcase, along with his passport. He had but one possible ally now, and that was the new Pan American Airways. He would approach them in London. He had already made a reservation on a seven-o'clock flight to Heathrow. If he could save them, perhaps they might be persuaded to return the favor.

Friday, March 24, 9:00 a.m.—Seattle

BRIAN Murphy found Bill Conrad in the upper first-class lounge of Ship 609 as it sat behind the closed doors of the Seatac hangar.

"We've been over all four engines, Brian, and the electronics and baggage compartments. They're starting on the interior. I told my people we think someone's likely to try to blow this bird out of the sky on Monday between Seatac and Kennedy. If anything's been planted on this ship, we'll find it. You still going to captain it?"

"Since I'm the one who predicted the attempt, either we cancel the flight or I'm honor bound to fly it."

Conrad got up and walked over to one of the windows. "Jennings thinks all this is nonsense, but I could care less."

"Bill, did you ever order a rubber stamp? You know, like one with your signature on it, or something?"

"I suppose I have at one time or other. Why?"

"I found out how easy it is to get creative with rubber stamps. For instance, I get your fingerprint, have a stamp made, and instead of ink, I just rub my hand on it to get it full of natural oils, and then I press it down on, say, a manila folder. Someone comes along and finds the print. Could they tell it wasn't you in person?"

Conrad turned from the window and stared at Brian. "What're you driving at?"

"Suppose someone did that with Marvin Grade's index finger?"

Bill Conrad sat down. "They only found the print for Grade's index finger, right? And that's the sole reason they maintain Grade was the saboteur?"

Brian was nodding energetically. "On my pilot file folder and on the circuit board, that's right." He pulled a small, red-handled stamp from his coat pocket, rubbed it with his hand, and pressed it onto a glass inlay on one of the teakwood tables. The clear image of a fingerprint was left behind.

"That's my fingerprint, by the way. I had it made yesterday to prove the point."

TEN miles to the north, at Swedish Hospital, Pan Am President Ron Lamb looked up from a stack of papers and focused on Public Affairs Vice President Ralph Basanji's worried expression. "Ra—Ralph get me th—the computer."

Basanji picked up the small laptop from an adjacent table and placed it on Lamb's lap. Ron's left hand flew over the keys.

> Jennings is ruining us! Why didnk . . . didn't Taylor fer . . . fire him after the newspaper/tv attack on the big guys?

"I don't know, Ron, but he's so busy playing games with this issue of who's after us, he's doing nothing about the real problem. Elizabeth Sterling is somewhere trying to get us the money."

Ron Lamb resumed typing.

> its easier without trying to hit upr case. elizabeth's good person . . . capable and smart. if anyone can do it she can, but we need to know what's going on with her, who she's talking to daily.
>
> get joe taylor in here to see me. i want jennings out of my office. i intend to resume my duties as pres. find elizabeth for me too please. tell her to call me here. we're not going to let all these years of hard work go to hell without a fight!

ELIZABETH had just cleared customs when Creighton MacRae appeared at her side, scooping up her bag and smiling at her.

"I've brought a legal team along, Elizabeth: Jack Rawly, your general counsel, and another attorney he's retained in New York. They're waiting for us across the field on board Jack Bastrop's Falcon Fifty, which will go back to New York in thirty minutes."

He took her arm gently and guided her through the throng of passengers, brushing past a balding man in a business suit who turned and called out to Elizabeth, "Excuse me. Ma'am?"

Creighton stopped as Elizabeth turned.

"I'm Jim Cleghorn, Pan Am's London station manager. Ms. Sterling, would you have a moment to come to my office and help me out with a slightly odd situation? I've got a fellow in my office, a well-spoken gent who wants to relay some information to us that he says is urgent, but he'll only speak with a corporate officer."

Creighton shook his head openly and looked at Elizabeth. "We really don't have time, Ms. Sterling."

She smiled. "I'm sorry, Jim. We have a private plane waiting for a transatlantic flight."

"Not to worry. I'll take care of it."

Creighton led the way to where a black Bentley was waiting to take them to the aircraft. "I know you're probably exhausted."

"Not really. I'm okay."

"Good. I thought we could work and plot strategy aboard."

"Any word on Jason Ing?" she asked.

Creighton shook his head as they pulled up to the airplane.

Less than a mile across the airport, in the main Heathrow terminal, Jim Cleghorn glanced at the distinguished-looking man seated on the other side of his desk. "I'm sorry, sir, but it would really be helpful if you told me what this was about."

"I cannot. Only to an officer."

"I ran into our chief financial officer just a few minutes ago in the terminal, and if I could have told her what you wanted—"

The man lurched forward in his chair, his eyes flaring. "Your chief financial officer is here?"

"*Was* here. She's headed for New York, I think, on a private jet."

290

The man rose to his feet. "Will you send a message to your people in New York that I must speak with her? This is vital for your company. It is so important that I will fly there at my own expense to speak with her."

Cleghorn looked up at the man. "Okay. I'll let them know." He pulled a pad of paper across the desk. "Your name, sir?"

"Jacob Voorster, formerly of Van Zanten and Vetter."

Saturday, March 25, 7:00 a.m.—Hong Kong

NICOLAS Costas gripped the balcony railing of his multimillion-dollar apartment on the mid-level slopes of Victoria Peak, staring at the harbor as he ground his teeth.

Two very alarmed men stood in the shadows of his living room expecting the worst, one of them the British expatriate chief operating officer of ITB, the other the head of ITB security. Neither of them had ever met the third man in the room, whose name was Choi. The leading member of a powerful Kowloon underworld family, he stood to one side looking quietly comfortable and waiting for Nick Costas to come back in.

Costas returned to the room, eyes ablaze with fury as he looked at his two employees; he then softened his expression and turned to face Choi Hee. "How bad is your guest feeling?"

Choi smiled an evil smile. "He'll live."

Costas nodded. "It would be appreciated if he were to remain your guest until Monday evening."

"I believe those wishes can be accommodated. On the subject of what he knew, we don't believe the woman told him anything of substance. All he seemed to know was that she was flying back to San Francisco, as we told you."

"He fooled you, I'm afraid. I had one of my people meet that flight in San Francisco. She wasn't there. This is the second time she's slipped out of the net."

Choi bowed and left. Costas waited before turning to the two bank officers, his voice at high volume. "You two idiots better be telling me the truth about the files."

The chief operating officer nodded furiously. "We know she looked at the files. But the security system would have erased them when she tried to download."

291

"Hell, she probably knows now that I own the bank."

"Nick, if you—"

Costas grabbed the man's tie with the quickness of a striking snake and jerked him viciously. "Where is she?"

The phone rang, and Costas released the man as he moved to answer it. After a brief exchange he replaced the receiver.

"Well, she showed up in London and got on a private jet bound for New York a while ago."

"What are you going to do?" the man asked.

Nick Costas turned back to the balcony. "What I should have done to begin with. But it's probably too late."

Friday, March 24, midnight—Seattle

WHEN his panicked client had finished talking, the man replaced the telephone handset and returned to his makeshift workbench.

He shook his head and chuckled to himself. So the airline was bending heaven and earth to keep anything from happening on the round-the-world inaugural aircraft as it flew from Seattle to New York. So what? A small change in plans he could easily handle.

The man slowly inserted a battery and carefully soldered the positive wire to the positive terminal. With the wires in place, he checked to see that the enabling switch was in the off position and began to pack it in a video camera battery case.

Once finished, he placed the package in the bottom of his camcorder case before peeling off his latex gloves. It was time to shave off the mustache, change his hair color, and pop in a set of blue-tinted contact lenses.

Pan Am's head of maintenance and its chief pilot were trying to play detective and find him, he knew. So far neither was getting close. But both men were wild cards in a deadly game.

And wild cards had to be neutralized.

Saturday, March 25, 10:30 a.m.—JFK Airport, New York

JACOB Voorster was astounded and angry.

"You are telling me I was misled in London?"

The Pan Am passenger service agent smiled a rueful little smile and shrugged her shoulders. "Sir, Ms. Sterling is based in Seattle."

"You must help me reach her or your president or someone in

292

authority by phone," he said. "This is an emergency. Your airline is under financial attack. If I do not reach the right person in your company, you will have no company. Can't you understand that?"

She drummed her fingers on her desk, then spoke. "Okay. If you'll wait in the outer office, I'll find someone of corporate rank, and we'll see what can be done."

"Thank you," Jacob said.

Thirty minutes later the agent emerged from her office with a notepad and a smile. She handed him a Pan Am ticket envelope and another slip of paper. "Our flight to Seattle leaves tomorrow at eight a.m. I've got a round-trip pass for you in this envelope. I'll put you up tonight at a hotel at our expense. Mr. Chad Jennings, the vice president of operations, will be at the airport on your arrival in Seattle. When I told him what you told me, he was very eager to meet you. He says you've found the right officer."

JACK Rawly looked at the paper-strewn table of the ornate conference room, the battlefield of nearly eight hours' work. In reality it was the living room of a Manhattan hotel suite, but it had served as the Pan Am war room since the airline's general counsel had assembled with three New York–based attorneys just before noon.

Elizabeth had departed in midafternoon to make a series of calls to Seattle and continue her last-minute efforts to secure a loan. By 6:15 p.m. she was back, relaying word that Chad Jennings had been relieved of his temporary post as acting president by Ron Lamb, who was running things from his hospital room.

"Any word from Hong Kong?" Rawly asked.

"Jason Ing is still missing, and his company is unwilling to transfer any funds without him, even if we resolve our problems with U.S. approval."

"So it's the courts or nothing." Jack Rawly got to his feet suddenly. "Right. Okay, I'll summarize." He walked to a large white posterboard propped on an easel and examined the different boxes representing such players as Nick Costas, ITB, the lenders, and Irwin Fairchild. "We have the connection and money transfers from Costas to Fairchild down cold. Now, thanks to Creighton MacRae's work, we also have a clear trail of the huge sums of money sent to our revolving-loan lenders from Costas' bank in

Hong Kong and pretty good circumstantial evidence that those sums were always to be passed on to Pan Am as a loan."

"So what do we do?" Elizabeth asked.

Rawly sighed. "We desperately need more evidence, but in the meantime, what we're going to say to the judge is that our lenders, by actively trying to destroy our ability to repay their loans, have breached the loan contract. Since they breached the contract, they can't declare us in default, and we would appreciate a temporary restraining order to prevent them from doing so."

"Have you called the judge?" one of the other attorneys asked.

Rawly nodded. "He'll see us at five p.m. sharp tomorrow."

16

Sunday, March 26, 5:00 p.m.—Federal Courthouse, Manhattan

AFTER reviewing the available evidence, Judge Walter Hayes agreed to sign a temporary restraining order blocking any attempt by Pan Am's lenders to declare the airline in default.

Elizabeth relayed the news to Ron Lamb and Brian before going to a victory dinner with Jack Rawly and Creighton. They were all profoundly relieved. But Jack Rawly sternly cautioned them that the battle would be joined within twenty-four hours, when the lenders, under the name of Intertrust Bank, would be formally served with the restraining order.

Elizabeth searched his eyes. "How will they respond, Jack?"

"They'll immediately try to get a hearing to vacate the order. They want to shut us down tomorrow, when the media is set to watch us anyway on the round-the-world inaugural."

"But can they succeed?"

"Let's put it this way, Elizabeth. If there's any way you can make that payment, make it. If we hand them the one hundred forty million, they can't do a thing until the next repayment is due."

IT WAS 11:00 p.m. Sunday in New York when Jeremy Ing, Jason's brother, contacted Creighton to say Jason had been dumped in a wooded area near the Chinese border. Badly beaten, he had staggered to a highway several hours later.

"In his conscious moments he's frantic to know whether Eliza-

294

beth Sterling is okay, but he's unconscious right now," Jeremy told Creighton. "I'm with him here in the hospital. When he's awake, he keeps saying he has something important to tell you, Mr. MacRae."

"Elizabeth is fine. Tell him that when he wakes up next time. She got away safely, thanks to him. She's with me in New York. But please tell him Pan Am still needs that loan most desperately."

Sunday, March 26, 11:45 p.m.—Near Kennedy Airport

JACOB Voorster turned off the bedside light in another room of the same hotel he had occupied the night before. Sunday morning he had gone to the Pan Am terminal only to find that his flight had been canceled. He had agreed to stay over another day and meet with Chad Jennings in Seattle on Monday instead.

As Voorster drifted into sleep, a few miles away at the international arrivals terminal used by Lufthansa, two neatly dressed men stepped off a flight from Frankfurt. Once they had cleared customs, they quietly began going down the list of airport-area hotels.

The Airport Ramada Inn was the thirteenth call they made.

"Excuse me, I am looking for a Mr. Jacob Voorster. Is he registered in your facility?"

The clerk grabbed a printout he assumed was current.

"Yes, here he is. Oh, wait a minute." The printout was for the night before, but the registration had been for one night only. "I'm sorry, sir. He checked out this morning."

Monday, March 27, 8:00 a.m.—New York City

CREIGHTON MacRae awoke to a ringing phone. It was Jeremy Ing, calling from Hong Kong. Jason was stable and had been conscious long enough to tell his brother to go ahead with the hundred-forty-million-dollar loan to Pan Am.

"It is nine at night here. We cannot finish the deal until tomorrow, but I will work on it."

"Should I have Elizabeth Sterling call you back?" Creighton asked, knowing this meant the funds would not arrive in time.

"Yes, but in the morning. In the meantime, tell her that Jason is afraid for her life."

"What do you mean?"

"The people who kidnapped him were looking for her. They

295

believed that she had something, some information they wanted."

He had barely replaced the phone when Jack Rawly called with the news that Intertrust Bank, as expected, had scheduled an emergency hearing to attack the temporary restraining order.

"When, Jack?" Creighton asked.

"Ten a.m. They want the appeals court to force Judge Hayes to throw out our TRO. So we go to the seventh floor of the Foley Square courthouse and fight it out before three circuit judges."

Two television camera crews and a handful of print reporters were waiting for them in front of the Foley Square courthouse at 9:55 a.m. Creighton MacRae was shown walking just behind Elizabeth up the courthouse steps, both of them identified—mistakenly in Creighton's case—as officers of Pan Am arriving to fight a last-ditch attempt to rescue the airline from an immediate shutdown.

A battery of three attorneys and the chief operating officer of Intertrust Bank were waiting inside with the grimmest of faces when the Pan Am contingent walked in. Neither introductions nor words were exchanged before the three appeals court circuit judges entered and took their places in the marble-and-granite courtroom.

Monday, March 27, 9:57 a.m. — JFK Airport

JACOB Voorster found himself seated in a compartment of a 747 now getting ready for departure for Seattle. Noticing the personal entertainment system, he tuned across several TV stations and settled on one in New York that was covering some sort of trial.

Suddenly Pan Am's name caught his ear, along with the chilling explanation that Pan Am's lenders were preparing to find the airline in default and seize all its aircraft.

The face of an attractive blond woman moved past the camera, and the newsman identified her as Elizabeth Sterling, the corporate officer Jacob had been told was in Seattle and the one he had barely missed in London.

Jacob grabbed his briefcase and rushed to the door, which was closing. "Stop! I must get off."

With some puzzlement the flight attendant pushed the door open to let Jacob escape up the Jetway. He raced for the terminal entrance, passing a host of curious passengers and startling the two men who had arrived from Frankfurt the night before in search of the person they now saw climbing into the back seat of a New York taxi.

Together they ran for the curb, shoving their way past a line of people and into another waiting yellow cab. Pulling a gun on the driver, they told him to follow the previous hack.

Monday, March 27, 10:10 a.m.—Manhattan

THE attorney for Intertrust, Sol Moscowitz, a senior partner of the heavy-hitting firm of Shearson, Moscowitz, and Katz, went through the background of the arguments used by Pan Am for the temporary restraining order before tearing into each allegation. No one in their bank or their lenders' consortium, he claimed, had any knowledge of any actions taken against Pan Am by Nick Costas or anyone else.

Moscowitz, a stubby, well-dressed man, waved his glasses as he warmed to his argument with restrained outrage.

"Your Honors, we request that you overrule Judge Hayes and vacate this ridiculous TRO so that we may hand them here and now their notice of default."

Jack Rawly took the three judges through the evidence again, reminding them that Pan Am stood on the brink of imminent destruction. "We need time to provide evidence that proves the nefarious relationship between ITB and Intertrust and justifies an injunction. But in the interim we need the relief provided by the temporary restraining order."

Chief Judge Richard Kenton sat back for a moment while the other two judges listened. He moved forward again suddenly.

"Very well. Mr. Rawly, I'll give your client until five p.m. this afternoon. But I will reverse Judge Hayes and vacate his TRO at that time if you fail to present the additional evidence."

Monday, March 27, 7:30 a.m.—Seatac Airport

As ELIZABETH and the Pan Am team were leaving the courthouse in Manhattan, Brian Murphy taxied from the gate at Seatac to the end of Runway 16 Left for takeoff. The passenger load was light for a 747—only one hundred forty-two people—but the aircraft was booked full out of New York for their first round-the-world flight.

Brian glanced up at the stream of cirrus shooting by in the teeth of the jet stream high overhead, the only cloud formations in an otherwise crystal-clear sky. With light winds from the south and mild temperatures, it was a perfect day for flying—despite the gnawing worry about possible sabotage.

Ship 609 had been all but disassembled and reassembled, and had been kept under twenty-four-hour guard in the hangar. Brian was confident no saboteur could have slipped through the net. But there was a nervousness in the pit of his stomach when he thought about the tempting target they made. He'd be relieved when at JFK he could safely turn the ship over to the crew flying to London.

His thoughts turned to Elizabeth, as the first officer called for takeoff clearance. After the inaugural ceremony, he planned to monopolize her for the rest of the evening. They needed time together.

And he needed to buy a ring.

"Clipper Fifteen, cleared to go, one six left."

"Clipper Fifteen's rolling."

Monday, March 27, 11:00 a.m.—New York City

DIETER Hoffman, the cabby driving Jacob Voorster, had heard the words "federal courthouse" and driven straight to Brooklyn. The surprise at finding another Dutchman in his cab was pleasant but short-lived; the fellow seemed preoccupied and only marginally responsive.

"Are you in trouble?" Dieter asked him after a long silence.

"*Ja*," he said. "I have lost my freedom and my job."

Dieter pulled up in front of the courthouse. He wished the man well and pointed the way to the courthouse entrance. Then he settled back to wait for another fare.

ONCE inside the courthouse, Jacob stuck his head in several offices, asking for the court where the Pan Am matter was going on. Eventually he reached the office of the chief clerk.

"Oh, the Pan Am matter on TV a while ago? You're in the wrong place. That was the *Southern* Federal District Court of Appeals, on the seventh floor of the Foley Square courthouse. This is the *Eastern* District. You want to go into Manhattan."

THE SQUEAL OF BRAKES CAUSED Dieter Hoffman to look up. Another cab had stopped inches from his rear bumper. It was being driven by a man with swarthy features, whose two fares were spilling out of the back seat and moving in Dieter's direction.

Both of the men appeared at his driver's window as he rolled it down. "Did you just drop off a man named Jacob Voorster?"

Dieter nodded before thinking.

"Which entrance did he take?" the taller man asked. A twenty-dollar bill was tossed unceremoniously through the window.

"The main entrance—there." He pointed at the building.

The two men stepped back and lapsed into German, in which Dieter was completely fluent. Their words chilled him.

"We can't kill him in a federal courthouse. They have guards. I'm not even sure we can get our guns in there," the tall man said.

"You take my gun, then. I'll go through security and find Voorster and get him to come out the same entrance. We'll get him back here and find another place to dispose of him."

JACOB got out of the elevator on the ground floor just as another elevator door closed next to him. It would be easier, the clerk had told him, to cross the main avenue to the east to catch a cab into Manhattan. He headed for the exit. Outside, he pulled his overcoat around himself more tightly and walked briskly toward the curb.

DIETER negotiated the intersection and turned north toward the bridge, driven by the urgent need to put distance between himself and the killers at the courthouse.

The image of a tall man wearing an overcoat and carrying a briefcase shot by on his left as Dieter passed the crosswalk.

It was Jacob Voorster.

Dieter pulled across two lanes of traffic toward the curb. He opened the door and yelled at Voorster, "Get in!"

They were halfway across the bridge to Manhattan before Dieter finished blurting out the story, noticing the haunted look on Jacob Voorster's face.

"I must go to this address," Jacob said.

Dieter looked at the slip of paper. "Don't go to the courthouse. Go to the police."

Jacob shook his head. In his mind, Pan Am's assistance was the key to getting his job and his freedom back. Without them, being stalked by hired killers seemed immaterial. It was 11:40 a.m. With any luck, the Pan Am officers would still be there.

Monday, March 27, 10:30 a.m. — In Flight, Clipper Fifteen

BRIAN left control of the Clipper Fifteen with the first and second officers and returned to the cabin for a private telephone call to Elizabeth in New York. He was hoping for good news.

He didn't get it. The sound of her soft voice carrying tones of inevitable defeat broke his heart. He longed to hold her. With less than three hours' flight time left before landing at Kennedy, they tried to arrange a time and place to meet.

"I was going to be there for the send-off ceremony," Elizabeth said, "but it looks like I'll be in court, hoping Jack Rawly can produce a miracle. Call me about five thirty, okay?"

"Okay, babe. Keep your chin up."

He didn't want to return to the cockpit just yet. He had already decided not to tell the others how grim things were looking.

Brian strolled toward the back of the main cabin. He uttered a few words to a passenger here and there, and stopped to chat with one who had an open video camcorder case on the seat next to him. Something about the fellow seemed familiar. *The way I feel right now,* Brian cautioned himself, *my memory is not reliable.*

He said a few falsely encouraging words to the worried flight attendants before retreating to the flight deck, feeling like a liar.

Monday, March 27, 12:35 p.m. — Foley Square, Manhattan

JACOB Voorster had gone straight to the seventh floor of the court-house. At last the young man behind the counter in the clerk's office turned his attention to Jacob.

"Excuse me, please. It is urgent that I speak with the corporate officers of Pan Am who are here for a hearing."

"I'm sorry, sir, but they've all gone. Hours ago."

"How do I find the Pan Am people, then?"

"You could call the law firm representing them in New York." He looked around, trying to find the records.

Another clerk turned toward him. "That was Sol Moscowitz's

case. His office is in the MetLife Building—the old Pan Am Building—by Grand Central station. I'll give you the location." The clerk grabbed a memo pad embossed with the court of appeals name and Justice Department logo and began writing.

ON THE western perimeter of Foley Square, Dieter Hoffman sat parked facing the courthouse, waiting for Jacob Voorster.

Within minutes another taxi screeched to a halt in front of the courthouse—the same cab, Dieter saw, that had brought the two gunmen to Brooklyn. The two Germans scampered up the steps and into the building. Seconds later Jacob Voorster emerged from the same entrance.

Jacob had spotted the two men and managed to evade them. Now he found a pay phone and dialed the number on the memo paper, relieved that the court clerk answered so quickly.

"This is very important," he said. "I came to your office a few minutes ago, looking for the Pan Am lawyers. My name is Jacob Voorster. There may be one or two men coming in there shortly looking for me by name."

"One of them is already here. Do you want to talk to him?"

"No. Listen very closely," Voorster continued, "and answer yes or no only. Have you already told him where I am headed?"

"No."

"Then don't. The man in front of you has a partner. Both are hired gunmen. They intend to kill me. When the man leaves, if you can alert your security police to catch this man downstairs with his partner, you'll find that at least one of them has a pistol."

"Okay, I, ah, thank—thank you. We'll handle it."

Jacob hung up and returned to his taxi, relieved to find Dieter still where he'd left him. Within ten minutes they pulled up to Grand Central station.

THE shorter of the two Germans had acted innocent when a team of security guards surrounded him in the lobby of the courthouse. He was carrying no weapon, and his passport seemed in order. It would have ended there except for the decision of the lead guard to walk the man to the exit by holding his upper arm lightly.

The German's accomplice, outside the security checkpoint,

looked up to see his partner apparently in custody. The accomplice pushed his hand in his coat and fingered the .38. When the guard and the short German closed to ten feet away, the accomplice pulled his gun free, took careful aim at the guard's head, and squeezed off two perfectly placed rounds.

The shorter man abandoned the dying guard and sprinted toward the security point, broad-jumping the table as his accomplice dropped a second guard. The two men fled the courthouse and leaped into a waiting taxi.

"Drive!" The taller gunman shoved the barrel of his gun into the back of the driver's neck.

"Where do we go?" the driver asked in a tense voice.

"The woman in the court office mentioned the Pan Am Building when I walked in. We go there."

IN THE elaborate waiting room of Sol Moscowitz's office, Jacob Voorster approached the receptionist. "Tell Mr. Moscowitz, please, that I have come from Amsterdam with vital information and evidence involving the Pan Am case."

Within five minutes he was shown into an even more sumptuous office, where a short, fierce-looking man stood in front of his desk.

"I'm very busy, Mr. Voorster. What is this evidence you mentioned to my secretary? Kindly give it to me in summary form."

Jacob briefly described his years with VZV first. "In short, Mr. Moscowitz, I have proof that VZV hired Mr. Nicolas Costas and his company to put Pan Am out of business, and VZV also supplied the money to do that. Nearly five hundred million of that money was loaned to Pan Am as their revolving credit line after we laundered it through several financial institutions, including one in Hong Kong and several banks here in New York."

Sol Moscowitz leaned against his desk and looked hard at the ramrod-straight way Jacob Voorster sat in his chair.

"What," Moscowitz began, "is the name of the lead New York bank in that revolving loan you mentioned? And were they innocent bystanders?"

Voorster shook his head in the negative. "Intertrust Bank here in New York. And no, Intertrust is one of our indirectly owned institutions. VZV pulls the strings."

Sol Moscowitz stood up. "Mr. Voorster, those are potentially slanderous allegations. Do you have any proof at all?"

Voorster snapped open his briefcase, handing over a thirty-page report that Moscowitz scanned quickly, his face becoming more ashen with each page. He handed it back then and walked to his window. For several minutes Moscowitz stood in silence before turning to fix Jacob Voorster with an unyielding stare.

"You've made an unfortunate mistake, Mr. Voorster. You're the Yankee pilot who's landed his fighter on a Japanese carrier."

Voorster looked lost. "I beg your pardon?"

"I am the lawyer for Intertrust Bank. From what you've told me, I think you were trying to find the lawyer representing Pan Am, and I'm going to give you his name, address, and phone number."

Jacob nodded and retreated in confusion after Sol Moscowitz handed him a piece of notepaper. On it was the name of Bill Phillips, an attorney at the New York law firm retained by Pan Am.

"Call them, Mr. Voorster." Jacob turned toward the door as Moscowitz addressed him one last time.

"Tell them, Mr. Voorster, that I play by the rules."

17

Monday, March 27, 1:40 p.m.—New York City

DIETER Hoffman heard the news flash on his AM radio just as he finished dropping off a fare on the East Side. The words "federal" and "courthouse" riveted his attention. The report that the gunmen had last been seen rounding the corner in a taxi caused him to race back to Grand Central station.

JACOB boarded the elevator and started down to the lobby of Moscowitz's building and then took the escalator to the main concourse of Grand Central Terminal. Looking for a public phone with some privacy, he found one at last and dialed Bill Phillips' number. When Phillips answered, Jacob Voorster told him the story in capsule form. Then he asked to speak to Elizabeth Sterling.

"I'll do better than that," Phillips said. "I'll connect all of us on the same line." Motioning to the others, he activated the speakerphone; introduced Jack Rawly, Creighton MacRae, and Elizabeth;

and asked Voorster to repeat who he was and the information he had.

Jacob Voorster took a deep breath and went through it again, mentioning the report that summarized it all, with attachments that provided proof of VZV's intent and involvement.

"Where are you?" Elizabeth asked.

"Somewhere in Grand Central station," Jacob replied.

"We'll be there in fifteen minutes." She told him where to wait on the street, before Jacob interrupted to tell them about the two men who had been chasing him with guns.

"Okay," Elizabeth told him. "Go to the bookstore on the eastern side. Stay tucked away in the far corner. I'll find you."

Jacob left the phone booth and looked for the bookstore. But the entrance eluded him. He stopped near a stairway, wondering where to go for information.

A FEW moments later Dieter Hoffman was racing into Grand Central after leaving his cab at the curb. He spotted Jacob Voorster near the information booth, standing with his briefcase in hand. Dieter began moving toward him, his glance flickering across the faces of several people at the far end of the terminal. Two of them looked familiar, and his heart leaped into his throat as he realized who they were.

These men were killers. They had not yet sighted their target, but Dieter broke into a run nevertheless. He wanted to yell, but the noise might alert the gunmen. Just in case they had noticed him, too, he altered course to the south side of the booth to confuse them. Dieter let the structure's bulk mask him as he slid to the side of it. He reached around and grabbed Jacob Voorster's sleeve just as the two Germans spotted Voorster.

"The gunmen! They're here, and they're coming for you!" Dieter gasped to Jacob, whose eyes flared in fright as he turned and saw the two killers now running toward them.

"When I hit them, run as fast as you can to the nearest exit," Dieter said.

Dieter left Jacob and began moving toward the two men like a train passenger in a hurry. As expected, they parted to let him pass.

Dieter knew he had to time it just right. He dropped to his knees with his arms out, catching the legs of both men as they charged forward, bringing them down hard on their faces. He heard the sound of a heavy metal object hit the floor and skitter across it. A nearby passenger gasped as she saw it was a gun.

Dieter clambered to his feet before either of the killers could regain theirs. He kicked the taller man in the side of the face with every ounce of strength he had, then turned toward the other one, who was crawling for his gun. Dieter, realizing the killer's intention, closed in on the weapon, too, intending to kick it out of harm's way.

To Dieter's utter surprise, the gunman reached out at the last second and yanked the cabby's legs from under him. Dieter had no time to raise his hands to protect his head from crashing against the marble floor when he fell. Everything faded as he lay helpless on the terminal floor.

The killer got to his feet and scooped up his gun. He wildly cast his eyes around the terminal, looking for Voorster. In the distance to the right he saw Voorster disappearing through the gate for track number 32. The assassin broke into a dead run.

Jacob kept a death grip on his briefcase and raced with all his might down the ramp between two waiting commuter trains in the great dark expanse of the terminal. Both of them had their doors open. Jacob darted into the second car of the train on his left.

The conductor had opened the door on the opposite side to examine something on the adjacent track. Jacob moved instantly. He brushed past the conductor, leaping out the open door into the gravel and dirt between the tracks.

An oncoming train was less than a hundred feet away. If he timed it right, he could lose the gunman by appearing to go one way while darting another. He hoped the headlight would blind the gunman and obscure his own desperate move.

Something pinged and whizzed above him. Then another bullet slammed into the concrete wall next to him.

He's shooting at me!

He would jump in front of the train when twenty feet remained.

Now! Jacob darted to the left across the track, his right foot clearing the rail easily. His left shoe caught, however, and his entire body began to rotate downward. He grasped for balance as he fell.

The huge train was mere feet away. With one final effort Jacob leaped to the right. The right edge of the lead car brushed his feet

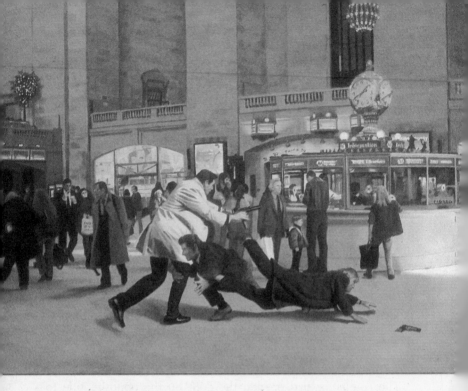

as the trunk of his body cleared the track. The impact spun him into the gravel. Somehow he hung on to his briefcase. He jumped up in an instant and darted in the opposite direction, moving up the long black tunnel from which the train had come.

He could hear the cars screeching to a halt beside him as shouts echoed behind. On impulse he turned and looked back. The gunman hadn't been fooled. He was now on Jacob's side of the train, moving in his direction.

Jacob instantly resumed his dash up the feeder tunnel. He ignored the reflection of a bright electrical flash behind him before stopping in a small recessed doorway. The door was ancient and wooden. He tried the handle, astounded when it responded. He pushed the door open slowly.

The sound of a male voice from the darkness caused him to jump. "This is my hidey-hole, brother. But I guess there's room."

What looked like an old utility shed was dimly lit, and a large man

lounged along the opposite wall, regarding him from beneath a frayed gray watch cap.

Jacob was panting for breath, his words coming hard. "Someone's . . . chasing me . . . with a gun. Is there a way out of here?"

"There's a way out. Hold on. I'll show you."

The homeless man got to his feet, then motioned for Jacob to follow. The man led Jacob through several foul-smelling passageways before showing him a rusted metal ladder.

"Okay. Climb up here and open the manhole cover, and you'll be out in an alley behind the station. Don't hang around here."

"Thank you . . . thank you," Jacob said huskily.

"Ain't no problem, brother. Have a nice day, as dey say."

Jacob clutched his briefcase securely to his chest. Then he began climbing. When he reached the manhole cover, he found it harder to move than he expected. But he finally shoved it up and climbed into daylight in an alley four blocks north of Grand Central.

ELIZABETH HAD BYPASSED THE commotion at the main booth in Grand Central, moving to the bookstore where she was supposed to meet Jacob Voorster. Creighton joined her later, looking grim.

"Elizabeth, I think that mess at the booth involves our man."

They walked over to where the investigating police were located. Creighton took an officer aside and spoke earnestly with him for a few moments.

He returned to Elizabeth. "He says the man over there on the floor was carrying a gun with a silencer. He's dead. Looks like a broken neck. The other guy sitting up and holding his head is a cabdriver who tackled the dead guy and one other."

"The two gunmen Mr. Voorster mentioned."

Creighton nodded. "There's also been an accident on one of the tracks. The policeman doesn't know who, but someone touched the electric rail and fried himself."

"If that's Voorster down there, we've got to get his briefcase. He said he had a report, Creighton. That's the key to everything!"

It was twenty minutes before the body of the dead man was pulled from the tracks. They found no briefcase and little I.D. The word was relayed to Creighton that the man had died with a gun in his hand. Witnesses said he'd been shooting at another man, who'd disappeared behind one of the trains.

"Then where is Voorster?" Elizabeth asked, with tears of frustration hovering at the corner of her eyes.

"Call Bill Phillips," Creighton said. "If our Mr. Voorster called him once, he'll no doubt call him again."

Monday, March 27, 3:00 p.m. — Kennedy Airport

BRIAN Murphy taxied Clipper Fifteen smoothly off the runway after an almost perfect touchdown at Kennedy.

The crew wore smiles at the gate until all the passengers had disembarked. Then they cornered the station agent to hear the latest word on their company's fate.

"You see those men in trench coats through the terminal window?" she asked.

They nodded.

"They're all equipped with repossession papers. I understand the sheriff will be out here to seize this airplane at five."

The crew was scheduled for a layover in New York. None of them wanted to go to the hotel until they knew what was going to happen. They reboarded the aircraft to wait for the outbound crew.

Brian left the others in the forward section of the plane and wandered back, wondering what he would do if the company folded. He was deep in thought when he glanced down at a row of seats near the tail. He realized he was looking at the video camcorder case of the man he had talked to during the flight.

Didn't that fellow say he was getting off in New York? Brian reached down and opened the case, finding the camera and one extra battery still inside. He closed the case and carried it to the rear, where the caterers were loading the galley for the flight to London.

Something familiar about one of them caught his attention.

With a shock Brian remembered where he'd seen the man before. He was the passenger Brian had talked to, the one who owned the camcorder—the one he was holding right now!

"Hey, you there! Excuse me." Brian saw the man's head snap up. "Didn't you just come in on this flight? Isn't this camera yours?"

"I wish it was, mate," the man in the coveralls said, "but I can't afford one." The accent was Australian, but it sounded false. Brian knew Aussies too well to buy the flawed inflection.

Before Brian could make a move, the man dropped something into the wastepaper slot of the galley.

"I think I've got it fixed," he said as he slid a food cart back into position and turned on the internal heater.

One of the other caterers was arranging empty carts in the front of a truck body that sat level with the 747's doorway. Brian walked across the narrow metal bridge and tapped him on the shoulder.

"Have you ever seen that guy in the galley before?" Brian asked in a low voice as he gestured toward the airplane where the man was standing at the door.

"No, but he said he's a repairman. He didn't come with us."

Logic told Brian he had identified a saboteur. Instinct told him to hide that recognition. He turned to the man in the doorway. "Sorry to hassle you. Can't be too careful, you know."

"Quite all right, mate." The man looked at the other caterer in the back of the truck. "Okay if I ride back with you guys?"

The caterer hesitated, then shrugged. "Sure."

Brian took the camcorder around the corner into the galley and opened the case again. Then it hit him.

The battery. When he had seen the case opened in flight, there had been two batteries. Now there was one.

He pulled out the remaining battery and slipped it into his pocket. Leaving the case in the galley, Brian returned to the rear door. The driver was preparing to disengage the truck from the aircraft. The passenger-cum-repairman was standing on the platform just inside the truck body when Brian waved him forward.

"Excuse me. One more thing."

The man walked forward, stopping on the bridge, which was now bare of its protective railings. Brian pulled the battery out of his pocket and held it up. He watched the man's expression freeze as he calculated what Brian was going to do with it.

If this is a bomb, Mr. Saboteur, you're not going to want it to hit the ground, are you?

"You left this behind."

Brian tossed the battery to the man.

The battery sailed through the door and off to one side of the truck as the man clawed after it in midair, before realizing that he had leaned too far and was falling. He reached for a handhold, but it was too late. He fell thirty feet to the concrete below.

Brian climbed down the ladder on the outside of the truck and rushed to the body. He found no pulse. The shocked caterers called for an ambulance. Brian unzipped the top of the man's coveralls, revealing the shirt and tie he had seen him wearing earlier. As sirens approached, he located the man's billfold and looked inside. He found a Washington State driver's license with the saboteur's picture, except that in the picture he had a mustache.

Several Pan Am mechanics had run to the scene. Brian turned to one of them now. "We've got a bomb on board, in the rear galley area. Clear the airplane immediately and call the bomb squad."

The mechanic nodded and pulled out his handheld radio. Brian continued to search through the man's pockets for any additional clues. He was about to give up when his fingers contacted a plastic bag. He removed it and found himself staring at a small piece of molded latex, rounded and slightly ridged. He pulled it from the bag and examined it, finding a perfect replica of a single fingerprint.

THE receptionist at Jamison, Reed, Owen, and Phillips wasn't sure what to make of the disheveled man in the gray overcoat, so she called Bill Phillips on the intercom.

Phillips shot out of his chair. "Jacob Voorster is *here?*"

Phillips appeared within seconds, pumping Voorster's hand and assuring him he had found the right place at last.

Elizabeth's cellular phone suddenly rang in the middle of Grand Central. She quickly relayed the news to Creighton that Jacob Voorster—and his briefcase—had surfaced. Creighton pointed out that they now had less than ninety minutes to halt the seizure of Pan Am aircraft worldwide.

Elizabeth and Creighton dashed by cab to Phillips' office, while Bill Phillips requested a hearing before the three-judge panel for 4:15 p.m. Other members of his firm now labored to prepare new court orders for Judge Hayes to sign. When they arrived at Phillips' office, Jack Rawly gave them a capsule account of how the hearing would be handled.

"Okay, here's the deal. Intertrust, the holder of the revolving loan, took us to court this morning to kill the TRO, and as you know, we were given until five p.m. to find new evidence, or the appeals court would sweep the TRO away. Thanks to our newfound best friend here, Jacob Voorster, we now have that new evidence. I expect the appeals court to deny Intertrust's motion. The problem is, the airplanes themselves are owned by Empire Leasing, not by Intertrust. To stop them from any cowboyish repossessions, we need Judge Hayes to slap an additional TRO on *them*. Someone in authority is going to have to deliver the order in person at Kennedy while we do the appeals hearing. I don't see how anyone can get out there in time."

"I've got an idea," Elizabeth said, and headed for the phone on an adjacent desk. Within two minutes she was back.

"I don't have to be at the appeals hearing, so I'm elected to deliver the TRO. My former partner, Eric Knox, is going to fly me out in his helicopter."

Jack Rawly looked relieved. "That's great!"

They gathered Jacob and began moving rapidly to the elevator.

AT THE FOLEY SQUARE COURTHOUSE, Judge Walter Hayes ushered the team in immediately at 4:15 p.m., questioned Jacob Voorster for less than five minutes, and glanced over the report that had so disturbed Sol Moscowitz.

"Where's the order?" he said.

Jack Rawly slipped two court orders across the desk. One extended the TRO against a declaration of default by the revolving-loan lenders headed by Intertrust. The other ordered the leasing company not to repossess any Pan Am aircraft until the entire matter could be brought to a formal injunctive hearing.

As his pen scratched along the signature line, Judge Hayes shook his head. "You've got a lot of work ahead of you, Counselor. You've got so many targets to sue, it boggles the mind. This is going to be a political thunderclap as well, if it turns out the motive of this Dutch company is what you think it is."

"Excuse me, Your Honor, I don't understand," Jacob said.

Judge Hayes looked at Voorster. "What I was referring to is Mr. Rawly's theory that your former employer has somehow secretly bought illicit majority interests in the big three airlines in North America and manipulated the voting stock to decrease competition among them and produce ever higher profits. It's what we call combination in restraint of trade."

"Oh, that is exactly what's happened," Jacob said quietly.

Judge Hayes studied him. "How can you be sure, Mr. Voorster?"

"Because you are speaking with the architect of that plan. I spent the last five years putting it together very quietly from Amsterdam: setting up the intermediary corporations all over the world, transferring money with great stealth from VZV to those holding corporations, and then arranging for them to buy the airline stock. In a few years the profits would have been unbelievable—that is, if our managing director had not used criminal means to try to destroy a competitor."

The judge's chambers were electrified by this admission, which fully explained why a corporation such as VZV would want this man dead. But there was no time to consider the implications.

Judge Hayes broke the spell. "I'm staggered, Mr. Voorster. But"—he turned to Elizabeth and inclined his head—"you've got a helicopter to catch, young lady."

ERIC WAS WAITING WHEN ELIZABETH reached the heliport by the East River. As soon as her door was closed, he lifted the turbine-powered helicopter into the air and headed for Kennedy.

A short while later JFK appeared in the distance. Elizabeth checked her watch. It was 4:46 p.m.

Pan Am's station manager had hurried the TV crews to the departure lounge in time to catch her arrival. With the bomb search of Pan Am Flight 1 now successfully completed, the cameramen focused on the Jet Ranger as Eric brought it delicately to the ground, aft of the giant Boeing.

Brian was there to open the right-hand door of the chopper and help Elizabeth out. She smiled and showed Brian the court orders as he briefed her on the successful search for the bomb.

"It wasn't a bomb at all the guy planted. It was a firestarter—an incendiary device designed to set the galley on fire and cancel the flight. The man threw it in the wastebasket in the aft galley when I first confronted him."

The ringing of her cellular phone interrupted them. It was Jack Rawly, calling from the hallway outside the appeals court.

"All done, Elizabeth. The appeals judges dismissed the action. The TROs are as good as gold. How're *you* doing?"

She looked at her watch. Five minutes remained.

"I'm on the ramp by the airplane, Jack, about to stuff a turkey with a court order."

"Oh, by the way, Creighton's headed out there for the ceremony. He's going to be heading back to London tonight."

With Brian standing beside her, she thanked Jack and rang off. Then the two of them walked slowly toward the men from Empire Leasing. The head of the contingent extended his hand, and Elizabeth slapped the court order in it.

The time was exactly 5:00 p.m.

ELIZABETH prudently omitted the details about the shocking revelations Jacob Voorster had brought from Amsterdam, as she briefed the media in the boarding lounge.

"Today," Elizabeth said on camera, "we have utterly defeated what has been a major coordinated campaign by offshore corporate interests to put Pan Am out of business. We're here to stay, with the best service in the world, and the flying public is the beneficiary."

She smiled and stepped away from a barrage of follow-up questions as the outbound crew appeared. She took the chance to slip away with Brian, who had already borrowed the key to a small V.I.P. room down the concourse, with privacy in mind.

He locked the door behind them, then drew Elizabeth into his arms in a long embrace, which evolved into a deep, passionate kiss filled with stored-up longing. She responded in kind.

They sat on the couch then, Brian touching her cheek lightly with his fingertips. "Elizabeth, let's start over again. We got off to a rocky start with all the pressure, and I—"

She pulled him to her, speaking low in his ear. "After I see Mother and Kelly, the first night back in the condo is ours, and the phones will be turned off."

He laughed. "I'll look forward to that, but you don't have to do that. I just have to get used to things." He pulled back and looked her in the eye. "I *am* getting used to things, like the fact that you're the most capable executive we've got, and I'm proud of you and I love you."

"I love you, too, Brian."

He sighed. "I have to rush back to Seattle. This isn't over yet. There's at least one more rat in the woodwork."

"Rat?"

"Within the company."

"Can't the FBI handle it?"

He shook his head. "I found something on the body of that guy I caught on my plane today—a business card from a condominium rental agency in Seattle. If I'm right, that card—and the address written on the back—could lead to whoever hired that bastard."

"You think he was a hired gun?"

Brian nodded solemnly. "I think he's the one behind the computer dirty tricks, all the sabotage, and that explosion."

"Promise me you won't take unnecessary risks."

"I promise."

ELIZABETH had agreed to substitute for Ron Lamb at the formal initiation of the new service. Speaking to the crowd was the last thing she wanted to do as she watched Brian wave good-bye and hurry toward his Seattle flight. She forced herself to say the appropriate words before cutting the ribbon to launch Pan Am's first round-the-world flight service. But the sight of Clipper One, pushing back on time with a full complement of eager passengers on board, was beautiful, and she was teetering on the verge of tears when a large, gentle hand closed softly around her right shoulder.

"That 747 you've launched represents the salvation of your whole airline. You did it, Elizabeth. Congratulations!"

Creighton MacRae was smiling broadly as she turned to him.

"I have a message for you from Jason Ing," he said. "He's recovering quite nicely. He thanked us for the small florist shop you sent, and he said to assure you that the papers for the one hundred forty million have already been faxed to Seattle as per your instructions."

Elizabeth was regarding him quietly. "Creighton, you've been so invaluable to us; it almost scares me to have you leave."

"I've got to get back. I have a meeting in London tomorrow."

She looked down and placed her finger on his chest. "I couldn't have done this without you, you know."

He cocked his head slightly. "It did work out rather well, now that you mention it. Why don't you walk me to my gate, Elizabeth Sterling, C.F.O. Unless you've got something else to attend to."

"I wouldn't think of letting you depart without waving goodbye." She took his arm as she walked with him.

"Jacob Voorster wants to see the cabdriver who saved his life," he said. "So Jack Rawly is planning to arrange police protection for Mr. Voorster and take him over to the hospital."

"How's the cabby doing?"

"Brave fellow. Nothing wrong but a mild concussion."

All too soon they were standing in another departure lounge, watching the last of the passengers board a British Airways 747 to London. Creighton took his boarding pass from the gate agent and walked with Elizabeth to the door.

She was having trouble meeting his gaze, and he gently raised her chin until their eyes were locked on each other.

"Scotland's rather beautiful in the early spring, you know."

She smiled. "Yes, I do know."

He looked at her in silence again, his smile slowly fading, his carefully guarded emotions finally overwhelming his resolve.

"Elizabeth, come with me. This shouldn't be good-bye."

"Creighton, I have a commitment in Seattle."

"No strings, Elizabeth, just an open invitation."

She knew the invitation was permanent, as he leaned down to kiss her.

Epilogue

Tuesday, March 28, 11:00 a.m.—Seattle

BRIAN Murphy sat quietly facing the door, listening for the sound of footsteps in the hallway of the condominium in the Redondo Beach area, a few miles southwest of Seatac. The recipient of the single-page fax he had sent should be arriving any minute.

Brian looked around at the expensive interior. For an attempted mass murderer, the renter of the condo had shown elegant taste. It was hard to believe such a man would be careless enough to leave the address of his base of operations on the back of a card in his wallet. But he had done exactly that. It had been simple for Brian to obtain a key, using a carefully constructed lie to the rental firm.

He had entered gingerly, just as unsure of what to expect as he'd been in Marvin Grade's house, but here there was a world of difference. The condo was full of electronic equipment—computers, printers, electronic components and tools, and a fax machine with ten memory buttons. The fax memory provided a record of all the numbers to which documents had been sent in the previous few months. One number in particular kept reappearing time and again.

Its owner hadn't been difficult to trace, but the realization of who it was had provided quite a shock.

The distant slamming of a car door filtered into the darkened room. Brian felt the switch on the power cord he'd connected to several floodlights on a stand.

The wording of the fax had taken some time, but Brian had decided to strike the greatest amount of terror into the heart of the co-conspirator—a co-conspirator who also carried a Pan Am I.D.

We've got major problems that could lead right to your door-step. Meet me at the Redondo location at 11 a.m. I'll leave the door unlocked. I'm not answering the phone, so just be there.

Urgent, rapid footsteps thudded down the hallway now. Suddenly they stopped. He heard the sound of the doorknob turning.

The door to the condo opened and then slammed shut. The man moved into the room, suspecting nothing until Brian snapped on the bright lights.

The man stood in the entryway, holding his hand over his forehead, trying to peer beyond the glare. "Turn those lights off!"

Brian altered his voice before speaking in an approximation of the saboteur's voice. "I've got a loaded Uzi aimed right at you. Answer me yes or no. You hired me to screw up your airplanes, cause delays, and make your airline look incompetent, right?"

"You've already been *paid* for all that! *Now* what do you want?"

"You didn't tell me your chief pilot was gonna play detective. I got jumped yesterday at Kennedy."

He seemed stunned. "What were you doing at Kennedy? I told you the job was over. I told you we had gone too far with the airplanes. What's with these lights?"

Brian snapped the lights off and watched as Pan Am's vice president of operations, Chad Jennings, stood in complete confusion, his eyes focusing at last on Brian Murphy.

"You're right, Chad. It's all over."

Four FBI agents who had been waiting in an adjacent room entered, guns and handcuffs at the ready.

Friday, March 31

FAX COVER SHEET

From: Jack Rawly
To: Ron Lamb
Subj.: Further newspaper clippings, as promised

SECRET AIRLINE CONTROL SCHEME UNRAVELS
INDICTMENTS PREPARED AS DUTCH AND AMERICAN
OFFICIALS PRESS INVESTIGATIONS

(Washington, D.C.—Special to the *Times*) Pan American Airways, Inc., filed numerous federal lawsuits here this morning against a long list of defendants, including the principal lenders and the lessors of their air fleet, seeking damages that could theoretically run as high as $3 billion. The massive civil action charges the defendants with various acts of sabotage and criminal conspiracy designed to bring about the destruction of the year-old airline through purposeful financial interference and direct criminal acts against its aircraft and computer systems. The Pan Am move comes amid a burgeoning investigation of a giant Dutch multinational corporation, Van Zanten and Vetter, Ltd., which is suspected of illicitly trying to buy into and manipulate the North American airline market.

According to court documents filed by Pan Am, the scheme went so far as to "plant" an insider in a high position at Pan Am to oversee an internal sabotage campaign. The vice president of operations, Chad Jennings, the corporate officer allegedly responsible for the campaign, has been arrested and charged with numerous criminal violations, but is said to be cooperating with federal authorities. More arrests are pending within the United States and the Netherlands in a dragnet that is expected to result in indictments against several high-level financiers.

Wednesday, April 12

UPI—(Miami) BULLETIN

Fugitive financier Nicolas Costas, former chairman of defunct Columbia Airline Systems, was arrested early this morning by federal agents after attempting to leave the United States in his private jet. Costas was forced down by air force fighters after his aircraft blundered through restricted airspace near Hurlburt Air Force Base, Florida.

John Nance grew up with the romance of flying. As a boy in Dallas, Texas, he heard the stories of his father and uncle, both pilots during World War II. His aunt took him on his first commercial airline flight at the age of five. "It was a big, big deal," he recalls. Soon he was riding his bike out to the little local airport, where he would sit wistfully beside the runway. If he got lucky, a friendly pilot would say, "All right, I'm sick of sitting there watching you watch me. Why don't you hop in and I'll give you a ride."

In those days Nance discovered another interest—writing. At age eleven he had a column in the local weekly newspaper, and before long he had, as he says, "wormed" his way into the title of aviation writer. While attending Southern Methodist University, he got his pilot's license. After graduating with a law degree in 1970, Nance joined the air force and flew transport planes in Vietnam. He then became a com-

John J. Nance

mercial pilot for Braniff. *A Splash of Colors,* Nance's nonfiction account of Braniff's demise, won critical praise.

Today Nance is an air safety consultant who has made many appearances on television shows like *Good Morning America* and the *MacNeil/ Lehrer Newshour.* One of the emergencies he describes in *Phoenix Rising*—his third novel—is loosely based on a 747 emergency that occurred south of Honolulu. The details of the fictional accident differ, says Nance, who has taught about the real one all over the world. "But the reactions of the crew are very very consistent with reality."

This multitalented pilot/reporter/lawyer/air safety expert/nonfiction writer/novelist lives with his wife in Tacoma, Washington.

Max Apple

ROOMMATES

My Grandfather's Story

When Max Apple was five, he brought his pillow and his comic books upstairs and staked out the other bed in his grampa Rocky's room. Unlike the rest of the family, Max *enjoyed* being with the contrary old man. And so they became roommates, and friends. Theirs was a special bond, strengthened by tragedy and blessed with love. And it was to last for many more years than either would have dreamed.

Chapter 1

I HAD come to nominate a President; so had seven or eight hundred other hippies, yippies, pacifists, Black Panthers, macrobiotics, and assorted nonbelievers in the two-party system.

It was 1968. There were already five hundred thousand troops in Vietnam and more on the way. On the grass of the University of Michigan student union, Lyndon Johnson hung in effigy. On the stage of the second-floor ballroom, where Eldridge Cleaver spoke about peace, his Black Panther bodyguards pointed machine guns at the audience. Every time there was applause, I started to duck.

"Are you a faster?" someone asked me.

She wore a black T-shirt with a picture of Jimi Hendrix. Her sunglasses hung from a string around her neck. She was barefoot, and her blue jeans had a few tears around the knee.

If I had seen her on the street that evening, I wouldn't have been surprised if she'd asked me for spare change. I would have given, and I would have remembered her.

"What's a faster?" I asked.

"If you don't know," she said, "then you're not one."

She looked at Cleaver; I looked at her.

"If you're just going to stare," she said, "I'll be happy to let you hold my driver's license photograph."

"No picture," I said. "I prefer the real thing."

"Well, the real thing is a lot messier."

"I'll take my chances," I said.

"Suit yourself," she said.

I followed her out of the ballroom. In the hallway there were at least twenty tables filled with propaganda leaflets. She stopped to pick up a pamphlet from the macrobiotic table.

"Why are you following me?" she asked.

"I'm not following," I said. "I came to get a pamphlet, too. You're not the only one interested in macrobiotics."

"Ask one of those guys." She motioned toward two young men in sunglasses who stood behind the table. Then she slipped back into the crowd and headed toward the staircase.

I pushed a shirtless delegate out of my way to catch up with her. "Hold on," I said. "Don't run away. We've just met."

"I'm sorry," she said, "but I'm busy. I'll see you around."

She walked quickly down the big marble stairs, and again I followed. She noticed me at the first landing.

"Hey," she said, "you're getting to be a pain."

"If you'd stop running away, I wouldn't have to follow you."

"Okay," she said. "What do you want?"

I introduced myself; so did she.

"I can't really stop to talk," she said. "I'm in a hurry."

"I'm not," I said. "Can I come along?"

We walked down University Avenue. She stopped at a yellow Plymouth convertible and got in. The back seat was full of clothes and boxes. We hadn't said another word, but we both understood that I was going along. She leaned over to unlock the passenger door.

"Do you always carry so many changes of clothes?" I said.

"I've been looking for a place for my stuff for two weeks. It's no problem to find a place to crash somewhere for a night, but if they give you a closet, suddenly they want you to sign a lease."

She turned up Hill Street, lined with sororities, fraternities, and large houses that the university owned. She parked in front of the multicolored Victorian headquarters of the Rainbow People's Party.

"I'll see if I can store my stuff here. It's my last hope."

She got out and closed the car door, and walked toward the house. I watched her reach the purple steps, stop, then turn back. She squatted by the passenger door so she could look me in the eye.

"You can sit here if you want, but I might be a while."

"I'll wait."

"When you do get tired and decide to leave, please keep your finger on the button so the door will stay locked." She lowered her dark eyes. I had the feeling that she really didn't want me to leave, no matter what she said.

"It's a guy I'm going to see in there. That's why I can't take you inside. It would spoil any chance I have." She stood up and ran toward the house.

Mentioning the guy had done it.

"I've got a closet," I called out. "It's yours if you want it."

"Why didn't you say so?" she said. She ran back to the car even faster than she'd hurried away.

In the car she was a little suspicious. "Are you holding out while you decide how much rent to charge?"

"No charge," I said.

"You're sure?"

"Positive."

"One other thing. I want you to get this straight up front. It's just the stuff—not me."

I ASKED her to speak softly when I unlocked the apartment door. It took us only two trips from the car. Her clothes and books, stacked neatly on the floor, required less room than I thought.

"Let's put it in the closet," she said.

"It's a mess now," I said. "I'll put everything away in the morning."

She looked around the apartment—the two stuffed chairs, the wooden dinette table, the wall-to-wall carpeting. "This doesn't feel like a student apartment," she said.

I pulled out my wallet and showed her my I.D.

"That's not what I mean. The place is so clean."

I turned on the TV to divert her. The ten-o'clock news was already over. She plopped down next to me. The weather and sports were on when I put my arm around her.

"How come you live so far from campus?" she said.

I thought I heard something, so I didn't answer. I was thinking about how I'd explain the stacks of books and the clothes.

"You sure you don't want me just to go?" she said.

I must have been quiet and straining to listen longer than I realized. She started to move away.

"No," I said. "Please stay. We'll watch the late movie."

"You're sure?"

"I'm sure."

I was thinking about what she had told me—just the clothes, not her. But when I put my lips in front of hers, she didn't resist.

When I looked up, John Wayne was shooting at someone on my black-and-white Philco portable. This time I did hear a noise.

I heard footsteps. A door closed, and then the toilet flushed.

I sat up quickly and moved away from her. She didn't seem surprised at all.

"Your roommate?" she asked.

I hadn't said anything about a roommate.

"Yeah," I said. "That's why I wanted to be quiet and not put your stuff in the closet tonight."

She moved close to me again, but I was no longer comfortable.

"You want something to eat?" I asked. I stood up.

"Do I have bad breath?" she whispered.

"No," I whispered back. "I don't want to wake my roommate."

"Do I kiss that loud?"

I sat back down and kissed her again. "Yes, much too loud."

"Maybe it's you," she said.

"Can't be," I said. "I practice silence all the time." Then I kissed her again to keep from talking.

From the bedroom we heard a high-pitched wheeze, followed by a fluffy noise of flesh—as if the lips were clapping hands. There was another wheeze and clap of the lips, and then a curse in a powerful, grunting whisper.

She laughed. I stood up and started moving her clothes to the other side of the couch, where they wouldn't be so obvious to someone emerging from the bedroom behind us.

It was a mistake. I carried a stack of books, supporting the top one with my chin, and a Modern Library edition of *The Rise and Fall of the Roman Empire* fell. As I reached for it, the whole stack hit the carpet. Debby tried to catch them and fell off the couch. That's when my roommate ran in from the bedroom. Debby's clothes were spread around her, and she lay among a pile of books.

Debby and my roommate eyed one another. She was surprised but tried to act as if meeting an old man in long underwear could hap-

326

pen to anyone. "Hi," she said, "I'm Debby. I'm sorry we woke you."

His blue eyes showed no hint of tiredness. He had snow-white hair, was five feet tall, and weighed one hundred and ten pounds. He attacked.

"Ger out from here," he said. He grabbed an armful of clothes and carried them to the door. I hurried to the hallway to pick them up, but he had already tossed out another armful.

"I get the message," she said. "I can take the stuff out myself if you'll give me five minutes."

"Now," he said.

I met him at the door and caught the next load. Debby had picked up as much as she could carry and was at the door.

"Ger out," he grunted again.

"I'm gerring," she said, meeting his fierce look with one of her own. While they stared each other down, I was in the hallway picking up shoes and shirts.

She grabbed them out of my arms, and some fell. I gathered them up and followed her outside. She was fighting back tears when I stopped her at the wheel of her convertible.

"I should have warned you," I said. "It's my fault."

"Will you bring the rest out?" she asked. "I don't want to see him again."

"I can explain. . . . Leave everything."

"Please," she said. "I wanna get out of here."

I didn't have to go into the apartment; her things were all in the hallway. I reloaded her back seat.

She blew her nose and regained her composure.

"He's not always like this," I said.

"Even if he's paying more than half the rent," she said, "you're getting a bad deal."

Chapter 2

THAT roommate who chased Debby out of our apartment had been looking out for me all my life. Our bond began one night in January, 1936, five years before my birth, when my grampa Rocky, his son Max, two female cousins, and Rocky's son-in-law Sam—who was my father—were in Max's new black Chevrolet, returning to Grand

Rapids, Michigan, from a wedding in Detroit. Max was at the wheel.

Max was twenty-three and not too experienced at highway speeds, but he wasn't going too fast—he couldn't. The wind blew blinding snow at the car, and beneath the snow lay the dangerous black ice of Michigan winters.

Somewhere near Lansing, the Chevy skidded on one of those ice sheets and began to cross the median. Max hit the brake; the car spun off the road into a healthy elm tree. The passengers were all thrown from the car. The steering wheel kept Max inside, but the pointed Chevrolet insignia penetrated his chest.

The two women were killed instantly. Rocky and my father were battered but conscious. When the ambulance arrived, they watched the two medical workers load Max onto a stretcher.

The ambulance, because of the treacherous weather, had to travel far slower than usual. The emergency medic put oxygen over Max's mouth and held a stethoscope to his heart. A few minutes from the hospital he removed the oxygen. "I'm sorry," he told Rocky. "He died." Rocky pushed open the door and tried to jump out. The medic and my father barely kept him from doing so.

Rocky never told me that story, never mentioned his son at all. What I know of my uncle Max comes from my grandmother, who never stopped mourning him, and from my mother, who even years later, during my childhood, still visited the cemetery so regularly that tombstones with Hebrew lettering are my earliest memories.

In many families there is a single defining event that changes everything. This was ours. Five years later, at my birth, my parents, grandparents, and my two sisters were all living together—a band of survivors. My arrival, I think, finally turned them toward forgetting. No one could replace their loss, but I entered the world loaded. They named me Max, and everyone had an equal share in me.

In a big gray clapboard house in the industrial district of Grand Rapids, my family, like many immigrants, put all they had into their children—in our case, the grandchildren as well.

At home we spoke Yiddish, but at school my sisters and I hung on to English like the life raft it was. Once we had the language, we polished it. The girls became paragons of fluency, high school debate champs. Around the kitchen table the adults spoke Yiddish and talked about the czar and pogroms—but in the dining room, only the issues of the day passed my sisters' lips as they practiced debate before a large gilded mirror. My father carried their trophies in his truck to show to the purchasing agents and plant managers who sold him scrap steel and other metal.

"You'll be a speaker, too," my mother promised me, but I didn't think so. I gravitated instead to an older set of debaters—Rocky and my grandma—who wished upon one another cholera and ague. If anyone gave out trophies for Yiddish cursing, they would have been daily winners.

Gootie, my grandma, was a short, large-boned woman who made the kitchen her kingdom. She entered the living room only on special occasions—like Monday night to watch *I Love Lucy*. She had fallen from a freight train in Russia during World War I, and her broken leg, never properly set, left her dragging a stiff limb for the rest of her days. Slow and careful in everything, she was the exact opposite of her speedy husband. They were the marriage of thought and action, and in constant conflict.

Rocky was a whirlwind and the family pioneer. He came to America on his own in 1914 and began to work sixteen-hour days so he could bring his wife and two children, Bashy—my mother—and Max, to Michigan. During what he called "the first war," none of his letters were answered. He didn't know where his family was or even if they were alive. But he saved his money, and he kept writing.

After the war, when Gootie, Bashy, and Max returned to their village from Odessa, where the Russian government had shipped them, their house was a ruin and their German and Lithuanian paper money worthless. A few letters were waiting for them.

In Michigan, Rocky went to night school, where he learned to read and write English. The only thing he did at less than top speed was sign his name. He braced himself with his left hand on the writing surface, checked the position of his thumb and forefinger on the pencil or ballpoint, and then executed the curves of "Herman"—the American name that an immigration clerk had given him because Yerachmiel was too hard. The men who worked beside him at the American Bakery were smarter. When they couldn't say Yerachmiel, they called him Rocky—the name that stuck.

I never missed an opportunity to watch him sign "Herman." It was regal. When I learned cursive in fourth grade, I filled notebooks practicing my name and his. "Max Apple" never got beyond a scrawl, but I could do "Herman Goodstein" like a master forger.

Gootie never learned English. That lack kept her housebound more than her lame leg did, but she made immobility a strength. She liked the rest of the family to report our experiences to her, and she rewarded us with ironic commentaries. A coffee cup always in front of her, her bad leg propped on a stool, she made her spot at the kitchen table the center of the household. She kept a big white rag beside her to wipe her eyes, which regularly leaked tears of laughter. She had two big things to laugh at—America and her husband.

What she knew about America she learned from looking at pictures in the newspaper, watching people on the street, or picking up the news and gossip that the family brought to her. Her longest field trips were our walks to the neighborhood supermarket. She liked to go with me because I had the patience to read labels and explain what was in the cans and packets that were new and usually amusing to her. I could read by five and liked to show off.

We didn't go to the A&P to buy—my parents did that once a week. Gootie and I went for entertainment. She liked to watch people load up on absurdities, like tissues and deodorant. She could look at the shopper, the contents of the cart, and then imagine the life. She had no experience with romance, but liked it above all else. When we saw a couple call one another "honey" or "sweetheart" and exchange a little kiss near the door, she mimicked them. At home she would give me a soulful look, purse her lips, and call me "sveetheart honeydear" until neither of us could stop laughing.

In Lithuania her parents had a small store where she had sold bread and produce and liquor by the glass to barefoot peasants. She wanted me to own a store someday.

This was a subject of dispute between my grandparents. Rocky didn't want me primed for storekeeping. He had bigger plans. He'd take me to various teachers—men who he said knew what to teach a boy like me—and he'd introduce me in the same way to each wise man: "Do something. Teach him. He's growing up like a goy."

I don't know what any of these men might have done. As I think of them now, they were probably bigger disappointments than I was. The itinerant teachers and rabbis who passed through western Michigan in the late 1940s would no doubt have preferred to be elsewhere. The ones who tutored me made up a kind of pony express of teachers who alighted for a while in the provinces, all the while praying for a better life in a big city.

I would sit beside a Hebrew book and a glass of tea while a wispy man in his thirties would say, "So we'll begin."

We never got beyond beginnings. My heart was too American. While they helped me read and translate Hebrew and Aramaic prayers, I was thinking of baseball.

Rocky didn't take out his anger and disappointment on me, but it became part of a constant feud with Gootie. There was no suspense in their disagreements—Rocky always lost.

My father stayed out of the squabbles, but my mother had inherited Rocky's quick temper and used it against him. She inevitably sided with Gootie. Because the war had separated her parents, when my mother came to America at twelve, someone had to tell her who the dapper fellow in brown-and-white shoes was. In a way her father remained more a stranger to her than to my sisters and me.

If an argument with Gootie was serious enough, Rocky responded by storming upstairs. The house was a triplex. We lived downstairs, and there were two apartments above. The heat from the coal furnace was almost nonexistent on the second floor, although with a wall heater, the back apartment was warm enough to rent.

Rocky slept in the front apartment. This gave him the privacy he needed to keep his hours—to bed at eight thirty, up at four.

To go from the warm, crowded downstairs to the cold, empty upstairs seemed to me a terrible punishment. Usually, after an argument with Gootie, he would retreat to his bedroom but return in an hour or so. When his anger didn't abate, my job was to coax him downstairs, back into the bosom of the family.

Gootie never stayed angry. When he didn't come down for a meal, she worried. So did I. I would put on my coat and go upstairs. He was usually sitting at a wooden table covered with a white crocheted cloth, reading the Talmud.

At four and five years old I was like a little lawyer going to question the prisoner in his cell. On the first trip I would merely listen—let him get out his rage and state the justice of his case. On the second trip I would bring food prepared by his enemy wife. He would refuse to touch it.

Then my work began. I had to charm him into eating. He was stubborn and not always hungry. Sometimes I failed.

On one occasion the dispute stretched into a second, and then a third, and a fourth day. That battle concerned a housepainter. Rocky had promised the job of painting our house to Ed—one of his Polish co-workers at the bakery. Gootie had struck a deal with Mr. Cooley, a retired man who lived across the street. She had made the deal in Yiddish; I had translated, so I felt partly responsible.

For Rocky more than honor was at stake. Ed was one of three people who could squeal to the union, which had forced Rocky to retire. He continued to work, secretly. His cousin Phillip, who owned the American Bakery, kept him on part time. Going to the bakery with him was a kind of espionage mission. We knew the union spies might be anywhere.

Phillip was taking a big chance, Rocky told me. If they caught him, the union could shut down the bakery. I never went in without looking around for the union men. While Rocky worked, I would have a doughnut and a glass of milk, and all the time keep a lookout.

There were two other bakers, Joe Post and Ed Wizneski—the one who moonlighted as a painter. Joe weighed over two hundred pounds and tossed seventy-five-pound sacks of flour like marbles. But when he decorated a cake, he held the long tube of artificial color delicately, like a paintbrush, and made tiny green and red flowers, even when Rocky was yelling at him to go faster.

Ed teased Rocky about turning him in to the union. "What's your hurry?" he would say. "You're not even working. You're not here—you're retired." Rocky tried to ignore the teasing, but he took it seriously. He probably considered the housepainting job as a kind of bribe. I tried to explain all of this to Gootie and my mother—it didn't help. They wanted Rocky to retire. Even part time, he was still working thirty hours a week. I understood more than they did how much he loved the bakery.

On cake days he stayed late. Rocky and Joe Post were both cake men. They used a different kind of flour, and on cakes, even Rocky slowed down. When they made fresh frosting, I always got a taste.

"You gotta know what you're doing when you bake cakes," Rocky said. "Cakes aren't like cookies or doughnuts."

When there was no one else to do it, Rocky made doughnuts, but he hated it. He drew the line at cookies. I'd seen him storm away once, when Phillip asked him to make ten dozen coconut spots.

"Don't be so stubborn," Phillip said. "Just ten dozen—how long will it take you?"

Rocky took off his apron and threw it on the table. "C'mon," he said to me, and left. I ran to catch up.

"I'm on your side," I told him. "I want Ed to paint the house."

At home I lobbied Gootie. She was ready to give in, but my mother hardened her heart. "If you'll stop bringing him his food, he'll come down when he's hungry," she said. "Leave him alone."

On the fifth day of the dispute, my mother gave up. "Tell him that Ed can paint the house," she said. "I can't stand it anymore."

I ran upstairs to tell him the good news, but he wouldn't budge. His anger had separated itself from the cause. Propped up on the huge pillow that kept him almost sitting while he slept, he told me he was never coming downstairs again. I believed him. I went down and returned with my pajamas, two Archie comic books, and my pillow. He told me to go downstairs, but I refused.

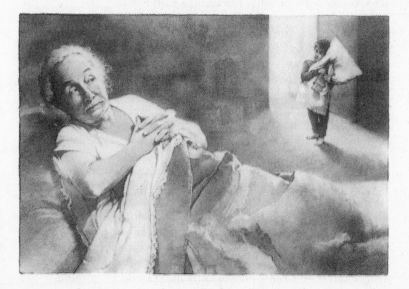

The bedroom had been a kitchen and still was. A porcelain sink separated twin mahogany beds. I settled in across the sink from him. Even though the room had some heat, I could still see my breath. In a few minutes Rocky was snoring.

The next morning he ordered me downstairs. "It's too cold for you up here," he said.

"I like it," I told him, and the next night I was back.

When he saw that I meant business, Rocky relented. He let me carry messages back and forth. For two days the bargaining continued. Then we reached a settlement: Ed would scrape the house; Cooley would paint. As chief negotiator, I named my price and I got it—I stayed upstairs. Rocky had a roommate.

Chapter 3

WHILE I lingered in the Old World, my sisters went headlong into the melting pot. Maxine rose to captain of the Turner School safety patrol. Bailey became a junior high student-council officer. Encouraged by their examples, my parents urged me to take a big step into America. Reluctantly I became a Cub Scout.

Mrs. Clark came to our second-grade class to recruit for a new den. I knew her. She was the cashier at the Red and White, a small grocery store four blocks from our house.

Mrs. Clark was a very heavy woman with blond hair and red lipstick. Her son John was in my class. He had been a Cub Scout the year before in another den and liked it so much that Mrs. Clark wanted to offer all of us the same opportunity.

I joined, but there was only one problem. Our den would meet at the Church of St. Peter and St. Paul. Rocky forbade me to go.

"A Jew," he said, "doesn't go to a church."

I argued. "It's not a church; it's a meeting room in a church. And there's no priests or nuns, just Mrs. Clark, the den mother."

"First they tell you den mother; pretty soon they'll start talking about a Holy Mother. I know. It was like that in Lithuania."

"They didn't have Cub Scouts in Lithuania," I argued.

"You're right. We didn't waste time on such things. We studied."

He refused to give his permission, but with my parents and sisters and even Gootie encouraging me, I stood my ground.

My father drove me to the meeting in his truck. I didn't even tell Rocky I was going. I walked up the steps and into the yellow brick building, as wary as if I were entering a prison.

When I found the room, I opened the door and saw only Mrs. Clark and a few boys in uniform, not a roomful of nuns and priests. I relaxed. There were chairs and a blackboard, and on the table a kite-making display.

"Hi," Mrs. Clark said, "I'm glad you could make it." She knew, I think, because I had ordered only a cap and a compass instead of a full uniform, that I was on shaky ground. "You like kites?" she asked. "I hope so. We're having an interesting demonstration."

"Outside?" I asked, hoping I could tell Rocky the whole thing took place outdoors.

"No!" Mrs. Clark said. "Right there at the table. But next week, after everyone makes one of his own, we'll go outside together and fly them. You'll really like that. Everyone does."

We all pledged allegiance to the flag and recited a Cub Scout pledge. Mrs. Clark wrote our new pack number on the blackboard so we could write it down and buy shoulder patches.

"You're in for a special treat tonight," she said. "I told you that we'd be doing kites, but I didn't tell you that we'd be learning from a master kite maker. Let's give him a big Cub Scout welcome."

We did. I clapped as hard as anyone until the side door opened and a priest walked in.

"This is Father Dembrowski," Mrs. Clark said. "I know some of you boys go to church here and know him very well. We appreciate your coming in to spend some time with us, Father."

"It's my pleasure, Mrs. Clark," the father said.

I recognized him from the bakery. He was a heavyset bald man, about fifty. This was the first time I'd heard him speak English. In the bakery it was always Polish. Rocky had talked to him lots of times. I looked down in case he might recognize me.

"Kite making," the father said, "is a challenging and wonderful activity. I've been doing it for many years. A well-built kite can give you hours and hours of pleasure, so let's get started."

He walked to his worktable, where there were sticks and paper and string. We all watched as he tied the plywood and then stapled thin paper to the wood. It took him only a few minutes.

"When you make them at home," he said, "don't worry about the stapling. I can do that for you here."

Each of us got a little kit of plywood, string, and paper. After the meeting I sneaked mine into the house and hid it in the bottom of the drawer where my shirts and Rocky's long underwear lay side by side. I took it out only when I was sure I would be alone.

I was certain that I could make a good kite. The priest's instructions were clear. But every time I started to tie one piece of plywood against the other, I didn't see a kite; I saw a cross. The more solidly I tied the sticks, the more guilty I felt. I angled first one stick, then another. The shape I finally tied into place was closer to an X than a cross.

Rocky didn't mention Cub Scouts. I think he assumed I had never gone. The next week I sneaked the kite out and walked to the church.

Mrs. Clark had my hat and compass waiting for me. "You can order the rest of the uniform whenever you want," she said. "This is enough to make you official." She put the hat on me. I remained a proud Cub Scout for about fifteen minutes.

But when I brought my frame to Father Dembrowski for stapling, he shook his head. "You'll have to redo this," he said. "It will never fly. Don't you remember what I showed you last week?"

His fingers went at my knot, and before my eyes my kite became a crucifix. I ran for the door. I was up the stairs and out of the church before Mrs. Clark could move from her chair.

At home, I found Rocky cleaning the birdbath. I confessed. "I went to church," I said, "but I didn't make a cross."

He put down the hose and stopped scrubbing the ceramic bowl. I told him about Father Dembrowski and the kite.

"You became one of them?" he asked.

"Just a Cub Scout," I said, "not a goy."

"And you want to do this?"

I nodded. "Everyone in my class is in the den."

"C'mon," he said.

We walked back to the church. I wouldn't go in. Rocky did. "I thought we weren't supposed to go in," I reminded him.

"We're not, but if you're wearing a hat, it's not so bad."

I sat on the steps and waited for him. Mrs. Clark came out first. She put a big arm around me. "I'm sorry, honey. I didn't know. Your grandpa and Father D. talked it all out in Polish. Father D. didn't mean anything about religion. He was just talking about kites."

She waited on the steps with me until Rocky and Father D. came out. Behind them marched my den, everyone carrying a kite. John Clark handed me mine, bent back to my original X.

We flew the kites on the church parking lot. My misshapen one got into the air, but as I ran to give it space, it sank and stuck on the antenna of a 1947 Plymouth—the priest's car.

A few weeks later I bought the trousers and shirt and an official whistle. That year I made a straw broom and a lamp, and I learned to climb a rope, hand over hand. But I never forgot the kite. The next year, when it was time for Boy Scouts, I stayed home.

WHEN I was twelve, Rocky gave up on my intellect. My approaching bar mitzvah made him face reality. I would become a man, but not a rabbi.

Tenderly he gave me the news that was not news to me. "Not everyone can do it," he said. "In Europe you would have had a chance."

"In Europe," I reminded him, "I would have been dead."

He had an alternate plan. He believed in apprenticeships. "You can be a professional man. You'll never have to work nights."

He walked a block with me to the Rexall drugstore. I waited at the soda fountain while Rocky talked to the pharmacist, a man I knew as Doc. Doc had two gold teeth, like fangs, that showed when he opened his mouth to warn us not to read the comic books. A tall man on level ground, Doc was a giant when he stood in the pharmacist's booth, his eyes more observant than today's electronic cameras.

He stepped down from his perch; he and Rocky walked toward me. I sat on a round stool trying to look as professional as I could.

"Your grandpa tells me that you want to be a druggist."

Rocky had coached me in advance. "If he asks you something," Rocky had said, "just say, 'I'm ready to work.'"

I nodded.

"Can I trust you around the comic books?" Doc asked me.

"I'm ready to work," I said.

"Sick people come in here," Doc said. "You'll be exposed."

"I'm ready to work."

337

"You may be ready, but you're too young. It's against the law."

"Give the boy a chance," Rocky said. "I want him to be something."

"I told you, I can't hire him, but maybe . . ." He stared at me.

"I'm ready to work," I said.

"You can hang around," Doc said. "You can learn the ropes."

He walked behind the soda fountain to the stainless steel surface where the soda flavorings and the milk shake machines were. He handed me a damp red rag.

While I wiped the sticky surface of the soda fountain, Doc went back to his druggist's perch, and Rocky, accepting my limitations, walked to the American Bakery, satisfied that he had done what had to be done. I would be a professional man.

At the Rexall store I also swept the floor, straightened the shelves, and stayed alert for the secrets of the druggist's trade.

"If you're a good worker," Rocky had told me, "he'll take you in the back and show you how he makes the medicines. Once you know that, you'll understand science."

I waited, but science eluded me. Doc didn't fill that many prescriptions. Most of the time he worked crossword puzzles from the magazines on the rack. After tearing out a puzzle, he'd put the magazine back for sale. "Nobody'll miss it," he said.

Though I was careful not to risk my job by reading comic books, Doc didn't seem to mind if I read the paper or the magazines. Since I was about to become a scientist myself, I began to notice how often Albert Einstein appeared in the news. Reading about the great physicist whetted my appetite for understanding prescriptions.

One day I finally asked Doc when he was going to show me the compounds.

"Okay," he said. "You wanna know medicine; I'm gonna show you."

He told Jerry, the fountain worker, to watch the store. He led me into the backroom, where there were boxes full of cigarettes and candy and toothpaste alongside the glass bottles of medicine.

Doc opened a bottle and put a blue-and-orange capsule into my hand. "Look at that," he said. "Know what you're holding?"

I didn't know.

"Penicillin," Doc said. He took the capsule and dropped it back into the bottle. "I've seen you reading about Einstein."

I nodded.

"It's all baloney. I mean, he might have invented the atomic bomb all right, but it wasn't the bomb that saved us. It was penicillin. The Germans had a plot to give everybody the clap. You're too young—I'm not gonna tell you how. But once they knew we had penicillin, they called it off. So what do you think is more important—the bomb or penicillin?"

"Penicillin," I said.

"Don't forget it," Doc said.

I tried not to, but all the magazines had pictures of the flash of light and the mushroom cloud. Doc's blue-and-orange capsules couldn't compete with all that power.

When I read that Einstein didn't believe in God and never went to synagogue, it strengthened my own resolve. One Saturday when Rocky was hurrying me to get ready for synagogue, I dropped my own atom bomb. I refused to go. That afternoon we had it out. With Einstein in my corner, I denounced religion.

Rocky stopped talking to me. He didn't wake me; he didn't take me to the bakery. The rest of the family wisely stayed out of it. It complicated matters that I was preparing for my bar mitzvah. I certainly intended to go through with that. I wanted the presents.

"Have a bar mitzvah," Rocky said, "but I won't be there."

We went down to the wire. Nobody could convince either of us to give in. Ten days before I became a man, the drugstore got its first shipment of 3-D comic books. Other than the bar mitzvah, nothing excited me more. Sharkey, who distributed magazines and tobacco, had seen one. "Superman looks like he's flying off the page," he said. "You've never seen anything like it."

In the weeks of my apprenticeship at the Rexall store, I had never opened a comic book. The day the 3-D's arrived, I bought one for a dollar—ten times the price of a regular comic. Mighty Mouse did me in. I wanted to see the red line that signified his speed in three dimensions.

When Doc caught me, I had opened the cellophane packet that contained the red-and-blue three-dimensional glasses, and I was holding the comic at an angle to feel the full force of Mighty Mouse coming off the page.

Doc yanked the comic out of my hands. I held on so tightly that one of the pages ripped in half. He pulled the glasses off my face.

"Get out," he said. "You know the rules."

I ran home and went to my bedroom before I started to cry. When Rocky came in, I was really sobbing. He still wasn't talking to me. He left the room, but in a minute he came back.

"What happened?" he asked.

"Doc kicked me out," I said. I told him why.

Later Jerry told me what happened. "Rocky went at Doc with his fists. It was the funniest thing I ever saw. Doc didn't want to hit him, so he just kept running around the Hallmark card display, and finally he yelled for me to watch the store and he ran out the door."

I was still crying when Rocky came home.

"It was his fault," Rocky said. "The druggist put Einstein into your head. I'm glad you won't be a druggist."

He rubbed my back until I stopped crying.

At my bar mitzvah he sat in the first row and motioned for me to sing louder. He corrected my four mistakes in the Hebrew reading. I gave my speech in Yiddish. I spoke about the atomic bomb. I compared it to the Flood in Noah's time and reminded my audience that nobody promised rainbows after bombs.

After the bar mitzvah I didn't flaunt Einstein, and Rocky was equally discreet about God. For prescriptions we went to the Cut-Rate store on Leonard Street.

Chapter 4

THE way Rocky had blazed our trail in America, my sisters led the way in education. First Bailey, seven years older, then Maxine, two and a half years ahead of me, won scholarships to the University of Michigan, in Ann Arbor. My parents expected me to follow in their footsteps.

Their success gave me greater responsibility. When I was a high school senior, Bailey was already working in Detroit. Maxine had a boyfriend and would clearly be moving far from home when she graduated. I felt the burden of my grandparents' loneliness. If I went away to college, my parents would miss me, but they had other things to do. Rocky and Gootie didn't. The thought of leaving them made me ambivalent about college.

Instead of meeting that subject head-on, we discussed food. At that time there was no kosher food regularly available at the university. At home our meat came every month from Detroit, and Rocky baked the bread. Our packaged goods carried the little circled U that identified it as rabbinically approved. We never ate out.

My sisters began to eat nonkosher at college. "You can, too," my mother said. "You have to."

My break with God had been easy—merely a spiritual matter. Forbidden food was another story. When it came to eating, I remained observant enough to be a rabbi.

As unhappy as Gootie was with the idea of my leaving, her greater fear was that I would starve. At seventeen I had already reached my full height—five feet four inches—but my weight lagged. On a good day I could top one hundred pounds. My admission and the scholarship to the University of Michigan put flesh on her theoretical worries.

In the summer before my freshman year, I went to Ann Arbor for three days of orientation. I took a Greyhound bus. I promised Gootie that I would eat everything.

I stayed in a dormitory and thought I smelled pork everywhere. I took tests in math and Spanish and English, but my anxiety was about the dining room, not the classroom. For three days I ate only breakfast cereals. I came home pale and hungry.

"That's it," Gootie said. "He can't go to college."

I was ready to agree. I was so worried about what I could eat that I did badly on all my exams. The counselor assigned to me told me he didn't know how I'd gotten a scholarship. He advised me to go to Grand Rapids Junior College and take remedial English.

"You're going to Ann Arbor," my mother said, "and you'll eat like everyone else, and you'll be smart. What do tests know?"

Gootie plugged for junior college. "You can go there," she said, "and come home for lunch."

As I struggled to decide, my father reminded me of what happened when he took me to my first big-league game. I was ten, and we went to see the Tigers play the Red Sox. We left home at six a.m. so we'd be in Detroit early enough to watch all of batting practice.

It was a five-hour drive. I carried my glove and my Scripto pencil for autographs, just in case I ran into Al Kaline or Ted Williams in the parking lot. I left my lunch at a rest stop. I wanted to go to my

341

first big-league game without the burden of a half-pound tuna sandwich on yellow challah. I wanted my hands free for pop fouls.

By the time we got to the stadium, it was the fast of Yom Kippur in the back seat. My father circled Briggs Stadium, looking for a parking place. "There it is," he said. Weak and dizzy, I looked up to see the dark green stadium.

My fingers were hardly strong enough to unlock the door. "You've got to eat something," my father said. He turned away from the stadium and stopped at a kosher-style deli.

The waiter told me the hot dogs were kosher, but I would only order a Coke. My father, almost in tears, begged me to eat so I could enjoy the game. The waiter gave me a "Let him starve" look and returned to the kitchen.

Then a waitress came through the swinging doors. "Honey," she said, "come with me," and took me into the kitchen. She let me watch while she put two kosher hot dogs into a thick plastic bag and then boiled them in that bag. She produced a packaged rye bread and pointed out the vegetable shortening. She brought out a side dish of vegetarian baked beans and sat next to me while I ate.

"You almost spoiled it for yourself by being so stubborn," my father said of that incident. "That was just a doubleheader. This time it's your education. You'll have the rest of your life to keep kosher, but if you don't go to college now, you'll never go."

He walked me outside to his Dodge truck. He unlocked the cab and opened the glove compartment. He took out the pair of tiny yellow mittens that I had prized when I was about five.

"My work gloves," I said.

"They remind me that I don't want you to be a truck driver."

In September my parents drove me to Ann Arbor. They helped me unload my belongings in South Quad, and then, for the first time in my life, they took me out to dinner.

My mother had done some research. She asked my sisters and the parents of children who she knew had gone to Michigan. She wanted the name of the best restaurant in town.

My parents didn't tell me until I was in the car that our destination was the Sugar Bowl in downtown Ann Arbor.

By the time we got there, about eight, the restaurant was empty. I later learned it usually was. The Sugar Bowl was a huge high-ceilinged place, with plaster columns and walls of two-tone green. A Greek family owned it, and they all worked there. Demetra, our waitress, ushered us to an eight-person booth. All the booths were that size or larger. My feet barely touched the ground.

I had, of course, been in restaurants—the coffee-shop variety— but I'd never had to face a menu. Now the pressure was on. My parents tried to pretend it was an everyday event, just an American mom and dad taking their college boy out to dinner.

"He'll have a steak," my mother said, "the best one you've got."

They worked at being casual. My father talked about the Michigan football team, about the beautiful dormitory my sister Bailey had lived in. We killed time while in the dark kitchen of the Sugar Bowl my steak sizzled.

Demetra finally arrived with my dinner beneath a steel cover. She laid the meat in front of me, surrounded by steaming mashed potatoes and green beans. I had heard of T-bones, and now I saw one. I recognized the T, surrounded by fat and gristle.

"It looks delicious," my mother said as she sipped her juice.

My father raised his coffee cup. "*L'chaim,*" he said.

Their bravery put a lump in my throat. My father's grandmother returned to Poland in the 1880s because she didn't trust the kosher food in America. Gootie's stepgrandmother lived in Brooklyn beyond the age of one hundred without ever tasting canned food. Our family history was studded with such culinary denial.

I caught my mother staring at the steak. That T-bone was not meat; it was a border. She and my father and all my ancestors sat on one side of the table—the steak and I on the other.

"Don't let it get cold," my mother said.

I cut, I bit, I chewed. My mother held her breath. I swallowed. After the first bite, I ate everything on one side of the long bone. It was a love feast. I did it for them; they did it for me.

They drove home satisfied that I would not starve in college. In the dormitory I unpacked my clothes and didn't vomit.

My roommate, a sophomore from Detroit, had spent the evening in one of the lounges playing bridge. About midnight he returned.

"What did you do?" he asked.

"My parents took me out for a steak dinner."

"Lucky you," he said.

343

As an undergraduate I had, for the first time, roommates my own age, and I did not starve. I began graduate school at Stanford in September 1964. In October my father suffered what he said was a mild heart attack. He hired a driver to help him on his scrap metal rounds, but he expected to be at full strength in a few months.

When I came home for winter vacation in December 1965, he looked well. My first night home, we watched a Michigan basketball game together. The Wolverines had a great team that year.

That September my father had driven to California with me, and we'd spent one night in Las Vegas. He'd won two hundred dollars shooting craps and another hundred at blackjack. He'd enjoyed the game, and we'd talked about going again the following fall. He didn't understand exactly what I was doing at Stanford, where I had entered the Ph.D. program in English.

"What does a doctor of philosophy do?" he'd asked.

"They teach in colleges," I'd said. I was a little tentative because I wasn't sure if they did anything else. I intended to be a writer, but I didn't know how to become one. I thought that getting a Ph.D. would at least keep me close to books.

I was upstairs shaving when I heard my mother scream. I ran to their room. My father was on the floor struggling for breath. His back was arched, his fists clenched. My mother called an ambulance. I put my mouth over his and blew with all my might. From the back of his throat I heard a sound like a handful of those Las Vegas chips clinking against one another. It was the death rattle. I blew it away.

In a few seconds his lips moved. In a minute he tried to sit up. By the time the ambulance arrived, he didn't even want to go to the hospital. But he did go and he stayed, and in the next seven weeks there were two more such episodes.

I didn't return to Stanford. I stayed home to do his work and to visit him in the hospital. Although I had almost tasted his death, I knew my father would recover and live for a long time. He looked fine, and he didn't want me to stay away from school.

"The scrap business isn't for you," he said. "Go back to California. I'll be okay in a little while."

He wasn't okay in January or in February. He remained in the hospital, and on the last day of the month, just after midnight, his heart stopped. He was fifty-nine.

Rocky, who fought with everyone else, never had a run-in with my father. He lost another son.

Gootie survived my father by just over a year. I took over the truck, shoveling up steel and aluminum shavings in machine shops in Big Rapids and Lakeview or standing by the loading dock at the Kysor Heater factory in Cadillac, Michigan, while union men loaded our truck with barrels of brass shavings and used radiators.

By then the girls were married. Maxine lived in California, Bailey in Minnesota. My mother, Rocky, and I remained in an empty house full of memories. My father's months in the hospital, and then Gootie's, were uninsured. I had to keep working on the truck. In the glove compartment the yellow mittens were still there, but I didn't need them to remind me that this wasn't what my father had wished.

I hated the small talk with the workers in the machine shops and garages. The various grades of aluminum and brass and bronze all looked to my eyes like what they were called—junk. My year and a half at Stanford seemed like paradise. The only thing that gave me satisfaction that year were my daydreams, the unwritten stories that kept me company between Grand Rapids and Cadillac.

About six months later my mother tried a daring experiment. Our business was teetering. Competitors understood my inexperience and offered higher prices to our customers.

While my father was alive, the customers were secure. His honesty was beyond doubt. Some of the factories didn't even weigh what they sold to him, and the men on the shop floor knew him as their friend. He spoke their language; I didn't.

One Monday my mother and Francis, our driver, secretly arranged to start early. At three a.m. she stepped up into the cab of the truck to sit beside Francis and ride north. By five, when my alarm went off and I read her note in the kitchen, she was well past Big Rapids and busy studying a list of metals and prices. That day a fifty-seven-year-old, four-foot eleven-inch grandmother oversaw eleven tons of mixed metals and steel scrap.

She went out of her way to greet every one of my father's friends at Kysor. She told the purchasing agent that she knew others were trying to take our business and asked him to give us time to learn what we had to do. Her hair was as white as Rocky's, and she had

345

his energy. On the loading dock the men had to keep her from trying to move the barrels by hand.

When she came back with the load of metal, she drove a hard bargain at the junkyard. She asked the manager to write out the price of every metal; then she took out the list the purchasing agent had given her—the prices our competitors were offering.

She came home after fourteen hours, with smudges on her slacks and grease under her nails. She had new prices—a penny and a half raise on metals, five dollars more a ton on the steel. Her earnings were about three hundred dollars more than mine would have been.

"Go back to school," she said.

I waited a few weeks to make sure she really could run the scrap business; then I left not for California, but to go back to Ann Arbor, and I took along my old roommate, ninety-three by then.

He was happy to accompany me. At home he had outlived his town and his time. He had been among the founders of the synagogue in Grand Rapids, but to the younger members he was merely a weird old man sitting in the last row, chanting prayers that long ago had been removed from the liturgy.

Yet at ninety-three he was scarcely different from the way he'd seemed to me all my life. It was as if his body had reached a permanent seventy. His white hair thinned but stayed. He had good color and muscle tone. He didn't wear glasses. He was strong. He wanted to work.

In Ann Arbor I rented better housing than I could afford—a suburban garden apartment close to a bus stop and far from the campus, teeming in those years with antiwar protest.

When I met Debby, Rocky had already been in Ann Arbor with me for a year. He sometimes walked the three miles to campus. He made friends at the synagogue and in the apartment building. He baked for neighbors in the complex. When she could get away, my mother spent weekends with us. I felt lucky to have been able to return to a version of the life I wanted without abandoning Rocky. I didn't want to change the way things were.

By the time I walked back into my apartment that night in 1968, he was asleep. There was one item Debby had left behind—a silky striped robe. I tiptoed into the closet and hung it on my side.

In the morning he did not mention the girl. I'm sure he considered the matter finished. When I got out of bed at seven, he had already baked a dozen rolls, cleaned the kitchen, and taken out the garbage. I knew he was angry, because he was reading the Help Wanted section of the Ann Arbor *News*.

Whenever he was mad at me, he looked for a job; and whenever I was mad at him, I delivered a lecture. These were our styles—and neither one worked. But that didn't stop us.

There were no "good mornings." The minute I stepped into the kitchen, he headed for the bedroom—not to avoid me, but to make the bed. He loved order. I often thought, when I was a teenager and wanted on vacation mornings to luxuriate in my bed, that he wouldn't have minded my sleeping if only he could have made up the bed while I was still in it.

He would stand for no impediments to his sense of the way things should be. And where girls were concerned, until Debby, I had not tested him.

I hardly knew Debby, yet I had brought her back to our apartment. Maybe I had already decided in the crowded ballroom that she was the one, and maybe he suspected as much when he saw the living room full of her clothes. Of course he hated the disorder. But a girl in my life would be the greatest disorder of all. I should have understood that and searched for some way to reassure him. Instead, between bites of cinnamon roll I explained modern romance.

"First, there is nothing wrong with bringing a girl to your apartment. Second, everyone is entitled to privacy. Third, under any circumstances you don't throw a person out."

"You're lucky," he said, "that I woke up, or she'd be here right now with a policeman."

"A policeman?"

"Yes, a policeman. You bring a girl into your house and carry her clothes in, and then you don't marry her—they'll put you in jail for breach of promise."

"This is not 1910. There's no such thing as breach of promise, and anyway, I was just giving her a place to store her clothes."

"She needs storage," he said, "they got lockers at the bus station. She won't sue the bus station." He left for his morning walk.

"It's not over," I yelled to him as he slammed the door, and I hoped I was telling the truth.

347

ALL THAT SUMMER I WAS STUDYING for my preliminary exams. I had
to know English literature from Chaucer in 1400 to Henry James in
1916. My reading list was nine single-spaced typed pages.

Of course it was impossible to know it all, but three or four
months of solid reading wouldn't hurt my chances. That was my job
for the summer—to lie on the gray vinyl couch, a thick book resting
on my belly and a yellow highlighter in my right hand every once in
a while darting toward a line of Shakespeare or Ruskin.

Rocky couldn't take it. "Lazy good-for-nothing," he called me.

"It's my job. I'm getting paid to do it." It was true. I had a
summer study fellowship.

"You lay there doing this. . . ." He imitated with his finger my
gesture of underlining. "Look, I'm working, too." He mimicked
me, underlining the empty air.

What I was doing did not to him constitute a job. Every day I
woke up, ate, showered, and went to the couch. I liked to stick
around in the mornings to keep him company. After his TV shows
he would make lunch for me, usually herring and onions and coffee.
I had been eating that for so long that it didn't seem strange to me,
but every now and then, when he packed me a lunch, I noticed
people moving away when I spread my feast on the lawn or at a
crowded table in the student union.

It finally got through to me that he was happier if I left. When I
ate the oatmeal as fast as I could, almost chugged the hot coffee,
loaded my briefcase, and hurried away, he believed I was working.

I would stay away until suppertime. We'd watch the Walter
Cronkite news together; then he'd cook soft-boiled or scrambled
eggs and start to get ready for bed. He was always asleep by eight
thirty and usually up by four. He kept his bakery hours.

Twice a week I helped him take a bath. Tuesdays was a quickie,
just for hygiene; the main bath came on Friday afternoon. In honor
of the approaching Sabbath, Rocky soaked. Tub lifeguard was a
new job for me. At home, in the big claw-footed bath, he had been
confident. The apartment tub, though half the size, required him to
enter at a steep angle, and there were no sides to grab.

The bath relaxed us both. While he splashed in the warm water,
I teased him about how good he looked after the hair washing.

"Let it grow over your ears," I suggested, "and you can be like the Beatles. There are no Yiddish rock stars; you'll have the market all to yourself."

I stretched a few white hairs to the tip of his ear. "You'll look ten years younger," I said.

"I don't wanna look younger. I wanna get dressed and make *Kiddush*."

After I helped him dry his back and legs, he put on the clean union suit that he had carried all rolled up, his socks in the middle, and placed on the back of the toilet Friday morning.

I knelt to put on his socks; then he slid his feet into sheepskin slippers at least a size too large. I held his arm as he crossed the slippery bathroom tiles, but at the safety of the dark green carpet he always broke free and hurried to his bed, where the brown suit and a clean shirt had also been waiting since morning.

Though I was the one who went out after he slept, he was the one who dressed and went to the party.

He lit the candles and said *Kiddush,* the prayer over the wine. When he pulled the white cover from the warm challah, he held it up to admire his work before he sang out the blessing. He waited for me to tell him how good the bread tasted. I made him wait a few seconds until I approved. Then, in a ritual no less sacred because no prayer preceded it, he grabbed the back of my neck, pulled me closer, and kissed me.

"Good *Shabbes*," he said. "Now eat."

Chapter 5

I STARTED going to every peace rally I heard about, hoping to run into Debby. I wanted to see her again. Although the university had about thirty thousand students, it wasn't that hard to find someone.

After our first meeting I expected to find her the next day, just by sitting outside in the middle of campus, but I didn't see her. By the third day I even wandered into the Rainbow People's house. Nobody I asked seemed to know her. She wasn't at the coffeehouses or bookstores, either; not in the student union or on the diagonal—called the diag—the grassy green by the library where everyone congregated on summer days. I studied in the library, and on frequent breaks I looked for her wherever I happened to go.

I didn't mention her again to Rocky, and he didn't ask. He liked to think his actions were final. When he ordered someone out, only an act of God could bring them back. He did, however, find me another companion.

I had been up very late studying. I was still asleep when he shook me one Thursday morning about seven thirty.

On Monday and Thursday mornings he went to the campus synagogue. They needed ten men to hold services, and it was always a struggle to get people to come at that hour. I refused, and he didn't press me. Anyway, he didn't need me. He made new friends there—most of them graduate students in philosophy. That Thursday, as he shook me awake, he meant to please me.

"I found someone like you," he said, and he stepped back to produce a slightly familiar face—a fellow graduate student whom I had seen but whose name I didn't know.

The thin, sandy-haired young man stood near my pillow. I rolled over, hoping they'd leave.

"Get up and talk to him," Rocky said. "You can sleep later." When he started pulling the bedspread up, I understood that I had no chance to escape.

As soon as I stepped out of bed, Rocky had the bedspread over the pillow. The graduate student stuck out his hand. "Joel Kerner," he said. "I've seen you lots of times, but I never knew we had so much in common."

Five minutes later, while Rocky poured coffee and Kerner praised the cinnamon rolls, I learned what we had in common.

"Your grandpa says you're having some problems understanding Shakespeare. He asked me to help."

I gave Rocky my best imitation of his own "I'll get you for this" look. It didn't bother him.

"You don't have to be ashamed," Rocky said.

"I wrote my M.A. on *Antony and Cleopatra*," Kerner said modestly. "If I can help with anything . . ."

"I don't need help," I said to Rocky, ignoring the guest.

"Don't be so stubborn. It's no sin to ask someone who knows more."

"You don't think that I know anything about Shakespeare?"

"If you did, you'd go on to something else."

I literally threw up my hands. "What do you think I do for twelve or more hours a day?"

"That's what I've been trying to figure out," Rocky said. "You sit there, and nothing goes in. If a druggist reads something and he doesn't understand, he calls the doctor and the doctor tells him."

I looked at Kerner, who was keeping a very serious expression. "And you're the doctor?" I asked him.

"M.A.," he said, "from Johns Hopkins."

"Okay," I said. "Tell me about Shakespeare."

Rocky nodded and sat down to listen.

Poor Kerner. He was two years behind me. His eyes blinked rapidly, and he stuttered a little. "I didn't bring any notes. I wasn't expecting . . . But if you want to discuss individual plays, I know the tragedies best."

"Okay," I said. "Explain *King Lear*. And do it fast."

That was the kind of direct question Rocky liked. It wasn't fair to do this to Kerner, but I wanted to teach Rocky a lesson.

"Lear was a foolish old man who learned the limits of his power through tragic experience. In the end he is redeemed by love."

Kerner took a big bite of cinnamon roll so he could chew for a while without having to explain more. I started to feel sorry for him. Suddenly, watching him chew and sip coffee as he thought over the explanation of *King Lear*, I burst out laughing.

"He tells you what something means, and you think it's funny," Rocky said. "That's why you'll never be anything. To you, laughing is more important than understanding."

"Right," I said. "King Lear was the same. He liked to kid around so much that he hired a professional joker. They called him a fool; he's one of the most important people in the play."

"If he was still a king," Rocky said, "then you wouldn't have to worry. You'd get that job." He looked at Kerner. "Does he know enough Shakespeare?"

"I think so," Kerner said.

"Good," Rocky said. "Now go learn something else."

That afternoon in the library Kerner found me. "I've been thinking about you and your grandpa all day," he said. "I'm really fascinated by Rocky. Would you mind if I came over again sometime?"

"You wanna teach me some more?"

"No," he said. "I want to learn."

Rocky obliged him. One morning, when I came into the kitchen for breakfast, I found Kerner, literally bound in leather.

The tefillin—two leather bands with wooden boxes on each—were all over his arm and neck. Rocky, in a hurry and assuming Kerner had more knowledge of the procedure, had tangled the Shakespeare man in the paraphernalia of prayer. I helped untangle him.

"Seven times you wind it around your arm, and then you do this." Rocky whipped the leather band into a shape around his hand. He had been doing it every day since his own bar mitzvah some eighty-one years earlier. He wouldn't slow down for Kerner.

"It's not so hard," he told Kerner. "Even he learned how. Maybe he still remembers."

I did, and I demonstrated for Kerner, slowly. "Now we're even," I told Rocky. "He taught me Shakespeare; I taught him tefillin."

"Not even," Rocky said. "Shakespeare's not important—this is."

Kerner bought it. A few weeks later he was spending more time on Hebrew than on *Hamlet*. He was around so much that I began to like him. He was twenty-four and a seeker who had discovered his Judaism on a visit to Israel the year before.

Kerner's mother had died when he was six. His father and older brother raised him to become a businessman, a good citizen. The trip to Israel had opened his eyes, and now Rocky was opening them wider. Kerner's father insisted that he finish his education, but Kerner himself wanted to immigrate to Israel immediately.

"Two years," he said. "I promised my father that I'd stay two more years, and that's it. Then I'm moving to Israel."

While the two of them discussed religion and Zionism, I kept looking for Debby, but after a month I gave up. I knew that if she was in Ann Arbor, I would have seen her. Her memory drifted away. I realized that even if she had been available, I was so occupied with studying that I wouldn't have had time for her.

I did, though, make some time for the Detroit Tigers. They were in the midst of winning their first pennant in my life as a fan. The televised night games were my reward for a long day of study. And if the Tigers made it to the World Series, I wouldn't have to miss a thing. My prelims would end the week before.

In the world, big things were happening. Robert Kennedy's assassination, the riots at the Democratic Convention, Lyndon Johnson's decision not to run for reelection, and, above all, the ever escalating war in Vietnam. I did not shut my eyes to the news; Rocky wouldn't let me. His friend Walter Cronkite told us the way it was each day, but I was so immersed in my reading that the events of the day seemed no more immediate than the 1666 fire of London.

The Defense Department broke through my barrier of books. In the mail came greetings from my draft board. I went to the graduate dean, who told me that all graduate students in good standing received automatic deferments. I didn't have to choose between serving my country or my conscience. I just had to stay in school.

THE warmth I felt against my knee surprised me. Who expects a dog in the general reading room? It was the day before the prelims, and I was more than ready. I was daydreaming about the World Series, so when I felt the dog's tail and bent down to see him, I was more amused than distracted. But others were more disturbed, so I led him out the front door. I watched him sniff the air, look around among the guitar players and Frisbee throwers on the diag. I watched him run right to a girl in a brown sack dress. He jumped up to lick her face. She laughed as he almost knocked her down.

I ran almost as fast as he did.

"Remember me?" I said.

"Oh, yeah," she said. "The guy with the friendly roommate." There were hundreds of people around and her dog was barking at me, and there was someone standing next to her, talking to her—but I only noticed her.

"I looked everywhere for you," I said.

"I've been gone. I had to stay home the rest of the summer."

"I missed you," I said. "Give me another chance?"

The person she was talking to, a dark-skinned man in a suit, coughed. "Excuse me," he said, "we were talking."

"This is Bijan," Debby said. "He's from Iran."

"Let's go have coffee," Bijan said. He took her arm.

"I'm sorry that I was so rude," I said to Bijan. "I know I'm barging in, but I've been looking for her. I can't let her get away without knowing where she lives."

Debby borrowed a business card from Bijan. On the back she

wrote her address and phone number. The two of them and the dog walked across campus. I stood there watching.

They were almost at the corner of State Street where the green ended and the stores began. Bijan crossed the street while Debby and the dog turned back to campus. The dog got to me first and slobbered my cheeks. Debby came running and called him off.

"How'd you know I was waiting?" I asked.

"I didn't," she said. "I was just hoping."

She had coffee with me instead of the foreign student. I learned she'd had a run-in with her mother. Her parents had taken away her car and demanded that she stop being a hippie.

"Did you?" I asked.

"Of course," she said. "I joined the D.A.R. and had my nails done. My mother was so impressed that she allowed me to return to Ann Arbor under the condition that I do nothing to stop the war or help the poor. I am only to study."

"Boring. That's all I've been doing since I saw you."

"But you have such an exciting homelife. When it's his turn, does he cruise the old-age homes and then you get to throw the ladies out? No kidding. Do you go through this a lot?"

"You're the first. I hope it doesn't start a streak."

She loved it when I told her about breach of promise.

"He's a gentleman after all. I like that. So if I ever do go back there, you have to marry me—right?"

"Let me pass prelims first; then we'll discuss it."

We were in a dark green booth in a restaurant called Drake's. In her dress and expensive sandals Debby seemed so unlike the barefoot girl in ragged jeans. Yet even dressed like a sorority girl, she looked like a waif. Her sad brown eyes filled with pleasure when I held her hand. We discovered that we were both from Grand Rapids—not such a rare coincidence, but I was willing to read it as a good sign. Through the window her dog, George, watched every move. He couldn't take his eyes off her. Neither could I.

On the day of my first exam Rocky pulled out his king-size thermos and had it ready for me at the door. It was probably made in the '30s—real glass and a stainless steel cup. He took it to work every day and used to let me sip from the cup. When I saw the bottle at the door, it was the first time I knew that he took my studying

354

seriously. I realized that Kerner had probably gotten through to him.

He couldn't have given me a better gift. I never opened it, but having that thermos in front of me was the best lucky charm I could have received. I brought it all week, with the original coffee.

I DIDN'T see Debby that week, but every night after each of the four prelims, I talked to her. We had a date for Saturday night.

I had a note in the mail from Kerner wishing me luck on the exams. It turned out he was the one who needed it.

I knew something was wrong when Rocky came home from the synagogue on Saturday and didn't yell at me because I was still in bed. I had finished prelims on Friday and was treating myself to a sleep-in morning. When he didn't come in to make the bed, I worried and went out to the kitchen.

"We said *Tehillim* for Kerner," Rocky said, referring to readings from the Book of Psalms. "They say he won't live through the day." That was all he knew.

The University Hospital operator wouldn't tell me if Kerner was a patient, but around noon I got a call from an intensive care nurse.

"Mr. Kerner asked me to call you," she said. "Could you please come over quickly?"

She told me he had been shot the night before in front of the library. The bullet had entered his neck, and he was awaiting neurosurgery. His family was on the way.

"He wants you to pray with him," the nurse said.

"Is he going to live?" I asked.

"Get here as quickly as you can," she said.

The war, which I had tried to avoid all summer, had made an unscheduled appearance. On the diag, where Debby's dog and a dozen others chased Frisbees, where lovers held hands, and in view of a dozen bystanders, Kerner had walked past an angry drunk.

The man had been standing in front of the library, harassing passersby. Nobody took him seriously. He was a corporal who was AWOL. A crazy soldier with a gun. How free and easy the students must have seemed to him that night—carrying books, laughing, not even noticing him until he yelled and shoved a few, and even then they just walked away from him. Kerner had tried to walk away, too.

The nurse took me right to him in a tiny room off the intensive care unit. "We're getting him ready for surgery," she said, "but he wants to see you. Please hurry." She stood next to me. "Don't touch him. We don't want the slightest movement."

I waved to him—I didn't know yet that he couldn't wave back. I had to bend down close to his lips to hear his voice. His face looked good. There was a small bruise on his forehead. That was all. I wouldn't have been surprised to see him stand and walk away.

"Help me say the *Shma*," he said.

I opened the prayer book I had brought along and read aloud the Hebrew creed—which, though said at other times, too, is what believers utter with their last breath. Then the nurse tapped my shoulder, and the surgical team wheeled him away.

I went home and told Rocky all that I knew. I omitted just one thing. The nurse had told me that the spinal column had been cut. If Kerner survived, he'd never again have use of his arms or legs.

Rocky prayed for him from one of his oversized books from Lithuania. The bindings had broken many times, and he'd repaired them with Scotch tape, masking tape, and black electrical tape.

At five o'clock Kerner's father and older brother called. They didn't know anyone in Ann Arbor. The nurse had told them that Joel had called me. They were in the surgical waiting room. I telephoned Debby. She wasn't home. I left a message canceling our date and drove to the hospital.

Joel's father, his brother, and I waited until the surgeon came out at about eight thirty. The news was as good as it could be. He would be able to breathe. "He should be able to move his neck, too," the doctor said.

"What else?" Kerner senior asked.

"Everything above the neck—his eyes, his face."

I couldn't look at his father when he heard. I excused myself. I didn't know whether to pray for Kerner's recovery or not.

As I walked down the steps of the hospital, George ran up to greet me. On a bench beneath a lamppost, Debby waited.

"How'd you know?" I asked.

"You left a message, and then I heard it on the news. By now everyone knows. They already caught the guy who did it." She put her arms around me. "I'm sorry," she said. "I really am."

The Tigers beat St. Louis in seven games. I caught only fragments. Instead, I spent most of that week looking at a little screen in the intensive care unit that recorded Kerner's heartbeats. Every day he got stronger. When the doctors told him he would be a quadriplegic, he surprised everyone. He still wanted to live.

Once Kerner was well enough to be moved to a ward, he wanted to study, but the staff was not pleased. There were sixteen people on the ward. A few had use of their arms; none had use of their legs. Visiting hours ended at seven because the nurses had so much to do, even though the early hours inconvenienced lots of families.

"Nobody's here for a short stay," Helen, the head nurse, told me. She had worked on that ward for a decade. Nobody argued with her. "They can learn to work around the hours; so can you."

When Kerner told the neurosurgeon he needed time to study for his prelims and needed someone to read to him, the doctor got him special permission. Each evening someone could read to him. Everyone in the English department volunteered, but after a few days Helen called a halt. "They're not studying; they're visiting."

Kerner worked out a compromise. Someone could help him study from seven to nine, but it had to be the same person every day. That, Helen said, would avoid the temptation to do more than study.

Kerner asked for me. We developed a routine. I came home earlier to have dinner with Rocky. Rocky baked something for Kerner and sent it with me. While I read to Kerner, Debby studied in the hospital cafeteria and George waited for us out front.

Rocky visited Kerner from time to time, though by mutual agreement they put off the Hebrew study temporarily.

Debby and I didn't go to many movies and never had time for bars or parties. Sometimes after the hospital we stopped at the library. Then, as quickly as we could, we went to her apartment.

In February the man who shot Kerner was sentenced—three to five years.

Chapter 6

ROCKY knew something was up. He noticed that I didn't come home sometimes until one or two or even later, although none of his realizations stopped him from waking me at seven.

No matter how tired, I had to get out of bed, eat oatmeal and a roll, take my herring or smoked fish or boiled chicken lunch, and hurry out of the apartment. Sometimes I managed to get in a few hours at the library before I collapsed; other days I didn't even try. I just went right to Debby's apartment and slept until ten or eleven.

Debby didn't understand why I put up with it. Filial affection was not her strong point. When I met her mother, I understood.

When Harriet walked into Debby's apartment, she took two steps onto the cracked linoleum and stopped abruptly, as if to await a bellhop with her bags. She looked around the living room/dining room/kitchen, taking in everything slowly. I stood in front of the three-legged couch, near the books that supported the load of the missing leg. Her eyes passed me by as if I were a sign at a bus stop.

Debby had told me that her mother was almost fifty, but her figure had remained girlish. Even her face, aided by light makeup, had aged without losing its beauty. She had bleached hair and wore an off-white suit that would show spots if she sat down anywhere in the apartment. She demonstrated no inclination to sit. After her visual scan she walked quickly into the bedroom, then turned her eyes from the bathroom as if she couldn't stand any more.

"Why didn't you tell me it's a basement?" she said. "Rats live in basements." She nodded to me as if I were the doorman. Debby didn't let her get away with it.

"Hello, Mother," Debby said. "This is the person I told you about. You could at least be civil enough to greet him."

Harriet extended her fingertips to me, then pulled them away from my sweaty grip as fast as she could.

Nothing satisfied her. The refrigerator motor was too loud. The faucets leaked. The mattress was soft, the linoleum filthy.

Finally Debby stopped her. "Did the housing bureau send you?" she asked. "Or is this a friendly visit?"

"Everything I do is friendly," Harriet said. She was opening the closets. "And where are your things?" she asked me.

"At my house," I said. "You don't think I'd live in a place like this, do you?"

From the kitchen Debby bit her cheeks to keep from laughing.

"What do you study?" Harriet asked me.

"Literature."

"Is that practical?"

With a look Debby encouraged me to take her on. "Of course," I said. "Some of the most successful people can read and write."

She chose to ignore me. She pulled out her checkbook and wrote six separate postdated checks as she stood.

"This is for the rent."

"So you approve after all," Debby said.

"No," she answered, "but you signed a lease, and I believe that a promise is binding. I hope you remember your promises."

"Of course I do," Debby said. She looked at me. "Have I done anything to stop the war?" she asked. I shook my head. "And if you don't believe him, just keep watching the news. The bombing, the napalming—it's right on schedule."

"I'm sure my daughter has convinced you that I'm a warmonger," Harriet said. "I want peace as much as any of you, but I don't want her getting arrested every two weeks."

"C'mon, Ma," Debby said. "Where else am I gonna meet such interesting guys?"

Harriet looked at me as if to decide whether I really might be interesting. I asked if she'd like coffee or soda.

"No, thank you," she said, "but if Debby will change her clothes, I'll be happy to take both of you to lunch."

Debby had dressed in preparation. She wore a white blouse and a flowing Indian skirt—even a little eye makeup. She went to the bedroom and returned quickly, wearing jeans and a T-shirt.

"All right," Harriet said. "Wear what you had on."

Debby changed back to her original outfit, and they both seemed satisfied, as if they could relax now that they'd had the necessary face-off.

In the restaurant, Harriet seemed almost pleasant. Debby didn't talk back. Neither did I. After Harriet paid, she pulled two credit cards out of her wallet and handed them to Debby.

"Saks," Harriet said, "and Jacobsen's—I didn't know they had a store here. Ann Arbor has finally improved a little."

Debby accepted the cards.

"Use them," Harriet said.

That night, when we were lying in bed reading, Debby opened the drawer of her bedside table and threw the cards in. There were at least a dozen others already there.

"Do you ever use any of them?"

"No," Debby said. "She'd get too much satisfaction. Her aim is to have me spend and then to hold it over my head for control."

"I used to envy the rich. You're making me change my opinions."

"I'm not rich," Debby said. "She is."

Partly, I think, to convince me that she was serious about breaking away from her parents' financial domination, Debby got a job. She supervised the Burns Park Elementary School playground during lunch for children in nursery school and, after three, for the older children who stayed late.

When I could, I joined her on the playground. I loved the way the fourth graders in the outfield would yell "He's up!" when I grabbed a bat, and the way they would move back almost against the wire fence barely one hundred feet away.

If Debby was pitching, as she often did, she didn't make it easy. She could throw the ball at least as well as I could, and when I came to the plate, she switched from underhand to sidearm. She played for the girls, and I for the boys. The boys had always won until Debby showed up; now the nine-year-old males counted on me to return them to constant victory.

Debby was a half-inch shorter than I and about the same weight, but more agile. She moved effortlessly, not only when she pitched but when she swam or jogged or threw a stick for George. She wasted no movements.

When she pitched, she kept her hair in a short ponytail that stuck out of the back of her baseball cap—a light brown one that bore the logo of her father's factory.

"Ready, Mr. Rotten Apple?" she liked to ask. The girls took up the chant: "Mr. Rotten Apple, Mr. Rotten Apple . . ."

When my team tried to rile her, they yelled, "We want a pitcher, not a belly itcher." The more they yelled, the more she taunted the boys by scratching her stomach before she turned to lob one down the middle to them.

WRITING a dissertation, followed by fun on the playground by day, reading to Kerner in the evening, and going to Debby's at night gave my life a new fullness. But someone was left out.

He never said anything; I didn't even see him reading the want

ads. When I felt guilty for spending less time at the apartment, I told myself he was probably happy because I was working so hard. I didn't try to incorporate him into the life I was living, the life in which Debby, not Rocky, was now at the center.

Though I hated to bring him up, I told Debby one evening how guilty I felt for leaving him alone so much of the time.

"Guilty," she said. "You set the clock for three and drive across town so that he can wake you up at seven, and you feel guilty toward him. How do you think I feel when you tiptoe out to Grampa?"

"You've got other things in your life," I said. "He doesn't."

"What about the synagogue?"

"He already goes there every hour it's open."

"What about a hobby?"

"He doesn't have hobbies. People like him only understand work. He wouldn't know what a hobby is."

"I think you're his hobby," Debby said. "A full-time one."

I DIDN'T TELL DEBBY THAT I wanted to marry her; I told Kerner. He had amazed the medical staff by going at his graduate work a month after being shot. They thought he was the most dedicated student on earth. I knew better. We only talked literature when we had to. Whenever a nurse was suspicious, Kerner, who knew a lot of poetry by heart, would break into quotation. When Helen, the head nurse, was on duty, we had to be extra careful; sometimes she actually stood at the foot of the bed to listen.

When Helen wasn't there, we talked openly. "I don't want to be an English teacher," he said. "I never did. I'm just going through the motions. Whether or not I get a Ph.D. didn't matter before. Now what difference can it make?"

"It will help you get a job."

"Getting a job," he said, "will be the least of my problems. What about you? What will you do when you finish?"

When I told him I wanted to marry Debby, he had only one question: "What will Rocky do? Will he still live with you?"

"I don't know," I said. "He could go back to Grand Rapids, but the synagogue isn't Orthodox anymore and all his friends are dead. He'd just be waiting to die; he'd have nothing to look forward to."

"What about Israel?" Kerner asked. "I'm going. Why can't he?"

"I want him a little closer than that."

"It's hard for you, isn't it?" he asked. "Do you and Debby talk about it?"

"I don't mention him unless I have to. He's not number one on her list. But I'll have to think of something."

Rocky had been thinking, too, and he made the first move. Instead of looking for a job, he decided to find a new place to live.

"I've been looking," he told me one night. "You got no time to keep running out here to me. And you're never home. It's a waste of money. I don't need such a big apartment."

His solution—we'd split up. He'd get a single room on campus, and so would I. It was a more elegant plan than any I'd thought of.

"When will I see you?" I asked.

"Whenever you want. You're the one that's busy, not me."

I thought he was merely using the suggestion to remind me to spend more time with him. I was wrong. He meant it, and looking for a room put him in such a great mood that I didn't protest. He rode into campus with me in the morning and began walking along the street where the Victorian houses mingled with ugly, expensive apartment houses. In the old houses you could sometimes get a bargain.

As I thought about it, the room might not be so bad. He'd be on campus in the middle of things. He could even sit in on classes if he ever wanted to. Instead of seeing him at seven and briefly for dinner, I could pick other times, maybe four to six every day. Best of all, it would free me to move in with Debby. She had offered.

I already kept a few shirts and trousers there. Not moving in would be silly. She didn't hide our living together—I did.

LOOKING for a room occupied Rocky and relieved me, until he walked past the elementary school. He had answered an ad in the *Michigan Daily* that offered a garage apartment in return for lawn care and general handyman work. I can imagine what the couple, expecting a student, thought when Rocky rang their doorbell.

Being turned down must have been especially disappointing to him, because he was in a foul mood when he walked past the schoolyard. I didn't see him approaching from behind home plate.

I held the bat in my hand. The outfield was deep, and there were boys on base. Debby glared at me, took off her cap to wipe her brow. I waved the bat. The kids loved it when we went through the big-league motions. She ran her hand through her fine brown hair, which hung straight and then curved just below her ears. Half-inch bangs slipped down her forehead. She tanned easily and was already nut brown, even in early spring. She rubbed up the tattered softball, pounded her glove, eyed the plate, gave me a mean look. I knocked the flattened milk carton that served as home plate.

"Put it here, belly itcher!" I yelled.

She came in with a high fast one. I swung and missed—and not on purpose. I struck out. The girls were going wild, mobbing Debby. The boys were already thinking about next time.

"Lazy good-for-nothing." I heard the gruff whisper. His face was against the chain-link fence. "This is how you're working."

Debby freed herself from the girls and walked to the fence.

"Hi," she said, "you want a turn at bat?"

Rocky spit and literally ran from the park.

I waited until dinnertime, then drove home. There was no meal, and he had already packed the duffel bag that I'd bought for him when he moved to Ann Arbor.

"If you'd listen," I said, "I could explain."

"You listen," he said. "I got a new place."

"All right," I said, "but there's something more important. I don't want to hide this from you any longer. I have a girlfriend."

"So does every dog on the street," he said.

"So I'm a dog on the street because I play softball for an hour with some kids."

"You're no good," he said. "After tomorrow you won't see me."

He went to his room and slammed the door. I called Debby to tell her that I was going to stay home that night.

"He has a tantrum, spits at me, and you reward him."

"Lay off," I said. "He's moving out tomorrow. I want to spend his last night here with him. I'm sorry he spit at you. I apologize for him. What more can I do?"

I didn't sleep that night, and neither did Rocky. At three he went to the kitchen to boil water, and he was in the bathroom when the kettle started to whistle. I ran out to stop it. He came out of the bathroom and drank hot water into which he squeezed half a lemon. I sat across from him, drinking instant coffee.

"Go back to sleep," he said.

He didn't have to wake me. At seven his duffel bag sat against the door. He had tied his favorite shoes—brown-and-white wing tips—around the canvas handle to keep them from being crushed.

He was dressed for the move in his brown double-breasted suit, which was much older than I was. His white hair was combed, and he wore a dark brown tweed cap almost the color of his suit. Only the blue Adidas running shoes that I had bought him kept him from looking like a distinguished retired executive.

At 7:05 he was out the door, pulling the heavy bag down the hallway. I hurried out to help him load it into the car. He sat in the back seat like a passenger in a taxi and kept silent. I didn't start the engine. Finally he broke the ice.

"C'mon," he said, "or I'm going to the bus."

"I'll go," I said, "when you tell me where."

He handed me an address written on the back flap of an envelope. I had no trouble finding the street. It was around the corner from Debby's apartment. I carried his bag up the porch steps and into the entryway of the old Georgian mansion. He walked behind me, aloof and formal.

"Where?" I asked.

He pointed to a room to the left of the staircase, took a key out of his zippered change purse, and tried to unlock the door. In the kitchen four Chinese men, their faces close to their steaming bowls of rice, put down their chopsticks to stare at us.

He couldn't get the door open. One of the men who seemed to be my age or older rose to help. His English was halting.

"Excuse," he said. "I assist."

I introduced myself. Rocky didn't. Once the door was opened, he dragged in the duffel bag. There was an iron bed and a chair. That was it. No lamp, no table, no dresser. I looked around for a closet—none. The room was about three times the length of his duffel bag.

The man who helped us with the bag, Richard Huang, seemed embarrassed by the inadequacies of the room.

"Small," he said, "but maybe very comfortable."

Rocky had already put his two-tone shoes under the bed. He unzipped his bag and held a handful of socks and underwear. He walked around looking for a place to put them. Finally he laid them on the bed. Then he stopped.

"You can go," he told me. "I'm all set."

He almost pushed me as he closed the door. I stood in the hallway with Richard Huang. The three men in the kitchen who had gone back to their meal looked up again to contemplate me. Richard invited me to the kitchen to join them. They fitted me in around the small table. They were lab assistants and math grad students who were hoping to learn English. The landlord had sublet Rocky's room when one of their colleagues went back to Taiwan. Everyone in the house was Chinese.

"He student?" Richard asked me.

"No," I said. "He's my grandfather."

"Small room," Richard said.

"Small room," I echoed.

The lab assistants finished their breakfast. By eight they had all gone off to work.

I dozed off at the kitchen table, but I heard Rocky when he opened his door and looked for the bathroom. There wasn't one on the first floor. He had to trudge upstairs. Before I heard him flush the toilet, I peeked into his room. He had put everything back into the duffel bag. The two-tone shoes were tied around the handle again.

He went outside and walked to the corner.

I put my head on the kitchen table and slept until I heard a door slam. It was ten fifteen. I washed my face with cold water at the kitchen sink to wake myself, then dried it on a paper towel. At ten thirty I knocked on his door. He opened it.

"How much are you paying?" I asked.

"Twenty a week," he said.

"What do you think this is—a hotel? For twenty a week you can get a private bath and a kitchen. The landlord took you."

"He knew I was desperate," Rocky said.

"You told him you needed it right away?"

He nodded.

"You were on the way back from the playground?"

He gave me an angry look, but he nodded again.

"Did you sign a lease?"

"No," he said.

"How much did you give him?"

"Two weeks in advance," Rocky said. "Forty bucks."

"If you let me, I'll write the guy a letter on university stationery and tell him he has to give you back your money. I'll tell him there's housing codes. Every room has got to have a closet."

"Tell him," Rocky said, "to lower the rent for the Chinese guys, too. They don't know the laws—he's probably taking everyone."

I already had my hand on his duffel bag. He didn't stop me.

"I'll get your money back."

"You keep half," he said. "A lawyer would charge that much."

Chapter 7

HE MOVED back, but it wasn't over. He had made up his mind to leave. That afternoon, when I expected a reprieve, he handed me a slip of paper from his wallet—the address of the Jewish Home for the Aged in Detroit.

"Give me a break," I said. "Relax for a while."

"I'm not relaxing," he said, "until I get out from here."

He dictated:

Dear Head of the Home,

I'd like a room there. I'm independent. I get $120 Social Security every month. I'm right now living with my grandson in Ann Arbor, which is close. I can be there in an hour if he takes me or maybe two or three hours by bus. What street is the closest bus stop?

My brother used to own a bakery on Livernois Avenue so I know Detroit. Call me at my grandson's to tell me when I should come there.

Then he'd signed the page with his florid "Herman Goodstein." I folded his letter and put a different one in the envelope. "Please send me an application for admission," I wrote. Then I copied his signature. I didn't mail it. The letter sat on my desk. When he talked about a room on campus, I thought it might have worked, at least for a while. But a home was something else—a bureaucracy with all sorts of procedures and rules. I knew he would hate the home and probably try to leave within a week.

"What'll you do," I asked him, "if they let you into the home and then you want to leave?"

"I'll leave," he said.

"Where will you go?"

"That's not your worry."

"I'll have to forward your mail," I said. "What if the Social Security check comes to me, or your life insurance bill?"

"I'll let you know where to send everything."

When I understood that he was not going to let it drop, I mailed the letter, no more certain than he was where it would lead us.

Debby laughed when I told her about the boardinghouse. "You should have left him there for a week or so," she said, "to teach him a lesson."

"I couldn't do that to the Chinese guys," I said.

She didn't storm around the way Rocky did, but in her own way Debby was also putting me through a test. We all knew that this threesome wasn't going to last, but neither of them knew who would be left out. I tried to tell Debby that it wouldn't be her.

367

"He's not an old girlfriend," I said. "I don't have to break up with him."

"I wish he was an old girlfriend; then I could be angry and jealous without feeling guilty."

"You feel guilty and you don't even like him. How do you think I feel?"

"I know it's hard for you," she said, "but I've got to decide what to do about me. When I graduate, if I don't have a job or a place to go, they'll get on me to come home. You know what that will do to me."

She told me a week later, nonchalantly, in her apartment. I was working on my dissertation, a study of a seventeenth-century book on melancholy. She waited until I looked up from the table where I sat, and she pulled herself up to a window ledge across the room.

"I told my friend Barbara that I'd go to Chicago."

"I'll drive you to the airport," I said. "When are you going?"

"Not for a visit. To live. After graduation."

"Where does that leave me?"

"Wherever you want it to."

"What's that supposed to mean?"

She hopped off the ledge and came close. "Come with me."

"Just like that—come with you?"

"Why not," she said.

"You know I can't," I said.

"I know you could."

"Lay off," I said. "I can't decide anything yet."

"Maybe you can't," she said, "but I have to make plans."

"And I'm not in them?"

"Don't be stupid."

"That's what it sounds like."

"It doesn't have to sound like anything. I'm only telling you what I have to do. You decide what you have to do."

I closed my book, packed up my papers.

"What do you expect?" she said.

"I expect you to talk to me, to tell me things, to decide together— not just tell me you're moving to Chicago. Aren't we a couple?"

"Sometimes we are, but most of the time it seems like you and Rocky are the real couple."

I slammed the door as I left.

The next day I didn't go home for dinner with Rocky, and I didn't call Debby or go to her house. I stayed in the library until midnight and then went home to sleep.

I was fed up with both of them, but more angry at Debby. I knew how to handle Rocky. I had spent my life living around and with his ways. He wasn't just in the apartment; he was in the air around me—an angry, opinionated fairy godmother-grandfather, who gave me not only my wishes but his, too. From him I expected opposition, and coping with it had formed me. He could get away with most anything; Debby couldn't.

The next day, when she called me, I blamed her for overreacting to the spitting incident at the playground.

"He'd just been turned down for that handyman job. For three weeks he'd been frustrated trying to find a room. Then he saw me playing instead of working, and he got a little wild."

"I don't want to hear excuses. I don't care who he is or what he does. I just want him to leave you alone—to leave us alone."

"You don't just walk away from your family."

"My mother is family. Wouldn't you agree that it's smart to get away from her?"

"That's different. She's got money and influence—real power in the world. Rocky's got nothing. He had his work; now he's got the synagogue three mornings a week and he's got me."

"Well, he doesn't have me," she said, "and he's not going to."

When she hung up, she called Chicago and told Barbara she'd arrive the day after graduation.

NINETEEN seventy, my last spring in Ann Arbor, happened without me. Usually when the weather turned, I couldn't stand to stay cooped up in the dry air of the library. Life was outside on the diag. By the dozens, classes moved outside—all on the new grass. That spring I stayed in the library. During the first two weeks of glorious sunshine I wrote two chapters of my dissertation. I didn't see the sun, and I didn't see Debby.

When Rocky received a letter inviting him for an interview, I drove him to the Detroit Jewish Home for the Aged. He wore his brown suit and a dark red tie. I took it as a good sign when he told me twice that I was going the wrong way on I-94.

The home we looked over that day in late April was a red brick building with trimmed hedges. The rooms were doubles—utilitarian, but they had carpeting, desks, lamps, closets, and bathrooms.

Rocky knew that it was merely an interview, but he insisted on taking his duffel bag along. "What if they get an opening while I'm there?" he said.

"Then you'll go on the waiting list. They don't just let in whoever happens to be in the office."

"That's what you think," he said. "If there's a room and they see you can take care of yourself and probably won't eat too much, you slip them a ten-spot or a twenty and they let you in."

I didn't tell him that slipping someone a ten might not even get you a good seat at a Tigers game anymore. Rocky lived outside the flux of money, mostly because my mother and I protected him by paying for almost everything. But it went beyond that. He never let the country get too big. He kept everything on a local scale—the way he had in his Lithuanian village. Rocky never had a bank account. He paid his bills by walking to Wurzberg's Department Store or the gas company. He counted out dollars and change to the penny.

I was exhausted from carrying his duffel bag all the way from the parking lot. In the lobby I put the bag down so I could rest while he walked into an office to announce his arrival. I felt foolish standing there with seventy pounds of clothing and the Babylonian Talmud.

A half-dozen residents sat on the leather couches. A man approached slowly from the men's wing. When he came to a spot about ten feet from the couch, he grabbed his trousers just above the knee, as if he wanted to keep them from getting wet in a puddle. I knew who he was. At our house he used to grab his pants as soon as he walked in. I think he did it to keep the creases straight. I had no idea he was still alive.

"Mr. Schneiderman," I said, "do you remember me?"

When I told him my name, he did. Rocky, standing near the administrative office, called out for me to come in.

"Rocky," Schneiderman said, "you old s.o.b. You're still alive?"

Rocky stared at him. "I forgot," he said, "that they let you in here." Schneiderman walked over to greet his old acquaintance.

Rocky waited, let Schneiderman shake his hand. When Schneiderman tried to embrace him, Rocky stepped back. "I gotta go," he said. "Be well, Schneiderman." I followed Rocky down the corridor.

The director of admitting, Mrs. Okrent, was a pleasant woman in her early fifties. She laughed when she saw me with the bag.

"I'm sorry," she said. "Didn't the secretary tell you this was only a preliminary interview?"

"The secretary told me," I said, "but try telling him."

As she walked us through the building, Rocky was not only polite, he was courtly. He motioned for Mrs. Okrent to lead the way; he opened doors; he praised "the good paint job" in the rooms.

When we returned to her office, Schneiderman was there, along with a man in the kind of gray felt hat that 1930s gangsters wear in the movies.

"Harry Zeff," the man said. He was about five feet five and wore a silky gray suit that must have fitted him once, when he was heavier.

"Harry Zeff," Rocky repeated. I couldn't tell if he was pleased or not. I remembered the name, but not the person.

"And this must be the little kid," Zeff said, looking me over. "I had a Henry J. convertible—remember that?"

I did.

"And you were little—maybe five, six years old—and you kept bothering me for a ride."

I remembered.

"But the mother, the grandma, Rocky—they wouldn't let go of you even to ride around the block. They said you'd catch a cold in the convertible. You still a mama's boy?"

"We didn't let him go," Rocky said, "because we didn't want him in the car with you, and we were right. You're a regular gigolo."

Mr. Zeff had dated one of Rocky's cousins, a bosomy widow named Bashel. Now and then they took a Sunday drive all the way to Grand Rapids to see us. About Bashel and Zeff I recalled only the names, but the Henry J. . . . I could still see its chrome-tipped fins.

Mrs. Okrent tried to make peace. "Please, Mr. Zeff," she said, "would you mind waiting outside? We'll be done in a few minutes."

Rocky turned to Zeff. "Are you still selling dead men's clothes?"

"What does he know?" Zeff said, addressing the rest of us. "I had a war-surplus store; he thought I robbed graves. You spent too many years with your head in an oven, Rocky. You got nothing upstairs, and you never did."

371

"I know a crook when I see one," Rocky said.

"Enough," Mrs. Okrent said. She walked out of her office. Rocky hurried after her. I grabbed the duffel bag and followed.

Zeff stuck his head out of the office door. "I hope you come here, Rocky, and live a long time. That's the worst I can wish for you."

Mrs. Okrent walked us to the car. She was trying not to laugh.

"Throw him out," Rocky said, "or I'm not moving in."

"We can't do that. There are policies, procedures. Anyway, it's a big place. You wouldn't have to see too much of him." She said we'd hear from the admitting committee in about a month.

When we got back to Ann Arbor, I dropped Rocky at home and went to campus. In my mailbox there was a note from the rehabilitation ward of the hospital. "Mr. Kerner," the note said, "will be able to leave the hospital for a brief outing Saturday night. Will you be able to take him?" It was the last day of April. He had been shot in early September. He hadn't been outside the hospital grounds for eight months.

UNABLE to reach me that day, Kerner had the nurse try Debby's apartment. I hadn't told him that Debby and I hadn't been speaking to one another. He was too persistent and questioning.

Debby called me. "Are you gonna take him out somewhere?"

"Of course," I said.

"Can I come, too?"

"Sure."

"Are you still mad at me?"

"Yes," I said.

"I'll try to stay out of your way, then. I just want to be there. It's so exciting after all these months."

Debby had only met Kerner once, when I wheeled him down to the cafeteria. The two of them spoke for a few minutes, awkwardly. Even before he was shot, Kerner made people uncomfortable. He would ask you something like what mattered most to you in the world, after he'd known you for five minutes. When he asked Debby, she pointed to me.

Where to take Kerner and how to do it occupied me, but I thought about it even more because I could hardly wait to see Debby again. Kerner had asked our mutual friend Alan Perlis to come, too. In addition to his being a close friend, the muscular New Englander could help us with the big wheelchair. Perlis, the star of our department, had given up his time off on a Ford Foundation grant to teach Kerner's classes. He worked without pay so that the university could give the meager salary to Kerner.

When Alan and I asked Kerner where he wanted to go, he told us to surprise him. We didn't want to surprise ourselves. We borrowed a wheelchair from the hospital and practiced taking it apart. It wouldn't fit into the trunk of Alan's Volkswagen Beetle, but in my Chevy we could squeeze it in. We decided to take him to a movie and went two days ahead of time to the State Theatre to request special parking and to look over the layout. Alan and I wanted this first outing to be as flawless as possible.

I didn't consult Debby; I was still playing my angry role. She called me on Friday. "I got tickets to a concert for all four of us."

I had thought of it, too. Every spring Eugene Ormandy and the Philadelphia Orchestra came to Ann Arbor. Kerner loved music.

"It must have cost a fortune," I said.

"It did, but that's what credit cards are for."

"Forget it," I said. "I don't want your mother paying for this."

"It's all right."

"Fine," I said, "until she sees the bill; then she'll make you pay in other ways. It's not worth it. We'll go to the movies. I already figured out a route and have special parking."

"Hold on," she said. "My mother offered to pay. She suggested it."

"Okay," I said. "Mom treats. Is this a date for us?"

"Do you want it to be?"

"I don't know," I said. "There will be Kerner and Alan; you're not crazy about it when there are other people involved."

"Other people don't bother me, with one exception. But do we have to fight about that again? Let's just take Joel out. That's enough for one night."

Alan and I scouted out Hill Auditorium. It was more accessible than the State Theatre. There was a ramp as well as special parking.

Helen, the enforcer, was on duty when we came to the ward at six thirty to pick Joel up. She made us wait until exactly seven. Debby and Alan had never seen her before.

"She acts like it's a prison, not a hospital," Alan said.

"Have him back at ten," Helen said. I pleaded for an extra half hour in case there were multiple encores.

"Ten thirty," she said. "No later."

When we got there, all our plans fell apart. In the traffic we couldn't get anywhere near our special parking place. When we did, it was occupied. Then when I finally parked, we couldn't open the trunk. A strap from the chair had jammed the lock.

The crowds walked past on their way to the concert. Kerner sat in the front seat and watched the passersby. Alan and I struggled with the trunk.

Kerner pleaded with us to stop. "Don't waste the tickets," he said. "The three of you go. Nothing's gonna happen to me."

Finally at eight, a half hour after the concert began, Debby took out the back seat and crawled into the trunk. Using a screwdriver, she pried open the lock. We cheered as if it were a football game. Alan pulled out the chair; Debby followed. Her face was sweaty and streaked. Trunk dirt decorated her light yellow dress.

By the time we got to Hill Auditorium, it was after nine and the intermission was already over. The ushers wouldn't let us in. Debby was furious. She wanted us to muscle our way in.

"I don't care if the whole orchestra has to stop," she said. "We're going in." Kerner ignored us. Seated in his chair on the broad porch, he looked up at the Doric columns and beyond at the spring sky.

"Just leave me here," he said. "I haven't seen the sky for eight months."

We sat on the steps next to him and waited. He was glad to be where he was—outdoors and alive. "I don't need a concert," he said. "This is a concert." We believed him, but we still felt as if we had failed.

"Where else do you want to go?" Debby said.

"If it's not too much trouble," Kerner said, "I'd love to go see Rocky."

It was already nine thirty, an hour past Rocky's bedtime. Before I could say so, Debby started pushing the chair toward the car.

"Sure," she said. "No problem."

I caught up with her and just shook my head. I didn't want to explain to Kerner. She ignored me. "Anyone," she said, "would rather see Rocky than the Philadelphia Orchestra."

"I would," Kerner said. "I really would."

She got a running head start trying to push the chair up Hill Street but still needed Alan's help for the steep grade.

I got her alone when Alan took over. "Why are you going along with this?"

"I'm not going along. Once you get in the car, I'll go home. Rocky won't kick him out, will he?"

When Debby didn't join us, Kerner began to figure things out. By the time we reached my apartment, he was actively meddling.

"I'll talk to him," Kerner said. "Rocky listens to me."

"Please," I said, "he's okay now. Let's not get him started again. Just let him enjoy seeing you."

Alan and Kerner waited in the hall while I woke Rocky. He came running out in his long underwear to embrace Joel. Once in the apartment, he started to pull Kerner out of the wheelchair into the red-and-white easy chair near the window. It hadn't occurred to Alan or to me that our friend was not glued to his wheelchair. He enjoyed the easy chair and the cinnamon rolls that Rocky heated for him after he got dressed. Rocky even put on a tie—in honor, he said, of such an important guest.

He pulled out a prayer book and helped Kerner recite the prayer of a person who has lived through a life-threatening experience. "Blessed art Thou, Lord our God, King of the Universe," Kerner read in slow Hebrew. Rocky corrected every mistake.

"Louder," he said. Kerner continued. "Who bestows favors on the undeserving, and has shown me every kindness."

Rocky said, "Amen." Alan and I had tears in our eyes. When I could, I reminded Joel about his curfew.

"Forget it," he said, so I did.

Alan and I took a walk, telling one another how wonderful it was to see Kerner so much himself in spite of everything.

When we came back to the apartment, Rocky was holding a cup of coffee to Kerner's lips. He'd already spilled a lot on Joel's shirt, but it didn't seem to bother either of them. On his own, Rocky had transferred Joel back to the wheelchair. They were having a good time.

We stayed at the apartment until almost midnight. When Alan and I wheeled him into the ward, Helen walked quickly toward us.

"Leave," she told Alan and me. We were helping Kerner into bed.

"You're almost two hours late," she said. "I've had hospital security looking for you."

"Did you think I'd been shot again?" Kerner asked.

"You're not funny, and you have no respect for authority."

"You're right," Kerner said.

She glared at me. "You're responsible. You can't come here to read to him anymore—not that you've been studying. I know you've just been visiting him."

"What's so terrible about visiting?" Alan asked.

"If they hadn't put you in bed," Helen said to Kerner, "I would have made you sit in your chair all night—to teach you a lesson."

"If you ever do that," Alan said, "I'll break *your* neck."

She ordered us both out again. We were already at the far end of the ward when we heard her scream. She had bent to straighten Kerner's pillow. When he had a good angle, he had locked his teeth onto the starched white shoulder of her uniform.

Helen called the resident to give Kerner a sedative. In the morning a psychologist and a social worker came to visit. All three told him that a graduate student should know better than to bite.

I was banned for a week. The social worker made it the goal of Kerner's therapy to have him apologize. The hospital called a family conference. His father and brother flew in from the east coast.

Joel treated it all like a comic episode. He had something bigger in mind. "I knew that night," he said, "that I was ready to leave. I talked it over with Rocky."

The Helen episode gave the hospital a reason to speed up his exit. When his father and brother visited, he told them his plan: after Passover he was going to Israel, and so was his ninety-five-year-old buddy.

Chapter 8

IN MAY I received a graduation announcement from Debby. Since we still weren't talking to one another, she didn't know that I would be there anyway. Writing furiously, I would finish my dissertation before the deadline. I, too, would graduate in June.

I called to thank her for the announcement.

"Are you gonna be mad at me forever?" she asked.

"I'm not mad," I said. "You made your decision about Chicago. That told me everything."

"You're really pretty stupid," she said. "If this was happening in a book, you'd know what the guy's supposed to do."

"I'd read the last page to find out."

"Then you'd miss all the fun. You're missing it now, and so am I. Will you meet me for coffee?"

We sat in one of the dark wooden booths at Drake's again, and George watched us through the window.

"Why are you so stubborn?" Debby said. "You're not even giving me a chance."

"You made up your mind."

"So what? Make me change it. What do you want me to do?"

"I want you to marry me," I said. "You know that."

She moved over to sit next to me. "Okay," she said, "I will."

We were kissing when George sneaked in as someone opened the door. Jealous, he jumped between us. The manager made us leave.

We walked the streets of Ann Arbor, too happy to talk about it. As if he were announcing it, George ran ahead, barking. I walked Debby to the playground, where she was still working. We told the kids. They started calling her Mrs. Rotten Apple.

We decided not to discuss the problems. "We'll deal with all that later," she said. "Let's just be happy now."

I went back to spending most of my time with Debby. Rocky didn't seem to mind my absence. He had his own little secret.

He and Kerner had made their deal that night in our apartment. Kerner had asked him to keep it quiet until everything was arranged and he had the tickets in hand.

Rocky announced it to me casually. "Right after Pesach I'm going to Jerusalem." I thought he was speaking metaphorically, announcing his death.

"Are you sick?" I asked.

"I'm not sick. I'm going to help Kerner." I didn't believe him, but that night at the hospital Kerner confirmed the statement.

"I need an attendant," he said. "The insurance company will pay for someone. Why not Rocky?"

"He's not strong enough to push your chair and to pick you up."

"Actually he is," Kerner said, "but my brother's coming, too. Rocky wouldn't let me buy him a ticket until I told him I needed him. He'll only come if he can call it a job."

I called my mother. Together Bashy and I worried. We knew that Rocky would try to do all the physical labor—a danger to him and even more to Kerner.

"He can't go," Bashy said, "unless you go along to keep him under control."

I wanted Rocky to see Israel, but not as much as I wanted to marry Debby. "I can't do it," I said. I told her half the reason. "I've got to finish my dissertation."

When I explained all my reservations to Kerner, he understood. "Can Bashy go, too?" he asked.

On her trips to Ann Arbor my mother would always visit Joel in the hospital. She was very good at helping him. Kerner, motherless since he was six, let her be as maternal as she wanted.

"She'd have to make arrangements for someone to take care of the business, but she probably can."

"Good," he said. "Then they'll both come with me."

"It's too expensive," I said, "to take them both."

"Not too much at all," he said. "It's cheaper than hiring people."

When I still hesitated, Kerner settled it. "Think of it as a wedding present," he said.

Bashy came to Ann Arbor, and I drove the three of them to the airport. Joel's brother would meet them in Jerusalem.

I helped Kerner onto the plane. My mother sat next to him. Rocky, at the window seat behind, his running shoes not quite touching the floor, could hardly wait for the takeoff. I strapped him in and kissed each of them good-bye.

"Thanks for the wedding present," I told Joel. "I hope he doesn't drive you nuts."

"According to the hospital," Kerner said, "I'm already nuts."

In June, while I marched up to receive my degree, Rocky was in an apartment on Jabotinsky Street in Jerusalem. I even got a letter from him. He told me that he was coming back because he was too old—he was ninety-four—but if he were younger, eighty or so, he would stay and work on a kibbutz.

378

With Rocky in Jerusalem and all the test taking and writing finally behind me, for the first time I had entire days to spend with Debby. We jogged together through the arboretum; we bicycled to the malls, went to three or four movies a week. The only problem was our marriage—Debby told her family.

Her father, Ben, a businessman who specialized in avoiding family life, had his usual no comment.

Harriet first took our announcement as a sort of April Fools' joke. When Debby persisted, she switched tactics.

"You're not getting married and that's final," she said.

"Mother," Debby said as I listened to the telephone conversation, "I am getting married. I'm not asking for your permission."

"And you're not getting it—or one penny, either."

"Good," Debby said. She knew the money threat was coming. That was Harriet's usual opener.

"How will you support yourselves?"

"He'll sell drugs; I'll work the streets; and when the children come, they'll beg."

"It's all a game to you, isn't it?" Harriet said. "You'll learn that life is not a game."

"Look, we're getting married," Debby said. "I'm sorry you're not happy about it."

"You're twenty years old," Harriet said. "You'll meet other men."

"You mean richer men."

"Yes, and better-looking and smarter and everything."

"Thanks, Mom," I said from the extension. She paid no attention.

"If you don't do better, you can always marry him. He'll wait."

"If that's all you've got to say, I'm hanging up," Debby said.

"Wait a minute," Harriet said. "Is he still on the line?"

"I am."

"Forget all of this," she said to me, "and I'll put a check in the mail tomorrow. Ten thousand dollars—all yours."

"You're even worse than I thought," Debby said. She hung up.

"Well?" Harriet asked me.

I hung up, too.

The next Sunday Debby's father invited me out for lunch. He had to be in Detroit for business. He didn't invite his daughter; it was going to be the two of us, man to man.

"He'll offer the money again," Debby said. "Maybe he'll up it—I'd guess he'll go to twenty."

"I'm holding out for fifty," I said.

"Don't joke about it. It's not funny to me."

As it happened, he didn't mention money or Debby or the marriage. He was a quiet, darkly handsome man. Uncomfortable with words, he would have preferred to have had his wife take care of our meeting. I could tell that this was his assignment.

He started by talking golf, as if I were a stranger who had a particular golf course in common with him and not a particular daughter.

"I don't play golf," I finally told him.

He understood that this meant we needed a new subject. I read a mild panic in his eyes. He didn't have another subject—at least not for me. He was no fool. In his steel business, Debby told me, he had made millions. But when he wasn't talking about plate or sheet or reinforcing bars, he seemed to draw a blank. Only once, at the end of the meal, did he even come close to our subject.

"Women," he said, "can cause a lot of trouble."

"Are you referring to your wife," I answered, "or to Debby?"

"Women in general," he said; then he started telling me about the high-quality rebar that came from Mexican minimills. He called for the check. I thanked him, and we shook hands.

"Our family is divided in an exact way," Debby told me when I tried to explain the emptiness of that lunch. "She's in charge of everything; he supplies the money. He'll do anything to avoid getting into it with her. I'm sure he likes you. He's a sweet man, and he likes things to stay on an even keel. He's happy when he's at the shop."

Harriet telephoned twice a week and never asked about the wedding. Debby advised me to ignore her parents. We planned our own wedding, on July Fourth, at the playground. I wrote to my mother and Rocky in Israel, realizing how lucky I was not to be telling him in person.

A few days after my proposal we had decided what we'd do about Rocky. He would stay in the apartment; I would move to Debby's, but I would come over every day for at least one meal. If he spoke to Debby and acted decently, he could come to her apartment, too, whenever he wanted.

"Don't count on it," I said.

Technically he was still waiting to hear from the Detroit Jewish Home, but I knew that after his run-in with Zeff, he'd never go. I was in the process of applying for a teaching job. If I got one, we'd have to move; then it would be his choice. If he wanted to come along, he would live not with us, but close by. Debby and I each gave in a little. With Rocky in Jerusalem, planning his future and ours seemed a lot easier.

When Debby finally gave up the idea that there was a chance to have me without him, she was philosophical. "No place is perfect. There are earthquakes in California, tornadoes in the Midwest. . . . I'll just try to think of him as a natural disaster."

"I'm sure he'll do the same for you."

"Too bad we can't buy insurance against one another."

Rocky returned from the Holy Land on July 1. When he came through customs, he handed me a plastic garbage bag of dirt almost as heavy as his suitcase.

"For my grave," he said. "Put it in."

I knew what he was referring to. All pious Jews want to be buried in Israel, but a symbolic bit of earth from the land of Israel is the best that most can do.

We left him to watch the luggage while Bashy and I went to get the car. I finally had a chance to ask her how he'd responded to the news of my wedding.

"I didn't tell him," she said. "What would I have done if he got mad and said he wasn't coming back with me? I was going to tell him on the plane, but I didn't want him to make a fuss there, either. Anyway, I thought, in a few hours he'll be home and you can tell him. You can handle him better than anyone."

"This time I was hoping I wouldn't have to."

"You shouldn't have to," she said. "Thank goodness you didn't let him get in your way. I don't know what he's got against Debby."

A few hours later I found out. I gave him time to sleep off his jet lag, put his Holy Land dirt in his underwear-and-socks drawer, and have his coffee-and-herring lunch. Then I told him.

He picked up the newspaper, went to his chair, and began to read. I waited a few minutes.

Finally he spoke. "I'm glad you're getting married," he said. "I want you to get married. I got married, your father got married—that's the way it should be. Only not her."

"Okay," I said. "Why not her?"

"She stuck out her tongue at me."

"You threw her out of the house."

"I had a right to throw her out. She moved in like a gypsy in the middle of the night."

"She didn't move in—I invited her. Don't forget that."

I went to the kitchen to think of a better approach. What we were talking about had nothing to do with Debby. I wanted to let him know that I understood how this must feel to him.

I stayed in the kitchen, as if the twenty feet that separated us as he sat in his easy chair would give me the distance I needed to talk about what neither of us had ever put into words.

"I'm not going to get married and forget about you. Wherever we live, there's always going to be a place for you."

He didn't look up from his paper. "Don't worry about me. I can live wherever I want."

I let him have his bravado. "Sure you can," I said, "but what about me? What am I gonna do if we live far apart?"

"You'll write letters."

"I could write every day and call, too, but you know that's not enough. I wanna see you every day."

"Then marry somebody else and I'll come over."

"You keep coming back to silliness."

"You want her," he said, "forget about me." He tossed his paper onto the coffee table and stormed outdoors.

When I told Debby, she said that Harriet had told her almost the same thing when she agreed to give us a wedding.

"All right," Harriet had said. "If you're going to go through with it, I'd rather have you get married in our house than on a playground. But why does it have to be him?"

Harriet's objections were pretty straightforward. She wanted a son-in-law she could be proud of, someone rich or likely to be. Instead, Debby chose "a bookworm who lives with his grandpa," and even worse, because I was from Grand Rapids, too, some of her guests would know me. She wanted her daughter to do better.

Rocky wouldn't admit to anything that rational. He stuck to the mysterious tongue complaint. I felt foolish, but I finally confronted Debby with the charge. She didn't laugh.

"What will satisfy him—cutting off my tongue?"

"He's just grabbing at straws," I said. "He doesn't have an objection, but he's taken his stand and he won't back down."

We tried to make peace. First an apology. Debby agreed to try.

"Dear Rocky," she wrote, "I'm sorry if you think I stuck my tongue out at you." I made her leave out "if you think."

It didn't matter. Rocky threw away the note.

"What more do you want?" I screamed. "She apologized. Now you can be a mensch, too. Stop torturing me about her tongue."

"Do whatever you want," he said. "Forget about me."

"I will," I said, and for the next three days I tried to.

Harriet hadn't spoken to me, but I understood that when she agreed to the wedding, she was compromising as much as she could. Debby and I decided to match her gesture. We let her plan the ceremony just as she wanted it, allowed her to limit our guests, pick the flowers and Debby's dress.

I did my best to please her. One of my friends, Stanley, a lawyer in Washington and an excellent dresser, selected a gray Brooks Brothers suit for me. I had my curly electric hair cut bridegroom short and tried to look as much like a doctor or a lawyer as I could.

On the day before the ceremony Rocky and I drove to Grand Rapids. We spent the night in our old bedroom. It was going to be a small family wedding in Harriet's living room, but in the morning, when faced with glorious sunshine, Harriet decided to set up the chairs in the yard. Bashy left the house early to play with my sister Bailey's two sons. Bailey and her family were staying with one of Bailey's friends. At noon my other sister, Maxine, sent her own family ahead, and she waited at the house to drive Rocky. We decided it would be best to let him stay home until the last minute so he wouldn't add to the already tense atmosphere.

I tried to read, but couldn't concentrate. I retied my tie a half-dozen times. I didn't want to get to Harriet's house too early, either. At one o'clock Maxine ran up to my room. She was crying.

"He's not going. I had him almost to the car, and then he ran into the basement. He locked himself in. What shall we do?"

I tried to stay calm. "Leave him to me," I said.

"You shouldn't have to do this," she said. "Not on your wedding day. I can't believe he's doing this to you. You know how much he loves you."

"That's exactly why he's doing it." An hour before my wedding he was making me play my oldest role. I would have to placate him, bring him not downstairs, but this time upstairs into the warm and now widening world of his family.

Maxine was still crying when she got into her rented car.

"I'll be there in a few minutes," I said.

It was a few minutes after one as I stood outside the basement door. He had snapped the security latch from within, so there was no way for me to enter. To see into the basement, I would have to get down on my knees to look through a little window that hadn't been cleaned in years.

If I was going to be on time to my wedding, I had about twenty minutes to lure him out. I started out gruff, businesslike.

"C'mon," I said, "we haven't got much time."

He didn't answer. I yelled, "Do you hear me?"

"I hear you," he said. "I'm not going."

I put a piece of newspaper down on the bare dirt near the window so I wouldn't stain my trousers. Through the clouded glass I saw him sitting on a wooden chair. Above him glared an un-shielded hundred-watt bulb. He looked like a prisoner in solitary confinement. He wore everyday clothes: a short-sleeved blue shirt, patterned blue trousers, and the Adidas running shoes I had given him. The clothes told me he meant to stay put. He liked to dress for occasions; today he had dressed for the basement.

"Look at you," I said, "sitting there like a prisoner in a cage instead of coming to my wedding. Is this what you want?"

"Yes." He didn't look up to see me peering into the window.

"No matter who I'm marrying, if there's anybody in the world who should be there, it's you. Don't do this to yourself."

He didn't answer. I didn't have any more time. "You'll be sorry for the rest of your life," I said, "and you're not going to stop me."

"Go ahead," he said. "Do whatever you want."

When I left the basement window, I sat in the car for a minute or two, thinking he might come out. I knew that if I could get my

hands on him, the contact of the flesh would do what words couldn't. He would not have resisted the tears streaming down my cheeks. He knew that as well as I did, and he stayed in the basement, keeping his feelings and himself hidden.

At a quarter to two I drove to my wedding. In the pictures I'm smiling as I sign the marriage document, shake hands with the rabbi, hug my best man, and pose with Bashy and my sisters. In the pictures you can't see what's missing.

I didn't see Debby that day until she walked down the little cloth aisle spread over the grass of her backyard. She asked me with her eyes where he was. We'd had no rehearsals, but he was supposed to stand beside me. Debby looked, in her white gown and tiara, so beautiful and bridelike that I was glad we were in a more conventional setting than home plate on the school playground.

I was marrying the woman I loved, and not even Rocky could stop me—but he could and did keep me from enjoying it. When Debby asked me again with her glance where he was, I stuck out my tongue.

During the ceremony all I thought about was that stubborn old man in the basement. I felt more angry than married.

At the reception, as Harriet and Ben's friends shook my hand and occasionally slipped an envelope into my pocket, I kept checking the door to see if maybe he had come late by cab.

We went to Stratford, Ontario, for our honeymoon. It was the least expensive place that still felt like going away. It was only a three-hour drive, but you had to cross the border.

We had been married two days and were canoeing on an artificial lake near an imitation of Shakespeare's Globe Theatre. The lake was full of mosquitoes. People who looked as if they were enjoying themselves kept rowing past us.

Debby knew what was wrong. "Maybe he would have come to the ceremony," she said, "if you had invited him along for the honeymoon, too. That's probably what he was holding out for."

"I'm sorry," I said. "I just can't stop thinking about him. I never thought he'd do this."

"Seems in character to me," she said.

"You're probably right. I'll try to be better company."

We rowed for a few more minutes.

"Is this a honeymoon," Debby asked, "or a school trip?"

"I vote for school trip."

"Me, too," she said.

"Shall we call it that and have a honeymoon some other time?"

"Great idea," she said. We packed and drove home. In the car I could hardly wait to give Rocky a piece of my mind.

"I've gotta settle things with him before I can relax and feel officially married. If I don't have it out with him now, I don't know what I'll do. I may start being mean to you."

"Do me a favor—don't confuse us. I'm your *new* roommate, the one who spits less."

At the border the customs inspector took our car apart looking for drugs. He even checked the air filter. We had left before noon and didn't get home until six. It didn't help my mood. I took a quick shower and was ready to go see Rocky.

"What are you gonna do?" I asked Debby.

"I'll go pick up George at Nancy's. Maybe after you give Rocky hell, we can go to a movie or something. Even if it's only a school trip, we can still liven it up a little."

He was watching the news when I walked in. He offered me a cinnamon roll and coffee. I shut the television off and was ready to tear into him, but he disarmed me. On the kitchen table in front of him, next to his soft-boiled egg, was the old book of great speeches. He had it open to the Gettysburg Address.

"You still remember it?" he asked.

My father, now and then, used to come across books in scrap piles. If they were fairly clean, he would bring them home. We didn't buy books—there was a public library for borrowing. The ones my father found became our private library. Reader's Digest Condensed Books dominated, along with stray volumes of various encyclopedias and home-improvement manuals. We kept anything that had a solid binding. When he brought in a volume of *Great American Speeches*, Rocky and I read the Gettysburg Address. He didn't know all the words, and I didn't know what Gettysburg was, but if Abraham Lincoln spoke it, that was enough for us.

Lincoln was Rocky's only postbiblical hero. In kindergarten I knew the address by heart. Every few years he'd ask me to recite it—partly to make sure I hadn't forgotten, but also, I think, to give him the pleasure of hearing Mr. Lincoln's words spoken by me.

"I remember it," I said.

"Say it, then."

"No."

"What will it hurt you to say it? I'll tell you the words if you forget some." He picked up the book.

"Why should I recite the Gettysburg Address? You didn't even come to my wedding."

"What's that got to do with the Gettysburg Address?"

"Everything," I said. "You undermined everything you've done for me by hiding in the basement. I'm not gonna forgive you."

387

"I'm not asking you to," he said.

"You're worse than a Republican," I shouted. "I don't trust you anymore."

He slammed the book shut and went to the bedroom.

"Get out," he said.

"Why should I?" I asked. "It's my apartment."

"Then I'm going."

He walked outside. I didn't follow him, but I was still raging, getting ready to attack him again when he came back.

When it got dark, I went out to look for him. The grocery store at the top of our small hill looked closed, but sometimes he sat on one of the benches near the free scale. I didn't find him.

In the other direction, farther downhill, Milford Road turned briefly woodsy. I hoped he wasn't there. I stepped in among the trees and called to him.

"C'mon out. I've got more to say."

I was sorry I said it that way. I was already more worried than angry. It was eight o'clock, almost his bedtime. I started to fantasize that he'd decided to sleep outside because I had reminded him that it was my apartment. I looked under trees, calling his name.

I came out of the woods running, and checked the apartment. He wasn't there. I went back to the woods to look again.

"Rocky," I yelled, "I'm sorry. Come in the house."

By nine I was frantic. I decided to drive through the main streets of the campus in case he had walked there. Then I would check the synagogue.

In the car I found him, asleep in the passenger seat.

" 'Four score and seven years ago,' " I yelled, " 'our fathers brought forth on this continent a new nation . . .' " I went on to the end.

"Good," he said. "The Gettysburg Address is always beautiful."

We walked back to the apartment together. Even though it was late, he seemed alert after his nap. We were both calm.

"I'm going to the home," he said. "This time for sure." He turned on the television.

"Will you have a TV in your room at the home?" I asked. "Otherwise you can take this one."

"What'll you use?"

"My wife has one," I said.

It was the first time I had called Debby that. I said it with extra emphasis, trying to make my point without yelling at him.

"All right," he said. "As long as you don't have to waste money on a new one."

A call from Debby interrupted us. Rocky listened to my end of the conversation.

"Someone stole the dog?" he asked.

"Can you believe that? Nancy, the girl Debby left him with, says he's half hers. They used to own him together; then Nancy moved to the dormitory last year. They wouldn't let her keep the dog there overnight, so she gave him to this woman, and now the woman and her kids won't let him go."

"What are you gonna do?"

"Debby's gonna sit on the woman's porch. She's not leaving without him," I said. "I'm going there."

He didn't even ask—he just followed me out the door. He got into the back seat.

"Get in the front," I said.

"No," he said. "That's for your wife."

When we arrived at the house where George was being held captive, the front shades were down and the porch light was on. Debby ran to the car, but she stopped when she saw Rocky in the back seat. She gave me a mean look. "It's confusing enough," she said. "Let's not make it worse. I just wanna get George and get out of here."

"Nobody can give away what's not theirs. That's what the Communists do," Rocky said.

Debby nodded. She didn't know whether he'd blow up if she spoke to him.

"Let me try," I said. I walked onto the porch and rang the bell. No one answered. I rang a second time, then a third.

"Get out of here," a woman's voice yelled, "or I'll call the cops."

"I'm not leaving without our dog."

"I mean it," she said. "I'm calling the cops. All of you sitting on my porch—you're scaring the kids."

"I'm sorry," I said. "Give us the dog and we'll go."

"Listen, I'm dialing right now, and I'll press charges."

"So will I," Debby said. She and Rocky had joined me on the

389

porch. Debby, more bold now that I was there, walked to the side of the house to look in the windows. She found a shade that wasn't down.

"George," she yelled, knocking on the window. "Over here."

I ran to the window. A boy about eight held George on a leash. The dog barked wildly. A large woman in her mid-thirties saw us and hurried to pull the window shade. Then she ran to the front door, unbolted it, and yelled, "The cops are on the way." She didn't know Rocky was on the porch. "Who are you?" she said.

"Never mind. The dog is theirs." George broke away from the boy, and the woman turned to help her son catch him. Only a light screen door kept us from George.

Rocky pulled it, kicked it, then pulled again. The eyehook pulled through the molding. The door came off in Rocky's hands.

"George!" Debby yelled. "C'mon, boy."

Trailing the leash, he came flying off the porch steps.

The woman screamed when she saw Rocky holding her screen. She slammed and bolted the inner door.

By the time the Ann Arbor policeman arrived, Rocky had put the door on its side and examined the damage.

"Cheap labor," he said. "She probably put it in herself."

The woman opened the door a crack for the policeman. Her three children huddled near her. I almost felt sorry for them.

"All I want to know," the cop said, "is, who does the dog belong to?"

As if he were King Solomon himself, the officer directed the woman to stand at her door. He sent Debby across the street. He pulled George over to the police car, then let go of the leash.

"Okay," he said. "Both of you call him."

George, a black mutt of no particular distinction, perked up his ears. Debby called for him in a plaintive wail. The mother, joined by her children, drowned her out. George ran straight to Rocky.

Rocky reached into his pocket. "Here's a ten-spot," he said to the officer, "so she can fix her door and buy her kids a dog." He took out another bill. "And for you—go buy yourself a beer after work."

Rocky led the dog to my car. The cop, too surprised to respond immediately, took a minute before he gave Rocky back his dollar. By then George was in the car and so was Rocky.

"Thanks, Rocky." Debby extended her hand. He shook it.

"Come over," he said. "I'll give the dog something. Who knows whether they even fed him."

George had a pack of hot dogs; Debby and I ate herring. She closed her eyes and swallowed a few bites. After that, I felt really married.

Chapter 9

When I received a job offer to teach English in Houston at Rice University, I asked Rocky what he wanted to do.

"I'm staying in Ann Arbor," he said.

"Bashy's moving to Houston with us."

"Who needs her?" he said. "I'm staying here. I'll get a room."

After my failure to convince him to come to the wedding, I had lost some of my confidence, but this time it seemed to me that he was making a rather tame last stand. He was willing to talk.

"What's the difference," I said, "if you live here or Houston? You'll have a synagogue there, too, and Houston's a lot warmer."

"I've been in Michigan . . ." He stopped to count. His lips moved silently. "Fifty-five years. How am I gonna move at my age?"

"You already moved at your age when you came here."

"That was different. I could come by bus."

"So you'll move, but only to places you can go by bus?"

He nodded.

"Then it's settled. You can take the bus to Texas."

"If I go," he said, "I'm taking all the furniture."

Ever so subtly, he had changed the terms. He wouldn't go without a fight, but the fight was going to be about furniture. I had him.

Bashy, ready for a new start, wanted to give the heavy couches and the dining-room table and china closet to the Salvation Army. She thought of Texas as a gigantic patio furnished in rattan, chrome, and glass. I took up my old job as mediator. The couches stayed in Michigan; the dining-room set came to Texas.

Rocky and Bashy moved to a one-story tract house two blocks from where Debby and I bought a house. Rocky moved out on the first day because of the air-conditioning. He showed up at our front door, ready to join us if Debby and I would turn off our air-conditioning. The temperature was in the nineties, the humidity just as high. I understood that the chill affected him, but I couldn't make life unbearable for the rest of us. At his house, I shut off the vent to his room. At our house, there was a glassed-in porch that had no air-conditioning, so he had a hot room in two houses. Yet he took up his primary residence at a location he chose himself. He sat under a chinaberry tree in front of his house for most of the day.

He moved a table and a lawn chair outside. For about five months every year the chinaberry tree served as his study. He came in for meals and his nap. The rest of the time he read the oversized, fixed-by-Scotch-tape volumes of the Babylonian Talmud. For most of the day George sat at his feet. People who drove by grew accustomed to seeing the old man and the dog outside. Rocky's skin tanned evenly, emphasizing his bright blue eyes even more. He looked like a yeshiva cowboy.

He said he would never stay indoors for long, but two things made him change his mind. First, we had a baby. If there were any bad feelings left from our premarital days, Jessica's birth drove them away for both Rocky and Debby. Watching Rocky and Jessica, I realized how it must have been for me when I was a baby. Rocky became Jessica's living playground—his ears, his hair, his animated face, his polished shoes. He lay on the floor and let her explore.

The second event that brought him indoors for a while was the Watergate hearings. He watched all day at his house and then came to our house for the repeats on public television. I turned the thermostat way up, and Jessica sat with him for hours.

His grudge against Nixon went back to 1923. Rocky had worked for nine years, saved enough money to bring his wife and two children to America, and a month after their arrival, creditors took away his house and furniture. He moved his family to a few rooms above the bakery and began all over again, but he carried the memory of that injustice, and fifty-one years later Nixon was paying for it.

I tried to set the record straight. "Nixon had nothing to do with your house on Lane Avenue."

"People like him did it," Rocky said. "The ones that take advantage of the workers."

"Nixon should be tried and convicted only for what he did, not for what people like him did. There are millions like him. Do you want to put them all in jail?"

"Yes," he said.

Jessica clapped. Her hero could say no wrong. Rocky stood her on a stool, gave her a small rolling pin, some flour, and dough, and let her work alongside him.

There were fewer breads and rolls that summer, Debby noticed.

"Is Rocky feeling okay?" she asked. He usually baked so much that we had to give the overflow to our neighbors.

"He only bakes while the Congressmen go to lunch; he doesn't want to miss a minute of the hearings."

Debby was not as happy during that year as Rocky. We had decided to have children quickly so she could later have a career uninterrupted by childbirth.

Motherhood plus moving to a new city confined her. The transition from hippie to housewife was too much to do in a flash. We were used to dropping in on friends unannounced, going to movies at the last minute. With my university job came a whole series of rituals—dinner invitations a month in advance, departmental gatherings, teas. She was restless and found it hard to make small talk with my middle-aged colleagues.

"I know they mean well," she said, "but when they start talking, I feel like I'm back in class and should be taking notes."

To counter some of the routine of childcare, Debby enrolled in a filmmaking class at the university. The use of an 8-mm camera came with the class.

While she filmed and Rocky and Jessica watched Watergate, my writing career began. I sold a story and received five hundred dollars. Rocky couldn't believe it. I had to show him the check.

"Someone paid you five hundred dollars for a made-up story?"

"That's right," I said.

He considered it an act of divine mercy.

For one brief period Rocky, Debby, and I were all working in separate but connected ways. Debby, now into our second pregnancy, started it by opening a store. Ever since we'd been in Texas, she'd wanted to work, but she felt guilty about leaving Jessica, even with baby-sitters like my mother and Rocky.

We were bicycling home from the ice-cream shop one day when we stopped to have a look at an old house that was being remodeled. We met the owner—a wiry, nervous man named David. He said the house was going to be a craftsman's mall. He had one space left—the glassed-in ten- by fifteen-foot upstairs porch, almost hidden in branches and gleaming in the late afternoon sun. We couldn't resist. For one hundred dollars a month we rented a tree house.

Debby turned it into a tiny health food store. She also stocked wooden toys made by a few local people who let us sell their goods on consignment. David operated a restaurant downstairs, and the former upstairs bedrooms now housed a potter, a jewelry maker, and a leather worker. On our porch Debby installed the toys alongside herbal teas, spices, scented soaps, peas, beans, and lentils.

Jessica was her assistant. My mother and Rocky donated the crockery jars that Gootie had carried from Lithuania and had used to make mead, a kind of honeyed beer. Debby filled them with lima beans and Texas reds. Rocky also donated himself as a worker, though retailing was not his strength.

It was rare enough that a customer ventured upstairs, still more rare that anyone went beyond peeking in the door of our shop. If someone actually stepped in, Rocky would growl, "What do you want?" If the customer didn't answer specifically and right away, he wanted nothing to do with them. When I tried to give him lessons in salesmanship, Debby agreed with Rocky.

"He's still gotta be polite," I said.

"Why?" Debby said. "The ones that just wander around and sniff at things don't buy anyway. If he gets rid of them, I can read."

From the restaurant, David, who had no experience in the food business, constantly called on Debby to help. He had a long lunch menu and a cook who regularly didn't show up. He would come up and beg Debby to close the shop and help in the kitchen.

"You don't have customers anyway," he would say.

Debby liked that kind of bluntness. She would go into the kitchen and, holding Jessica, would look for what they needed to fill an order. If the ingredients weren't in the kitchen, David would apologize to the customers, wring his hands, and urge them to walk through the shops. Then he'd run to the supermarket to buy what he needed.

After four years of being a housewife and mother, Debby was back in the kind of chaotic atmosphere she liked. We never quite made the one hundred dollars a month for the rent.

"Do you care?" Debby asked me. "I hate to lose the money."

"It's an investment," I said, and it was. She had an eye for absurd detail. Almost daily she came home with good stories. I let them expand in my imagination. I sold one about a fervent vegetarian. This time Rocky decided that I had discovered something.

"If they'll pay him five hundred dollars again for a story," he told Debby, "they'll pay me five thousand dollars." He went to work.

"How many pages do I have to write?" he wanted to know.

"You've got to write until you come to the end of the story."

"What I write won't be a story," he said. "It's all true, and so many things happen that it could go on for years."

"Good," I said. "Let it go on—the longer the better."

I was happy that it kept him occupied. He wouldn't tell me what he was writing; he just announced page quantity every few days.

"Twenty," he said. "Is that enough?"

"I can't answer unless you let me read it."

"You wouldn't understand this."

Of all the things he did, nothing amazed me more than the way he went at writing. He was almost one hundred and had a total cataract in one eye. He had refused surgery because he still had the other eye, but it, too, was clouded over.

"How can you write when you can't even see?" I asked him. "I have a friend who's an eye doctor; he says he can do the operation in a half hour. One night in the hospital, and that's it. You'll see fine again, and you'll write ten times as much."

"I see plenty now," he said.

He sat at his desk with the same kind of attention he gave to Watergate. Sometimes, when he came out of the room, I saw a look I recognized—the one that keeps every writer going, the one that shows you've pleased yourself.

"It's going okay?" I asked.

"You can take the money," he said. "Once I'm finished, it's yours."

Eventually Rocky came around. He decided one afternoon when he couldn't read his own writing that he'd have the cataract out. "Call your friend," he said.

"When do you want to do it?"

"Tomorrow," he said, "in the morning."

I should have known that he'd want it immediately. Whenever he bought a pair of trousers and wanted them hemmed, the clerk would look at the calendar, Rocky the clock. If the salesperson couldn't get the tailor to do it on the spot, Rocky wouldn't buy.

I did call my friend, and I did ask him for the next day.

"First, I'm booked for the week. Second, I wouldn't touch a hundred-year-old guy. Take him to the medical center."

I made an appointment there for the following month. Rocky grumbled, but I reminded him that he had waited himself, so he couldn't complain.

With one eye he continued to write, and just before his cataract surgery he handed me the manuscript—ninety-five pages in Yiddish. He had written on unlined white paper. His rows were quite straight and the Hebrew characters all legible.

I shook his hand and hugged him. He moved away.

"Let me congratulate you. It's no small thing to write ninety-five pages."

"When it's in the magazines and they pay you, then you'll congratulate," he said. "It's not as easy as I thought, but making a good dough is even harder."

I tried to prepare him for disappointment. "You know, most writers don't sell the first thing they write. You might have to work on it some more. Change it a little."

"I don't change. It's all true."

"Okay," I said, "then maybe you'll start another one."

"Nah," he said. "That's your job."

HE STAYED in the hospital three days, because the doctor wanted to be extra careful. Then he wore a bandage for two more weeks.

While he recovered, I read his manuscript. The hero was a great rabbi of Dubnow, a city in Poland. In the eighteenth century he traveled throughout Poland and Germany, and everyone knew him as the Magid (the preacher) of Dubnow. He was such an excellent speaker that wherever he went, the synagogues were filled. Rocky emphasized the preacher's learning; by the age of eighteen he knew nine tractates of the Talmud by heart.

The Magid's piety was also exemplary. He put on his tallith—a prayer shawl—and tefillin in the morning, and he kept them on all day. On Mondays and Thursdays he fasted. He gave good advice and helped people to observe the law. Whenever the Magid traveled, he changed lives.

In the moral tales of this preacher, I recognized a lot of what Rocky admired—piety, learning, and big crowds at the synagogue.

I thought that one day we'd sit down together and translate it into English, but he never asked for it, and soon after he finished, I forgot his work. Too many bigger things took over.

A PERMANENT contact lens solved the problem of Rocky's left eye; then a few months later he had surgery for bowel cancer. He was home in two weeks and at our house the next day, pulling the garbage to the curb by eight a.m. But I worried.

"He used to have it at the curb by six," I told Debby.

"They don't pick it up until four or five in the afternoon. He's still eight hours ahead."

"He's not the same. He takes a nap in the morning and one in the afternoon."

"He's one hundred years old and recovering from surgery—what do you expect? He's entitled to slow down." She was right. I started to prepare myself for the inevitable.

Debby tried to take photographs of him, though he rarely let her. She got a few beauties—one of Rocky and Jessica baking together. He is wearing her plastic apron with the ABCs. It ends above his waist. Jessica smiles shyly at the camera, as if she's doing her best to make up for the angry scowl that her great-grandfather is giving her mother as she photographs the two of them.

There's one of Rocky holding our second child, Sam. Sam, a hundred years younger than his baby-sitter, has his lips on Rocky's cheekbone. With his tiny hands he's going for the cap—as Jessica did, as I remember doing. The children helped him fight the lethargy that was overtaking him.

Sometimes Bashy would call to tell me that he wouldn't eat. I would bring Jessica and Sam. Each pulling him by an arm, they could get him into the kitchen to eat a soft-boiled egg or herring and bread.

He had lived to become the favorite of his great-grandchildren and to see me established in a teaching career. He had overcome cancer and partial blindness and thirty years of forced retirement. He had moved twice in his nineties and made new friends in each place. He still had the energy to go to the synagogue to study. Debby was right; what more could I expect? A four-generation family living so closely together. I knew what a rare thing I had.

In the 1970s I saw myself change from a rebel to a father and a professor-writer, and when the children were both in school, Debby started teaching in a community college. The next stage of her life had begun, too. "I want more children," she said, "but I need a while to recover. Give me a decade to think about it."

It was fine for us to think in decades, but not for Rocky. The clock ticks for everyone, but for him it boomed.

Occasionally he'd mention it. He liked clothes. Over the years I had bought him dozens of caps and shirts and trousers, but shoes were harder. He wore a size six, and most men's sizes began at seven. One day I found a size six in a modern version of his ancient favorites, the brown-and-white cordovans. I couldn't resist.

I tore off the price tag, but he knew they were expensive.

"Take 'em back," he said. "I don't need 'em."

I knew he'd say that, so I countered with the truth. "It's so hard to find your size that I would have bought almost any style. But this one, that I know you like—how can I take it back?"

I helped him step into the stiff, thick leather. He looked down and liked what he saw. Then he used one shoe to kick off the other before I could bend to help him.

"Take 'em back," he said. "I won't live long enough to get your money's worth."

When I refused to return the shoes, he started wearing them daily instead of saving them for Saturday. He was doing his best to get his money's worth. Every time I noticed the shoes, I thought of his mortality.

"You know," Debby said, "you're talking yourself into something. He just felt sorry for himself for a few hours, that's all. This guy is not about to leave us. He needs more to keep him busy."

The next morning, when he came out to pull our garbage to the curb, Debby was waiting. She told him she had a problem.

"I hate to bother you," Debby said, "but I need a little help. If you can, I'd like you to stick around Tuesdays and Thursdays from, say, one to five. I'll be here, but if you're supervising the children, I'll be able to prepare for my classes. When you need a rest, just tell me."

After his first week of "supervising," we both noticed that he'd perked up.

"It was a great idea," I said.

Saturdays the synagogue kept him busy, and Sundays, when Debby and I jogged together, we did so at the university track so he could watch the children. Jessica and Sam played in the sand beneath the pole vault; Rocky sat on one of the judges' seats; and George ran ahead, sniffing the cinders for enemies.

The children liked to meet us at the finish line, holding paper cups of water. Debby always beat me by a step or two. "Yeah, Mommy!" the children yelled. She was their hero.

Day by day I knew how fortunate I was to have Rocky so old and still so able. When I ran, I sometimes jogged to a silent rhythm, a kind of prayer that came from my pounding heart and my quick breath. I prayed for him—for more strength and a painless end.

As it turned out, I should have prayed for another.

Chapter 10

WE WERE at the movies watching a cult film that one of Debby's students had recommended. Most of the audience seemed to love it, but we didn't. I was dozing off when Debby poked me in the ribs.

"How many people do you see on the screen?"

"One," I said.

"You're sure?"

"Of course I'm sure. How many do you see?"

"Two," she said. "It's been like that for about five minutes."

"Probably your contacts," I said. She closed one eye, which solved the problem, but we left because we didn't like the movie.

It started that simply. At first we both joked about the effects of a bad movie. Debby went to the eye doctor to check her contacts. He found nothing wrong, but suggested a dentist. He thought that tension in the jaw might be causing her vision problems. The dentist found no tension in the jaw and recommended an ear specialist. Her ears were fine. Debby went to a neurologist, who hospitalized her for tests. A brain tumor, he said, could be the cause.

We sat in the X-ray room waiting for Debby to be called. We were both terrified.

We leafed through magazines together until Debby went for her X rays and CAT scan; then, in the evening, when the neurologist walked in, he told us right away. "It's not a brain tumor."

"Thank God," I said. I kissed the top of her head.

The neurologist wasn't as happy as we were. He kept her in the hospital to test for hepatitis and meningitis; then he checked her spinal fluid and scanned her bones. The tests were all negative, although by the time we received that verdict five days later, Debby had become so dizzy that she couldn't stand up without help.

"I'm certain," the neurologist told us, "that it's multiple sclerosis. The only way to diagnose it is to rule out everything else. We've done that."

"What is it?" Debby asked. I didn't know, either.

The doctor spent the next half hour telling us about myelin, the white fatty substance covering the nerve fibers of the central nervous system. When myelin wears away, some nerve impulses can't get through. Multiple sclerosis, he said, is the name of the disease that causes myelin to degenerate.

We asked all the questions we could think of, and there were no answers. Nobody knows what causes MS, and there is no treatment. He gave us a thick pamphlet so we could read about it. "It could go away and never return," the doctor said. "Or it might come back in a year or five years, or it might never go away."

"You mean I might always see double?" Debby asked.

"Right now it's affecting your optic nerve. It could let up."

"But you don't know if it will?"

"No," he said, "I don't. I wish I could tell you things with greater certainty, but MS follows no absolute pattern. Why don't you read the pamphlet, and then we'll talk again." Debby had it open to a page that showed a photo of a man in a wheelchair.

"Will it do this to my legs, too?"

"I can't make any predictions," the doctor said. "I can tell you what will happen in a thousand cases, but not in one."

Unlike that doctor, I can only tell you what happened in one. It has taken a long time for me to forget the medical facts, to put them enough out of mind so that I can recall the Debby who was not defined by a disease.

Debby came out of the hospital determined not to give up any-

400

thing. She was in the midst of making a slide show for the end-of-year party at Jessica's kindergarten.

She had a plot taken right from life—a dognapping—and two stars, Jessica and George, who got along well. Jessica, posing in front of a huge glass candy-corn container, was already a heartbreaker. Stuart, her little co-star, looked longingly at either Jessica or the candy. The bad guys—five-year-olds chomping on rubber cigars—chained George in a garage. But in the plot that Debby and the kindergarten teacher, David, wrote, the good children won. George, released from captivity, had dinner at an expensive restaurant.

The five-year-olds loved best of all the slide in which George, seated at a table, scanned the menu. He looked up to make a choice. Debby couldn't. She held the slide viewer to one eye, but couldn't raise her head. "Is it in focus?" she asked me.

Section by section her body deceived her. She lost feeling in part of a toe, in the bottom of her left foot, in the side of her face, in her bladder, in her scalp. Some of the losses were fleeting; some stayed. When her balance faded, she bought a bright red cane. On the bumper of her two-tone Plymouth she put a sticker that said FIGHT THE GOOD FIGHT. For two and a half years she did.

I had one big job during those years—I looked with her at a tiny screw that held the glass globe of our bedroom ceiling light in place. I stared at that screw as a sailor adrift might scan the horizon for some hope of land.

As the dizziness increased, Debby spent more of her time in bed. Since everything awful had started with her double vision, I pinned all my hopes on a return to single vision. If she saw one screw, I was convinced our life could go back to the unity of the past.

She thought so, too. We were surrounded by friends: by our neighbor Marcy; by Jane, our car pool friend; by Debby's racquetball partner, Meryl; by Cookie, our PTA friend; by half a dozen great people from the English department who came to read to Debby. But we were not wholly in tune with any of them. The two of us were adrift on our innerspring mattress, looking up at that screw, which had become our North Star, our guide through the darkness.

Debby's mother telephoned daily and refused to call the disease by name. Harriet referred to it as a virus, which some researchers thought it was. If calling it a virus instead of MS seemed to make it more understandable, I didn't argue. I couldn't worry about names; I had my hands full trying to keep our life from crumbling.

While Debby lay in bed waiting for the double vision and the dizziness to pass, strangers entered our lives: a string of house-keepers and baby-sitters—one less reliable than the next—and the nurse's aides who helped Debby bathe.

As Debby's disease progressed, I spent less time with Rocky. I took the children to his house, but he didn't come over as often. He didn't know what to do. No matter how often I tried to explain it to him, he couldn't understand what was happening.

"How can there be something wrong with her brain?" he asked me. "She knows everything."

"It's like a light switch that doesn't work," I said, using one of the analogies I'd read. "You can turn the switch on all day, but if the signal doesn't get through, the light won't go on."

"It must be cancer," he said.

"It's not cancer."

"Then when is she gonna get better?"

I had no patience for him when he started asking me the medical questions. I had read everything I could about multiple sclerosis, and I had no answers. I understood why the neurologist had been so vague. Rocky didn't. He had lived his century in the world of absolutes. If you were sick, you either recovered or you died.

"I'm not going to tell you a hundred times," I yelled. "The trouble is in her brain. Nobody can tell you when she'll be better."

"And what about you? What's the matter with your brain? You're the one who's acting crazy."

"What do you want me to do?" I said. "Jump for joy because the Astros won or the temperature didn't hit ninety?"

"You don't have to jump for joy," he said. "Just take care of your children."

"The children are fine. They go to school; they have a baby-sitter."

"You don't need the baby-sitter," he said. "I can do it."

Because we always reached a dead end when we talked about Debby's illness, both of us took out our anger on the baby-sitting.

Sam was three when Debby's sickness began. We could explain to Jessica why she couldn't jump or even sit on Mommy's bed, but Sam wouldn't listen to explanations.

Rocky was there watching once when Sam ran to Debby, and even while I screamed for him not to do it, he jumped onto her bed.

"I want a story," Sam said, "like you used to tell me."

He was burrowing under her arm to hide from me. Debby's face had turned pale. The dizziness was more than she could bear. I grabbed Sam, screaming, and threw him to the ground.

"Don't you ever jump on Mommy's bed!" I yelled.

He raced past me and tried to reach her again. I carried him howling down the hall and threw him into his room. Jessica and Rocky watched.

"You got no business doing that to the baby," Rocky said. "He's not hurting her."

"He is," I yelled. "Don't stick your nose into what you don't understand."

"You're the one who doesn't understand," he said. "Go take him out of the room. Tell him a story."

"He'll stay there until he listens when I tell him something."

"I'm going to get him," Rocky said. "All he wants is a story." He walked toward Sam's room. I blocked the way.

"He'll get it," I said, "when I have time."

"You never have time," Rocky said. "You sit in there like you're afraid someone will steal her. Pay attention to your children."

I took my hand from the doorknob. Sam ran out, right to Rocky, and climbed into his arms. I tried to help Rocky lift him, but they both pushed me away.

"I'll tell you a story," Rocky said as he carried Sam to the living-room couch, "about the bakery in Beaver Falls when I first came to America."

He kept Sam on his lap. Jessica sat beside the two of them.

I went back to our room. Debby was staring at the bottom of the light. Her face was more pale than I had ever seen it. Silent tears were streaming down her cheeks.

I asked my daily question. "How many do you see?"

"Three," she said. "Leave me alone."

BETWEEN 1978 and 1980 Debby's condition deteriorated, and Rocky, who had seemed as if he had one foot in the grave at one hundred and two, bounced back into action. He was too busy to die.

We worked out an agreement on the baby-sitting. He didn't do primary care of Jessica and Sam, I kept the baby-sitters, and Bashy helped enormously. But Rocky became what Debby had called him, a supervisor. No detail was too small for him.

He complained because I bought Sam Velcro-snap shoes just when he planned to teach him to double-knot; he told me I should be taking Jessica for violin lessons instead of to baseball games. Above all, he started to focus again on the longer range rather than on wearing out a pair of shoes.

He went to school with me to find out why Sam's teacher recommended that Sam wait a year before entering kindergarten.

"What's the matter?" Rocky asked her. "You don't think he's smart enough to be in kindergarten?"

I had explained to him that I wanted to keep Sam back a year anyway. His birthday was in November. He could be either a few months young in one class or a few months old in another.

"What did he do wrong?" Rocky wanted to know. "When I cash my Social Security, he counts the money perfect, and he knows the ABCs and a lot of Hebrew songs."

"He's a smart boy," Mrs. Shaw said, "but he has trouble cutting."

"What do you mean, cutting?"

"Cutting with a scissors." Mrs. Shaw made a scissors of two fingers on her right hand to demonstrate.

"What kind of school do you send him to?" he asked me. "Are they teaching him to be a tailor?"

Mrs. Shaw laughed. "He's just a little behind in manual dexterity. Most boys his age are."

"What does he do wrong?" Rocky pressed the issue.

"He doesn't cut straight."

"Who cares," Rocky said, "if he's not gonna be a tailor?"

"Enough," I said. "I want to keep him back anyway."

I thanked Mrs. Shaw and pulled Rocky out of her room. It was the end of the school year, and lots of mothers were in the hallway emptying their children's supply buckets, packing up the leftover crayons and wide-lined paper. I didn't know any of the mothers in Sam's class and hadn't made any play dates for him.

Jessica had lots of friends. After the last day of kindergarten Jessica had spent a summer being invited out. Her popularity continued into first grade, but in second grade she stopped going to the houses of her friends. She just wanted to stay home.

I saw her becoming more isolated, but I didn't do anything about it. She played with Sam. She taught him jacks, and I bought them a little trampoline and baseball gloves and plastic bats and a battery-operated pitcher who lobbed Wiffle balls at them.

Debby had been sick for so long that all of us forgot what it had been like before. I stopped asking how many screws were at the bottom of the bedroom light fixture. Debby struggled to get out of bed. Instead of just reading to her, she asked her friends to help her go to the store. She fell often, but she kept trying. Because she couldn't use her eyes, she began to listen to classical music. At night we talked about the children, the way all parents do.

I had given up the innocent hope that things would go back to what they had been. Debby was sometimes depressed, but she was still Debby—until that, too, began to change. Within a period of weeks she lost interest in everything. She stopped pushing herself to get out of bed. Throughout the illness she had always forced herself to get up, especially in the morning to see the children before they went to school. But in the spring of 1980 I had to coax her to arise even at ten. Sometimes I had to wait for help from her friends. She didn't resist; she just became more and more passive.

When Rocky and I came back from the conference with Mrs. Shaw, I had the last two weeks of Sam's classwork to show her—seven drawings and the obviously uneven cutting.

"Picasso probably couldn't cut straight, either," I said as I held up the preschool artworks. It was past noon, and she was still in bed. Her look was so far away that it scared me. It wasn't only passivity; something else was wrong, too.

I put down the drawings. Almost in a whisper I asked her, "Do you know where I've been?"

She hesitated for a minute; then she looked at me. "Alabama."

I showed her more of Sam's work, then called the doctor. I told the nurse the symptoms, and she gave me an immediate appointment.

The neurologist examined Debby in his office, then called the hospital to order a room. "I'll have to take some tests," he said, "but it appears that the disease has affected her thinking." He said he wanted to call in a psychiatrist, too.

Debby continued in that dreamlike state. She didn't ask about the children, but on Sunday I brought them. Jessica kissed her, but Sam—fearful that I'd pull him away—stood far from the bed until I carried him over. Rocky and Bashy came in the afternoon and then drove the children home.

Bashy had recognized for weeks that everything had changed. Wisely, she didn't question me. Rocky wanted explanations.

"Why doesn't she talk? What happened?"

"I don't know," I said. "When I know, I'll tell you."

I had lost my patience. When I had a call from someone who introduced herself as a nurse at Methodist Hospital, my heart raced and my mouth went suddenly dry. "We're having a little problem with your grandfather," the nurse said.

"What happened?" I screamed.

"Don't worry, he's fine," the nurse said. "I'm sorry to alarm you. He's angry, but we really can't let him contribute."

"What?" I asked. "What's he doing?"

"He's at the blood bank; he wants to give a pint of blood to your wife. The technician tried to explain that we have regulations. He's listed his age as one hundred and three. Is he really?"

"He is," I said.

"I thought," she said, "that maybe he was a little confused."

"Is he still there?"

"Yes," she said. "That's why I called you. He refuses to leave."

"I'll come get him. I can be there in a few minutes."

She had called me at my university office, across the street from the medical complex. I jogged to the blood bank and was a little winded when I reached the waiting room, but Rocky was standing at the door. I snapped at him for pulling me away from my job.

"I didn't tell them to call you," he said. "How can blood be too old? If it still works, it's good."

"They're not gonna take any from you," I said. "They just want you to go home. . . . Please, I don't have the strength to argue."

He let me guide him to the door. Before he left, he said, as loudly as he could, "If you don't want people to give blood, don't say you do on the television."

I waited with him at the bus stop. "Debby doesn't need blood," I said. "Her blood's fine."

"It can't hurt to try. When you talk to the doctor, ask him to give her some blood."

When the bus came, I held his elbow as he climbed the stairs, but he pushed my hand away.

I did speak to the doctor that night, but not about blood. He was with three other doctors and clearly in a hurry.

"I don't have any new information," he said. "All the test results will be in by next Tuesday." We made an appointment to meet at the nurses' station on Debby's floor at three that Tuesday.

During the entire time of Debby's illness only one part of my life had stayed the same. Every day at noon I ran with Huey, a Chinese physicist who also taught at the university. He was a much better runner but kept my pace, so he always had the breath to answer my endless physics questions. He had some problems with English, but in three miles he could explain an electron microscope.

After the exercise and a shower we would drive a few blocks to the Cultured Cow and eat tuna sandwiches. The run and shower and lunch altogether took us an hour and a half.

Huey, who was doing experiments in biophysics, knew what was happening to Debby; he also knew that the constant repetitions of her problems didn't help. "Try to think about something else," he'd say, and he could make me do so at least for that hour and a half.

But during that late spring, as Debby faded, I couldn't talk about anything else. Huey tried to switch the subject from Debby's brain to the brain in general, but I couldn't listen. I didn't care about anyone else's brain.

"Wait until the doctor explains to you," Huey said. "Don't try to understand it by yourself."

On that Tuesday, as I awaited the doctor's explanation, Huey left for Ireland to attend a physics conference.

At the gym I took my wire basket to a locker, as I always did, unrolled my shorts and socks, and headed for the street. I only ran a few steps. Without someone to talk to, I had only the constant dialogue about Debby in my head. The three miles that I covered every day seemed as impossible as running to California.

"Too hot for you today?" the woman at the desk asked when I walked back inside.

"Yes," I said.

Instead, I got into my car and drove. I had no destination in space, only in time. I had to get from twelve until three. Downtown Houston looked absolutely foreign. I parked and wandered into Foley's, a six-story department store.

I spent a long time at the Hello Kitty collection—Jessica's favorite. On all the objects, a red-and-black kitty almost smiled. She decorated watches, pens, pencils, stationery. I bought a Kitty key chain and held it clamped in my fist like a worry bead.

For half an hour I rode the escalator. I looked at everything—a two-second view of each floor. I was an astronaut among things that used to be familiar—buttons and sunglasses, fur coats, vacuum cleaners, chandeliers. The world lined up before my passing glance and then slipped away. I had to force myself from the escalator.

I was better by the time I arrived at the hospital, and I already knew what I was going to hear.

At three fifteen I sat in the cubicle that belonged to the nursing chief of 5N. The doctor had just arrived from his own office. I saw him slip on the white hospital coat with his name sewed on in blue. He carried a thick notebook—Debby's chart.

He shook my hand, offered me coffee in a foam cup. He put the chart on the desk in front of him. I didn't know what words he would use, but by that time I didn't need him for the bad news. I only wanted directions on how to find her.

He opened the chart. "These are the results of the personality test. They're not as precise as we'd like, but they do show what I suspected. In Debby, the disease has progressed to the point where there's no way to distinguish between her brain and her mind."

"What does that mean?"

"It means that she's not likely to come out of this. We will of course try everything. We'll see if drugs or behaviorism can bring her back somewhat, but I think it's neurological. Her mind can only be what the brain still allows. It doesn't go this way very often."

Suddenly my vision was very blurred. The doctor reached across the desk to hand me a little gray box of hospital tissues.

"You have a lot to cry about," he said. "I'm sorry. I'll ask the nurses if you can stay here awhile."

He closed the door quietly. He had left Debby's medical record, but there was nothing in it I wanted to read.

In a few minutes I walked down the corridor to Debby's room. "I went to Foley's today," I told her. "I got this for Jessica."

I held up the key chain with the ceramic Hello Kitty. I put it in her hand. She seemed asleep, or maybe she wasn't. I didn't know how to recognize the difference.

Chapter 11

JESSICA and Sam slept at Bashy and Rocky's house every Saturday night. Bashy pushed twin beds together and joined her grandchildren in a slumber party. Sunday mornings Rocky walked them home and the fighting began.

Sam watched cartoons nonstop. *Transformers* was his favorite show, but he watched *Tom and Jerry, Bugs Bunny, Flintstones,* and *G.I. Joe.* Between the three UHF channels he had all-day coverage. Jessica wanted to watch baseball.

"You always let him hog it," she complained.

Sam had his standard reply: "She can listen to the radio. There's no cartoons on the radio."

Rocky sided with Jessica, I think, because he liked baseball.

"She has to watch," he told Sam. "She'll be an announcer someday."

"She can be a radio announcer, too," Sam said.

"Maybe I'll just buy another TV," I told Rocky, "a small black-and-white."

"It won't help," he said. "They'll fight over who gets the color. What you should do is get the little one away from the cartoons."

I knew he was right, but I didn't have the energy to make any changes. The cartoons kept Sam occupied; that was enough.

"It's a shame," Rocky said. "PeePee needs the television. She tells me what they're gonna do next. She could be the manager."

Rocky called Jessica PeePee, his version of Fifi, her own name for herself when she was a toddler. Fifi stuck—Sam and I still used it—but PeePee was only Rocky's.

He was right about her, too. She followed the games closely; not only the games, she followed innings. On her notepad she put little gold stars beside the ones she wanted to narrate to me.

Sometimes when I would come home from the hospital at eleven or so and open the refrigerator to look for something quick to eat before bed, I would hear her door open. "Can I come out, Daddy?"

I knew I should say no, but I was so happy to hear her voice that I rarely did. Instead, we went through a little charade.

"Is it important?"

"Yes."

"Can it wait until morning?"

"I guess."

She'd start to close her door, then give me one last chance—a burst of information. "We lost in the eleventh. I want to tell you about it. Then I'll go right to sleep."

Baseball was working for both of us. For some reason, although I'd lost my taste for almost everything else, the fate of the Astros' pennant drive held my attention.

"Five minutes," I'd whisper, and that was all I allowed. But those five minutes redeemed the day.

She held her notepad and read from it. She didn't know how to keep score; instead, she wrote out a narrative of what happened in every inning. I only let her read me the exciting innings. She didn't write out the great plays. She just drew a star at that spot in the text and told me from memory.

Her five-minute sports report did more than bring me up to date—it brought me back. Every day I hurried home from the hospital and had dinner with Jessica and Sam; then at six thirty I drove back. Rocky, Bashy, or the baby-sitter—sometimes all three—put the children to bed.

Sam went to bed early but woke up at night between two and three. He didn't ask permission; he just sprinted down the hall to my room. At first I'd walk him back and tuck him in again, only to have him return in a few minutes.

I gave up. I put an old mattress at the foot of my bed. He slept there like a pet. In the morning I'd step over him and go out to pick up the paper. I'd read about the Astros first, enjoying another version of what Jessica had already highlighted.

There were lots of wins that summer. The Astros had great pitching and played tight defense.

So did we. Jessica defended herself with baseball; Sam used cartoons. For me the best defense was order.

I had a schedule. I would comb Debby's hair, try to feed her, hold her hand, and read the paper aloud. As much as Debby, I settled into a small room in Methodist Hospital with a fourteen-inch TV, an adjustable bed, a tray table, and an excellent reading lamp. It was cozy in its way, even romantic. We were more than alone.

Everything else in my life—my students, my work, even Jessica and Sam—were offstage, in the wings. I waved, I threw kisses, I checked in. I read stories at night, paid the baby-sitter, bought the groceries, but the only intense life I had was in that hospital room.

To accommodate us, Rocky had changed his schedule. He took his naps when I was home so that he could be alert when I was at the hospital. While the children and I ate, he snored on the couch. I would shake his shoulder at six twenty and have some coffee ready, which he drank while watching either cartoons or baseball.

I was about to buy a second TV when Huey, during one of our runs, had an idea.

"I have a broken one," he said, "a nine-inch. It jumps all the time." He showed me with his hands.

Jessica and Sam both complained, but I stored our twenty-one-inch color set in my office and installed the vertically disordered black-and-white.

Rocky had to close his eyes as he listened to the news. Jessica switched to radio, but Sam continued to watch television.

For about a week he continued his daylong vigils. Then, Rocky told me, he started shutting off the television himself. He still watched his favorites, but he transferred some of his attention to the hallway.

As a fourth birthday present our neighbor Marcy and her family had bought Sam a set of racing cars—two- and three-inch speedsters that operated on push power. I added a gray Plymouth like the one that I drove.

I noticed that he played with the racers in the hall. Lots of evenings, as I was leaving, I had to step over his parking lot to get to the door. One day in July I heard something. He was on his knees, making an engine-revving noise with his throat. I kissed the top of his head, the straight soft brown hair so much like Debby's.

"See you in the morning," I said.

I was already out the door when he stopped revving his Chevy. "You never play with me," he said.

411

"I heard that," I said. I pushed the mail slot open with my finger so he could see me. "I'll play with you more soon."

"When?" he asked.

"Pretty soon. You'll see. . . ." I walked fast so I wouldn't hear any more questions. As I backed away from the house, I saw Sam's eyes following me through the mail slot.

I was already at the hospital garage and had taken my punched card at the automatic gate when I decided to turn around. I drove back through and paid fifty cents to exit. I drove fast.

When I got home, it was seven fifteen and I walked into the Indianapolis Speedway. All the cars were lined up at one end of the big hallway. Sam knelt beside them. At the other end, sitting cross-legged on the floor, his back against the wall, Rocky waited. He held his cap in front of his legs—a target for the cars.

Jessica, taking a break from baseball, kept score here. She listed each vehicle—Fiat, Chevy, Oldsmobile, truck—and kept track of how often each one sped directly into Rocky's cap.

"What's this?" I said. "Sam and his pit crew?"

"Be careful," Sam said. He slid quickly to his left to keep me from stepping on his cars.

I sat down to join him. "Can I play, too?" I asked.

He didn't answer; he just slid back to make room for me. His shoes and socks were off; his little toes squeezed the floorboards. He was all business.

"Are you gonna push or catch?" Jessica asked me.

"I'll push," I said, "but you'll have to teach me the rules."

I kicked off my shoes and sat down. I picked up one of the golden Pontiacs.

"Be careful," Sam said. "That one can really go."

"Let's see," I said. I pushed the golden racer, and it sped straight across the floorboard into Rocky's cap.

"Mazel tov," Rocky said.

"You didn't think I could drive straight?"

"I didn't think you could think straight."

When he started to stand up, he had to get on all fours first and hold on to the wall. Jessica and I ran to help him.

"Now you catch," he said. "I'll sit down."

"Have you been catching cars every day?"

"No," he said. "Sometimes he bounces those little Super Balls into my cap. The cars are easier to stop."

Sam ran to his closet to get his Super Balls. "I've got a whole collection," he said. Vaguely I knew it, but I hadn't sat down with him to appreciate all the colors and sizes.

While Rocky rested on the couch, I played Super Balls. We measured the bounce of every ball in Sam's collection.

Rocky went to sleep, and Jessica brought out her Barbie dolls and treated me to a fashion show.

That evening I was their special guest. Sam went deep into his closet, brought out all the collections. Some were his exclusively; others they shared—rubber bands, colored paper clips, disposable spoons, marbles, the paper flowers from get-well cards. They had salvaged what they could. In the hospital room I had felt that Debby and I were stranded on an island, but as I examined their treasures, I began to understand who the stranded ones really were.

ONCE I missed that first night at the hospital, it was easy to miss others. I still spent my afternoons with Debby, but the evenings belonged to Jessica and Sam and, when he chose to join us, to Rocky.

In August, while the Astros and Dodgers jockeyed for the division lead, I began to realize why Jessica had become such a baseball fan. It wasn't only Rocky and me; the other regulars in our house were also sports nuts.

Joel, Debby's cousin, stopped by every day. He was twenty-four, a salesman, and single.

The other regular, David, was Jessica's former kindergarten teacher. After Debby's slide show for the kindergarten, he had become one of our closest friends. When I was still going to the hospital every night, if I came home early enough, I'd find everyone in front of the TV—Jessica taking notes, Joel holding the remote control so he could click on other games, David watching the game while he played cars with Sam, Bashy trying to straighten out the kitchen, Rocky snoring from his spot on the big red chair.

"Except for Bashy and the baby-sitters, Jessica's surrounded by men," I told Rocky, "and all she hears is sports talk. I want her to be interested in other things. She's eight years old; she should do what other little girls do."

"You're right," Rocky said. "I'm gonna take her shopping."

A few days later Jessica came home wearing a flowered dress and a bonnet. She ran into her room. "He embarrassed me so much," she said. "I didn't want this stupid dress and hat, but he liked it, so I let him buy it. It was a lot of money, too. Twenty dollars."

"Don't worry," I said. "I'll pay him back."

"He won't let you. He took his handkerchief along. If I knew he was going to do that, I'd have never gone. First he told the saleslady that it was way too expensive and asked her when it would be on sale. Then when she said it wouldn't be, he counted out his money right to the penny and then knotted the handkerchief up again. Everybody was watching."

"That's nothing," I said. "Probably nobody even noticed."

"They did, too," Jessica said. "And then he called me PeePee in front of everybody. I'm never going to go back to Penney's."

"Let's make a list of some other things you'd like to do."

"I want to go to ball games—that's enough."

"What about going to the movies with your friends?"

"I don't have any friends," she said.

I started naming them. "Hilary, Ilana, Rebecca, Sarah . . ."

"They used to be my friends. They're not anymore."

"Why?"

"I just don't like them."

"Do they ask you about Mom?"

"Sometimes," she said.

"So it's hard for you to talk to them?"

She nodded.

"I know," I said. "It's hard for me, too."

I didn't press her that day, but I did what I'd been considering for some time. I telephoned a psychotherapist. As briefly as I could, I told Joyce what had happened to Debby.

"I know Jessica's lonely," I said, "and I know there are things I can't change, but I want to help her. I hope I haven't waited too long."

Later that week Joyce spent two hours with me at her office; then she went to the hospital to see Debby. By the time she met Jessica, she was ready. She took Jessica to Pizza Hut and then drove her home. Joyce was talking to me when Joel came running into the house holding a napkin as if it were a hundred-dollar bill.

"You won't believe this," he yelled. "Look what I got for you."

He opened the napkin on the floor, held Sam back to keep him from trampling it. "To Jessica," it said, "Joaquin Andujar." Andujar was one of the Astros pitchers.

"He just wrote his name at first," Joel said, "but I asked him to make it personal. He was at McDonald's, just sitting there with his own kids. Excuse me," he said, noticing Joyce for the first time.

Jessica brought out a baseball card and compared signatures to convince herself that it was really Joaquin. She and Sam both examined the napkin like detectives. They agreed it was real and gave Joel high fives. "Gotta run," Joel said.

Rocky kept his eye on Joyce. "Are you a doctor?" he asked.

"No," she said. "A psychologist."

"There's nothing wrong with PeePee," he said. "Her father is the one who's nuts."

Joyce stayed an hour and a half. The next day she suggested that both children begin therapy. Sandra, her partner, would take on Sam.

"Jessica has had a big loss," Joyce said. "It's harder to cope with than a death because there is no finality. She doesn't know what she's supposed to do."

415

"Why is she so stuck on baseball?"

"It gives her a way to reach you," Joyce said, "a way not connected to Debby or anything else. Baseball is a straight shot to you."

"She wants to hang around with me all the time."

"Of course," Joyce said. "She doesn't want to let you out of her sight. It's almost like an infant's fear that Daddy will never return when he leaves the room. Jessica calms that part of herself with baseball. While you're gone, she's got that, so she's not afraid."

"I guess it makes sense."

"It's a long, slow process," Joyce said. "She'll have to learn to trust the world again so she can let go of you and baseball."

"What can I do to help her?"

"I can't say for certain," Joyce said, "but from what I've seen, I'd guess you've got some letting go to do as well."

JOYCE had two specific suggestions—a cat and Brownies, the younger Girl Scouts. I resisted the cat; Jessica vetoed Brownies. She also tried to convince me that seeing Joyce was a waste of time.

"She's not fun to play with," Jessica said, "and she always asks me, 'How do you feel about this?' Why is that her business?"

"That's her job," I said, "finding out how you feel and helping you to understand your feelings."

"I understand how I feel without her," Jessica said. "All she does is snoop around. If you really wanted to make me feel better, you'd fire her and buy season tickets with the money you'll save."

She'd guessed right to remind me of the cost. Jessica had two appointments a week with Joyce; Sam, three with Sandra. Once a week the two therapists met with me. They agreed about the cat.

"She's lonely and she loves cats," Joyce said, "and we can learn a lot from the way she relates to the cat."

"Can't we learn just as much from the way she relates to George?"

"I don't think so," Joyce said. "George is the family pet, not really hers. I think she needs to connect to something that's completely separate from everything else that's going on."

"I'll think about it," I said. George convinced me more than the psychologist did.

I knew what bothered the dog. He looked everywhere for

Debby. He crawled under the bed and tore open the bags full of spices—all we had left from the store. He howled in the kitchen. In the yard he uprooted the azaleas and dug into the ground as if he could find Debby if he went deep enough.

One Sunday afternoon on the hospital lawn Jessica and Sam and Rocky held him on a leash, and I brought Debby to the window. We were five floors up, but Jessica and Sam could see us. Jessica held George by his paws so that he stood on his hind legs. Rocky kept trying to keep the leash from getting tangled in Sam's feet. I could read the children's lips as they called out to Mommy. Hearing that word must have made George bark. He bounced around on his hind legs.

"George is going nuts. He wants to see you. Can you wave?"

I held Debby's hand in the air and pressed it against the window. I supported her in that position for a minute or two—long enough for everyone to wave and throw kisses to her.

Three weeks earlier the doctors had switched Debby to psychiatry to see if anything in that department could help. They gave her drugs that made her sleep and caused her body to become rigid. When that didn't help, they decided on behaviorism.

"The reward system might pay off," the psychiatrist had said.

"She doesn't ask for anything," I said.

"We'll deny some of the things she's getting now, then give them back if she responds."

We started by denying Debby her mail. Every day I used to bring something from the children. Jessica wrote notes to her mother, decorated them with flowers and trees and birds. The colors were bright; the words were what they had to be: "Get well, fast," "I love you," "I miss you."

I didn't tell the children that under the doctor's direction I was now withholding Jessica's letters and Sam's drawings. I kept their work in a bag at my office. Debby didn't respond, but her room, without the children's decorations taped to the wall, lost its only brightness. As another experiment in denial, I stopped reading aloud and the room lost its sounds. Nothing else changed.

We stopped the experiment. I taped all the letters and drawings that I'd collected to the wall beside Debby's bed, and I decided to bring George—my own experiment.

417

When I came downstairs to the lawn near one of the parking lots, the dog was loose and about to attack a security guard. George wanted to find Debby. He had bared his teeth. His backbone stiffened. The security guard had removed the billy club from his belt and held it in his right hand.

"Don't hit him," Jessica yelled to the guard. Rocky tried to get the leash back on, but George was too quick for him. He kept moving away, circling ever closer to the guard.

I saw what was happening as I ran out of the building. I grabbed George's collar, but he snarled and tried to fight me off. When he fell to the grass, I grabbed his choker and pulled as hard as I could.

"Stop it, Daddy," Jessica yelled. Sam held on to Rocky. George tried to bite my hand so that he could get to the guard. I tied the leash around his jaws like a muzzle, then pulled him toward the car. He was shivering and so was I.

"That's a mad dog," the guard said. "I would have shot him if the kids weren't here. If I were you, I'd have him put away."

In the car we had to wait a long time until George was calm enough for me to begin driving.

"Would the policeman really have shot him?" Sam asked.

"I don't think so," I said.

"George doesn't like policemen," Sam said.

"That's not why," Jessica said. She had her hand on George's head and opened the window a little so he could hold his nose out and sniff the air.

I waited for Jessica to continue. When she didn't, I asked, "Why do you think he was so angry?"

"Because," Jessica said.

That night I called Joyce and okayed the cat. On Saturday she arrived with Snow, a white Siamese whose previous owner had given her away because she couldn't be housebroken. Joyce didn't tell me that. By the time I figured it out, it was too late—Jessica already loved her.

"Okay," I told Jessica. "I gave in on the cat; you can compromise on Brownies."

"I'm not going," she said. "I don't have to do everything Joyce says."

"I want you to go. I think Brownies will be good for you."

We were sitting in a booth at the Pizza Inn. Rocky drank coffee and kept his eye on Sam, who liked to push the buttons on the jukebox.

"You're always on Joyce's side."

"PeePee's right," Rocky said. "You don't need those women to play with the kids. Let them get a real job."

"And he's always on your side. But let's get back to Brownies. What have you got to lose by giving it a try?"

"I don't want to," she said, "and you can't make me." She left her slice of pizza half eaten and walked to the car.

"Leave her alone," Rocky said.

"Just don't try to talk her out of it."

"I don't even know what it is," he said.

"It's Girl Scouts for younger girls."

"Like what you did? The Cub Scouts? You didn't have enough yourself—now you want it to happen to PeePee?"

He stormed out to join Jessica in the car.

"I know why Rocky doesn't like Girl Scouts," Sam said to me. "It's because they make cookies, isn't it?"

THE Brownies, of course, also met in a church—St. Anne's. Jessica went to the meeting only because I bribed her. After the meeting I promised I'd take her to a ball game.

"Is Nolan Ryan pitching?" she asked.

"He's scheduled."

"All right," Jessica said. "I'll go to Brownies, but only if we get to stay for the whole game, even if it's extra innings."

Rocky stayed with Sam. I didn't tell him we were going to a church, but I wore a hat—my blue Astros cap with an orange star.

The troop had already been meeting throughout the school year. We were late. When we entered St. Anne's recreation room, the girls were sitting in a circle. Kay Randall, the troop leader, was holding her hands out from her chest. She looked at her fingernails as if she were checking to make sure they were all the same color.

"Ready?" Kay Randall asked. She didn't wait for an answer. "Close your eyes," she said, "and bridge."

Kay breathed deeply as she put her fingertips together. The girls imitated her. Jessica and I sat on folding chairs and watched.

After about thirty seconds Kay stood. "Five-minute break," she said, "a quiet one." She came over to us. I had spoken to her on the phone. She shook my hand and Jessica's. Then she held Jessica's hand and walked her across the room to join the other girls, who were eating Ritz crackers and drinking half-pints of milk through colored straws.

"I know we're joining late in the year," I told Kay, "but I hope Jessica can still benefit from being part of the group. She knows most of the girls."

"Of course she can," Kay said. "Not everyone has to start at step one. It's not the army."

"She tends to be a loner," I told Kay. "The group might help."

"We have a lot of shy girls," Kay Randall said. "Scouting brings them out."

"That's why I want her in Girl Scouts. I want her to go to things with her girlfriends instead of always hanging around with me."

"I understand," Kay said. "It's part of bridging. It's what we were doing when you came in."

"I wondered what it was," I said.

Kay raised her fingertips to eye level. "This is a bridge," she said, "a symbolic one. There are five levels of scouting, and we bridge between each one. These girls are coming close to the end of their Brownie experience. In the fall they'll be Junior Girl Scouts. Bridging is a way to get ready for what comes next so it won't be so scary."

She raised the whistle that hung around her neck, blew one short blast. The girls returned to the circle.

"Are we gonna do projects now?" one of the girls asked.

"No," Kay said. "We'll finish bridging, but first let's welcome Jessica." The girls held hands and swayed from side to side. "Hello, hello," they sang. "Hello to Jessica." She sat on the floor between Sarah and Rebecca. Kay raised her hands, and twenty girls in white shirts and brown sashes held out their chewed fingertips and made bridges. Jessica kept her hands at her sides.

When Kay lowered her arms, the circle broke up and the girls went to a long table where buttons of all sizes were laid out. There were also rubber-tipped bottles of glue and thick paper.

"Crafts," Kay told me. She helped the girls get started. Jessica picked an assortment of buttons and began to arrange them.

When Kay asked me if I could help out, I volunteered.

"Katherine's mom helped all year," she said, "but they moved to St. Louis. It's hard for one person. But if you're too busy . . ."

"I can do it," I said. "One night a week is okay."

After the meeting, while I helped Kay carry the supplies to her car, Jessica didn't jabber with any of the girls. She just went right to the car, strapped in, and braced herself for destruction.

I WAITED until the sixth inning to say anything about Brownies. Nolan was throwing nothing but smoke and had only given up an infield single. I tried to give her my new information in the best possible moment, while Nolan still looked great.

"I'll be going to the Brownies meetings, too," I told her. "I volunteered to be Kay's assistant."

"You're off your rocker," she said. "I'm never gonna go again."

"All right," I said, "suit yourself. Don't go. But I said I'd be an assistant and I will."

"I know why you're doing this," Jessica said. "You think that because I don't have Mommy, Kay Randall and the Girl Scouts will help me. That's crazy. And I know that Joyce is supposed to be like a mother, too. Why don't you just leave me alone?"

In the seventh inning Nolan gave up four hits and a walk. Although Jessica had made me promise to stay into extra innings, she wanted to leave after the eighth.

In the morning she told Rocky that I had joined the Brownies.

"You don't have enough on your hands," he said, "you got to join clubs."

Jessica smiled as she ate her cereal.

"If Jessica doesn't want to learn things, I still can," I said.

"Sure," Jessica said, "go ahead. Learn how to make a necklace out of safety pins."

"Nobody's forcing you," I told Jessica. "You do what you want, and I'll do what I want. A promise is a promise. I signed up to be a leader, and I'm going to do it with you or without you."

Every Tuesday, Rocky would stay with Jessica and Sam while I went to the Brownies meetings. We talked about field trips and how to earn merit badges. The girls giggled when Kay pinned a promptness badge on me—my first.

Jessica thought it was hilarious. She told me to wear it to work.

Chapter 12

AFTER the behaviorism failed to change anything, the hospital started to pressure me. Sharon, from the counseling office, came up to see me one morning.

"Can I buy you a cup of coffee?" she asked.

I suspected what it was about. Sharon was a woman in her mid-fifties, whose hair had gone past gray to white and cushioned her long face. She reminded me of the good-hearted neighbors in movies, the ones who come over after the fire and, without asking, begin to help you rebuild the barn.

Until she came into the room, I had been feeling pretty good. It was my morning for Sam's car pool. He didn't sit next to me in the front seat; he wanted to be in the back with Kevin and Brad. Two months of therapy with Sandra, a broken TV, and fifty or so hours of rolling cars in the hallway had made a difference.

"The staff doesn't think you've faced everything," Sharon said. "You have a big decision coming up. I know you're trying to avoid it. I don't blame you. It's your decision, of course, but I've compiled a short list of nursing homes. . . ." She handed me a packet.

"They're for old people," I said, "not for Debby."

"They're for people who need them," she said, "at any age."

I shook my head. "How much longer can she stay here?"

"We decided that she could be released immediately. But she can stay until you've made arrangements—up to ten days. Sometimes," Sharon said, "a person is so close that they don't see."

"I *see*," I said. "It's one thing to see, another to do."

"That's true," she said. She handed me her card. "I have an appointment now, but anytime you want to talk some more, please call me."

Sharon was wrong. I hadn't avoided the issue. I had thought about nothing else.

I had the pamphlets Sharon left for me in a manila envelope when I drove up to our house. Sam and Rocky were shining shoes. Rocky sat on the lawn chair. He splattered liquid polish onto Sam's white canvas shoes. Sam, holding the brush, waited for the shoes to dry.

The trash cans were at the curb, the animals' dishes clean, the driveway swept. Jessica came running out with a message.

"When Sandra dropped off Sam, she said you should call her as soon as you get home."

"I'll call her," I said, "but I need my hug first." When she felt like it, Jessica added to my hug a bonus—a little tickle with her long hair against my cheek.

When I reached Sandra, she was still at her office. "I'll wait for you," she said, "if you can come over right now."

Only two months earlier I'd had to drag Sam literally howling into her office. Now he looked forward to seeing her and sometimes chose the games he wanted to play with her the night before.

She was a tall, slender woman, almost too glamorous looking to be on the floor playing with Sam. She had been patient and kind to him even when he was hysterical and throwing toys at her. She usually made me feel better about Sam. This time she didn't.

Harriet had been in town for the weekend. She had taken Sam and Jessica to Toys "R" Us and loaded them with gifts.

"Sam told me about his grandma's visit. Did you know they went to the hospital to see Debby?"

"Yes."

"Did he tell you what Grandma did?"

"I don't think so," I said.

"She put him on Debby's lap and told him to kiss Mommy and that would make Mommy better. Then she told him that Mommy did talk to her and told her what to say to the children. He wants to know why Mommy can talk to Grandma and not to him."

"She wants it so badly," I said, "that she's making it up. She doesn't mean any harm."

"She may not mean any harm," she said, "but she sure can do some. If I had to come up with a scenario designed to create psychosis in children, this would be it. They're getting the message that it's their job to save Mommy, and now they've got a translator, someone who understands Mommy and knows what Mommy wants. Have you told the children how bleak Debby's condition is?"

"Not in exact words, but we always talk about it."

"I think it's time," she said, "to put all the cards on the table. Sam is already worried that he can't save Mommy and that Grandma is going to be mad at him. I asked Jessica about what happened, and she told me the same story."

"I can't stop Harriet from saying what she wants."

"If you can't, who's going to protect your children?"

WE WENT to the coffee shop at Penney's. It seemed like the right place. The children were there so often with the baby-sitter that the waitress called for two cheese sandwiches as soon as she saw them walk in. Rocky came, too.

I reassured Jessica and Sam that Debby wasn't talking to Grandma Harriet.

"If she could talk, she would talk to you guys. The other thing you have to know," I said, "is that you didn't make Mommy sick, and you can't make her better. No matter how much you want to, no matter how much you love her, you can't make her better."

"Who can?" Jessica asked.

"Nobody."

"The doctors can't do anything else?" Rocky asked.

I shook my head. I hadn't directly told him so, either. The children ate their sandwiches.

"I've known for a few months that Mommy's not going to change. The doctor told me, but we still wanted to try everything, in case there was a chance."

"Why didn't you tell us?" Jessica asked.

"I wanted to protect you a little longer. I should have told you."

"I knew Grandma Harriet didn't really talk to her," Sam said.

When we got home, I gave Sam an early bath. When I dried him, I saw the curve of Debby's toes in his. I put him into his Green Hornet pajamas. He carried Snow around in his right hand, chanting, "One-handed Snow." The cat purred to the rhythm.

In the backyard I saw Jessica. She was picking up pebbles and throwing them. She wound up like Nolan Ryan but threw the pebbles straight up into the air. Rocky had gone outside with her and was dozing on a lawn chair a few feet away.

I watched her throw the stones, one by one, taking aim and then firing with all her might. She owned a mitt, a hard rubber ball, and lots of tennis balls. I picked up my glove and a ball and went outside.

"Wanna play catch?" I asked.

She shook her head.

"C'mon," I said. "You can be Nolan Ryan and throw all fastballs."

She shook her head again. She wasn't just idly flipping the stones; she was concentrating hard, the way she did when she printed her letters carefully. I watched her aim at the sky and throw a half dozen more. It was starting to get dark and looked like rain.

"Aiming at something?" I asked.

Jessica nodded.

"What?" I asked.

"God," she said.

I watched her throw for a few more minutes. The little stones fell back close to where she stood. I came over and picked one up. We took turns. I threw mine as hard as I could, too. When it started to rain, we woke Rocky and went into the house.

WHEN Jessica stopped going out for recess, Mrs. Klein, her teacher, called me in for a conference.

"I offer her the use of the library, or even the cafeteria," Mrs. Klein said. "Not all eight-year-olds love to play. . . . But Jessica doesn't want to read or have a snack. She just takes out those baseball cards and thumbs through them. I thought you should know."

"I know. She does it at home, too," I said. "She's updating the statistics on the cards. It's probably my fault. I taught her how to figure out batting averages so she could enjoy long division, and now she keeps track of everything."

"It may be a useful hobby," Mrs. Klein said, "but missing recess, coupled with her lack of interaction with the children . . . You know, it worries me even though I understand the situation. My son kept up with baseball cards," she added, "but he was thirteen or fourteen. Isn't she too young for it?"

"I've taken her to a lot of games, and she listens every day."

"I know," Mrs. Klein said. "I've warned her about listening during class. You've seen the note."

"I have, and I back you one hundred percent. She's not allowed to take her radio to school."

"I'll just continue to monitor the situation," Mrs. Klein said, "and we'll hope things get better. She's an excellent reader and speller, and the math, well, with all that practice I guess it's no surprise."

FOR HER NINTH BIRTHDAY I surprised Jessica. I invited all the girls in the class—fourteen of them—to a party. Jane, one of Debby's best friends, brought some tapes. I pretended that we were going to the movies to celebrate. On our way I turned back because I forgot my wallet. Sam never let out a peep.

When we walked in, the girls were all hiding in the bedroom. On the table was a surprise for me, too. I expected a birthday cake.

"You like it?" Rocky asked Jessica.

"It's so beautiful," she said. "I don't think we should cut it." She ran over to hug him.

Rocky had made a three-decker wedding cake. Instead of a bride and groom he'd put the figure of a ballplayer on top. Jessica was still hugging him when the girls ran out yelling, "Surprise!"

I was sorry the minute I saw the look on her face. The cake was plenty. When Jane put on a tape and all the girls went into the living room to dance, Jessica went to her room. Rocky followed her.

"Is she coming out?" Jane asked me.

"I don't think she liked the surprise. Go ahead, entertain the rest of them." When I knocked at her door, Jessica was lying on her bed, facing the wall. Rocky was rubbing her back.

"I thought you'd like a surprise party," I said.

"I didn't want a party. I just wanted to go to the movies."

"Do you want me to send the girls home?"

"I don't care; they're not my friends."

"They sure sounded like they were. They were all excited to come. And you," I said to Rocky, "you pulled the biggest surprise of all. Why didn't you tell me what you were baking?"

"Because you'd say no."

"That wouldn't have stopped you."

Jessica smiled.

"Are you gonna come out to cut it?" I asked. She looked at Rocky.

"Sure she'll cut it," Rocky said. "A cake is to eat, not to look at."

Jessica washed her face. When she and Rocky walked to the cake—they came down the hall as if he were walking her down the aisle—the girls stopped dancing. She wore blue jeans and white Keds and a striped sweater, but the cake made her as much a bride as a birthday girl.

The dancers sang "Happy Birthday" quietly, and everyone stood

near the cake. Rocky had arranged nine candles on the second tier and one to grow on, at the top, next to the ballplayer. "Be careful," Sarah said when Jessica took a deep breath. "Don't get any spit on it."

I cut. Jessica gave the first piece to Rocky. Every girl took a big piece. Sam ate three flowers, and there was still three quarters of the cake left.

When everyone left and I began to help clean up, Rocky covered the third tier of the cake in aluminum foil. I pulled the foil apart to look at it. The ballplayer and the candle were gone, but the white fluting on the sides and the frosting were untouched.

"Take it to Debby," Rocky said.

While he wiped away ice-cream spills, I kept my eyes on the cake. It was ten years late and missing the bride and groom, but he hadn't only baked this cake for a birthday.

I said that to Debby when I put the cake on the table in front of her. "Rocky told me to bring you the crown," I said. "I think he's trying to tell us he wishes he had baked it for our wedding."

I put a bit of the frosting to her lips. She made no attempt to eat any. I tried again with a piece of the cake; then I wiped her lips clean and cut the cake in fours for the duty nurses.

In October, Mrs. Simmons, the principal, called. Mrs. Klein had caught Jessica in spelling class listening to the World Series through an earphone. Rocky took the call.

"Jessica understands school policy," Mrs. Simmons said. "We confiscate radios and send the child home. I've called her father at his office, but I haven't been able to reach him. Is there anyone else who could pick her up?"

Rocky walked the five long blocks. When he got to school, Jessica was sitting on a bench outside the principal's office.

Rocky took her hand. "Where's the radio?" he asked.

Jessica motioned to the door marked PRINCIPAL.

"He knocked," Jessica told me later. "He didn't just walk in and yell at her. Anyway, I don't think she understood him, so I told her what he was saying."

Rocky wanted the radio.

"I'm sorry," Mrs. Simmons said. "The radio has been confiscated. She can have it returned after a seven-day period."

"I bought her that radio," Rocky said. "I've got the receipt to prove it." He fished it out of the zippered change purse that the children and I bought for him last Father's Day.

"Nobody is taking the radio. She just can't use it for a week."

"Are you in the union?" Rocky asked.

"I am a member of the teachers union."

"Is that where you learned to steal, or were you a crook before you joined those robbers?"

"I tried to pull him away then," Jessica said, "but he wouldn't move."

"Give her the radio," Rocky said, "or I call the Labor Department. You union people think everything is yours."

When he grabbed the radio from her desk, Mrs. Simmons didn't try to stop him. "Her father will hear about this, and so will her teachers," she said, following them out the door.

"Good," Rocky said. "I'll tell all the people I know, too."

When Mrs. Simmons did reach me, I went right to school. By then she was calm. She went out of her way to let me know that she wouldn't hold Rocky's behavior against Jessica.

"I know it's her grandfather," Mrs. Simmons said, "but he had no respect for school policy."

"Actually," I said, "he's her great-grandfather, and he doesn't have respect for very many policies, but I apologize for anything he said or did."

We agreed that Jessica would stay home from school the next day to reprimand her.

When I came home and broke the news, Jessica screamed with pleasure. "I'll be able to watch the seventh game!"

"You see?" Rocky said. "The principal knew she was wrong."

ON THE morning of the seventh game it was eighty-five in Houston and our air conditioner didn't work.

"Good," Rocky said. "Now we can watch the game in peace."

I had decided to wait until spring to repair the air conditioner, so I spent some time on the phone trying to price a fan that would cool two rooms and the long hallway. When the game began, Jessica had the starting lineups in front of her on three-by-five cards.

Rocky and Jessica were arguing about who would win when the phone rang.

"If it's the school," Jessica said, "I'm still being punished."

"It's probably someone calling back about the fan."

I had a pencil in my hand and a piece of scratch paper near the phone so I could write down the model number and price.

"I'm at the hospital," my caller said. "I'm taking Debby out. If you want to see her, get here right away."

I knew Harriet was coming, though not the exact date. A week earlier, when I had made my decision, she had made hers, too.

We were now enemies—a situation Debby would have approved. It started when I phoned Harriet after I told the children what Sam called "the whole truth." I told her she had to stop confusing them.

"You can believe whatever you want, but don't tell Jessica and Sam things that are only fantasies. They have to know what's real; it's the only way they can face it without ruining their lives."

"So," she said, "you're joining the doctors and the witch doctors and giving up on your wife."

"I'm trying to protect our children, that's all. They know the truth. Don't confuse them."

"The truth," she said, "is that the doctors have made her worse. As soon as she gets home, she'll be fine. The children will make her better."

"No, they won't," I said. "Children can't cure this kind of disease. You can't put that pressure on them."

A few months earlier I wouldn't have argued. But now I knew— not because of what the doctors said or what Harriet demanded. I knew from Debby.

For almost three years she had fought the good fight. Partial vision and shaky limbs and devastating dizziness had not overwhelmed her. But in the last six months something had. I couldn't pretend that there was still a Debby who understood.

"I'm making arrangements," I told Harriet, "to move her to the Jewish Home."

"Never," Harriet said. "My daughter will never be in a home."

"It's not a prison. If she gets better, she'll come home."

She knew my weakness and went for it. "You didn't put the old man into a home," she said. "How can you put your wife there? She's not like those old people."

It was true. Debby wasn't like them. On the day I visited, I envied most of the retirees. They played checkers, went on bus trips, complained about their meals. Debby would be housed not with them, the director told me, but in the hospital section. I was no happier about it than my mother-in-law, but I didn't know what else to do.

I had told Jessica and Sam that Grandma Harriet would be coming to Houston to take Mommy to her house for a while. They were prepared, and I thought I was, but my hand shook as I hung up the phone.

"How much is a fan going to cost?" Jessica asked. The game was in the middle of the fourth.

"It was Grandma Harriet," I told her. "She's come to take Mommy to Michigan." I picked up my car keys.

"You want me to come?" Rocky asked.

430

"Stay with Jessica," I said, "and wait for Sam's car pool. I don't know for sure how long I'll be gone."

Jessica put down her pencil and scorecard.

"You don't have to go," I said. "You just saw Mommy on Sunday. Nothing's changed."

"I still wanna go," she said.

Neither of us spoke on the drive to the hospital. I pretended I was listening to the game. I thought Jessica was paying attention.

"What's the score?" I asked when we pulled into the garage.

"I don't know," she said. She held my hand in the elevator. The door to Debby's room was open when we arrived.

Harriet had brought a helper with her, a woman in her twenties. Harriet didn't speak to me, but she hugged Jessica. She had dressed Debby in a red-belted dress, one I had never seen.

The attendant stood by, not sure what her role was supposed to be. "You'll see," Harriet told her. "In a week Debby will be doing everything herself. And will she ever let us have it if her canopy bed isn't in her room just like it used to be. This morning that was the first thing she asked me about."

Jessica looked at me. She knew it wasn't the truth. She looked at me for help, but I couldn't give it. I needed help myself.

An orderly pushed Debby's chair down the hall. Harriet and the attendant followed, and Jessica and I trailed them.

Outside, Ben, Debby's father, was waiting in a rented Buick. He nodded to me and waved to Jessica. The attendant helped Debby into the car; then they strapped her into the front seat.

I leaned down so I could kiss Debby's cheek. I smelled her perfume, saw the rouge and lipstick.

"Come kiss your mother," Harriet said. Jessica leaned her face quickly toward Debby.

Harriet and the attendant went back inside to get the packet of medications that they'd forgotten in the room. Ben rolled up the window so the car would stay cool. Debby stared straight ahead. Jessica and I looked at her through the glass.

"Mommy doesn't wear lipstick and makeup," Jessica whispered to me. "Why did they do that?"

"Grandma Harriet wants her to look good."

"But Mommy doesn't like it. Make them take it off."

"You're right," I said, "but I don't want to get into an argument about it. Let them do what they want. It's not hurting her."

We waved until the Buick was out of sight. In our car we forgot to turn on the radio. We stopped at Sears to pick up a fan. I bought the biggest one they had—a fifty-eight-inch oscillating model that sounded like a hurricane.

I paid in cash and had fifty dollars left. I gave it to Jessica and told her to buy anything she wanted.

"Whenever you're sad, Daddy, you want to buy me things." She put the money back in my hand. "It won't help."

At home I had no energy even to take the fan out of the box. I carried it in and left it for Rocky and Jessica. Nothing had changed. Debby hadn't been home since late spring, but that afternoon I couldn't stand to stay indoors. I sat on Rocky's aluminum lawn chair watching the tennis courts across the street. Sometimes Debby and I would lie in bed at night reading, while tennis balls from across the street softly hit the cement. "Fault," she would say if I dozed and the book fell to my chest.

Rocky came out. He carried a paper cup full of ginger ale, his version of medicine. Whenever he didn't feel well, it was the first thing he asked for.

"I'm okay," I told him.

"Drink it anyway," he said. "You'll be more okay."

"Daddy," Jessica called, "are you coming in?"

"Pretty soon," I said.

"Sit," Rocky said. "I'll take care of her. When the car pool comes, I'll take Sam, too."

I drank the ginger ale. I could tell time was passing, because there were at least three different sets of players on the courts before I stood up to face what was the whole truth—my life without Debby.

As soon as I opened the door, I smelled the aroma. Jessica was standing on a chair holding a star cookie cutter. She licked chocolate chips from her fingers.

"Do you believe it? Rocky's helping me bake cookies."

The erstwhile cake man, his sleeves rolled and flour up to his elbows, had three sheets of stars and one of chocolate chips cooling on the counter. I smelled more in the oven.

"We'll have enough for a bake sale," Jessica said. "We can set up a table outside. Shall we charge a dime apiece?"

"Too much," Rocky said. "A nickel is plenty."

When the car pool dropped Sam off, Jessica and Rocky had already carried the coffee table to the curb. Jessica was laying out Toll House cookies on white paper towels. Sam ran to the sale table.

"Rocky baked cookies," he said. "How come?"

I took out two nickels, bought one from Jessica and one from Sam. Though the bitterness at the back of my throat did not leave then or for a long time after, on that day I still could taste the sweetness.

Chapter 13

THE leaders of troops 114 and 226 and Kay and I were planning the Brownies' final event—a daylong picnic and flower gathering at a ranch. It was a seventy-mile trip, and we tallied supplies for the busload. Kay, like Harriet and Terry, the other two leaders, had been on the same outing numerous times.

"The girls will all pretend they're glad to leave Brownies," Kay said, "but every one of them, years later, will still have her little notebook of pressed flowers. It's a big event for them."

Kay gave me the easiest job—cold drinks and snacks for sixty-two.

"Jessica is welcome," Kay said. "Even though she hasn't joined, she might still want to go on the picnic."

"Believe me," I said, "I've invited her."

"I admire you," Kay said, "for sticking with it. Jessica might get something indirectly through your experiences."

"I don't know about that," Terry said. "All my husband says he gets from Brownies is cold suppers."

Kay poured coffee as we traded stories about our troops. It felt so ordinary that I could hardly believe I was part of it.

In the past few weeks, when the girls put their fingers together to bridge, I joined them. Bridging was quiet, just an awkward pose of nine-year-olds uncertain about what would happen next. I felt like one of them.

At home, I showed Jessica. "I'm bridging," I said.

"So is everyone in my class. It makes me sick."

"The picnic is the last event. You used to like picnics."

"I'd go with you and Sam and Rocky," she said, "but who wants to go with all of them?"

"If Rocky goes on the picnic, will you go?"

"He'll never do it," she said.

I thought she was right, but I gave it a try.

He answered with a simple no and went back to reading his Yiddish newspaper. "It's important," I said. "If you go, maybe she'll go, too."

"She can pick flowers and get sunburned in the park," he said. He held up his newspaper so he didn't have to look at me.

"I'm not talking about across the street. I'm talking about out into the world to be a little girl, to have a childhood."

"All right," he said. He put down his newspaper. "I'll go, but I won't pick any flowers."

Jessica was more stubborn. "I don't know how you tricked him," she said, "but I'm still not going."

I was sure she'd change her mind. "Why are you making such a big deal out of it?" she asked when she went to the store with me and helped me load three cases of Coke and one hundred and twenty-four lunch-size bags of chips into the trunk. "It's just a dumb old picnic."

"You're right," I said. "But we've gotta start someplace."

Until picnic morning I expected her to come; so did Rocky. He made her a peanut butter and honey sandwich and wrapped some herring for himself in waxed paper. All morning she stayed in her room and wouldn't come out. Sam had spent the night at his friend Brad's house and would remain there all day.

"We can't leave her," Rocky said. "I'll stay."

"You said you were coming. I'm counting on you."

"I was coming so PeePee would go, not to sit on the bus with your wild gang."

He put his lunch back in the refrigerator and turned on the television. I went to the phone. Juana, our cleaning lady, was home and said she could baby-sit all day. Rocky trusted her.

"She'll be okay with Juana," I said. "You know that."

He didn't answer. A few minutes later he took his lunch out of the refrigerator, then put it back in. He wanted me to give him an absolute reason to go, something powerful enough to counteract his desire to please his PeePee.

"All right," I said. "If you're too lazy to go on the trip, stay home. I'll do it alone."

"What do you have to do?"

"You know—the cases of Coke, the potato chips, all the food other people are bringing. You think a picnic is easy? The girls will be playing; somebody's gotta do the work."

When Jessica came out of her room, I showed her the waffles in the waffle iron. Rocky picked up his lunch and went out to the car.

"If you want anything else, just ask Juana."

"Juana doesn't speak English."

"Honey, I told you, you can come; there's plenty of room on the bus. It's not too late for you to change your mind."

"It's not too late for you, either. There's going to be other leaders there. You don't have to go. You're just doing this to be mean to me. And taking Rocky is supermean."

I was ready for this. I had spent an hour with Joyce the day before, steeling myself. "Before she can leave you," Joyce had said, "you'll have to show her that you can leave. Nothing's going to happen to her. And don't let her be sick that day, either."

Jessica was too smart to pull the "I don't feel good" routine. Instead, she became silent. When I left, she didn't say good-bye.

Rocky didn't talk to me on the hour-and-a-half trip. When we got to the ranch, I grabbed the heavy cases of Coke. He handed me the potato chips, then stayed on the bus with the driver while I ran out into the field with the Brownies.

I pointed out the names of various flowers to Carol and JoAnne and Sue and Linda and Rebecca. The Girl Scout flower book had very accurate photographs that made it easy to identify the bluebonnets and buttercups and poppies.

Everyone had collected lots of flowers by the time Kay blew her whistle. She signaled for us to gather at the bridge, a twenty-foot wooden semicircle that passed above a rocky creek as it ran through the meadow. The bridge was only wide enough for one person to cross at a time—perfect for what we needed.

Terry stood on one side with a paper bag full of Girl Scout wings. The girls were ready to cross. Carol went first. She put down her

435

flowers, stepped to the creek side, and looked into the shallow water.

" 'Twist me and turn me and show me the elf,' " she chanted in a singsong rhythm. " 'I looked in the water and saw . . . myself.' " Then she walked to the bridge, clenched her fists, and crossed over. On the other side Terry pinned the Girl Scout wings to her collar.

" 'I will do my best,' " Carol said, " 'to be honest, to be fair, to help where I am needed. . . .' "

The girls were all quiet; there was no pushing in the line.

Rebecca poked my arm and pointed. Far from us, near the gate, Rocky was bending, picking flowers. I backed away slowly so I wouldn't disturb the ceremony; then I ran across the meadow.

I was out of breath when I got to him. "Let me do it," I said. "I don't want you to bend."

He pushed me aside. "Look at you," he said, "running around like a nine-year-old, and PeePee is home. It's upside down."

"You're right," I said. "That's why it has to change."

I walked back to the bus with him, watching from the distance as the girls, one by one, went from elf to winged being.

Rocky and I were on the bus, waiting, as the Junior Girl Scouts marched on, carrying wildflowers.

He was asleep already. He snored on the bus—the whistles followed by the puffs that had been the music of my childhood. A few of the girls who walked past giggled when they heard those noises coming from the first row, but most were subdued. They were showing their wings.

Kay came over to check. "Is he okay?" she whispered.

"Yes," I said. "It's just his time to nap. He'd do it at home, too."

I believed that, but one of these days I'd be wrong. When I had taken him for a routine chest X ray before his cataract surgery, I got tense when I saw the doctor look at the film for a long time.

"Is it normal?" I had asked.

"I don't know," he had said. "I've never seen an X ray for someone over a hundred. I don't know what normal is supposed to be."

I didn't wake him until we arrived at St. Anne's and unloaded. I said good-bye to Kay and to the troop. I picked up Rocky's cap and pulled on his left earlobe. He sat up in a hurry and wouldn't let me hold his arm as he stepped down from the bus.

"Thanks for coming along," I said. "I hope it didn't tire you out."

"I'm not tired," he said. "I'm worried about PeePee."

When I opened the door to the house, I could smell the taco sauce that Juana had made. Jessica was in her room. She came running to the door when she heard us.

"We had a lot of fun, honey, but we missed you."

"The Astros lost five to four," she said. She tried to act as if everything were fine.

"Next time," Rocky said, "you're going, not me."

"No, I'm not," Jessica said. "I hate all of that."

"Then you can try other things," I said. "It doesn't have to be Scouts, but I'm not gonna let up."

"Tell him to leave me alone," she asked Rocky.

He handed Jessica the flowers he had picked. "Here," he said. "The other girls all had flowers, so I got you some. I don't know what you're supposed to do with them."

In the driveway Brad's mother sounded her horn. Rocky went out to claim Sam. Jessica held the flowers like a shield.

"Are you still gonna take me to ball games?" she asked.

"Of course, but I want you to start bringing a friend along."

"When you were little and Rocky took you places, he didn't make you bring a friend, did he?"

"That was his mistake." I laughed. "Look at us now, still hanging around together."

"I don't think it was a mistake," she said.

"Maybe not, but guess what—I'm no Rocky."

"I know that, but when you're real old, maybe you will be."

"I'll try, but I want you to promise something, too."

"What?"

"Try to have fun." She couldn't hold back any longer. She dropped the flowers and cried against my shoulder. I felt like holding her the way I used to when she was an infant, the way I rocked her to sleep. But she was a big girl now and needed not sleep but wakefulness.

We heard Sam and Rocky open the gate to the backyard. George ran to them.

"I'll try," she said. She wiped her eyes. "Don't tell Sam I was crying." She went to the kitchen for a vase. After she'd put the flowers in, she turned to me. "Did Rocky do all that bridging junk?"

437

"No," I said.

"I knew he wouldn't."

"He didn't have to," I said. "He's done it lots of times. Who do you think showed me how?"

WHEN he was eighty-nine, Rocky had developed a growth on his vocal cords. It annoyed him enough to go to the doctor.

"In that spot and with his symptoms, I'm sure it's cancer," the doctor told me. "You've got to tell him the truth. He needs surgery."

"I'll tell him," I said. "I'll just use a different word."

I picked a good one—boil. In Yiddish a *geshvir* could be a wart, a pustule, an annoying everyday malady, but not a killer.

"If you don't let them take that boil out," I told him, "the cough will never go away."

The cough bothered him so much he agreed to the operation.

It was scheduled for eight a.m. a few days later. He spent the night before in the hospital. So did I, on the floor beside his bed. He was up at four and was ready. By six he had put away his tefillin and read the paper. At eight he was standing at the door. At eight fifteen he walked to the nurses' station to ask where the doctor was. The nurses told him it was not unusual for the surgeon to be late.

"He told me eight," Rocky said. "Eight is eight."

By nine thirty he was dressed and about to walk home. When I blocked the elevator, he headed for the stairs. "That doctor's a liar," he said. "I don't want a liar operating on me."

We were on the landing of five, two flights from where we'd begun, when a nurse yelled down that the doctor was ready. Then I heard the doctor's voice.

"I'm very sorry to keep you waiting," he said. "I had another operation, and it took much longer than I thought it would."

"Why?" Rocky yelled up. "Did you make a mistake?"

His knuckles were white as he gripped the rail. For the first time I saw that he was afraid. I put my hand over his and loosened his grip. Slowly we walked up the stairs.

The doctor and two assistants waited outside the room while Rocky took off his suit and put on the hospital gown. He was still angry when he got onto the stretcher and an orderly wheeled him toward surgery. I walked alongside.

"Do you remember," I asked him, "when I had my appendix out? I was on the stretcher, and you came running down the hall."

"I remember," he said. "I was scared."

"So was I until I saw you."

When he had caught up with me at the edge of anesthesia, he was sweating and red-faced and out of breath.

"Mein kind," he asked, "are you sick?"

"No," I said, answering him with one of his own phrases. "I'm fine, but the doctors need to make some money." I fell asleep laughing.

The orderly interrupted us. "You'll have to wait out there," he said. I hadn't even realized until I started to back away that Rocky and I were holding hands. He held on and propped himself up on one elbow.

"If I die," he said, "you can have all my suits."

"None of them fit me," I said.

When the orderly wheeled him through the operating room doors, I was smiling.

The cancer was completely removed, but the doctor wasn't certain how much of Rocky's voice would return. He spoke in a whisper after that, but in therapy sessions he learned to breathe from his stomach so his voice could be stronger. He didn't need a mechanical assist. His whisper was more emphatic than most voices.

Later there were more "boils"—this time on his colon. First one, and then another that became malignant.

"Just a boil," I said, "but if you don't take it out, it could kill you."

"You're telling me," he said. "What's a person? A feather? You can die from a toenail. Let's go."

After each operation Rocky was home in two weeks and fighting me to let him pull the garbage to the curb.

When he was about one hundred and five, he stopped walking over to our house, but by then Jessica and Sam were old enough to visit him. Most days, when I stopped to see him, he was in his usual spot on the front lawn, reading one of his volumes of the Talmud.

When Rocky was one hundred and six, I received an invitation to visit Brazil as a literary lecturer for the United States Information Agency.

Since the onset of Debby's sickness I hadn't written anything. For a few years I had neither the time nor the peace of mind. My storytelling went entirely to the children. Jessica and Sam got five stories a night—all made up on the spot. Sometimes it would take me an hour and I'd leave their room sweating, but once in a while, when a bedtime story engaged me, I missed my old work.

The invitation to Brazil came at a time when I wasn't getting others. The trip itself wasn't important, but for me it would be a first step, a way to return to my life as a writer.

"I can take care of the kids," Bashy said. "Go ahead."

Everyone I talked to encouraged me, yet as much as I wanted to go, I kept hesitating. Finally, as the commitment deadline closed in, I realized that it wasn't Jessica and Sam who held me back.

When I sat on the lawn beside Rocky one day in 1982, I was both a forty-one-year-old man talking about a trip to Brazil and a five-year-old boy asking if I could go across the street.

Rocky was not in good shape. He was losing weight. His hollow cheeks made his nostrils seem larger. He had one leg thrown over the armrest of his lawn chair, and he pulled his cap down a little to shade his eyes. I asked, as always, indirectly.

"If I go to Brazil," I said, "can I get you anything?"

He thought about it for a minute. I waited, not for his words, but for the look in his eyes, his false bravado, his impatience, the signs I had been reading all my life. I would know if my old roommate thought he could give me up for two weeks.

"Maybe you can find me a pair of yellow shoes down there," he said. "Look around."

I did. In Rio and São Paulo and Brasília, when I wasn't talking to students or being escorted to literary groups, I was sticking my head into shoe stores, looking for yellow size sixes.

The shoes were his gift to me. He used yellow shoes to tell me that he wasn't going to die while I was on another continent—not if he could help it.

I came back loaded with souvenirs. For Bashy I bought a purse and a lapis necklace; for Jessica and Sam, wallets. And in Recife I found a pair of yellow canvas shoes, size six. Rocky wore them proudly to the synagogue, and a few months later, before he went into the hospital, he put them away in his closet with newspaper stuffed in the toes to hold their shape.

This time there was no further medical help; his entire body was failing. In the hospital we could only wait. Bashy slept beside her father on the vinyl armchair that unfolded into a bed. I prepared Jessica and Sam, told them that Rocky was very very sick, but they didn't believe me.

On Sunday they came to see him, elated that they were sneaking in, though the hospital prohibited visitors under twelve. An intravenous solution had strengthened him temporarily. When Jessica and Sam came in, he raised the electric bed so that when they stood on a stool, they could lean over the guardrail to kiss him.

"Your mustache tickles," Sam said. He was almost seven.

"Don't squish his mouth when you kiss him," Jessica said. She took her turn on the stool and delicately offered her cheek.

"Don't forget," he told me. "On Tuesday take out the garbage."

When Bashy took the children to the cafeteria for ice cream, he motioned for me to lower his bed. I leaned over the guardrail, and into his ear I yelled in words what he had taught me with his life.

"*Shtark zich* [Strengthen yourself]!" I yelled it so loudly that a nurse hurried in. I waved her away.

He shook his head, and I put my ear close to hear his whisper. "*Ich ken shein nicht* [I can't anymore]."

He was sleeping when Bashy and the children returned. In the cafeteria Jessica had made a discovery.

"Rocky is more than half as old as America." She showed me her figures on a cafeteria napkin: $1982 - 1776 = 206$. Sam wanted me to double-check.

"It's true," I said.

On the ride home we continued to talk about Rocky's age in relation to America's. The children seemed dazzled by the idea that their country wasn't even twice as old as their great-grandfather. It made history seem so close. I was thinking about it, too, when a few hours later, Bashy called to tell me he was going fast.

I left the children with Marcy. In the hospital elevator a sleepy young man handed me an "It's a Boy" cigar. I was holding it when I walked into Rocky's room, just seconds after he died.

Because Jewish tradition forbids embalming and encourages immediate return to the dust, we buried Rocky in Houston, far from his wife and son in Michigan. We buried him in his shroud and his tallith and with his bag of Jerusalem dirt, but on the wooden coffin

441

I poured the symbolic first shovelful of Texas soil and then laid down the shovel to fulfill the role I'd been born to. As his son, I stepped forward to say the *Kaddish*, the mourner's prayer.

The rabbi held out a book, but I shook my head. I knew the words by heart, yet I was sobbing too much to say them. The small crowd waited—Bashy, my sisters and their families, a few neighbors, some of the old men from the synagogue. I wanted to get all the words right. Rocky didn't like mistakes. *"Yisgadal, v'yisgadash,"* I said, almost in a whisper. . . . I couldn't go on.

Jessica and Sam, through their own tears, were watching as I took a deep breath and looked up past the solid tombstones and the gardener's cottage to the high arc of I-45, where lines of traffic bent toward Dallas and Galveston.

Shtark zich! I told myself, and I did.

In the land of Washington and Lincoln, on a patch of grass not even visible from the highway, I prayed, thinking of another great American, my little Rocky. My voice steadied, and I made no mistakes. By the last stanza everyone could hear.

Epilogue

AFTER years of lingering, Debby died in her parents' home.

George, the dog, lived to seventeen—in dog years, the children told me, older than Rocky.

Jessica is in college.

Sam is a high school senior.

Joel Kerner is married and lives the life of a pious scholar. Some consider him a holy man.

On a sabbatical year in New York, I met and later married a woman who studies Talmud. We have daughters, three and two.

ABOUT THE AUTHOR

"I loved writing this book," says Max Apple. "It was like having Rocky and Debby back again—all the happy times." According to the author, the memoir was a long time taking shape. He first wrote it as an essay, then as a somewhat fictionalized screenplay. (The movie is scheduled for release in late 1994.) Apple says he had been hesitant to write in depth about the painful period of his first wife's illness, and it wasn't until after Debby's death in 1989 that he felt he could tell the whole story. Even then, he was afraid that sad memories of her illness and his grampa Rocky's death would come flooding back. But to his surprise this wasn't the case. "I felt buoyant. It was wonderful."

Max Apple

Apple is the prolific author of numerous articles, short stories, essays, and a novel. He continues to teach English and creative writing at Rice University in Houston, where he lives with his second wife, who is a historian, and two small daughters. Jessica and Sam, Max and Debby's children, are now both at the University of Michigan. Bashy, Max's mother, still lives in the same house that she shared with Rocky.

Not surprisingly, Rocky remains very fresh in the author's mind. "There's a picture here right now of him scowling at me," Apple remarked during a recent interview from his Houston office. In a fitting coincidence the book was finished on the anniversary of Rocky's death. No doubt the old curmudgeon would have been pleased.

WHITE HARVEST

by
Louis Charbonneau

The Alaskan tundra: a vast land, rich in beauty, teeming with life. To John Mulak it is home. Here he has fished and hunted for all of his many years. And he cherishes its wildlife as dearly as he does his own family.

Now others have come to this place—men who want only one thing: to get rich by poaching walruses, magnificent animals whose tusks are worth a fortune in distant lands.

John is determined to stop them. It means risking his life. But for the sake of everything he loves, he must try.

PROLOGUE

AT THE edge of the world, where the barren sweep of the Alaskan tundra met the gray waters of the Chukchi Sea, a finger of a peninsula hooked outward to form a buffer against the icy winds and the smashing waves. Over countless years the pounding of the surf had pulverized the base of the bluff, creating a rocky shelf within a sheltered cove, protected from the sea's unending blows and the blasts that roared unimpeded across the Arctic wastes to the north.

For three days in mid-September this northern Alaskan coastline was buffeted by high winds and rain. In the early hours at the end of the third night the storm pattern broke. When the winds subsided and the sea grew calm, a deep crashing sound jarred the small cove, as if a giant beneath the waves were hurling himself against a massive door. For several minutes the heavy knocking continued. Then, after a brief silence, a strange song began. It rose and fell, echoing eerily off underwater rocks and the submerged cliffs that formed the seawall, as if bells were tolling below the ocean.

The belling ceased. Within the cove the sea heaved upward beside the shelf of rock. A huge walrus hauled himself out of the water. Weighing at least two tons, he dragged his great bulk onto the rock by hooking his long tusks over the edge of the shelf. This habit was responsible for the walrus's scientific name, *Odobenus,* the Tooth-Walker. His thick skin, normally a deep rose, was white from the near freezing cold of the water. In the pale morning light he looked like an enormous ghost of the sea.

447

Young walrus bulls in a herd practiced their mating song for hours in the night, but they invariably swam in packs of four or five, belling in chorus. The huge old bull swam alone and sang alone.

Eskimos who had seen the great bull estimated his age at no less than thirty years. He was larger than any other bull in the herd, with magnificent tusks—four and a half inches in diameter at the jawline and nearly five feet in length—extending almost straight downward from his jaws. They were so long that he could lie comfortably only on his back or on his side. The tusks of the mature males in the herd averaged from two to three feet in length.

The Eskimos who inhabited this northern Alaskan coast had caught glimpses of the huge bull many times. Old men told stories of their attempts to hunt this great prize. His skin carried the scars of a score of bullet wounds. To the awed hunters he seemed impervious to their weapons, as if he were invincible, a god of the sea.

The natives called him Muugli. The Great One.

In the morning, fog shrouded the cove where the male walrus herd had paused in its fall migration. But at midmorning the fog lifted. A pale, late summer sun bathed the rocks in its soft light. The shelf seemed to come alive, for it was covered by the massed bodies of the walruses—about two hundred of them. The old bull slept by himself, undisturbed, on a separate table of rock.

For some time the shelf stirred with activity. There was steady grunting and snorting. Barks and bellows shook the air. Some of the mature males jousted, using their tusks as weapons. Others slipped off the rocks into the sea, where they scoured the muddy bottom for the clam beds. But as the day warmed, almost the entire herd piled back onto the narrow shelf. Some lay on their backs, their flippers languidly waving. Others sprawled on their sides or draped their heads over the armored backs of neighbors. They pushed and shoved, and settled down and slept.

There was nothing to disturb them within the sheltered cove: on the landward side the steep cliffs thrusting seventy feet high made the shelf inaccessible. The walruses' only enemy from the sea itself was the killer whale, which stayed in open waters. Their real enemy was man. And the cove was hidden from human hunters by the jutting finger of land.

AT THE BEGINNING OF THIS century the walrus herds of the North Pacific had numbered more than two million. Arctic Eskimos—the Inupiat and the Yupik—hunted them, but only for need. A single walrus might serve a native family for a full winter, providing food, skins for their boats and for making ropes, and ivory for carving and trading. Then a different kind of hunter came—light-skinned, hunting not for subsistence, but for ivory or, more perversely, for sport. In the annual slaughters that followed, the very survival of the species was threatened. Laws were finally passed against the wholesale killing. Only Eskimos' traditional subsistence hunting was allowed. So was their sale of small quantities of carved ivory. Poachers quickly exploited this breach in the law, using Eskimos as cover for illegal ivory harvesting. The slaughter continued.

During the summer, female walruses and their calves remained in Arctic waters near the pack ice in the northern Chukchi and Arctic seas. Male herds scattered, riding drifting islands of ice southward to choice sea-bottom feeding grounds. Some ventured as far as two thousand miles to the southern Bering Sea. It was during these few months that the males built up the thick layer of fat that would enable them to survive winter.

In the fall, males traveled north to meet the descending pack ice and to reunite with the female herds. Together they traveled to breeding grounds in the northwest sector of the Bering Sea. For Muugli's herd the arduous northern journey of over fifteen hundred miles was near its end.

The cove seemed safe. Even if hunters had discovered the herd, the shelf was normally impossible to reach in small boats because of the turbulent sea outside. At peace, the walruses dozed in the sun.

A MILE from the cove, on orders from white hunters, the outboard motors powering two long Eskimo skin boats shut down. Although walruses have no external ears, they can hear fairly well in the open, and remarkably well underwater, where motor sounds easily travel a mile or more.

There were five natives in one boat, six in the other. One white man crouched in the stern of each boat, hunched against the wind. The open sea was rough, the current strong enough to make the Eskimos working the oars grunt and strain.

The boats were umiaks—narrow, open, about twenty feet long, and covered with walrus skin. They were remarkably durable and seaworthy, but Billy Mulak, in the second boat, knew that the weather could change in an instant. Five-foot waves could become towering walls of water, swamping them.

The appearance of the sun that morning had brought the boats out. The white men had been three days at the village, while rains and heavy seas battered the coast. They wouldn't listen to the possibility that this morning's break in the pattern was only a lull. They had to go after the walrus herd that had been spotted from the air just a few days ago, before the storm.

This was no ordinary hunt; they were after Muugli, Billy reminded himself. The name, with its weight of legend, brought an exhilarating edge of excitement to the hunt.

Billy thought of the reward Travis Mayberry, the white hunter in command of Billy's boat, had promised for the Great One's tusks.

He brushed off a flicker of guilt. Billy had been taught to hunt by his father in the traditional way of his people. They killed only for need. They respected, even revered, the animals that provided them with their means of survival. For them the seal and the walrus were gifts of God. In consequence they did not kill wantonly or for sport or to prove their mastery of nature.

The white men didn't hunt in the native way. They brought many weapons with great firepower. They did not honor or respect their victims. They did not care how many were killed.

This morning all of the men carried weapons. Travis Mayberry and one of the natives, both in Billy Mulak's boat, had Chinese-manufactured AK-47s—assault weapons that fired a hail of bullets. Billy, armed with the rifle his father had given him when Billy was still a boy, envied the villager who had been given the AK-47 for this hunt. And yet . . . Although his stomach churned at the prospect of the carnage that lay ahead, he thought again of Mayberry's promise. Nothing else mattered.

The first boat was nearly level with the last rocks. Billy could see an edge of the cove just around the tip of the peninsula. At a signal from Wolf Simpson, the white hunter in the lead boat, the natives working the oars kept the umiak in position, waiting until the second craft was almost abreast.

THE OLD BULL LIFTED HIS massive head. A feeling stirred within him—an old instinct of danger. But the sun was warm, and he was sleepy. Normally he could smell humans hundreds of feet away, but the wind was carrying their scent away from him. Although the sky was black against the horizon, the sea remained calm. A group of four walruses swam across the cove toward the shelf after feeding. With their keen underwater hearing, they would have sensed any threatening sound. The Great One let his long tusks drop over the edge of his bed of rock.

The boats appeared without warning at the mouth of the cove. Even as Muugli bellowed his warning, one of the men was clambering up on the rocks, from which he could look straight down at the herd. The bulls near the edge of the shelf lunged for the water. In the manner of their kind, they turned to face their enemy together, presenting a wall of tusks.

The men were standing now in the boats. From the rocks, Billy Mulak trained his rifle on the old bull at the end of the shelf. He was awed by the bull's size, the magnificence of his tusks, the defiance of his roar. Anxiously Billy took aim. He mustn't shatter the tusks, he'd been told. He must shoot to kill.

For the next ten minutes the cove was bedlam. The crack of rifle fire punctuated the harsher rattle of automatic weapons. Densely packed onto the shelf, the walruses were trapped. Scores died in the first volleys of fire; some wounded reached the water to die; others were cut down before they could cross the shelf. There was a ceaseless din of roaring and bellowing from the wounded walruses. Outside the cove the wind had picked up, unnoticed by the hunters, and ten-foot waves slammed against the walls of the peninsula.

Billy Mulak stood frozen, unable to move. Travis Mayberry was screaming at him. Wolf Simpson shook his fist. Billy was certain that his first shot had struck the huge old bull. Simpson had fired simultaneously, yet the bull was lumbering across the shelf toward the water. Billy fired again as the big walrus tumbled in.

Was he badly wounded? Billy stared down in rising panic. He waited for the bull to surface. Tales of Muugli's capacity for survival jabbed at his memory. The waters that had closed over him were darker now, red with blood.

Below Billy some of the other Eskimo hunters had leaped from the boats onto the shelf. They fired quickly, usually stopping one of the mammals with a single shot. One of the AK-47s rained bullets in a scythelike sweep across the shelf.

And at last the panicky bellowing was silenced. More than a hundred walruses lay dead on the shelf or in the roiling waters.

The Eskimos went quickly to work using razor-sharp knives and short-handled hatchets to chop the tusks free or sometimes to sever the entire head from a carcass. On a traditional hunt they would have paused to cut off a hunk of black flesh and thick white fat to drop into the sea as a tribute to ancient gods. Now there were no such offerings. There would be no taking of walrus meat for the winter. The carefully piled stack of tusks at one end of the shelf grew larger. The shelf itself was awash with blood.

In the noise and excitement, no one at first had paid attention to the darkening of the sky overhead or heard the rising winds keening in the rocks—least of all Travis Mayberry. He had been too choked with elation over his success in actually hunting down the legendary Muugli. The old bull's tusks were even more spectacular than Mayberry had imagined—priceless!

When the first heavy raindrops lashed his face, Mayberry turned toward the sea and gaped. His heart thudded. A black wall of rain marched toward him across the water. The waves in the open sea were already heaving twice as high as his head.

On the shelf the Eskimos abandoned their work almost as one and scrambled toward the boats. Mayberry yelled at them, ordering them back. They ignored him; they feared his anger, but they feared being caught by the storm even more.

"Muugli!" Mayberry screamed. "Where's Muugli?"

It was too late. The hunters were all in the boats. Mayberry had to follow. The curtain of rain reached them as they cleared the tip of the peninsula, racing for their lives before the storm.

ONE

FROM the office above his Front Street saloon Travis Mayberry looked out at the Bering Sea through rain-streaked windows. It was a week since the richest harvest of ivory he'd seen in years had been aborted by a series of storms. The view suited his gray, angry mood.

Mayberry was a powerful chunk of a man. His thick forearms, chest, and shoulders were covered with curly black hair. His face was square with wide-set brown eyes and a full mouth that could settle into a deceptive appearance of geniality. Although many of his activities were illegal—the saloon being an exception—in the hierarchy of the citizenry of Nome, Alaska, Mayberry ranked near the very top. The city's tradition of tolerance for drunkenness, gambling, and violence had begun with the 1899 gold rush, and it was still said to be a good destination if you were running from the law.

Nome, whose principal street comprised one sorry row of buildings, was home to fewer than four thousand residents, three fourths of them Eskimos. It stood at the edge of the continent and was usually shrouded in fog or rain or sleet. The climate was abysmal—dusty, windy, and rainy in the brief summer months; cold, windy, and foggy in winter. The terrain was bleak and barren in every direction, the nearest tree about eighty miles inland.

Travis Mayberry didn't think of himself as a criminal or even as a particularly violent man. He had a temper, sure; rock-hard fists; and was rumored to have killed more than once. But Mayberry considered his activities normal. He was doing what a man had to do when he didn't have life handed to him on a platter.

Mayberry had fought in Vietnam. He'd tried his hand at peddling drugs in the Lower 48 but had run into trouble with dangerous gangs. Drifting north to Alaska, he had encountered Delbert Hicks, a seller of illegal ivory, who took a fancy to him. Hicks had long since disappeared under mysterious circumstances, which Mayberry was careful not to inquire into when he met Hicks' boss, Harry Madrid, a kingpin in the North American traffic of ivory and other exotic items. Mayberry guessed Hicks was a victim of his own greed.

Mayberry had found his calling. He was a poacher, supplying Harry Madrid with walrus ivory, polar bear pelts, the gallbladders of brown bears—regarded by some as a cure for impotence—grizzly claws, and anything else in Alaska, from eagles to snowy owls, that was exotic enough to bring a good price.

The past year hadn't been good for Mayberry. Poachers caught in a U.S. Fish and Wildlife Service sting operation, including two who worked for him, had gone to trial in Anchorage. Then something happened that looked as if it would turn Mayberry's year around.

For years poachers dealing in walrus ivory in Alaska had heard Eskimo tales about an enormous old walrus with monstrous tusks that were—depending on the teller—four, five, or even six feet long. He was called Muugli, the Great One. The stories had been brushed off as native legend, but they were not forgotten.

Then, in June of this year, during the summer migration of the male walruses from their winter breeding grounds, a wildlife photographer flying over a small island in Bristol Bay snapped a picture of a walrus herd with a telephoto lens. In one corner of a tiny strip of beach, lifting his head toward the plane, was a huge old bull with enormous tusks. When the photo was published—ironically in a small magazine devoted to ecological concerns—it was possible to estimate the size of the tusks with a fair degree of accuracy. The measurement left no doubt: Muugli was more than legend; he was alive.

In late July a copy of the magazine reached Hong Kong, center of the hugely profitable international trade in ivory and exotic animal artifacts. At the heart of this traffic was the Chang family, one of two powerful Chinese families that dominated the illegal trade. The picture in the magazine was spotted by Deng Chang, youngest son of Madam Lu Chang, the matriarchal ruler of the organization.

At sixty, Madam Chang was as renowned for the cruel efficiency of her methods as for her delicate, parchmentlike beauty. Deng waited to approach her until after her morning massage, when she was usually in a good mood. It was a warm, bright morning, and she was on the terrace of her hilltop estate overlooking the crowded heap of skyscrapers below and Hong Kong's glittering, teeming harbor. Her cheeks and lower eyelids had been carefully rouged, making the pale skin appear almost translucent.

With a small smile she watched Deng's approach. "What is it, my son? You have something that would interest me?"

"I am sure of it, honorable Mother."

He handed her the magazine, opened to the photograph of the walrus on the beach. She studied it, tracing the outline of the tusks in the photo with a three-inch carmine-colored fingernail. Deng saw a flicker of emotion in his mother's black, almond-shaped eyes.

The walrus tusks were magnificent—at least as large as many elephant tusks. If they could be captured intact, there would be nothing to compare them with in the world. Madam Lu Chang's clients included a rich Taiwanese collector of rare ivory and an equally affluent Japanese with the same passion. The two could be played off against each other.

"You have done well, my son," Madam Chang murmured.

That afternoon Madam Chang placed a call to a New Jersey warehouse, the office of one Harry Madrid. The effect was electrifying. Yes, Madrid had men in the field in Alaska—the very best poachers. The search for the walrus with the extraordinary tusks would begin at once. If the animal was anywhere in or near the Bering Sea, they would find him. Madrid guaranteed it.

Harry Madrid's call to Travis Mayberry, in Nome, if not as terrifying as a personal call from Madam Lu Chang, nevertheless built a fire under the poacher. The hunt began at once.

For the next month Mayberry and his agents scouted the male walrus herds that thronged islands and shores of the Bering Sea. The hunt was exhaustive, but there was no sign of the walrus the Eskimos called the Great One.

The hunters intensified their search. Under pressure from Madrid, Travis Mayberry even took his own plane up, while Wolf Simpson, his second-in-command, flew with a hired bush pilot in a chartered plane. With summer's passage, time and patience were running out. Winter would soon make observations by sea or air impossible.

In the first week of September the bush pilot's plane, with Simpson aboard, quartered the rocky coastline in the northern reaches of the Bering Sea. After a fruitless morning it continued northward to the edge of the Chukchi Sea. The grizzled pilot, an Alaskan veteran named Les Hargrove, kept a close eye on his fuel gauge. In the early afternoon he told Simpson their run was over for the day. The poacher, nursing a hangover, didn't argue.

As he flew closer to the mainland, Hargrove's eye was drawn toward an odd crook of land to the north, extending into the sea. The pilot glanced again at his fuel reading. Close call, he thought, but what the heck. "No risk, no gain," he muttered.

Acting on a hunch, he flew toward the peninsula. He came in low over the bluff and passed directly over an inlet rimmed by a narrow rock shelf. The shelf was completely covered with walruses.

Scanning the scene through binoculars, Wolf Simpson felt astonishment, then elation. He gave an involuntary whoop. "It's him!" Simpson yelled. He pounded Hargrove's shoulder. "Look at the size of him. It's Muugli!"

REMEMBERING the scene in the cove, Travis Mayberry flushed with renewed anger. He had been so close—close enough to measure Muugli's tusks with his eyes. But Simpson and the native kid had bungled the hit. Both claimed to have got in clean shots. The old walrus had been wounded. There was blood on the rocks to prove it. But somehow he had managed to slip off the shelf and out of sight. Then the storm had struck, and the hunters had to flee.

That had been a week ago. The storm had battered the coast relentlessly since then, and the sea remained too rough for the boats to gain access to the cove and haul the ivory out.

Mayberry swiveled his chair away from the windows at the sound of footsteps on the stairs to his office. He glared toward the open doorway, as if he were ready to pounce. Wolf Simpson's lean, long face peered around the edge of the doorway, followed by his thin whippet's body with its narrow shoulders and bony chest.

Simpson's given name was Clyde, though few people knew it. He had acquired his nickname from his predatory enthusiasm for hunting wolves from the safety of a helicopter, a sport that had in times past been popular in Alaska.

Satisfied when his appearance did not spark a tirade, Simpson sidled into Mayberry's office. "Uh . . . we got a problem, Trav."

Mayberry glowered at him. "I don't need any more problems. This storm is enough problem." When Simpson was prudently silent, Mayberry said, "Seven days we've been sitting here doing nothing, while the biggest fortune in ivory we've ever seen is sittin' out there where you let it get away."

"I hit him, but I didn't have a good angle from the boat," Simpson whined. "The Eskimo kid had the shot. Up on the rocks, lookin' right down his sights at Muugli. No way he could miss."

"He says he didn't, but neither one of you stopped that bull goin' in the water."

"He was hurt. He wasn't goin' anywheres. We get back there, I guarantee you we'll find him tossed up on those rocks."

"Well, we're damned sure gonna find out in a hurry. This storm is breaking up. I want Hargrove here early tomorrow morning."

"Hargrove's gone—that's the problem."

"What do you mean, gone? I know he went back to Anchorage. Get hold of him and tell him to sober up and get back here."

"That's what I'm tryin' to tell you. Hargrove's bailed out. He's gone back to the Lower Forty-eight. Said he'd had enough."

"That's crazy." Mayberry scowled in disbelief. "You ever hear of one of those old bush pilots could walk away from it?"

"Hargrove did. Said he was gonna go and lay on some beach in California. He's gone, Trav. He recommended this other guy he knows—lives over in Fortune, flies a Cessna."

Travis Mayberry was sifting the news, examining it cautiously. He didn't like unexpected changes. In his business, changes in personnel were the most suspect. "What's his name, this pilot?"

"Robie, Rorie—something like that. Jeff Rorie, I think."

"These Alaskan bush pilots—they're all a little crazy," Mayberry said thoughtfully. "And they're a fraternity. The guy's been around, Hargrove would know him."

"That don't mean we can trust him."

"You got any better ideas?"

Simpson argued that he ought to check the new guy out, that another few days wouldn't make any difference. Mayberry said it couldn't wait. First chance, he wanted a flyover to see if the giant walrus could be spotted. Simpson could check on the pilot later.

"Hargrove wouldn't vouch for the guy if he wasn't right," Mayberry said. "Get hold of him. Tell him to be here at six in the morning." He swung his swivel chair toward the rain-smeared window. "Dead or alive I'm gonna find that long-toothed s.o.b.; then maybe *I'm* gonna go and lie on some sunny beach."

"Is one pair of tusks worth that much?"

"Not just any pair of tusks," Mayberry said, swiveling back around. "Just the biggest walrus tusks in the whole world!"

WHEN Wolf Simpson left, the angry optimism Mayberry had summoned while talking to him faded away.

Harry Madrid had called twice when Mayberry was out, both times leaving urgent messages. Mayberry hadn't told him about having to leave the ivory. Madrid, who shuttled between his million-dollar condo overlooking Central Park and a seaside villa on Key Biscayne, didn't understand about weather in Alaska. He didn't understand that flying a Cessna into an Arctic storm or trying to maneuver an Eskimo boat in those raging waters wasn't a walk in the park or a trip to Disneyland. He didn't even want to hear about such things. All Harry wanted was his ivory.

In a way, Madrid was like a spoiled child, Mayberry thought sourly. If he didn't get what he wanted, he threw a tantrum. The only time Mayberry had ever been physically present when Madrid had a tantrum was when Madrid paid an unexpected visit to Nome and caught Delbert Hicks keeping two sets of books—one for the stuff he sold Harry and another for a small portion of ivory and other items Hicks had set aside for himself. It didn't amount to much, no more than five percent of the illegal plunder Hicks provided to Madrid. But after Madrid took Hicks for a heart-to-heart talk out on the tundra, no one had ever seen Hicks again.

That was, in fact, how Travis Mayberry came to be promoted to Madrid's number one man in Alaska.

Mayberry stared glumly at the phone on his desk.

He knew he couldn't be out if Harry called a third time.

TWO

A HUNDRED and fifty air miles north of Nome, the week of persistent storms brought hard winds and rain lashing inland from the Chukchi Sea. The nights dipped below freezing, and the rains turned to sleet, which formed a frozen crust on the single muddy street of the Yupik village on the river.

When the sky cleared and the temperature climbed, the crust thawed and the street turned to an ooze that sucked at John Mulak's boots as he plodded toward the river. A short, blocky figure, he wore L.L. Bean rubber boots and a plaid hunter's cap with earflaps turned up. His quilted nylon parka had a sealskin fur cape sewn onto it, matching his handsewn sealskin pants, which were worn over thermal underwear from a Sears catalogue. His was an incongruous mix of traditional native garments and others that were manufactured in what he thought of as the Outside, a world he had seen only on television.

Head down in gloomy thought, he did not glance at the modern government houses on either side of the street. Mulak had spent his childhood in a sod house with dried seal gut over the one window, a mud floor in the single room where the whole family slept. The government houses, products of the prosperity brought by the Trans-Alaska Pipeline, changed village life forever. Each house had three bedrooms, a furnace, stove, washer, and dryer. An electric generator provided power for the entire village. A disk antenna brought television to every living room, dominating family life.

A blare of sound from a log house at the center of the village, a relic from earlier times, caused Mulak to lift his head. Even at this early hour the village's recreation center, with its wall of arcade games, would be crowded. Mulak supposed that was where his son, Billy, had gone when he stormed out of the house.

Mulak welcomed the clear day. It gave him a chance to get away from the village to hunt or fish. His daughter, Ruth, along with his brother's family, were off berry picking, a favorite activity.

The quarrel with Billy had started over the berry picking. Mulak had said that Billy should go along with Ruth. His son refused.

"You want some berries, pick 'em yourself," he had cried.

Billy was nineteen, and in the last year he had changed. His moods swung wildly from exaggerated laughter to sullen irritability. He spent most of his time at the arcade or at the village airstrip, waiting for the plane that would bring the white men seeking ivory. They paid Billy and a dozen other young men to hunt with them—paid them more than most of them had earned in their lives. These whites ignored the Eskimos' subsistence-hunting rule, which was not spelled out in the law, but was left to the natives to enforce.

Reaching the riverbank, John Mulak pulled the tarpaulin cover from his kayak and dragged it to the river. Although the kayak was nearly four times his size, he handled it easily.

Mulak's father had built the kayak with his grandfather, Eli, a hunter of whales. It was twenty feet long and about three feet wide at the center. Its whalebone frame, which was covered with seal-skin, had been reinforced over the years by wooden supports. The deck was completely covered except for the cockpit, and even here John Mulak had a skin shirt, inherited from his father, with fringes that laced into the edges of the opening, sealing out the water.

He pushed off the bank into the swift current. It was good to feel the pull on his back and shoulders. His paddle flashed silver in the sunlight with each stroke. But he did not find his usual joy in his boat and the river. Billy had been moody and sullen since the last hunt with the white men, just before the storms. Some of the hunters bragged that Muugli, the Great One, had been slain in the hunt, but no one knew if this was true. Whatever had happened, Mulak thought, something was wrong with his son.

LATE that afternoon, far north along the coastline, John Mulak worked his kayak skillfully through rough water. He rounded a pile of rocks fingering out from shore and, entering an unexpected cove, came upon the carnage without warning. First the bloated body of one walrus, headless, lying against a pile of rocks; then others, piled like driftwood along a rock shelf or lumped in shallow water. The long shelf was dark with blood, and the familiar sea seemed menacing. Mulak thought he heard the bellowing and roaring of the dying mammals, their clamor so real that he sat motionless in his skin boat, appalled, listening.

Only the waves beating against the shore. Only the screams of scavenger birds, frightened by his passage, wheeling overhead.

He paddled toward the shelf. Here the walrus colony had dozed in the sun, heedless of danger. Riding up onto a flat rock, Mulak jumped out with an agility that belied his sixty years. He pulled the kayak halfway out of the water. The blood was pounding in his head, a drumbeat of shock and anger. And fear.

For a half hour Mulak walked along the shelf, picking his way among the dead bodies like a stray soldier blundering upon the scene of a recent battle. He counted the bodies of the dead until, after the first fifty and more, the numbers became so great his mind rejected their grim reality. This kind of killing was the gussak's way, Mulak thought. But the knowledge that white men were responsible did not ease his mind. White men might have organized this hunt, but when Mulak pictured the hunters, he saw them with brown faces.

Eskimos did the gussak's hunting now—the young, restless ones who were no longer content with the ways of their elders; those who had lost their jobs on the pipeline but had become accustomed to thick rolls of money in their pockets.

Even, Mulak thought with anguish, his son, Billy.

The poachers had abandoned the shelf in haste, Mulak decided. But they had completed much of their work before they were interrupted. There were at least a hundred pairs of tusks, he guessed, stacked like wood against the wall of the bluff. Alongside them were a dozen severed walrus heads, saved because they carried the longest, most valuable tusks. After a week on the shelf the roots would have begun to lose their grip, and these tusks could be pulled out without the risk of damage.

In the shadow of a small pile of rocks outside the cove, beyond the tip of the peninsula, some movement caught Mulak's eye. He walked to the end of the shelf to see better and climbed the rocks until he was close to the end of the finger of bluffs. Now he saw the small pile of rocks more clearly, a tiny island little more than a hundred feet from the peninsula. Surf spilled over the top of the rock pile and cascaded in foaming rivulets along the seams and cracks—and over a pair of huge tusks that gleamed like a monstrous smile, mocking him from the shadows.

Mulak stared in wonder. The huge old walrus appeared to be the only survivor of the slaughter. He did not plunge into the sea, which suggested that he might be wounded. He did not bark or bellow, but seemed to glare at Mulak accusingly across the narrow bridge of water that separated them. Mulak was transfixed by his tusks, larger than any he had ever seen, so large as to confound belief.

"Muugli," he whispered.

Although Mulak had never before seen him, Muugli had long been part of his life—the hero of countless stories, the object of dreams. When the word came to the village that the walrus herds were migrating—always a time of great excitement—tales of the Great One resurfaced. Mulak had always known he was there, sharing the harsh life of the North, a part of the Eskimos' world.

Mulak waited motionless as the wind and waves pounded the bluff. He was captive of the awe he felt for this wondrous creature. After what seemed a long time, Muugli moved, drawing deeper into the shadows of his little island, until he could no longer be seen.

Turning away at last, Mulak stared at the greedy slaughter on the shelf behind him. He began to shake with anger.

Mulak was not an impetuous man. Like his ancestors, he was

461

prudent and wary, not given to needless risk. But Mulak's decision had been forming as he counted the tusks on the shelf. The sight of the Great One, wounded and mourning, brought an overwhelming sadness, confirming his resolve.

It was a decision that would make him an outlaw, for which no word existed in the Yupik dialect of his village.

He had to work quickly. The poachers would have to take the ivory harvest out by air or sea—there was no overland road within a hundred miles. He decided they must have been driven from the scene by the storm that had blanketed the area for the past week.

The passing of the storm had brought Mulak out in his boat to fish. The ivory hunters would not be far behind. Was that why Billy could not go berry picking? he wondered. Was he waiting for the white men to return?

Most of the traditional kayaks used for centuries by Mulak's people had room only for the paddler in a round cockpit near the boat's center. The cockpit of Mulak's boat held two people. The design suffered little in loss of maneuverability, and the larger cockpit made an excellent cargo hold. Into it Mulak carefully placed several of the severed heads bearing the largest tusks, handling them with something like reverence. Then he crammed in as many of the other tusks as he could.

When he left the cove, the kayak, overloaded, rode very low in the water. Digging hard with his broad-bladed paddle, Mulak worked through heavy surf for a mile north of the inlet until he reached the mouth of the river. From there he turned inland, and the going was easier, even though he was paddling upstream. He left the river and threaded his way through tidal flats laced with marshes, ponds, creeks, and streams. Mulak knew them as he knew the veins and scars on the back of his hands. The fog closed in behind and then enveloped him.

Though he continued inland for most of an hour, Mulak was never lost for a moment, always knowing exactly how far he had come, how far he was from his village.

Once, he spotted two brightly colored tents pitched near the river. Obscured by brush along the bank, he drifted by, paddle still. There was no one in sight. A gussak camp, he thought, wondering what white men were doing here this late in the year.

Not long after, he came to the spot he had chosen. He left the kayak wedged into the bank of the stream and, in a series of trips, carried the ivory across the tundra into a cave located in some low foothills. Beyond them, their tops lost this afternoon in a mantle of low clouds, loomed the formidable crags of the Brooks Range. The tundra appeared to be covered only with low grasses and brush. It was, in fact, very difficult terrain for walking. The hummocks of grass twisted underfoot, and the boggy ground between the tufts sucked at his boots. In spite of his age and his burden of tusks, Mulak moved back and forth from the hills to his boat without pausing to rest. Only when the last of this load of ivory had been safely stored inside the cave did he stop to look out over the tundra toward the ocean.

Though the escarpment on which Mulak stood at the mouth of the cave was less than a hundred feet above sea level, it offered a view in every direction. Nothing within his sight moved but the grasses stirring in the wind. No one had followed him.

It was late afternoon when Mulak returned to the walrus cove. Even though he had seen no one, he approached the inlet cautiously. He knew the white men who were responsible for the slaughter were cruel beyond imagining and would not value the life of an old Eskimo who attempted to interfere in their plans.

He searched for Muugli on the little island, but there was no sign of him. Mulak prayed that Muugli would leave before the white poachers returned to search for him.

Once again, Mulak loaded his cockpit until the kayak rode dangerously low in the water. Always he watched and listened for the drone of an aircraft approaching. He was a man who had never stolen a thing in his life or even thought of it. Goods were shared in his village. No one needed to steal. Now, in spite of his anger, he felt like a thief. It was an uncomfortable feeling.

He made four trips before full darkness came. Each trip took well over an hour of punishing labor, paddling the overladen kayak first through the surf and then among the twisting warren of creeks and streams. Each time, he drifted silently past the gussak camp, and once, he glimpsed a slight figure in a red parka trudging across the tundra toward the camp, accompanied by a large dog.

Though he had begun in the late afternoon, he gave no thought to how long he was laboring into the night. For an Eskimo, to use every minute of summer's light was common; such times were too precious to waste. A little over a month ago, in early August, the sun had stood above the horizon for twenty-four hours of the day. This night there would be four or five hours of relative darkness. By late December there would be no sun at all, only the endless darkness and the cold.

He slept just inside the mouth of the cave. By then he had moved most of the ivory there. Perhaps two more trips, he thought.

He prayed again that Muugli would escape, because there was nothing he could do to save him. He was a Christian, but at moments like this, ancient beliefs of his people resurfaced, and he hoped the god of the sea would intervene.

He also hoped the bear in whose cave he slept did not decide to return before morning.

THREE

AROUND two in the morning a smothering fog lifted over the tundra, revealing a small camp with two bright yellow tents pitched a short distance from the river. Here, north of the Arctic Circle, the September darkness was not yet total at this hour, relieved by a kind of halo visible above the horizon, where the sun rolled just out of sight. With the absence of the foul weather that had battered the tiny camp for the past week, a deep stillness settled over the scene.

In that stillness a wolf howled.

Kathy McNeely woke suddenly, disoriented. As she shook off the clinging webs of sleep, she thought it was the unusual silence that had awakened her—the absence of tearing winds and pelting rain. Then she heard Survivor whimper. The husky preferred the cold air, sleeping just outside the entrance of her tent, to the relative warmth inside. Kathy reached out to open the flap. Survivor was on his feet. She saw a tremor pass along his flank.

The wolf howled again, startlingly close. The sound rose and peaked and died away. This time smaller yips and cries formed a muted chorus to accompany the soloist's soaring call. Kathy felt the hairs rise on the back of her neck, and a chill trickled along her spine. She peered out of her tent and froze in place as the wolf's long, haunting howl poured over her.

The first thing she saw in the pale light was a man standing naked at the edge of the river, a bar of soap in one hand. Like her, Jason Cobb was transfixed, his head tilted slightly as he listened to the cry of the wilderness. Kathy stared, no more capable of averting her eyes than of closing her ears to the wolf's call.

Cobb was a tall man—over six feet—lean, handsome, and fit. Kathy thought of a nineteenth-century painting of a lone naked savage pictured in the vast beauty of the western wilderness, an idealized canvas so extravagant and romantic as to seem unreal.

The silence returned. Across the thirty yards between the tents and the river, Jason Cobb's eyes met hers.

Kathy ducked back, shivering with sudden anger. He had deliberately chosen to make her uncomfortable. She was annoyed with herself for the strength of her reaction. Annoyed with Cobb for choosing to bathe so openly without forewarning her. Annoyed with herself again for the logic that told her he'd bathed in the middle of the night precisely to avoid such discomfort. Such moments were inevitable in their situation. You coped, that's all. She was compelled to admire Cobb's fortitude. My Lord, the river was freezing!

At length she began to smile in spite of herself, struck by the ridiculousness of the situation and her reaction.

She had first met Cobb on a flight from Seattle to Anchorage in the first week of June. The Alaska Airlines 747 flew low enough to offer breathtaking views of the unfolding panorama below—dense green forests yielding to snowcapped granite peaks; and the stunning vista of sea-flowing glaciers, great rivers of ice flowing between the flanks of mountains toward the ocean.

Captivated by the spectacle, Kathy had been aware of someone taking the empty seat beside her and peering past her shoulder. "There's your twentieth-century view for you," a deep, confident voice said. "Antiseptic, remote, and safe."

"It's still beautiful," Kathy replied, controlling a slight irritation.

"But not very personal." When Kathy glanced toward him, she recognized Jason Cobb instantly. She had met him briefly at the airport but knew him well by reputation. He was one of the driving forces behind ASSET's Alaskan expedition.

Cobb smiled. "I'm thinking of John Muir approaching one of those ice massifs in an Indian canoe a hundred years ago, listening to the crack and roar of ice slides, chunks of the glacier sheering off; feeling the ocean move; not knowing if he was going to get away alive. And still forcing his Indian guides to take him closer." Cobb paused. "Not quite the same, is it?"

He was in his early forties, tall and broad-shouldered. His dark hair was gray at the temples, and he wore a short, neatly trimmed beard that was mostly black, with clearly marked crescents of gray framing his chin. Very effective on television, Kathy thought. Cobb was an environmental scientist at Berkeley, one of those who were frequently trotted out as experts on television news whenever an environmental crisis made headlines. He had become a media favorite largely because of his telegenic looks, she thought. She was instantly uncomfortable with the glib assessment. That was one trap she, of all people, should avoid. Her own brief media fame, stemming from a widely publicized Antarctic adventure, had earned her some gratuitous sniping by jealous colleagues.

Staring through the window, Cobb added thoughtfully, "They say if you can get there by car or even on foot, it will never be a genuine wilderness experience. For the real thing, you have to fly in and have the plane leave so you're alone in the wild. If you meet a wolf or a bear, it's on his terms—and his turf."

"That's what we're here for, isn't it?" Kathy murmured. "To try to help preserve one small corner of the earth where man in the twenty-first century will still be able to have that kind of experience?"

"Of course, Doctor." The environmental scientist seemed amused. "We're fortunate to have the Bird Woman with us—someone who's been out there on the edge."

Kathy sensed the hostility within his words. The Bird Woman was a nickname she had accepted amiably enough at first, until, in the aftermath of Antarctica, it became a media catchphrase. She had degrees in marine biology and ornithology, but the former didn't lend itself quite as well to catchy capital letters. And birds were the reason for her Antarctic journey, prompted by a colony of penguins caught in an oil disaster on that continent.

"Antarctica isn't Alaska," she said. "And we're all fortunate to be taking part in what we hope to accomplish this summer." He's one of them, she thought with sudden prescience. One of those who opposed having me join the expedition.

"Of course," Jason Cobb said again, with a sardonic smile.

To her relief he returned to his own seat. Her thoughts strayed to the spring visit from a delegation representing ASSET—the Association of Scientists to Save the Environment. She had sensed even then that the decision to invite her had not been unanimous—and not entirely motivated by her credentials. But the chance to come to the Alaskan wilderness on a mission she wholeheartedly supported had been immediately tempting. If it hadn't been for Brian Hurley, she wouldn't have hesitated for an instant. But he had made her decision easy.

She had first met Brian at McMurdo, the U.S. station in Antarctica, during a Christmas break. Kathy had gone to the continent at the bottom of the earth with a group of other scientists to investigate unexplained oil damage to a colony of penguins. Brian was an adventurer, training a team of huskies for a one-man dogsled expedition to the South Pole. His attempt at a record-breaking run was being filmed for U.S. television.

They met again when Brian brought a dog with a broken leg to Kathy's tent. In Antarctica's severe conditions, survival seemed improbable. Kathy had fought to save the dog, setting his leg under primitive conditions while a blizzard roared outside. Surprisingly the husky had pulled through, earning the name Kathy gave him: Survivor. Kathy had won Brian Hurley's admiring attention, and she knew that what had started between them was more than a holiday fling.

At the age of thirty-one Kathy had a life that met her priorities. Brian threatened to change that. She was back at work at the university when he came to Santa Barbara for another Christmas holiday—and stayed on, turning her career-focused life upside down.

She had been approached by ASSET in April. The activist group was organizing an expedition of concerned scientists to dramatize the damaging environmental impact of a proposed new Alaskan oil pipeline that would bring oil from a new field on the North Slope over the Brooks Range, and across the unspoiled tundra to the Chukchi Sea. Congressional hearings on the pipeline were to convene in Anchorage in November. ASSET's goal, through field research along the pipeline route, was to identify, catalogue, and dramatize the reasons for its opposition to the pipeline. Kathy was a professor of marine biology at the University of California at Santa Barbara. Her area of interest was seabirds. Something like ninety-five percent of all the world's seabirds were in Alaska and would be threatened by the new demands of an oil-hungry civilization.

She had agreed to talk to the delegation from ASSET because an old friend and mentor from U.C.L.A., Carl Jeffers, was on the committee. The group had arrived in Santa Barbara on a Thursday late in April. They all had dinner together. Brian Hurley, one of the party, was withdrawn, listening thoughtfully and saying nothing. On Friday, Kathy spent most of the afternoon with the committee in her campus office, discussing their proposal. And resisting it: It would mean putting her own research on hold. And it would mean separation from Brian.

Carl Jeffers did much of the talking for the ASSET committee during that spring meeting. "They're planning another rape of the Alaskan wilderness," Jeffers had argued with typical vehemence. He had laid out all the arguments for the expedition. Its purpose was to stop further exploitation of the last accessible American wilderness by focusing publicity on the pipeline project and exposing its potentially devastating effects on wildlife and wasted wetlands favored by millions of birds. "You can help document the impact on one of the largest and most varied concentrations of birds not just in North America but on earth," Jeffers pointed out.

"I'll support you any way I can," Kathy had said. "But why me? I can think of a dozen others with better credentials."

"No," Carl said bluntly. "There's no one else. And Kathy, you'll not only be helping us, you might have a chance to look into the poaching business up there."

Jeffers had touched a nerve. Kathy had recently published an article on worldwide poaching activities that had touched upon the recent increase in illegal poaching of walrus for ivory in Alaska. Even though the focus of her study had been statistical, Kathy recognized that the lack of firsthand field observations was a weakness.

"What Dr. Jeffers is trying to say," a marine biologist named Berwanger commented, "is that you can make a unique contribution to the public side of our expedition."

"I'm not sure what that could be."

469

"You can get us some media attention, Doctor. Let's face it," Berwanger said, "after that Antarctic affair, you're a sort of celebrity. More to the point, an antidevelopment icon."

Kathy tried to control her temper. Her investigation of the oil injury to penguins in Antarctica had led to the discovery of an accidental oil spill at a remote research site. A development company's overzealous field agents had tried to stop her dogged probing. When Brian Hurley abandoned his polar run to help Kathy expose the truth, the story acquired a romantic twist that made headlines.

She tried to brush her feelings aside. Although she wasn't comfortable with the notion of being used for publicity purposes, she was realist enough to admit that was how the world worked.

"Think about it, Kathy," Jeffers urged. "Give it a chance."

Six weeks later she was in a 747 bound for Alaska with Jason Cobb and the rest of the ASSET team of scientists, a collection of fifteen men and one other woman.

During the busy days in Anchorage, in addition to the complicated logistics of obtaining food, supplies, and transportation for the expedition, there had been endless briefings, meetings, and conferences. Kathy had had little personal contact with Cobb. And when the expedition went into the bush and set up its base camp in the foothills of the Brooks Range, near the pass where the proposed pipeline would cross the mountains, the size of the group meant limited direct interaction.

Then, the first week of July, the members of the expedition got their individual assignments. Kathy was to travel downriver toward the coast to document the varieties and numbers of birds that might be adversely impacted by the proposed invasion. The scientist who would supplement her observations with his own assessment of the environmental impact upon the land and its wildlife was Jason Cobb.

After ten weeks Kathy's feelings about Cobb remained ambivalent, but they had worked out unspoken accommodations that allowed for privacy, and they functioned well in the field together. They were building impressive documentation, Kathy felt, for the devastation that the pipeline would bring. Habitats would be bulldozed out of existence. Near the coastline—breeding and nesting grounds for millions of birds—there would be huge storage facilities, refineries, service roads. From the pass over the mountains to the sea, a raw scar several miles wide and nearly four hundred miles long would forever alter the wilderness.

Once, Cobb had pointed out some parallel depressions in the tundra that ran for miles. They were vehicle tracks, probably made a half century ago during World War II, going no one knew where. Over time the tracks sank down and water filled them. In the permafrost above the Arctic Circle the scars would never heal. "It's called a green wound," Cobb said.

In time Kathy accepted the fact that Jason Cobb was more than a television showboat; his passion for the environment was genuine.

KATHY must have dozed, because she sat up with a start. It was light inside her tent. How late had she slept? Why hadn't Cobb awakened her?

Frowning, she dressed quickly and emerged into the first blaze of dawn. The sight of sunrise over the tundra stopped her in her tracks. It began with a backdrop of light, reflected from the clouds above the eastern mountain peaks. The light slowly brightened, like the controlled illumination behind a stage set. It turned from pale pink to fuchsia to red. The red glow leaped from the clouds to the snowy peaks below them, lining their jagged outline as if they were on fire. In all that splendid vista nothing moved. A great stillness poured around the rapt observer.

She looked around the camp, eager to share the wonder of the moment. Jason Cobb was nowhere to be seen.

She saw that he had built up their fire and put coffee on. No doubt he would be back soon. They would have to take advantage of the day, which was clear and bright. Though the morning air was cold and the offshore wind carried a bite, the warmth of the Arctic sun made a tremendous difference.

Kathy walked down to the river, Survivor trotting at her heels. The shallow water was so clear she could see the varied colors of the gravel bed.

While she crouched there on the riverbank, half hidden by brush and bunchgrass, Survivor lifted his dripping muzzle, suddenly alert. Kathy stiffened, remembering the wolf cry. The husky growled.

471

Something large slid by them on the river. Kathy was able to catch only a glimpse of the pointed stern of a native kayak before it fishtailed around a gravel bar and disappeared downstream. It had bobbed lightly on the water as it slipped past, she noted—not the way it had ridden by the previous day. Then it had seemed over-laden, riding so low that its deck was only a few inches above the water. She had marveled at the lone paddler's expertise, progress-ing upriver against the current more rapidly than she had been able to walk on land.

She wondered where he had been and where he was going. She and Cobb had passed no Eskimo camp or village on their way downriver. The nearest village that she knew of, having flown over it on her way to ASSET's base camp, was far to the south. Glimps-ing this Eskimo for the second time in two days, her curiosity was piqued.

Outside her tent, Kathy was munching a granola bar and enjoy-ing a cup of coffee in front of the fire when Survivor's sweeping tail announced Cobb's return. He seemed animated, and his dark eyes warmed when he saw her.

"Good morning, Dr. Cobb," she said. "You were up early."

"Couldn't sleep." He grinned. "All that howling. I found the tracks of a mother wolf and cubs. I think she's been watching us."

"I wish I could see her."

"Not much chance of that unless she wants us to. But I don't think we have to worry." Cobb helped himself to coffee and stood beside the fire, sipping from his mug and looking down at her.

"I did see that Eskimo again this morning."

"Your mystery man in the kayak?"

Kathy nodded. "I'm sure he's the same one we saw yesterday. What do you suppose he's up to?"

"Fishing, I suppose. Or hunting—last chance before winter sets in." Cobb brushed the question aside. She saw a gleam of excite-ment in his eyes. "I have a surprise. Spotted it while I was searching for our wolf." He waited, savoring her curiosity. "How would you like to see a snowy owl in her nest, Kathy, up close and personal?"

Only later, as she eagerly followed him across the tundra, did the thought strike Kathy that it was the first time Jason Cobb had called her by her first name.

FOUR

A SMALL cluster of bars, a hardware store, beauty salon and barber-shop, a drugstore, market, bank, and a combination city hall and jailhouse composed the town center of Fortune, Alaska, along a single dirt road forty miles north of Anchorage. East and west of town the dirt road was flanked by a collection of houses that looked as if they had been built on impulse with whatever materials were handy.

West of the houses, the forest crowded close. On the east side, however, was open meadow, where a collection of small planes and helicopters were parked. The meadow served as the landing strip.

The fact that four fifths of Alaska was wilderness meant that many areas were accessible only by air. The state had more pilots per capita than any other state or country.

Jeff Rorie was one of them.

He was a compact man, not big, but well made, with the slightly bowed legs of a man who'd spent his boyhood on a ranch and spent a lot of time in the saddle. He had clear blue eyes and light brown hair and wore a short beard. He whistled softly to himself as he stood behind his shack and squinted at Mount McKinley, one hundred and twenty miles distant. He always looked at the mountain first thing when he stepped outside. It was almost a religious thing. To say that McKinley is the tallest peak in North America did little to suggest the mountain's immensity or its emotional impact.

The morning was crisp and clear. Rorie was relieved. He couldn't stall Travis Mayberry another day if he wanted the job.

Mayberry had wanted him in Nome yesterday. It was clear in Nome, he said. But it hadn't been clear in Fortune, and Rorie had a bush pilot's respect for Alaskan weather.

He walked toward his yellow Cessna 185, feeling the lift of plea-sure this workhorse utility plane always gave him. It wasn't as pretty as some, or as fast, but its two-hundred-and-sixty-horsepower fuel-injected Continental engine enabled it to climb more than a thou-sand feet per minute—often crucial in mountainous territory. It had a STOL package—Short Takeoff and Landing—that enabled it to take off and land in places that lighter aircraft had to pass by, and Rorie had had it fitted with amphibious floats to allow him to land on grass, glacier shelf, and mountain lake alike. The aircraft was nicked and scarred, but it always got him where he was going.

This time he was going into unknown territory, and he needed every small reassurance he could find.

THE small plane climbed slowly toward the pass. As usual, Rorie felt dwarfed by the peaks surrounding him—Mount Hunter at fifteen thousand feet and Mount Foraker, seventeen thousand feet high—soaring towers of snow and rock, yet mere satellites to the mighty McKinley, whose mass seemed to push against the tiny aircraft struggling past it.

Three hours out of Fortune, Rorie began to feel the first twinges of anxiety. The clear, sunny sky disappeared. Clouds piled, tier on tier, as high as McKinley. He couldn't climb over them. Alaska had done it to him again: he was flying into rain.

"I'D ABOUT given you up," Travis Mayberry said.

"When that first squall hit, I was thinking I wasn't much better than a lottery pick," the pilot said. "Lucky it didn't last."

"I was expecting you yesterday."

Rorie shrugged. He didn't seem ruffled, Mayberry thought. In fact, like most bush pilots, he acted as if he didn't give a hoot.

Mayberry studied Rorie appraisingly from behind his desk. "You knew Les Hargrove?"

"We flew some together last summer up around Prudhoe Bay."

"You flew those oil people around?"

"The pay's good, and you can't beat the food." Rorie grinned.

"Hargrove tell you much about my business?"

"Not much. He said you paid on time and didn't cheat him."

"Good," Mayberry said. "Lemme show you around. I got a trophy room downstairs. You'll get some idea."

Wolf Simpson had been leaning against the wall by the window, watching the newcomer with narrow-eyed skepticism. He was aghast. "You're not showing him—"

Mayberry stopped him. "Keep your pants on, Wolf," he said. "Rorie doesn't seem like he'd get skittish seein' a polar bear skin."

"You got a fireplace to put it in front of?" Rorie grinned again.

"Not in the trophy room," Mayberry said.

They went down a narrow back stairway off Mayberry's office. It led to a windowless passageway that ended in a steel door. Mayberry opened a padlock. Rorie was aware of Simpson scowling in disapproval behind him. You'd better watch your back with that one, Rorie told himself. He doesn't like you much.

The steel door swung outward. Mayberry flipped on a light switch as the pilot stepped through the doorway. Rorie jumped.

Mayberry whooped and laughed. Even Simpson snickered. Recovering, Rorie stared up at a stuffed bald eagle that, hanging from the high ceiling, seemed to swoop toward him. Wings spread as if in full flight, the bird of prey had a span of six feet.

"That thing's real enough to make you duck," Rorie said. He was looking around, taking inventory of the remarkable trophy display. Every inch of the room was crammed with wall mounts, bear and wolf rugs, piles of horns, deer and moose antlers. He saw a box of whale's teeth, a stuffed Arctic fox. Wooden crates were piled to the twelve-foot ceiling. And, as if allotted one corner of the room to themselves, a heap of walrus tusks, maybe two dozen pairs. The room had strong, pungent animal smells mingled with the smells of blood and rot. Death smells, Rorie thought.

He didn't have to guess what Mayberry's business was.

Mayberry was watching him, his eyes all business.

Rorie whistled softly between his teeth. "You hunt a lot?"

Mayberry chuckled. "You might say that. Natives sell most of this stuff to us. I got no need to do any huntin' myself."

"Isn't some of this stuff illegal?" Rorie asked.

"Depends who's asking. That bother you?"

"I'm not looking to go to jail." Rorie grinned suddenly. "You must sell this stuff on the Outside. I mean, there are tourists, but you got a lot of goods here. How do you ship it? You must—"

"You don't need to know."

"If I'm going to be carrying anything illegal, I do need to know. I mean, it makes a difference what I'm getting paid for."

He saw the glint of satisfaction in Mayberry's eyes. He'd said the right thing.

"If I was to charter your plane to fly a load of contraband out of Alaska, that'd be a separate deal, okay?" Mayberry said. "Right now I need you to fly me and Wolf here down the coast to this village. Nothin' illegal about it, okay?"

"Sounds good to me. When do we leave?"

"That little squall chased you in here, looks like it's blown over. We got an empty sky and three, four hours of good daylight left. That's enough to get us there."

Travis Mayberry didn't waste any time, Rorie thought.

IN 1971 THE Alaska Native Claims Settlement Act brought to a conclusion the claims of Alaska's natives against the U.S. government for its ancestral lands. The Eskimos received a total of one billion dollars and forty million acres of land. For a time all Eskimos benefitted, and their lives were altered dramatically.

Ruth Mulak, at twenty-six, remembered those early years after the settlement. She had watched new homes being built to replace shacks and sod dwellings, in which the villagers had always lived. The village acquired a generator to produce electricity. Ruth remembered her mother's joy when a washing machine was brought into their new house, even though she did not know how to use it. It was a symbol; everything would be better now.

Ruth's mother had been dead for seven years. Now the house had an oil furnace, a bathroom with tub and shower, even a freezer as well as a refrigerator. Sometimes, when taking caribou or seal meat from the freezer, Ruth would think of how much her mother would have liked the freezer. But if she could visit the village now, Ruth wondered if she would still think everything was better than in the old days.

"Ruth, come and watch," her father called from the living room. "It is time for *Magnum*."

"I can't, Papa. I'm fixing dinner. Where's Billy?"

"I don't think he will be home for dinner," John Mulak said after a moment. "He and his friends are having a meeting."

Ruth walked slowly over to the kitchen doorway. Her father was in his recliner chair in front of the television set. He had been one of the great hunters of the village and was still honored for his skill, but his eyes were no longer keen. Cunning and experience were what enabled him to hunt successfully now.

"What is it, Papa? What's wrong?"

"Why do you ask such questions?"

"You know why. Billy's been acting . . . He's not himself."

Her father was silent, still watching *Magnum* on the small color screen. Hawaii was so beautiful it seemed unreal, and the stories were like fairy tales of good and evil. Her father loved them.

"Something went wrong on the hunt," John Mulak said.

"But that was more than a week ago. Billy and his friends took their boats out yesterday right after you returned from fishing. It was only when he came back that he acted so crazy. What's wrong? You and Billy both are acting so strange."

"Sometimes there are things a woman shouldn't be involved in. Your mother wouldn't have asked such questions."

"I'm not my mother."

Her father nodded, as if this were something undeniable. Unlike most of the villagers, Ruth had studied not only in the village school. Sponsored by her government-assigned teacher, she had been sent to Anchorage for high school and also for two years of college. When she came home, she was restless. An unimagined world had opened up to her, and she dreamed of seeing the people and places she had read about. She was the village teacher now. She felt important, needed. And stifled.

Her father had caught some fine whitefish on his trip, which she grilled in seal fat and seasoned with fresh herbs. But they ate in unnatural silence; the old man was lost in his own thoughts.

They were just finishing eating when Mulak tilted his head alertly, listening. Ruth heard it then—the buzz of a small aircraft. For some reason the familiar sound brought a tug of apprehension.

Her father was at the front window, peering out. Some of the youngsters and young men of the village ran toward the flat strip of tundra that served as a landing area for the regular mail-and-supply planes. It was an old Cessna, painted yellow. She couldn't see who got out of the aircraft, but she felt her father's tension.

"There's trouble, isn't there, Papa?" she asked softly.

"Yes."

"Does it have to do with the white men?"

"It's always the white men," John Mulak said.

"What do you mean, the ivory's gone?" Travis Mayberry said in a terrible voice.

"We went out in boats yesterday," Kirfak said. He was one of the

477

natives who had participated in the slaughter of the walrus herd. "It was the right place. The ivory is gone—all of it."

Mayberry stared at him, then at the others, disbelieving. There were villagers all around, including women and a flock of children.

"We can't talk here," Mayberry said. "You," he said to Kirfak. "Is that storeroom open?" Mayberry's glance picked Billy Mulak out of the crowd. "You, too. This can't be happening. We gotta talk."

The log storeroom, one of the oldest buildings in the village, was once home to a large Eskimo family. It was now used as a storage shed. Mayberry waved the two natives into the building, along with Wolf Simpson and Jeff Rorie.

After shutting the door, Mayberry stood for a moment in silence. He was breathing hard, his rage threatening to explode. "All right, let's have it. What's happened to that ivory?"

Kirfak shrugged helplessly. "We went to find it as soon as it was safe for the boats. It's gone. That's all I can tell you. We weren't meant to kill so many. The seas took the ivory back."

"Don't give us that superstitious bull," Wolf Simpson said.

"No, it's gone! Tell them, Billy. You saw. None of us believed it could happen, but it did."

Mayberry glared at young Mulak. "You're the one we were told was the best shot with a rifle. What about Muugli?"

"He was not there," Billy said anxiously. "But I know I hit him. Twice. I'm sure of it. He is wounded. He could not go far. Or if he's dead, he would wash up on the rocks. We can find him."

Billy felt desperate. Now the white men would withhold what they had promised. Billy was trembling, not so much in fear of the white men's wrath as from his own craving.

There was a long, prickly silence. In the cold shed the men's breath made little white puffs of moisture in the air. For Mayberry the enormity of the loss was sinking in. He had built up the size and value of the white harvest to Harry Madrid, at the same time minimizing any problems in bringing it in. And he had assured Harry that the giant tusks—the prize of prizes—hadn't been lost. He felt the cold inside the storage shed touch the back of his neck.

"I don't buy any of this," Simpson said. "That much ivory didn't just float away."

"No," Mayberry agreed. "That means somebody else took it.

Maybe we got some entrepreneurs trying to muscle in on the ivory business. Maybe some Eskimo has some big ideas of going it on his own. Whichever, we got to find who it is. And find that ivory." He fixed his gaze on Billy Mulak. "I want Muugli. Whoever finds him for me, I'll take good care of him. You understand?"

"Yes," Billy whispered. "I promise I will find him!"

KATHY McNeely and Jason Cobb made detailed observations of the animal presence as they walked across the tundra. They noted the sign of ptarmigan, lemming, fox, and, of special interest after the night's concert, a wolf pack.

"Only one adult," said Kathy.

"Yes," Cobb agreed. "For some reason she's alone with her litter."

"Why was she howling last night?"

Cobb shrugged. "Perhaps for our benefit. Or to let other wolves know that this was her territory. Or even to attract a male. I wondered if Survivor might be a puzzle to her."

"Survivor?" Kathy stared at the big husky, who had spent ten minutes eagerly sniffing at the wolf tracks. "My Lord."

As they moved on, Survivor ran ahead, conducting his own inventory of the terrain, exploring fascinating new scents and tracks. The fact that they had not yet come across any bear sign, Cobb observed at one point, offered no certainty they wouldn't encounter one. The entire region was grizzly territory.

They were moving west, toward the sea, and Kathy's excitement grew. In the past few days alone she had observed an astonishing variety of birds. But she had yet to see one of the tundra's most spectacular residents—the snowy owl.

It was almost noon when Cobb gestured to her to stop. He pointed at Survivor. Nodding, Kathy ordered the husky to lie down beside a soft hummock of grass. "Stay," she said quietly.

Cobb led the way up a gentle rise. They crawled the last few feet. Cobb pointed. Silently Kathy took her binoculars and swept the area Cobb indicated. "I don't see—"

She broke off, her heart leaping. What she saw was small, brown, almost perfectly camouflaged, and nearly hidden by grasses and low brush. "I can just barely see. . . . It must be the nest and the chicks, but I don't see the mother."

"She's probably off foraging for food."

"The chicks will be demanding food all day long," Kathy agreed, just as they began a shrill, plaintive whistling.

"Here she comes!" Jason Cobb exclaimed.

Suddenly Kathy saw the snowy owl, hawklike in flight except for the distinctively larger head and heavier body. The bird was a brief dazzle of mottled white as she swept in low above the grass. With a swift, astonishing spread of her wings—the span was five feet—she skidded in the air and slipped lightly to the turf.

Anyone would have found the sight breathtaking. For Kathy it crystallized years of study into a single unforgettable moment.

The snowy owl was one of the few birds known to nest in the open tundra, perhaps because she was large and aggressive enough to defend herself and her young against predators. The female's white plumage was accented by blackish brown bars, and her coloring enabled her to blend almost perfectly into the background.

Kathy's heart still beat rapidly from the elation of that vision of the owl as she braked in midair. Like a reflex, Kathy felt another quickening—this one of anger that such a creature could be not only an object of awe and delight but a mercenary hunter's target.

"How could anyone kill a creature so beautiful?" she whispered.

"Because she is so beautiful," Cobb replied in the same hushed tone. "That's what makes her valuable to poachers."

Kathy knew this bitter truth. The wing and tail feathers of the owl were prized on the black market, like those of the bald and golden eagles. Whole specimens of a snowy owl could fetch as much as five thousand dollars in the Hong Kong or Taiwan underground.

Kathy picked up her binoculars again, trying for a more intimate view of the owl at her nest. She could see the mother's white head bobbing as she offered up lunch for her chicks.

They fell silent. While Kathy was completely absorbed, Cobb's gaze strayed across the sweep of the tundra toward mighty crags mantled in snow, their peaks disappearing in mist. The mountainous mass seemed to fill up the sky.

"Magnificent, isn't it?" Cobb murmured, half to himself.

"I think it's the scale of it all, you can't be prepared for. I know I wasn't. Valleys so long you can't see the end of them, and huge mountain ranges dwarfed by others, one after another."

Kathy's eyes lit as she spoke. Cobb was moved. More and more frequently these days he found himself covertly staring at this young woman who shared his days and nights. At night, in his solitary tent, he had no trouble calling up the picture. Her dark, curly hair, cut short, framed an appealing face with a straight, no-nonsense nose; lively, intelligent hazel-green eyes; and a generous mouth that seemed always on the verge of a smile.

He felt wry chagrin over the fact that he was one of those in ASSET who had opposed including Dr. McNeely in the expedition. Well, he didn't mind admitting he'd been dead wrong.

Watching her rapt expression as she focused on the snowy owl, Cobb found his thoughts stumbling over a hard fact: McNeely hadn't been alone in Antarctica—or in Santa Barbara, for that matter. That adventurer, Brian Hurley, was part of the picture.

But Hurley was at the other end of the world. Cobb and Kathy were here. And ASSET's expedition was far from over.

A shadow passed swiftly over the tundra. Black clouds tumbled toward them, driven by high winds, where moments earlier there had been clear skies. To the west they could see the brush bending and whipping before the gusts.

"Time to call it a day," Cobb said quickly.

They moved carefully down the knoll and rose to their feet, Survivor joining them. They climbed into low foothills and were about four miles from their camp when the full force of the storm reached them and the long gray twilight darkened into premature night. The temperature dropped twenty degrees.

The rain enveloped them as they were working their way back down a long slope toward the level tundra. The descent was not difficult except for the footings. In addition to the thick tufts of grass that yielded and twisted underfoot, there were patches of loose shale. Survivor found these hikes a lark, regardless of the conditions. But for Kathy and Jason the going became increasingly laborious as the ground quickly melted into muck.

Near the bottom of the slope, Cobb's foot slipped on loose wet gravel. He caught himself, bracing one arm against the ground to avoid falling, but his ankle twisted. Pain shot up his leg.

In the tumult of wind and rain, Kathy did not hear Cobb's scuffling struggle or his gasp of pain. He limped, twenty yards behind

481

her now, breathing hard, his heart thumping. The wind-driven rain formed horizontal strings that cut where they lashed across his face.

Cobb's startled cry cut through the wind. Kathy whirled about. Favoring his ankle, he had tripped over a thick tussock. As he struggled to keep his balance, his feet skidded out from under him. He fell hard, sprawled on his back, his face turned up into the rain.

Kathy was at his side, alarmed. "Dr. Cobb, are you all right?"

For a moment he couldn't speak. When she tried to help him sit up, he made a hissing sound and pushed her hands away.

"Sorry," he gasped. "I . . . I can't move."

"Don't try. Just lie there."

She thrust her pack under his head. It was then she discovered he had landed on the hard protrusion of a large, concealed rock.

"It's my back," Cobb said calmly.

"We'll get you back to camp and call the base for help."

"That may not be so easy, Doctor . . . Kathy." There was a glitter of pain in his eyes. "I'm afraid something's broken."

FIVE

HARRY Madrid was his own creation. He had erased all evidence of a Peapack, New Jersey, street kid's speech, appearance, and style, and replaced that with the polish of a sophisticated New Yorker who moved easily in the most cultured settings. He lived on Central Park South, wore custom-tailored suits and English wing-tip shoes, and was a dealer in fine arts and collectibles.

The kid Harry had once been had started out stealing hubcaps when he was ten. He had graduated to stealing and stripping automobiles, then to peddling crack for small-time street dealers. He learned quickly.

Harry rarely thought of his petty criminal past now. Nevertheless, his early lessons on the street had helped to shape the man he had become. Perhaps the key lesson Harry retained was that you didn't try to cross the heavy players; you worked for them. Their muscle became your muscle.

Harry's art dealership was a legitimate business, but it was essentially a front, a way to launder money otherwise obtained. It created a plausible reason for shipping and receiving goods to and from the far corners of the earth. Harry's real business—which would have astonished any number of Manhattan hostesses, but not agents of the FBI or the U.S. Fish and Wildlife Service—was trafficking in exotic animals and their pelts, tusks, and horns.

On this September morning, across the river from his just off Park Avenue store, and a world away, Harry was expansively introducing a group of potential buyers to the abundance of illegal goods he had in stock. The shabby exterior of the old brick warehouse near the docks didn't suggest the presence of anything valuable. And the devastated area approaching the warehouse caused uneasy murmurings among the three Japanese in the back of Harry's Mercedes limo. He smiled. A few moments later, when the heavy steel door clanged shut behind them and Harry flipped on the banks of fluorescent lights illuminating the main warehouse, the uncertainty gripping his guests turned to awe.

HARRY Madrid got his start in the poaching business by default. A man named Louis Durand, from the steaming bayous of Louisiana, had hinted around the New York waterfront that he had alligator skins that needed to be sold in a discreet way.

Initially dubious, Harry became very interested after talking to Durand for three hours one night in a waterfront bar. Harry didn't even know that alligators were an endangered species and therefore both killing them and selling the hides were illegal. The Japanese, Durand said, were the largest buyers, and they were not overly concerned about the hides being illegal, as long as the transaction could be carried out without publicity.

That was how it started. Before long Harry was handling not only alligator skins but bear, otter, and wolf pelts, eagle feathers, rhinoceros horns, and—especially—ivory.

Ivory, in the international market, was number one. The demand was insatiable, especially in Japan, Taiwan, and China, and the profits were enormous. The more Harry learned about the trade, the more he saw it as a vacuum that had been waiting for him.

At about that time the Convention of International Trade in Endangered Species put the African elephant on its list. Harry didn't see that as a major concern; laws against poaching would actually work to his advantage, throwing the whole ivory business up for grabs. Harry heard there were some major dealers linked to Asian buyers, but he would set up his own pipeline. However, since the major buyers were in the Orient, Harry decided to go where the money was. In this case, that meant Asia.

Obtaining the names of potential sources proved to be surprisingly easy. Harry Madrid was becoming known in the business.

Thus it was, four years after meeting Louis Durand in a dingy Brooklyn bar, that Harry Madrid found himself flying to Taiwan. As the Singapore Airlines jet landed at Taipei's international airport, Harry felt he was going big time for the first time in his life. He checked in at the Hilton and waited impatiently for a phone call.

The call came the next morning. A name was mentioned—the only one Harry had yet heard: Chang. A meeting was arranged. A taxi would pick him up at his hotel at exactly eight p.m.

Taipei surprised Madrid. With its bright lights and its glut of modern high-rises, it was much like New York. The driver, a young Chinese, also drove like a New York cabbie. He shot from zero to fifty miles an hour as if he were doing a road test for *Car and Driver*. An hour later, having left the neon lights behind, the vehicle nosed through the narrow, twisting streets of Quanzhou, an ancient seaport on the island that was formerly known as Formosa.

Harry was beginning to feel uneasy as he rode along a rickety wooden pier. There were dim lights strung along posts, but the night was overcast and the darkness thick beyond the feeble glow of the lights. The harbor was clogged with junks, and it seemed you could step from one to the other without getting your feet wet.

His guide stopped beside a boat and beckoned Harry to follow him into the cabin. In the orange glow from two lanterns, three men stared at Harry in silence. Two of the men were smoking.

"Which one of you is Chang?" Harry asked truculently. He didn't think he was being treated like a major player.

None of the men answered. They looked like thugs, Harry decided. He turned. The Chinese driver was blocking the stairs.

"What's going on here?" Harry blustered. "If you think you can muscle me without it raising a stink—"

"You have no reason to be concerned," the young man said in clear, polite English.

He didn't look like the others, Harry realized. They wore long, baggy black overshirts and rubber boots—fishermen's outfits, he thought. The taxi driver wore a pair of Dockers pants and an open-necked white shirt.

"My name is Deng Chang," Harry's guide said.

Harry tried to hide his disappointment. He hadn't come all this way to do business with a kid.

"Madam Chang will be here very soon."

Harry stared at him. *Madam Chang?*

A moment later Harry heard light footsteps coming down the stairs. He watched small feet appear, clad in black slippers, followed by a long silken red dress embroidered in gold thread.

She was a diminutive woman—less than five feet tall and very slim. She appeared fragile, like a porcelain figure. Her hair was as black as night, caught up in a tight bun at her neck. Her features were delicate and flawless. Harry's first thought was that she was the most beautiful woman he had ever seen. His second thought was that she had the coldest eyes he ever wanted to see.

"I am Madam Lu Chang," she said in a thin singsong voice. "You are Mr. Madrid?"

"That's right," Harry said, recovering. "Harry Madrid."

"We must talk," the woman said.

"I understand you need ivory," Harry answered smoothly. "I can supply as much as you want."

She glanced sideways. A chair was instantly brought for her. She sat erect on the chair. The slit on the side of the red dress revealed a perfectly shaped ankle and slender calf. The men in the cabin stared at her as if she were the Queen of England, Harry thought.

"Let me speak plainly, Mr. Madrid. I considered having you killed without discussion. You are interfering in my family's business affairs. However, my son suggested that you might not be aware of the nature of your transgression. That is why I agreed to this meeting."

Harry's mouth fell open. He couldn't believe what he was hearing. *Killed without discussion!*

"I'm not trying to interfere with your business; I'm here to negotiate a deal. I have a pipeline set up in Africa—"

"Allow me to finish, Mr. Madrid." Madam Chang cut him off in an icy tone. "The ivory business in Africa is my family's business.

485

There are others who buy and sell ivory in Asia, but not in Africa. We have permitted you and a few petty thieves to make minor arrangements, particularly for sale of small quantities of ivory in Europe and the United States. But now you wish to intrude directly into my family's affairs. That is unacceptable."

Her cold black eyes fixed on Harry's, holding him captive. He thought of a snake's eyes. He was sweating. Suddenly he knew that he was in over his head.

"I thought you wanted . . ." Harry floundered.

"There will be no negotiations," Madam Chang said. "My son has suggested that you might prove useful to us—not in Africa, but in the United States. You have established shipping and storage arrangements. If you wish to work for us, it is possible that an association may be mutually beneficial."

Her words brought a flicker of hope.

"I can see where I might have made a mistake," Harry said, almost fawning. "I don't see why we can't have an . . . association."

Madam Chang offered him a very thin carmine-colored smile. "I'm afraid so ready a concession cannot be trusted."

"Hey, Harry Madrid's word is good."

"We will see." She gave the briefest of nods. Before Harry knew what was happening, two of the heavily muscled thugs had wrestled him over to a narrow bench and shoved him down. One arm was twisted behind his back; the other was jerked forward, and his hand was slammed down onto the table in front of the bench.

Harry couldn't move. He was terrified.

"Permit me to make your choice clear, Mr. Madrid," Madam Chang said coolly. "You may work for the Chang family if I so choose, while carrying on your own affairs, as long as they do not interfere. Or you will die."

"There is no need for this," Harry said. "I made a mistake. I didn't know— You have to believe me!" He was babbling.

Madam Chang stared at him for a long minute in silence. Then she turned toward the third of the thugs, who had been watching quietly, and gave a brief nod. He stepped over to the table, drawing from a scabbard at his waist a long, sharp knife.

Harry Madrid began to jerk convulsively, trying to free himself. The steel fingers on both arms were unyielding, digging into his flesh.

"You must understand, Mr. Madrid, that if you were permitted to challenge the Chang family in its enterprises, others would perceive this as a weakness. It is necessary to send a message. I will permit you to join our organization. However, there must be a penalty, a visible sign. I think, perhaps, the small finger. . . ."

Before Harry knew what was actually happening, the little finger of his left hand was pinned to the table and struck with the knife, as simply as severing the head of a carrot.

Harry went limp. His head swam. He was dimly aware of someone packing the wound to stop the flow of blood. Deng Chang placed some kind of ointment on the stub and bound it tightly.

Madam Chang was talking to him, Harry realized. It became desperately important for him to listen to her. "Our association can make you a very rich man, Mr. Madrid. But you must never think that you are beyond my reach. Do you understand?"

Harry Madrid understood very well.

THE Japanese buyers exclaimed over Harry's showpieces—a magnificent polar bear rug, an eagle-feather headdress spectacular enough for a Sioux chief, and a stack of tiger hides. But they were most excited by the ivory samples he displayed. They wanted raw ivory—a lot of it. Ivory to be carved into figurines, jewelry, Japanese signature seals, canes, fans delicately carved in filigreed panels, and more. Much of the ivory Harry sold now was ivory that he and his accomplices had bought or otherwise obtained, without any help from the Chang organization. No matter. There was a poignant reminder of the bargain Harry had made with Madam Chang: he remained only the middleman, not the major player he had hoped to be. His share of the spoils had made him comfortable, but not really rich—and never in control.

"We would like perhaps to see more ivory," the Japanese spokesman said. "Our order is a large one—ten thousand pounds."

Harry had to swallow his reaction. That many tusks accounted for more than three hundred slaughtered elephants or seven hundred walruses. By Harry's reckoning, even at fifty dollars a pound the Japanese order came to a half million dollars. And Harry might be able to jack the price up to sixty dollars.

"I don't have that much ivory in this warehouse," Harry said. And

487

then smiling, he added, "But it is available—at the right price."

He showed them a room filled with African ivory. The room held most of the elephant tusks Harry had in stock. A little over half the order, he estimated. Mayberry would have to come up with the rest in Alaska.

"I also have a large supply of excellent walrus ivory. It's being shipped to me now," Harry said, stretching the truth.

The Japanese buyers exchanged glances and a rapid volley of Japanese words. The spokesman bowed. "We are satisfied," he said.

THERE was a message from Travis Mayberry when Harry and his clients returned to his Manhattan office. Harry had to ignore it while he took care of business. An hour later the Japanese had agreed to pay him fifty dollars a pound for ten thousand pounds of raw ivory for delivery within thirty days, including both elephant and walrus tusks. Harry bowed them out of his office; then he put the call through to Nome, Alaska.

"It's about time you got back to me," Harry said without preamble as soon as Mayberry answered. "I've just got a big order. You'll have to go to the secondary storage." The latter was Harry's code for the remote cabin where Mayberry stored the bulk of the walrus ivory awaiting shipment. Harry did not wholly trust the feds not to tap his telephone. "We're probably going to need all that new stuff, too. And Madam C. is champing at the bit to get those big ones—you know what I mean. The special order. She's making it personal." Harry had received a hint of just how personal. The bidding for the legendary Muugli's mammoth tusks was rumored to have started at a quarter of a million U.S. dollars.

"That's what I called about," Mayberry said. Harry went very still. He had a survivor's instinct for something going bad, and he felt the foreboding now. "It's missing. Gone. All of it."

Harry's mind refused to believe what he was hearing. "You can't be serious!"

"I'm telling you," Travis Mayberry said, "someone's stolen it."

Harry lost it then. He forgot all about the federal agents who might be listening. "Who is it?" he demanded. "Who'd do it?"

"I don't know," Mayberry admitted.

"The feds? They could have a plant in your organization."

"Why would they take it? They'd rather catch us with it."

Harry Madrid's mind raced, sifting possibilities, rejecting them. "Someone's trying to cut into our action."

"Could be. But if there'd been strangers around—white men—the villagers would have seen 'em, unless they came and went by boat."

"Who knew?" Harry said coldly.

"Nobody else. Just me and Simpson . . . and the natives."

There was a prickly silence. Mayberry waited it out uneasily. He hoped Harry Madrid didn't decide to make a personal visit to Nome, the way he had once come to check on Delbert Hicks.

"Find out who," Harry said, "and make an example of them. I don't care how you do it, Mayberry. And find that damn ivory!"

SIX

AFTER leaving Simpson at the Eskimo village to begin interrogating the natives, Mayberry flew back to Nome to report to Harry Madrid in New York.

"If I get hold of Madrid right away, Rorie and I will be back tonight," Mayberry had said to Simpson before he left. "Tomorrow we start hunting for that ivory."

Simpson started easy. He made it a social occasion, all of the men from the hunt gathering together at the village school. It was late afternoon, and classes were over for the day. He had unloaded a case of vodka from Jeff Rorie's plane.

Eskimos, like most North American Indians, easily acquired a craving for alcohol once it was introduced to them, but had little tolerance for it. They got drunk quickly, Simpson knew. He poured generous splashes of vodka into small paper cups. He got the Eskimos talking about the hunt and how much money and whiskey they were all going to have when the ivory was found.

After a while Simpson singled out the hunter called Kirfak, older than the others. After only two drinks Kirfak's speech stumbled.

"You think that much ivory could've just washed off that shelf?" Simpson asked him, earnest and friendly.

"No way," Kirfak blurted. "Too much ivory!"

"Well, if it didn't wash away, I mean, what happened to it?"

Kirfak grinned. "The sea . . . take it all back."

"We went over that," Simpson said. "There aren't any sea gods out there protecting the walruses. If there were, we wouldn't have been able to kill so many, would we? What I figure is, maybe some of you hunters went back for the ivory. Am I right?"

Kirfak looked wobbly. He shook his head. "I think . . . gonna be sick." The Eskimo stumbled and weaved toward the restroom.

Simpson kept digging. Three hours later, with only a few hunters still able to string intelligible words together, his patience was running out. He glared at one Eskimo who hadn't been on the walrus hunt, but was only there to cadge a free drink. Simpson was about to throw him out when he thought of a key question.

"Did any of the men go fishing or hunting during the storm?"

The Eskimo shook his head. "Not safe. You got good vodka?"

"Maybe, if you tell me something interesting. Did anyone leave the village right after the rains stopped?"

The native licked his lips. "Some go out, sure. When storm is over, even the women and children go. They go pick berries."

Simpson poured vodka into the last of the paper cups he had. He held it for a moment, out of reach. "You remember who went?"

"Sure. Mulak go fishing. He likes to go alone."

Simpson turned quickly, trying to find Billy Mulak. The young Eskimo had stumbled out of the school about an hour earlier, he remembered. "Billy Mulak? He went fishing alone?"

"No, not Billy. John Mulak. I saw him go down to his boat."

Simpson pushed the cup of vodka toward the eager Eskimo and hurried from the building.

HE FOUND Billy Mulak huddled on the steps outside the school-house. Stains on his parka showed he had gotten sick.

"I've gotta talk to you," Simpson said.

He hauled Billy roughly to the storage room in the rear of the building. Simpson turned on an overhead light and closed the door. "You sober enough to know what's goin' on?" he asked.

"Sure. I got a little sick, that's all."

"You could get sicker fast. I thought you told me no one left the village before you and your friends went back for the ivory. You was lyin' to me, Billy. Tell me about your father. He went fishing alone before the rest of you."

Billy looked disconcerted. Not scared, Simpson thought, watching him narrowly; not worried yet.

"Well, yeah. Pop isn't scared of anything. He'll go out in his boat when nobody else will. But that doesn't mean anything."

"You should have told me, Billy."

"He wasn't even with us on the hunt."

"I hear he's the great walrus hunter of the village."

"But he knows nothing of the hunt or the ivory."

"And you never mentioned such a successful hunt to him? Seems kind of funny. You shot Muugli, the Great One, and it wasn't important enough to mention to your old man?"

Billy averted his gaze, uncomfortable with the question. "I could not tell him. My father would not approve."

Wolf Simpson had one of his intuitions then—a little nudge of inspiration. It was like when he was hunting a wolf from a chopper, harrying him back and forth. Sometimes he would get inside the wolf's head until he would actually know which way the wolf would veer. And when the wolf did what Simpson knew he would do, Simpson would have his sights already lined up, waiting for the kill.

"I tell you what, Billy. We should have a talk with your old man."

AFTER Cobb's accident on the way back to camp, Kathy made him as comfortable as possible. His injury was in the lower back or hip. Knowing the risk of moving anyone with a back injury, she eased him onto more level terrain and used a plastic tarpaulin from his backpack to shield both of them from the rain. Their condition remained cold and miserable.

After an hour the rain swept on.

"I have to get you back to camp," Kathy said.

"I don't see how. Better get back yourself. Call for help."

"It's going to freeze tonight. You can't stay here."

Neither of them mentioned the possibility of predators. During the course of that day, they had seen the tracks of a wolf pack.

"There's no point in two of us being in jeopardy," Cobb said.

"You're in no position to argue," she replied.

She had both a knife and a small hatchet in her pack, but there were no real trees that she could see. There appeared to be shrub growth in the foothills not far away, even a few substantial willow thickets. But how far? The massive thrust of the mountains, like the vast tundra, altered perspective. Distances were dwarfed.

"I'll be back," she said. "Survivor will stay with you."

She ordered Survivor to stay, then set off without another word. She didn't look back.

The tangled shrubs that had caught her eye proved disappointing when she reached them. Even the thickest stems weren't large or strong enough for what she had in mind.

She glanced north, up a barren slope toward a few thin willows. How far? Another mile?

Fifteen minutes later she reached the first of them. She selected four willows about the size of tall Christmas trees. From these, after trimming off all the branches, she fashioned four slender poles, each a little over eight feet long, tapering from about an inch and a half at the base to a thin, flexible tip. She needed only two, but spares were necessary.

It took her forty minutes to return to the river. She overshot the point where she had left Cobb, and felt panic; then she spotted the husky near the riverbank a hundred yards to her right.

Jason Cobb looked pale and drawn when she reached him. He stared at the poles. "I suppose you know what you're doing."

"Yes, I do," Kathy answered, more cheerfully than she felt.

She worked quickly, not sure how much twilight was left. Two hours at most, she thought. She used two straps from her backpack, along with Survivor's collar, to rig a harness to hold the heavier ends of two poles. Then she folded the plastic tarpaulin into a long panel draped over the poles and tied at the ends.

"What do you suppose you're making?" Cobb asked finally.

"The Indians used to call it a travois. Survivor is used to pulling. You should be no problem for him at all."

"I'm not riding on that thing. Something's broken in my back."

"You're not walking," Kathy said, feigning indifference. "You can't stay here, and I can't carry you. That means you ride."

She gingerly wrestled Cobb onto the crude stretcher, his head at the forward end. She lashed the spare poles to the sides. Survivor acted excited to be back in harness, prancing and whining eagerly.

"I don't think he can do this," Jason Cobb said, paler than before.

"Piece of cake for him," she answered. "But I have to tell you, Cobb, you're going to hurt some."

"No kidding."

Kathy led the way. Most of the time, she sought out the most level terrain, though it meant constant detouring. But for Cobb every bump or lurch sent pain rocketing through his hip and lower back. No matter how carefully Kathy tried to pick their route across the tundra, there were no smooth, level stretches. The hummocks seemed to reach out to grab the trailing tips of the side poles.

A tearing sound. Something gave way beneath Cobb. One of the poles of the travois twisted to the side, and the improvised stretcher collapsed. Cobb cried out as he slammed to the ground.

It was a moment before he could talk. Kathy tried to ease him onto his back again before inspecting the damage to the travois. He pushed her away angrily and swore. "I told you this thing wouldn't work!" he said. "What I don't need is some amateur playing games with a broken back. My leg is numb. I can't feel anything."

"I don't think your back is broken." Kathy's face was as pale as his. "And I'm not playing games, Dr. Cobb; I'm trying to help."

"You could help a lot more if you went ahead and radioed for someone competent."

She stopped trying to repair the stretcher and glared down at him. "You listen to me, Doctor. I know this isn't fun. And there *is* some risk in moving you. But I couldn't leave you back there. The base is going to have to call for an emergency plane, and who knows when that will get here. Have you really thought what it was going to be like alone out here? Not just for a few hours, but all night, in the freezing cold? I know you like to prance around naked in icy rivers, but—" She broke off, her face flushed. "I'll compromise with you, Doctor. We're only about two miles from camp. If I can't get you there, I'll bring the camp here."

"No," Cobb said tersely. "Fix this thing and let's get going."

They studied each other. Cobb thought she looked especially beautiful in that moment. "I guess I don't have any more secrets from you," he said.

"Not a one."

"Okay. What can I do to help?"

"Just be quiet. And pray a little."

In a matter of minutes she had the stretcher more securely fastened to the twin poles and secured to Survivor's harness.

"My Lord, look at that!" Cobb said, his voice oddly strained.

She turned to follow his gaze. The cloud cover to the north had lifted completely, and a vast portion of the sky was dancing with light. Swirls of color ebbed and flowed, twisting ribbons of pink and lavender and green and yellow. They were witnessing the aurora borealis, a phenomenon of the Arctic night.

"Is this a sign?" Jason Cobb said. "Are you some kind of witch doctor, after all?"

Kathy grinned. "You'd better believe it."

WITH the passing of the squall, the sea became calm, and within the sheltered cove there was a stillness. Just outside the cove, on the tiny island, something stirred, a shadow so bulky it appeared as if a portion of the island were breaking away.

Muugli slipped quietly into the water.

A day earlier he had heard and smelled the hunters when they returned, and he had not moved; he was hidden within a cup of rock shaped by the relentless pounding of the waves. The hunters in the boats did not see him.

He was weak from loss of blood, but the wounds themselves had closed, healed by the freezing water. Now he was hungry, and the cove floor was a banquet of mollusks. He would eat, storing the prodigious quantities of fuel he needed to regain his strength.

Afterward, when he was rested, he would turn north. The ice was coming. He would find his own kind, and he would survive.

If the hunters did not find him first.

"HE JUST wants to talk to you, Pop," Billy Mulak said nervously.

"He is a friend? I would not refuse to talk to your friend."

"Not here," Wolf Simpson said. He was standing in the doorway of John Mulak's house. Simpson wanted to unsettle the old man, to have him nervous and rattled. Right now he was much too calm. "We're having a meeting. I figure the great hunter Mulak might help us. Come along, Pop."

At that moment Ruth Mulak appeared from the kitchen, hearing voices. She was startled. "Billy! Papa— What is this?"

"I am going to a meeting," John Mulak said.

"You don't have to go with them, Papa. They have lost their ivory. The talk is all over the village. It has nothing to do with us."

"This is not for you to say. I will speak with Billy's friend—"

"He's not a friend—not to any Eskimo!"

"I will talk with him about the hunt, and the ivory that is missing, and the killing of the great Muugli," he told his daughter. "It is right that I should know about such things." John glanced at Billy. What is the hold they have on you? he wondered.

John Mulak followed Simpson and Billy out the door. To Billy's surprise Simpson didn't take his father to the schoolhouse, where many of the village men still sprawled, but to the log building that served as a cold-storage shed. At the doorway, Simpson grinned. "Go get yourself a drink, Billy boy. I got to talk to Pop."

Simpson flipped on the single overhead light in the shed and shut the door in Billy's face. He grinned at the old Eskimo, who regarded him impassively. "Billy tells me you weren't interested in the hunt for the Great One. That puzzles me, Pop."

"I don't hunt in your way."

"Yeah. Billy says he didn't tell you about the hunt, because you wouldn't approve. Made me wonder what you would do about things you didn't like. Steal the ivory so we wouldn't have it?"

"How do you know your ivory didn't wash away in the storms?"

"Why would it do that?" His suspicions fastened on Mulak's question. "How come you know it was where it could wash away?"

"I know you killed many walruses and stacked the ivory on a shelf in a cove. And you shot Muugli, but he escaped. I know these things because I was told about them."

He didn't act guilty, Simpson observed, scowling. He decided to push a little harder. "I think you're lying to me, Pop."

Simpson drew a narrow leather pouch from one of the deep side pockets of his parka. It was about eight inches long, filled with coins. A thong at one end slipped over Simpson's wrist. "I think you have something to tell me, Pop," he said, adding, "It's cold in here. The colder you get, the more it hurts if you get hit with something hard." He reached out, jerking one of Mulak's mittens off.

The old man reacted. He tried to shoulder Simpson aside. Simpson brought the loaded pouch around in a swinging arc. It slammed

495

into Mulak's shoulder blade with such force that it knocked him against the wall. Simpson swung again and struck the back of the Eskimo's bare hand. A bone broke. Pain rocketed from Mulak's hand to the back of his brain. He sank to his knees.

Panting, Simpson stood over the old man. "You're gonna talk to me, you stubborn old coot. Sooner or later you'll talk!"

TRAVIS Mayberry returned to the village late that evening in Jeff Rorie's Cessna. He found Wolf Simpson in a sour mood. His interrogation of the villagers had gotten nowhere.

"Nobody knows anything. I tell you, though, I think Billy Mulak's old man knows more than he says. I got a hunch he knows where that ivory is. He went out in his boat before the others."

"Billy's father?"

"Yeah. He's supposed to have been a great hunter in his day."

Mayberry looked at him, sensing something. "Where is he?"

"I got him locked up in that log storage shed. I wanted to give him time to think things over."

Mayberry sighed. "You worked him over? Is he hurt?"

"Hey, he'll survive."

Mayberry didn't like being heavy-handed with the Eskimos. It could backfire on him. At the same time, he had to have the missing ivory. "It's cold in that shed," he muttered.

"He's an Eskimo," Simpson said. "He's used to being cold. Besides, he gets cold enough, his answers might get warmer."

Jeff Rorie wandered over from tying down his aircraft. Mayberry didn't think the bush pilot had been close enough to monitor the conversation, although sounds carried remarkably in this brittle air.

"Man, it's cold," Jeff Rorie said. "Where are we supposed to bed down tonight? I don't suppose there's a village Hilton."

Mayberry grinned. "No. But there's an empty house we can use. Got two bedrooms. The locals use it to put up visiting relatives." He pointed the house out to Rorie, a frame building about thirty yards up the street. "The door's open. I'll be with you in a bit."

Simpson frowned as he watched the pilot trudge through the freezing mud toward the one-story house. "I don't know about him," Simpson said. "I still want to check him out."

"He's okay," Mayberry said. "And I need him. Where's Billy?"

"In the school."

Billy Mulak was obviously agitated, Mayberry saw as he entered the schoolhouse. "My father knows nothing," Billy mumbled.

"You're sure? You know where your father went in his boat?"

"He brought home fish. He was fishing, that's all."

"I know what you need," Mayberry said quietly. "You need to calm down, kind of look at this thing the right way."

He fished a zip-lock plastic bag from his pocket, opened the seal at the top, and extracted a hand-rolled cigarette.

"Here you go, Billy."

When the young Eskimo reached for it, his hand trembled. Mayberry snapped open a battered lighter to light it. After a moment Billy leaned back against the wall of the schoolhouse, inhaling deeply. The pinched look around his eyes began to ease.

"Nepali gold." Mayberry chuckled. "Best grass in Alaska."

He waited a moment, watching the youth. He knew that Billy had an even stronger craving.

"I tell you what, Billy. I've got a little white powder with me, a little coke. I know you didn't earn it—not until we find that ivory—but that's okay. You do a little something for me, I do a little something for you. If your old man knows anything about that ivory, he has to tell you or you're in big trouble. You have to make him understand, Billy. Either he talks to you or he talks to Wolf. Either way, eventually he has to talk."

Billy stared at him. He took another drag on the marijuana cigarette. His actions were in slow motion. His hand no longer shook.

SEVEN

THE strange luminous darkness of the Arctic night closed in during the last weary quarter mile, but by then Kathy had spotted the two yellow tents that identified their camp. She got Cobb inside his tent and lit the Coleman stove, which also served as a heater. She built a roaring fire near Cobb's tent.

"We have to get you out of those wet clothes," she said.

"Heck of a time to make an offer like that."

"Uh-huh. I guess you're not in such bad shape."

She was able to pull off his parka and sweater and found scissors to cut away his wet shirt and slacks. To her considerable relief his thermal underwear seemed reasonably dry.

When she had the wet clothes off, she wrapped him in a blanket, topped by her own down-filled sleeping bag.

"Where are *you* going to sleep?" Cobb said.

"I guess I'll just have to stay in here with you and keep warm. I don't plan to sleep much, Dr. Cobb."

She left him alone while she used the shortwave radio to raise the ASSET base camp, two hundred miles upriver. There was a long delay before a voice answered: "ASSET base. Come in."

"Riverboat One," Kathy said, using the call name she and Cobb had been given. "This is Dr. McNeely."

"Dr. McNeely! We tried to call you earlier, but there was no answer. Have you seen our incredible light show? Some of—"

"I'm sorry." Kathy cut him off. "There's been an accident. Dr. Cobb is hurt. We need to get him to a hospital."

"Oh, my gosh. The plane isn't here, Doctor, but I think it's supposed to be back tomorrow. I'll get right on it. We'll get you both out of there as fast as we can."

"Just Dr. Cobb," she said. "I still have work to do."

At that moment, from the shadows of the tundra nearby, a wolf howled. Kathy looked up toward the spine-tingling sound.

She saw the wolf then for the first time, standing on a mound about a hundred yards away, her head lifted. She was large—at least as tall as Survivor—although she appeared to be thinner. Her coat was almost pure white. It seemed to Kathy that she looked directly toward the camp for a moment, then threw her head back and howled again.

Survivor, his hackles rising, moaned deep in his throat.

Cobb was watching Kathy when she reentered his tent. "You should get out of those clothes, McNeely. I won't mind."

Kathy grinned. "I've heard about troublesome patients. My sister's a nurse."

"Occupational hazard. You go around saving people's lives, you have to take the consequences."

"I didn't save your life, Dr. Cobb. I'm not even sure I did the right thing."

"I am, and you did."

Cobb was silent for a moment. Kathy was aware of a difference in their relationship—a subtle, unspoken alteration from working colleagues to friends.

"What's with this guy Brian Hurley?" Cobb asked finally. "Are you in love with him?"

"That's . . . personal."

"But if everything were perfect, I think you'd say so."

"We have a ways to go," she admitted. "But we're working things out. I've never been very good at relationships. It's something I have to learn."

"I don't believe there's anything you're not good at—not anything important. And if you were my girl, I wouldn't be off in Antarctica chasing rainbows. I'd be wherever you were."

Kathy smiled. "Well, you're here now, and a lot of good you are to me. Anyway, Brian isn't chasing rainbows. A dream, I guess, or a challenge he couldn't pass up. Brian's going to race to the South Pole, trying to set a record. I think it's something he has to finish or he'll always regret it."

"And after that?"

"After that . . . we'll see."

She remembered the last angry exchange with Brian. It would have been different, she'd argued, if he were going wherever his work took him—Hurley's training was in archaeology—even if it meant having him go off to Borneo or Tibet. But he was going to the bottom of the world just for kicks, she'd said. On a whim.

It was the word "whim" that got him. It wasn't a whim, Hurley raged. It was something he'd given several years of his life to. It mattered. He wanted to do this better than anyone had ever done before him. It was the worst argument they had had, and the timing couldn't have been worse, coming the night after the ASSET committee arrived in Santa Barbara to talk to Kathy about the Alaskan expedition. They had got over the anger, but they hadn't resolved the conflict; there hadn't been time.

She stood, feeling tired and clammy in her wet clothes.

"I'm going to change into something dry, but I'll be back."

"Good. I don't fancy being alone tonight."

In her tent, she recalled Cobb's last words with a grin. The formidable Jason Cobb was vulnerable, after all.

INSIDE THE STORAGE SHED JOHN Mulak sat on top of a crate, with his legs drawn up close to his body for warmth. He kept his left hand under his parka. After Simpson left, Mulak had retrieved his mitten to cover the broken hand. Warmer now, it didn't hurt as much.

Mulak had encountered anger among his own people, but he had never known or even witnessed the calculating vicious cruelty Simpson seemed to enjoy. What was it in the white man's nature that made such indifference to the humanity of others possible?

Mulak thought about what he had done to create his present predicament. The white man was right: he had stolen what was not his, and he had lied about it. Both actions were alien to his nature, but he had seen no alternative. He saw none now.

They had sent Billy to gain the answers Simpson could not get. His son, but a stranger. There was a brightness in Billy's eyes that was not normal. When he entered the storage shed, he spoke excitedly, pacing back and forth, not looking at his father directly. "If you know where the ivory is, Pop, why won't you tell them?"

Mulak would reveal nothing to this stranger.

Billy talked about the hunt, about how exciting it was to see Muugli. How the men had killed great numbers of walruses.

"What do the white men give you for this killing?" Mulak said.

"They'll pay us, but only for the ivory. Do you know what happened to it, Pop? Without it we get nothing."

"This hunt," John Mulak said after a moment. "Is this a story you would tell your children and your grandchildren? The white men are not hunters, they are butchers. This isn't the Eskimo way."

"We've always killed the walrus for ivory."

"Only what we needed," his father said simply.

The stubbornness in John Mulak's face increased Billy's desperation. "You've got to tell them what you know, Pop. You don't know them. You don't know what they might do."

"Yes, I know them."

Billy didn't know about the bone in his father's hand broken by Simpson's blackjack. He didn't know about the painful bruise on Mulak's shoulder. But he saw the bruises on the old man's face, the cut and swollen lip where blood had dried. Billy began to tremble.

"Tell them whatever it is they want to know, Pop. Do it for me."

"I *am* doing this for you," Mulak said. "And for our people."

He saw the shock of his words register in Billy's eyes. His son whispered, "You did take it. You stole the ivory."

"Go away," John Mulak said. "I will not talk to you anymore. Tell your bosses you learned nothing."

Hours later the white men had not returned to the shed. Mulak wondered what Billy had told them and what they had given him in return. He thought he understood now what had changed his son. For the past year he had heard talk in the village about some hunters selling ivory for the white powder called cocaine. Mulak knew about cocaine from watching TV. People would destroy their lives to possess it. They would destroy even their families.

Mulak remembered Billy as a boy, eager to learn everything his father taught him. He had been a cheerful child. His mother was alive then. Her laughter filled the house, and it made everyone around her happy. The house was always full of people eating and laughing and telling stories.

Mulak thought about what the white men were doing to his son, and he knew that he would never tell them where the ivory was.

He dozed for a while, his bones and muscles stiff and aching. A rattling at the door awakened him suddenly.

The door was secured by a sliding bolt and a sturdy padlock on the outside. He heard a scratching. Simpson was returning.

In spite of himself, Mulak felt a twisting in his belly. He steeled himself against the fear. And waited.

The crack was so loud it caused Mulak to jump. He slid off the crate he was sitting on, jolting his wounded hand. His heart pounded.

Nothing happened. The door didn't fly open. No one was standing there to confront him. Nothing. The night silence returned.

After a moment Mulak approached the door. It was no longer firmly shut. He tested it, and it swung open slightly.

Someone had pried open the wood frame to which the lock and the sliding bolt were secured. A crowbar lay on the ground.

Mulak pulled the crowbar into the shed. The white men might think he had found it there and pried open the door himself.

He stood beside the building, under the shadow of the roof overhang. The village street was empty. Who had broken the lock? Who other than his son? Mulak felt a surge of renewed pride in Billy. He didn't like leaving him to face the suspicion of aiding his

501

father's escape, but remaining at the village would mean even more trouble—for himself, for the entire village.

Mulak angled toward the river. On the narrow beach where he had pulled his kayak out of the water, he paused. There was no other hope of escape. How far could he travel on foot across the open tundra before searchers in an airplane found him?

He slid his kayak into the water. He couldn't grip the paddle firmly with his injured left hand, but he could use light pressure to guide the paddle, relying on his good hand for strength.

He glanced for the last time toward the sleeping village. He saw no one, but the sensation he felt was inescapable. From the moment he left the storage shed, someone had been watching him.

RUTH Mulak was up early as usual. She often used these hours to work on one of her crafts. She had learned basketmaking from her mother and had been laying in a supply of wild rye grasses for the long winter nights when she could work on a basket while watching television. A store in Anchorage paid fifty dollars for her smallest baskets and twice as much for the larger ones with lids.

Ruth also practiced other traditional skills. She had filleted and salted most of the fish her father had caught on his last fishing trip, for example, and hung it on the fish rack behind the house. The dried fish, oily and chewy, was an Eskimo delicacy.

She also had three sealskins stretched on racks. Two of these her father would use this winter to re-cover his kayak. The third—soft and pliable—would be used in her skin-sewing class.

Billy entered the kitchen silently as Ruth was wrapping the tanned sealskin in a cloth. She was going to show her students how to make a pair of knee-high waterproof boots called mukluks.

"Why do you bother with such things?" Billy said suddenly. "No one needs them anymore."

"I don't see you throwing away your old boots, Billy. Anyway, this is to show the children how Eskimos have always made boots."

He watched her fold and wrap the sealskin. "Why do you live in the past? That way is dead. You're like our father. He doesn't understand we live in the white man's world now."

"We still live in our own village, with our own people," Ruth retorted.

"Don't tell me you're happy here. You wish you could go away, be like the gussak women you see, with their fine clothes and their cars and all the rest. You envy them just like I do."

"No, I don't! I would like to see more of the Outside. There are so many wonderful things I've never seen, so much to know. But I wouldn't live there; I belong here. So do you, Billy."

"You think I want to stay here all my life? I want more than this."

Ruth asked now, "What has this to do with Papa? He didn't come home last night."

Billy became evasive. "It's not your business."

"He's my father. What have those white men done to him?"

"Nothing. They locked him in the storage shed to teach him a lesson. They think he stole the ivory from the hunt."

Ruth was shocked. Her father locked up like a criminal! "Papa's not a thief."

"If he didn't take it himself, he knows what happened to it." Billy's tone became sullen. "He's a foolish, stubborn old man. If he doesn't tell them where the ivory is, we will all suffer."

"Did you help them? Did you turn against your own father?"

She saw that the accusation was truer than she had guessed. Billy became agitated, as if looking for escape. "You don't understand—"

A fist pounded hard on the front door. "Mulak? Are you there?"

Apprehensive, Ruth went to the door. Three white men stood outside, two of them on the porch, the third hanging back.

"Where's John Mulak?" Travis Mayberry demanded.

"I don't know," Ruth said. "You took him away last night."

Billy appeared at her side. There was consternation in his face. "Pop's not here." He looked past the men, in the direction of the log storage building. Disbelief replaced the worry in his eyes.

"He's gone," Mayberry said harshly. He glared at Billy with suspicion. "Somebody broke the lock. You wouldn't have started feeling sorry for your old man, would you, and let him out?"

"No. I swear it!"

"Well, Mulak took his boat. He's gone."

Ruth's elation was banished by the white man's next words.

"You're coming with us, Billy. You know where he'd go. Him running away clinches it. That old man took the ivory for himself. And he's gonna give it back, or this whole village is going to pay!"

503

THAT MORNING JASON COBB FELT much worse. All movement was painful, but he was not—as he had feared the day before—paralyzed. He was able to move the leg that had felt numb.

Kathy brought him some crackers and cheese and a mug of hot coffee. "When's the plane going to get here?" he asked.

"Soon, I hope. I talked to base an hour ago. The regular supply plane is in Anchorage. But they talked to a pilot who's picking up some sport fishermen this morning at a lodge in the Brooks Range. He's going to divert this way for you."

"Great. I'll listen to fish stories on the way to the hospital."

"Stop complaining. It'll take your mind off things, like missing all this camp food."

He studied her quietly. Her face was flushed from the cold outside. He thought that what he was going to miss most was not the camp food, the incredible scenery and wildlife, or even the work he had come to do, but the growing intimacy between himself and this sensible, caring, desirable woman.

"Kathy—"

"Don't, Jason. Don't say anything you'll regret later."

"I'll regret not saying anything."

"But I'll feel better if you don't. Anyway, it's not as if we're not going to see each other again. You'll be on your feet in no time."

"Maybe." His disappointment was plain. He covered it by saying, "I heard you talking on the radio last night. You aren't serious about staying here alone!"

"Survivor and I will be fine. We haven't finished what we came here for, Jason, and we're running out of time. Those hearings in Anchorage are only about six weeks away."

"It's too dangerous here. That she-wolf, for instance . . . She was back last night. I don't like that."

"You weren't worried about her before. She's not threatening us. Anyway, I'm sure our colleagues will send someone to join me or insist that I pack it up. I'll be fine for a day or two."

"Stay close to camp; stay out of trouble."

"You sound like a parent," Kathy said, amused.

"I care about you, Dr. McNeely."

"Yes," Kathy said, "I know."

It wasn't long before the floatplane appeared. It made a couple of passes over the camp, then landed roughly in the middle of the river. It taxied toward them, working gradually closer to the shoreline, and stopped a few feet from the riverbank.

"Need a lift?" the bush pilot called out.

EIGHT

"FELLA back at the Nome airport was telling me Mayberry has some wings of his own in a private hangar there," Jeff Rorie said.

Wolf Simpson's suspicion flared. "Yeah? What's it to you?"

"Wonder why he needs me if he's got wings of his own, that's all. I wasn't lookin' for just weekend work."

Slightly mollified, Simpson glanced toward Mayberry, who was talking to some Eskimos near the river, and grinned. "He cracked up about eighteen months ago. Got hit by a crosswind touching down, and it blew him off the strip into a ditch. He walked away from it, but since then, he hates to fly on his own. He'll take her up when he has to, but not when he can get a chauffeur."

Rorie wondered what those trips might be that Mayberry had to take on his own, even though he hated flying solo.

Mayberry joined them, with Billy Mulak in tow. "Let's get her up. That old man's got a good start on us."

Taking off, the Cessna felt the tug of southerly side winds, but the landing strip ran east to west. Rorie had no choice but to ignore the winds and point the aircraft's nose to the east, in the direction of distant purple mountains.

Once airborne, the airplane headed out over the coastline and, at Mayberry's direction, turned north along the rim of the Chukchi Sea. Rorie scanned the horizon to the west. The gray cloud cover extended to the end of the world. He didn't trust that sky.

The Cessna 185 was a six-seater. Rorie had removed the two rear seats to create storage room. Simpson sat in the front next to Rorie. Behind them were Mayberry and the young Eskimo. The kid was troubled, Rorie thought. And scared. The four men were packed so close together in the little cabin that Rorie could hear most anything that was said, especially since speakers had to raise their voices close to a shout to be heard over the droning of the engine.

"Where would the old man go?" Mayberry asked Billy. "Are

there any other villages, friends, or relatives he'd likely run to?"

"He knows many people, he has many friends, but their villages are all inland, not close. He might have gone that way."

"I think his hand's hurt," Simpson shouted. "No way he's gonna paddle a hundred miles upstream with one hand. I say he's stashed that ivory and that's where he'd run to."

There was a silence for a while. Rorie hadn't wanted to inquire too closely into what ivory they were talking about.

"Where does he like to go fishing?" Mayberry asked Billy.

"There are several places. I'm not sure which he likes most."

"Don't hold out on me, Billy!"

Billy Mulak cringed. He wished desperately that his father hadn't done this stupid thing. Stealing from men like Mayberry and Simpson was crazy. It would be better for all if the ivory was found. They wouldn't care about an old Eskimo then. And they would pay what they had promised.

Billy felt jittery this morning. When he was able to get the white powder, like the sample Mayberry had given him last night, he was on top of the world, up there all by himself where nobody could reach him or sneer at him or make him feel as if he were nothing. But the mornings were always worse after being up so high.

"There's some creeks just ahead there." Billy pointed toward a broad sweep of marshland. "And there's another river to the north, past the walrus cove, where he catches big whitefish."

"He bring any whitefish back from that fishing trip?"

"Yes."

Mayberry grunted. He tapped Rorie on the shoulder and pointed. "Take us down, and cruise along as slow as you can."

"You've got it."

"I know that river he's talkin' about," Simpson shouted at Mayberry. "Maybe the old man's got a place where he could've stashed the ivory. He had to have some place to hide all those tusks."

KATHY McNeely watched the small rescue plane carrying Jason Cobb dwindle into the far distance. At last she turned away. Until someone from ASSET joined her, she was on her own. She could set her own priorities. With a colleague, there were always adjustments, compromises. Today she could do what she wanted.

The sense of freedom was overwhelming, like the space around her. Perhaps it was true, she thought, that you couldn't have a real wilderness experience unless you were alone.

She thought about that Eskimo who had slid by on the river in his kayak. He belonged here like the fox, the wolverine, the snowy owl, and the ptarmigan. Like that female wolf and her pack.

Where had the Eskimo been going, always with his boat laden down with cargo on the way upriver? As long as she was documenting this habitat anyway, it made sense to discover what he was up to.

She recognized that she was rationalizing a decision she had already made unconsciously, perhaps from the moment she knew Jason Cobb had to be flown out to a hospital. Cobb had dismissed the Eskimo; Kathy couldn't dispel her curiosity.

"We're going for a walk, Survivor," she murmured.

She took along a light pack, including some food, a knife, a flashlight, and a ground blanket. She didn't intend to stay out late, but over the past two months in the Alaskan wilderness she had learned not to count on anything going exactly as planned.

As she walked along, she gave herself to the land and the sky, savoring everything she saw and heard. The fascinating bird life of the northern tundra was more than she would have seen in a lifetime in any other place. Being able to document the potential damage to the birds' habitat from the proposed pipeline was a bonus.

She stopped to rest in the early afternoon and had some of her nuts and raisins and a granola bar. She let the sense of space pour around her. The sky remained overcast, gray to the horizon. Did that mean another storm? She told herself the Eskimo couldn't have gone much farther. Had she missed the signs along the river-bank where he might have come ashore? She didn't think so.

She walked on, captivated by the sense of being little more than another stem in a universe of brown and beige and red grasses bending before the wind.

Several times during the afternoon, she thought of turning back, realizing that she had perhaps come too far to make it back to camp before dark, but her stubbornness drew her on. Another mile, she told herself. She was making notes as she went. Nothing she saw would be wasted.

Kathy almost missed the tracks. They had filled with water from the rain and hardly looked like human footprints. She followed them to the river and saw where the Eskimo had drawn his kayak onto a narrow beach.

The tracks led inland, away from the river. The land rose, gradually at first, then on a steeper rise toward a broken crest. She followed. Here and there she lost the tracks, but each time found them again, climbing higher. Near the crest they vanished.

Kathy examined the ground carefully, frowning. The Eskimo didn't just vanish into the earth. But where could he have gone?

Survivor, trotting ahead of her, was sniffing at an opening into the hillside, half covered with stunted brush. She realized that there was a flat spot just inside the opening, a kind of level ledge. The hole was much larger than it appeared from above.

She felt tense as she bent to peer into the hole. It was dark inside. She fumbled for her flashlight and clicked it on.

The yellow beam startled her. It leaped into a cavern at least a dozen feet across. It was a natural cave with a floor that was several feet below the mouth. Heart hammering and stomach quivering, Kathy slid down this short ramp into the hollow in the hillside.

Old, dried animal droppings covered much of the floor. One corner of it, to the left of the opening, was elevated where a large burrow had been dug out several feet higher than the floor. An animal's bed. My Lord, she thought, a bear's!

Fear seized her. She had to fight it back. There was no bear here now; she hadn't followed the tracks of an animal, but those of a man. There was nothing to be afraid of.

She turned her attention toward the back of the cave, which had remained in gloom, shined her flashlight toward it, and jumped a foot off the ground. Heart pounding, Kathy McNeely stared at rows of walrus tusks, scores of ivory teeth arrayed along the wall in a monstrous grin.

IT WAS afternoon when the Cessna flew over the walrus cove. The group had spent hours exploring every stream that wound into the tundra from the coast, examining any creek where Billy remembered his father sometimes fished.

Mayberry had Rorie circle low over the cove. The pilot saw the lumpy walrus carcasses, like large sacks of grain, on a rock shelf

along one edge of the cove. A congregation of scavenger birds wheeled and scattered before the noisy airplane.

Mayberry had him come about for another pass, then a third. He had his binoculars fixed on the scene below, scanning the rocks and the shoreline and the surrounding sea.

"What are we looking for?" Rorie shouted.

"Biggest walrus you ever saw," Mayberry shouted back.

While they were circling, Rorie spotted a small boat to the south. Mayberry waved him toward it. Flying over, Rorie recognized the umiak from the village. The hunters had caught up.

"Any place you can set down around here?" Mayberry asked.

Rorie considered. He wasn't going to try to land in heavy seas, and there was no suitable stretch of beach. "I could put down on a tundra lake, but you'd have to wade through wetlands."

Mayberry scowled, but didn't push it.

They flew north after that, checking every slab of floating ice Mayberry spotted. "If Muugli is hurt and there's ice to be found, he'll hitch a ride," he argued, half to himself.

"I say he's dead," Simpson answered. "He'll pop up on a beach somewhere sooner or later."

"Harry Madrid wants those stupid tusks. I never should've told him about them."

"We find the rest of the ivory, he'll simmer down."

Late in the afternoon Mayberry, whose mood became more savage as the fruitless search continued, turned on the Eskimo. "Where on earth is this river your old man goes to? The one where he catches the whitefish?"

"We're almost there." Billy pointed. "Look. You can see it."

The river was a gray ribbon at the edge of an infinity of marshy tundra. To the north the land climbed through rounded foothills toward craggy mountains whose peaks were invisible.

"Flying this slow, we've used up more than half a tank of gas," Rorie stated reasonably. "That river might have to wait."

"I'm not waiting. The old man's got to be there somewhere."

"He could be anywhere. I doubt he'd have got this far."

"I'm payin' you to fly, not argue."

At Mayberry's demand Rorie was flying over the network of creeks near the coast when the first snowflakes smacked the

Cessna's windshield. Rorie knew instantly that he had been paying too much attention to Mayberry and not enough to his own instincts. He hoped he could outrun the storm, but it was moving very fast. He could feel the tension inside the small cabin.

A downdraft pushed the plane toward the ground like a giant fist. It dropped five hundred feet in seconds, to within a hundred feet of the ground. Then an updraft threw the Cessna skyward like a toy balloon. Rorie was anticipating it, but his passengers weren't. Billy Mulak screamed in panic. On the seat next to Rorie, Simpson was swearing steadily, savagely.

"Get us out of this!" Travis Mayberry raged at the pilot.

"My sentiments exactly," Rorie muttered, not caring if Mayberry heard. It was a big front and incredibly deep. He was not going to fly out of it going up. He knew he could probably get out of it if he flew inland long enough. But there were mountains that way, and closer to the north. Heading south offered no better alternative. For fifty miles he would be over nothing at all if he had to set down. He raised his voice. "I'm going down to find that river."

He was talking more to himself than to his passengers, but Mayberry heard him. "You're gonna get us all killed."

"Shut up!" Rorie's control momentarily snapped. He knew he was going to have to concentrate, using every trick he knew about flying, and he couldn't do that with someone yammering in his ear.

Simpson stared at him with his mouth open. Mayberry, who actually seemed to have some common sense, fell silent. Rorie shut out the sound of the young Eskimo's whimpering. Then there was nothing but the airplane, of which he was a living part, and the whirling snow through which he flew on blindly.

He dropped back down below a hundred feet, then fifty. Not much room to maneuver. Was he above the river? Was his compass reading accurate? He kept looking for a shine of water, a glimpse of brush, anything to tell him where the river was—if he was still near it.

A gap tore in the curtain. Rorie saw two bright patches of yellow on the tundra. Tents! And a gray worm of river beside them. He dipped toward the river reflexively. He was going down.

The real world reappeared suddenly. He was over the water. The tents he had glimpsed were ahead and above the left bank. The river was shallow and about fifty feet wide, but he didn't need much water for his floats. He throttled back, aware of the stall indicator blinking, of the snow streaming past his windshield like white water. He remembered to keep the nose up.

Water was as hard a landing surface as any airport tarmac. Rorie felt the first jolt as the floats struck the river. He fed a little more gas and rode through some hard, choppy pounding. But the aircraft was still all in one piece and under control.

He taxied toward the splash of yellow above the riverbank. Cutting power at the last moment, he ran out of water and onto mud, anchoring the floats in the riverbank.

In the sudden muffled silence, Rorie heard the metallic ticking from the hot engine and the hoarse rattle of someone breathing hard. He couldn't control the grin that spread across his face.

KATHY McNeely was not aware of the storm when it began. She was so absorbed in her assessment of the awful harvest she had stumbled on that she didn't sense any change in the atmosphere. When she finally did, what she noticed was silence.

Moving quickly to the mouth of the cave, she was stunned by the sight of snow falling thick over the tundra, isolating her.

She thought of trying to make it back to camp. Then she realized that with visibility only a few feet, she might easily become lost.

She turned reluctantly back into the cave. She was sheltered here from the storm. She had food and water for herself and Survivor. Like it or not, this was where she would spend the night.

THE old walrus heard the droning of the aircraft engine long before it passed overhead. He was riding on a cake of ice in open water. He was not yet at full strength and was slow to react to the droning sound, which was different from anything that had previously threatened him directly.

He lumbered toward the edge of the ice cake. The noise was louder now, resembling the rasp that came from boats. Two tons of ungainly flesh, the walrus would never make it to the edge before the plane passed directly overhead. But a gust of wind brought a whirl of snow between them, a white curtain blowing in the wind.

The walrus lifted its whiskered head and hooded eyes, peering up into the snow as the droning engine passed overhead.

NINE

KATHY McNeely woke to a feeling of claustrophobic panic. She was in some kind of earthen hole, walls closing her in on three sides.

Awareness came in a rush. She remembered the blanketing snow that had forced her to stay the night in a bear's den. And she remembered the astonishing hoard of ivory forming a bulwark several feet high and nearly twenty feet long at the back of the cave.

She rose, stiff with cold. The cave floor caught a spill of light flooding in from the opening. She suddenly realized Survivor was nowhere in sight. She heard a muffled sound. "Survivor?" she called.

Kathy stepped toward the den entrance, which was almost at eye level. A man crouched on the flat ledge at the opening, his bulk filling the hole. His brown face was unsmiling, the black eyes that studied her unreadable. He had a swollen lip and what looked like dark bruises on one cheek. She was jolted by the realization that he blocked the only way out of the cave. She was trapped.

Survivor's big head appeared beside the Eskimo. The husky looked happily into the man's face, gave a tentative lick, and accepted a pat on the head. Kathy felt immense relief. She trusted Survivor's instinctive judgment of a stranger.

"Who are you?" Kathy asked.

"I'm a human being." An Eskimo did not readily identify himself by name to a stranger.

"I can see that," Kathy said dryly. "Is this your cave?"

"This is a bear's cave," the man said seriously. Then, after a pause, "You're not a bear."

"No, I'm a human being, too."

The native nodded. "You are a hunter of ivory?"

"No. I . . . I watch birds. And study sea animals."

He was silent. She wasn't sure if he found her answer perfectly reasonable or preposterous. He was short and sturdily built. His age was indeterminable—anywhere from forty to sixty. He did not appear threatening, but he had not moved away from the cave mouth.

"There aren't any birds in the cave," he said. "And no sea animals, either."

"No, there aren't." Kathy become bolder, encouraged by the ironic humor in the Eskimo's words. "But there's a great deal of walrus ivory. It's yours, isn't it? I've seen you before. I saw you in your boat on the river."

"I didn't expect anyone to see me." The Eskimo nodded appreciatively. "I remember passing your camp, and once, you were there beside the river with your dog. You are a good watcher."

"Your boat was very full each time you came this way."

He nodded again. "There are many dead to make so much ivory."

Kathy was appalled. "You killed them all?"

"My people don't kill that way." For the first time the native's voice roughened with anger. "That is the gussak's way."

"The gussak?" White man, she thought. "I don't understand. If you didn't kill for the ivory, how did you get it?"

Instead of answering, the Eskimo slid down into the cave, bringing with him a small avalanche of snow. Kathy could smell the snow and vague smells of fur and leather and sweat from the man who now confronted her. Survivor scurried after him, gave Kathy a perfunctory greeting, and eagerly turned his attention back to the stranger, who took off one mitten to scrub the husky's head.

"So much ivory has to be illegal. Where did it come from?" Kathy asked quietly. "Do you know?"

"Yes." The Eskimo's expression became brooding as he peered toward the small fortune in walrus tusks in the back of the cave. More comfortable now, he said, "I am John Mulak. I come from a village on another river, a half day's boat ride to the south."

Kathy speculated over what lay behind the Eskimo's somber mood. Poachers, she thought with a spurt of anger. But how had the old man come into possession of this bloody harvest? My goodness, he must have stolen it!

She studied the bruises on his face, the puffy mouth. He had also winced when he took off his mitten, favoring his left hand. He had been beaten. Her anger deepened.

"Are these gussaks searching for you?" Kathy asked.

"They have been hunting me, and they are close. But they didn't see me on this river. And there are no tracks now, only snow."

No tracks, she thought. "How long have you been here?"

"I came before the snow stopped. You were sleeping." He spoke with simple dignity, as if the answer were self-evident.

"Are you hungry, Mr. Mulak? I have a little food."

He smiled. The suggestion was one an Eskimo might have made. Instant hospitality to strangers was a tradition among the people. "I have not eaten. I left my village in a hurry."

She had eaten most of her raisins and nuts the previous day, but she still had a can of Spam and some water crackers. She dumped the contents of the can onto the metal plate she carried in her pack, and opened the crackers. "We'll have to share," she said.

"Of course." Mulak beamed.

When the Spam was gone, and most of the crackers and the last of her chocolate bars—which she also shared—she said to him, "Tell me what happened to you. Tell me about the ivory."

Expressing his thoughts carefully, he told her about the great hunt, occasionally lapsing into brooding silence. This was personal and painful, she learned. "The walruses were in a protected place near the edge of the sea. The hunters, who included my son, Billy, came in their boats and found them sleeping. There was one very old walrus among them who is famous among my people. He's called Muugli, the Great One. He has the largest tusks any of us has ever seen. The hunters were all excited about seeing Muugli."

Mulak was silent so long Kathy thought he wasn't going to finish the story. Then he said softly, "The white men brought guns that shoot many bullets very fast. They sought to kill the entire herd of walruses. There was much ivory taken—all you see here. But they had offended the sea from which the walruses come, and a storm came. The hunters had to leave the ivory behind.

"The storm went on for many days. When the rains stopped, I was the first to leave the village. I wasn't looking for the walruses or the ivory, but I found them. The killing was done without respect. I saw all these tusks, and I became very angry. I thought there should be no reward for such killing. So I became a thief."

"You took it . . . alone . . . and brought it all here in your boat," Kathy said. The prodigious physical effort involved in what the Eskimo had done strained credulity. How had he done it? But she had seen him on the river. And she had no doubt of his honesty.

"It's not the way of my people to take what isn't ours."

"I know that. But what you did isn't stealing; you did what was right. Slaughtering all those walruses was illegal. These white men are poachers. They can be arrested."

515

Mulak looked at her skeptically.

"Some poachers were caught selling illegal ivory in Nome over a year ago," Kathy went on. "They were brought to trial. That can happen to these men, too. Do they know you took it?"

"I think so. That's why they locked me up."

Kathy McNeely's outrage was growing by the minute. "They locked you up? How did you escape?"

For the first time Mulak seemed puzzled. "Someone broke the lock. I think it could only have been my son." The pride in the old man's voice was restrained by anguish. "The gussaks have given him whiskey and drugs to hunt for them. They have changed him. But perhaps he could not accept that his father would be put in a cage. They are searching for me now."

"Listen to me, Mr. Mulak. These men have broken the law. We can have them arrested. They won't be able to touch you."

Mulak studied Kathy. "This may not be easy," he said. "When the snow came yesterday, I passed your camp. I was coming to the cave. I heard the airplane behind me, and I hid to watch. The airplane landed on the river near your camp. The pilot is very good."

"What!"

"I believe they are staying there until it is safe to fly again. I don't think they were following me. I believe they landed because of the storm. The airplanes don't come to our village when it snows. It's dangerous for them." He paused, observing her consternation. Then he added simply, "So you see, it may not be easy to arrest these gussaks. And my son is with them."

Mulak glanced around the cavern, and as he did so, his expression changed slightly. Kathy thought of someone in a church gazing at an altar. "This is a very old cave," John Mulak said. "I have known it since I was young, but the bears have known it much longer."

"Grizzlies?"

"Yes. That's your gussak name for them."

"This bear's cave is about to become a famous place, once I get through to my people and tell them what's here."

"You must be careful," Mulak said. "These are bad men."

"There's no way they could guess I know anything about the ivory unless they can track me back to this cave after I leave."

"There will be no tracks," the Eskimo promised. "It is snowing

516

again. It is light, but it will fill your footsteps quickly, and mine, long before you reach your camp."

"What about you?" she said, worrying. "I'll contact my people by radio as soon as the men leave my camp, and they'll get in touch with the authorities. But you won't really be safe until the government steps in. Will you stay here, Mr. Mulak, where you'll be safe? I'll come back as soon as I can."

He was silent for a time, weighing her arguments. When he spoke, he said, "I'll meet you here in the bear's cave. But first I have to go to my village. I must know that nothing has been done that's harmful to my daughter and my son. I don't want to bring them harm through what I've done."

"You can't go there!" Kathy protested. "Someone is sure to tell the poachers. And you said your son is with them. He—" She broke off, seeing the pain in his eyes.

"They forced him to go with them," Mulak said stubbornly. "But he helped me get away. Why would he betray me now?"

"If the weather clears, they'll be up in the air again, searching. They'll see you before you can reach your village."

"This is my country," the Eskimo said, "my home. It has many paths. There is a fork in this river where it meets another, smaller river. That river will take me to a place from where I can walk to my own house. I will come there when it's dark."

Kathy saw that nothing she could say would dissuade Mulak. "Can you meet me here by tomorrow night?" she asked anxiously.

"I will come to the cave."

"Then we have a deal, Mr. Mulak. And some nasty men are going to be in for a nasty surprise."

THE weather cleared before noon, and Jeff Rorie began preparations for taking off. It was going to be chancy—there was ice floating in the river—but Rorie thought there was enough open water to get airborne.

He had spent the night in the aircraft with the heater on—more to keep his plane's engine warm and to prevent its oil from freezing than for his own comfort. Simpson and Billy Mulak had shared one of the empty tents in the camp, Mayberry taking the other.

The camp did not appear to have been abandoned—there was

food in sealed animal-proof lockers, along with clothing and the usual camp gear. They had been speculating all evening about the whereabouts of the campers: two people—a man and a woman. Who were they? What had they been doing here?

Now eager to be under way before the Arctic weather took another of its capricious turns, Rorie removed the wing covers he had put on the night before.

"Hey, what have we got here?" Wolf Simpson called out.

Rorie followed his gaze. A figure in a red parka had appeared around a bend about a quarter mile upriver, trudging through the six-inch layer of powder snow that covered the tundra. A large husky trotted alongside.

"It's a woman!" Simpson exclaimed.

She had seen them and waved.

As the pair neared the camp, the dog bounded ahead. Simpson backed off, as if he confronted a known enemy. The dog was instantly wary, slowing to a stiff-legged pace, his ears pricked. A low rumble started in his throat.

Reaching the camp just behind the dog, the woman took hold of his collar. "He wasn't expecting strangers." She offered an apologetic smile. "I hope you helped yourself to anything you needed. I was caught by the storm and couldn't get back."

She was cool and relaxed, Jeff Rorie thought. A slender, attractive woman, thirtysomething. He wondered why, beneath her surface composure, he sensed a thread of tension.

"I'm Travis Mayberry," Mayberry said genially, approaching her. "This is my associate, Mr. Simpson, and that's our pilot, Mr. Rorie. We had to set down in the river last night when all that snow blew in. I hope you don't mind. We took advantage of your tents."

"No, of course not. I'm Dr. Kathleen McNeely. I'm with a scientific expedition called ASSET. We're doing an environmental impact study here in Alaska. . . . It's a long story."

Mayberry glanced at the two yellow tents. "You're alone?"

She smiled. "At the moment. My colleague was injured and was flown out yesterday." She hesitated. "Some other people from ASSET will be coming down from our base camp today."

She's afraid of us, Rorie thought. She knows something. The perception confirmed his hunch that the woman had not been surprised to find strangers here. But how could she have known? Rorie himself had not known where he was going to land.

"Do you mind my asking what you're doing here, Mr. Mayberry?" The scientist sounded naturally curious.

"We're looking for a renegade Eskimo," Mayberry said. "He stole some valuables from a village south of here, and the Native Council asked us to look for him. You happen to see anyone?"

She glanced curiously at Billy Mulak. The young Eskimo seemed mesmerized by her. She shook her head. "No. Dr. Cobb and I hadn't seen another human face for weeks until yesterday when the plane arrived to fly him out."

"He might be dangerous," Mayberry said. "He's an ivory poacher."

"I assure you, if I run into any ivory poachers, I'll notify the authorities immediately."

"That might not be such a good idea," Wolf Simpson said.

Mayberry cut in. "What Mr. Simpson means is, this Eskimo is on the run and you shouldn't give him any reason to be afraid of you." He smiled easily. "I bet you're hungry."

"I'm starved!" Kathy said. "I hope you had something."

"We helped ourselves to some hash for breakfast."

"I can do better than hash if you've time to stay for lunch."

"I don't know. I think our pilot wants to get in the air."

Jeff Rorie had come over to the big husky, who had relaxed somewhat as his mistress talked amiably with the strangers. The dog sniffed Rorie's boots and, as Rorie squatted beside him, nosed and pushed against his offered hand.

When the woman mentioned bacon and powdered eggs and canned tomatoes, Mayberry decided they would stay for lunch. Rorie put the wing covers back on the Cessna, even though he hoped to be leaving within the hour. Although the snow flurries had let up, the temperature was well below freezing.

From the aircraft, he watched the others at the camp: Billy staring covertly at the woman while she went about her meal preparations with economy and efficiency; Simpson hanging back with an uneasy eye on the husky; Mayberry talking to Dr. McNeely, asking her about her work along the river. It was an unremarkable scene, but something about it didn't ring true. Dr. McNeely knows something, Rorie thought again. It bothered him that Mayberry

519

might have had the same perception. Otherwise, why had he stayed for a meal when he had been so anxious to leave an hour ago?

Rorie wished he could have a chance to talk to Dr. McNeely. She might not understand the kind of men she was dealing with.

The opportunity came unexpectedly after they had finished their bacon, eggs, and fried tomatoes and were preparing to leave. Simpson and Billy Mulak had boarded the Cessna, and Mayberry was standing by to cast off the last of the tie-down lines. Rorie walked back to the campsite and squatted beside the husky to say good-bye. As he patted the dog, he murmured, "I wouldn't stay here long, ma'am—not alone."

"I'm sure you mean well, Mr. Rorie," Kathy said. Then she added coolly, "Your friends are waiting for you."

Rorie stood up and smiled. "You take care of yourself, ma'am," he said, loud enough for Mayberry to hear him.

He went back to the plane. Mayberry climbed aboard, and Rorie taxied out into the river and turned into the wind. He picked up speed until the aircraft was skimming the water, a tail of spray boiling up behind. Then suddenly the river released its grip. They were in the air, lifting, flying free.

KATHY watched the floatplane lift cleanly from the water, feeling sharp relief as she stared after its shrinking silhouette.

Before leaving camp, she had stored the shortwave radio in one of the lockers. She wasn't sure what that bush pilot had been trying to tell her—his words had sounded almost like a warning—but she intended to waste no time alerting the people at the ASSET base.

Her thoughts froze. Her mind went blank.

She stared at the remains of the radio. There would be no immediate rescue, no federal agents scrambling to respond.

The radio had been deliberately, systematically smashed.

TEN

HARRY Madrid stared unseeing from the window of his New York apartment. The little finger of his left hand—the finger that wasn't there—ached the way it sometimes did before rain. He absently touched the small rounded stub.

Two calls from Madam Lu Chang in a month. Her tone increasingly impatient. She wanted confirmation of Harry Madrid's assurances that the huge walrus tusks would soon be in her possession.

Harry couldn't bring himself to tell her that the tusks were missing. Instead, he offered details of the Japanese order for five tons of ivory: sixty percent of the order had already been shipped; the rest was being assembled from his most reliable sources.

"That is excellent, Mr. Madrid," said Madam Chang, who knew all about the Japanese buyers' negotiations. "But I must also have those special tusks. You will inform me as soon as you are certain that they are in a place of safety."

"Yes, yes, of course," Madrid said. "My people are working on it."

The Chinese matriarch paused a moment, then added, "There is another matter I would like to discuss with you, Mr. Madrid. It concerns my youngest son. . . ."

AFTER breaking the telephone connection to America, Madam Lu Chang sat in silence for several minutes smoking a long, thin cigarette. She pressed a button fitted into the arm of her chaise. A white-suited servant appeared instantly. Madam Chang glanced pointedly at her empty champagne flute; then she asked that her youngest son be summoned. She waited while she sipped the champagne that had hastily been poured into her glass.

Deng Chang appeared at her side. "Honorable mother."

"I have spoken to the American, Harry Madrid. The splendid tusks you brought to my attention have become increasingly valuable. You did well."

Deng said nothing, waiting, his manner subdued.

"I believe there may be a problem with the tusks, however. Mr. Madrid sounds anxious. After assuring me that the old walrus had been hunted down and killed, he is now being evasive."

"He wouldn't lie. He wouldn't dare risk your anger."

"Perhaps not," said Madam Chang. "But I think it is time, my son, for you to go to America."

Deng Chang nodded, as if the startling decision had been expected. He was maturing, his mother thought, watching him. Except for a barely noticeable flicker in his eyes, there was no sign of his reaction to say whether he was dismayed or elated.

"I have another reason for sending you. The time may have come for us to consider a different arrangement with Mr. Madrid. You will be my eyes and ears. You will tell me what I need to know."

HARRY Madrid, when he spoke to Travis Mayberry on the phone, was in no mood to hear excuses. "I've been talking to my people in Hong Kong," he said. "They want to know whether there's a problem delivering the goods I promised."

"I'd call it a temporary hitch," Mayberry said, "not a problem."

"I see. Does that mean you've found the goods?"

"Well, not exactly. . . . But we'll get the ivory. It's just taking a little longer than I thought."

"I don't like using that word over the phone."

"Yeah, well, I guess you want that other order—the one that's been in storage."

"That would be nice. When can I expect it?"

"It'll go out this week."

That was as explicit as Mayberry could be. He had various sources for shipping illegal goods out of Alaska. Some, labeled as office supplies, went through the U.S. post office with the help of a cooperative postmaster at Clark's Crossing, a small town on the Yukon. Even federal agents could not tamper with the U.S. mail. The bulk of the shipment would go by airfreight through Fairbanks, where another man on Mayberry's payroll worked as a freight handler.

"I guess that'll have to do," Harry Madrid said to him. "But I need those oversized pieces also—and as soon as possible."

"Yeah, I know." Muugli, Mayberry thought. "We're looking."

"Find them," Madrid said, "or I'll find someone who can."

The threat evaporated from Harry's mind as soon as he broke the connection; he was thinking of the second reason for Madam Lu Chang's latest phone call. Why was she sending Deng to America? Harry remembered the slick, arrogant young man, in his American Dockers, whom he had met in Taipei. Harry's street smarts made him wary. He didn't want Deng Chang looking over his shoulder. Maybe Deng was the heir apparent in the Chang dynasty, but he wasn't going to take over Harry Madrid's life and times. Not now.

The game wasn't being played out in the Taiwan Strait this time. It was in Harry's ballpark.

THE MORNING AFTER RETURNING with Mayberry and Simpson to that bleak outpost on the edge of the Bering Sea, Jeff Rorie left Nome. Mayberry wasn't too happy about it, but Rorie had told him of a charter he couldn't get out of. It would only be for a couple of days. In fact, he could be back the second night.

After Rorie left, Simpson went to Mayberry's office. Mayberry had been dourly uncommunicative since talking to Harry Madrid shortly after returning to Nome.

"What'd Madrid have to say this time?" Simpson asked.

"The same. He wants ivory."

"Yeah, well, we got our hands on the best haul in two years—"

"And we lost it," Mayberry interrupted curtly.

"We'll get it back. I tell you what's bothering me more than that ivory," he said. "It's this hotshot pilot. I don't like him. There's something wrong about him. I want to check him out, Trav."

"Yeah, sure. But I need you to follow through with those Eskimos first. Find that old man. I've got to do some of my own flying."

"You're going up to the cabin?"

"That's right."

The storage room in the back of the saloon held only a small quantity of Mayberry's poached goods. For security the bulk of the raw ivory was stored at an isolated mountain cabin in the appropriately named Raw Mountains, north of the Yukon River and northeast of Clark's Crossing. The cabin stood at the edge of deep woods, overlooking a small lake—the only place Mayberry would land his plane since his accident. In the summer Mayberry's plane, a Piper Super Cub, was fitted with floats. When the lake froze and there was snow cover, he switched to skis.

"Madrid has this big order from some Japanese buyers, and the Chinese are breathing down his neck to get it filled. We've got nearly two hundred tusks in the hideout. I'll have to ferry 'em out myself and get 'em shipped. It'll take me at least three trips. That'll have to hold Madrid until we find the other tusks."

"You're not going to wait until Rorie gets back?"

Mayberry stared at him. "Nobody knows about that cabin except for you and me and those two brain surgeons I have baby-sitting it, unless I want him to know."

Simpson had no comment. The two baby-sitters were Phil Tor-

rance and Lester Paley, who had been under investigation by the
Fish and Wildlife Service a year ago for poaching activities but had
slipped through the legal net. Since Mayberry needed someone to
guard the storage cabin anyway, he had sent Torrance and Paley up
there to keep them out of the way until the feds forgot about them.

"Look, Trav, let me check Rorie out," Simpson argued. "I can't
do anything until he comes back anyway. So let me tag along after
him and see if he's what he says he is."

Mayberry swiveled around in his chair toward the gray sea. "You've
got two days," he said. "It'll take me that long to move the stuff. When
Rorie gets back, you and him go back to the Eskimo village, find the
old man's son, and use him. You know what he likes. Let him see a
nice fat packet of the white stuff. Let all those natives know there's
something extra for them if we find those tusks."

SIMPSON caught a scheduled Alaska Airlines flight out of Nome
for Anchorage, departing at eleven that morning.

Rorie's flight was booked by Far Eyes Charter Tours at Anchorage's Lake Hood, home of the world's largest floatplane airport.

Simpson rented a Ford Escort and, after booking a hotel room
downtown, drove out to Lake Hood.

It was a bright autumn day in Anchorage, with the temperature
just at freezing. The storm that had battered the northern coast,
blocked by the towering Alaska Range, had not reached this far
south. The snow-covered mountains ringing the city to the north,
east, and west stood in sharp relief against a brilliant blue sky,
except for majestic Mount McKinley, whose upper reaches were
lost in clouds.

The floatplane airport was a jumble of small hangars, fuel-storage
tanks, Quonset huts, and offices, including those for a number of
charter services. Simpson found a pay phone and called Far Eyes. A
woman answered. He asked for Jeff Rorie.

"Mr. Rorie is due in at any time. Can I help you?"

"I was thinkin' of booking a plane, and I was wondering if Rorie's
available the next few days. A friend of mine recommended him."

"I'm sorry. He's booked for tomorrow, and he's also been hired
on an independent long-term contract. We have several other fine
pilots available. What kind of trip were you thinking about?"

"It's not set yet," he said. "I just wanted to find out about Rorie."

Simpson checked the area out, looking for a place to observe activity without being noticed. He found it in the parking lot of a used-plane outlet across the lake from the Far Eyes office.

When Rorie's Cessna landed, Simpson watched the pilot go into the charter office. An hour later he saw Rorie emerge from the Far Eyes office and climb into a red Ford pickup behind the building.

He expected the pilot to head north on Glenn Highway toward Fortune, the small town Rorie had given Mayberry as an address. Instead, to Simpson's surprise, Rorie drove to a small motel on the outskirts of town. There the pilot booked a room, had dinner at a nearby coffee shop, and walked to a bar for a beer. Then he returned to his motel. The television set flickered inside.

Simpson spent a restless night in his hotel room fretting over the possibility that Rorie might leave during the night. Up at dawn, he sat for over an hour outside Rorie's motel before the pilot checked out and drove back to the Far Eyes office. Simpson followed.

Rorie's charter passengers were already there and waiting. They were a couple of jovial, hearty types, loaded down with gear. Simpson could hear their laughter drifting across the lake in the early morning stillness while they helped Rorie load the Cessna. A half hour after Rorie's arrival his aircraft took off and turned north.

Simpson knew he should return to Nome. He had found nothing about Rorie that didn't ring true. But he still wasn't satisfied.

After asking questions about Rorie all over town, Simpson found a bar amidst the clutter of buildings at the floatplane airport. It was called The Bush League. It smelled of stale beer and cigarettes. A half-dozen men sat drinking on stools, and a television set was suspended over one end of the bar, next to a mounted moose head. Simpson slipped onto a stool and ordered a Beck's.

He wasn't sure exactly why he had stopped at The Bush League, except that in his gut he knew he was right about Rorie.

He was nursing his third beer, thinking about leaving, when the man on the stool beside him, a pilot, said, "What're you flyin'?"

"Huh? Oh, I'm not a pilot. I was just here lookin' for a guy. Jeff Rorie. You know him?"

The man frowned in concentration. "Yeah, I remember Rorie. New guy. Worked for Far Eyes this summer."

"That's right," Simpson said. "And last year he was up at Prudhoe Bay with Les Hargrove, flying people around for ARCO."

The pilot stared at him. "What'd you say about Les?"

"You know Hargrove?"

"Heck, yes. We've flown together a thousand times."

Simpson felt a nibble of excitement. "Buy you a beer?" he asked.

The pilot didn't mind if he did have another. After some small talk Simpson said, "What were you saying about Hargrove?"

"It wasn't what *I* said, it was what *you* said—about Les flying with this guy Rorie up at Prudhoe Bay. Les was one old-time sourdough who hated the pipeline. He wouldn't have been caught dead flyin' for ARCO or the Trans-Alaska or for British Petroleum or anyone else had anythin' to do with it."

Wolf Simpson heard. After a moment's careful thought he murmured, "So why did Hargrove take off for California?"

The pilot shrugged. "You're in this business, you do a little finaglin' here and there. Maybe Les did; maybe he didn't. But my guess is, somebody got to him. He didn't leave Alaska because he wanted to—not someone like Les. He left because he had no choice."

Simpson sat very still, a smile growing on his face. "Bingo!" he whispered to himself. He had been right all along. Jeff Rorie had lied about working with Hargrove. He was a plant.

And unless something was done about him, Simpson and Mayberry were in trouble.

THE two tourists sat in the back during takeoff and stayed there while Rorie headed north toward Fort Yukon. The noise inside the cabin during the climb precluded easy conversation. A half hour out of Anchorage, Bob LoBianco, one of the passengers, clambered into the seat beside the pilot. "How's it going, partner?" he asked.

"So far, so good," Rorie said. He grinned, relaxing. It felt strange to let down his guard. He was so deep into his cover it was unsettling to surface, however briefly.

Like Rorie, his two passengers were Fish and Wildlife Service agents. Everett Sanderson was tall, wide-hipped, and heavy without being fat, like an NFL linebacker. His light brown hair was an inch-long brush cut. His habitual walk was an amble, and he spoke at the same pace, in a lazy South Carolina drawl. Bob LoBianco was wiry, compact—a volatile Italian with the sound of Brooklyn in every word. He had thick, wavy black hair, and eyebrows that met to form a ridge above his dark brown eyes.

Rorie knew the risks involved in working undercover for a prolonged period. There was always the chance of slipping up in some small way. For this reason, like most undercover agents, he said as little about himself as possible. His current role, built up over the past year, was that of an easygoing live-for-today bush pilot who, if he wasn't actually bent, had a careless attitude about activities that were either openly illegal or skirted around the edges of the law. He was certain that Mayberry had bought the story.

"What about this search for the ivory? How do you figure in on that?" Sanderson was concerned about the narrow line between allowing a criminal to commit his crime and entrapment.

"I'm just the pilot," Rorie said. "I don't tell them what to do."

Rorie was not an undercover agent by choice. His superiors had simply discovered that he was good at it. There was something believable about him. The people he became involved with tended to trust him—even those whose business made them inherently cautious.

"What's your line on Mayberry?" Sanderson asked.

"You went fishing with him or met him over drinks in a bar, you'd get along with him fine," Rorie said. "Simpson's a slimeball, but Mayberry you could almost like."

"Don't start liking him too much," LoBianco growled. "He's dealing grass and worse to the Eskimos for ivory."

"There's something you should know, Jeff," Sanderson said. "We've turned up a haul of bear hides and raw ivory at a Fort Yukon trading post. Not just a couple of tusks somebody had in a closet, but twenty-six pairs of high-quality walrus tusks and about a dozen polar bear skins. They just walked in out of the cold."

The owner of the trading post had purchased the bonanza from a man who was so anxious to sell he took a lowball offer, Sanderson explained. Afterward the buyer realized that he was almost certainly dealing with illegal goods. Worried about keeping his license, he contacted a Fish and Wildlife Service agent in Fairbanks.

Rorie thought it over. What Sanderson described sounded like the product of large-scale poaching. Rorie didn't think that could be going on in Alaska without Travis Mayberry's knowledge or involvement. Then he remembered Mayberry's need to make special trips in his own plane.

"I think Mayberry must have a secret cache," Rorie said. "If he's the main source of Alaskan ivory for major dealers like Harry Madrid or for the big Chinese cartels, then he has to have a lot more of it than what he keeps in that back room of his."

"That ties in," Sanderson said. "One of our agents showed the trader in Fort Yukon some mug shots. He nailed one—Lester Paley, a minor player on Mayberry's team—right away. There was another guy with him when he sold the ivory. We don't have an I.D., but Paley used to hang with another creep, named Phil Torrance. Both did some poaching for Mayberry and dropped out of sight after our sting operations last year."

"So what's going on?" Rorie wondered.

"Mayberry's dumping inventory," LoBianco suggested.

Rorie shook his head. "No. He needs everything he can put his hands on. I don't have all the details, but he's got a big order to fill. He wouldn't be unloading tusks at a low price in Fort Yukon."

"They're freelancing," LoBianco ventured. "If what you say is right—about Mayberry having a big shipment to get together—these punks have to be selling without him knowing."

"If we can pick them up before they leave Alaska," Sanderson speculated, "we have a link to Mayberry that'll hold up in court. But finding them won't be easy. If they've hijacked Mayberry's cache, you know they're going to try to get lost in a hurry—not because of us, but because of Mayberry."

"Yeah," LoBianco said with a wry smile, "Mayberry finds 'em, they could disappear for good."

"This could play into our hands," Sanderson drawled. "From what you've heard, Jeff, Mayberry needs a lot of ivory. He's had this big harvest stolen there on the coast. Now he'll find out he's been ripped off a second time by his own people. That will make this missing ivory you've been hunting even more important."

"The Eskimos will feel the heat," Rorie said. "Especially the old man who got away from them."

"You really think the old Eskimo stole that haul?"

"It's a good bet." Rorie had been as impressed with John Mulak's quiet dignity as he had been disgusted by the son's betrayal.

"Maybe the old guy wants to sell it himself," LoBianco suggested.

"No." Rorie was emphatic. "He took it so Mayberry couldn't have it. Because that kind of killing violates everything the Eskimos believe about themselves and nature."

The other two agents regarded him quizzically. And after a silence, Sanderson said, "We want to shut Mayberry down up here, but we want Harry Madrid even more." Sanderson leaned close to be sure he was heard clearly. "We've got a blanket over every possible way Mayberry can ship his stuff out of Alaska. We want to find the hideout, sure, but we'll let Mayberry take what's left. We'll track it wherever it goes. Our guess is a warehouse in New Jersey. If we can follow it there, then maybe we really get lucky."

"What if we find this other harvest—the big one?" Rorie asked.

"Call for backup," Sanderson said, "and we take him down."

Rorie was frowning. There was a rogue factor, an element he hadn't yet figured out. He told the other two agents about the scientist alone at her little camp on the river. He outlined his concerns. Why had Dr. McNeely been so cool to strangers, barely concealing hostility? A woman alone in the wilderness would naturally be cautious, but Rorie sensed there was more to her hostility.

"You think there's any way she could know something about the missing ivory?" LoBianco asked.

"That's what I've been wondering," Rorie said. "And there's only one way."

"What's that?"

"She's met John Mulak."

And if the possibility occurred to him, Rorie thought to himself, it would occur to a frantic, increasingly desperate Travis Mayberry.

THERE was no way of knowing when Mayberry would be back, and Wolf Simpson knew that Mayberry wouldn't be happy on his return if he discovered that Simpson had sat around waiting for him instead of going after the missing ivory. The fact that Simpson had discovered something about Les Hargrove and Jeff Rorie wouldn't cut any ice. That problem could be taken care of after the ivory was found.

For now, Simpson needed Rorie and his plane. The pleasure of dealing with him could wait.

Planning ahead, Simpson knew how to work it: he would leave Nome with Rorie, fly to the Eskimo village to pick up Billy Mulak, and take care of business.

Afterward the pilot wouldn't be coming back.

ELEVEN

THE night John Mulak returned to the village, the temperature plunged below zero with a windchill factor of minus thirty. Although there was no fresh snowfall, driving winds hurled the dry powder into miniature storms of whirling snow. Blinded by the whiteout, Mulak huddled in a nest of rocks northeast of the village.

He had left his kayak on a narrow gravel beach two hours earlier. Head down, he had plodded across the tundra on improvised snowshoes he had fashioned with willow struts. He was less than four miles from the village when the winds forced him to seek cover.

Until now, hunched inside his fur parka and sealskin pants, he had kept warm. His head had been covered not only by a baseball cap but also by the fur-lined hood of his parka. Only part of his face had been exposed. Now, waiting in the nest of rocks, his cheeks felt dangerously cold. A frosting of ice crusted on his eyebrows and clung to his lids. More ice froze in his nostrils, and he had to breathe through his mouth. His puffy lips were cracked from the cold.

He did not let himself think about his warm house, now so close that, through gaps in the whirling snow, he imagined he could see a halo of light over the village. He knew that such visions could be false in whiteout conditions, like a mirage in the desert.

Sometime later he sprang to his feet in alarm, realizing he had dozed. His cheeks were numb. He could rest no longer; he had to keep moving. If he slept again, there would be no awakening.

WHEN she saw her father in the doorway, Ruth burst into tears. Quickly she pulled him inside and closed the door. He moved stiff-legged, with his arms away from his body.

One look at his blue cheeks told her that he had frostbite. She heated a pan of water and began to bathe her father's face. Mulak flinched, but did not pull away. He was still bundled inside his fur parka and sealskin pants, and he was still shivering.

The ice that had clogged his nostrils and rimmed his eyes melted quickly in the warmth of the house. Water ran down his face.

All this time he had not spoken.

Ruth retreated to the kitchen, where she began to heat some leftover stew. By the time it was ready, Mulak had stopped shivering. He took off his parka and sat at the table. His hands trembled, and his fingers seemed thick and clumsy. He ate slowly, chewing each mouthful of stew methodically. Ruth cringed when she saw how badly his lips were swollen and cracked.

She watched him in silence, her heart aching, until he had finished eating. Only then did she trust herself to speak. "The gussaks have left the village."

"They will be back."

Tears returned as she studied him. Where had he been? What had he been doing? How far had he come on this cold night?

"You can't stay here," she said. "They'll look for you here when they come back."

"Where's Billy?"

"He . . . he's with some of his friends. He doesn't sleep here in his family's house. I think he's ashamed."

"He shouldn't be ashamed. He helped me to get away."

Ruth looked at him, puzzled. "You're sure it was Billy?"

"Who else would have tried to free me?"

"I don't know, but . . ." Her next words came reluctantly. "Billy went with the gussaks to find you. He was helping them."

John Mulak considered this and nodded with understanding. "He could do nothing else. They would have punished him."

Mulak did not tell his daughter where he had been or about the white woman he had met or anything about the ivory he had stolen. It was better for her not to know.

In the comfortable warmth of the house his fatigue began to crush him. He would rest for a while. The white men would not return tonight. Later he would talk to his son—

The old man and Ruth heard the footsteps outside at the same time. Running steps, thudding on the porch. They both looked toward the front door, Ruth's expression suddenly anxious. The door burst inward, and Billy Mulak appeared in the doorway, dusted with snow. The bitter cold blew into the room with him.

531

"Pop! Someone said they saw you. I couldn't believe it!" Billy glanced back over his shoulder. He closed the door quickly, afraid someone might have followed him. "The white men know you took the ivory. If they find you . . . I don't know what they'll do."

"How can they know it was me?"

"There's no one else." Agitated, Billy began to pace the room. "Why did you run away? You can't keep hiding from them."

"Then why did you break the lock on the cabin?"

Billy's face registered incredulity. "I didn't break the lock; I thought you did it yourself." He dismissed the puzzle. His arms flailed the air, his movements were jerky, and his eyes darted about. "You've got to tell them where the ivory is, Pop, don't you see that? Or tell *me* where it is so I can take them to it."

John Mulak felt many things in that moment. Confusion, disappointment, sadness, dismay, as Billy's words sank in. Billy hadn't helped him escape. Then who? He had no answer.

Billy had told the gussaks where they might find him. Billy knew that he fished in that river, that he went there often. That was why the airplane had flown over the river not far from the cave, why it had come so close to discovering him.

Ruth saw the understanding in her father's eyes and the grief it awakened. Her anger erupted at Billy. "What did they promise you to betray your father? Tell us that!"

Billy became sullen. "You know nothing about such things."

"I know about loving my father," Ruth retorted scornfully. "I know enough to see how much it hurts him when he sees that his son would sell him for the white men's drugs."

Billy glared at his father. "What am I supposed to feel when my father is a thief? That ivory was *ours!* It wasn't yours to take."

"No," John Mulak said heavily. "You've become more white than brown. You no longer think like an Eskimo."

"If you mean I think there's more to life than seal blubber and berries, you're right." Billy's words turned bitter. "The white men have everything. We have nothing. We would still be living in mud huts if not for the gussaks."

"We have ourselves. We have a good life," his father said. "The white men I've met are not happier than Eskimos. You won't be happy trying to be one of them—trying to be something you're not."

"I know the truth," Billy said. "This isn't about me at all. It's about you. You wanted Muugli's tusks for yourself."

"Billy!"

Wearily, John Mulak waved away Ruth's protest. "Go," he said to his son. "Go to your white men. Tell them they'll never find the ivory—not even with you helping them. And tell them their bullets will never kill Muugli. He's not dead. He is part of our lives; he belongs to the people."

The old man turned away. He did not look up when Billy stormed out of the house.

In that moment her father's slumped figure seemed smaller, frailer, and Ruth had a frightening vision of the house without him. She shivered, hugging her chest with her arms.

"You must get some rest, Papa," she said softly. "I'll have some food ready for you to take when you go. But you must be gone in the morning, before the gussaks come back." Ruth had a sudden inspiration. "You can take the sno-go. There's enough snow on the ground." The snow machine was one marvel of the white man's world that had been enthusiastically adopted by the Eskimos. A hundred-mile journey across the frozen tundra could be completed in less than one day in good conditions. "You could get far away."

John Mulak's puffy smile was heavy with irony. "No," he said. "Billy is right about me. I will go my own way. The Eskimo way."

THAT same night, in the river bottom, where the two yellow tents stood out sharply against an endless sea of white, was the coldest Kathy McNeely had experienced north of the Arctic Circle. The Coleman stove struggled, winds tore at her tent, and the flapping and keening kept her awake. She could not get warm.

The darkness and cold and, especially, the fierce winds transported her in her thoughts to Antarctica—and Brian Hurley.

Seasons in Antarctica were the opposite of those in the Arctic. Where winter was setting in for her, Hurley was now experiencing spring on the ice. His dogsled run was planned with the goal of reaching the South Pole before Christmas.

He would be there now, she thought. Too busy to send a radio message. She'd had no word from him the past two months, not even while she had had a working radio. Lying alone in her tent, she felt impossibly remote from Hurley. The feeling unnerved her.

She heard the wind scouring the snow-covered tundra, prowling outside her tent like a malicious force, every sound magnified. She found herself lying rigid, listening tensely. Something rustled just outside. But Survivor slept there, having dug out his own shelter in the snow. He would sense another animal's presence.

Stupid to start feeling vulnerable because she was alone. No comforting male presence in the next tent or in her bed. No Jason Cobb to challenge her. No Brian Hurley lying beside her.

And no radio.

Kathy was uncertain why Mayberry had felt the need to isolate and silence her, unless he had guessed that she might somehow have linked up with John Mulak. Or maybe the poacher was simply a careful man, leaving nothing to chance. Either way, he would be back, and she didn't want to be here when he came.

She thought of the old Eskimo. In less than twenty-four hours Mulak would be returning to the cave where the ivory was hidden, relying on her promise to meet him there, her confident assurance that she would notify federal agents of the stolen ivory and Mulak's dangerous situation—a promise she could no longer keep.

She would wait at camp until noon, she thought, on the chance the ASSET plane would arrive. No later. If it didn't come, she would go to join Mulak, and . . .

She didn't really have a plan two.

IN THE morning it was still fiercely cold, Kathy's thermometer registering twelve degrees below, but the winds had died. In their place was a dense fog that obliterated the mountains to the north.

Kathy waited through the morning, increasingly ill at ease. No cavalry arrived. If the fog persisted, no plane would come.

At noon she heated a can of chicken chili and tried to think of a plan two. By this time her ASSET colleagues would be concerned over their inability to establish radio contact. She knew that the supply plane would be dispatched with a rescue team as soon as it returned to the base camp. Even if the plane were grounded somewhere by bad weather, or delayed by other demands on its services, the ASSET group had a large, sturdy Kodiak rubber boat that had proved itself in Alaska's rivers. By air the downriver trip was a short two-hour flight. By boat, however, with floating ice escalating the normal hazards of river travel, it would be a journey of several days.

She couldn't count on an early rescue. She would have to work something out with John Mulak. The old Eskimo knew the land, the rivers, the wilderness. He also had his kayak, roomy enough for two people. But it would also make the two of them visible from the air if the poachers returned. Their pilot, Rorie, seemed more than competent for such a search.

Kathy frowned as she thought of Rorie. Something about him was missing. What was he? Simply a man who sold his services, no questions asked? Something tugged at her memory. She couldn't quite pin it down. What had the pilot said just before he left? *I wouldn't stay here long, ma'am—not alone.* In retrospect the words sounded even more clearly like a warning.

After lunch she cleaned up, packing everything away that she couldn't easily carry, and filling her backpack with lightweight foods—dried fruits and nuts, freeze-dried eggs, M&M's, oatmeal, crackers, cocoa. She added such necessities as a flashlight, change of socks, her folded tent, and sleeping bag. It made a bulky but manageable pack. Survivor, who had been watching the preparations, pranced around her eagerly. He was a traveler. Ready to go.

She started east toward the cave, following the general course of the river while picking her way across the tundra. In a way, she was grateful for the fog. It was thick enough to make her invisible from anything but a low-flying plane passing directly overhead.

Ten yards ahead of her, Survivor suddenly stopped at full alert. He stared off to the left. Following the direction of his stance, which was like a hunting dog's point, she felt her heart thump.

On a rise to her left, some forty yards away, was the gray-white female wolf. She stood immobile, while her pack of adolescent pups milled about her. One of them, the largest male, was already almost as big as his mother.

Kathy's heart beat faster. Even that gangling youngster was about Survivor's size. She could hear the pups yipping, but their mother continued to stand motionless, looking toward the intruders.

"Easy, Survivor," Kathy murmured. She reached the dog's side and seized his leather collar. She could feel the tension in his neck, the faint quivering in his powerful body. They walked on.

Her mittens were stiff with cold, allowing minimal sensation, but she became aware of something—a wedge of paper dislodged by her grip and working loose from under Survivor's collar. She plucked it out and stuffed it into her pocket, her attention on the wolves.

They were following a little behind, keeping to the higher ground. Sometimes Kathy would glance back and find they had disappeared from view, but as soon as she began to relax, they were back. She wondered what she would do if they came closer.

Odd, that piece of paper. How had it got caught under Survivor's collar? She realized suddenly why it hadn't worked loose earlier: it had been *stuck* there. A piece of gum now adhered to the tip of her mitten. She wanted to stop and dig out the wedge of folded paper, but the urge wasn't strong enough to override her nervousness over the following wolf pack. These wolves were not running or hiding from a human threat, but following.

Stalking?

Kathy shivered. Her skin prickled with gooseflesh.

The strange procession continued through the afternoon. The cave was not far from her camp in miles—no more than three or four on the river, though nearly twice that overland. Near the end she was laboring, her backpack a monstrous burden. She felt her legs quivering with strain, but she resisted the urge to stop and rest.

When she finally paused, dismay threatened to overwhelm her. She was convinced she had come far enough. She had thought she would be able to recognize landmarks—the thicket of blueberry bushes near the bend in the river, the profile of the ridge to the west of the cave, the strip of beach where Mulak had drawn up his kayak. But even though the fog had lifted, the snowfall had changed everything. It blurred outlines, altered contours where drifts had piled up, turned the entire landscape into a homogeneous sea of white.

Kathy stared back along the path she had followed and saw the clear trail she had left behind her. She might as well have been sending up signal flares for the poachers to follow!

She wondered how she could have overlooked something so obvious. Her only consolation was that it was already late in the day. By morning, especially if the night winds moved the snow cover around, her tracks would no longer be as obvious.

As Kathy stood there chagrined, her eye was drawn toward a

brow of rock a quarter mile north of the river, at the crest of a rise made smooth by its covering of snow. She hadn't recognized it in passing. Now she did: the overhang was a few steps from the entrance to the invisible cave.

By the time Kathy climbed up to it an hour later, she was near exhaustion. She dragged herself through the mouth of the cave, too tired even to look around for the she-wolf and her brood. Survivor preferred to linger outside, but she lured him in with chocolate, for which the husky had developed a craving almost as great as her own.

There was no sign of John Mulak.

The stack of ivory gleamed as before at the back of the cave.

Kathy ate a cold meal of dried fruits and peanut butter sandwich crackers. Would the old Eskimo come tonight? Had he run into trouble with the poachers at the village? Did he trust what she had told him? And what would she do if he didn't return at all?

She suddenly remembered the wedge of paper that had worked loose from under Survivor's collar. She fumbled in her pocket, unfolded it, and saw a hasty scrawl in pencil on a page torn from a small notepad. She dug out her flashlight, flicked it on, and read the words. "Don't stay in this camp. Not safe. Contact Fish and Wildlife if you know anything about poachers, esp. missing ivory. J.R."

Rorie! It was but a short leap to the conclusion that the pilot of Mayberry's plane was himself an undercover Fish and Wildlife Service agent trying, at considerable risk, to warn her.

While she stared at the note, a long, spine-tingling howl rose in the stillness outside the cave. The cry, deceptively mournful to human ears, rose and fell and became a chorus so close by that it filled the night with its outpouring of sound. Survivor was on his feet, an answering moan in his throat.

Kathy and the husky had indeed been followed to the cave—not by poachers, but by the she-wolf and her pack.

TWELVE

JOHN Mulak read the signs of impending snow in the thick pileup of black clouds over the Chukchi Sea. He wanted to be gone before the snow came. It would hide his trail.

The old Eskimo rose quietly. The house was still; Billy had not returned during the night, and Ruth, exhausted, still slept. Peering outside, Mulak saw thick fog—a welcome sight.

He did not awaken his daughter. Instead, he made a bundle of the food she had fixed for him to take, shrugged into his heavy parka and boots, and prepared to set off. He slipped on his best snowshoes, handcrafted of a willow frame and tough sinew.

A mile from the village, he knew that he was being followed.

Mulak continued inland for another half mile, where he diverted toward a cluster of cranberry bushes near the river. For the next half hour he picked berries until he had enough to justify his morning walk; then he returned to the village.

The storage shed behind his house offered a clear view of the eastern end of the village. From there he saw two men trudge into view, coming from the same direction Mulak had taken. They had not, he knew, been picking berries.

His son no longer cared to pick berries, but he would follow his father, as a hunter stalked his prey.

John Mulak decided he would wait for darkness; Billy would not expect him to travel over the snowbound tundra at night, especially during a storm. And even if Billy anticipated such a move, Mulak was too old a hand at the hunt to be easily tracked in darkness.

"WE'RE grounded," Jeff Rorie had told Simpson curtly that morning, frowning at the fog John Mulak welcomed.

"What's the problem? You're supposed to be the hotshot pilot."

"Good enough to know better. Getting us smashed into a mountain isn't going to get your ivory back."

The fog, frustrating Simpson's plans to get back to the Eskimo village as soon as possible, seemed to threaten his new spirit of agreeability. But after a moment of glowering, the poacher nodded and stalked upstairs to the office over Travis Mayberry's saloon, leaving Rorie to have breakfast in the bar.

The pilot was puzzled by the joviality Simpson had displayed toward him since his return to Nome—because Simpson had put his suspicions to rest? The uncertainty made Rorie uneasy.

After breakfast Rorie went to check on his Cessna. The evening before, he had rented a hangar for the aircraft. The hangar was unheated, but it was sheltered from snow or rain. Standing by its doorway, he could see Mayberry's private hangar. He talked casually with a mechanic who sometimes worked on Mayberry's Piper Super Cub, learning that Mayberry had taken off earlier for the interior, after having the aircraft fitted with skis.

"He give you any idea when he'd be back?" Rorie asked.

The mechanic peered at him. "When he's ready to, I reckon."

Rorie turned away. Mayberry's town, he thought. Rorie wasn't comfortable not knowing where Travis Mayberry was, or about the outcome of his solo expedition to the mountain hideout. The pilot had stayed in Fort Yukon with his fellow Fish and Wildlife Service agents only long enough to learn that one of Mayberry's baby-sitters, Phil Torrance, had been picked up in Anchorage. Since then, nothing. Rorie knew only that he was to stay on top of the search for the missing ivory. If the ivory was found, Rorie was told to act on his own initiative—whatever that meant.

THREE thousand miles away, Harry Madrid alighted from his Mercedes limousine near the entrance to his New York City showroom. He ducked inside. There would be little action today; it was a chilly, forbidding morning. Harry was surprised to see his manager, Paul Kaminski, talking to someone in the gallery. The client, whose back was to Harry, was slender and well dressed, his glossy black hair pulled back into a ponytail. Harry peeled off a glove as he walked toward his private offices at the rear of the building. Just before the customer was cut off from view, the man turned around.

Harry dropped the glove. Reaching for it, he felt as if his stomach were on the cold tile floor with the glove. He covered the trembling of his hands by removing his other glove. The smile on his face as he straightened felt carved in ice. "Mr. Chang, what a pleasant surprise! I wasn't expecting you until the end of the week."

The young Chinese wore a dark gray pin-striped suit, a white silk shirt, and a floral tie. He carried a camel's-hair coat draped over one arm. He looked like some Ivy League playboy, Harry thought.

"It has been a long time, Mr. Madrid. You are looking well." Deng Chang made the compliment sound like an insult.

"Yeah, well, we didn't meet in the best circumstances."

Chang raised an eyebrow. "I trust that what occurred in the past will not be a hindrance to our working together, Mr. Madrid."

Working together! There it was, right out in the open. The heir apparent to the Chang dynasty had come to stay.

Harry was still smiling. "Hey, we've been doing all right by each other, haven't we? I told Madam Chang I could deliver, and I have. We've both done okay."

"As you say," the Chinese agreed. He glanced around. "Your gallery is most impressive."

"Wait'll you see our real operation. I'll show you this afternoon."

HARRY took Deng Chang to The Four Seasons for lunch. The maître d', who knew Harry, found them a good table in the packed grill. Harry pointed out a few celebrities in the room. Chang seemed particularly interested in the model Niki Taylor. When Harry said he would see if he could arrange an introduction, Deng's dark eyes for the first time held a hint of respect.

When they drove over to Madrid's warehouse in New Jersey that afternoon, two bodyguards accompanied Deng Chang. They were burly men—short but powerfully built—and they sat stiffly on the backward-facing middle seats of Harry's limo, their expressionless faces making him uneasy.

Chang didn't trust him, which was okay, Harry decided; the feeling was mutual.

They spent the afternoon at the warehouse. Deng wanted to see everything. He shook his head in world-weary resignation over U.S. environmental laws designed to protect everything from bald eagles to small stream wrigglers. He asked seemingly innocent questions about Harry's sources in Africa and South America, as well as markets in Europe. Madrid smiled, answered politely, and seethed.

The young Chinese dropped his indolent air when they talked about walrus ivory from Alaska. Harry showed Deng the records for the recent large sale to the Japanese buyers, but Deng brushed these aside. "It was I who showed my mother the photograph of the old walrus with the magnificent tusks," he said proudly. "We're delighted that your source was able to find this walrus."

"Yeah," Harry said, resenting Deng even more.

"Do you know when these tusks will be arriving from Alaska?"

"I'm waiting to hear from my man. Should be any day now."

"Any day?" Deng prodded. "You are not in close touch with him?"

"Alaska's a big place. And we have to slip our goods past the federal agents. It is not going to do us any good if the government ends up with those tusks."

"That would be most unfortunate," Deng murmured.

It was at that moment that Harry knew he was going to have to go to the mat with the Chang family. He discovered that he wasn't as scared as he thought he would be. He found himself looking at a thin, cocky young man, with soft hands and a punk's grin, who wouldn't have lasted a week in the old neighborhood. Instead of shaking in his boots, Harry was looking forward to going eyeball to eyeball with Madam Lu Chang's heir apparent.

Harry had a score to settle.

NIKI Taylor was tied up that evening, Harry told Deng Chang regretfully. But one of the other models who worked for the same agency was free as a bird and would be delighted to start out an evening at the "21" Club with a visiting prince of the powerful Chang family of Hong Kong. Harry's limo was at Deng's disposal.

When Chang returned to his hotel, eager to prepare for his date, Harry tried to call Travis Mayberry in Nome. Mayberry wasn't there. Harry left a coded message on the answering machine: The buyer from Hong Kong was becoming impatient. When could Harry say the goods would be delivered?

Mayberry would read the message between the lines: What the devil is going on? Where are Muugli's tusks?

WOLF Simpson played the message back when he saw the red light blinking on Mayberry's answering machine. He knew what Mayberry would say: Forget about fog. Get off your rear end and get down to the Eskimo village and find that ivory!

Simpson went down to the saloon and found Jeff Rorie enjoying a beer. Rorie didn't look enthusiastic about having company, but the new, friendlier Wolf Simpson insisted on buying another round. The fog had thinned out, Simpson said, and they were leaving for the Eskimo village at dawn, weather be damned. Mayberry wouldn't stand for any more foot-dragging.

Rorie didn't comment. He wondered when Mayberry would contact Simpson, surprised that it hadn't happened already.

Over Moosehead beers Simpson shared his plans. Starting early next morning, he'd have the natives scour the coastline for Muugli while he and Rorie hunted down the fugitive old Eskimo. They'd take his kid along. John Mulak had to have his boat: he wasn't going to get far on foot, and the ice spreading through the wetlands near the coast would limit his options. "It's like when you're hunting a wolf," Simpson said eagerly. "Once you find out where his territory is, you can zero in on him. Then you work him into the open, where he doesn't have anyplace to hide. You chase him down, tire him out, close in on him. He'll snarl and show you his teeth, and if you get close enough, you'll see the hate in those bright eyes. But he won't be able to do a damned thing."

Rorie liked it better when Simpson didn't confide in him.

The pilot declined another beer and stepped outside. On Front Street he felt the full force of the wind driving inland from the sea. Great black clouds filled the sky. They appeared ominous, but the weather forecast was for brief snow flurries passing through overnight and clear, cold weather behind them. Good weather for flying, Rorie thought—and for hunting.

MULAK had spent the rest of the day in the village, staying indoors much of the time, offering no visible sign of his concern, which was chiefly directed toward the white woman who was a watcher of birds and sea animals. She would be at the cave to meet him tonight, and he would not be there.

The night was very dark when Mulak slipped from his house by the back door. The wind had quickened, and Mulak could smell snow coming. He thought of it as an old friend. It would hide him in its shroud and fill his footsteps over the tundra.

Ruth, her protests unavailing, watched anxiously until she could no longer see her father's dark shadow in the lee of the shed.

THE fog that lay over the north Alaskan coastline that day had not penetrated to the interior, and even though the sky was overcast, Travis Mayberry had been able to take off immediately after breakfast. Visibility was twenty miles or more, and when he reached the vicinity of his mountain cabin, the first inkling he had that something was wrong was the absence of smoke.

In the clear Arctic air, even on a cloudy day, the stain of woodsmoke spreading against the sky was visible for many miles. Mayberry searched the horizon, squinting and scowling.

Why was there no smoke? Torrance and Paley wouldn't be doing without a fire in freezing weather. What was wrong?

There were any number of reasons why the two men he had left at the hideout might be outside—hunting or fishing or cutting wood. . . . Besides, where could they go?

From the air he could just make out the cabin at the northern rim of the lake. Built of logs, it was camouflaged by a stand of spruce behind it. He flew over the cabin. The men should have been outside by now; no one in the wilderness ignored the buzz of a small plane passing close by. Mayberry's nervousness fueled his speculations—the two men had been attacked by wolves or, more likely, a bear; they were too sick to get up from their cots; they had run out of food and were too weak to respond.

The notion that they might have deserted the cabin flicked through his mind. But they knew better than to cross him.

After another pass over the cabin, Mayberry decided he saw no sign of immediate danger and he had to land. He hadn't come all this way, sweating out every mile in the air, to leave without the ivory he had come for.

This was the moment he had come to dread most of all. He made his approach tentatively, sweating in spite of the cold in the cabin. His hands shook, and perspiration dripped into his eyes.

The skis touched, the aircraft floated a little, the skis found snow again, and he was down. Feathery arcs of powder snow flew up in his wake. The plane slid effortlessly across the expanse of white, as sleek as a skate on ice. Mayberry taxied back toward the cabin.

No one came out to greet him.

When he opened the aircraft's door and stepped out onto the snow, Mayberry had a Heckler & Koch HK-91 military assault rifle in his hands, ready to fire.

THIRTY minutes later Mayberry's rage had simmered down enough for him to assess his situation rationally. Trashing the cabin's interior had vented his anger, but it didn't solve anything.

As soon as he discovered that the hideout was abandoned by his two baby-sitters, Mayberry counted the remaining tusks in the storage room beneath the cabin. There were ninety-three tusks. Mayberry estimated that he had had nearly twice as many stored there, which meant that his loyal employees had stolen nearly half the ivory, along with some bearskins and other items.

How had they managed it with no transportation? Mayberry hoped they'd been caught in the last storm and frozen to death. But that wouldn't bring back his ivory. And the remaining tusks wouldn't be enough to placate Harry Madrid. He would have to locate the harvest from the recent hunt. He would have to find where Muugli's body had washed ashore. If he didn't . . . Madrid would likely come visiting.

MAYBERRY hauled most of the ivory and all of the polar bear skins aboard the Piper Cub. It was overloaded by three hundred pounds, maybe four. The workhorse airplane was famed in the bush for its ability to haul far more than the factory estimate—but a four-hundred-pound overload? On a short field with thirty-foot trees climbing the side, and snow-covered ridges above the tree line?

He would never make it.

Mayberry retraced his steps to the cabin, replaced the floor-boards to conceal the storage area beneath, and sat at a wooden table with a tumbler of whiskey, pouring from a bottle that Torrance and Paley had left behind.

Everyone was ripping him off. No longer did he doubt that John Mulak had been involved in the theft of his ivory. Mayberry might not be able to run Torrance and Paley down quickly, but he could sure as heck find the native who had stolen from him.

He thought of the woman camped by the river. He wondered what it was about her that nagged at him. John Mulak's son, Billy, had led them to that river, a favorite of his father's. It was not far from the site of the walrus hunt, which made it a logical route for the ivory thief or thieves to have taken with his stolen goods. The woman claimed not to have seen anyone. Why would she lie?

Mayberry could not see her as someone eager to make a few quick bucks on the side, smuggling some ivory tusks out of Alaska along with her scientific gear. But he could imagine her siding with an old Eskimo who told a plausible story about evil white poachers.

Something about her hadn't rung true. She had been evasive. Mayberry had sensed it strongly enough to take the impulsive precaution of disabling her shortwave radio.

Simpson and Rorie should be at the Eskimo village by now. Tomorrow they could head for the scientist's camp. Mayberry could also approach from the interior. Between them they could scout the whole length of the river. If Mayberry's gut instinct was correct and the woman knew anything about Mulak and the ivory, the tusks had to be hidden close by.

Within walking distance, he thought—where she had been before she came strolling back to the camp where they waited? She had been gone overnight. And she hadn't seemed surprised to discover four strange men standing beside her tents.

He should have acted on his instinct then. But messing with scientific or environmental groups was a touchy business. Anything happened to a woman like that, there would be a major flap. He had been too cautious, he decided. The next time they met, he was going to enjoy asking that lady some tough questions.

After a while the smoldering anger drove him to his feet.

The engine was still warm enough to start instantly. He taxied slowly to the beginning of the natural runway of snow and ice.

He was forced to abort his first attempt at takeoff when he ran out of room. Throttling back, Mayberry swung out over the frozen lake and taxied back to the starting point. The second time, before he released the brakes and the small plane lurched across the snow, he revved the engine until it was screaming. The distant line of trees rushed toward him. He could feel the overburdened Piper Cub straining to gain enough speed and lift. The cacophony of engine roar and wind and the pounding vibration from the undercarriage overwhelmed his thoughts, drowning his fear. Suddenly the skis broke free of the snow. He was in the air.

He peered through the windshield, and his heart seized. The tree line rushed toward him. The little plane seemed to crawl upward, like a climber clawing at a wall with his fingernails.

Suddenly the trees were in front of his eyes. Mayberry felt the jolt as one of the skis hit the tip of a spruce. The aircraft wobbled, threatening to careen out of control, then straightened. A tiny bug droning in that vast wilderness, it began to climb and flew on.

MOMENTS AFTER THE PIPER Super Cub cleared the trees and swung west, heading for the pass through the mountains, two men stepped out of the woods behind Travis Mayberry's cabin. They walked down to the edge of the frozen lake.

"I didn't think he was going to make it," Bob LoBianco said.

"I believe he spit out some pine needles," Everett Sanderson drawled. "He must be under some heavy-duty pressure to deliver."

"Yeah." LoBianco fidgeted, stamping his feet in the cold. "You think we made a mistake lettin' him go?"

"We can always pick him up," replied Sanderson. "Mayberry's not leaving Alaska."

"But the ivory might."

"It'll be tracked, and we can identify it now." Sanderson spoke with satisfaction. He *wanted* the ivory to be shipped out of Alaska. He wanted it to go all the way to Harry Madrid's warehouse in New Jersey. Catching the poachers in Alaska wasn't enough. The Fish and Wildlife Service was now hoping to hook even bigger fish.

The agents had had their first real break when Phil Torrance had been picked up in Anchorage after a dealer reported that he was trying to unload a dozen pairs of raw ivory tusks.

Torrance denied selling ivory with Paley at the trading post in Fort Yukon. But agents had quickly discovered an airfreight shipment outbound on Alaska Airlines to an address in Seattle belonging to Torrance's brother. Confronted with the information, and eyewitness testimony that he had indeed been with Paley in Fort Yukon, the poacher had decided to make the best deal he could for himself. That meant informing on Travis Mayberry's entire operation. He identified several of Mayberry's clandestine shipping arrangements. And Torrance's directions had led Sanderson and LoBianco to Mayberry's cabin.

The two federal agents had been dropped off at the lake three hours ahead of Mayberry, in a Fish and Wildlife Service floatplane. They found the hideout unlocked; Torrance and Paley had left in a hurry. According to Torrance, their primary motivation had not been to steal from their employer. The problem was that Paley was going crazy from isolation. He told Torrance he was bailing out. Nothing would dissuade him, and Torrance couldn't face staying alone. They had taken the ivory only to provide a needed stake.

"Once we walked out on Trav," the poacher said, "we had to leave the state. There wasn't no other choice."

According to Phil Torrance's confession, he and Paley had hauled out seventy-six walrus tusks—all they could manage in two trips overland to the Yukon, where they had hired a boat. The rest of Mayberry's stock they had left behind.

Following the poacher's directions, Sanderson and LoBianco took up the floorboards in the cabin and found the remaining tusks. They also found dead eagles, a stuffed polar bear, ten polar bear skins, and a barrel filled with bear claws and assorted teeth. Working quickly, they marked everything with an invisible marker that would show up under infrared light. Then they left the cabin as they had found it and retreated into the woods. They had less than an hour to wait before Mayberry's Piper Cub climbed into view.

Sanderson surveyed the lake. He could see the path Mayberry's skis had left in the snow. The small plane had been overloaded, all right, and for a moment Sanderson had feared that Mayberry wasn't going to make it and the whole operation was going to crash with him.

"Better alert the boys at Clark's Crossing that our man is on the way." Agents were on standby in Clark's Crossing, Fort Yukon, and Fairbanks to monitor any shipments Mayberry made. Everything would be allowed to go through, but it would be tracked at every step. Meanwhile, other agents would be dispatched to impound the hideout, remove the illegal goods, and seal the building.

"Where do you think Mayberry's going from here?"

"My guess is, he'll head straight for the coast soon as he drops off his cargo," Sanderson said. "He needs more ivory. It's on Rorie's shift now. I just wish we didn't have to play that scenario out."

"Why not? It's one more nail in Mayberry's coffin."

"As long as it's not Rorie's coffin," Sanderson said.

A HALF hour after leaving the cabin behind, Travis Mayberry cleared the last tier of mountains and came into view of the Yukon River valley. Clearing the mountains greatly improved the probability of clear radio transmission to the coast.

He raised Jeff Rorie—who happened to be at the hangar checking out his plane—on the third try. By then Mayberry was approaching Clark's Crossing. "Where you guys been?" he demanded.

"Grounded by fog. But it'll clear tonight, and we're taking off at first light. How about you? Are you coming back to Nome?"

"I'm coming over your way in the morning. We're gonna find some ivory." Mayberry's voice was flat, cold. "Get Simpson. I want to talk to him."

"Trav?" Simpson's voice over the headset caused Mayberry to jerk in his seat. His nerves were frayed, and he faced another tricky landing.

"You alone?" Mayberry snapped.

"Better believe it." Static crackled over the headset, and Simpson's voice faded a little before coming back. ". . . like I told you. Our pilot's a plant."

Mayberry was silent. He could see tiny figures on the ground now, his arrival a moment of excitement for the isolated river settlement. "We still need him—for now. I'll be with you tomorrow. We can handle it then. We need to coordinate."

"Sure, Trav. You want to meet us at—"

"No names, okay? No specifics. You learn anything new from those natives, you let me know. Otherwise, we go back to where we stopped on the river overnight. We'll go from there. Understand?"

"You thinkin' about that woman—"

Mayberry cut him off. "I said no details. Just be there."

The landing strip at the edge of Clark's Crossing was a field of snow. Mayberry came in wobbly, scared, light as a snowflake.

THIRTEEN

IT HAD snowed during the night, but the morning was another world—clear, bright, and cold. Kathy McNeely woke to sunlight pouring in through the entrance to the cave.

Silence clotted her ears. Something unnatural about it struck her. Kathy's pulse quickened.

She rose, shivering, and called out, "Survivor?"

Kathy squinted at the cave mouth, trying to remember if she had packed her dark glasses when she abandoned her camp.

She called the husky again. "Survivor?"

It wasn't unusual for the dog to be awake ahead of her, prowling around outside. But this morning was different. As soon as she understood why, she turned back into the cave, fighting off alarm. She searched the interior quickly. The husky was not there. And there were no tracks in the fresh fall of snow outside the cave.

Sometime during the night, Survivor had gone.

SURVIVOR paused at the edge of a bluff, heaving. Below him broken scree formed a ragged slope leading down to the tundra plain. His mouth was open as he panted, and his tongue licked ice crystals from his muzzle. His legs quivered from the long run.

A few yards away the female wolf had flopped onto her belly in the snow. She, too, was exhausted, but she watched him with the glitter of excitement still bright in her eyes.

Their romp had begun before dawn.

Survivor had heard the wolf pack prowling close outside the cave during the night. Once, a shadow fell directly across the mouth of the cave, and he was instantly on his feet, snarling a warning. The answer, moments later, was a long, soaring howl.

The howling awakened a song in his blood, ancient and long dormant. He glanced at the woman, who slept undisturbed. The call came again. It compelled him toward the exit.

He stepped out, wary and alert. The darkness was not total, and he saw the she-wolf instantly, not twenty feet away. Behind her other shadows writhed, low figures slinking back and forth. Survivor took a few steps toward her, stiff-legged, ears and tail up, hackles rising. The smaller figures—her pups—retreated hastily, scattering across the snow, but the female stood her ground.

Then, as Survivor drew close, she began to squirm, lowering herself closer to the snow. She began to whine. When the husky stopped a few feet away, she pulled herself closer. Finally she dropped onto the snow and rolled over, her belly totally vulnerable.

The age-old message meant the same to dog or wolf, and Survivor's spring-loaded muscular tension eased. His muzzle approached the wolf's, tentatively sniffing.

Out of the shadows in a rush the largest of the pups charged the husky, lips drawn back in an erupting snarl.

Survivor's early upbringing had been that of a contentious trail dog. Fights for position and role were common. The weeks on the tundra had hardened his muscles. He was on the young pup in a flash, pinning the lighter animal to the ground, his jaws raging.

It had happened too quickly for the other pups to join the fight. And suddenly it was over, the ferocious snarling stilled, the figures of husky and wolf frozen in place.

The husky stepped back, and the young wolf who had tried to claim his place as the alpha male beside his mother slunk away. The adult female came squirming toward Survivor again, a whine in her throat. Their romp began shortly thereafter.

It was not the female's time for breeding—that would come in early spring—but she was alone, except for her pups. Wolves are sociable, and she had fixed upon the husky as a suitable male to run beside her, to hunt and race and howl against the night. His quick, ferocious quelling of the young male's challenge had settled matters.

She led the way toward the mountains. Sometimes the pack ran snarling and yipping across fields of snow in sheer exuberance. Sometimes they stopped to howl in a chorus that was not mournful, but joyous. And at other times the female led them in a steady, purposeful trot across low plains and over rounded foothills, gradually climbing toward higher ground. The miles vanished underfoot, and as the day came bright and clear, they had traveled miles north and east of the bear's cave. They came to the rocky outcropping the female had chosen as a winter den. She stopped there. Here you can stay with us and lead us, she seemed to say.

After resting awhile, Survivor rose and trotted off alone. A half hour later he reappeared, carrying not one, but two dead rabbits by the ears. He presented them to the female wolf. She ate a little, quickly and voraciously, before sharing most of the small feast with the hungry pups.

Survivor rested happily, surrounded by the wolf pack. It was an hour before a restlessness began to disturb him. He gazed back along the flanks of hills, and a familiar longing grew within him. The strange, exciting song that had lured him this morning was quiet now. He was remembering other mornings, other attachments forged over months of companionship.

A distinct sound brought him to his feet, alert. He lifted his nose to the wind, as if it might confirm what his sharp ears recorded. Sounds carried great distances in the silence of the wilderness.

When the sound came again, reverberating across the tundra,

the husky began to growl. The female wolf heard him and watched, as if she sensed the conflict within him. Survivor glanced at her, but after a moment's hesitation he turned away.

He trotted off once more. This time the female was on her feet, watching him go.

JEFF Rorie was tired of watching Simpson hustle and bully the Eskimos and of being unable to do anything about it. Seeing young Billy Mulak tiptoeing around, high on cocaine on the morning he was to lead a search for his father, was more than Rorie could watch. He walked out of the recreation center, where Simpson was pumping Billy and several other natives about John Mulak's reappearance in the village the night before last and how he had stayed for over twenty-four hours before leaving again.

Simpson followed the pilot to the Cessna. "You got a problem?"

"No problem. I'm just the chauffeur, remember? This stuff you're into . . . it's not my business."

"You work for Mayberry, you better make it your business."

Rorie said nothing for a moment. It wasn't a debate he could safely get into. "That's a big country out there, looking for one Eskimo," he said finally. "What makes you think we have a better chance of spotting him this time than we did before?"

Simpson's smirk turned sly. "Because I learned something in there, Rorie, after you went soft on me and walked out. I learned old John Mulak didn't have his kayak when he came back this time. He was on foot. So we're not gonna be searchin' along the whole damned coastline. We got a trail to follow."

Rorie managed to conceal the thread of tension that ran through him like a hot wire. "Billy knows where he went?"

"That's right. You can start warmin' up this beat-up old flyer. And lemme at that radio. I gotta raise Mayberry."

FROM the small shelf before the entrance to the cave, Kathy McNeely surveyed a scene of breathtaking beauty. The dazzle of new-fallen snow was everywhere—drifting on islands of river ice, lying in seamless blankets of white over empty miles of tundra, and rising along sweeping slopes toward the hills and mountains—a universal whiteness, pure and unmarked.

The air was so clear that the view, with no trees or other familiar objects between land and sky to give it scale, seemed to stretch to infinity. The overwhelming sense of limitless space all around her was magnified by Kathy's feeling of being completely alone, without even the company of Survivor.

And there was no sign whatever of John Mulak.

She searched the surrounding emptiness for some evidence of the dog. She walked along the spine of the ridge above the cave, calling, "Survivor! Survivor!" The name echoed over the tundra.

She would have to leave the area of the cave to search. There had to be tracks somewhere.

She plodded through knee-deep snow toward the river, pausing every few minutes to survey the empty wilderness. The stillness was so absolute that her attention strayed. She almost missed the rustle of color and movement in the brush down near the river.

Shielding her eyes with one hand, she searched for a repetition of that fragmentary glimpse. Then she saw it again.

A short distance to her right—no more than fifty paces—a dense thicket of cranberry bushes sprawled along the river. Suddenly small clouds of snow erupted from the brush; something silvery gray moved within the tangle. Survivor? A wolf? She had the sense of a creature larger than either. What—

The bulky shape reared up, taller than a man. "My Lord!" she whispered aloud.

A huge male grizzly swung his massive head around slowly, as if sensing another presence.

AIRBORNE, Billy Mulak sat in the back seat behind Rorie, looking as if he was already coming down from his temporary high. Simpson was in the front passenger seat, a Remington .30-06 rifle propped beside him. Rorie had a government-issue Smith & Wesson .38 automatic taped to the underside of his seat, but he hoped he wouldn't have to dig it out in a hurry.

"Where to?" he asked once they were in the air.

"You tell him, Billy boy," Simpson ordered.

Speaking in a jerky monotone, Billy directed the plane inland, then onto the tundra plain, here threaded with a network of waterways, most of them frozen solid. Less than ten minutes from the village, Billy saw a larger stream—through which a gray ribbon of water was visible—and a fingernail-shaped gravel beach.

Billy pointed at the beach. "That's where he leaves his boat."

"Where does this river go?" Simpson pressed him.

"There's a fork not far from here where the big river meets this one. Our people go there to fish for salmon."

Simpson studied the empty white plain beneath them. If they spotted the old man now, he was thinking, there'd be no place for him to hide. The thought shot a jolt of adrenaline into his bloodstream. "We get to that fork, we'll swing back toward the coast."

"Maybe he went further inland," Rorie suggested.

"He's goin' for the ivory. And he wouldn't have ferried that much ivory so far upriver. He didn't have time."

Rorie reluctantly accepted Simpson's logic. Ahead of them the fork appeared. Rorie circled the area briefly before turning the Cessna's nose toward the coastline.

He could feel Wolf Simpson's excitement, and it brought a rising tension into the small cabin. "We're getting close, Rorie," Simpson said to him. "You know what I told you about a wolf on the run? I can feel him down there. And this time he's mine!"

STANDING erect and looking around, the grizzly seemed almost human. Kathy estimated him to be at least eight feet tall. The sight of him took her breath away. Her heart raced.

Random details from the briefing given by one of the wildlife specialists to the ASSET scientists before they went into the wilderness tumbled through her mind. This was grizzly country. If you encountered one, there was one cardinal rule: Don't run. Running simply brought you to the bear's attention and stamped you as prey. Grizzlies had poor vision, Kathy remembered. Could he see her at all at the distance of a quarter mile? Or was she only an inconsequential blur as long as she didn't move?

Grizzlies made up for poor eyesight with sharp hearing and a keen sense of smell. But she was downwind of him, and he had not caught her scent. The bear was drifting up the slope.

What had brought the bear to the river? With the arrival of cold weather, had the grizzly returned to the vicinity of his cave? If so, Kathy's presence near it would be an immediate challenge.

She began a cautious retreat. Instinct told her to withdraw upslope. The ridge that formed a brow over the cave's entrance would soon shield her from the grizzly's view.

The bear reared up again on its hind legs, and Kathy stopped to stare. She was filled with admiration. He was a king. This was his territory, and she was the intruder.

Suddenly she realized that, pausing on the ridge, she was silhouetted against the skyline. The bear had seen her!

He didn't hesitate. He broke out of the brush and lumbered up the slope toward her, gathering speed. The snow, which seriously hampered her every step, seemed no impediment to the bear. He plowed up the slope like a runaway bulldozer.

A shout startled her and stopped the grizzly in his tracks.

"Hallooo! Mr. Bear!"

It was a moment before Kathy located the source of the cry. A stocky figure stood near the riverbank in plain view. Recognition cut through her fear. The figure began to flap his arms and shout. "Here, Mr. Bear! I am here. Mulak the bear hunter!"

Kathy was astonished as much by the quirky humor in Mulak's cries as by his attempt to divert the bear's attention from her. The huge grizzly stood irresolute for a moment, his head swinging back and forth. Kathy remained downwind; her human scent was carried away from the grizzly, and he could see her only vaguely. The Eskimo, on the other hand, was upwind. The grizzly could not only smell him but could also see his dancing, taunting figure. It charged straight for him.

Kathy couldn't tear her gaze away. Why didn't Mulak run?

The gap between the charging bear and the Eskimo shrank swiftly. Then something in Mulak's shouts caught Kathy's attention. He was yelling at her! "Bird watcher! Go now. Hurry!"

The words shattered her trance. She floundered up the slope.

Climbing out of a hollow into full view of the river below, she saw the grizzly almost on top of Mulak. He had waited too long. The Eskimo scrambled behind some brush at the edge of the riverbank, and she saw the dark spearhead of his kayak slide into view. Mulak was in the boat, paddling furiously.

A roar of frustration thundered up the slope and reverberated over the tundra. The grizzly waded into shallow water, breaking through the shore ice in pursuit of the kayak. But Mulak was into the current now, and as the bear's paw slapped water at its stern, the narrow boat shot clear and sped away.

Kathy began to breathe again.

And in that moment she heard a sound that made her throat catch: the drone of a small aircraft. A rescue flight? Her hope was dashed as she recognized the poachers' plane.

JEFF Rorie had grown more hopeful. The farther they went without spotting the old Eskimo, he felt, the less chance there was.

"Not so fast, Rorie," Simpson said to him. "We could miss something. And take us lower. Like to a hundred feet."

"That's too low," Rorie objected.

"Don't give me that bull," Wolf Simpson said. "Take it down."

It was an order. Rorie dropped to an altitude of a hundred feet, throttling back to seventy mph. The little plane seemed to crawl over the limitless white landscape. At Simpson's direction, Rorie followed the twisting course of the river.

They had been flying seaward for about twenty minutes when Simpson suddenly exclaimed, "Look at that!"

Tilting on a wing, Rorie saw a thousand-pound grizzly, alarmed by the low-flying aircraft, run with surprising speed away from the river. As if in reflex, Simpson's rifle appeared in his hands. "Take us back," he ordered. "I want a shot at that big creature."

"Then do it in your own plane," Rorie said, "not in mine."

All the hostility that had lately been missing blazed in Simpson's eyes. His hand went to his side and reappeared with a short-barreled Walther PPK .380 automatic—there was no room within the narrow confines of the cabin for his rifle—and he thrust it toward Rorie's belly. The vindictiveness in Simpson's expression confirmed Rorie's suspicion that the poacher knew something about him.

Rorie could feel Simpson's hard stare as the poacher debated with himself how far to push the confrontation. He was still hesitating when Billy shouted, "There's Pop! On the river!"

In an instant the grizzly was forgotten. "I see him." Wolf Simpson pressed his face close to the window, a vicious grin distorting his mouth. "Stay with him, Rorie. Don't lose him now!"

555

Mayberry had left Clark's Crossing at dawn in his Piper Cub, having made arrangements for two boxes of ivory to go out parcel post on the next mail pickup. A larger consignment would go by boat to Fort Yukon and, from there, onto a short flight to Fairbanks, where it would be loaded as airfreight bound for the Lower 48.

He had stopped to refuel when he received Simpson's message that he had discovered John Mulak's route on leaving the Eskimo village. Simpson sounded eager, excited.

The pieces were falling into place. Mayberry had the feeling that this day would bring him a break. They were closing in. An hour later Simpson radioed again. "We got him, Trav. We got him!"

Mayberry thumbed the speaker switch. "Mulak? You're sure?"

"It's him, all right. Where on earth are you, Trav?"

"I don't— Wait a minute. I think I see something ahead. It's a big fork in the river."

"That's it!" Simpson yelled. "You're just east of us. Haul your ashes and you can still get in on the fun."

"I'll be there."

This was sure going to be his day!

Retreating up the snow-covered slope away from the river and the grizzly, Kathy quickly lost sight of both the bear and Mulak's kayak. Soon even the river was cut off from her view, and the rasp of the aircraft engine faded away. Through heavy snow that dragged at her knees and thighs, she fled eastward, away from the cave and its treasure, into the emptiness of the alpine tundra.

Finally she stopped, shaking with exhaustion. How far had she gone from the cave? Half a mile? A mile? Given the twists and turns of her panicky flight, she had no way of judging.

She saw the river directly below. No sign of Mulak and his boat. She could hear the buzz of the aircraft in the distance.

No sign of the grizzly.

Then, thin and sharp, an alien sound racketed across the white wilderness: the unmistakable crack of a rifle shot.

The Cessna quickly overshot the kayak, and Rorie swung into a steep turn. As he leveled out, he throttled back close to a stall. He glimpsed the long, narrow skin boat shooting a strip of white water.

A face in a fur-lined hood turned upward. Torn between his sympathies and the constraints of his secret role, Rorie brought the
Cessna around behind the kayak. He flew back and forth, a maneuver designed to harry the boater and to stay behind him.

But a low bluff worked against the strategy. It forced a sharp
bend in the river and caused Rorie to climb quickly to three hundred
feet. He swung left to intersect the river again, and Simpson began to
swear. "Where'd the fool go? I told you not to lose him, Rorie."

Rorie could sense Billy Mulak—silent since spotting his father
on the river—trembling in the seat behind him, his eyes wide with
fear. Or was it the drugs? Rorie wondered bitterly.

Rorie was the first to spot the kayak again, no longer in the river,
but paddling along a narrow creek. Maybe Simpson wouldn't see it.
The Eskimo was in trouble, slowed by his struggle to break through
surface ice.

Then Simpson spotted Mulak. "There he is!"

Simpson kicked open the right side door. Shoving the automatic
pistol under his waistband and grabbing the Remington, he braced
himself at the opening, half sitting and half kneeling.

"Are you crazy?" Rorie shouted. "If you shoot him, you'll never
find the ivory."

"I can wing him. He's not getting away this time."

Billy, shaking, his face sickly pale, stared helplessly at Simpson as
the poacher took aim at the old man in the kayak.

"Even if you only wing him, he could die out here," Rorie
shouted. "You can't risk it!"

Rorie reached for the panel-mounted microphone, flipped the
speaker switch. Before he could speak, Simpson swung the butt of
his rifle, two-handed, smashing it into the black box. Plastic splin-
tered, and sparks sizzled.

Rorie stared at the radio. "Mayberry will skin you alive."

"Who cares about Mayberry!"

There was a glitter in Simpson's eyes that didn't answer to reason, and Rorie realized that the poacher was so caught up in the
excitement of the moment that he was beyond caring about the
consequences of his actions.

The slam of the rifle filled the small cabin as Simpson fired at the
fleeing Eskimo.

A BURST OF STATIC ON HIS HEADSET was so loud that Mayberry jerked the set free. Suddenly it went silent.

He thumbed the SPEAKER button. "Simpson? What's going on?"

In the normal tumult of noise inside the Piper Cub's cockpit, the abrupt radio silence seemed ominous. He peered ahead through the windshield. The Cessna had to be nearby.

A moving speck, laboring through deep snow, caught his eye, took human shape. A face turned upward, a hand waving.

It was the woman from the camp. To Mayberry that meant only one thing: Let Simpson take care of the old Eskimo. *She* would lead him to the ivory.

THE shock of the distant gunshot pulsed through Kathy's mind. It seemed incredible that the poachers would shoot Mulak, their only link to the missing ivory. But if the Eskimo was under fire, she had to do something. Surely a witness would make the poachers hesitate. She had to find a way to get back to Mulak without crossing paths with the grizzly. The Eskimo had been carried downriver, while her flight took her in the opposite direction.

The growl of a small plane came again, closer. Kathy squinted skyward. She saw that the aircraft's landing gear were skis not floats. This was not the poachers' plane.

As the aircraft passed overhead, she waved frantically. Just when she became convinced the pilot had failed to see her, the plane began a wide circle, turning back.

Elated, certain that the plane had come from the ASSET base camp to search for her, Kathy plodded up an incline. She reached the lower side of a snow-covered meadow as the plane began its descent. An ASSET rescue plane changed everything. It meant the poachers would have to pull back from any open attack against the Eskimo. And the plane made an air search for Survivor possible.

As the aircraft taxied toward her across the open expanse of snow, she could see a goggled face behind the windshield—one face only—which surprised her a little. But the aircraft's cabin was small, and her colleagues would have expected Survivor to be with her.

The plane was within twenty feet of her before it stopped, the propeller wash creating a blizzard of snow. The cabin door opened. Kathy started forward, grinning through cracked lips. Then something about the man stepping from the cabin stopped her.

She stared at the pilot as he clambered down. There was something familiar in the heavyset body and aggressive thrust of the head. She knew who it was even before he pulled up the big sun goggles and the brown eyes stared at her above a disarming grin.

Even before she saw the weapon in his hands.

She began to run back the way she had come, the snow dragging at her legs. Before she had covered twenty yards, she heard the airplane taxiing after her, growing closer and closer. It cut in front of her and swung around. She ran back, the aircraft dogging her.

It drew alongside of her and pulled slightly ahead. Once more it stopped. The door popped open. Kathy veered away, stumbling in the knee-deep snow. The hard slam of a single gunshot was so shocking that it dropped her to her knees.

Mayberry climbed down from the Piper Cub. Kathy turned toward him and stared at the ugly assault rifle in the poacher's hands. "That's what they call a shot across the bow, Dr. McNeely," he said, his tone almost genial. "Give it up. You've got no place to run. I've been lookin' forward to meeting you again. I think you have somethin' that belongs to me."

FOURTEEN

"Slow down," Simpson yelled. "He's gettin' away."

"This isn't a helicopter!" Jeff Rorie yelled back.

A hundred feet below, the kayak veered suddenly, and the Cessna roared on by. The maneuver had become part of a pattern. The Eskimo was like a rabbit eluding a pursuing dog. The dog was faster on the straightaway, but it couldn't make a ninety-degree turn like the rabbit.

For Wolf Simpson this kind of pursuit—like the wolf hunts that had given him his nickname—was the ultimate high. Such hunts were usually carried out in a helicopter, but the added difficulty of pursuit in a conventional small aircraft added zest to the game. He kept up a fevered commentary. "There he goes. . . . After him, Rorie. . . . Left, left! . . . He's looping back. . . . Slow down, slow down. . . . Good. Get on top of him. . . . Come on, baby, give me one clean shot, that's all I ask. . . ."

559

Rorie, walking a tightrope to avoid giving his own game away, was doing his best—with small nudges and twitches of operating stick and wing flaps—to prevent Simpson from getting a direct shot.

Even before accepting his undercover assignment, Rorie had thought about the kind of dilemma he faced now. He knew he couldn't let Simpson shoot Mulak in cold blood. He kept hoping that the poacher would cool off enough to see reason. They needed to question Mulak, he kept insisting, not fish his body out of a frozen creek. Simpson ignored him—and Rorie knew he was running out of time and options. He had allowed the Cessna to bounce and rock in imaginary turbulence too many times.

"Now!" Simpson gloated. "You thievin' old man—gotcha!"

Rorie had nudged the Cessna to the right, spoiling Simpson's angle of fire, but unexpectedly the kayak had changed course at the same instant and in the same direction Rorie took. Suddenly Mulak was in Simpson's sights.

Rorie flattened the manual flaps. The aircraft's nose lifted a moment before Simpson fired.

The poacher spun around. "You did that on purpose."

"I don't know what you're talking about."

"Take us down!"

"Don't be stupid. There's no safe place to land."

"You can find a place. You're good, Rorie. Ain't that why they picked you?"

"Who? What are you talking about?"

"The feds, who else? The same ones who got Les Hargrove to disappear."

"You're hallucinating, Simpson." Rorie wondered how much the poacher really knew and how much was a bluff.

"Take us down."

"No," Rorie said. "You want to kill all of us, pull that trigger."

"He's—he's stuck!" Billy Mulak's anguished cry broke through the deadlock between Rorie and Simpson. Both men followed Billy's gaze. The kayak was hung up, wedged in the grip of thick ice. The old Eskimo in the boat battered at the ice with a paddle. He peered upward. Rorie thought of one of Simpson's exhausted, helpless wolves at the end of his desperate run.

"Take us down," Simpson raged. "You hear me, Rorie?"

"I heard you, and you can go stuff it."

Simpson swung the rifle—not toward Rorie, but at Billy. In the tight limits of the cabin the muzzle stopped inches from Billy Mulak's chest. "He goes first. We're not on the way down in three seconds, you're gonna have a messy cabin to clean up. Do it!"

KATHY McNeely stared at the weapon in Mayberry's hands. "Are you out of your mind?" She looked at him in disbelief. "You can't go around shooting at people."

"You gave me no choice, Doctor. You have some ivory that belongs to me—or at least you know where it is."

"I don't know what you're talking about."

"I think you do. If I had any doubt, you took care of that when you tried to run away. What reason did I give you to run?"

She met his gaze. "You might as well know I won't do anything to help you, and I don't believe you're prepared to shoot me and face the consequences."

"I wouldn't be so sure about consequences," Mayberry said. "We're a long way from civilization."

She stared at him in silence, sobered by the realization that he was right. He could do anything he wanted.

"You must think me some kind of monster, Dr. McNeely," Mayberry went on. "Who put such ideas into your head? That old Eskimo? A thief hardly makes a good witness."

She refused to rise to the bait. No way he could know about her and John Mulak. She wasn't going to give information that easily.

"That gun you're carrying gives me a clue," Kathy said. "It's what they call an assault rifle, isn't it? Hardly the kind of weapon a legitimate sportsman carries in the wilderness. What do you propose to do with it, Mr. Mayberry, slaughter more walruses?"

He smiled. "I can see I'd better not get into a debate with you, Doctor. But this weapon has an unfair reputation. On semiautomatic, the way I have it now, it fires only one bullet for each squeeze of the trigger—no different from a dozen semiautomatic hunting rifles no one tries to outlaw. It's a Heckler and Koch HK-91, a superior gun."

"It must make you proud."

Mayberry's good humor vanished. Adjusting his sun goggles, he

561

turned to peer off across the tundra. "I think we'll walk. I doubt we'll need the plane right away."

"I won't tell you—"

"You don't have to tell me anything. We'll just follow your tracks." Kathy wasn't quick enough to conceal her dismay at that, and Mayberry smiled. "Once I have the ivory, you'll be free to leave, Dr. McNeely. I really mean you no harm, you know."

"Leaving me free to tell the authorities what I know?"

"It won't matter. The authorities already know I deal in native artifacts, including ivory carvings."

"Dealing in *artifacts?* Is that what you call killing an entire walrus herd?" She was stopped by Mayberry's satisfied grin.

"So, Doctor, you *do* know all about the ivory." The poacher clicked his tongue against his teeth, mocking her. "Who can a fellow trust anymore?" He gestured with the rifle. "Shall we stop playing games and get started?"

Kathy saw there was little to be gained by refusing to go with him.

"There's something you should know," she said suddenly.

Mayberry waited, eyes hidden behind his goggles.

"The ivory is hidden in a cave—a grizzly's cave," she added pointedly. "The bear wasn't there when the ivory was taken to the cave, but he's there now. I saw him this morning." She nodded toward her path in the snow. "That's why I'm out here in the middle of nowhere. I was running from him."

Mayberry seemed to weigh her words, then smiled and shook his head. "That's very good, Doctor. But you can hardly expect me to believe you."

"I'm not lying," Kathy said. "Going back there now is dangerous. He . . . he's huge. And he was angry."

"Well then," Mayberry said, impatience resurfacing, "I'll be glad to have this handy-dandy version of a machine gun, won't I?" He pointed to her tracks. "After you, Doctor."

RORIE tried to guess how crazed Simpson was and whether he would carry out his threat against Billy Mulak. There wasn't time to calculate the odds; he simply couldn't take the chance.

He shoved the stick forward, and the Cessna started downward. Rorie couldn't see enough open water to gamble on. He would have to come down on the snowpack. "Better hang on!" He raised his voice so Billy Mulak could hear him.

He saw a level stretch of tundra—no way of telling what treacherous holes or bogs or creeks might be hidden under the snow. Lining up his landing area, he came in nose-high, at full flaps and close to a stall, at under fifty knots. At the last moment, Simpson put his rifle aside and grabbed his seat with both hands.

Kissing the snow, Rorie dumped his flaps and killed power. Then the edge of the floats dug into the snow a little and Rorie was fighting for control. He braked hard. The aircraft tilted up, settled back, then came to rest in a pounding silence.

Rorie had hoped that at the moment of shutdown he could lunge for Simpson's rifle, but the poacher was ready for him. His Walther pistol was back in his hand, pointing at Rorie's chest.

IN HER flight from the grizzly it had seemed to Kathy as if she were crawling across the tundra. Now, with Mayberry behind her, the distance seemed to fly. Ten minutes after they set out, she was recognizing landmarks. She scanned the snowy slope angling down toward the river, searching for the grizzly, the berry patch, Mulak.

The bear's presence would change everything. Once Mayberry actually saw him, for all his confidence in his assault rifle, he would, she hoped, think twice about approaching the cave.

"How much farther?" Mayberry grunted.

She squinted against the snow glare, uncertain. The profile of the ridge slightly below them, perhaps two hundred yards ahead, seemed familiar. She wasn't anxious to reach it. Could she stall?

"How far?" Mayberry repeated impatiently.

"I'm not sure. I was running scared." She glanced over her shoulder, trying to refresh her memory of the terrain, and gasped aloud.

Mayberry jerked around, instinctively raising his rifle.

"Don't shoot!" she called out.

"What the— What is it? A wolf?"

"No. It's Survivor. My dog!"

The husky had burst over a rise in the distance. Spotting them immediately, he raced toward them.

"He'd better stop or—"

The roar behind them chilled Kathy to the marrow. She knew

what it was even before she spun around. She and Mayberry had been distracted by Survivor's sudden appearance; they hadn't seen the grizzly climb onto the ridge above the cave. Not sixty feet away, he rose to his full height—a thousand pounds of massed bone and muscle. Mayberry's jaw literally dropped as the bear roared once more and charged.

"Nice work, Rorie," Wolf Simpson said. "You're good—good enough to keep me alive and get you killed."

"What are you going to do, Simpson, walk out? You need me alive."

"Mayberry will find me. And you're a dead man."

Simpson hadn't been paying attention to Billy Mulak. He had written the young Eskimo off as a nonperson, someone easily controlled. Without warning, Billy threw himself over the front seat at Simpson. Momentum carried the two partially through the open door, Billy awkwardly on top, Simpson sprawled halfway out. The gun in the poacher's hand went off outside the cabin, tearing a hole in the high wing. Billy was screaming incoherently. "Gussak! You never said nothin' about killing him. I won't let you!"

By this time Rorie had dug his gun out from under his seat. He lunged across the cabin but moved too fast, and when Simpson kicked out in his struggle to free himself from Billy, his boot caught Rorie in the head. Blood gushed. A red haze filmed Rorie's eyes.

Simpson and Billy Mulak thrashed around at Rorie's feet. Pushed out through the doorway, Billy grabbed a wing strut with one hand. Simpson clubbed at him with the automatic pistol. His finger was still on the trigger, and the handgun fired on impact. The explosion must have momentarily stunned Billy, because his grip on the strut slackened. The poacher fired again as Billy fell.

Raging, Rorie dove into Simpson from behind. The tackle carried both men out into the snow. In the fall from the cabin, Simpson lost his gun. He scrabbled in the snow, digging for it, and the delay gave the pilot the moment he needed. Rorie had only time enough to wonder if the snow clogging the muzzle of his Smith & Wesson would cause it to misfire.

He felt the gun kick in his hand, saw the surprise in Simpson's eyes turn to bewilderment and then, like a curtain rising over an unpainted wall, to a gray emptiness.

"YOU'RE JOHN MULAK," RORIE said to the gray-haired Eskimo.

"Yes. Were you the one who broke the lock on the storage shed and let me get away?"

"Yes. I hope I did the right thing."

"I was glad to get out." Mulak paused. "I thought it was my son who did it."

"Your son saved my life," Rorie said. "But I believe he was trying to save yours."

Billy rested with his back against one of the aircraft's pontoons. Simpson's last bullet had gouged a furrow in Billy's right shoulder, missing bone as it passed through.

"He is my son," the old Eskimo said. "He lost his way, but he is still my son."

Both men stiffened at the crack of another rifle shot rolling across the tundra. They exchanged glances.

Rorie was already moving toward his plane. "You stay with Billy. I'll be back. I think I know who the hunter is. I have to find out what—or who—he's hunting."

THE charging grizzly completely unnerved Travis Mayberry. In his panic, he forgot to click his weapon over to full automatic. A full burst might have stunned the bear, but Mayberry fired only a single shot. It struck the grizzly high on his massive chest, but didn't even slow him down; it merely increased his rage.

Mayberry glanced at the assault rifle in disbelief and stumbled backward a step before the grizzly got to him. In one sweeping blow the bear's six-inch claws tore through Mayberry's layers of clothing and ripped flesh away to the bone, from his right shoulder to his waist. His scream was lost in the bear's thunderous growl.

As she tried to run, Kathy floundered in the snow and stumbled to her knees. Scrambling back to her feet, she slipped and fell on her back. She looked up as the grizzly's attention turned from the rag doll he made of Travis Mayberry toward this other intruder. At that moment Survivor reached the front of the ridge.

Attracted more by a moving object than by a stationary one, the grizzly focused his attention immediately upon the dog. Survivor circled the bear, barking furiously, darting forward, dancing back. The husky's actions drew the bear away from Kathy. She got up unsteadily and backed away. Wrong! The bear saw the movement. His massive head swung from the dog toward her. He hesitated, deciding between them. At the same moment, Kathy heard the rapidly approaching snarl of a small aircraft in a dive.

Rorie's Cessna pulled out of a steep plunge directly over the ridge, the engine's scream bottoming out like a small explosion. The size, speed, and thunder of this unknown thing hurtling toward him out of the sky was too much for the grizzly. He turned and ran down the long slope to the river, plowing a small highway in the snow. He never looked back.

"This is becoming like an emergency hospital flight," Jeff Rorie said. "I don't think there's room for everyone."

Travis Mayberry was alive, but he had lost a great deal of blood. If he lived, Rorie speculated, he would probably lose his right arm or the use of it. Though in much better shape, Billy Mulak needed emergency care. Rorie had taken out the Cessna's rear bench seat so the two wounded men could be on the floor. That meant only the seat next to the pilot remained, leaving one person out, and the husky.

"I will wait with the dog," John Mulak said. "He will be good company, I think."

Rorie had contacted the ASSET base camp over the radio in Mayberry's Piper Cub and been told a rescue team should reach the area by the following day.

"I want to be here when they arrive," Kathy said. "I'll stay, too. Mr. Mulak will be good company."

"I'll get back as soon as I can," Rorie promised. "But I don't think staying near the cave is such a hot idea with a wounded bear around. Your old camp makes better sense. Your people will be looking for you there."

"How badly do you think the grizzly's hurt?" Kathy asked.

"They're hard to kill," Rorie said. "My agency may want to send someone up here to look for him."

"If he comes back before you do . . . Well, as far as I'm concerned, he can have the ivory!" Kathy said.

"He will take good care of it," Mulak said. "I think, when he leaves in the spring, he will not care if we come back for the ivory." Mulak studied the Fish and Wildlife Service agent, not sure of his reaction. "It belongs to my people. I took it from the white hunters, but they won't get it now. I never wanted to take it from my friends."

Rorie looked at him for a long moment. If agents recovered the ivory, it would be evidence against the poachers. But they already had the ivory Mayberry had shipped as evidence. Simpson was dead, and it would be a very long time before Mayberry recovered enough to stand trial. Besides, Rorie had never actually seen the white harvest.

Aloud Rorie said, responding to Mulak, "Neither do I."

MUUGLI raised his head when he heard the drone of Rorie's aircraft flying south. It reminded him of the buzz of an outboard motor in the water, a grimly familiar threat.

Beneath the smothering fog over the straits and the coastal shelf, the temperature had risen slightly, and ice that had piled up near the entrance to the straits broke loose and drifted on the current. Muugli had been imprisoned at the ice barricade for nearly two days. Now his island moved slowly but steadily southward toward the Bering Sea.

Although he had not regained all his strength, his wounds had healed. What he suffered now was a malaise that time and nature alone could not heal. Walruses were sociable creatures. The herd instinct was strong, and Muugli's herd had been destroyed.

The old walrus drifted through the afternoon and into the lengthening night. Sometime in the darkest part of the night he was awakened by another sound. Something stirred in him. He listened to the continuous crunch and rumble of ice, the roll and crash of the sea. Then his head tilted, as if to hear better.

A tolling, as if bells boomed in the darkness of the sea. Muugli's response was instinctive: he bellowed at the night again and again. Other voices answered him—first one or two, then more—in a strange bodyless thunder that filled the darkness.

When the first pale light of dawn filtered through the mist, Muugli saw that another large cake of ice, perhaps forty yards across, had bumped into his own during the night and they had drifted together. Dozens of reddish brown bodies lay on the adjoining island; other individuals swam in the water nearby; and other groups were scattered about on smaller ice floes. There were females as well as males, the former surrounded by the smaller shapes of their calves. The barking and bellowing began again.

Muugli's voice, the oldest and deepest of them all, became the centerpiece of a raucous celebration of reunion.

Soon some of the walruses hooked their tusks over the edge of Muugli's island of ice and heaved their heavy bodies onto it. Using their powerful flippers, they walked across the ice toward the huge old walrus. Their bodies gradually surrounded him. Grunting and snorting, they lay close together, some back to back or lying across other bodies or piled two-deep.

Muugli rested in the center of the herd, at peace. The weight that had lain across his spirit dispersed as light as the fog, which lifted slowly to unveil the white splendor of the Arctic sun.

EPILOGUE

ONE cold morning in early November, Harry Madrid hurried out of his apartment building. His limousine was waiting. Harry was startled when the man who jumped out to open the door wasn't Sal, his regular chauffeur. "Sal's sick," the man mumbled.

Harry ordered the driver to the Waldorf to pick up Deng Chang, who had been delighted to hear that a substantial shipment of ivory had arrived from Alaska. Chang chattered happily all the way to New Jersey. His bodyguards sat facing Harry and Chang, their faces expressing nothing.

They reached the warehouse shortly before ten thirty. The Mercedes slid through iron security gates into a walled yard. The gates were automatically swinging shut when Harry stepped out of the car and glanced around the yard. Nothing out of line: a few cars parked near the entry, a truck backed up to a loading dock. Good. Nothing to make Chang or his goons suspicious.

Harry walked briskly toward the entrance. "I'll make sure those boxes have been brought down for you to look over," he called over his shoulder. He wanted to be inside, out of the way, while Chang and his men were still in the open. Fish in a barrel, Harry thought.

He had the morning's second small jolt when the door opened and he saw another unfamiliar face. The man had knee-breaker written all over him. Someone Tony—his foreman and primary heavy-duty muscle—had recruited for the occasion, Harry decided.

Seeking reassurance, he glanced down the hallway, looking for more of his own men. No one in sight. Through a half-windowed wall to the right of the corridor he could look directly into the main offices. Surprisingly they were empty.

Harry quickly turned. Three wrong notes in one morning were too many; there should have been some action behind him by now. Chang and his goons had to be taken quickly, by surprise.

Chang stood smiling in the doorway. "You were expecting some-one else, Mr. Madrid?"

"Huh? Yes—no! What are you talking about?"

"My mother has spoken to your principals. They are in agreement."

"What's that supposed to mean? I don't have any principals."

Chang smiled. "I doubt very much you intended that as a joke, Harry, but it's a good one. What I mean, of course, is that you could not operate on the docks without the cooperation of . . . certain people of influence. But you should have understood that Madam Chang has long had an arrangement with them. And you were trying to act on your own initiative, without seeking their approval for what you planned to do to me."

"You been sniffing too much opium, Chang."

"*No.*" The Chinese spoke sharply for the first time. "You planned to kill me. Your men have been removed. Most of them went willingly. Your foreman, however . . ."

"Tony? What's happened to Tony?"

"He resisted. Most unfortunate."

Harry saw his future opening up before him like a deep black pit. No way to escape it, but at least he would take Deng Chang with him.

Harry's shoulders sagged, as if in surrender. He turned away and reached for the gun in his shoulder holster. He actually got his hand on the pearl handle of the Beretta .25 automatic before a bullet from a much more powerful gun struck him in the back.

DENG Chang spent the rest of the morning in Madrid's office. He was anxious to inspect the newly arrived shipment of walrus tusks from Alaska, which had provided Harry with the excuse to lure Chang into a trap. Chang had the boxes brought to the offices and opened up. The contents—handsome walrus tusks packed along with several polar bear hides in mint condition—were impressive in themselves but disappointing in light of Deng Chang's expectations. The spectacular tusks of the huge old walrus were not there.

Harry Madrid had lied.

Deng placed a call to Hong Kong and was informed that Madam Chang would return his call shortly. While he waited, Deng heard a commotion near the front entry and saw several men push through the doorway.

Chang was on his feet when two men reached his office. One was large, heavyset, and slow moving; the other, small and energetic.

"What is the meaning of this?" Chang asked. "Who are you?"

"We might ask you the same question," the big man drawled. "We're looking for Harry Madrid."

"You will not find him here." He realized now that the two men had the unmistakable demeanor of policemen. "Mr. Madrid is no longer involved in the business. My name is Deng Chang. I represent the Chang Asian Import-Export Company. Our main offices are in Hong Kong."

The two men looked at each other. Behind Chang the telephone rang. He ignored it. He was perspiring slightly.

"You've taken over?"

"That is correct. Now, if you'll tell me your business with Mr. Madrid, perhaps I can help."

Another exchange of glances. The smaller man produced some papers from his suit pocket. "Then these are for you," he said. "We're with the United States Fish and Wildlife Service, Mr. Chang. That's Mr. Sanderson there, and I'm LoBianco. We have a warrant to search these premises and to impound any illegal goods found." He paused. "I think you'd better call a lawyer, Mr. Chang. From where I'm standing, you're gonna need one."

The telephone kept ringing. Deng Chang, the reality of his situation becoming clearer by the second, made no move to answer it.

ANCHORAGE lay under twelve inches of new snow that first week of November. Outside the windows of the television studios, in a high-rise building in the heart of the city, the peaks of the Alaska Range were crowned in white.

Alaska's governor, Tom Brady, turned away from the view and

took his place on the set, facing a local news anchor. He smiled automatically at the young woman sharing the hot seat with him on *Alaska Speaks*. A scientist, Brady had been told, part of the ASSET group that had spent the summer conducting environmental impact studies near the Arctic Circle. The governor hated these TV debates, but with a congressional subcommittee convening hearings the next morning on the proposed new North Slope oil development, he couldn't risk turning down the invitation.

"How would you sum up your view of the proposed new oil pipeline, Governor Brady?" the anchor asked.

The governor turned toward the woman beside him. Dr. Kathleen McNeely seemed to be ill at ease facing the cameras. To the television-wise politician, she looked like an easy target.

"Alaska is incredibly rich in natural resources," the governor intoned in his rich baritone. "Not to develop those resources would be both shortsighted and incredibly wasteful."

"Aren't you being the shortsighted one, Governor?" Kathy McNeely cut in quickly. "You're talking about oil and mineral resources. How long are they going to last before being exhausted? Twenty years? Fifty years? What is Alaska going to be left with at the end of the next century?"

The governor smiled indulgently. "We're talking about carefully controlled development that will benefit us and those of you in the Lower Forty-eight who still want to drive around in your automobiles and live in your air-conditioned houses." He leaned forward, his professional smile suggesting tolerance for an opponent who didn't know any better. "What we here in Alaska can extract from those mountains and from the North Slope will help make it possible for millions of people to continue to enjoy their way of life."

"It will also destroy the habitat of millions of birds and animals that have been thriving there for centuries," Kathy shot back. "ASSET's report will be released tomorrow. It documents the serious impact of the development not only on birds but on scores of land and sea animals, the fish in Alaska's river systems along the route, and on the land itself. I think you'll find our report a revelation, Governor. I'm sure the subcommittee will."

The governor flushed. He had the feeling he'd been sandbagged. "What we don't need in Alaska," he snapped, "is another spotted-owl controversy that stops development and drives business away."

"That's the heart of the matter, isn't it, Governor? The development you're so anxious to see will also make some individuals a great deal of money. Isn't that what it's all about?"

"You're darned right it is! It will bring jobs here for Alaskans, like the first pipeline. It will benefit this state and the United States."

"The way the pipeline benefitted Prince William Sound?"

The governor's red-faced reply was lost in the general uproar as the studio audience reacted. The news anchor tried to intervene while Kathy and Brady talked over each other. Watching from the control room, the producer of *Alaska Speaks* grinned with delight. Tonight's show was going to be a ratings bonanza.

JASON Cobb limped up to Kathy McNeely. She turned away from a couple of spectators who were ready to continue the televised debate. Her eyes sparked with pleasure. "Jason! They told me you'd gone back to the States."

"The Lower Forty-eight, you mean. I did. But I wouldn't have missed your show today for the world."

She made a small grimace of discomfort. "That's the problem. Instead of addressing the issues together, we were competing for points as if this were a Nintendo game."

"You're not going to change politics overnight—or TV." Cobb grinned. "Not even you, Kathy."

She looked at him with obvious affection but, he regretted to note, with nothing more.

"You're looking great, Jason. I expected to see you in a wheelchair or at least limping around with a cane."

Cobb shrugged. "It turned out I fractured my pelvis. The doctors had me walking in two days."

"I'm glad. I was afraid I'd crippled you for life, hauling you all that way over the tundra."

The noisy confusion in the emptying television studio swirled around them. Cobb saw Alaska's governor, still obviously angry, stalking toward an exit with a phalanx of aides.

"I heard what happened with those ivory poachers," Cobb said. "Someday I'd like to hear the whole story. What about the poacher who was attacked by the grizzly?"

"His name is Mayberry. They say he'll recover. His trial has been postponed indefinitely, but I understand Fish and Wildlife has impounded all the skins and ivory he had."

Cobb studied her admiringly. "You do seem to be a lightning rod, McNeely, as His Honor the Governor discovered. The people who wanted you for ASSET's expedition weren't wrong about you."

Some well-wishers interrupted them, one congratulating Kathy on her television confrontation, another wanting to talk about her encounter with the ivory poachers. Finally, when they were left alone again, Cobb cleared his throat self-consciously. "Have you heard . . . that is, from Brian Hurley?"

Kathy brightened. "Someone handed me a note just before the telecast, saying there was a radio message for me."

They saw Kathy's old friend Carl Jeffers moving through the crowd toward them, a broad grin on his face. He thrust a Teletype into Kathy's hand. "What you've been waiting for, my dear."

Kathy's hand trembled a little as she took the message. It read:

I HAVE THE D.O.P. ON THE WAY HOME. I LOVE YOU, BRIAN.

"The D.O.P.?" Cobb murmured. "What . . . ?"

Jeffers laughed. "Damned Old Pole. It's what Admiral Peary put in the telegram he sent after he returned from the North Pole in 1909."

Watching Kathy closely, Cobb could not miss the glow in her eyes. It answered the question he had been unable to ask. Nothing left to say but "Congratulations . . . to both of you."

Kathy looked up at him quickly. "You are . . ." She seemed to grope for the right word, then impulsively stepped close and hugged him. He felt the warmth and strength in that slender body, and his regret deepened.

"A prince of a fellow," he said, and turned away.

The destruction of wilderness and wildlife has been a recurring concern in the books of Louis Charbonneau. Condensed Books subscribers will no doubt remember the heroine of *White Harvest,* Kathy McNeely, and her loyal husky, Survivor, from Charbonneau's 1991 subzero thriller, *The Ice.* In that book the author focused on the despoiling of Antarctica. His next book, already in the works, will center on the plight of the Siberian tiger. Ironically enough, the Siberian tiger is no longer protected as it was during the communist era, the author explains. In the former Soviet Union "poaching has become epidemic," he says, "partly because people are hungry and partly because there's no one to control the poachers effectively in the preserves."

Louis Charbonneau

The author's love of animals is not limited to endangered species. At his home in Lomita, California, he has "a number of dogs and cats—two dogs and eight cats, actually," he says, laughing. "We've rescued a cat here and there, and somehow the number has grown."

A World War II veteran and former teacher, columnist, and editor, Charbonneau these days devotes himself full time to fiction writing. Whenever he can, he also travels with his wife, Diane. Most recently they took an extensive tour of Civil War battlefields and Appalachian craft fairs, a distinct pleasure for the author's wife, who is a traditional basketmaker. As for wilderness adventuring, Louis Charbonneau prefers to leave that to Kathy McNeely and his other fictional creations.